I0635846

Alice Was Not Her Name

Alice Was Not Her Name

A Novel

P. K. Kilcullen

Grateful acknowledgement is made to the following for permission to reprint previously published material:
Excerpt from ELSEWHERE: A MEMOIR by Richard Russo, 2012 by Richard Russo. Used by permission of Alfred A. Knopf, an imprint of the Knopf Doubleday Publishing Group, a division of Penguin Random House LLC. All rights reserved.

Paperback edition printed and bound in the United States.
ISBN 979-8-9895176-0-2

For
Jean, Conor, Celia, Kat,
and Kieran

In Memoriam
James J. Gillespie
John Vincent Kane

The mechanism of human destiny—that intricate weave of chance and fate and free will, as distinctly individual as a fingerprint—is surely meant to remain life's central mystery, to resist transparency, to make blame a dangerous and unsatisfactory exercise.

Richard Russo
Elsewhere: A Memoir
2012

Prologue

In her bedroom, she rubs a towel on her hair, grateful to muffle that loud male voice downstairs in The Grotto. She was at first horrified and is now indignant that he was in her home, intruding where he'd never gone before. She knew he would interfere, but she hadn't expected he would show up here, especially at the last moment.

Barefoot in a tee shirt and underpants, she stands before her full-length mirror, preparing to confront him. First, the tremors in her breath and in her fingers. Not fear, but adrenaline. Deep breathing through the nose, exhaling through the mouth. Using the rush, energizing her control. Then, steady fingers on the instruments at the sink, up to the face, quick delicate touches, brushing the thick dark brows into submission, dabbing the cheeks with blush, powdering the shadows under the pale green eyes, shading the lids with a soft hue, nothing needed for the long lashes, but a defining line around the orbs required for clarity, for penetration, which he will get from her, like it or not.

She swipes a stripe of rose on her lips and runs her fingers through her short auburn hair to even out the curls. She shrugs at her good fortune—hair that takes care of itself. Who does she owe that to? Her mother? Who would know?

She pulls off her tee shirt and searches her dresser for a bra. She spills underwear onto the floor, cursing to herself, and then turns to look at herself again in the mirror, this time covered only by the pastel blue bikini underpants. She ponders her body, its condition, the signs of her life there, the toll she has inflicted. Despite her best attempts to destroy herself, she decides she was dealt a durable body, an athletic form with smooth, toned, unblemished skin that she wonders about—the strength and resilience likely from her father, but no real idea what her mother might have looked like before she was ill, certainly not underneath all that bedding or in old photos under all those clothes she'd worn—who knew what women looked like naked back then, what they hid from the world. Why? Everyone knows why.

She grabs a bra from the pile on the floor, straps it on and pauses in front of the mirror. It's another one of those damn torpedo devices—how many does she still have? Who thought two missiles aimed at you was a good idea? She doesn't know, of course, but she's certain he never tried one on.

She casts about in the pile, then straightens up before the mirror, pulls off the torpedo and puts on a beige bra—a newer type without the underwires and frilly decoration, more like a simple layer of skin. She finds a red silk long-sleeved shirt and, as she fastens the pearl buttons from the bottom up, she stops to consider her cleavage in the reflection and then decides to button the shirt all the way up to her neck. She pulls on a pair of loose-fitting black slacks and tucks the shirt into her pants, and then untucks it, then tucks it in again. She sighs in exasperation and stares at herself for a while, listening to the rise and fall of the voice downstairs, unwilling to know what he's saying. She whispers to the mirror, "What is left of me? What has he not taken away? Nothing. Absolutely nothing."

She looks at the painted face, the covered body. "No. I will present myself, finally, as just that. Nothing. He'll have to peel the skin off my face and body if he wants any more of me."

She rips open the shirt, pearl buttons popping off the reflecting glass. She tosses it on the floor and pulls off her pants, unsnaps her bra, shakes it off and pulls down her underpants, kicking them at the mirror. She stands naked before the mirror and takes in the form in a fog of disassociation, the entire shape before her a vague apparition in a soft blue cloud, a sallow moth too close to the light.

She blinks away the aura, focuses on the image and begins to scrutinize. She assesses the neck and chin: tiny suggestions of wrinkles but no sag yet, here on the threshold of forty; the arms and shoulders: still solid, muscles holding on, protecting the torso; the hands, long and slender, someone called them piano hands, and she's kept that thought for years; the breasts: subjects of nurture, objects of desire, lower now than in the torpedo shackles, but in the natural place on her ribs, still proud, still standing at attention, whether required or not; the hip points, once prominent over concave slopes toward her mons, but now softer-edged and filled in, youth gone; the thighs long and lean, always an inch or so apart even with her knees touching; the calves strong and toned— these sturdy legs still holding her up, despite her best efforts to knock herself down. The feet: are there such things as piano feet? Yet, these look more weathered than the hands, squished at the sides from years of binding shoes, sore around the perimeter.

Then, turning around and looking over her shoulder, her back: in a flash from another dimension, she sees a fresh wound surrounded by scars from earlier stabs, but, in this conscious life, she sees smooth skin, shoulders and wings toned and strong, again thanks to someone before her, the father? The waist is soft in the back, but the rear is reliably solid, like her breasts, defying gravity's angry pull here at the literal end of her young years.

Turning around again, she hears his voice rising, and she feels her heart thrum; her lungs fill, her breath escaping as she looks at her middle, once so lean and tight and now fragile, her waist softer than it ever was, bearing the punishment of her drinking. She pokes two fingers there, still solid under an inch of fat. Her eyes fall to her pubic bone pushing out below her navel, naked of hair and revealing the cleft beneath it, reminding her of her child body. She laughs a little at the odd feeling. "Marte's idea. A present for me, she had said, but I know it was for her. So why do I still shave it?"

She makes a sweeping assessment of the face and body she'll present. "So, this is what I'll be—as untouched and innocent as the child I was born to be. And he will have nothing left to take from me."

She strides to the bathroom, the voice downstairs now louder. She scrubs off her makeup, runs her hands into her hair and stares at her face in the mirror. "Fake up, gone." She smirks at the image of her face. "Huh." She's heard others call her mouth puffy, but that always just made her laugh. Now those pillowy lips are pale, her eyes unburdened by goop, her dark eyebrows thick and feral, hovering over the wide green orbs, crystalline now, the pupils large, darkness at the heart of her light. Soft sweeps of tender skin underneath her eyes reveal her truth. And her hair? Ringing her face now like the mane of a wayward animal. No rules there, no boundaries; it goes its own wandering, swirling way, untamable.

She returns to her bedroom. She takes one more head to toe survey before the mirror and approves her presentation with a satisfied grin. "The original version. He'll be disarmed. But I won't be."

She steps to her closet and pulls on her silk red robe, the feather light hem tickling the tops of her knees. She ties the sash in a careful bow and turns back to the closet and begins rummaging on her hands and knees past shoes until her fingers touch the cool glass. Her courage. She grips the smooth neck, so familiar, an appendage of her need. Then she stops, lowers her head and shakes it slowly, closing her eyes, her hand letting go and dropping the appendage to the floor. Tells herself the bottle is vestigial, a phantom limb now. Her head lower still, she slowly shakes off the urge, the need. The body and mind must be in sync for this.

She shuffles backward out of the closet and stands up, adjusting and cinching her robe, pulling her wings down to stand taller, chest out, middle tight, head over spine, chin up. She goes to the bedside table, opens the drawer. She pulls out the shiny silver pistol Marte had given her, checks the barrel, drops it into her robe pocket and walks out the bedroom door.

Part One

1
Her Last Lecture

Late February 1969

With four days left in a brutal month, an unexpected thaw jolted the ice bound valley from its oppressive winter torpor. Runoff surged in the streets, starlings bolted drunkenly into the air, children slopped through muddy yards, mailmen wore short sleeves, and the low sun delivered much more heat than its dull glow promised. Afraid to celebrate their unaccustomed good fortune, the citizens of the valley greeted the sudden warmth with caution bordering on mistrust. Something weird was going on.

Jade's last semester at Ebonton High was well underway, and the proverbial light at the tunnel's end felt closer in this sudden burst of spring. But he, too, could not celebrate because Alice, as if aided by her own divination, had to come to life. Winter for her had been much longer, deeper, darker; it had lasted two years or more. Now, to Jade's astonishment, she was risen. He refused to believe it had anything to do with her long winter of prayers, her conversations with unseen spirits. The temptation to assign her transformation to the supernatural challenged his reasoning. Was it absurd to consider that her spiritual vibe had caused this atmospheric shift? Some magical, mystical intercession with her friends in the other world? A last gift of light before her darkness might consume her?

Whatever the source, Alice was suddenly and unusually buoyant. Jade wondered if she, too, had seen the light in the distance and would somehow stand in its way. In *his* way. Still, despite doubts, he was relieved. Alice was back. He even dared to imagine that her long day's journey into night was over at last.

In this sudden new season, Alice reversed her habits and became consistent. Up in the morning to get Jade breakfast before school, home in the early evenings, pleasant, chatty about nothing, even surprising him once with dinner and a bouquet of flowers on their kitchen table. She seemed more coherent, less disheveled than she had been in months. Her hair, her skin, her eyes—there was a freshness, a luminance about them. She still wore men's clothes around the house, but, lately, her sweatpants, flannel shirts, and tennis shoes looked new, almost stylish. One evening, she announced in the kitchen that she was going to resume a role she'd adopted during Jade's last two years in elementary school through his first year in high school. She would be his unsolicited literature adviser.

It was a Tuesday evening. She had come home early, wearing new clothes, all black—a turtleneck sweater under an open trench coat, fitted slacks, and Chelsea boots. She'd gotten her hair dyed black and cut in a boyish style, and she wore no makeup; but if her intention was to look mannish, it wasn't working. She could no more hide the silky skin and delicate structure of her face than she could mask with her trench coat the obvious curves of her body. And yet, her look was purposefully counter-fashion, unisex. She looked hip. She could be in a band.

Her pale green eyes danced at him, her full smile unbound—the one he remembered from his childhood. She bit her lip mid-smile. She had something up her sleeve. He'd forgotten how much he loved this way she had, this look that told him excitement was imminent. He dared to ask himself the question: Could it be that she was happy? Why? How? After so many seasons in the dark, how could her long-dormant magical light so suddenly return?

She greeted him with a kiss on the cheek and then dashed upstairs. Jade had just returned from his after-school stint at Wally's Diner, and he was sorting through his homework at the kitchen table. Alice bounded down the steps into the kitchen and, in a haughty tone, but with a smirk on her face, she announced that she would be augmenting the literature he'd been assigned by his English teacher, given that his school reading requirements, in her opinion, had declined after he'd left Pell Academy. She'd supplied him with novels regularly in elementary school, and now she felt the need to resume that practice. She declared that her past approach of giving him random single titles would change to multiple novels, in tandem, that would fall under certain categories. She reminded him that, at Pell, he had been assigned novels that were complementary. "For example," she said, "debut novels: Lawrence's *Sons and Lovers*, Joyce's *Portrait*, McCuller's *Lonely Hunter*, Lee's *Mockingbird*, and, of course, Salinger's *Catcher*."

"At Pell," she said, "that practice had continued through your second year with 19th century European debuts, but, at Ebonton, your required reading has provided no such contextual benefit. So, I will assert one. We will move into modern America, the New World of pre- and post-war breakthroughs. And I will bring you outside into the fresh air, to breathe in ideas beyond the same old stale breath of men choking our imaginations. Dead White men. Their rule is ending. Now."

6

Jade sighed and closed his eyes. He craved this new brightness in her, but he could feel her moving into his own path, his own light, the one that beckoned him at the tunnel's end, his freedom. From Alice, he had acquired an interest in literature, but now he was more interested in surviving the final months of high school than he was adding to his reading assignments. Plus, it was a bit late for Alice to be imposing new standards on his Ebonton education. He'd be graduating in three months.

"Why are we doing this, Alice? I'm not planning to go to college."

"College is in your future, young man, if I have anything to say about it," she replied. "But, for the moment, college is secondary to the matter at hand." She began to pace back and forth, looking like a nightclub performer in her tight black outfit and hard-heeled boots, but sounding more like his private professor. "Reading is the matter at hand. I'm talking about your education for the rest of your life. College, or no college, you shall continue to advance your reading. That's my principal demand of you. If you do not advance your reading, you will fall dumb, like so many men around you, everywhere. Illiterate men in this country are falling from trees like an endless rain of acorns in the autumn of our nation's life. You need to be the enduring trunk, my son, not the finite fruit. Reading is the source of enlightenment. Would you prefer to stay in the dark? Underfoot, on the cold ground, rotting and dumb with the rest of them?"

Jade knew too well that his dedicated reading habits had been established under Alice's guidance. She'd been unreliable in so many other ways, but, on this mission, she had been steady—perhaps the only anchor she'd ever dropped on their itinerant voyage together.

"I've set your sail," she said, reading his thoughts. "Now, it is up to you, not fate. You are master of the steerage of your course."

Jade was tired from school and a busy evening at the diner. "I have homework to do, Alice. I haven't even broken the binding on *Invisible Man*, and Mr. Heath's test on it will be first thing Friday morning."

"Ellison! My goodness! Not a woman, alas, but at least not another dead White man. Mr. Heath must have channeled my new path for you, bless his stunted heart."

Alice resumed her pacing, charging now with her chin out, her finger in the air. "We can stay in that category—novelists from other races and cultures. After Ellison, let's go with *Native Son*. That one shook the world to its core. Next, you should try Alan Patton's *Cry, the Beloved Country*. Then, we'll go to Baldwin. Perhaps, logically, *Another Country*. Talk about another culture, a country within our own country, real life choices American publishers hide from us! Bisexuals in puritanical America! Imagine!" She stopped and made a prim face at him. "Shocking," she said in a faux-British accent. "Someone should be arrested!"

Jade let go a snort of laughter and shook his head, closing his eyes and quietly reveling in the joy of her theatrical bursts, especially her mimicry of the Brits, as she'd called them.

She leaned back against the kitchen sink, smirking at him, subsuming his collusion. She reached over to pick up a screwdriver and a faded brass hinge that had been lying next to the sink unattended for months. She began poking at the hinge with the screwdriver. "Then, once you have Baldwin in your skin, son, we'll get daring. We'll get real. We'll read Malcolm X. His personal history inside a Black body. His autobiography."

Jade broke her spiel. And her spell over him. "Alice. Look at my eyes. Are you sober?"

She stopped her tinkering with the hinge and stared at him, her knuckles turning white around the screwdriver. A moment passed between them—the sweetness and sadness of their life together, the thrill of their tiny world at the beach, just the two of them in their endless game of catch with a hardball at dawn on wide hard sand, and the long evenings of playing—acting parts after a trip to the movies, laughing until they cried. And then, the hostile grip of her spasms with booze and, of late, her religious ranting, her visions, her rage unbound and mysterious, her long disappearances. All of it, a bond and yet a lost trust, hope entwined in wariness.

She put down the screwdriver and held out her hand toward him, her fingers steady, her eyes holding his.

"I could do surgery right now," she said, taking his accusing gaze and molding it to her own, their eyes nearly identical, a single set of four verdant windows on the world. She gave a little huff and started again at her fix-it work, using the screwdriver to pick with precision at the rusty hinge. "Back to the issue at hand," she said. "With Malcom, we're breaking out of fiction, yes, but we'll explore Black non-fiction a bit, then back to fiction. Essays, too. Poems. Criticism. Women, for a change, Parker, Woolfe, Lessing. *The Grass is Singing.* Ever hear of it?"

Jade sighed and shook his head. "Teachers at Ebonton say 'Negro' or 'Colored,' not 'Black,'" he said. He'd begun to fade from her spell over him.

"How enlightened." Alice said. "Underscores my point. Ebonton High is a cultural and literary backwater. I should not have encouraged your departure from Pell Academy. Mea culpa, mea culpa, mea maxima culpa," she said in rapid-fire, her soft fist tapping her chest. "I promise I'll make it up to you. We'll work on your reading together. I'll get you a copy of Malcolm X. After that, we'll take a break from the weight of our broken culture and have some fun in outer space. How about *Stranger in a Strange Land?* You've heard of Heinlein, I assume. Sci-fi man? The writing is a mess but it's fun."

8

"I don't know." He pulled a notebook from his pile and sighed. "I don't think he's been mentioned in English class. Would you like to teach the course, Alice?"

She laughed in a single-note shout.

"Of course I would! You know it. And I would enlighten you and your fellow students to ideas you will never hear from teachers in that dull place."

"So, I guess I'm about to be enlightened," Jade sighed, then chuckled. He set his pen on top of his notebook and turned his upper body toward his mother, anticipating one of her rounds of mental gymnastics, a practice from her clear days, before the booze took over. Jade was relieved to let his defeated mood evaporate, replaced by an unexpected surge of pride. The old Alice was back. He loved her like this. He could no longer restrain his grin. He let the feeling take over.

"Fiction, Seamus Dellworth Flynn, is more real than life itself." She smiled at him, her electricity on, her teenage smart girl charm in full display. She had him. She returned to fiddling with the rusty hinge, reasserting her professorial tone, but looking up at him between sentences, holding him in her spell. "It's the life of the mind, Seamus. The expression of the complex and mostly ineffable conscious dreaming we all experience but deny in favor of the safe, prosaic existence we inaccurately call reality." She stopped tinkering for a moment and smirked, watching Jade nod, then setting his head back, anticipating more lecture and giving her his own wry grin. It was the bond he loved between them, listening to her opine in her haughty way, his undivided mind intertwined with hers for the duration. He'd once lived for these moments. Now, in her sudden resurgence, he made a concentrated effort to capture every thought, every utterance from her—to freeze her in his mind, to prevent this old magic from disappearing again into the void of the toxic life she'd lived over the past two years.

"We love predictability," Alice continued, "that trait which we believe, wrongly, separates us from all other forms of life insofar as we make predictions from observed patterns, while we assert that other living creatures simply follow their own patterns without consciousness. It's wrong and cowardly to think that other beings cannot anticipate where combined patterns of their own behavior will lead them. This is the safe route, living in predictable reality. The far more interesting one is to live with an awareness of your dream life, figuring out without logic or reason where and who you are."

"And this has to do with reading, exactly how?" Jade the student said, a smug smile for his professor. "It's Jade, by the way. Not Seamus. Remember?"

It had been her idea to change his name from Seamus to James when they'd first moved to the Black Diamond Valley. He was nearly twelve and about to enter the tail end of seventh grade in yet another new school in a long, disconnected line of them. She'd said the locals would mangle the pronunciation and spelling and that James was the anglicized version, not that they'd landed in England, exactly, she'd said in her mock-accent. She'd also instructed him to call her "Alice" going forward, never Mother or Mom. She'd said she was setting a new course for them in this less welcoming place, but it was she who later fell back on calling him Seamus or Shay, especially after he changed James to J.D., for James Dellworth, and then much later when his new girlfriend shortened that version to Jade, which he loved and which Alice hated, calling it a mangling. The nicknames, she'd said, were too unique. These would distinguish him, make him stand out in a place where anonymity was preferred.

Names were a form of protection, she'd told him at the outset of these mandated changes, and when he'd asked what they needed protection from, she'd said assumptions, exposure, and liabilities in this gossipy valley. He was twelve and wasn't sure what she meant by all that, but, a few years later, he thought she resisted calling him Jade because she didn't trust his girlfriend, even though she'd never met her.

"It has to do with all art, Seamus," she declared, ignoring his correction on his name. "Especially first efforts, where art is unencumbered by judgment, where the artist is alone, embracing doubt, informed by the imagination, the unconscious, the living being within all of us—mammals, creatures around us, the sky above us, the air we breathe." She set the hardware on the edge of the sink and walked toward the second-floor stairs. She turned in the doorway in a dramatic twirl, waving her arm in a semi-circle at him. "The random novelists that your class is unwittingly exploring are all examples of artists taking to the public stage their own inner consciousness. You should take note."

She paused and locked her eyes on his, raising her index finger like a wand. "Now! I will return in a moment with a special gift for you. It's not a novel by a woman or a Black writer, alas, but it's almost as revealing, almost as misunderstood. It is a very public exploration of the inner consciousness unlike anything before it." She lowered her hand and bowed her head in a quick nod, indicating intermission. Then, she clambered up the steps like a child at Christmas.

Some of this lecture made sense to Jade; some of it did not. He was almost 18. He had other distractions. He loved the performance by Alice in this, her magical state; but her theories begged for clarity at the edge of his reason. Her declarations seemed to make sense but, then again, not entirely. It reminded him of a man on a street corner he'd witnessed in New York City, the one and only time his mother had taken him there, to see *Carnival!* at the Imperial Theater, when he was 10. The man was standing on a fruit crate next to a phone booth near Times Square and had caught Jade's eye in the midst of making loud proclamations to the passing crowds. To Jade, the man seemed to be making perfect sense, as if he were talking just to Jade. But when Alice tugged his sleeve to make the street crossing, he heard the man's words drift off into an incoherent series of broken phrases and non-sequiturs, for anybody to hear. Alice now sounded a bit like that, but Jade was happy for her anyway. She was sober, and she loved to talk about books. And miraculously, at least for now, she was her old self.

He heard her new boots on the steps. She appeared in the doorway with her hands behind her back, an impish grin on her face. Her eyes were alive with the light of her surprise for him. He held his breath.

"Guess what it is," she said, her cheeks blushing, the teenage girl inside her bursting. Jade grinned at her, shaking his head. He was afraid the gift itself would not rise to the level of this moment he so desperately wanted to retain—this butterfly of anticipation. He closed his eyes, trying to stop time, to keep Alice here like this with him, for good.

"Ready?" she chirped, unaware that he was not ready, not willing to break this rare charm, this fluttering heartbeat, this magic that could not get better than now.

She stepped toward him and stood close. He could smell the familiar scent of her skin, feel the heat from her.

"Open your eyes." She was inches from his face, her breath sweet and her eyes on fire.

She slapped a new hardback on the table in front of him, next to his homework pile.

"Just out," she declared, sounding like a radio announcer. "The most publicly castigated novel in years, the wildly revealing Jewish boy confessional—something every Catholic boy and girl should read." She pulled back her chin, her face tilting away from him. "Not that you're an actual Catholic boy. More so one by osmosis. But you should still read it."

He looked down at the book. The magic gone. He sighed, reminded again that with Alice the anticipation was always the best part. He recognized the title. It had been talked about at school in hushed and tittering conversations in the halls, but no one had read it yet. No one he knew.

"You've heard about it, no doubt," she blurted before he could react. She was excited, as if it were her own novel. "Everyone's talking about it. The Sheldon library wouldn't order a copy, so I had to special order it on the sly." She stepped back from him. "Shay, it's not just about masturbation, but you must read this. It's a breakthrough for men. It's a subject Mary McCarthy's novel has opened up, so to speak, for women, but here, remarkably, a man has confessed to an obsession over it. A confession of his own humanness. Or perhaps human mess."

"What are you talking about?"

"Sex, Jade. And self-love, too. It's a natural obsession, you see. A necessity. A need that alleviates anguish. It's nearly 1970, for God's sake. It needs to be talked about! It's not all about masturbation, but that subject is presented in this book in a vivid way, nearly an obsession. Why? Because people are appalled by this subject and all that it implies, and yet they're clucking like stone Pilgrims behind their false faces, knowing that everyone does it. Women masturbate, too, did you know that?"

Jade stood up from the table and grabbed his pile of homework. "Alice, I can't talk about this with you. You're supposed to be my mother!"

"Exactly! Who else can you talk to about it? Your father? Haven't seen him lately. Your girlfriend? Janey, or Lacy, or whatever her name is?"

"Lucy."

"Lucy. You think Lucy doesn't masturbate? She does! And so do you."

"Jesus, Alice. This is crazy. And no, I don't! I don't need to. I have a girlfriend. And she definitely doesn't need to."

"Why? Is she around every time you feel the urge? No. Are you there with her every time she feels it? Do you even need to be? Absolutely not!" Alice put her hands on his shoulders and looked him in the eye. "Jade, what I'm telling you is that it's ok. We're all humans. Sex is not shameful. It's private, yes, but it's—"

"I'm not listening to this anymore," he blurted and pulled away from her. "You sound like one of those loopy California hippie chicks. You're not making any sense." He headed for the stairs and pounded his way up to his bedroom.

Before he slammed the door, he heard Alice sigh with heavy exaggeration. "My dear Mr. Roth!" she shouted. "You think *you're* misunderstood!"

A week later, Alice, still sober, approached Jade with another book. She was more tentative this time, no introductory lecture. He could see she was as uncertain now as she had been certain before.

"This is a book I found in our library. It's unfinished. We're not sure who the author is—someone calling herself Jeannette Robbins. An unknown. Written sometime in the last few years, as far as we can tell. It's interesting. I'd like you to give it a try. Let me know what you think. It's an unusual story."

It was hardly a book. It was a black three-ring binder filled with typed pages. As Jade leafed through it, he noticed penciled notes, paragraphs crossed out, and sentences edited in longhand.

"Is this another first novel, Alice?" Jade smirked at her from the kitchen table where he'd been studying. He couldn't read her face now. She was neither the pedantic professor nor the untethered, unsober clairvoyant. Her look was reticent, almost defensive.

"Why was it at your library?" His smirk gone, his voice flat, edging toward suspicion.

"There's a closet there filled with odds and ends, mostly out-of-date books." She blinked rapidly while talking, the light still in her eyes, but it was refracting, dodging. "But there are a few notebooks, handwritten, that people left behind, or donated. None of it is organized. But this one is typed, easier to read. I'm curious what you think of it."

Jade sighed. "Is it another sex manual?"

Alice smiled, less guarded. Her eyes were steady again. "No, don't worry. There is some sex, but nothing like the Roth story. It's from a woman's point of view. So the sex is less overt, more subtle, and, naturally, more complex. But the story is curious. I think it's worth your while. You haven't read many women authors."

"There's no title, no date, nothing," Jade said, flipping to the front of the binder.

"Yes. I think that's the exciting thing about it." Her voice lifted; she was selling now. "Jeannette Robbins is—or was—an unknown. No evidence why she wrote it, or how it got into our library closet. You're jumping off a cliff with this story, Shay. No famous name on it. As you say, not even a title. If I could give it one, I might say it should be called 'A Fall from Grace.' Perhaps with a subtitle, 'The Rise of The Interloper.' I think you'll find it compelling, an adventure into the unknown."

"I'm way behind in schoolwork, Alice. I have a French test on Thursday. Plus tons of Math homework. I don't have time for this." He pushed the binder toward her.

"Just give the first thirty pages a quick read," Alice pleaded, pushing it back to him. "Thirty pages, that's all I ask. I think you'll be surprised when you want to read more."

Jade flipped to the back of the binder. "324 pages to this thing, Alice, and you said it's not even finished. Why would I want to read it?"

"Thirty pages, honey. That's all I ask. I know that's not too much for you. You're a fast reader. Please. For me." She put her hand on his shoulder.

Jade looked up at her. He knew this woman—at least what he hoped was the best of the many versions of her—and yet he couldn't read what was in her eyes now. "You sure you don't know who wrote it?"

Alice squeezed his shoulder and smiled, her eyes softening. "I wish I did." She leaned down and kissed his cheek. "Thirty pages, sweetie. You can do it."

She disappeared up the second-floor steps. Jade put his head down on the black binder and fell asleep.

Two weeks later, on a Thursday, he came home from Wally's and found the house empty. He'd had a full meal at the diner, so he decided to crack the books for Friday's tests. In the pile on the floor, he found the black binder. Deciding it would make a suitable distraction from homework, he read the requested thirty pages quickly and moved on to the next section. He was surprised to be even remotely interested in what started out as a boring account of a girl's life.

Jade found the writing uneven and the story more of an amateur diary than a novel. Yet, he was compelled by a prurient curiosity. Secrets of a teenage girl had to contain something he needed to know.

In the first section, the writer seemed childlike, gushing over the memories of her perfect life as the youngest in a large wealthy family who lived like European royalty in a massive home and exclusive estate grounds somewhere in the mountains west of New York City. The author, Jeannette Robbins, described her parents, Angus and Isobel, as distant and formal, her mother, often ill and bed-bound, and her father, dark-tempered and frequently away on business. There were more servants and groundskeepers on the estate than family members. Her older siblings attended boarding schools or private colleges, and most lived abroad during the summer months. In June and July, when the family gathered— at least those stateside—they shuttled back and forth between their summer estate on The Gold Coast and hotel stays on Block Island. It was the only time the author saw much of her father. She remembered those summer excursions as rare periods when his dark mood abated and he gave her special attention, holding her forth to his visiting friends and business associates as a prodigy in athletics and the arts, and a natural beauty on top of it all. The Renaissance Girl, he'd called her. From these rare moments of paternal interaction and praise, Jeannette deduced that she was not just her father's youngest and most promising, but his favorite among his eight children.

Jeannette's life at the estate involved mostly adults; she didn't mention friends her own age. In the opening section of the story, her favorite memories were reserved for her in-home educators who became her best friends—the live-in servants, nannies, tutors, groundsmen, equestrians, and visiting athletic coaches. At an early age, she learned to ride and jump horses, play tennis, target shoot, and to swim and dive in their indoor pool. She even tried her hand at fencing and discovered she was good at it. Her teachers and craftsmen praised her as dexterous, artistic, athletic, an intellectual wunderkind—a section of the story Jade found difficult to abide, as it seemed braggadocious, if not unbelievable. She claimed to have easily absorbed everything she was taught—from literature, singing, dancing, piano, and painting with visiting New York tutors, to steeplechase and polo, water and snow skiing, chess, cribbage, and billiards, and even down to the rudiments of auto mechanics that she learned from the Italian garage hand who was in charge of the family's fleet of automobiles at a time when most families had none: the 1930s. Her account of her siblings was incidental. She breezed over the few times

Elspeth and Kelvin—her older siblings closest in age to her—were at home, reporting only their frustration at being bested by Jeannette in riding, shooting, tennis, and swimming.

In the second section, the author's tone changed. She wrote from an adult's viewpoint, judgmental and critical, as if the idyllic life she'd just described was, as Jade had suspected, pure fantasy. Her voice became grim as her family story darkened.

Mining her memories, Jeannette revealed she'd had little interaction with her mother. She recalled Isobel lying in her canopied bed most of the time, either asleep or in a deep haze. A nurse sat sentry at her bedside, the heavy drapes always closed, a dim light revealing on a side table her mother's litter of small brown medicine bottles. The room always smelled of licorice, and when Jeannette was allowed to visit, her mother seldom spoke, just nodded at the girl's precocious chatter and attempted a smile. The nurse would usher Jeannette out of the room when her mother began her fitful coughing, a sound that often filled the second-floor hallways around the master suite.

Less than a year after her mother died in spring 1939, Jeannette's father brought home a new wife, his third. Along with the haughty and indifferent Mhairi Flannery—the widow of prominent politician Michael Flannery—came her son, Carlon, an only child a year older than Jeannette and described by the author as a physically aggressive and emotionally childish nincompoop—and now a competitor for the prized position in the family that the author had once claimed.

Two years earlier, after Jeannette's older sister, Tara, had died, the family curtailed their summer vacations, and her father's special regard for Jeannette began to wane. She'd gone to him for consolation after Tara's death, but was told instead that Tara had disgraced the family and that her name should never again be mentioned. Upon the arrival of Mhairi and her son, Jeannette noticed the extra attention her father began to give Carlon, and for the first time she felt threatened. Once the Renaissance Girl, now she was second fiddle to a brutish lout. The Intruder. The Interloper.

By this point, Jade had had enough of this girl's family melodrama. He'd read more than twice the number of pages Alice had asked him to read. The next morning, before he left for school, he put the binder on the kitchen table, with a note: *Alice, I read 70 pages. It's interesting, but not that interesting. I guess there's a reason we've never heard of Jeannette Robbins.* — Jade (not Seamus).

A week later, the spring tease was over, the entire valley buried under a foot of snow. The heavy pall of winter returned: relentless wind, a low slate sky, skeins of dark ice coiling in the frozen streets. Alice didn't mention the binder again. And, just as suddenly as her mood had brightened weeks earlier, it plunged untethered into swirling darkness.

She went deeper than ever before. She stayed in her bedroom, crying endlessly, wailing. Jade couldn't get her out of bed, couldn't feed her. She slept long hours, awakening in the night with a high-pitched keening squall. Startled the first few times, Jade would rush to her side, the wailing only intensifying. She was inconsolable.

He knew now that Alice's unusual mood boost and the unseasonal atmospheric change in late February had not been codependent through some spiritual invocation, but had been merely coincidental. Something else had caused her sudden brightening for weeks and then her equally sudden descent into this hell where she now howled. Amid the weeping and bawling, he heard just one word, over and over. A name? Martin?

By mid-March, Alice shifted from mourning and sleeping to drinking and praying.

2
The Orb

March 1969

A lice and Jade lived in a narrow, two-story wood frame house. From the street, the house looked exhausted. Even on a bright spring morning, the gaps in the brown shingle siding looked like dark sores on the matted hide of a weary animal. The comically tilted, cracked cement chimney seemed a trick of the eye, its imminent collapse moments away.

There was no porch on this flat-faced little house. The front door listed off its frame toward Reston Street just ten feet away. On both sides, and all along this section of Reston, other narrow, exhausted little houses seemed to lean toward each other and collectively sag. Reston was the main drag in Mell Hollow. It was a two-lane state road built over a once-wooded footpath along a narrow river that for most of the previous eighty years had served as an open sewer and a silt spill for coal mines.

Jade was about to turn 18, and he was beginning to step back from his own shadows, to lift his nose from his navel and notice a world beyond himself, other possibilities. As spring approached, with more light in the sky, he often found himself, on early mornings, standing across the street from their little house imagining what he would think of the place if he did not live here, if he had just landed in this spot, dropped here in a dream, an alien passing through this world. He would have telepathic powers, of course. He would see through walls. What would he think about the people who lived in such a house? Would he think they could be happy? He would laugh his alien laugh, some kind of insect sound, perhaps. A haughty, reedy noise. Could these creatures in this little hovel so much as comprehend the meaning of happiness? Did these mortals know the difference between a few moments of bliss and the emotional security of true happiness? Among the three triumphs of life in this place called America, could that third lofty goal—the pursuit of happiness—ever be realized in such a place?

Happiness, Jade had figured out by then, even without the insight of his alien personality, was more of a fleeting sensation than the enduring state of mind about which Americans had long fooled themselves. Despite the classroom indoctrination of Life, Liberty and the Pursuit, Jade had finally realized, here at this prolonged pause in his wandering life with Alice, that happiness was unplanned. It occurred unexpectedly, infrequently, and it nearly always disappeared as soon as he became aware of it. This was one of his epiphanies during these self-awareness exercises he'd started that spring, out in front of his crooked little home. It was a realization born of a first-ever introspective look at his childhood years, his eighteen years with the inscrutable, excitable, unreliable, spontaneously inspired, theatrically didactic, sometimes tender, often absent, and always mysterious Alice—who was now, the mostly bitter, magically mad, and sadly sotted Alice.

Jade began to understand that he'd been living with his head down, in the shadow of Alice and their squandered little life. He had three friends, including a girlfriend, but none of them was asking the questions that needed to be asked. They were living teenagers' lives, moment to moment, insulated self-absorbed worlds. Despite an unraveling society beyond the valley—and, for them, the vague possibility of joining that grand rebellion—their own sense of the future, beyond today or tonight, had not been considered at all, by any of them.

So, when he began drifting into these new solo reveries at dawn in front of his little house, Jade started to wonder if he could belong somewhere else. Beyond his friends and this crumbling abode. Beyond this dank and smothering valley. Beyond Alice.

As he stood in his alien's shoes, Jade would tune out the sporadic rumble of traffic in front of him and look above the little house and its tilted chimney to the other dark sagging rooftops on this side of the river and then up to the black coal breaker on the hill a quarter mile beyond the neighborhood. He imagined the stranger from the dream being curious about this monstrous black specter, how it hovered on stilts on the smoky hillside like a giant praying mantis singed to a charcoal standstill in mid-stride by some great fire from above. Or, more likely, from below. It seemed as if the great mantis, like the chimney on his house, might crumble in a cascade of brittle splinters at any given moment, at an errant breeze, a whimsical wave from a fickle god.

He imagined the alien trying to make his way down to the narrow river behind the cluster of colorless homes and then, daring to cross that maligned moat, to stumble through the littered, rodent-infested shoreline and up the hill through the slag-choked collection of wiry vines and scrub trees, to see about that black monster on stilts. And when he got there, would the alien know what a coal breaker was? Of course he would; he was the omniscient alien. But would he be surprised to see that, although the breaker appeared to have been abandoned for years, no one had bothered to tear it down? And would the alien smirk haughtily at the hillside adjacent to the old breaker and chuckle to himself that the hill was not only barren, but actually on fire, smoldering beneath its crust? Heavy bilious clouds of pink and black ash oozing into the air like pus from an eternally infected wound. Just like that other burning hill of culm a half-mile away and within sight of this place. Hills on fire? Humans living amid them, smothering themselves? Why? Even the alien would be flummoxed.

The alien would be a master of logic, of course, and find it irrational that the people who lived among these smoking hills would not try to extinguish the fires. Surely, they'd noticed by now. Is it possible they'd gotten used to this wasteland they called home—this choking miasma of sulfuric soot, the river black and foul, cluttered with tires, coal dust, human waste, dumped refrigerators, the rusty shells of cars? A river long ago named The Philomena, but to most here, especially the children banished from its shores by adults, it was now known as The Filthy.

On every one of these occasions, Jade would implore the alien, "Take me with you when you leave!" After a few of these vigils, that hopeless intercession would make him sigh in resignation as he realized that no one was going to take him anywhere. That he would have to make that happen on his own. Alone.

As the pall of culm smoke robbed light from the murky morning air around him, Jade's eyes were drawn upward, above the black breaker and the burning hills, to the dim orb directly overhead. He craned his neck and squinted to make out the definition on its surface—the face that mythically looked back at earth. But the air was thick with sulfurous smog; he could barely see the perimeter behind the haze. Yet its glow was irresistible. It was an omnipresence, a guiding light for his alien self. He'd been distracted at first, but then excited by the ubiquitous talk of that orb—in the hallways at school, in the booths and kitchen at Wally's, on street corners, in his ruminations with Lucy. Would it really happen?

If a man could walk there, Jade now mused aloud to himself, this young man could walk away from here. He could even fly. That close to the cool moon, his wings would never melt.

3
The Ex-Pells

March 1969

Jade was an awkward sight. Barely 18, he looked more like 15, with certain incongruous adult features that made him seem out of focus to the casual observer—the nose of a man surrounded by the face of a boy, feet too big for his long spindly legs, hands too big and arms too long for his sleeves. He was slight in build, more wiry than just skinny, with a head full of unruly curls that failed to make an intended statement about the changing times—too long in the front, too short in the back. In the midst of a late growth spurt, his narrow frame had elongated, allowing him to catch up, finally, to his peers—at least in height. He was a hair under six feet tall but weighed no more than 150 pounds and appeared to be a threat to no one.

Other guys his age in this hard knocks valley were already men, muscled and menacing. To ward off attacks, Jade had to rely on his easily provoked internal rage in lieu of physical strength. When he was much younger, Alice had had enough of his temper and, rather than trying to suppress it she channeled it, teaching him how to use his rage.

"No one has your back, you know," she told him when he was 10, when she still called him Shay. He'd been getting pummeled on occasion by the migrant kids and White farm boys in central Jersey. "Sorry about that, but it's true. You don't have a big brother, or a cousin, or even a big friend."

"Or a father," he said, looking up at her accusingly.

"Correct," she said, dousing the inference with a wave and a shrug. "You know I don't like violence. In fact, I hate it. But sometimes you just have to throw yourself into a fight, because if you don't, you're going to continue to get hurt. That nose of yours...good God."

She hugged him for a moment, then pushed back and stood up tall in front of him, taking a wide stance, one foot back and the other forward, her shoulders loosening, her fists in the air in front of her.

"Ok, here are the rules. Don't start a fight you can't finish. Don't look for fights, avoid them if you can. But if you cannot, and you know someone is coming for you, it is absolutely imperative that you hit him before he hits you. Let your anger help you. Use it. The instant you feel it rise, get in those first two or three punches," she said, her voice louder, as if she herself were getting angry.

He wasn't sure how she knew anything about fighting, but he knew she was strong and that she was agile and was likely sure of herself when she was young. By the way she held herself before him, he was certain she'd defended herself more than once.

"Swing fast and don't stop," she'd told him, jabbing her fists toward him. "Use those long arms. Go for his nose first, then his teeth." She emphasized each of these with a hard jab that stopped just short of Jade's face. He stepped back. She bounced on her toes. "No matter how big they are," she said, breathing harder now, "guys hate to get hit in the nose 'cause it hurts like hell. Stuns them." He could vouch for that observation, having been stunned by more than his fair share of direct hits to his beak. He just figured it was because his nose was hard to miss.

"And if you hit 'em in the kisser, he'll stop dead for a moment," Alice said, pausing her jabbing dance, "because guys know that missing front teeth won't get them very far with the girls. So, when the guy pauses to check his teeth, that's when you hit him hard in the gut or, better yet, in the sternum. Knock the wind out of him. In either case, don't wait a single second!" She demonstrated another power punch that ended just inches from his chest. "And after that, if he keeps coming, kick him in the balls and run like hell."

She pantomimed how that was done and Jade covered himself instinctively, shaking his head. "No! I'm not doing that!" he protested. "No way."

But she insisted. She crouched down in front of him so their eyes were at the same level. "It's your last resort, Shay. Your final bullet. If your first punches don't stop him, you must go for the balls."

Then she gave him a soft poke in the forehead with her fist and watched his rage rise quickly. "Remember this," she said. "It's not the size of the lion in the fight; it's the size of the fight in the lion." Just from that one tap to his head, she could see the lion in his eyes.

Also, thanks to Alice, all was not lost in the appearance game for Jade. He had an incomplete version of her features, her Made in America look. Square jaw, strong chin, wide forehead, high cheekbones, full mouth, thick hair. His was reddish brown and wavy, unlike Alice's now, but she'd said his hair color was what hers looked like at his age. His skin had an olive tone, while hers was pale pink with a faint sprinkle of freckles. His nose was also a mismatch for hers—the pert little button above her full lips. His was a bulbous thing with a slight bump on the ridge. Skin and nose—no doubt leftovers from whomever his father was.

Still, Jade did have Alice's defining feature—large, wide-set, pale green eyes under a ridge of dark eyebrows. She called them cat eyes, but Jade wouldn't let her say that in public. In Alice, that combination of light eyes and dark hair often distracted passersby, and Jade had long ago noticed the same effect for himself. People stared a little too long. As a young guy trying to stay out of the limelight, he would never get used to the awkward gawking.

"You look like an alien," Rocco Bondagio told Jade more often than he cared to hear it. Rocco had the same entitled perspective as Jade's other pal, Free Freeman, but his delivery had an off-putting edge to it, unlike Free's toothy, honest ignorance. Ever since the three boys met at Pell Academy, Rocco had been attempting to fill the role of ringleader—the one with his own car, the self-appointed idea guy, the first to speak up in every situation, the leading edge of the group of three. By far the shortest of them, Rocco was always the first up for action—a joy ride, a provocation, a fight. On the inspiring front, though, he fell short, not just in stature, but in temperament. He wore the short man's burden in the thrust of his jaw. A bitter guy who jumped at every chance to elevate himself by putting down someone else, even a friend, even one of his two best friends. A plumber's son with a new '69 Chevy Camaro, Rocco lorded over Jade with his family's newfound suburban status, but he couldn't rid himself of the valley thug that lurked in his own shadow. Rocco was always getting in the way of his undeclared mission in life—to prove that he was tougher and smarter than his father. Jade had no such burden.

Free, on the other hand, was a native of the burbs and a perfect fit for his nickname. Robert Freeman, Jr., an oversized, occasionally bright, but mostly lazy, thick-armed, red headed fun boy, born and raised in The Highlands. His dad was a second-generation insurance business owner at a time when America was made for insurance. Like Rocco, Free looked just like his dad, but he wasn't out to top his father's success. He just wanted to coast in his shadow. Booted out of Pell along with Rocco after sophomore year, Free continued on his chosen path of least resistance, confident that his dad would take care of him—his Junior, his namesake.

Free and Rocco were inseparable—now living in the same neighborhood, their fathers in the same country club, their matching failure at Pell a bonding moment that sealed them together in a crucible of infamy. Early in the summer of '67, when they had learned that their sometimes Pell friend Jade Flynn had decided not to return to the private school that they had been ejected from, they recruited him with gusto into their ex-Pell club.

"Get it?" Free had declared as if Jade were a stone. "Expelled? Ex-Pell?" He'd jumped around in a circle, waving his thick arms, flopping his head back, howling at his own idiotic enlightenment.

"Jesus Christ, Free, they should've kicked you out in first year," Rocco had cracked, while trying to wedge his boot under Free's giant feet, to trip him in his circle dance.

By the fall of '67, Jade was relieved to be part of this gang of two, now three. All of them were ex-private school transfers, new guys at Ebonton High, entering in the difficult junior year. And while Jade was accustomed to being the new kid at a school, it was comforting to have comrades for the intimidating trial of breaking into a well-established clique-bound mob of hormone-infused public high school students. Ebonton had three times as many students as Pell, the atmosphere was much less restricted by the rules and discipline of a private school, and the mix of students was far more eclectic.

First and foremost, there were girls. Lots of them. Seemingly everywhere. After two years at an all-boys high school, it was mesmerizing for the three Ex-Pells, especially Free, who was immediately drunk with the joy of being surrounded by all kinds of females—girls his age, girls younger, and girls older. Three hundred sixty degrees of girls. It didn't matter to him what they looked like or said; he was simply ecstatic in their company. And, of course, they loved him. He was big and just smart enough, but silly and carefree, all about fun, which the girls found endearing, a few of them more intimately than others. Rocco was more soldier-like in the presence of so many females for the first time since elementary school, especially the fully developed versions. He behaved more like a cold-hearted dad than a hormone-infested boy. He considered the Ebonton girls frivolous and petty, even unnecessary. It gave him new opportunities to ridicule Free, who took the little general's verbal taunts with abandoned laughter, further endearing Free to the girls and compounding Rocco's frustration.

Jade was quietly awed by the girls' casual familiarity with other boys. He very much wanted to be in the shoes of one of those lucky guys, but he was far less openly propelled by his urges than Free or any of the other boys, mainly thanks—or no thanks—to Alice. Over the years, she had taught him way too much about girls—biological details that took some of the excitement out of the mysteries of the female, and plenty of lessons about respecting girls' intuition, recognizing their positive traits, and understanding the unfairness of society's limitations over them.

All of that made sense to Jade, but in the presence of so many new girls all around him, he knew he could never fully understand Alice's ministrations until he got to know at least one of those girls. Their very presence was such a stirring distraction that he simply could not wait to have a girlfriend. More than anything, Jade was relieved that he was released from the prison of Pell, where access to female humans was limited to two opportunities: finding an excuse to go to the campus library to stare in awe at the middle age librarian's very much covered but quite large and pointy breasts, or waiting for the rare occasions to interact with the mostly shy, reserved students from the all-girls Catholic school seven miles away.

At Ebonton High, there was also a lot more hair. It was 1967, and while the national unraveling of community standards had not yet hit Ebonton, there was ample evidence at the high school that the revolution was coming. At Pell, the boys couldn't let their hair grow much longer than a military cut; but at Ebonton, boys grew unkempt bangs, their ears covered by hair, lips topped by attempts to grow moustaches, and curly hair wildly breaking out of its age-old restraints among both girls and boys—most prominently among the small contingent of Negro students. That, too, was something new for the Ex-Pells—Negroes. Also, Puerto Ricans, and a few Orientals.

At Pell, the students came from rising middle class and upper middle class White families. Jade had been the partial exception—White but not rising anywhere. At Ebonton, the Ex-Pells found students from all economic strata and races—although still predominantly White—and a clear division into social castes: the jocks and cheerleaders, the academic nerds, the arts and theater crowd, the loners and shadowy types, three small and separate groups of non-Whites, and, most prominently, the hard knocks leather and chain set, the White boys who were already angry and dangerous men, and the girls who clung to these malcontents—tough, sulky, sinister girls who'd threaten to rip the face off anyone who looked twice at them.

The Ex-Pells knew they did not fit into any one of these cliques, so they had to form their own—an ad hoc nameless alliance, unannounced and publicly identified only by their traveling emblem of presumed superiority—Rocco's shiny new faux-leather-topped '69 Camaro coup, a modestly trimmed suburban car, with standard-looking suspension and factory wheel covers, but secretly harboring four on the floor, a Weber downdraft, Shaeffer magnetos, four-part Hobart fuel injection, and a 327 V8 monster under the hood.

The day after the start of fall semester, the leather boys smelled a challenge when Rocco rolled onto campus in his rich-kid machine. They lurked and shifted their bodies away from the car, heads turned toward it but eyes averted, muttering to one another. One of their Harleys barked into life and a surly, leather-bound, grease mopped guy sat up high on it, revved the engine with a sudden explosion, and then shouted something nasty to one of the gang's girls. The leather bad boys were primping—but they were watching, too.

Rocco held his chin as high as he could stretch it during the Camaro's inaugural slow-waltz entry into the school parking lot. He was proud of the discreetly hidden weapons of power he'd installed under the Camaro's hood. He pushed in the clutch and hammered the accelerator. The Camaro roared a blast of bass-rattling response to the Harley that felt like a jet breaking the sound barrier. Jade hoisted himself as tall as possible in the coup's hunched back seat. Free rode gun, his big red hairy arm hanging out the open window, his fist flexed.

"Blood will spill," Rocco declared.

Jade wished the Ex-Pells had some bonding experience that tied them intrinsically together, something other than their ignominious exits from Pell and an enviable set of wheels that didn't belong to him. But the Ex-Pells were simply the remainders of a less than subtle social division. They were the latecomers who didn't factor in to any group, the former private school preppies who weren't welcome to the commoner fold, who were assumed by the public school kids to think of themselves as above the masses—a false distinction that threatened to derail Jade's enthusiasm for his new crew of three.

The war with the leathers never came. Weeks of machine roaring in the school parking lot simply filled the already sick sky with more smoke—nothing else. In the end, the two sides declared a bloodless truce, leaving Rocco's prediction precisely where his other leadership attempts had landed. The unspoken agreement that ended the confrontation unraveled in an unexpectedly, unintentionally courteous fashion.

Rocco later told the story that he and Leather, whose name turned out to be Bob, decided to settle it without an audience. They drove their hot machines to the quarter-mile strip behind the Gulph Mill culm dump and took three runs at drag racing each other—each guy driving the other guy's machine. Leather Bob won two out of three. Then they switched back to their own vehicles, and Rocco took two out of those three.

For the next hour, Rocco and Leather Bob stood in the smoldering shadows of the culm dump, inspecting each other's engines with the camaraderie of two soldiers who'd just won a battle together. Rocco reported to the Ex-Pells that he'd never ridden a motorcycle until that day, and, for once, Jade considered the possibility that Rocco might have a leadership role to play yet, someday, somewhere.

The Ex-Pells never heard what Leather Bob told his own crew, but from that day forward, over the final two years of high school, neither side spoke to each other nor ever acknowledged each other again.

When Jade brought Lucy Melburn into the collection of odd-men-out, Rocco and Free were thrilled to have a new audience. Lucy socialized on the high school fringes, but, like Jade and his pals, she was an outcast, for reasons at first unclear to the Ex-Pells. She was female, of course, utterly confounding them and creating a new reality that brought out in the boys a clumsy theatrical playfulness, soon pivoting into combative divisiveness. Three fools stumbling over one another to please Lucy, to make her laugh, to impress her with their physical and not quite intellectual prowess. After their boyish antics subsided and the reality of Lucy's relationship with Jade began to set in, Rocco and Free grew hostile toward one another for a period, and sometimes toward Lucy. Their ambivalence and frustration about this fourth member of their outcast crew were exacerbated by Lucy's undeniable beauty, her brutally cutting wit, and her mysterious air—as if she were hiding something. She was unlike any of the girls in the various cliques.

Her appearance played havoc on the boys—long, silky black hair; dark, wide-set eyes; flawless skin that seemed permanently tanned; a perfectly proportioned body. All these distractions were disabling to the Ex-Pells when Lucy's acid tongue let loose. She had more street smarts than all three of them, and she was tougher. Buried anger. Repressed terror. She held it all in, barely. When Rocco started mocking her by singing "Lucy in the Sky with Diamonds" in a fake drugged chant, she cut him down in a single droll comment. "Rocco, you're not just a physical midget, you're a mental one."

By the boys' senior year, and Lucy's junior year, the four friends settled into their respective roles—Lucy tacitly in charge, Rocco further embittered, Free freer than ever to chase other girls, and Jade bouncing on a string between ecstasy and misery, both lucky and unlucky to be the one who was Lucy's boyfriend.

In Jade's dream plan in spring 1969, he saw himself parting ways with these fellow misfits by summer's end. Free was off to a private Connecticut college in the fall and, around the same time, Rocco would turn his summer stint at his father's new plumbing supply company into a full-time job. He said his dad had greased somebody's palm and got him out of the draft. "Set for life," he told his pals.

But Jade was the one who would be set, or so he believed. After a summer of full-time work at the diner, he'd have enough money to be on his own, to be rid of all his burdens—his drunken mother in their falling-down house, his gorgeous but sullen girlfriend, whose seesaw moods reminded him too much of his mother's swings through booze binges and sobriety lapses—and his pals, Rocco and Free, whose feet of clay secured them to a long local life that he could not imagine for himself. In his alien's mind, his dreamer's insight, Jade had a visceral sense of eternal sadness about this valley, with its befouled earth, broken souls, and certain doom. He decided he would be gone from it by summer's end—if not sooner.

4
The Offer

Jade was bussing his last table in Wally's Diner on a cold evening when two men pushed through the front door. The place was empty, all the regular hangers-on had bolted after the furnace failed to fire up. Dee was at the register cashing out for the day. She tossed a glance Jade's way before slamming the drawer shut with a ring and offering a flat welcome to the two late arrivals.

"We're closing, fellas, but I can get you some lukewarm coffee while we wrap it up here." To Jade, her usual effervescent lilt could not have been more absent.

The men ignored her and took a booth against the far wall with a view of all doorways and the front parking lot. They kept their trench coats on and the older one, in his Bogey fedora, nodded to Dee. She turned her back to them at the counter and splashed coffee into two cups.

"You Flynn?" the younger guy called out across the diner. It was more of a threat than a greeting.

Jade set the dishpan on the counter and wiped his hands with a rag. He nodded.

"Come on over here, son. Take a seat. Need to talk to you." This was the older guy. A shade more pleasant than his punk partner.

The older guy faked a smile to Dee as she plunked the coffees on their table. "We only need a minute here, honey."

Dee smirked at him and went back to work at the cash register. Jade could feel her eyes following him as he walked toward the men. He glanced at her and confirmed his suspicion. This did not look right.

The older man spoke first. "James Flynn?" The man's fedora was tipped at an angle over one of his eyes. He peered at Jade with the uncovered eye. Jade returned the stare in silence. This guy was no Bogey.

Jade smiled to himself when the guy took off his hat, uncovering a head full of silver hair slicked straight back.

"Something funny, son?" the man said, freezing the hand holding the hat.

Jade wiped the smile off his face with his wrist and shook his head, still holding the man's stare.

"Sit down, boy." There was appeasement in his tone, and he feigned a doting smile, his dull eyes wrinkling with the effort.

The younger guy shifted over to let Jade sit next to him in the booth. "Fuckin' freezin' in here," he muttered. He crooked an arm over Jade's shoulder and breathed on him through an upside-down grin. Cigarettes and whiskey, sallow teeth, slimy lips. "Keep me warm, honey," he said, and puckered the slippery mouth. Jade recoiled, pulling out from under his grip.

Whiskey Breath barked a laugh at his own hilarity. He fished his coat pockets and tossed a pack of filterless Camels onto the table. His fingers were covered in silver rings, the skin mottled green under the cheap ornaments. Both men looked uncomfortable in their white shirts and ties. Especially Whiskey Breath.

"We have something you're going to like, kid," Silver Head said as he plucked a Camel from the pack and with a flick of his wrist popped open a gold Zippo. "But the thing is, we need to know *now* if you want it." His partner leaned into the flame with his own cigarette.

Jade glanced over his shoulder to see if Dee was still there, and then turned back to look Silver Head in the eyes. "Who *are* you?"

Silver Head and Whiskey Breath tilted their heads back and exhaled simultaneous clouds of smoke, as if they'd practiced the bit. The younger guy pushed his last puff out with a punchy laugh.

"There's a job waiting for you at the Macson plant, if you want it," Silver Head announced. "Hard work, eight-hour day, morning and afternoon breaks. Best wage in the valley. A shot at union scale if you're good." He squared his shoulders and lifted his chin to look down at Jade. "And, on top of that, you'll be doing something for your country. Helping us keep those Commie slope heads off our shores."

"Why me?" Jade lifted his frame to meet Silver Head's, and then turned to glare at Whiskey Breath, who was leaning too close again.

"Cuz you're perfect for the job, tough guy," Whiskey sneered. "So big and powerful and *scary*. Woo." He forced a laugh over Jade's head, took another drag on his Camel, and spit a fleck of tobacco off his lip in Jade's direction. Jade felt heat rising in his neck and face.

"Our boss says you'll take the job, son," Silver Head said. It was his turn. Good cop. This time, to Jade, he sounded like Ward Cleaver, trying too hard to be a dad. "He knows you want college in the fall, son, but you can't get there working here. Not enough money. You met our boss a few years ago. Mr. Hafferty."

Jade was about to say he was not going to college, and that they had the wrong guy, but he hesitated. "The Commissioner?"

Silver Head nodded, grinning just like old Ward.

Hafferty's name had made the rounds every day in the diner chatter, which was mainly about local politics. The Judge and Jury, as Jade and Wally called the hard-core regulars, ruled the chatter from their corner booths. Depending on who had the floor, County Commissioner Hafferty was credited with or blamed for every event that happened in Ebonton, the county seat. When it was a negative, The Judge and Jury used the name with caution, and the other regulars muttered it with a reluctant reverence. The diner had eyes and ears.

Jade knew Hafferty long before he started listening in on the daily gossip at the diner. He had met him four years earlier, just as he was finishing up eighth grade, less than a year after he'd started at the diner. Hafferty came in at closing time. He sat in the same corner booth that Silver and Whiskey now occupied. Jade's first impression at the time had been that Hafferty was just another talking suit; but when he met him up close, he saw something else. The suit alone made him look like a movie star, with its fine cloth and tailored fit. His face was scrubbed bright pink, even his fingernails looked manicured. His smile had seemed permanently pasted on his glowing face, his teeth perfectly aligned, unnaturally. A gold circular pin with a small shield had gleamed on his lapel.

Across the narrow table from Jade during that short visit, Hafferty had loomed above him like a bird of prey, his smile freezing into a rictus of hunger, his eyes larger than real behind thick lenses. He made his point quickly. "Son, I'm here to congratulate you. You've won a scholarship to Pell Academy."

That night, Alice had said Jade could not accept the scholarship; she'd been adamant. She'd told him to stay away from *that man*. Then, a few days later, she'd changed her tune—suddenly weird with exaggerated excitement. Jade had seen her make an about-face a few times before, but this time it had been hard for her to hide her bitterness, despite her best attempt at a Pollyanna smile. He'd been certain she did not want this for him. Yet, somehow, the adult with the most persistent will her son had ever known had been made to change her mind against her wishes. "He's a big politician—the biggest around here—and he likes to help young people who don't have privileges," she'd told him, with an odd stiffness in her voice. "He shows up like this once in a while with a special offer. People usually don't refuse it." When Jade lasted four semesters and then bailed out of Pell Academy, Alice took him out to dinner for the first time since he was ten. For his third and fourth year, he attended Ebonton High, and was now six weeks from graduation.

"I remember him," Jade told Silver Head. "He was nice to me, not sure why. Got me to go to Pell Academy. Tried it. Wasn't for me."

"Yeah, we know all about that," Whiskey Breath snarled, smoke spilling out of his moist maw. "It was more like they didn't like *you*." He puffed the rest of the smoke toward Jade. "Now? Who knows why, but the Commissioner wants you to be a college boy. But you'll have to work your balls off for it first. So don't fuck up this time, asshole. Ask me? A scrawny shit like you will get eaten up in that bomb factory. You won't last a fuckin' week. I don't see college in your future, boy. You'll be dead before you get there." He snapped another drag on his Camel and poured a cloud into Jade's face. Jade backed out of the booth and stood up, his fists clenched in front of him.

28

Silver Head slammed his coffee cup on the table, and Whiskey ducked sideways to avoid the splash. "Shut up, Zulkowski! We have a mission to complete here. We offer this kid a good paying job, and if he doesn't accept, it's on you. Got it? You're a moron, you know that? The boss will not be happy with you." Ward Cleaver was off the stage.

Zulkowski's hand shook as he took another drag and turned away to blow his smoke at the closed window. Still standing, Jade glared at the back of Zulkowski's head and calculated that if his left fist made solid contact with that greaseball head, Whiskey Breath's bloody face would make a nice mess on the window. When he tightened his hand and set his knee on the seat for leverage, he felt a vice grip on his cocked left arm. Silver Head. Ward Cleaver's evil twin. Jade yanked his arm free and stood up again, but Silver's glare held him in place.

A car swung abruptly into the parking lot, and Whiskey muttered to the window, "Oh shit."

It was a new shiny black Fleetwood. Jade saw the back door open slowly and watched a man in an open trench coat over a dark suit step onto the parking lot. The man's eyeglasses caught the reflection of the setting sun as he looked directly at the three of them in the booth on the other side of the window.

"I guess Mr. Hafferty found the time to meet with you after all, son," Silver Head said. Ward Cleaver was back. He clenched a frozen smile at his partner.

In a single movement, Zulkowski doused his Camel in the ashtray, slid out of the booth, and leapt to his feet. "I gotta hit the head," he blurted. He grazed Jade with his shoulder and headed toward the restrooms.

Silver Head barked after him. "You better stay in there, Zook, if you know what's good for you." He crushed his cigarette in the ashtray and stood up next to the booth, squaring his shoulders and pulling down the tail of his shiny suit jacket. Jade turned around just as the front door swung open. Hafferty swept in like he owned the place.

"How are ya, dear?" he called to Dee, his teeth flashing as he strode toward the corner booth. "Coffee please, my love. Black, one cube." Dee moved quickly. Despite herself, she forced a smile, a subtle deference reserved for men of power and rank. Jade had seen this act from her, and it had always disappointed him.

"Stanley!" Hafferty announced. "How's our little deal going? Mr. Flynn ready to go to work?" He glanced at Jade as he held onto Silver Stanley's handshake, pulling the bigger man off-balance and leaning into his face. "Where's your sidekick, Stan? Behaving himself?"

Stanley teetered close to Hafferty and then backed away, his face assuming the guilt he'd been assigned. "In the...he's in the head," he stammered. Hafferty shot a glance toward the men's room door.

"Go get him. Bring him outside. Wait for me."

Stanley saluted with a short nod and strode toward the men's room. Hafferty turned to Jade, who was standing up straight next to the booth, attempting to minimize his size disadvantage. Hafferty, an inch taller but sixty pounds heavier, puffed up his chest, tilted his head back, and stared down his nose at Jade.

"Sit down, son," he said, flashing his neon smile. He took his time pulling off his trench coat and tossing it into the booth. He squared his thick shoulders and shrugged his suit coat into place. No hat for this guy, Jade thought as he sat down. A Kennedy wannabe. He'd spent way too much time oiling his coif to wreck it with an old-fashioned fedora.

There was a rumbling sound in the men's room and then a shout. Stanley emerged with Zulkowski in tow. Stanley held his head high as they paced quickly toward the front exit. Zulkowski's chin was on his chest. Jade felt the passive warmth of vindication, but he knew that guys like Zook resisted education. Whatever punishment he was to receive, Zook would absorb it only long enough to pass it down in a more primitive form to a weaker target. Kick a dog, beat up a younger guy, punch his girlfriend. Jade's warm righteous feeling faded. He knew he'd see this ugly man again.

Hafferty remained standing while his men waited silently at the door as Dee unlocked it, let them out, and locked it again. Without looking at Jade or Hafferty, she delivered Hafferty's coffee and disappeared into the kitchen. Hafferty took a deep breath, exhaled, and canvassed the empty diner as if there were a crowd awaiting one of his tumid orations. He unbuttoned his suit jacket, shook out his shoulders like he'd just finished a workout, and sat down across from Jade. He punched his left hand into the air over the table and glared at a massive gold and silver watch on his wrist. He wore thick horn-rimmed glasses, and he seemed to struggle focusing. When he turned from his Rolex, his eyes met Jade's—fuzzy blue blurs bulging twice their size behind funhouse lenses. The magnified orbs were ice cold and did not match his smile.

Under his dark suit jacket, Hafferty wore a bright red tie over a crisp white shirt. In his lapel, there was a new version of the disc Jade had seen four years earlier—this time it was a monogrammed gold circle—a large H in the middle, with a smaller M and D on either side. A matching circle was mounted on the gold horizontal bar of his tie clip and another on his gold cufflinks.

Hafferty thrust his thick right hand across the table. The proffered paw hovered palm down over Jade's, giving him no alternative but to take the inferior position. "It's good to see you again, son. I'm sure you remember me." The hand engulfed Jade's and squeezed. Jade gritted his jaw and tried to look unphased.

"Yes, sir."

5

The Seer

Jade remembered that it had happened in February, but he was haunted by the idea that there must have been something that led up to it, some change in her that he'd missed. It seemed to have come on too suddenly. Something—aside from the weird weather—had to have triggered her unexpected recovery and then the dramatic reversal. Almost overnight that week, Alice had switched from a long-practiced binge drinker to a sober, clear-eyed, younger version of her old self. And then, a little more than a month later, she fell off a cliff into a weeklong swoon, weeping and howling. And sleeping. Endless sleeping.

After that reversal, Alice had become a reliable drunk through the first few weeks of spring. Not a sloppy or nasty drunk, but a consistently overbearing one. Especially after a night with her favorite, Four Roses. She'd also started to smoke again and then quickly devolved into a chain smoker. Lighting filterless Luckies end to end, to keep what she claimed to be "offensive molecules of clean air" out of her lungs. "What difference does it make?" she asked him one night. "We inhale poison all day every day here. We live in the *real* valley of ashes, Seamus. Not the fictitious one." A fragment of allusion from the once clear-minded would-be professor.

She spewed her cynicism as if she knew the joke was on her. "Gotta die from something, dahling," she'd say, affecting her Marlene Dietrich pose—thick-lidded eyes, head tilted back, shoulders slouched, her elbow resting on her knee, her cigarette notched in her long fingers, a turned-down smile lingering on her pillowy lips. The act, at first, had made Jade laugh. Now, it was pathetic. He hated the smoking as much as the drinking, but he knew that it would be the steady drinking that would push their lives to the brink.

Alice was also a seer; at least that's what Jade had come to believe. She began seeing things sometime in late autumn. Then, there was the break of clarity during the late February thaw; but after her fall from that brief plateau, the visions returned. By the end of April, Jade wasn't quite sure how to decipher her clairvoyant messages, how to distinguish them from her drunken trances laced with her new religious incantations.

Alice's pious bent had come on just as suddenly as these other personality shifts. It was a mixture of explosive inspiration and indoctrinated ritual, resurrected somehow from a past unknown to Jade. One night, during a few days of sobriety in early April, she declared to him that she had evolved from mere prayerfulness into an alternative spirit, a direct connection to a Catholic saint from the fifteenth century. She did not offer a name for that saint. She just used the term reincarnation.

In her new sober and holy state, her religious fervor was manifested in icon worship, candle lighting obsession, a dependency on intercession through her fellow saints, and rote repetition in prayer, with what seemed to Jade a constant rattling of her newly acquired rosary, an absent-minded mumbling, a breathless swooning. But, just days later, when she reintroduced Four Roses to the mix, her elevated state became inflamed, her connections to other worlds feverish and uncontrolled, and, to Jade, incoherent and frightening—and very suspect. He was well accustomed to drunken rants by Alice, but this new combination was hard to follow. At times, he wasn't sure if she was talking to him or to someone in her visions. He was determined to resist alarm, to stay grounded, anchored by his sense of doubt, his instinctive caution, while he watched his mother, his only life companion, inexplicably drift away.

Still, Jade was certain there was a specific cause, a trigger for this cascade of personality changes, and he was sure it had come to a head at the end of that mysterious weather transformation in late winter. When he asked about the name he'd heard her calling out—Martin?—her eyes went blank, and the muttering of prayer resumed.

Jade was relieved when Alice announced one evening that she'd joined Saint John the Divine parish in Sheldon. He considered it a positive development, an anchor in reality for her new religious ardor. She did not suggest that he join as well, but he decided he'd do so if she did ask, just to keep her grounded, to help her get exposed perhaps to other religious people, who he assumed lived somewhat in the real world. But a week had barely passed before Alice quit the parish. Despite her outward adherence to Catholic rituals, her passionate expression of her very personal relationship with God conflicted with the new post-Vatican II ecumenical obligations of the parish. After Mass on the second Sunday of her new membership, she had an explosive argument with the pastor, who had been greeting departing parishioners in the nave of the church. The argument echoed throughout the cavernous building, she later told Jade, and was witnessed, she said, by a mob of sycophantic weaklings. "Pathetic sheep who understood nothing about the gift of my relationship with God and his mother," she proclaimed. Within days, Alice launched a worship of her own devising, formalizing it by converting their front parlor into a grotto of idolatry.

That was the term Alice used. The parlor was now The Grotto. The couch, coffee table, and sofa chairs had been moved into a tighter arrangement against the kitchen wall to make room for small tables and other platforms for statues of saints—Joseph, Christopher, Theresa of Avila, Benedict, and others. The main feature, a life size statue of the mother of Jesus—the Blessed Virgin, as Alice had called her—stood in the center of the room near the piano. Alice had built a short wall of neatly piled rocks surrounding the sides and back of the Virgin Mother and set a thick candle in red votive glass on a small altar at the statue's feet.

As May approached, Jade wondered if he'd ever figure out what had triggered Alice's fall from grace in March. If her visions and rantings continued, he realized he might never find out. And when he decided to accept Mr. Hafferty's offer to work at Macson Munitions—a decision Alice vehemently opposed—her exhortations increased in number and intensity. In her altered state, she had warned him about satanic fires at that factory, and that the war ordnance plant was the source of evil in the dark heart of Ebonton, which Alice called "Gomorrah." One night, her eyes huge with fright and her head convulsing, her wild Medusa curls wavering, Alice warned Jade, with a wide-eyed mask of certainty, that dark faces would both threaten and save him "in that place of wickedness."

Jade dusted off these desperate warnings as typical drunken ramblings from his mother, the reincarnated saint from the fifteenth century. But, as he would come to learn in June, after his first day on the new job, he would have to consider the possibility that, for the last few months, this woman with otherworldly connections may have been talking to him from a perspective he might consider taking a bit more seriously.

6
Unfortunate Son

April 1969

Jade was about to be free at last from high school and felt the end approaching to his relationship with Lucy, whose father, like Alice, was a drunk—a common adult condition that seemed difficult to avoid in this dark valley. There were just two other friends—Rocco and Free. The rest were acquaintances, schoolmates. As for the two guys, he would say they were boorish, and they'd say the same about him, if they knew what it meant. But Alice would disagree with them, should she ever meet them. She would say her son was civilized, and she'd say it as a matter of fact, not prejudice.

During their early years together, and even later, during her plateaus of sobriety, Alice had done her best to teach Jade a modicum of civility. She had rules. She'd introduced these to him when he was quite young, so, by now, he'd converted most of them to instinct. He not only had exceptional table manners, but he knew how to set a table, even for multiple courses, even though they never had guests and they'd never had more than a single course. Even so, Alice always insisted on him setting their table for the inconsistent dinners she shared with him. She also had rules for dealing with adults—rules she'd called "social decorum," encoded for him by the repeated word, "respect." He knew to stand when a woman came into the room, to shake her hand only if she offered hers first, to make eye contact upon introduction to an adult and to wait for the adult to be seated before he sat. He knew to hold the door for others before entering himself, to wipe his shoes at the threshold of a house and to doff his hat in others' homes and in places of worship—the latter experience having occurred just once so far. He knew how to listen and when to speak up. He knew when to defer and when to insist, but always with sensitivity to others' feelings, unless, of course, the other person was hopelessly uncouth. These were her basic rules, and, if given the opportunity, she would assert that there were other finer attunements beyond mere rules that she'd taught him, ways to develop empathy, to overcome natural selfishness, and to learn to adapt, if not blend, but to stand out when appropriate.

But Jade and his two friends were teenage boys, driven by their hormones to repel accepted behavior. So, he hid his civility from his pals. It was not difficult.

Imminent flight was also part of the teen code to which Jade and his two male friends subscribed. If you could see an exit, you'd take it, or at least feign in that direction, so your friends could be assured that your flight was inevitable. Like them, you had to announce regularly that you couldn't take another day among these people, in this school, this house, this town. For Rocco and Free, their determination to fly from their homes and towns was less authentic, less desperate than Jade's. Compared to life with Alice on Reston Street, their family lives in the Highlands on the other side of the mountain were cushioned cradles. Their futures were circumscribed. Jade's future looked like his present. His rebel's claim on flight was very real. He needed to get out. If not, he'd die young here; he was certain of it.

Thanks to the mysterious Mr. Hafferty, Jade's new job at Macson, the biggest factory in Ebonton—the largest city at the center of the old coal valley—provided grist to his plan. He would earn much more money than he could at Wally's—enough to afford his own place by the end of the summer, and then, in a month or two, take off for points west, which meant just one place—California Dreamin'. Don't look back. Goodbye, Alice. Goodbye, Lucy. Goodbye, Smell Hollow. That's what Free called Jade's smog bound valley town. From his perch in the fresh air burbs, Free could disparage the valley dwellers with cheeky confidence.

Jade's plan was flawed on two fronts. The first: Alice. She was on to him. She'd begun to lean on him over the last few years, and she wasn't about to let him go now, no matter what escape plans he might have in mind. She also loved him—inconsistently, perhaps, but there was no doubt. The shabby little house they lived in—given to them by her mystery donor—meant nothing to Alice. If one of those eighteen-wheelers thundering by the front door happened to veer off course and take out the front of the house, Alice probably wouldn't care. She might even be relieved. But, if that happened, Jade would be sure to fly away, and, without him, she'd be lost.

She'd told him so countless times that spring, as if the very persistence of that drunken repetition would cancel the plans she suspected he was cooking up. Once, in a holy musing in The Grotto, she shouted it out. She declared in a preacher's calling that the Lord, our God, and his holy and sacred Blessed Mother forbade him to leave her. Jade's plan was thus proscribed.

The second front was the one he'd been dismissing whenever Lucy or Rocco or Free brought it up. Vietnam. Hard to ignore. The war was on everyone's mind, in every conversation at Wally's Diner, in the classrooms at school, in the newspaper he read daily at the diner, and always on TV news, which Jade only occasionally witnessed since he and Alice hadn't had a working television in more than a year.

The news seeped into his reluctant consciousness through the chatter all around him—the gore and mayhem of a war without a goal, the body count like some sick sports game, the permanently ruined men returning home all over the valley. Despite the new President's promises to scale back U.S. forces in Vietnam, everything else pointed to escalation, an endless quagmire. There were 500,000 American soldiers there, and American deaths had reached 35,000, with thousands more wounded. After the Tet Offensive in 1968, Americans seemed to lose faith in victory, and now the feeling was contagious. Protests against the war were escalating across the country—college and high school students, radicals like the SDS and the Black Panthers, even Vietnam veterans. The push against America's war was everywhere—except in Ebonton and the surrounding Black Diamond Valley, a place that seemed not only abandoned by the hopeful, but lost in a time gone by, shielded from the rest of the world by its own willful absence from it.

When Nixon announced troop reductions in April, Jade was certain his luck was turning in his favor. Yet, he and his friends doubted Nixon would follow through on those reductions, especially since draftees were still being gobbled up all around them—guys Jade had met or knew about who'd finished school ahead of him, or guys Lucy, Rocco, and Free talked about. Worse still, dead soldiers were in the news every day, arriving *en masse* at airports in ominous flag-draped boxes. At the diner, Jade had heard dozens of stories of local guys who had come home in one of those boxes.

But Jade could not accept that his fate would be decided so randomly. He had a blind eye to his own vulnerability, and he couldn't be talked out of it. His pals and his girlfriend repeatedly warned Jade that if he did not apply to and enroll in a college for the fall, he'd be drafted. Jade's retort was that he was lucky. They would overlook him, he claimed. All 18-year-olds were not being drafted, just the unlucky ones, he'd say. When Rocco first told Jade he was in the unlucky caste of 18-year-olds, Jade just laughed. But Rocco wouldn't let it go at that.

"You're from the poor side of town, pal," Rocco, the self-appointed leader, said with authority. "The side where there are two choices: sign up or get drafted. The only way out is for your daddy to buy your way out. And last I checked, your daddy's not a rich guy."

Jade had a ready retort: "I don't have a daddy, asshole! And you know that. And guess what? It's an Army rule: they won't touch a fatherless son."

In the most recent version of this exchange, Rocco rejoined with something Jade hadn't heard about. "They won't draft the son of a fallen soldier, Jade. *That's* the rule." He turned his chin up at the taller Jade and pushed back his shoulders. "You don't even know who your father was! You don't even know his name! Was he a soldier? Did he die in Korea? Maybe he's still alive—and he's not a fallen soldier. You have no idea."

Jade felt heat rush into his face and took two quick swings at Rocco's nose but missed with both. Rocco was too fast, accustomed to dodging his own father's flying fists. He danced away from Jade and taunted him with a pointed finger.

"Better find a college, pal. If you don't, you'll be comin' home in a box." As Rocco turned and strutted away, his squealing imitation of Jade sent Free into convulsions.

7

The Librarian

May 1969

Jade lay on his bed in the fading twilight, watching a spider zigzag across the cracked, once-blue ceiling. Before he lay down, he'd opened his bedroom windows to test the air, hoping against hope, and he'd got lucky. No sour sulfur blast tonight. In its place, a rare floral aroma and a hint of freshness in the air, reminding him of a place he hadn't thought about in years. The seashore.

He and Alice had moved to Reston Street just before he'd turned twelve, but he had spent little time since then thinking about where else they'd lived. He knew the litany of places described often by Alice—Vermont, where he was born; two years in a cottage in "a rough little Connecticut town" on Long Island Sound; an unclear period of time in a cabin in the Catskill woods; a few years on New Jersey's Long Beach Island. He did not need her to recount or reinvent the last place they'd lived; he remembered it well. A little crossroads town in central Jersey farmland, where he had kissed a brown-skinned girl named Rosaria, who broke his heart when she did not return from Mexico the following spring. But he and Alice had moved so often that most of his memories of these places and faces were ephemeral—shadowy vestiges of another life lived by another self.

Now tired, his senses tweaked by the gift of fresh air, he let some of those dreamy memories wash over him. Running full speed on the wet sand, Alice hollering in pursuit as he bolted into the surf—Connecticut? Jersey? Sitting on the sand in the rosy sunrise watching Alice paint another oceanside scene—a closeup of dune life or a panorama of the ever-changing horizon. The paintings, in which no human could be found, accumulated as they drifted along their meandering journey from town to town, the watercolor scenes memorializing each location, sometimes in peculiar ways. He remembered a dead horseshoe crab she'd dwelled on for days, somehow capturing its decay in slow motion strokes of her brush. She hung that painting prominently in their various dwellings until one day it was gone.

As he drifted toward sleep, he heard the rise of voices amid flashes and blurs of images. Arguments on the baseball sandlot with friends, their shouts fading echoes in the tunnel of time. Gut laughter during pissing contests in the woods. Taunting and cheering over arm wrestling at a low wobbly table in a shabby makeshift fort. The flooding rush of warmth in his loins as Rosaria took his hand and held it to her heart. And then heated cafeteria shouting, his own voice arguing that Mays was better than Mantle. Then the sudden empty silence of an auditorium filled with mum students, as he stood on a stage after winning a spelling bee alongside a red headed girl he liked who wouldn't talk to him.

The girl turned to look at him, but her face wasn't hers, it was Alice's. She was trying to say something to Jade, but she was talking around a Lucky Strike in her mouth, and he couldn't understand her.

The next moment, he was sitting up in his bed. It was dark in the room, and he smelled smoke—not from outside but from somewhere in his house. He leaped to his feet and down the steps three at a time to the kitchen. Smoke was pouring from a pot surrounded by a flame on the stove. Jade flipped off the gas, wrapped a dish towel around his hand, and pulled the smoking pot into the sink full of dishes. The cold dishwater hissed, and a cloud of steam rose from the sink, the pot crackling and pinging.

"Alice!" Jade shouted. Tufts of thick gray smoke hovered at the ceiling. He strode through the kitchen door into The Grotto and found Alice face down on the couch, the butt of a lit cigarette about to burn her dangling fingers, and an empty cocktail glass on the coffee table. She smelled sour, moldy with booze. Jade woke her, propped her on her feet, and propelled her up to bed, Alice pitching off course most of the way, and Jade carrying her up the final few steps.

As he cleaned up the kitchen, Jade tried to forget about Alice by reconstructing the segments of his dream; but it was gone, all of it. He thought about the few times recently when Alice had reminisced in broken segments about those towns and hamlets where they'd started their life together. She made it all sound romantic, but she'd change each recollection depending on her mood or state of mind at the moment. In the telling, Alice would also switch around the timing of each location, leaving Jade struggling to distinguish his real memories from his imagined dreams of their life in these places. He most often conjured glimpses of their beach life. Those were the memories he tried to trick himself into believing were real. He'd pleaded with Alice to describe what their beach bungalow looked like, but she would always decline—politely, but firmly. Jade eventually stopped pushing the issue. He had to find contentment in his imagination. Most likely, the real version of their beach life would be a disappointment if measured against his own.

Their move to the two-story house on Reston Street was a step up from a tiny apartment or a cabin or a trailer; but Jade soon learned that Mell Hollow was a hellhole—the very worst among the places he could remember. Still, Alice seemed more settled here, if not simply resigned to a loss he could not decipher. She clearly had more money, yet their home life declined. Alice did increase the frequency and quality of groceries she had arranged for delivery by Wally's friend, Abe Lever. But, in other areas, she pinched pennies even more so than before, refusing to pay to have the television or the record-player fixed or fulfilling her long-standing promise to have someone tune the old upright piano that had come with the place and that she only ever played late at night when Jade was trying to sleep, the sour notes bringing a burst of laughter from her when she was deep in her cups. One cold day after school in early 1968, Jade came home to find all her paintings burning in the oil drum in their tiny backyard. For the remainder of their time on Reston Street, the shadows on the walls where the paintings had hung remained unfilled.

The story Alice stuck to in explaining her job in this godforsaken valley, as she'd called it, was that she was a librarian. Jade at first accepted the story at face value; but it wasn't long after they'd arrived on Reston Street—just as he was about to turn thirteen—that he began to doubt her story. As far as he knew, all her previous jobs had involved working on her feet, with her hands, restaurant work, odd labor jobs—work that had kept her restless athletic body in motion. Alice did not fit his idea of a librarian. She read liberally, but he would not consider her bookish, and he could not fathom Alice sitting still for long periods, as he imagined librarians must. Why move here—all the way to Pennsylvania—to take a job she'd never done before? And didn't seem qualified for or suited to? What about the regular cash payments she continued to receive? She'd admitted that the amounts had increased in New Jersey and then again after they'd moved here to the Black Diamond Valley. If so, was the amount of the new increase so significant that they had to leave the wide-open farm country of New Jersey and move to this desolate place? So she could get a job as a librarian?

During their first months on Reston Street, Alice had never talked about her job, except to say it was the reason she was often late or completely absent in the evening. Jade believed her, but wondered—a library open so late? His opportunity to investigate came unexpectedly when he was 13, toward the end of eighth grade. After the strange Mr. Hafferty had dropped in at Wally's and offered Jade a scholarship to Pell Academy, Jade rushed home to break the news to Alice, but she didn't show up until after he'd fallen asleep. The next morning, she was gone before he arose. But, that afternoon, his classes were canceled for teacher meetings, so he decided to surprise Alice at work. He took the Number 15 upvalley to Sheldon to share his good news about high school.

The Cairstine Morgan Memorial Library in Sheldon was not an imposing structure, but to Jade, it was impressive. He felt an unexpected surge of pride in Alice as he mounted the wide stone steps to the front door of the two-story limestone building, its slate roof and carved stone windows reflecting a bygone era of prosperity in the otherwise shabby little town of Sheldon, just another Mell Hollow along the old coal line and polluted river, another collection of sagging homes and broken spirits. The building seemed misplaced here, as if it were erected by mistake, belonging instead to a brighter much larger city. At the front door, Jade felt compelled to stop and read the bronze plaque; but he could not determine from the inscription what someone named Cairstine Morgan, described as an art collector, had to do with a library or with the town of Sheldon. When he pushed through the large wooden front door and saw huge oil paintings hanging below the balcony railing, he wondered if Cairstine Morgan had meant for this to be an art museum rather than a library.

The main floor was a mountain of books—aisles of shelves eight feet high, the far walls even taller, with ladders on runners along a bank of endless spines, and, in a far corner, a black iron spiral staircase leading to a balcony. A skylight decorated with what Jade thought was religious symbolism spilled daylight in dapples and sprays of color across the recessed wooden balcony and onto the main floor. The space felt grand—

much larger than it had appeared on the outside. Jade felt another surge of pride that his mother worked here; yet it seemed more a sense of his own belonging than hers. Restless Alice must surely be out of place here, quiet and sitting still among all these books, whereas Jade was glad for the solemn magic of this silent haven. Perhaps it was the cinematic columns of colored light from the ceiling or, more certainly, it was the books themselves, hundreds of them, waves of hills within the greater mountain of knowledge in this kingdom of the mind. He could work in such a place, surrounded by stories of other's lives, so much more exciting than his own.

Jade was suddenly conscious of the squeak coming from his right shoe, and he stopped what he realized was a circle he'd been turning himself within. Ten feet in front of him, a small middle-aged woman sat at a large wooden desk, the silent space around her appearing to have been carved by a glacier parting the great mountain of knowledge to create a special core, a secret cave, her own sanctuary of hidden truths. The woman's gray head curled upward from her work and her thin mouth grimaced at Jade's shoe, her concentration interrupted. She raised her eyes to meet Jade's, and her face softened into a smile.

"What is it, young man? No school today?"

"Is this the Sheldon library?" Jade asked, immediately realizing how foolish he sounded.

"This is the Cairstine Morgan Memorial Library and Gallery, as indicated above the front door. And yes, you are standing in the borough of Sheldon."

Jade smirked, feeling his face warm up.

"Is there something *else* I can help you to understand?" The irony in her voice reminded him of Alice. This woman filled the bookish profile that Alice did not; but her eyes had the same mischievous glint, giving him the weird feeling that Alice herself was looking at him, challenging him with one of her mind games.

"I came to visit my mother, Alice Flynn. Is she working here today?"

The woman's eyes narrowed, the spark disappearing behind a veil of caution. She turned her head to the side, looking at Jade as if he were pulling a prank on her. "Working? What do you mean?"

"My mother works here," Jade said. "Alice. Alice Flynn."

"Oh." She drew a sharp breath and made a little squeak in her throat. "Oh yes, um. Alice. Yes. Of course." The woman's voice was louder now, cheery, like a teacher introducing a new student. "Well, let's see now," she said, shuffling papers on her desk and standing up. She was quite short. Her heels left a heavy echo in the room as she came around to Jade, pushing out her chin to look up at his face. She offered her hand. "I'm Miss Filbert, head librarian. And you are?"

"Seamus. Um, James. James Flynn." He gave her a tentative handshake. Alice would have been disappointed.

"Well, Seamus. Or...James," she said, again turning her head to the side. "I didn't realize Alice had a son." She straightened her head and leveled her eyes at him. "You must be, what...a freshman or a sophomore in high school?"

"I'll be a freshman in the fall. I'm thirteen."

She nodded, assessing him quickly from head to toe. "Well, your mother's here often, of course. In fact, she's our best volunteer."

"Volunteer? She doesn't work here? For pay?"

Miss Filbert opened her mouth to speak and then seemed to struggle as if she'd momentarily forgotten how to breathe. "Why...yes, uh, James. Of course. She...a...well, she's quite an astute researcher, and, I must say, she's a prolific writer. Once she closes the workroom door upstairs, the typewriter never stops. So, yes, she does do some work for us. For me, that is. Um. Researching. And writing, of course. But it's um. Part time. Yes." She resurrected her smile and offered it up to Jade, with an extra pinch of her dimples.

"Part time?" Jade said, returning the smile. "So, she volunteers *and* works part-time? As a researcher. And...as a writer."

"Yes," Miss Filbert said, steady on her feet now. "And I believe she does some part-time work up in Monsey at their library, although she's here most of the time."

"So, she's here today?"

"Well, no, not at the moment," Miss Filbert replied, and glanced up toward the balcony. "She was here earlier, but she had to step out. I believe she went up to Monsey, but I'm not certain. She does come and go, and, well, I don't watch over her. I'm quite busy. There's just the two of us, really. And, of course, our other intermittent volunteers. And the building and grounds man downstairs."

Jade looked up at the balcony; no one was there.

"Is there a message you'd like to leave for Alice?" Miss Filbert offered. "Your mother, that is."

"Yeah. Uh. Well. Actually, no. I'll tell her when she gets home. It was just some news about high school."

"Oh, lovely," Miss Filbert said, brightening. She looked relieved. "I'm sure, with a bright-eyed young man like you, it will be good news."

"Yeah," Jade said, as he turned toward the door. "I think it will be." He turned back to Miss Filbert. "Well, thanks. It was nice to meet you."

She offered her hand again, and Jade shook it this time with a firm grip. Her hand was dry and tiny inside his, but equally firm.

"And you as well, James." She smiled, the dimples popping again. She turned toward her desk then back around again. "Oh, James. Um, if you wouldn't mind asking Alice—your mother, that is—to call me when you get home, I'd appreciate it. She has the number."

"Sure," Jade said. He didn't want to tell her that their telephone was not working. Another unpaid bill he'd have to take over from Alice.

That evening, he waited for her in the kitchen until 11:30 before trudging up to his bed. The good news about the Pell scholarship would have to wait.

8

Queen of Heaven

Saturday, May 31, 1969

She struggled to her feet, cold and bare on the wooden floor, and put a hand on the shoulder of The Virgin to steady herself. Her knees had gone numb as if she'd climbed a mountain on them, her head lost in a fog of exhaustion. With her other hand, she clutched the beads against her stomach.

"Regina Coeli," she whispered, struggling to speak any words beyond the rote chant of prayers she'd said aloud for hours. "There." She swallowed air, a knot in a frayed rope, and lifted her eyes to meet The Virgin's. "I've done it. All five Glorious mysteries." She coughed until she found her full voice, looking around for her drink.

"My dear Queen of Heaven, I've done what you expect in honor of your month, and that's the heart of what they taught me, drilled into me, kneeling before you, offering up my pain to you. Cleaning floors. On the knees again. And mending clothes and scrubbing stains from sheets and polishing already polished silver, and playing your music with numb fingers on their out-of-tune piano." She coughed again and sighed a weak laugh. "Just like mine, right here. Barely know what a chord in tune sounds like."

She dropped her hand from the Virgin's shoulder and let the rosary slip from her other hand, clattering at her feet like hail on a tin roof. She winced at the sound and then sat heavily on the piano bench and sighed, gathering her strength. She reached up to the lid for her drink and tasted it and winced again. Ice long gone. She opened the fallboard, her arm and hand shaking with electric numbness. She turned toward Mary and the other statues.

"I'll play it for you. Perhaps you'll sing the lyrics for us." She nodded a tempo for a moment, and then began to play *Queen of the Holy Rosary*, a soft touch on the keys at first, humming along with it, but quickly increasing the tempo, shouting, "Sing! Sing!" and then suddenly hammering the keys, her mouth a thin line, her eyes darting toward Mary and the saints, her head jolting in time ever so slightly, just like Sister Saint Joe and her army of sister supplicants, holy, reverent, but stoic in the deliberate cadence. Veiled soldiers in lock step but not marching; kneeling, not moving; just their hearts.

She hit one of the sour keys and flinched but played on. She stopped suddenly when she saw her drink on the piano top, chaos echoing around her until she released the sostenuto pedal. She reached up for the glass, her arm following its own advice, her hand seizing it. The glass warm, the brown tint now pale. She drained it in two great gulps.

"Okay," she said, announcing as she rose from the bench and limped with her glass to the kitchen, raising her voice as she lectured. "Since you won't sing along, and since you won't even talk to me any longer, like you used to, like you did before she disappeared and then wouldn't tell me where or who took her, like you did when I first brought you here and heard your words and saw your eyes smile at me as you explained my waking dreams." She bashed the ice tray on the sink, cubes clattering. "Since your silence—despite my continued reverence in this your month—has brought me to my knees in supplication but with no response from you..." She returned from the kitchen and took a slug from the filled glass and set it on the piano.

"For all this silence that you and your frozen saints maintain, like Sister Saint Joe and her cloaked comrades on their kneelers there in that musty old chapel, while I played their music of drones on the keyboard and then scrubbed the altar floor, the deck of that ship of damned mothers. Since you won't respond even to my insolence, I will just have another drink. Disappointing you, of course. Thy bell tolls for me!"

She raised her glass, took another gulp, plopped onto the bench, and turned to the statues once more before flexing her fingers over the keys. "And I will play actual music for you this time. I will play for you and your silent saints what my father used to have me play for his sotted associates in the drawing room at the end of an evening, after he would get them drunk and pry secrets from them and then put more logs on the fire until their eyes hung heavy and they could no longer lift their drinks, and he would say to me, 'Play it!', and there I would be, my young strong hands poised over the keys, and he would give me the nod, and off I would go. The first movement of Sonata 14, his favorite sleeping pill for his guests, those mighty men of power suddenly mollified and drained by the teetotaler's clever tricks. And he would smile at me, his hand swaying in a perfect metronome for the piece, his flouncy mustache fluttering with bursts of his sinister laugh."

She faced the piano and closed her eyes, her long fingers finding the keys and then drifting into the sonata, working around the sour notes, covering the duds without losing tempo, a piece she'd played once for

Seamus when he was younger, and he was not as impressed as she'd hoped he would be.

She'd played this movement hundreds of times, but this time she focused on the complexity of it, the pacing of the silence around the notes and the complications of control, the recapitulation, the point-counterpoint that her father, and, much later, her son, had not recognized. The old man had said it was a simple song, and the boy, separately years later, had said so too, and these memories reminded her that some people only see and hear in black and white and gray, poor things. There are so many more layers to sounds and sights that she sees and feels and hears but that no one else does. And Mother Mary won't tell her why.

She opened her eyes when her fingers stopped playing, and she reached up for the glass and emptied it into her wide mouth. She stood up from the bench and headed to the kitchen for another refill.

"Mother Mary," she called out, "you must know I'm seeing things, disturbing things, that I should not be thinking about. I've told you that often enough. But since you won't explain them to me any longer, I'm going to have to pursue my own course here." She returned to The Grotto, glass in hand, and began to pace among the statues.

It was mid-afternoon on a Saturday, she was in her nightgown, Jade was at the diner, and, before she prayed on her knees for hours, she had opened all the windows on the first floor, and now the outside air had long settled inside the house. She cringed at the stench of the culm dump and then lit a Lucky and sucked in the smoke, reveling in the weight of it on her lungs.

"There," she'd said, exhaling a long cloud and reaching for her drink. "He'll be pissed about the windows, but I will make it up to him."

As she paced among her silent saints and Virgin, she held her cigarette suspended before her face and raised the other hand, pointing at nothing in particular. "You must help me understand many things, Mother, and you too, dear silent saints. You must." She leveled her look directly at Mary's eyes and blinked away sudden tears.

"Glory be to the Father, and to the Son, and to the Holy Ghost. Ah-men."

She took a deep breath and exhaled. She sucked the last fumes of her cigarette and punched it out in the litter of butts on a dinner plate. She grabbed the flattened pack of Luckys, ran her fingers inside, crushed it, tossed it to the floor and took another gulp from the glass. She continued her barefoot march among the statues. "I must be frank with you, Mother. I'm tired of my journey. I'm spent, and I see what's coming. I've no one else to tell but you, now that Marte is gone, who knows where. Only you know my truth now. Unless you bring her back, which I'm assuming now you will not, in your silence, in your shutting me out.

44

"Can't you see, Mother, what Marte did for me? Did you not notice? She restored my strength, the body of my youth, she cut me from the drink, and recovered my confidence, my old wise-cracking self, my laughter, my concentration; she started me reading again with passion, new ideas, she did it for me, Mother, out of love, the kind of love I'd never known, and *you* let her go, let her be stolen away from me, let her die. Sam said someone broke into her place and took her away, the place was smashed up, he thought someone had been following her, and he thinks it could be really bad. And do you know what, Mother? I know who did it. I know who ordered it. In my heart of hearts, I know. I'm certain of it.

"It was the same certainty I had when I found Tara, my Tara. Yes, the one who taught me about you, about our Queen Mother in heaven. It was I who found her, as you certainly must know. She didn't show up at the pool for our lessons, so I went up to her suite, her bedroom was dark, she must have slept in. I drew the curtains and the daylight fell upon her in her bed, her nightgown, her eyes closed, such a peaceful face I hadn't seen on her in months. And then I smelled it. Licorice. And I pushed on her shoulders and watched her face fall to the side, and then I saw the bottles—little brown bottles—mother's bottles—on her bedside table, and I screamed; I can still hear my own screaming at our third-floor maid, Gertrude, who stood there like a statue in the doorway. I screamed, 'Help, Gertrude! Help! Get a doctor!' but she just stood there…"

She paused her march and stood face to face with The Virgin, her voice quavering in a breathless whisper, her green eyes accusing.

"And then Papa appeared. He *pulled* me away, out of the room, did not even look at Tara, the angel alone in her bed—and that's when I knew. I was just a child, and I did not understand, but I knew it in my heart. He was responsible." She gasped at the Virgin's face. "Just as I know now. Just as I know who took Marte. But *you* won't tell me where she is, and I know she's not alive, and I know who killed her. I know it in my heart. Even if you will not say it. *I know.*"

She turned away from the statue in disgust and grabbed her drink. She kept her back to the Virgin as she swayed on her bare feet and stared at the open window.

"I see the end on the near horizon, and I can feel it, and I'm sure you know all about it, Mary. Twenty years. God knows, I've tried. You know what I've been up against. The cross I've borne." Her breath came in sharply, her hand flew to her mouth, and she turned around to the Virgin, her eyes wide. "Oh no, I'm sorry. I cannot presume to have carried the burden your son has carried. No, certainly not. Of course not. But, dear Mother, it has been a long, long time, this lost voyage of mine. And now, like you, I see that I will lose my son.

"My tormentor, you understand, will take him away from me and then hoist me up on my cross and put a lance to me. I know it. And yes, that sounds blasphemous, you know, as if my pain were at a level of your son's, which it is not, of course, but this is the only life I've known, and, while it started out quite enchanted, it was brought to a halt just when I found love. It was long ago, long before Marte. I had found for the first time, real actual love—mutual love; not the silly romantic kind, but the love of two minds melding, hearts and bodies and souls entwined. That connection sustained us for a brief but glorious period and protected our true selves from a merciless world. But it was taken from us. It was my sin, they said. And, as you well know, I've paid for it ever since."

She stepped within inches of the Virgin, took a drink from her glass and gazed down at Mary's lifeless eyes. "You're not even listening, are you, Mary? Huh!"

She emptied the glass and set it on the coffee table and returned to face the statue, peering down at the blank face. "How tall are you, Mary? Because I think you should be much taller. Yes, I know, women and men were smaller in your day, I know that. But you should be taller. You're the Queen of Heaven, after all. You should be my height, at least. I'm what, five nine in bare feet? And you, in your bare feet—the thickness of the green snake underfoot notwithstanding—you must be five three at most." She sighed and stepped to the coffee table, reached for the glass, held it up, and then set it down and continued her pacing.

"They all said I should have known better, but the truth is I *did*. I did know better. I knew our love was my salvation, not only because of what it gave to us, the two of us, but also what it did for *me*—real world intellectual stimulation, not that fatuous classroom drivel—my kite and his clay in perfect syncopation, art and science in an exchange that no one then could even fathom, no one else. And liberty, finally! Freedom from the ridiculous plans my father had for me. I knew it meant breaking away finally from the reins of my family, my father in particular, but how would I know that he would swoop over me, tighten those reins around me again and hand them over to a diabolical reprobate?!" She clutched her abdomen and glared at the saints one by one. She charged into the kitchen for a refill and then resumed her march among the statues.

"I made my own choice, and the reprobate, the tormentor, decided I had no such thing as a choice over my life or my mind, or especially my body, my own strong body—able, certainly, to withstand the challenge before me.

"Fool that I was, it shocked me when the dim-witted reprobate took it all away. Everything. What did I think would happen? That I could prevail over a *man*? A post-war American man in 1949?! Even though he ducked out of serving his country, the impudent lump. To be a public servant, he said. Coward." She gulped from the glass and set it on the votive altar in front of the Virgin statue. "And so, he put me in an unholy prison with depraved women in dark cloaks and bonnets who sold orphans to donors of the faith, and then he drove me out on my own, onto a path filled with roadblocks, traps, and rejections, an endless series of landmines. For two decades! *For Christ's sake!*"

She stopped and put her hand to her mouth. "Oh, I'm so sorry," she muttered through her hand. "So sorry, Mary. So sorry. I'm just…I'm just in and out with this Catholic thing, you know. In fact, as you know too well, I was never *really* a Catholic. It was my sister, my Tara, who taught me about it when I was a kid, and she was, what, fifteen? So devoted, yes, but what could a fifteen-year-old teach an eight-year-old about an entire religion, other than the rituals and prayers? Which I loved by the way, because of Tara, because they reminded me of her, those rote prayers and dull hymns and sad holy cards. Until years later when Sister Saint Joe and her team of self-deniers taught me the true rigors of the faith—the chanting and praying and kneeling and scrubbing and cleaning until you can no longer feel your body—which was a good thing for me, of course, being so fat with child as I was. It really was an effective distraction. Pain and deprivation being what they are—techniques to numb the body and make silent the spirit."

She headed toward the kitchen, fumbling through drawers for cigarettes while still shouting.

"But that music, please! So sour and dour and then the endless silence! Always silent when not praying or singing those lugubrious songs. Dismal, joyless. And making me play them over and over and over and over again. *Christ!*"

She ripped open a pack of Luckys and set a match to one. She ran her hand through her hair and shook her head and opened the refrigerator, shouting to her audience as she scraped the last of the ice from the tray. "One more! That's it, I promise," she shouted.

She returned to the Grotto, sipping at the full glass, the burning Lucky in her fist, and then, after two slurps, she set the glass on the piano. "So, did you like my Ludwig, Mother? My Sonata?" She walked up to Mary and stared down at her. "No, I can see you did not. Too bad. Perhaps a bit too modern for your time, I suppose. Was he even a Catholic, old Ludwig? Probably not, as his music was too passionate, too full of life.

"But, Mary, the landmines that The Interloper set up to punish me at every turn for the sin of making my own choice. He is Lucifer, you *do* know that, Mother, don't you? *El Diavolo.* Mephistopheles. The Slanderer. The Manipulator. He's posing as an empathetic leader, a man who understands the plight of his people, but he actually feels nothing, Mother Mary." She held a hand to her chest and used the other to point into the distance, her chin in the air. "He is the painting of a sorrow, a face without a heart."

She dropped her arm to her side and bowed her head, chuckling. "Sorry, Mother. You wouldn't get the reference. You weren't around for the old bard, either. But you do know my tormentor is the face without a heart, the face of evil. And you know what he took from me, time after time, and now he is at it again. I'm certain he ordered Marte's disappearance. I know it. I *know* that she was murdered. And who else would order such a hideous act against her and against me? And now, he's after my very last connection to life. My Seamus."

She stood in front of the Virgin, swaying on her bare feet, drink in one hand, Lucky in the other, her eyes struggling to focus, her wild black curls bobbing.

"I need your help, Mother. I need you to help me stop him. I need your help to save my son. And yes, I know, you lost your son, too, but listen. And I mean no disrespect here. Maybe I'm too drunk, I don't know. But come on, Mary, please. Your son was *God,* after all! Or the Son of God, or whatever. It's confusing to an outsider like me, all this perplexing trinity nonsense. It's a twisted riddle, an M. C. Escher conception. I wish you'd straighten that out. But you know what I mean." She set the drink on the piano bench.

"OK, yes, I know, Mother, that I'm a little tipsy now, I'm sorry, I'll stop after this one, I promise. I'm so sorry. I think all that praying on my knees for...hours...I...I think it made me a bit dehydrated. Perhaps I should have drunk something less poisonous under that condition. But I *am* sorry. Truly, I am." She put her hand on the Virgin's shoulder again. "Please don't shut me out here, Mother. I am trying. You must know that."

She sighed. She wiped tears from her face and let her hand drop and then stood up tall and shook her head. "Please say something to me. Tell me who this woman is that I keep seeing in my daydreams. Or night dreams or whatever they are. She has a soft and lovely voice, so soft, she's trying to say something to me. She's young, her skin is night black. And golden beams are pouring a great light from her eyes. She's not like the other dark faces I saw—the ones that dance with my son at the edge of death. No, this one is full of grace, I know she is. I keep seeing her, and I think she's trying to help me. Give me a clue, Mother, please. Who is she? What does she want from me?"

She bowed her head and sobbed out a sigh, setting her hand on Mary's shoulder, the Lucky smoke shrouding the Virgin's face. "My God. Why won't you talk to me? I need to hear your voice. Why did you take Marte away from me? She was my salvation. My last chance. Why? And who is this other dark woman, not the angelic one but the one with her face all bloody and staring at my Seamus? Who are these dream visitors I keep seeing? It's why I drink, don't you see? They disappear only when I drown them out. Don't you see?"

She looked down into the empty eyes of the Virgin and felt a laugh rising in her throat and she let it out. She threw her hands in the air, took a drink and started to pace in front of the statue. "Okay. Okay, Mary. Here's what I think, booze talking or no booze talking. I'm not trying to be a smart ass here, but I'm getting tired of praying to you and the saints over here and getting nothing in response. I mean, when I first started this…this sanctuary…when you first came here, we talked all the time. Now you're freezing me out. I'm confused by your silence now, and so listen, I must tell you that I've already talked to your husband over there. Joseph. He says nothing. Ever. At least you've talked to me in the past, but this guy says nothing. So, I must ask you. Did he ever say *anything*? Tara taught me that he was a holy man, this carpenter. But it seems to me Joseph might just be a prop. You know? Something the holy men of the church made up to make it look like you needed a husband to depend on to get you through your journey. But we both know that you walked alone. *I* know that. I saw it in your eyes when you first spoke to me. You're just being nice about it now. But let's face it. And again, I'm not trying to be smart here. But Joseph is a straw man. I think you must know that. Now, I'm sure he had his difficult times, and that it was no picnic traipsing across that desert with you, but let me be clear about something. He wasn't pregnant. *You* were. And I'll bet those holy men scripted in a donkey for you to ride just to make you look fragile, but my money's on you walking the whole way. Pregnant! See, I know this because you are just like me, and I can hear your thoughts. Or at least I used to hear them. Now you're freezing me out, and I don't know why. Remember the last time, what was it, last week? When I heard you say to me that I didn't need Father Shanahan's permission to pray to you in his fancy Our Lady Chapel over there in Saint John the Divine church. He told me I was a distraction to his other parishioners who came to hear him sing and play the guitar up there on his altar like he was a folk hero instead of a pastor. Pete Seeger, the priest version. And he thought *I* was being disrespectful. Good heavens, you're the mother of God, and you certainly know better than Father Pete Seeger what's best for you and me and our relationship. That's why I listened to you and brought you here, along with the other saints. But I must tell you, I think Joseph might have to go. I mean, is there a statue of Mary Magdalene that I can buy? Wasn't she your comrade? Or your son's comrade? I'm a little rusty on the stories. I wish Tara were here to guide me. I miss my Tara, my poor Tara. Everything I know about you and the others came from her. Not from Sister Saint Joe. Jesus, that old witch was named after your straw man! Ha! That figures."

She felt a wave of lightness come over her and then let herself slip to the floor in a heap of nightgown and folded arms like broken wings, her head on the carpet, her eyes closing, the sound of her empty glass rolling away. "My son," she slurred. "So afraid for him. Need to help him. Keep him out of that place, away from that man. Tormentor. I need to find my strength. To fight like I did when I was young, so full, so sure, so strong. I depend on no one, and you know that. And don't tell me his money has sustained us, don't dare say that, because it's *my* money he's been paying me. Parceling out my own inheritance in tiny crumbs and acting like he's generous. The arrogance..."

She closed her eyes. She saw the face of Tara, then Marte. Both silent.

Just before the darkness, she saw the young Black woman again, her face radiant, the light in her eyes and then the sound of her voice. She couldn't make out the words, but the voice itself was a song.

9

Hizzoner

Friday, June 13, 1969

It was just after five on a sunny day at the end of Jade's last full week at Wally's Diner. The place was filling up fast, the regulars in their usual spots: The Judge and Jury holding court in their two catbird corner booths, the solo-flyers with their elbows out at the counter stools, the factory crowd in pre-party mode in the far corner booths, and the once-a-weekers bustling to grab the remaining counter spots. Wally's was the go-to diner for the after-work Friday crowd looking to fill their bellies with low-cost beer-absorbing fare before they scattered to the bars for the launch of the weekend. On this warm Friday evening, the joint was jumping. Wally's new table-side jukeboxes were in high demand, and the competing music of generations and the crowd's attempt to talk over it created a cacophonous clash. Dee and Brenda strained to shout their orders as they clipped tickets to the wire at the kitchen window. Cigarette and grill smoke competed for whatever oxygen wasn't consumed by the boisterous crowd.

Jade had a lump in his throat. Wally had given him the following Friday off to attend his pre-job interview at Macson and to buy new work clothes, so this would be his last evening with the diner's Friday crowd—the week's most spirited and entertaining. As he headed toward the kitchen to back up Wally on the grill, Jade paused to look around the diner at the familiar faces, wondering what would happen with these characters after he left. For six years, he'd cooked for, served, and cleaned up after this rowdy crew and he'd listened, always with mixed emotions, to their endless banter. He wasn't sure if what he'd learned from them would benefit or harm him, but he was certain he'd never forget them.

Jade was more at home here than in whatever temporary quarters he and Alice had shared over the years. With no siblings or cousins or even neighborhood friends in the Black Diamond Valley, Jade thought of the diner as the only place where he was part of a family—a hodgepodge of workers and customers whose lives had been open books for him every day after school and on weekends since he was 12. The diner workers were the tightest circle of that family. Wally and Wilma, not quite surrogate parents, more like caring and trusting uncle and aunt, whom Jade worried he'd betrayed by taking the Macson job; Dee, his favorite co-worker, would-be big sister and, recently, his on-again/off-again secret crush; Brenda, Dee's comrade in arms, whom Jade thought of as his doting, sharp-tongued older cousin; and even Gordon, the wall-eyed dishwasher and maintenance guy, whose unflappable spirit kept Jade's dark moods in perspective, if not in check.

The regular customers were extended members of this family. The generous, funny guys from the battery plant and the foundry, alternately teasing Jade and building him up; the sweet ladies from the silk mill, offering unsolicited oral history to his transition from a boy to a young man with their flirty hints of feigned desire; and, especially, The Judge and Jury in their prized booths, ever deciding the fate of humanity, a generally harmless but vocal group of older guys who paid little attention to Jade but taught him by example how not to behave in public.

Wally had bestowed the name Judge and Jury on this core group of six regulars one Friday night after they'd left, as he and Jade were cleaning up and laughing about the unmitigated confidence with which this collection of pontificators expressed their opinions. Jade disagreed with most of their loud declarations, but he marveled at the certainty of their assertions, how adept these self-appointed authorities were in proclaiming their well-worn ideas, as if each one was a new revelation. Wally mostly disagreed with them, too, privately characterizing the bloviating Judge and Jury as "seldom right, but never in doubt." But, like Jade, he laughed with them.

"What can I do?" Wally had told him in his heavy Polish accent. "They're always here, most pay their bills, they make free entertainment, and one of them helped defeat Hitler. Best of all, no fate is sealed by what this Judge and his Jury say."

The local newspaper was the source for most of the raucous discussions among the Judge's crew, often drawing shouted responses from other regulars scattered across the diner. Most of these unflappable men had a way of calling out their opinions without overtly offending anyone in the diner, but certain subjects brought out exceptions to this cordiality. These pontificators covered everything from local and national politics and sports to the dizzying pace of changing social issues to oversimplified solutions for complex problems. None in this crew would ever take part in the named solutions but the most vocal among them would sound off heartily on which solutions would work best—for someone else to carry out.

On this Friday, the back-to-back red-leather booths occupied by The Judge and Jury were at capacity—three men at each of two four-seater tables, a presumptuous occupation of extra space earned by a combination of seniority, sheer gall, and, in one case, an ever-expanding girth. The seating arrangements in the booths were loosely pre-ordained among the Jurors, but The Judge had a guaranteed spot on the "throne"— the center of the premiere booth, the one at the end of an open aisle that ran the length of the diner. There on his stage, with his back to the wall, The Judge could see everyone in the diner while keeping his eyes on both doors. The Judge—Robert "Red" Larkin—was a big man with a voice that was known among his Jury members as a "saw-mill whisper." Dinty Connolly once said that Red was so loud, you could hear him thinking when he was behind two closed doors on the can in the men's room. Red was a patient listener, but when it was time for him to make his stentorian judgment, it was clear there would be no other opinions rendered on the matter. His face would turn crimson—hence the nickname—and he would bellow his decision, scanning the diner for the challenge that would never arise. Earlier on this Friday, before the bulk of the crowd arrived, Red had presided over a discussion about new jobs at the Macson munitions factory.

"Goddamn Hafferty can't delegate a goddamn thing!" Red boomed, concluding the discussion and taking on a target deemed untouchable, even by Judge and Jury standards. Red's bold statement was met with frozen faces among his Jurors. He used his thick fist and index finger to punch out his points. "He controls every single federal job doled out, without giving the other Commissioners or the Mayor or the party bosses anything but his leftovers. It's gonna cost him in the '70 election, I'm tellin' ya. I, for one, will *not* be voting for him." The rest of the diner fell silent for a few icy moments, followed by tentative low chatter among the factory guys, tacitly acknowledging the Judge's final dictum and his implied permission to resume normal conversation.

Rondo "Bowl-and-a-Roll" Yanish started to say something, but Red held up his hand to render silence. The discussion would move on. Bowl-and-a-Roll was sitting across from Red with his back to the room. He was a small-framed middle-aged man who ordered a bowl of chili and a hard roll for dinner every weeknight except Friday, when he would switch the bowl to minestrone "in honor of Our Lord"—the only vaguely positive comment he'd ever offer. Bowl-and-a-Roll hated nearly everyone. But everyone loved him, because no one took his cynical comments to heart.

They merely counted on them. Especially Red, who usually waited for Rondo's dark pronouncements so that Red's final judgment would seem more positive, no matter how dubious or nasty it might be. For the Macson discussion, though, Red hadn't waited for Bowl's negative prompt. Everyone in the diner by that point knew Red was unhappy with Hafferty's silence in response to Red's recent inquiry to the Commissioner's office about a Macson job for his oldest son, Bobby. There would be no other opinion tolerated on this subject but that of the Judge. It would be thumbs down on Hafferty from then on.

Through the cook's window to the kitchen, Jade heard Red's pronouncement and felt his neck and face heat up. These guys knew everything. And that meant they—especially Red—likely knew about Hafferty's offer to Jade.

Next to Bowl-and-a-Roll in the primary booth was Phil "The Councilman" Koldaski, a cranky, bald-headed critic in his sixties with a chin like an anvil. The Councilman's vocal pitch imitated Red's and, also like Red, he made his declarations with a fist and finger in the air. The Councilman found fault with everyone, especially members of City Council, whom he heckled relentlessly every second Tuesday at their public meetings. Never having served on Council himself, the Councilman was nonetheless the Jury's authority on all things municipal. Every evening he dined on Wally's "Special" like a horse at a trough, his chin leading the way. He loved that Dee confirmed his importance by bringing the steaming dish to his spot in the booth at precisely 5:30 every Friday. Once, when Jade asked him if he ever ate a special he didn't like, the Councilman told him, "No. I know diners. If it's special, it's fresh." Jade acknowledged that he was correct, but the Jurors protested that the Councilman simply couldn't taste food, indiscriminate as he was about what he shoved into his massive maw. Dinty Connolly pushed the notion further, to the Jury's enjoyment, asserting that the Councilman had no taste whatsoever—in anything.

William "Dinty" Connolly usually occupied a spot in the Judge and Jury's secondary booth, with a limited side-view of the diner crowd. A well-done-burger-with-raw-onion guy, Dinty often reminded the diner audience that he was a veteran of the final Allied assault on Germany in World War II. He was also the self-appointed resident comedian—not a joke teller, but the deliveryman of the spontaneous one-liner. Dinty's vocal jabs often derailed the diner-wide discussions, sending conversations onto unrecoverable tangents. While many of his one-liners were off-color or offensive to just about every race and creed on earth, his jovial delivery overshadowed his narrow, trenchant ideas. Dinty's one-liners reminded Jade of the puerile humor he'd so often heard in the halls of Ebonton High but carried out here with a level of confidence that could be gained only through years of repetition. Moronic humor, Alice would have called it. Humor meant to elevate yourself by denigrating someone else. A shallow man's way to make himself feel bigger and better, she'd say.

Beyond the cover of his one-liners, Dinty often held forth on the rising anti-war movement. He stoked fear about the inevitable overthrow of the government by the "hippies and Black Panthers and college punks" who, in his opinion, "had been given far too much leeway these days in America." He believed the war in Vietnam was not only just, but that America should treat all of Southeast Asia as another Japan and drop an A-Bomb on it. But he couched these volatile notions in a comical, off-putting manner that defied challenge, expertly timing his comedian's punchline laugh to spark supporting laughter from the crowd. Still, Dinty's comments left no one uncertain about the right way to think—his way.

Dinty was always and conveniently flanked in the secondary booth by taciturn Jerold Kent, the loneliest mailman on earth, whose pale opinions were limited to the certainties in his own life—a steady paycheck, the promise of a good pension. Jerold seldom spoke up when the discussion vaulted into the high stakes realm of opinion occupied by Dinty, the Councilman, and especially the Judge. Instead, he'd nod and smile at the appropriate moments. He was more interested in simply being part of the crew. Jerold never ordered anything other than meatloaf, gravy, mashed potatoes, and black coffee.

Big Gino Mecca filled out the remaining spot in the six-man Judge and Jury quorum—literally. He took up an entire side of the secondary booth, opposite Dinty and Jerold. Dinty always said Big Gino "ate like he was going to the chair," and he regularly reminded everyone of Gino's weeks-long tab that only got paid when Wally would send Dee to Big Gino's booth with a meat cleaver. Dee, a natural actress in her own mind, would holler dramatically and hold the cleaver over Gino's table, announcing to all how much Big Gino owed Wally. Gino would protest with a feeble smile and a shrug, and Dee would threaten with much flair, and after a theatrical beat, Gino would always come up with the cash. Once, when Dee brought the cleaver down onto the table, very nearly chopping it in half, even Dinty had no comment. But, after that, Big Gino, unfazed, simply continued his deadbeat habits while Dee, by edict from Wally, was left to dunning Gino without weapons.

In the kitchen, Jade had taken Wally's place at the grill and was juggling a deluge of dinner orders, falling behind on this busy Friday. He sensed a change in the diner chatter from wise cracking to muttering complaints. Brenda and Dee started cajoling Jade to pick up the pace, threatening to call in Gordon, the dishwasher, to flip burgers. Ten minutes earlier, Wilma had called Wally away from the grill for what she called "important business" in the office, but Jade was starting to wonder what could be so important to take Wally away from his top priority—his customers' meals. Jade could hear Wally's voice in his head, chanting his mantra: "Three important things to know, son: customers first, customers first, and customers always first."

As if conjured by Jade's thoughts, Wally appeared at his side and began attacking the grill and pushing through set-ups. Wilma joined him, and Wally gently moved Jade aside. "Someone wants to see you right now in the office," Wally said. "Go. We will handle this. Customers first."

Jade was stunned when he opened Wally's private office door and found Commissioner Dennis Hafferty sitting at Wally's desk. Silver Head Stanley stood guard inside the door.

"Mr. Flynn! So good to see you again," Hafferty said. He put a cigarette in his mouth and Stanley flicked open his gold Zippo and lit his boss's Benson & Hedges. "I'd offer you a cigarette, kid, but I'm concerned about your health." He laughed at his own joke, and Stanley took his cue to chuckle and then stepped back to his sentry post. Jade was grateful that Stanley's psycho sidekick Whiskey Breath Zook was not on hand.

"Sit! Sit!" Hafferty insisted as he waved his thick bejeweled hand at the chair in front of Wally's desk. As Jade lowered himself slowly into the chair, he took note of the Commissioner's impeccable appearance. Same slicked back hair, same ice blue suit and red tie, gold tie clip and cufflinks, same shiny pink face and thick glasses, same enlarged gauzy blue eyes. The perfectly aligned teeth made a sudden blinding appearance as Hafferty tipped his head back and gave Jade his Commissioner smile. To Jade, it felt like someone had turned on a fluorescent flood light.

"Mr. Flynn, I'm looking forward to hearing good things about you at the Macson plant starting in what—a week? No, ten days from now. You know your intake meeting is next Friday morning with General Manager Jensen, and then you're in the thick of it the following Monday. But you already know that, don't you? Because you're a smart kid, and you paid attention to me. I just wanted to be sure you haven't backed out of our deal. You'll be on time for that meeting, now, won't you."

"Yes, sir. Thank you very much for the job." Jade glanced at Stanley, who offered a mirthless smirk that looked like a warning.

"You're very welcome, son," Hafferty said, exhaling a smoke stream that smothered Wally's favorite desk decoration—his globe of the earth. "I know you won't disappoint me." He stood up and came around to the front of the desk and sat on the corner, looking down at Jade.

"I came here this evening to pay respect to your boss. Wally's a great man, he is. His wife, Wilma, a princess. I'm taking away Wally's best young worker—you—and I wanted to let Wally know that I'm not leaving him in the lurch. I'm giving him a young guy to replace you. Timmy Larkin. You will start training him on Monday. He's only fourteen, but he's a smart kid, like you. He's Red Larkin's younger son. You know him?"

Jade shook his head. "I know Red. He's out there in the diner right now."

"Is that so?" Hafferty said and turned with a wide smile to Stanley, who chuckled, again on cue. "Imagine that, Stanley. Red Larkin is here tonight." He stood up and began pacing, holding his cigarette in front of him like a magician's wand.

"Do you know what I'm going to do, son?" The cigarette swirled in the air and then pointed at Jade. "I'm going to ask *you* to stand by my side out there in the dining room right now, as I greet all my friends and thank them for their continued support. I'm also going to tell them about Wally's new employee, young Timmy Larkin, and how he's going to be just as hard a worker as you have been for the last—what—three years?

"Six."

"Six years!" He turned to Stanley again. "Six years, Stanley! Christ, I'm going to have to report Wally on a child labor law violation!" Stanley tipped his head back for an exaggerated silent laugh.

Hafferty stood up and crushed his cigarette on the concrete floor with his shiny wingtip. He straightened his tie and then squared his big shoulders, flashing the fluorescent smile down on Jade. "It's showtime, kid. You ready?"

Out in the kitchen, behind the swinging door to the dining room, Hafferty held up his hand to halt his small battalion of Stanley and Jade. "Wally! Wilma! Get off that grill for a second and come with me. I won't be more than a minute. Have your dish guy there hold the fort. Come on! We have an announcement to make."

When he pushed the swinging door into the dining room, Hafferty nearly knocked over Brenda. Dee was behind her, hoisting a tray of dinners. Brenda gave a small shriek, and Dee backstepped and caught her tray just in time.

"Holy love a' God, girls, I almost caused a train wreck," Hafferty shouted, louder than necessary. "I beg your pardon, my loves. How are ya, Dee. I'd kiss you but your arms are busy, and you wouldn't be able to hold on. You look beautiful as ever." The buzz of the dining room lowered a notch, as heads turned at the counter and across the long room. Dee and Brenda moved aside as the Commissioner strode to the middle of the room, with Jade, Stanley, Wally, and Wilma forming a halting train behind him.

"Well, look who it is," Red Larkin boomed from his throne in the primary Judge and Jury booth, his voice deliberately louder than Hafferty's, and decidedly sarcastic. "Hizzoner, the Commissioner. What brings *you* here, all the way from the fancy suburbs? Ya lost?"

The diner went silent. Red's scarlet face froze in gleeful anticipation, his eyes scanning the diner for a laugh. Jade and the little train from the kitchen came to a halt. All eyes turned to Hafferty. Someone in the factory booths started to clap, and then a few more joined in, and, in a moment, the room filled with applause. Hafferty let the commotion build and then linger for a beat before he put up his hands to silence the crowd.

"Thank you, my friends! Thank you!" he boomed, smiling and waving his arms. As he headed toward the factory booths at the far end, he stopped along the way, shaking hands and calling out names. The applause resumed section by section as he passed through. "Hey, Jerry Schwab, how are you!" "Barney Phillips! Bethy Phillips! Good to see you!" "Gina Piccolini, how's that job at the foundry? You let me know if that Jim Harney pinches you, ok?" He laughed with her and then reached into the booths occupied by the factory guys and shook every man's hand. "Men of the bindery! Men of the foundry! Best of the best! Jimmy, Al, Coop, Carlo, Pauly, Peanuts, Duke. Good to see you all." The men beamed. As he moved away from their booth, they amped up the applause.

Hafferty swept along the length of the diner shaking hands, hugging women, patting the heads of a few young kids, shouting and laughing with the men. To Jade, he looked like a movie star in his impeccable suit hovering above his swooning commonfolk fans, reaching down from an invisible stage to let them touch him. He was mesmerizing. He seemed unreal to Jade, an apparition. He watched this super being with a new regard as Hafferty soaked up the gratitude and warmth of the crowd. Jade was still intimidated by Hafferty but now he felt less cautious about him, less suspicious. Hafferty was a man who clearly made people happy, made their lives better, merely by his presence, his aura. There was still something fake about him, but he had something else Jade instinctively knew that worked for people. In spite of themselves and their hard-earned cynicism, they were drawn to him. He had charisma. He had power.

Jade stood with Stanley, Wally, and Wilma at the cash register and watched the Commissioner make his way past them, heading toward the Judge and Jury. But as Hafferty finished greeting the booths on either side of the aisle, he turned around in front of the Judge and Jury, ignoring the reigning pontificators, and walked back to the cash register at the center of the room. He held up his hands and faced the crowd, turning left and right as he spoke. "My friends, I won't interrupt your dinner one more second, except to say thank you from the bottom of my heart to each and every one of you for your support in the last election and for your faith in me as I continue to serve God and to serve you here in the heart of our fine county. Lots of you folks have good jobs now, and most of you know by now that *more jobs are coming!*" His elevated cue was greeted by more applause. Jade glanced toward Red Larkin. Red's eyes were frozen, his mouth a rictus, his crimson cheeks glowing.

"Yes, that's right, folks," Hafferty continued. "You read it correctly in the paper. Thanks to my dear friend, Congressman Walsh, this valley will be seeing more jobs coming down the road through new factory grants, funds for rebuilding roads and bridges, millions for filling the mine voids, replacing our rundown city residences with modern housing, and making life better for *everyone* here in this city and throughout Yoakna County." Hafferty nodded and smiled as more applause filled the room. When he turned and gestured to Wally and Wilma to come forth, Jade saw him glance toward Red Larkin.

"As you all know," Hafferty shouted, his hands in the air, "next week we'll see forty-five new jobs start at our Macson Munitions plant right here in town. That's more than a hundred and fifty this year so far." As the crowd applauded, he stepped back and pulled Wally to one side of him and Wilma to the other, and he put his arms around them. "I came here tonight to personally thank the best diner owners in the Diamond Valley, our own Wally and Wilma, for letting me give one of their young workers a chance to move up in his life. Wally, Wilma, I'm here to apologize for stealing your young apprentice chef, Mr. James Flynn over there. Take a step forward, James. James will be starting a new job at Macson in ten days. He's been working here at Wally's Diner for six years, ladies and gentlemen. *Six years!*"

Hafferty leaned back and called to Jade above the applause. "Smile, son. Wave your hand. Acknowledge the love!"

Jade stretched a grin at the edges of his mouth and lifted his hand above his shoulder for a tentative wave. He glanced around the room, stopping helplessly at Red Larkin. The man's eyes were burning a hole into him.

"So, what happens to poor Wally and Wilma now?" Hafferty thundered. "Well, I asked myself that last week when I learned that young Mr. Flynn's application was accepted at Macson, and I came up with an outstanding solution. I've asked Wally if our own Red Larkin's young son, Timmy Larkin, just fourteen years old, could step into James Flynn's role here, and Wally gladly accepted the offer. So, we owe Red Larkin a gesture of thanks as well. Red has been a long-time customer of Wally's, and, well…" He turned to face Red for the first time. "Red, I guess you're gonna have to behave yourself here at Wally's now that your boy will be working here after school every day."

The room erupted into laughter. Red tried to expand his frozen smile, but he looked ill. His skin softened to pink then pale as he looked around the room at all the laughing and cheering faces. Someone in the factory corner hollered out, "Who ya gonna vote for Commissioner next year, Red?" The crowd responded with a burst of laughter.

The members of the Jury shifted in their booths, looking around haltingly at the laughing faces, then at Hafferty and Jade, and finally at Red. The Judge took a deep breath and leaned back in his throne, his nostrils flaring.

Hafferty broke in. "No, no! This is not about votes, my friends. This is about *jobs*. Red Larkin has always been a big supporter of mine, and I've always been a big supporter of *his*. We go way back, don't we, Red?"

Larkin nodded, his eyes still frozen, his smile erased, his head bobbing like a bowling pin about to fall.

"Oh, my God!" Hafferty erupted, his thick finger in the air. "I forgot an important detail, ladies and gentlemen." Turning to Red again and pointing at him, he said, "Red, your older son, Bobby—they call him Little Red, don't they? Hell, I met him this morning at the mayor's office, and I'll tell ya, he's bigger than you are. Maybe he'll be *Big* Red from now on." More laughter. Red leaned forward, gripping the edge of the table. He looked like he was about to stand, but Bowl-and-a-Roll was in his way.

"Red, I don't know if Little Big Red told you, but the mayor just made him a rig operator on the mine flushing crew up there on top of North Heights. That's a federal program grant through *my* office, of course, but your son will be working out of City Hall under the Mayor's payroll. So, today, ladies and gentlemen, is a great day for the Larkin family! Congratulations, Red. Let's hear it for Red, folks!"

The applause was obligatory, a hollow echo of the noisy effusion for Hafferty. As The Commissioner moved quickly to Red's booth, Red attempted again to stand up, but Hafferty held up his palms for him to remain seated and then reached in to shake his hand. "Red, best regards to your lovely wife, Rita," he said, loud enough for the diner crowd to hear every word. "And thank you as always for your continued, *faithful* support. Good luck with those boys. I'm sure they'll represent you well, especially young Timmy as your crew's *new busboy* here at Wally's Diner."

The crowd laughed and applauded yet again. Hafferty made a quick round of handshaking among the members of the Jury and then turned around. He raised his hands and stood in front of the Judge and Jury booth, obscuring Red on his withering throne.

"I apologize to everyone here for interrupting your dinner. My God, it must be like ice by now. Well, I'm going to make that up to you right now. You might have noticed that the girls have made their way around the diner and picked up all your food checks while I was talking with you. I asked them to do that because tonight, *your dinner is on me*! Everyone here! And if you want another warm meal, just ask the girls. Wally and Wilma, and our young James, here, and our beautiful Dee and Brenda will fix you up just right. No one leaves here without a full belly. *It's. On. Me!!*"

For this final curtain call, the applause was deafening. Men in the factory booths stood up clapping and cheering. Women edged out into the aisle to hug Hafferty as he made his way around the diner. Jade was awestruck. It was a perfect performance. Hafferty was being mobbed by the crowd as he pulled away to kiss Wilma, shake Wally's hand, kiss Brenda, hug Dee a little too tight for Jade's liking, and then turn to Jade.

He put his bear's arm around Jade's shoulder and pulled him along with him through the swinging doors and the kitchen to the back exit next to Wally's office.

"You did well out there, son." He put both hands on Jade's shoulders and looked him in the eye. "I appreciate your help with that crowd. But you need to learn to smile in public." He showed his fluorescent grid as an example. His googly eyes were dancing at Jade. "It's not easy at first, son, but when you hear that applause, well, it gets a hell of a lot easier. And they love you more if you smile to acknowledge their praise. It'll come to you, son. Just keep watching *me*. I'll show you how it's done." He patted Jade on both shoulders and started to turn away, then paused and clutched his shoulders again.

"You know what the truth is, don't you? The truth is that you're not just another constituent to *me*, James Flynn. I have high hopes for you. You're stepping up by taking that Macson job. It's not a friendly place like this diner. It's hard physical work, and the guys there are tough. *Really* tough. But I think you're up for it. You're older and more mature now than you were at Pell Academy. You blew that chance I gave you, but this time, if you hang in there, I'll make it worth your while. College is in your future, son. The alternative? You're a grunt in Vietnam. Nothing wrong with that. God loves those brave boys. You might want that chance—to serve your country. But I don't see it for you. I see you in college. I see you out on your own making big money, making things happen. Like me."

He pushed away from Jade and looked him up and down. "You're a smart kid, James. Soldier boy? College man? In the end, whichever way you go is entirely up to you."

He gave Jade a light slap on the cheek and left his hand there for a moment. Magically, the exit door opened from the other side. Jade recognized Stanley's thick hand holding it from the shadows. Hafferty turned in the doorway, smiled back at Jade, and pointed his finger at him.

"I know what you're wondering about, son. You're wondering what the hell happened back there in the diner. You're wondering how in the name of God did the Commissioner turn Red Larkin on his ass back there? Red Larkin, the king of Wally's Diner, no less." Hafferty showed Jade his broadest dayglow smile. His foggy blue eyes seemed to be laughing behind his thick lenses. "Eyes in the walls, ears to the ground, kiddo. You'll learn. You'll learn in that munitions factory, starting next Monday. Just be careful what you say. And *who* you say it to." He turned to Stanley. "Keep an eye on this kid for me, Stanley. And that's an order." He winked at Jade, and Stanley shut the door behind them.

10
Jew Hunting

Friday, June 13, 1969

That evening, Rocco and Free took Jade and Lucy on a joy ride through the hilly North Heights and almost wiped out a flock of kids playing in the street at dusk. It was their big night on the town. First celebration after graduation and it was the usual "double date," Jade and Lucy in the back seat, and Rocco and Free going stag up front. On this special night, Rocco announced, they were Jew Hunting.

"It's Friday the Thirteenth, boys and girls," he declared, barely containing his joy. "Time to scare the shit out of some Jew boys and then kick their asses."

Rocco's Camaro was in flight, the little pilot gleeful and pumped up. Free, at shotgun, leered at Lucy and Jade as he passed beers back to them, his eyes dancing with excitement. As Rocco flicked his Pall Mall out the window and exhaled a cloud of smoke that filled the back seat, he downshifted the Camaro to take on a brick hill that, from the approaching street, looked like a 200-foot wall.

"Thanks, Rocco!" Jade shouted, squeezing his eyes against the smoke.

The Camaro's front bumper caromed off the foot of the hill and Rocco slammed it into second gear. Everyone lurched forward and then back again.

"Rocco, Jesus Christ!" Lucy yelled. "My beer!"

She snapped her cigarette out Free's window and brushed her hand across her wet dungarees. Her breasts bounced as the car hit a dip in the brick road. Rocco cocked his head just in time to catch the bounce and then glanced at her wet pants. He turned back to the road, crowing a primal cackle, and gunned the Camaro up the hill.

The rumble and whir of tires on brick and the roar of the engine nearly drowned out Jimi Hendrix, his guitar wailing "Red House" on the eight track. Free belched over all the noise and shoved an empty pizza box out the shotgun window. Jade's throat launched a reflex gag at the mixture of cigarette smoke, Free's beer and pizza gas, and the swirling scent of burning rubber and engine exhaust filling the Camaro's back seat.

"You're disgusting, Free!" Lucy screamed.

Free turned all the way around in his seat and grinned, showing Jade and Lucy his cheese-covered teeth.

Lucy let out a gut laugh and fell backward in her seat and gulped a slug from her beer can. She yelled something else to Free. Jade couldn't make it out, but it sounded complimentary. He couldn't get used to how

Lucy seemed to love these idiots in an odd, almost romantic way. They were his comrades, but they were her anti-heroes, and, lately, the only subject she talked about with enthusiasm.

"Why don't you grow some muscles?" she'd recently told him, squeezing the wiry membranes at the top of his right arm and grimacing.

In one of her whimsical moments, she'd disclosed to Jade, as if he were one of her girlfriends instead of the guy who regularly explored her anatomy, that she liked "tough guys." She'd said, with a lusty laugh, that she had a thing for strongmen—"hulky, brash, mule-like, thick-chested louts." She wanted to rub their hairy chests and pound on them with her fists like Fey Ray on King Kong. The whole idea gave Jade a sour stomach.

A rusting assemblage of mine flushing equipment obscured the view of the crest of the hill, but Jade could see over Rocco's shoulder that a direct blast from the setting sun was going to greet them head-on.

"Over the fuckin' top, men!" Rocco shouted and the Camaro lurched into the air over the intersection.

"Yeeow!" Free screamed and flung a half-full beer can out the window and then yelped a second time as the can crunched with a whump against the trunk of a parked Dodge Dart. The Camaro touched down, front bumper first, and sparks flew off the pavement. They were blinded by the sunlight. The air in the car was suffocating. Jade grabbed Rocco by the shoulders. "Slow down!"

"Fuck off, man!" Rocco screamed and yanked his body forward. As the rear wheels touched down, he shoved the Camaro into third gear and the car jolted forward with a screech.

"I can't see!" Lucy hollered.

"You're not drivin'!" Rocco shouted and Free laughed.

"Slow down, man!" Jade yelled. "Kids up ahead!"

He could see the silhouetted figures of children playing a ball game in the next intersection. Free leaned out the shotgun window.

"It's Steve McFuckin' Queen, kiddos! Get the hell out of the way!"

The Camaro roared through the intersection with Rocco leaning on the horn as the kids scattered to the curbs, the older kids diving and rolling. Jade and Lucy ducked down in the back seat, unable to watch.

"Assholes!" Jade shouted to Lucy. She took a slug of beer and smiled. Even in the smoke and furor of the moment, he could see in her eyes that she wasn't with him.

They hunted for Jews over the next half hour. Jade and Lucy tried to discourage the hunters, offering to buy more beer and pizza and suggesting a drive-in movie instead. But Rocco and Free were determined to fight on this night. They needed at least two more victims, and they hadn't beaten up Jews yet. It was a personal goal for the diminutive Rocco. By graduation, he'd wanted to hit the cycle, but he was late, and he was pissed. He and Free had taken on a few colored guys, and, according to

Rocco, "kicked some queers' faggy asses," and now he declared that they needed to finish the cycle, graduation or no graduation. There were only a few Jewish families in this neighborhood, and Rocco suddenly seemed to know right where they lived.

After the Camaro turned right and then an immediate left uphill, Jade spotted two heavy-set teenagers walking up the steep sidewalk along a fieldstone wall that held back a pitched embankment in front of an old Victorian home. Both boys were dressed in white short-sleeved collared shirts, shiny black pants and thick shoes. Their yarmulkes were easy to spot as their heads bobbed forward into the steep climb.

"Jew beanies!" Rocco shouted as he slammed on the brakes and skidded to a stop opposite the targeted prey. The boys continued to walk but Jade knew they'd heard Rocco. An impulse struck him. He shouted out his back window.

"These guys wanna fight, boys. You better move out!"

The boys stopped and turned. One said something to the other, shaking his head, and then they started walking more quickly up the hill.

Free was the first to get out of the car. Rocco leaned on the horn and then opened his door and stood on the doorframe, his fist pounding the roof.

"Jewtelmen!" he announced over the top of the car, as if he were addressing a rally of political supporters. "Friends, Romans, Jewtelmen! Lend me some money!" In the back seat of the Camaro, Lucy spat a spray of beer and cackled and then slapped a hand over her mouth.

Rocco slammed his door behind him and pounced into the street. He looked much shorter standing next to the Camaro than he did behind its steering wheel. Jade knew Rocco kept the seat pushed all the way forward and he wondered if Rocco had trouble reaching the pedals. Rocco sucked hard on his filterless Pall Mall and then spit out smoke and bits of tobacco like dragon fire.

"Hey! Jew boys!"

The Camaro engine was still rumbling. The two boys continued to climb the hill.

"Hey!" Rocco shouted again. "I'm talkin' to you, Jew!" He squared up in the street and then hunched his shoulders and flicked his cigarette stub away in a spiraling trail of pink light in the gold-soaked air. Lucy leaned over Jade in the back seat, her knee digging into his thigh. She poked her head out Jade's curved window.

"Rock," she pleaded. "Leave 'em alone." Rocco turned to her, and she shifted her weight off her knee and drew back a few inches.

"Shut. The. Fuck. Up." He spoke the words through gritted teeth, his lips barely moving, his eyes black seeds of rage.

Lucy slumped back into the seat and reached for her Marlboro box. Jade turned to her, but she leaned forward to hide her face behind her veil of soft hair. Her hand trembled as she put a match to a cigarette.

On the sidewalk, Free had caught up to the teens and was walking alongside them, taunting. Jade could see that the boys were nearly as big as Free, but they looked soft and vulnerable in their formal clothes. Their pace had slowed, and they were talking to each other as if Free were invisible.

Suddenly, Rocco leaped from the sharp shadows of the sunset onto the back of one of the boys. In a flash, all four were sprawled on the sidewalk in a knot of arms and legs. Jade could hear a few punches land, but he couldn't tell who was making contact. Lucy pushed her body into his back and squeezed her head next to his in the small rear window frame.

"Jesus," she said.

Jade glanced at her and then turned back to the fight. In that moment, he'd missed a shift in the momentum of the brawl. Somehow, Rocco and Free were now on their backs, and the two Jewish boys were sitting on their assailants' chests, pummeling their faces with steady punches. Jade could see Rocco's fists shielding his face, but the hits were coming too quickly, and his fists turned limp and fell to the ground. The Jewish boys seemed to be casually practicing speed bag contact on Rocco and Free. Their arms moved with a practiced purpose, windmills in a storm.

Free's hands were at his side now, but he held his head off the ground, as if to facilitate the assault on his face. He couldn't bring himself to give up, yet he couldn't defend himself.

Rocco squirmed under his combatant's heavy body and relentlessly pounding fists. Jade saw an arc of blood from Rocco's mouth spray into the golden sunset.

Suddenly, the windmills stopped as if on cue. Rocco seized the opportunity to take a swing at his opponent, but it was more like an underwater hand signal than a punch. The boy moved casually away from Rocco's wave and stood up. His partner stood next to him for a moment, and then they turned and walked away, glancing over their shoulders as their attackers struggled to get up.

Rocco found his way to his knees and lifted his torso upright, looking even more childlike at half his height. In a gurgling voice, he called up the hill to the retreating victors.

"Fuckin' Jew cunts. We'll be back to kick your kike asses!"

When the bloodied fallen heroes returned to the Camaro, they collapsed into their seats, and Rocco gunned the Camaro's engine. He turned to Jade and Lucy, his face a puddle of blood and broken skin.

"You fuckin' tipped them off, Flynn! You're fuckin' done. Get the fuck out of my car."

64

Free had to get out and pull the back of his seat forward to let Jade and Lucy out, but she sat rigid in the back seat and looked at Jade, then at Rocco.

"Really, Rocco?" she said, shaking her head.

"No," he said. "You stay."

Jade turned to Lucy, but she lowered her gaze, leaned back in her seat, and crossed her arms. As Jade crawled over her to get out, Rocco growled at him. "Let the liar out, Free. We all know how he got that job at Macson. He's suckin' Hafferty's dick. And now he's a Jew lover. Get the fuck out of the Camaro! You're out for good."

Jade stood on the curb and watched Free pull the shotgun door closed and turn his head to look at Jade. Under a mass of blood and snot, Free's eyes were puffy slits. Still, Jade could see the anger, the betrayal.

The Camaro's tires smoked and screamed as Rocco the Hunter peeled out and thundered away. In the back window, Lucy looked out at Jade. She was smiling and giving him the finger.

11
General Patton

Friday June 20, 1969

On the morning of his scheduled meeting at Macson, Jade woke up at 5:00 and fidgeted for an hour about the job and how he'd got it. At first, neither the Ex-Pells nor his girlfriend had believed he'd been hired just by walking up to the gate and asking about openings, but that was his line. "No one gets a job that way," Rocco had said, "especially in Ebonton, and especially at the bomb factory. Those are plum jobs, and you gotta know someone to get one."

Jade stuck with his lie, but it didn't stick long with his friends. Everyone at Wally's Diner had learned about his new job at Macson, so Jade should have realized it was only a matter of time before Rocco, Free, and Lucy found out. He discovered the hard way, and Lucy's betrayal was his comeuppance. Rocco and Free were idiots who didn't deserve his honesty, but Lucy did, and Jade was now certain his breach was the tipping point for the decline of their relationship. He let a few days pass before calling to apologize, but she wouldn't take his calls. Now, it was a full week later, and he was resigned to his fate.

But it was Alice he was most worried about. She'd been out of her mind over his Macson job when he told her about it weeks ago. She'd cursed "that man" and then she'd cursed Jade. She'd seemed sober at the time, but she descended into a disconnected tirade that made little sense to him—something about being manipulated by the master and then her life in tatters and then Jade torn to bits by exploding bombs. When he'd told her that the bombs at the factory were not loaded, she ranted about making murder weapons for killing innocents in greedy men's wars. This went on for nearly a full day, and then she disappeared. Jade figured she'd gone on another binge, her usual way of dealing with life's insults. But, as the week wore on and she was still absent, he worried for the first time ever that he'd never see her again. When she finally returned, she hit the booze hard and only mentioned Macson when she was drunk and hearing voices. And her own voice warned him with eerie authority that he was walking into the mouth of Hell.

Working at the bomb factory would be a mixed blessing for Jade. Good money, but dangerous. That's what Rocco had said a few days after the failed Jew hunt when he stopped by Jade's house to harass him for lying. Rocco sat behind the wheel of his Camaro in front of Jade's house and taunted Jade while gunning his engine. Then he shut it down and changed his tone to offer fatherly counsel. He told Jade men were often maimed or even killed in that factory, that workers were treated like animals, and the place was known as a prison without bars. He told Jade his best bet was to simply not show up. Jade took the advice with a poker face, but he was unfazed by Rocco's feint, his attempt to diminish Jade's good fortune in the guise of wise counsel. He would tough it out. It would be worth it in the end. For the first time in his life, he'd have money, and then, his freedom.

The war in southeast Asia raged on with no end in sight, despite the rhetoric from Nixon. The proof of the war's escalation turned up close to home. In early May, the newspapers had reported that the Macson Munitions plant in Ebonton had received an unexpected Defense Department order for thousands of additional bomb shells. When Macson immediately ramped up hiring, Jade was somehow in the good graces of the man doling out the 45 new jobs. As Hafferty had told him, there was no job interview, just a sign-up meeting. He'd instructed Jade to report to the front gate of the Macson plant on the third Friday in June at 8:00 a.m. and ask for Mr. Jensen, the General Manager.

The guard booth was empty, its door ajar, and the plant gate was wide open. As Jade strode through the opening into the massive concrete yard, he heard a faint shout amid the factory's wall of noise. A tall guy with curly red hair was limping toward him, waving at him to stop. He plunked a misfitting cop hat on his huge red head and smiled as he hobbled up to Jade.

"You have to sign in, son." He yanked off his hat and pulled a handkerchief from his back pocket to wipe his forehead. When he turned around in the doorway of the booth with a clipboard in his hands, Jade told him his name.

"You're ten minutes early, Flynn. In this outfit, that means you're right on time. Sign here." He smiled as he handed Jade a clipboard. "Caught me with my cock in my hands. A guy can't even take a piss around here without an interruption."

Jade tried to laugh, but it came out like a squeak.

"Going to see Patton, huh?" He made a sideways laugh around an unlit Winston he'd jammed in his lips.

"Appointment with General Manager Jensen," Jade said. "Eight O'clock."

"That's General Patton, son," the guard said, around his cigarette. "Meanest mother fucker in this plant. Runs the place like he's head of Central Command. He says 'jump,' you say 'how high, sir?' He calls you a pussy, you say, 'No sir, I'm no pussy.' Then he orders you to do fifty push-ups to prove it."

Jade wasn't sure if he should smile or frown. "You're kidding, right?"

The guard lit his Winston, took a long pull and directed his exhale just over Jade's head. "Don't call him Patton, kid. By the looks of you, you're in for some pushups." He chuckled to himself and pointed. "Straight to that black door at the foot of the center building, the one with the Five Stars over the doorway. His secretary's off today, so you'll have to go right through to Patton's—eh, Mr. Jensen's office door. Knock real loud so he can hear you. Everybody's a little deaf around here."

Jade passed through the black iron gates into a vast concrete courtyard with light posts on cement blocks staggered across the open-air yard and a flagpole in the middle, a massive Stars and Stripes limp at the top. He saw two forklifts pass each other at the huge entrance to a sprawling brick building on the left. The building joined another one like it at the far end of the courtyard and that one joined a third building, forming a U around the colossal factory yard. Smokestacks over all three buildings spewed great clouds of soot into the crisp, blue morning air. A steady rumbling exhaled out of the cavernous opening on the left.

Jensen's outer office door creaked when Jade entered the tiny square room with an empty desk and a dirty porthole window overlooking the yard. The air was thick with the sour sting of cigar smoke. He repressed a cough and decided to breathe through his mouth.

He could see Jensen standing at a desk inside the next room, a much larger office. He knocked hard on the door frame. Jensen's head popped up from his desk, but Jade couldn't tell if Jensen was looking at him or looking over his head. The stub of a stogie was wedged in Jensen's puckered mouth. His face was pock-marked, pink, and puffy, and his head was shaved on the sides, the top covered in a short flat rug of wiry dark spikes. Jade could see through the haze that Jensen' eyes were black pinpoints, unwavering. Jensen shifted his gaze to something behind Jade in the secretary's office and his voice burst out of him like gunfire.

"This job's like a fuckin' wife!"

Jade turned toward the front office. It was still empty. He turned back to Jensen.

"Sir?"

Jensen stuck out his chin, still gazing past Jade. He was taller than Jade by half a head—a head that, to Jade, looked like an upturned bucket.

"Your paycheck is like gettin' laid by your old lady," Jensen shouted around his stogie, pointing at a chair for Jade to sit. "First couple times, it's worth puttin' up with her shit. After that, no matter how many times you get it, you're miserable for the rest of your fuckin' life."

Jade snorted a repressed laugh as he sat down, unsure if Jensen's humor was intentional. Jensen lowered his eyes and looked at Jade for the first time. He didn't know what General Patton looked like, but he imagined this man had earned the moniker.

"Think that's funny, son?" He grabbed the cigar from his mouth, his face frozen in a menacing scowl. Jade noticed a piece of tobacco on the man's lower lip, and, as if the man read his mind, Jensen spurted out a cloud of exhaust and, raising his chin, spat the piece of tobacco off his lower lip. Jade watched it come at him like a tiny missile and then drop suddenly to the desk.

"Shit, boy," Jensen said, with his pinprick eyes wide on Jade, his cigar hand pointing at his face. "You ain't even got your dick wet yet, have ya?"

"Sir?"

Jensen looked down at the papers on his desk, picked up one and flipped it into the air.

"What the fuck's he doin' sending me a fuckin' skinny kid?" He looked up at Jade. "You shave yet, boy?"

He shoved the cigar back into his mouth and dropped into his chair, shaking his head. Then he slid a form and a ballpoint pen in Jade's direction.

"If you want the wife, you gotta sign up for her."

"Sir?"

"Fill out the fuckin' form!" Jensen shouted.

When Jade was finished, Jensen leaned forward on his hairy arms and hissed out a cloud of dank breath. It smelled like the river behind Jade's house.

"I hope you work faster than you write, asshole," he growled. "Takin' up enough of my time."

He told Jade to be there Monday morning at seven, with steel-toed boots and a worker's attitude.

"No jerk offs or pussies in this place!"

When Jade stood up to leave, Jensen muttered something Jade didn't catch.

"Sorry, sir?"

68

Jensen lifted his chin, his brown teeth clenching the cigar.

"I said get down and give me fifty. NOW!"

Jade's arms trembled as he hit pushup thirty-five. He tried to focus on the numbers, but he heard Jensen's boots move around the desk; then he saw them slide underneath him. He felt the General hovering over him like a wolf over its prey. At number forty, Jensen's right boot left the floor. Jade's breath escaped in a huff as the boot landed in the middle of his back. When the General pressed down, Jade's arms gave way and his entire body flopped.

"I'm puttin' you with the nigger." He lowered his face to Jade's ear and growled, "Ya scrawny little pussy."

Part Two

12
Queen of the Four Roses

Monday, June 23, 1969

Jade sat at the kitchen table, adrift. It was a few minutes after 5:00 a.m. He was dazed from restless sleep, distracted by an emptiness that should have been the opposite—excitement about his first day on the new job. But now, what lay ahead seemed unreal, an unformed idea.

He made a few absent swings with his fork in a feeble attempt to joust with a house fly for domain over a plate of scrambled eggs and toast. Surrendering, he set the fork next to the plate. His stomach was a knot. The air in the kitchen was thick with dueling smoke from the hot frying pan and Alice's cigarettes. She'd returned on Sunday from another weeklong absence and the weight of her sour Sunday evening hung heavily behind closed windows. Jade scratched his smooth chin with a slow hand and watched the fly rub its front feet together and then scamper toward the runny eggs. When the little guy began to dig in, Jade fingered his fork and then let it rest. He set his chin into the palm of his hand, his elbow braced next to the plate.

"You don't like my eggs!"

It wasn't an observation; it was an accusation. It was Alice. Why was she here at this hour? Jade stared at her. She was sitting across the table from him in a black tee shirt and white bikini underpants, her gauzy cover-up hanging off her shoulders covering nothing. She had her foot on the seat of the chair, her elbow propped on her bare knee, her trembling hand holding a lit Lucky Strike.

She stared back at him through the cigarette fog and pushed her free hand through her hair. Short black curls sprung out everywhere. A soft gray saddlebag under each eye, her full mouth cracked at the edges.

Her arm convulsed as she brought her Lucky to her swollen lips and tilted her head back to take a pull.

"You never make eggs," Jade said, back to watching the fly on his plate. His voice was flat, alien to his own ears.

"I made them for you!" Alice shouted. "To give you strength!" She slammed a fist on the table, startling Jade from his emptiness. For a moment, Jade thought the wobbling red table with chrome edges was going to collapse, taking his plate of eggs with it.

He watched the fly resettle onto the scrambled eggs and then met Alice's glare again.

"You don't do food, Alice," Jade said, his real voice returning. He blinked and then deepened his focus, holding her glaring green eyes with his own. "Remember? You gave that job to me. Your job is to drink."

Alice held his challenging stare for another moment and then flinched. She tipped her head back and blew twin pipes of smoke from her nose. "You need to be strong for that new job…" She choked on the last words, coughing into her fist and shifting her eyes to his plate. "You need to eat."

Jade pushed away from the table in a burst and tossed his plate on a small stack of dirty dishes flickering in the sink under the broken rhythm of a fading fluorescent bulb. An empty bottle of Four Roses lay on its side next to the sink. A collection of damp, yellowed Lucky Strike butts littered the inside of the bottle.

"What's wrong with Wally's?!" Alice started again. "Why can't you go back there?"

"This place is a mess, Alice." Jade waved his hand around the room. "And I can't breathe in here." He strained at the kitchen window until it finally gave way with a groaning crack. He put his face into the opening and breathed, teasing his mind into wakefulness. The outside air tasted worse than the kitchen's mash of acrid scents.

"Wally loves you," she said. "God bless his heart."

"Wally's a Jew, Ma," he said as he stooped further into the window opening. "You used to tell me Jews don't have hearts! Now that I've finally left his place after six years, you suddenly love the guy?"

"I never ever said that about Wally! I said it about another man I knew. Bastard that he was. But Wally? I love Wally. Always will. He's been a father to you!" She pushed the cigarette into her mouth, her trembling fingers covering her lips. As her cheeks puckered, the tip of the Lucky lit up.

Jade pushed past her to the doorway between the kitchen and The Grotto and looked toward the front door. He turned around, passed her again, and stepped to the back door. He pulled the sagging red gingham curtain aside and looked out at their tiny backyard. The first sharp edges of sunlight danced on the battered rooftops behind the yard but the little square yard itself was in deep morning shadow. The old oil drum stood in its center, a lonely sentinel protecting a ten-foot square dirt patch in the gray darkness. Eight hours earlier, Jade had been burning trash in the old drum when Alice had appeared in the open doorway in her coverup, naked underneath the flimsy sheer. She'd waved her hands around the halo of her hair and called out to him in a distant voice, as if he were a mile away.

"Seamus! My son! Beware the dark faces ahead!"

Her eyes had turned gray and flat, unfocused. "One will bring death to you there in Gomorrah! Another will save you! But why, Shay? Why? Seamus my son, Mother Mary will be your guide! Take her hand, Seamus. Take her hand!" Then she held both arms out and with palms up she pointed with her right hand to something behind him. Jade turned and saw nothing but darkness. When he turned back to Alice, she'd disappeared.

Jade shook the memory away and turned around. She was still at the table.

"You were happy at Wally's, Seamus. You grew up there. That's your family!"

Alice had lit a new Lucky and was talking through a funnel of smoke spewing from her throat, her voice struggling against the competing cloud. She pushed back in her chair and, tipping her head backward into her shoulders, emptied the rest of her drag in a fog that shrouded the dim globe of yellow light in the center of the ceiling.

"I gotta go," Jade told her. "I can't be late on my first day."

He crossed the room in one motion, his heavy new boots pounding the floor. He stopped in front of a mirror just outside the kitchen door at the edge of The Grotto.

"You have two hours!" Alice said, her voice clear and childlike now. "Plenty of time, honey." She shifted around to face him, her bare legs sprawling and her chair squawking on the cracked and torn linoleum floor. She ran a hand across her forehead into her nest of curls. She smiled at Jade, but her eyes didn't match her mouth. She was still drunk.

"Get yourself cleaned up, will ya Alice?" He said this without taking his eyes off his own image in the mirror. "I'll be gone all day. You have lots of time to make that happen."

Alice stood up, her eyes ablaze.

"Gone all day! Gone all day! Mister Big Deal!" She was shouting and waving her arms. She took a long stride toward Jade and pushed her face up to his. On her tiptoes, her tiny nose was at the level of his chin. "Mister Big Shot!"

He winced at her breath and then smiled into the mirror, pleased that his head poked through the top of the frame.

"I am taller, you know," he said.

It was the boots—new, steel toed, black, shiny, thick soled. The salesman at the Army Navy Store confirmed what Jensen had commanded. "Gotta have steel toes, son. They'll save your feet. Every guy there has 'em." Jade hadn't noticed in the store that the boots gave him another inch-and-a-half in height.

Alice suddenly giggled like a little girl. She reached up and ran a hand through his hair.

"You are a big deal, Shay."

Jade turned and, without making eye contact with her, slapped a backhand against a framed photograph on the opposite wall.

"Just like Big Mack!" he said in a shout of sarcasm, his arms waving to no one. In the blurry black and white photo, a White man in a black suit, stiff white collar and black derby stood alone in an empty field. This was the only photo in the house. It had hung in every home they had lived in.

Alice frowned. Her face fell. A dark look descended over her eyes, and she hunched her shoulders away from him.

"You're no Big Mack, boy!" she wailed, snapping her head to the side. "No sir! You're nothing compared to him!"

"Man of Mystery!" Jade called out, rolling his eyes. He started toward the front door.

"He would've put manners on you!" Alice shouted after him. "No one talked back to my daddy!"

Jade turned the knob on the front door and shifted his body back toward Alice.

"I gotta go, Ma," he said. "Take a bath, will ya? You look like hell."

Alice charged at him and grabbed his shirt, spitting her words up into his face. "This is hell, Seamus Flynn! I live in hell! And if my daddy were here, he would've changed it all. Never would have let that beast get away with what he's done to me. The bastard!" She punched Jade softly on the chest and sobbed into his shoulder. "And he would have stopped you from taking that job, sending you to that living Hell, making bombs for more killing. He would have stopped you from leaving me here to drown in the sorrows of my suffering soul. I have failed you. I have failed you. You've been stolen from me."

In a deafening screech, a siren filled the room, rising to a maddening pitch, then falling away. Alice dropped to her knees and, in a single looping wave of her right hand, made the sign of the cross. As the siren wailed away in the distance, she grabbed rosary beads from a small table and wrapped them around her left hand and began to pray out loud in that distant voice that Jade had become oddly accustomed to.

"Jesus, Mary, and Joseph, save them!" she wailed. "Mother of God, Saint Christopher, Saint Michael the Archangel, watch over them! Saint Benedict, protect them from evil!"

Jade took a deep breath and blew it out, exasperated. He looked around the front room. Over the past six weeks, his home had been converted into a Catholic sanctuary. The Blessed Virgin stood in the center of what was once the parlor, now The Grotto. The altar candle at the statue's feet flickered inside its red votive glass. A framed print of the

Sacred Heart of Jesus hung over a closed upright piano against the side wall. Statues of saints stood in solemn watch on every horizontal surface in the small room, their pale faces flickering in the light of the votive candles at their feet. A crucifix hung over the doorway to the kitchen, another one over the front door with browned palm fronds jammed behind it, and one over every other doorway in the house, and on the wall over Alice's bed upstairs as well as Jade's. He wondered when she would erect a cross on their roof and make it official. The sanctum of Saint Alice. Or whoever she was.

She was still on her knees, striking her chest with soft blows from her clenched right hand and fingering the rosary beads in her left. Jade looked down at his mother.

"It's over now, Alice," he whispered. "Sirens are gone. C'mon, mom. Get up." He lifted her by the elbows to her feet.

"He ruined my life, Shay. Our lives. The monster." She was still trembling as she looked up at him with a vacant stare. Her breath was sharp with last night's booze and this morning's cigarettes. Her eyes, once so brilliant, were swimming in pink and yellow gauze. In that moment, Jade remembered her when he was a boy. The soft, smooth face he'd looked up to with hope when he told her he'd made the team. He'd been thrilled about this first big accomplishment, and she'd met his confident gaze with a warm, approving look. He'd felt connected to her, certain of her pride in him. Then, as if a hand had passed over her face, Jade had watched her eyes go suddenly cold, her face turn to stone. She'd told him, "No. You cannot play on that team." She'd held him by the shoulders and bent down to look him in the eyes. "We're leaving this place tomorrow. We're packing up today. Get your things ready."

Now her voice was nearly cracking. "Daddy would have killed him, Shay," Alice screeched, leaning heavily with her elbows into Jade's palms. "Daddy hated my brother. And he would have killed him if he ever saw what he did to me."

"Your brother." Jade shook his head and looked into her eyes. "Alice." He leaned his face down to hers. "You never had a brother. Or a sister."

"I had plenty of brothers!" she shouted inches from his face and then pushed away from him. She crouched in the middle of the room as if she were going to pounce. Her jaw hung low and her eyes narrowed. "My oldest brother, Junior! He was a war hero, Shay! Fought in The Bulge, then all the way through France into Germany. And they captured him. Tortured him. Then they killed him."

She held out her arms and gazed into a dream, whispering, "And daddy died with him…"

Jade sighed and nodded. He looked down at his mother.

"That's a new one, Alice. A brother? You told me your father died in a Nazi prison. Now you're saying he died in battle alongside his son? Your brother? Alice, you've seen too many war movies." He opened the front door and a wave of sunlight filled the dank room. "Stay off the sauce today, will you please? For me? Please?"

Alice threw herself on her knees again. "Please don't leave me, Seamus. You're all I have!" She burst into choking sobs, tears popping onto her cheeks.

"I'm not leaving, Ma. I'm going to work. Remember?"

"No," she said, holding out both arms to him and locking her eyes on his. "You'll be changed. That new job in that evil place, it will take you away from me. You won't come home at all! It's too dangerous!"

"Ma," he said. "I gotta go." He stepped outside and started to pull the door behind him when a truck roared by, filling the house with thunder, rattling The Grotto's wobbly floor lamp and threatening Alice's candles and saints. Her Blessed Virgin Mother.

"You'll go with that girlfriend," Alice called after Jade. "And you'll elope, and you'll leave me here." She was sitting on her heels now, her flimsy cover-up puddled around her bare legs. Jade stood on the threshold with the door half open and stared at her.

"I'm not going anywhere with her, Alice. If I go, it'll be on my own."

"You don't love her?!" Alice called out, her eyes like a child's.

"I gotta go," he insisted, but his shoulders dipped, and he stepped back inside, closing the door.

"You don't love me!?" Alice shouted, standing suddenly straight up. "You don't love me! You don't love her!" Alice lunged at him with her fists raised. "You love yourself!" She took a wide swing at Jade, missed, and fell to the floor at his feet. Before he could bend to help her, she scrambled to her knees, wrapped her rosary around both hands and looked up to him, her cracked lips trembling, her voice sputtering.

"Shay, for the love of God, please!"

"Ma," he said. Holding her cheek in his palm, he used his thumb to gently wipe away her tears.

"Oh, Seamus, please! Please don't leave. Please don't go to that evil place!"

"Pray for me, Ma," Jade said, as he stepped through the doorway. "I'll see you after work."

As he closed the door, Jade heard his mother chanting in her distant voice.

"Holy Mary, Mother of God, pray for us sinners, now and at the hour of our death. Ah-men."

13
Bum

Jade squinted into the shadows of a blinding morning sun as he made his way to the bus stop. Exhaust fumes and gutter dust scratched at his sinuses, but the air was lighter outside his house, the usual sour veil from the burning culm heaps having shifted to another neighborhood in a surge of sympathetic wind. He felt the onset of summer waking his senses at last. Spring had been a long battle for release from captivity, teased by hints of freedom and then engulfed by ice and gray snow and darkness again and again. By early June, resignation had settled into the voices and faces of the students and teachers at school, the customers at the diner, and strangers on the street. The valley's unmerciful cold firmament had stunned its inhabitants yet again into silent submission to their shuffling fate.

Finally, on this sunny third day of official summer, the longed-for break seemed possible. There was a floral sweetness to the generous unfamiliar breeze. Jade noticed moisture returning to his skin, an uncracking. He dared to part his lips to taste these teasing hints of what might come. In the gaps between passing cars and trucks, he could hear bird calls, chirps, whistles, insects whirring, the promise of the warm season at last. He wanted to believe in it, especially on this day.

As he approached the bus stop on Reston Street, Jade saw a man and three women in a row, holding their hands to their brows to shield the sunlight as they squinted in search of the Number 15. Although he preferred the full-on blast of a rare sunbath on his face, Jade felt compelled to join this military pose. He stepped to the end of the queue next to the third woman and, leaning out of her shadow, he joined the group salute to the unfamiliar daytime star.

The man at the front of the queue was tall and thick, his enormous head an inverted curvilinear triangle—a robot's head. He wore gray work pants draped over dark boots with steel toes peeking through torn leather. The big man turned from the sunlight to look at Jade. Most of his face was lost in hard shadow, but Jade could see the outline of oversized aviator glasses, the sharp point of the man's chin, and the matching hard corners of his crewcut. Jade thought of his alien alter-ego, his omniscient observer, and he imagined that this man was the alien's robot companion—Jade's own version of Gort from his and Alice's favorite sci-fi film. He looked down and saw the outline of a lunch pail in the man's right hand, and his gaze froze there. Jade had forgotten to consider lunch. He hadn't touched his breakfast. What would he do for food at work?

A queasiness seized him as he pondered the unknown job ahead. He'd worked for Wally for six years, first as a dishwasher, then busboy, and eventually short-order cook, standing by Wally's side, assistant to the man he most admired. But this new job was factory work, hard labor. Jade felt uncertain about what was expected of him, but quite certain that General Patton would attempt to make it as miserable as possible. His earlier confidence in front of the mirror evaporated in the bright blaze of daylight, his drifting thoughts disappearing into a dizzy void. As he leaned toward the street to watch the number 15 approach, Jade, for a moment, thought he might pass out.

The 15 was crowded with Monday morning workers. Jade had to stand in the aisle and hang on to a metal post. He could see Gort's huge metallic head nearly touching the ceiling at the back of the bus. The air on board was dank, a similar but less pungent version of Alice's kitchen. He'd spent six years riding this bus to Wally's, and the mixture of perfume, cigarettes, and booze breath embraced him like a musty old companion. He took shallow breaths through his mouth and lowered his head to watch the familiar scene along Reston Street. Most of the houses looked like his own, brown asbestos shingle or once-white aluminum-sided brittle boxes packed in together just a few feet from the curb like a refugee army embracing its defeat. Some of the homes had black iron fences with slumping gates left open. Many had religious statues on their humble patches of earth, and still others had peculiar decorations to which Jade had become accustomed but never understood. He was always puzzled in particular by a popular lawn ornament he'd often seen on this route—a concrete birdbath filled with a single giant pastel neon ball. Why have a birdbath, he thought, if the birds can't bathe in it? A wild idea popped into his head, answering his own question: what if these weird balls were signals, lunar transmitters, propped up by unsuspecting humans on behalf of an alien enemy? Guiding the Apollo 11 astronauts to the wrong moon. A secret alien sabotage hatched right here in unwary Mell Hollow.

Jade was jostled toward the back of the aisle as the 15 stopped every few blocks to pick up more passengers. With bodies pressing in on him, he found it more difficult now to bend and check out familiar sites along the route. He'd always tried to identify the towns, but it was a challenge. There was little difference among the tiny commercial centers with their indistinguishable flat store fronts, identical pizza shops, churches, bars, and funeral parlors. Jade wondered how anyone knew where one town ended and the next began.

A voice barked up at him. "I know you!"

Jade felt a tug on his shirt. He turned and looked down into the face of an old man seated on the aisle. The face was scarlet, the nose swollen and knotted, the open mouth cracked and gap-toothed. The man's dark

78

eyes, partly shaded under the brim of a sagging scally cap, looked blank, deadpan. His musty, acidic breath, hit Jade like a punch.

"I know who you are!" the man shouted. Then he bowed his head suddenly, let go of Jade's shirt, and hacked a long lung-burning cough toward the floor. The handful of passengers that had turned to look at him turned away again, some of them wincing. Jade tried to resume his window gazing on the other side of the street. The homes on the south side were bathed in dark shadow, but Jade assured himself from past experience that there were no aberrations from the street's theme until four blocks before Wally's Diner, where much larger homes were set back from the street, fronted by wide lawns with flowering trees and tall, neat rows of evergreen shrubs. As the bus passed the first of these homes, Jade strained to see buds on the flowering trees. When the bus reached Wally's, Jade stretched sideways to see if he could pick out a familiar face in the diner windows.

The stranger stopped coughing and barked at him again.

"Your old man's a bum!" the man said, louder than before. Jade turned to face him. "A sneaky Jew! Big shot reporter. Askin' too many questions, almost cost us our jobs. He's a liar! They canned him! Shoulda thrown him in jail. Jew bastard!"

Jade pushed away from the old barker and moved ahead of the passenger standing in front of him.

"You look just like him," the old man shouted to Jade's back. "And you're a no-good Jew just like him, too!"

Behind Jade, a woman squeaked a tiny laugh, and a man followed with an exaggerated cough. Jade stared straight ahead for the rest of the trip, his face hot, his eyes unfocused, his teeth clenched. When the bus reached the station in center city, he waited for the passengers in front of him to file off. As he moved slowly toward the exit, he heard a shuffling gait behind him, a coal miner's hack barking at his back. On the last step before the street, Jade turned around to meet the old man's sallow, beady eyes.

"I never *had* a father," he shot at the man's startled face. "Figure that one out, you miserable rotten asshole!"

14
Alone Together

She lay face down, her arms and legs spread wide, prostrated at the feet of the life-size Blessed Virgin. She had just completed one hundred Hail Marys. Her breathing was slower now, her heart relaxed, revived, a steady rhythm against the floor. Through her thin cover-up and tee shirt, she could feel the bristles of the worn carpet poking at her breasts and belly, her uncovered thighs and knees. She lifted her head off the bare wooden floor at the edge of the carpet and opened her eyes for the first time since he'd left. She could smell a sweetness in the room and remembered how her hand had trembled as she lit all the remaining candles after he'd slammed the door behind him.

"Glory be to God," she whispered. "Glory be to God." She picked up her head further and looked at Mary's pinkish feet, a green serpent curled under them. She thought she saw blood near Mary's ankle, but she blinked, and it was gone. She felt her heart racing again and put her forehead back onto the floor and began chanting another "Hail Mary."

Later, she lay on her back in steaming water, her head propped against the wall of the tub, the bottom ringlets of her hair submerged, her chin resting on her chest, her mouth at the water's edge. She stared at her nipples, bobbing on their islands of white blooms in this tiny sea, the rubbery purplish little pillars surrounded by imperfect circles of pink, rougher and darker than the rest of her breasts, the circles the texture of moon rocks. She thought it was funny that her breasts could float like this. She smiled at them, happy to see them so awake.

"My mother," she whispered. "She was an island. And so am I. Here we are, side by side. Alone together." She smiled, humming the melody of a pop song about being as alone in this world as a rock. She sang out, in a rasping falsetto, "My tits are i-i-i-islands!"

She burst into cackling laughter that echoed off the ceiling. She gasped, startled by the strange reverberating sound. She pulled herself up into a seated position, scooped water onto her face and shook her head to chase the echo, the sound of someone else's laughter. She closed her eyes and began washing her hair, humming a child's song whose lyrics she could not remember.

The sensation of her own fingers on her scalp set her memory astir. Tara had the softest touch, so she would only let Tara, and no one else, wash her hair. Once a week. Why couldn't she remember the lyrics Tara had taught her? The words were simple, rhyming. Why couldn't she remember? Annoyed now, she felt the bristling, forceful, angry fingers of

Sister Saint Joseph on her scalp, digging there, hurting her. She lifted her head out of the water and looked around the bathroom. What was wrong with her memory? How old was she now? Not the child, but her, now? Not at home, not at the convent, but here, now? How old? She couldn't remember. What year was this? What are moon rocks?

She slid her body forward, her knees coming up high and her head dunking backward under the water. She rubbed her submerged scalp, erasing the suds from her hair, pining for Tara's gentleness. But needle fingers Saint Joe came back again with a scolding vengeance, and for a long moment, she considered taking a breath under water. Just to see.

At the mirror, she stared at her wet head and then shook it like a dog just out of a lake. She barked, and then she laughed at the echo. "He will come back," she said to the mirror. "I will howl for him. And I will do a handstand. And I will hit him with pillows. And I will sing like Mama Cass. And he will laugh until he pees his pants."

She smiled at her foggy image. She still wasn't sure at that moment how old she was. Everything was unclear. Her mouth, her eyes, her cheeks, her chin. Wavering in a mist. She wondered if she could make up her face so he'd think she was young again. It would be easy, she thought. He'd be fooled, at least for a little while. He's so self-involved, hell, it might take him hours to notice.

Later, in bed, daylight stinging her eyelids, she thought she heard someone in the kitchen. She opened her eyes, touched her cheeks, remembering her makeup, hoping. Was it him? No. Not him. It was her. Could it be?

But she didn't get up to see. She knew her makeup would be smeared, her eyeliner running, her rouge blotchy. She would be a disappointment to her for trying to fake her face. She rolled over and pulled a pillow over her head.

15
Death Mask

Monday, June 23, 1969

Jade felt recharged after letting loose on the old man on the bus. He'd wanted to punch the foul bastard, but somehow shouting in his face felt better. And had a better effect. The man's tiny head had snapped back at Jade's fighting words, and, for a moment, Jade thought the old man might fall backwards, but he had not waited around to see.

In the rosy morning light, he shrugged off the confrontation and marched with purpose toward the factory, a man on a mission. He took long strides in his new boots, passing slower, less energized Monday morning workers ambling to their jobs. A soft breeze scuttled papers and cans along the Canton Avenue gutter and wide sidewalk, but it also washed away the sulfur stench that drifted daily into Center City from Jade's little burg, Mell Hollow. He breathed deeply, considering this a good sign. A fresh start. Literally.

A few cars and trucks passed by on the city's main street, quiet at this early hour. Trolley tracks ran down the middle of the wide avenue, a vestige of a bygone era. Jade smiled as he recalled his Christmas trolley excursions with his mother in a different town. He remembered her lipstick, red and shiny, and the look others had given her holding his hand and strutting forward with purpose. She wore a tan camel hair coat and narrow high heels that echoed on the sidewalk. Jade would tug on her hand and look up at her as they made their way through the close Christmas crowds. She would smile down at him, their eyes connecting in their private secret. He knew that she was smarter, more fun, and more beautiful than anyone in the world.

Sweet scents from a Canton Avenue bake shop brought Jade back to his mission. He picked up his pace, feeling the weight of his boots propelling him forward. He watched his image in the storefront windows, a quick-moving tall guy with a purpose in his stride. The breeze pushed his hair off his ears, the warm morning light giving him the cinematic look of Clint Eastwood. He pictured a dark cowboy hat on his head, a pencil thin cigarillo in his mouth, a scruffy beard. He was The Man with No Name.

He looked ahead and drifted into another daydream, this one about his job and the freedom it would bring him. He'd have more cash in his pocket and be able to move on with his life. With this job, he could complete the separation from his high school pals, his girlfriend, his old job at Wally's, his past. And Alice? It was time he moved on from her. He had been taking care of her more than she took care of him. With most guys, it was the other way around. By summer's end, he'd be headed west. No turning back. Alice would get along. The new job was the beginning of his new life. Doors would open, this one setting him free. He couldn't wait to leave behind this small stale broken life.

Jade heard a lock clicking, and he turned and saw the face of a shop owner staring at him from the other side of a glass door a few feet to his left. Something about the man's face reminded Jade of Lucy. The mouth was pinched, the eyes wide—the way Lucy looks when she's frightened.

Jade turned his gaze forward again just in time to witness a fast-moving car lurch over the curb onto the sidewalk and head directly toward him.

In mid-stride, he looked quickly left. No place to move. He shifted his body right. But the car, a bright red Mustang, was bearing down on him, and his move to the right into the street wasn't going to be fast enough. The car was upon him. His legs froze and his breath stopped. He closed his eyes, bracing his shoulders and his gut for the impact.

A booming explosion jolted Jade's head, and he felt a spray of tiny needles sting his face. A horn, blasting so close and so loud—inside his head. He ducked, pulled his hands to his chest, and crouched forward. After a long clenched moment, he realized he was still standing, alive, breathing, trembling. He opened his eyes.

The Mustang's front-end, hissing and smoking, had been reshaped into a "V," wrapped around a fire hydrant five feet in front of him. The car's horn seemed to get louder still, and a burning metallic smell assaulted him.

A face stared at him from the cracked windshield—wide-eyed, covered in blood, and shrouded in a cloud of dark curls. Its mouth was frozen wide in mid-scream. Teeth and tongue twisted in a red mass. The horn blared on, and on, and on.

16
On The Line

Monday, June 23, 1969

The guard on duty must have seen Jade approach the booth but he didn't acknowledge him standing on the other side of the window. Jade had heard the factory's first whistle just as the cops had arrived at the accident scene, and it was at least another thirty minutes before they let him go. They'd left him alone in the back of a squad car, dazed, watching the chaos around him, just a few feet from the wrecked Mustang, other cop cars surrounding the scene like a wagon train from the movies. But these weren't pretend cowboys, these were real cops and a few men in suits huddled around a smoking red car, shouting and shoving at onlookers and then crowding around the wreck, forming a blue wall. When two cops got into the car with him, he'd barely heard what they'd said to him. He'd already seen too much. He'd watched the ambulance guys pull the woman from behind the wheel. She was right there next to the squad car, next to him. He'd felt his stomach lurch as her limp body and her great thicket of bloodstained hair flopped onto the stretcher. He'd watched her last breath.

This grisly spectacle had been far worse than the terror of the impact. She'd died right in front of him. But for the hydrant, that corpse would have been his.

Jade knocked on the guard booth window. The man inside was not the friendly lumbering red-headed guard he'd encountered on Friday. This was a younger, smaller guy with pasty skin and thin crusty lips. He was slumped in his chair, paging slowly through a magazine with a blank stare and a turned down mouth. Lost in his loose-fitting uniform and oversized cap, he was a kid Jade's age playing cop. Jade could see naked women on the pages of the guard's magazine. The little guy looked up at Jade as if startled to find him there.

"Wadda *you* want?" the guard hollered at him from behind the glass, making no attempt to conceal the photos. His bony chin jutted forward, and he stood up without adding much to his height. He reminded Jade of Rocco. A short guy whose face had been punched so often that he dared you to take your shot; it wouldn't hurt him.

"I'm late," Jade said. "I was a witness to an accident, and I got held up."

"Late for *what?*" the guard snapped.

"For work."

"You don't work here!"

"I'm starting today," Jade insisted. He could feel the heat rising in his chest.

The little guard moved closer to the glass and ran his eyes up and down Jade. He shook his head in disgust, picked up the wall phone and looked toward the interior of the factory yard. Jade followed the guard's gaze toward General Patton's door at the far end of the yard. The massive smokestacks were chugging black soot, the buildings roaring their hot breath into the vast concrete yard.

The guard slammed down the phone and returned to his seat and his magazine. Jade knocked on the window.

"What!?" the guard shouted at him. The little guy's face was crimson now.

"Are you gonna let me in?"

The guard stared at Jade for a long moment then turned away, snapping his magazine straight with a flick of his wrists. He shuffled through a few pages and then unraveled the centerfold. "He's comin'," he said to the magazine.

"Who?"

"Why don't you just fuckin' wait 'n see, asshole!" the guard shouted, his lips curling into a pinched opening that suggested the very word he'd used. He stared at Jade until Jade turned and walked to the gate, sweat trickling down his sides. He looked back at the miniature guard watching him over the top of his dirty magazine. Jade held the little man's gaze, slowly raised his left fist, and popped up his middle finger.

By the time the foreman showed up, Jade was officially 55 minutes late for work. He'd started out from home with plenty of time to spare, but now he was not only late but owing time. The foreman wore a clean dark shirt and pants. He was Jade's height but at least 50 pounds heavier. Under his squared-off gray crew cut, he had a soft round face. He surveyed Jade from top to toe, as if deciding whether Jade was a bona fide worker or just a lost kid. Jade started to explain why he was late but the foreman held up his hand.

"Save it," he said.

"But I witnessed a woman getting killed."

"Where?"

"Canton Avenue, just two blocks from here. Her car ran up on the curb right in front of me. If it wasn't for a fire hydrant, I'd be dead right now."

"A lady, huh. Anybody else in the car?"

"Not that I could tell, but I saw the cops pull something out of the trunk."

The foreman raised his hand again and offered a half-smile. "We'll look into it, kid. Your time will start today when you punch in. Follow me."

As they approached the huge open doorway to the building on the left, Jade tried to reclaim the excitement he'd felt earlier about his new job, the lightheaded feeling along Canton Ave just before the crash. He tried to recapture his confident stride in his new boots, his Clint Eastwood persona. It was Monday, the raw unbroken part of the week, the beginning of a new adventure, his first summer after high school, the launch of his new life—his own moon shot.

But the feeling wouldn't hold. Now he was fighting two uneasy thoughts—the vision of the woman taking her last breath on the stretcher and the visceral memory of Jensen's boot on his back on Friday. And, mixed in with these unsettling thoughts, he was struck by a realization— the certainty that he was uncertain. What was he doing here? Was Alice right after all? He'd just turned 18, and he brought nothing to this kind of experience, nothing but his acquired sense of confidence that would be quickly unmasked in the first test. He'd try to puff up with the facade of the tough guy he thought he should be, but he knew it was a sham.

Jade's heart pounded as they approached the huge foreboding doorway, a blast of hot air pushing against his stride. Large indistinct dark shapes shifted inside the opening, swaying like angry trees in a night storm. The roar from within was palpable—mechanical shrieks that vibrated his skull. Groans from gasoline engines produced a steady ominous rumble, their fumes bitter in his mouth. This place was a single robotic being, its mechanical pulse feeding on fire tended by the humans in its grasp.

Jade was tempted to look back as they came to the threshold of the vast clanging cave. The memory of the sweet scent of this once-promising summer morning was smothered by smoky metallic air from within. He wanted to look back at the daylight in its brilliant morning sky, but he knew that if he did, he would run there. Away from this maw of mechanical madness, back into the arms of nature's offering, this first hopeful day. But he could not turn around; there was no place for him to go but backwards. He had to face this place that his mother had warned him against, and he had to prove to her, and to himself, that he would survive it.

The foreman showed him how to punch in, handed Jade ear plugs, and pointed at his own ears. The plugs were like candle wax, yellow and greasy. As he kept pace with the wide-stepping foreman, he could feel grit rolling under his new steel-toed boots, a thousand tiny marbles beneath each sole. The air was chalky, scratching at his throat and lungs.

"You'll get used to the noise," the foreman shouted, as they entered the depths, shapes of men moving in the near distance. No one was wearing goggles or scratching at their eyes. It's what Jade wanted to do— scratch his eyes with both fists, breathe fresh air, hear himself think, taste the new morning air again.

Two forklifts sped in opposite directions in front of them, and Jade realized these were the swaying trees he imagined he'd seen as they'd approached the opening.

"Here. Swallow these," the foreman shouted in Jade's face. He put two pills into Jade's palm. "Salt!" he shouted. Jade nodded as if he understood, and then pointed to the "Men's Room" sign at the top of a metal stairway, mouthing "Water" to the foreman. The foreman shook his head and pointed instead to a water fountain near the time clock on the main floor. Halfway to the fountain, Jade glanced over his shoulder. The foreman was shaking his head slowly, a cautionary smirk on his mouth.

Most of the heat and smoke seemed to be coming from a corner of the huge factory floor. "That's the Forge," the foreman shouted. As if on cue, a blast of flames burst from The Forge, filling the air with a blinding light, followed by a dense cloud of black smoke. Jade followed the cloud to the ceiling of the colossal building where it spread out, seeping toward narrow openings at the top of forty-foot walls. He could see a glimpse of the sky through the openings, and he realized these must be windows, shapeless under layers of soot and broken where the sky showed through.

The foreman gestured for Jade to keep up as they moved deeper into the factory, dodging two more speeding forklifts loaded with bombshells. The foreman grabbed Jade's arm and pointed toward an elevated area at the far end of the building. Jade followed him there. It was The Line. The foreman shouted an explanation of which Jade heard only parts. He said something about 120-millimeter shells coming from an adjacent building, and he pointed along a cluster of parallel conveyor belts, each moving at a different speed, ultimately delivering the shells to The Forge. Men on The Line seemed to be dancing over the moving shells. Some of them disappeared into the shadows where the yellow light from a series of suspended discs failed to reach, the men re-emerging magically farther along the highway of shells.

Jade noticed stacks of shells on the floor in front of The Line, and then he began to notice shells everywhere. In piles all over the floor, on the moving Line where the dancing men wrestled with them using metal rods, in eight-foot stacks on palettes carried by more forklifts, up on steel-girded pedestals in honing machines where the shells looked like giant bullets in revolver chambers.

At the foot of The Line, Jade and the foreman watched a young worker move gracefully across the conveyor belts crowded with shells. He stepped between the moving belts onto a mesh of steel crosshatches that separated each belt by a few inches—barely enough to get one foot between the moving conveyors. The worker had broad shoulders, and thick arms. He seemed to float across The Line, boosting himself along by stepping lightly on randomly moving shells. He pulled and twisted the shells from belt to belt using a metal rod with a hooked end that he slipped into the open nose or onto the nippled back end of a shell, maneuvering it into position with his steel-toed boot. This dance at first mesmerized Jade, but when he looked at the man's face, he was confused. The face didn't match the movements of the body, fluid and acrobatic, like a dancer on a stage. The man's face was frozen in a frown, the features pinched. His eyes were out of sync, as if his hands and feet were themselves machines and his mind had nothing to do with them.

"Wilson!" The foreman shouted. The frowning man made a quick movement with his feet, arm, and rod that re-positioned four shells almost at once. Jade got the sense that Wilson had heard the foreman but was ignoring him. Finally, Wilson looked up, took a long look at the foreman and Jade, and then sauntered toward them across the moving lines. He kept his eyes on Jade, walking through the moving shells without looking down, like a cat with footfalls instinctive and certain. Wilson pushed a red button in a box suspended over The Line, then flipped his steel rod over his head in an effortless motion, hooking it onto a pipe above him. The conveyors came to a screeching, clanging halt, and Wilson jumped down to the floor. He stood a few feet away and stared at Jade and then the foreman. He was at least three inches taller than Jade and thirty pounds bigger.

"So, now I get another skinny guy, huh?" he shouted to the foreman, but he kept his eyes on Jade's. Wilson looked familiar but Jade couldn't place him at first. Then it came to him. Roland Wilson, high school superstar athlete. He was famous in the valley, nearly notorious. A Black hero in a very White town. Of all places, what was he doing here?

Jade picked up on the use of the rod quickly, but his uncertain footwork and the intense heat conspired against him. After forty minutes on The Line, he still hadn't found the rhythm. Twice he stumbled over shells and fell. Both times, Wilson had to pick him up by the back of his shirt to save him from getting mangled by the conveyors. The third time Jade fell, Wilson leaped across the moving belts in one stride and shut down The Line by poking the red button with the end of his rod. As Jade struggled to his feet, he looked down The Line and saw the other linemen standing still on the halted conveyor, staring at him.

"You're weak!" Wilson shouted as he handed Jade the rod that had fallen out of his hand and had wedged in the moving conveyor. "And you almost knocked out one of our lines! You can't do this work!"

"I'm not weak!" Jade shot back and grabbed the rod from Wilson. "I *can* do this!" Jade had already discarded his shirt, and now his white undershirt was saturated with sweat, smeared with his own handprints. His face and hair were soaked. But he returned Wilson's fierce scowl with one of his own, and then he yanked a shell from a crowded conveyor belt to an adjacent one and spun his rod backhanded into another shell's nose.

"You fall down again, you're out of here," Wilson shouted. He glared at Jade for a long moment, then turned and restarted The Line.

At the mid-morning whistle, The Line shuddered to a stop. Nearly in unison, the men hung up their rods and jumped down to the floor. Jade watched them march in a loose phalanx toward the massive doorway that he'd entered with the foreman seemingly days ago. He was exhausted, and he'd only been working for an hour and a half.

Out in the yard, the men were huddled in groups of four and five, some with drinks, most of them smoking cigarettes. Several had gathered along the fence near the entrance to the yard and were hollering and whistling to someone on the street below. Jade noticed Wilson sitting by himself on the square concrete base that supported the forty-foot flagpole in the center of the yard. A soft breeze ruffled the flag against a blue sky fading to white. Jade breathed in the fresh air and, tasting a vague sweetness, closed his eyes and tipped his head toward the sun. For an instant, he fell asleep right there on his feet.

When he sat down next to Wilson, Jade's Line mentor did not acknowledge him. Jade looked up to Wilson's face in the sunlight. The man's eyes were closed.

"You're Roland Wilson, aren't you?"

Wilson did not answer.

Jade persisted. "Quarterback at Ebonton High. Forward on the basketball team. Ace pitcher, too. Big star, always in the papers, state champs."

Wilson continued to ignore him.

"Your father was my biology teacher," Jade said. "For less than a week."

Wilson opened his eyes and rolled them toward Jade, barely turning his head.

"I had him for three classes, and then he never returned. Quit his job at the school and went back to teaching college. I was relieved. Everyone said he was the toughest teacher in the school. Flunked fifty percent of his class."

Wilson sat up and faced Jade. "Pell Academy, huh? That explains why you won't be able to do this job. But it does not explain what the hell you are doing here."

"I'm an ex-Pell, just like you," Jade said. "You quit after the first year, I made it through two. And I *will* be able to do this job, just like you can."

Wilson allowed a smirk to crawl across his mouth, then he turned away from Jade again, tilted his head back against the flagpole and closed his eyes. "Still doesn't explain what a rich kid like you is doing in this place. You will *not* survive here."

"Who said I was rich? You went to Pell. Does that make you rich?"

Wilson chuckled. "Couldn't wait to get out of that damn place. Felt like a military camp. School without girls is just not natural."

"They said you quit because Pell didn't have a football team. They said you didn't want to be in your father's classroom in sophomore Bio."

Wilson laughed, his eyes still closed. "They certainly know a great deal about me. Those *they* people."

Jade was struck by Wilson's accent. It wasn't a southern or even a northern Black dialect; it was more like Jade's own, with a hint of British inflection. Wilson's father's accent. Jade's Pell classmates had said Dr. Wilson sounded just like Sidney Poitier, and Jade found Roland Wilson's voice lilting at the edges of that same sound. In the back of his mind, he searched for where else he had heard this guy's voice.

Wilson stood up and faced Jade, who had been sitting a quarter-turn away from him on the adjacent edge of the flagpole base. He stood in shadow; Jade couldn't see his eyes.

"You're Irish, aren't you?" Wilson said, that precise tone again teasing Jade's memory. "Irish are either big and dumb or small and smart."

Jade stood up to face him and realized too late he had been better off sitting. Wilson, in shadow, seemed a foot taller than Jade. "I'm American," Jade averred, trying to fight off a queasy sense of inferiority.

Wilson chuckled and turned his head toward the men at the fence. "Your name's Flynn, right?" he said. "So, you're Irish."

"Maybe. I'm not sure."

"Maybe. He says, 'Maybe.'" Wilson turned slowly to glare down at Jade. "I guess you're small and dumb. There goes my theory."

"I don't have a father. So I don't know for sure."

Wilson dropped his head and turned it slowly toward Jade. "You were conceived by a man and a woman. Whether or not you know him, Flynn is your father's name, correct? That's what we do in this country. We give the children their father's last name. It's called a surname."

His voice sent Jade spinning into the past. Wilson's words took on the exasperated tone of Dr. Wilson dealing with a slow student, an eerie sound and manner that brought Jade back to the Pell Bio class more than two years earlier. He remembered Dr. Wilson pausing when he came to Jade's name during roll call in the first Biology class. The imposing Black man in a dark suit and emerald green tie had stared at Jade as if he'd seen something sinister in him, as if he'd expected Jade to be a troublemaker in his class. After that long moment, Dr. Wilson did not speak to or even acknowledge Jade for the remainder of that class or for the two other two Bio sessions he taught before he disappeared from Pell altogether.

Stepping toward Jade and then walking around him so that Jade could now see his supervisor's face, Wilson continued the taunt. "So that makes you Irish," he insisted. "You like to drink?" Wilson's mouth grinned but his eyes remained fixed and expressionless.

"No."

"I bet you do."

"I don't."

"You're so skinny, one beer would put you down."

"I don't think so, man." Jade was heating up. He could feel his neck redden. He was very much in the present now.

"So, you do drink!"

"I didn't say that, man!"

Wilson chuckled to himself and turned again to watch the men at the fence. They had increased the volume and intensity of their catcalls to the street, likely in harassment of female prey walking outside the factory walls.

"Your long, stringy arms are going to snap like stretched rubber bands in there, Irish boy," Wilson said, still looking at the heckling men.

"My arms are fine, man." Jade's face was flushed, his breathing shallow.

Wilson turned his head and shoulders toward Jade. "I'm not 'man,'" he said, his dark eyes fixing on Jade's. "Just because I am Black does not mean you can say 'man' all the time to me. I don't say 'man' to you, do I? Perhaps I should say, 'boy.'"

Jade, red-faced, stared at Wilson. The big guy used a slow blink to shift his gaze back to the hecklers.

"You White people think every Black man is either Uncle Tom or Bigger Thomas. That he shuffles and talks jive, pimps whores, and sells death to junkies. Has a grandma in Mississippi, lives in a two-roomer with his mamma and ten brothers and sisters and no daddy." Then, he turned back to glare at Jade. "And says 'man' to everyone!"

Jade met Wilson's look with a vacant stare, his fury squashed. Wilson's voice, his accent. It wasn't just his father's didactic tone and haughty glower. It was something else, some*where* else. He knew this guy. He'd seen this face in person, up close, somewhere.

"Well, I am not 'man' to you, skinny boy." Wilson persisted, his head pitched back, his dark eyes peering down at Jade.

"It's Jade. Name's Jade, not Skinny!"

Wilson burst out laughing and shouted, "Jade the fade!" His laugh was throaty and spontaneous—the first unguarded sound Jade's Line supervisor had made since they'd met hours earlier. "Jade the fade. Because you will. You know that, don't you? You *will* fade."

Wilson was still laughing when the factory whistle pierced the sultry air. Jade was startled by the high-pitched assault, instinctively wincing and covering his ears. When the whistle stopped, he looked up to see the back of Wilson's head bobbing in his own amusement as he sauntered toward the dark shadow of the factory entrance.

Jade did not fall once between morning break and lunch at noon. But he was numb with exhaustion. His biceps and shoulders ached from lifting and twisting 30-pound shells on The Line, and his lower back burned from the times they had to stop The Line and unload excess shells onto the floor. And when production slowed at the far end, and the shell supply to The Forge thinned, the linemen had to jump back down to the floor and lift onto The Line the very same shells they'd hoisted to the floor just a half-hour earlier. To Jade, this was an uncoordinated process. The left hand not knowing what the right hand was doing. When he offered this observation to Wilson, the Line mentor scowled at him and shouted, "Keep lifting shells."

As the men sauntered toward the great opening at lunch break, Jade caught up to Wilson and asked him where he could buy some lunch.

"You didn't bring it?" Wilson asked without breaking stride or looking at Jade.

"I forgot."

"Bad move, Skinny. You've got a half hour, and the nearest place is two blocks away, and you're already behind the fifty other idiots who don't bring their lunch and have to wait in line at Ralph's for his overpriced slop."

Jade headed through the gates and trotted along the outside of the factory fence until it rose above him on a huge wall where the road pitched downhill toward the river. He was famished. His mouth was parched, his tongue swollen and wooden. He yanked out his wax plugs. His ears clanged, as if he were still captive inside those cacophonous walls.

He waited in line for the requisite fifteen minutes at Ralph's, then took five minutes to shove a steak and cheese sandwich and a pile of greasy fries down his throat, while he stood along a wall next to the sandwich shop, one of his steel toed boots braced on the wall to keep him from falling over with weariness. He wasn't going to risk sitting down.

He washed his lunch down with five great gulps of a Nehi orange soda. At the last gulp, the five-minute whistle jolted his body, and he dropped the bottle to his feet where it crashed into pieces. Two workers walking by laughed at him and told him to clean up his mess, or Ralph would be up his ass with a hot fork fresh from the grill.

Jade cleared the gate at the second whistle and trotted into the mouth of his dark workplace, nearly blinded by the transition from the June daylight. He felt his way to the time clock, punched in, and headed toward The Line. When his eyes adjusted, he could see Wilson watching his every step as he climbed up to his post.

Within an hour, Jade started to lose the energy from his lunch and his brief stint in the sun. He fought off the worry that he wouldn't make it to the afternoon break. As he slung shells from line to line and loaded them onto the floor and back up again, he recalled Wally's words when Wally finally stopped badgering him about quitting the diner for the factory job. "If you make it past the first week, you'll be alright, son. But remember, you're nobody in a place like that. Nobody but another cog in the wheel that feeds the war beast."

Jade had been tempted to say that working at the diner was also a form of feeding beasts, perhaps of a similar nature. War beasts. Most of the diner customers were men whose hopes had been worn down by failure, some by war itself. Others, a minority of them, were quite the opposite—strutting, chest-pounding, bloviating know-it-alls, showing off their prowess, their success in keeping the majority beneath them. An endless pissing contest of boys in men's bodies.

Yet Jade knew that Wally was referring to something much greater than the mini drama of the diner. Wally had lived through two wars, and Jade knew that Wally's family had been torn apart and slaughtered, his home and nation driven into the earth as if stomped under the colossal footfalls of those sci-fi monsters of film—a Godzilla of hate, a King Kong of oppression and obliteration.

Wally had been glad that Jade had found work with higher pay, but he'd been disappointed about the nature of that work. In early 1968, after Robert Kennedy had visited Ebonton, Wally found his own voice getting louder where it had always been hidden, suppressed by his past experience in a part of the world in which people were murdered for expressing their opinion. That spring, Wally began expounding on his opposition to the munitions factory and the war it supplied.

"We make death in that place," Wally had said to Jade in his thick Polish accent, long before Jade courted the notion of working there. "Death to thousands of innocent people. We are removed from it here, in our little town, in our bomb factory. We make mortar shells here, and, somewhere else, they put in powder and a firing cap. Then, on the battlefield, the cannon is a mile from where its targets lie, waiting to die. A soldier pulls a lever and releases the bomb. Somewhere in the jungle, bodies explode, souls die. We can grow numb when we are all so far removed from the killing we cause."

Wally leaned toward Jade, his thick arms on the tabletop. Jade could see the top edge of the blue numbers on the underside of Wally's forearm. "People die horrible deaths in war, Jade. It is wrong. For most of my young life, I lived with those deaths all around me, and it was wrong then, and it is still wrong now. Your New Testament, it is clear on one thing— lay down your own life before taking others. In my tradition, the Talmud says, "If I am not for myself who then will be for me? If I am only for myself then what am I? If not now, when?"

17
What Marte Would Say

Monday, June 23, 1969

There were new lines on her face now. Around her mouth. Outlining what she feared was a permanent pout. She dabbed at these intruders with a powder puff, erasing them for the moment. She was standing in the kitchen, using a small mirror over the sink, under the blast of fluorescent light. What the hell had she been thinking on that first day when she'd hung this mirror here?

"*Che scemo!*" she muttered, hearing an old voice. "Idiot! In this light, a child would look old."

She imagined what Marte would say about her face today. Despite the tiny lines, and the eyebags and bloodshot, the puffy cracked lips, the flaking over-scrubbed ridges on the forehead—despite these erosions, Marte would say she was lovely. Remarkably beautiful. In that accent, that lyrical improvement over flat Yankee intonation. Marte was always kind, even when kindness was feigned, a dodge in the shadows of truth.

Upstairs in her bedroom, in the dim yellow light in front of the more forgiving full-length mirror, she pulled a pale blue shift over her head and arranged it around her hips, the skirt falling in a gentle cascade to a respectable inch above her knees. She thought of the young girls now, who wear practically nothing to cover their private areas, skirts that look more like scarves wrapped around their narrow hips. No bras, tiny underpants. Legs that go on forever. How do they move without revealing every secret they have?

She needed to do something with the hair today. Her bath cleared away the cobwebs in her brain, but it did little to restore order to this unruly mop of bristly tangles. She knew the frayed ends were all about the booze working its destruction on yet another body part. No booze today. She could choose to do that, perhaps even two days of abstinence, maybe more. She still had her discipline, if not the pure beauty of youth, despite what sweet Marte would say. The kindest person she ever knew.

She decided she would be meeting *him* today, right there in his regal office. She would get what she wanted this time. Not just more money, but an admission of guilt. Ownership, for once, of the act he was so good at lying about. This time, she had leverage on him. Finally. She had evidence and witnesses. He would not be able to weasel his slick and slithering way out of this one.

She decided the hell with the hair. Use the blue cloche. It's always in style as far as she's concerned. Twiggy wears one, doesn't she?

18

Thunder

Monday, June 23, 1969

By the two o'clock break, Jade was suffocating in the factory heat. While the other linemen jumped to the floor at the sound of the whistle and sprang for the door, Jade moved in a fog. His knees weren't working, his head spinning. When he jumped down, he lost his balance and caught himself with one arm braced against the floor. Wilson had already marched out the door to the yard, but up on the honing machine platform, a plump bald guy stood watching Jade as he struggled to regain his footing. The bald guy smirked at him and nodded his head once. Then he shambled down the steps from his platform and waddled like a penguin out the giant doorway into the light.

In the yard, the air was heavier than it had been early in the day, but still cooler and brighter than inside the factory. Jade found Wilson in the same spot at the base of the flagpole. The flag was limp now, and the pavement gave off enough heat to steal away any comfort Jade had begun to feel in the open air. He sat down with a sigh next to Wilson and closed his eyes. The sun's warmth wasn't welcome this time, but Jade had little energy left to find shade. Within seconds, his chin rested on his chest, his head nodding. He was startled awake by Wilson's voice.

94

"Look, Skinny, you don't have to sit with me on break just because you work with me. Matter of fact, you should sit somewhere else. I see enough of you on The Line."

Jade snapped out of his siesta fog and sat up straight, staring at Wilson. "What's with you, man? What the hell did I do to you? I just came here to work and you're giving me all this shit like I did something to you."

Wilson turned to glare at Jade. "You did. *Man!* You showed up!" He turned away and leaned his head against the pole and closed his eyes.

Jade felt his face flush and his jaw tighten. He was on his feet pacing in front of Wilson. "OK, Mr. Big Shot," he barked. "Mr. Football Star, Mr. Baseball Hero. Mr. Big Dick! Just because you're pissed off that you have to work here instead of playing ball, that's not my—"

"I do play ball, Skinny," Wilson shot back, but his eyes remained closed, his head against the pole. "In the fall. And I work here because I want to, not because I have to."

Jade stopped pacing and stood still breathing hard, his hands knotted into fists. He knew he had a better chance befriending this guy than confronting him. And there was that gnawing familiarity in Wilson's voice. It was more than Dr. Wilson's accent. Jade felt as though he knew Roland from somewhere, and that he'd been the object of his wrath in the past, his bullying. No one at Macson was exactly welcoming, but Wilson's aggressive taunts seemed intentional, personal. Had Wilson been ordered by Jensen to drive Jade out? Or did Wilson recognize Jade from somewhere, setting off a grievance to settle? Jade exhaled and heard his voice come out calm and steady.

"What school?"

Wilson turned and gave Jade a quizzical look, then he smirked to himself. "Penn State."

"Scholarship?"

"Full ride."

"Football?"

"Academic. Sports are an add-on."

"Man!" Jade said and started pacing again.

"There you go again," Wilson said. He kept his head against the pole, soaking up the afternoon sun.

"Why aren't you at a training camp?"

"Because I'm not a pro athlete, and my father's a teacher, not a millionaire. I need spending money at school, money for books, money for extra-curricular activities."

"But why this place? You could score a better deal than this."

"This *is* a good deal. I'm already in the union, so I'm at scale right away. Best pay in the valley, and the work keeps me strong. And it's so damn loud in there that I don't have to talk to anyone."

"Except me," Jade said, smiling. He stopped pacing.

"Not for long," Wilson said, his eyes still closed.

"Why?"

"You won't make it."

Jade put his hands back on his hips and lifted his chin. "We'll see," he said, gritting his teeth, his rage rising again.

"Already seen enough," Wilson said just as the whistle blew.

Back on The Line, Jade found new energy, channeling his anger, as Alice would instruct him to do. He pulled on shells and danced The Line with sure movements, his eyes, arms and feet in sync. He found his rhythm through concentration. At one point, he saw Wilson smirk in his direction, perhaps surprised by Jade's sudden show of agility. Jade was determined to prove Wilson wrong. He would focus on what Wally had told him about making it through the first week. He would prove Alice wrong, too, although he was still troubled by her strange warning as he left home that morning. Already, he'd been brushed by death and saved from it by the lucky placement of a fire hydrant. And he could still see the dark face of that woman, smeared with blood and smashed against the windshield as if she were stuck in the porthole of another dimension. Her eyes wide open, mouth gaping in mid-scream, hair matted and tangled, the face framed in a halo of bloody cracked glass. Her dark face. As Alice had predicted.

Jade jumped to the floor to help Wilson and another lineman pull shells off The Line. As he hustled to their side, he nearly walked in front of a forklift loaded with shells and speeding from The Forge toward the main doorway. The driver saw him at the last moment and honked his double-pitched horn, a bleating sound that reminded Jade of a European ambulance siren he'd heard in war movies. As the forklift sped by inches from Jade, he felt the moving air in its wake and held his breath against the strong blast of exhaust fumes.

Pulling and stacking shells, he hustled to keep pace with the other two men. When they finished, he stood next to Wilson breathing heavily but pleased with himself. His arms and shoulders were throbbing, and he was grateful there were no more shells to lift; but he felt like he'd made the grade with these two guys. He'd done his fair share.

"Let's go!" Wilson shouted to him, pointing to The Line above them. Wilson hoisted himself with his arms in one movement onto the conveyor platform, and Jade followed him. His arms nearly gave way when he lifted himself off the floor, and he struggled to get his leg onto the platform and pull himself up the rest of the way. It was hardly the acrobatic motion Wilson had demonstrated, but in a moment Jade was standing on The Line reaching for his rod. Wilson was already dancing across the conveyor lines.

Jade's concentration started to slip. He became distracted by time. He could not see a clock from his post, but he sensed they were closing in on the four-thirty quitting time. He was thirsty and beyond tired, willing the wail of the final whistle.

Wilson barked at him and gestured toward the floor. The Line was backed up again. Further down the conveyor, Jade saw two linemen jump to the floor and begin pulling shells. Wilson hung up his rod and jumped to the floor.

Jade paused to steady himself. The thought of working this job every day for who knows how long struck him in the stomach, where most of his fears registered. He almost doubled over but caught himself. He had imagined his own apartment, his own spending money, his own freedom, even a glimpse of himself on a beach in California—but he hadn't fully considered what he would have to do every day to earn that cinematic dream. The idea of factory work was easier to trivialize from the comfort of his bed at night than it was now toward the end of a day during which he had worked his body harder than any other time in his life.

He suddenly found himself shoulder to shoulder with Wilson on the floor pulling shells from The Line and stacking them in neat piles. Had he blacked out for a long moment? He couldn't recall jumping down from The Line. He was a machine—reaching and pulling and bending and reaching up again, his mind disconnected, elsewhere. Empty. The incessant roar of the factory had been dulled by his ear plugs but now he could hear no noise at all. Only his breathing, arhythmic, raspy. Sweat pouring into his eyes, his shirt cold against his skin.

He backed away from the stack of shells and waved at Wilson who stopped his stacking and turned to him but said nothing. Wilson gave him a curious look, not the usual haughty glare.

"Water." Jade heard himself say, his arm pointing to the main doorway. As he turned toward it, he saw Wilson's mouth open wide, but Jade heard nothing. His feet were so far away. The water fountain. The clock.

That bleating European horn he'd heard earlier was now inside his head. He winced and jerked his head toward the sound. A mountain of shells as high as he could see was tumbling toward him in a wave. For a moment, he thought he was dreaming, a premonition that he would see these bombshells in his future sleep. Just as he thought he was there, in sleep, he felt his hips get knocked aside so hard they seemed to separate from the rest of his body.

He hit the floor. A mass landed hard on top of him. His breath vanished; he couldn't pull in new air. Eyes shut tight, mouth open, no sound. Then a thunderous roar and a screeching that seemed to come from deep inside his head.

The ground under him shook, hard thuds against the floor, and then a cascade of them. Falling? Exploding? Was he dead?

No. He could feel his eyes sealed shut. Smelled something metallic, the floor icy against his face and, at last, a wave of air entering his lungs. He heard something rolling in the distance, then an echo of pings, the last of them finding a resting place, a new grave. Then silence. Then nothing.

19

Good Riddance

Monday, June 23, 1969

It was the goddamn blue cloche. What had she been thinking? Blue sundress, blue cloche. She was a blue princess. Two days after the solstice and she was celebrating midsummer a month early with the dress and winter three months late with the hat. Mother of God, what was wrong with her? Playing right into his ploy that she was crazy. Why did she think the innocent princess routine would work to her benefit, especially with him? Just the opposite. Made him even more imperious, if that were possible.

He ran the gamut of his routine, brought on by her obsequious appearance and then her about-face brash accusation. First, he was solicitous, feigning meekness. Then, in rapid succession, he became defensive, then suddenly overweening, and finally he burst—a parade of chest-puffing, fist-clenching, arm-cocking, striding dominance—commanding her to heel, as if she were a dog. He frothed at the mouth as he lorded over her, the weak and dethroned princess. Yet again.

"Every Monday, I meet with people from this county who need my help. Regular people, good people. And I'm always there for them. And today, what do I get?!" he shouted. "You! The least significant of all my people! Why are you still alive?! I'm supposed to be at a luncheon right now, and where am I? In this stuffy office with you! A little blue fly in my fucking soup! Look at you! Pathetic in your little girl outfit, your stupid blue hat, trying to accuse me of bringing harm to your *what*? Your *girlfriend*? Your boyfriend? Which was it? *What* was it? Ah, that's exactly right. Not a he, not a she...it was an *It*. And now it's gone. Good riddance. And you want to blame *me* for its disappearance!"

He came around the desk and stood over her, his belly in the lead, his thick finger in her face, the stench of cigar on his bejeweled hand. "*You* accuse *me*?! What you have done, my dear...you and...and that...*thing*. What you have done is against the law! What you've done with her, with *it*...according to the *law*...means you are mentally *ill*!"

She bowed her head, and he leaned over her, his huge red face hovering, his spittle now falling on her cloche as he screamed. "If you *ever* make an appearance here in this office, or *any*where in my presence again, I will have you committed to the state institution at Valmore *for the rest of your pathetic life!* Do you hear me, girl? Do you understand what I am saying to you?"

She sat still and looked at his shoes. Rubbed and buffed to a sparkle early that morning, no doubt, by Lewis, his "shine-boy" in the grand lobby of the Sheeley Hotel. The gold buckle glistening, its monogrammed coin screaming his initials at her face.

She jumped in her seat at the sound of something smacking onto the linoleum between his feet.

"Pick it up!" he said. "It's what you came here for. It's all you ever want. Money for nothing. Just like your old lover boy's people. Leeches on society."

She reached down, took the thick envelope into her trembling hand, and stood next to her chair, three feet from him. She looked up into his googly eyes behind his Coke-bottle lenses. A seething blue sea of hatred. Years of resentment.

"Next drop is Saturday, your place, usual time. Keep up this act, Alice, and it will be your last. I'll send your favorite bagman this time, so dress like a real woman, sweetie pie. He has my permission to take a little extra if he wants it. And I'm not talking about a cut of the cash." His breathing had steadied, but now he was leering, his mouth in a frown, his nostrils flaring with each breath.

She dropped the envelope on the chair and finally found her voice, calm and empty. "I hope you die soon," she said. "But not immediately. Not without suffering for a very long and painful period that prepares you for your eternity in Hell."

He swung his hand back to strike her, but he held it there, cocked, his face flushed, his jowls trembling. She held both arms over the left side of her face and head, bracing for the blow. Like a boxer in a corner fierce with the belief that she could withstand a pounding from this monster.

He barked out a laugh and swept his hand over her head. She gasped, feeling the blow that never came, remembering yet again that he always got more pleasure out of threatening her. Aroused by her anticipation of pain.

She opened her eyes when she heard the jolt of his dark laugh so familiar, inflaming her blood. He was hovering over her, his arm now at his side, his other hand clutching his bulging waistline, his lips and chin glistening red with spittle.

"I saved your father's name from disgrace by changing yours," he snarled, leaning his foggy eyes closer to her face. "Best thing I ever did." He let out a hiss and pushed back his shoulders and tugged at the knot of his tie, composing himself for his curtain call on the stage of his imagination.

She stepped closer to him, her eyes wild on his. "You did not save his name, you *erased* it. You replaced it with your *own*. You're a charlatan. And a swindler. A coward. And a murderer!"

He flashed his automatic smile, his reliable weapon of diversion. He forced a low chuckle. "You *are* insane, just as I've always said. Jealousy has cut you up inside for twenty years and turned you into a *mental* case." He grimaced and leaned so close to her face that she could see the dark lines along the edges of his capped teeth.

"Well, here's the truth, darling, if you can even comprehend it. I'll tell you one more time before they haul you away in a straitjacket." His breath was fetid, his tongue glistening. "He rejected you for *me*. Because he could *trust* me. Because you defied his principles in the most vile way, and then you came back from your banishment and tried, with your second pathetic lover boy, to bring him down. Destroy his business, his reputation, his family. *Your* family!" He pulled back, straightened his shirt and tie, turned away from her and marched around his desk.

She wiped the back of her hand across her face to erase the noxious pall he'd left there, and then she shook her hand at him as if to shoo a pesky fly. Behind a coy smile, she veiled her seething hatred. She knew at that moment that she would never fear him again.

She grabbed the envelope from the chair and headed for the door. As she opened it, she stopped when she saw Louise sitting at her desk, pretending to read something. She turned back to him and chuckled. She yanked the cloche from her head.

"I know you covet my hat," she said to him, smiling. "Just like your real father would. And really, I'd like to give it to you. But I'm quite sure it won't fit your fat head. So I'll give it to Louise. She can wear it every Monday when you greet your *regular* people here in your pathetic little tower. It'll remind you of me."

She could see that he was looking at Louise, distracted from his own performance by the unspeakable reference. As she walked by Louise's desk, she tossed the hat on the papers the secretary wasn't reading.

"It'd be cuter on him," she said to Louise, "but you can pull it off, honey. Just remember: every Monday."

She left the office door swinging on its squeaking hinges, walked past the elevator, and pulled open the heavy stairwell door with ease. When she let it slam behind her, an echo reverberated down the stairway. It felt like thunder.

20
The Man in the Green Pickup

Monday, June 23, 1969

Jade trotted uphill toward Lucy's house, his legs nearly spent, his boots concrete blocks. Only the heat of embarrassment kept him going, his face burning, his thoughts branded by the hot iron of taunts from the Macson guys after he'd been nearly killed by the forklift's pallet of falling shells. Wilson had just stood there after saving Jade's life, listening in silence while the men had circled the scene, the foreman delivering his scolding and then opening the door to the rest of them by joking about Jade's brush with death.

"Too bad Wilson tackled you, kid," the foreman had said after his required pronouncements about safety. "Your family woulda collected a nice accidental death benefit. Been halfway to the Bahamas by now!"

The guys' laughter had seemed too hearty to Jade. It was as if they couldn't wait for the foreman to set them free to rip at Jade's tattered hide. Cackling hyenas, hungry for blood. The littlest guy had been the first to unload. He'd announced there was extra protection for new guys scared of bomb shells. "It's in the Ladies Room. It's called Kotex." The men had roared, including the foreman, and then the abuse piled on. They ridiculed Jade's lean frame, his skinny arms—"those toothpicks are cracked, boy!"—and warned him about looking both ways before crossing the street. Finally, the foreman had shouted them down and ordered a cleanup of the shells and a return to work.

Jade and Wilson had done most of the cleanup in silence, and Wilson hadn't spoken to Jade for the rest of the shift. He was three guys ahead of Jade at the time clock and out of the yard and through the gate before Jade could catch up to him. Jade shouted to him; he wanted to say thanks. Wilson either didn't hear him or chose not to.

Lucy lived in the Backend section of Ebonton, a few miles from the factory, straight uphill through the North Heights and down again into her neighborhood. High up on the hill a half century earlier, coal barons and their cohort had built massive turn-of-the-century Victorians and Georgians with ornate woodwork, filigreed iron balconies, Gothic pillars, and a few widows' walks with cupolas, even though the ocean was a hundred miles away. Built by immigrant craftsmen—Italians, Russians, Poles, Lithuanians—these mansions had steep banks of lawn guarded by concrete lions and eagles and bordered by ten-foot stone walls, iron fences, and gated circular driveways. The grand homes had been built close to one another on half-acre parcels that ran steeply away from the town center and the river, forming a rampart for the barons, a superior vista overlooking the smoke-shrouded valley of their conquest.

By the time Jade and Alice had arrived in the Black Diamond Valley, the barons of the North Heights had long since moved on, abandoning their depleted coal mines and leaving their mansions and once-regal properties to fallow. Real estate hawks had chopped them up into apartments, and, over time, the mansions had decayed into relics of their former glory.

Whenever he walked through this section, Jade sensed he was moving through ominous territory. The moldering grand homes were still intimidating, but the current residents, living in the crumbs of prosperity, gave off the dangerous scent of desperation. As if the ghosts of the barons were playing jokes on the squatters who now lived here, some of the grandest of these citadels were sinking into the earth where mine caves left malignant voids in the streetscape. As he passed by two idle encampments of government-funded equipment used to fill those voids—rickety towers of flushing rigs and thick ropes of crumpled hoses strewn along the street gutters like dead pythons—Jade pushed himself to get over the top of the summit and then down into Lucy's neighborhood, in the sudden dark valley behind North Heights.

But it wasn't the once regal now neglected neighborhood that hastened his pace that afternoon. It was the sense of panic, of his grand plans in a sudden and cataclysmic unraveling. Less than ten hours earlier, he'd been on the threshold of his new life, and now he was running away from a series of disasters that had turned his expectations upside down. He was running to seek consolation. He was running from the possibility of more disasters, and from the notion that Alice had somehow predicted these disasters through her visions and exhortations.

As he plodded uphill in his leaden boots, he told himself he would consider not returning to the bomb factory if Lucy would concur with that idea. They'd spent an hour on the phone Sunday evening trying to make up after a week had passed since the fiasco in the Camaro with Rocco and Free. Lucy had been evasive at first, then assertive in her denial of his "disloyal" accusation. "What is this, the army?" she'd shouted. "I'm not loyal to *any*one! You're the one who lied to me. To *all* of us. Who's disloyal now? And how the hell do you know that guy, anyway? He's a fat cat. Who are *you*?" Jade had been unconvincing in his reply. "He just appeared one day at the diner and offered it to me." Lucy had laughed at this. "He's probably queer for you." Finally, satisfied that she'd won the argument, she invited him over to her house. Jade took a cab. They had make-up sex on the loveseat in the den while *Mission Impossible* surged away on the fuzzy black and white Zenith.

On this once-promising Monday, the sweet morning air had turned sour and suffocating in the Macson factory, but now, up on the Heights, a steady breeze cleared the skies, as if in deference to the lords of the past. Jade decided to put this day behind him, to focus on Lucy. He picked up his pace. His boots created a rhythm of thuds as he punched his arms forward uphill and drifted away from himself, leaving his body. He scanned the passing scenery without reflection now, without judgment, his mind empty, exhausted.

He watched his boots lift over the uneven sidewalks as if someone else was operating them. Cars passed by and he fell into identifying them by their engine sounds—a habit he'd formed as a kid playing baseball in the street in some other town. Now, without looking, he heard a Ford, a Dodge, a Plymouth. Suddenly, he had to look to his left at an uncertain sound. A Corvette Stingray. Fire engine finish, silver spoke hubcaps sparkling in the sun, a smooth coupe top, and a rumble from the dual exhausts that gave Jade a rush in his loins. Lucy.

He slowed his pace. He would be soaked in sweat, and she wouldn't want him to touch her, and that was what he wanted most right now. He wanted to tell her he'd almost died, was almost killed twice on his first day on the job, and he wanted her to feel pity for him, to hold him, her breasts against him, her kisses, her neck, the sweet smell of her hair.

He picked up his pace again. His breathing came in gasps, part exertion from the climb and part fire for his destination.

A battered green pickup truck slowed down alongside him, keeping pace with his march. He looked over at the driver, meeting dark eyes straight on. The man looked frightened. He was alone. He appeared small as he clung to the large steering wheel.

"Need a ride?"

Jade ignored him and looked ahead at the hilltop.

"You're hot. You need a ride?"

Jade shook his head and kept his heated pace.

"You're all sweaty. Is someone after you?"

The pickup matched Jade's pace. He turned to the driver. The man attempted a smile but his mouth was shaking, his eyes now in shadow.

"Is someone chasing you? D'ya need a ride?"

"No." Jade slowed his stride and clenched his fists.

"I'll give you a lift up the hill. Wherever you wanna go."

Jade scowled at the guy.

The man's thin lips were trembling as if he were suddenly chilled. "Are ya sure?" he urged, his lips curling now into a liquid smile. "You're sweating."

Jade walked faster still, and the truck's engine sped up.

"Wherever you wanna go." The man's face glistened. "I could give you some dry clothes."

"Fuck off, asshole!" Jade shouted and then stopped to face the guy. "Fuck. OFF!" He started up the hill again in long, pounding strides.

The pickup sped ahead to the stop sign at the corner, and Jade thought the guy was going to get out. But when Jade reached the intersection, the man just sat there in his truck, smiling.

"One last chance, boy," the man said, his eyes clearer now and his voice steady.

"I said Fuck...OFF!" Jade hollered. The man grinned at him and revved his engine. He raised his eyebrows in some unknowable secret signal and the pickup coughed, and jerked away, a dark sooty cloud swirling behind it.

21
Why Love Lucy?

Monday, June 23, 1969

Jade was rattled by the time he made it to the top of the hill above Lucy's house. He'd worked himself into a lather again by half-running up the steep streets and looking over his shoulder for the green pickup. Alice's warnings continued to haunt him, and he wondered if the guy in the pickup was an Alice prediction he might have missed. He didn't realize what the man's motives were until Lucy clued him in later. "He's a faggot," she'd tell him, in her superior street-smart tone, mocking his naivete, his social isolation. "What the hell do you think he wanted? Just to give you a ride? Out of the goodness of his twisted little heart?"

At the top of the last hill, Jade took one more furtive look around for the truck and then pitched himself forward, down a steep brick street, over a wooden bridge straddling Rolling Creek, and then down into the shadowed neighborhood where Lucy lived. The brick hill felt more like a wall, with the creek serving as a moat around the once-grand homes at the top, a natural defense against encroachment by lesser beings. As he bounded down the hill in wide strides, Jade let himself go. Laughing out loud, hollering and flailing his arms, and barely able to keep his balance, he loped headlong downward, airborne at each swing of his boots, free-falling away from the choking hold of a failed day.

At the bottom of the hill, he stumbled over the tottering wooden bridge and lurched into the intersection, catching himself against a parked car with a thud. He lay on the car's hood, breathing in gasps and still laughing out loud. For that moment, and the last few moments of his free fall, the day's ghosts had vanished. His mother's desperate pleas in The Grotto, the gnarled old man on the bus, the bloody black face in the windshield, the pismire guard at the gate, Wilson's mockery, the broken bottle at Ralph's, the near-death incident with the falling shells, the sweaty little man in the green pickup. All of these hauntings, these embarrassments, these tests of his will and his ego—all of these had been let go in those long free moments, lifting him into a lightness of being. He lay on the car hood staring into new lime-green maple leaves and blotches of blue sky between them. At last on this long day, he felt free.

"Hey, douchebag! Get the hell off my car! Asshole!"

Jade was on his feet and running again. He cut through two yards and over a fence, then hopped the first of four railings onto the small porches of connected row houses, landing on the fourth—Lucy's porch—with two feet squared, facing her front door. He smiled and cocked his head, congratulating himself for his acrobatic arrival. He pounded on the screen door.

"What are you grinning at?" Lucy said, her mouth turned down, as she pushed open the screen to let him in.

Jade pulled her against him and tried to kiss her, his hands roaming.

"Eew! You're all sweaty!" Lucy said, pushing away from him. "You're disgusting!"

"I'm not disgusting," Jade laughed. "I'm lusting!" He lunged for her again, only to be shoved back, then kicked by Lucy's bare foot.

"Get away from me!" she squealed, and scampered toward the kitchen, half laughing. "You're a disgusting, smelly pig!"

Jade nodded and smiled at her backside and turned to the tiny den next to the vestibule. He plopped on to the loveseat opposite the TV console, his legs and big boots hanging over one end and his head and shoulders over the other.

"Don't you want to hear about my first day on the job?" he called to her.

Lucy crept around the dining room table and peeked in at him. Then she stood in the doorway and shoved her hands against her hips.

"Jade, get off the loveseat! You're gonna ruin it!"

Jade shifted his boots to the floor, sat up and smirked at her. He took a deep breath and sighed, dropping his face into his hands. He ducked his head, sweeping his hands through his wet hair, and then looked up at Lucy.

She was wearing a soft, flimsy miniskirt dotted with tiny blue flowers, and a plain white tee shirt, snug around her breasts. Her legs were long and smooth and already the color of honey, even though sunlight had been scarce. The toenails of her bare feet were lime green. She was ready for summer, as always. Her long thick wavy mane was the color of the summer sky at dusk—black infused with fire. She had it tied back in a ponytail, the peroxide-treated highlights framing her tawny cheekbones in feathery white wisps. She wore pale pink lipstick and too much blue eyeshadow and black mascara for Jade's liking. He thought her wide-set eyes were unique and certainly pretty enough by themselves that they didn't need all that paint. Hazel, she'd described her own eyes, but the word was limited; to Jade, her eyes shifted from green to gold to dark brown depending on the light. And her mood.

"OK," she said, hands on hips, feet apart. Her look was deadpan, her tone mock serious. "Tell me about your first day on the new job, mister bomb maker."

Jade dropped his eyes to her breasts and then to her legs and back up to her skirt, which was barely hiding anything. "C'mon over here," he said, "sit next to me, and I'll tell you." He moved over, patting the worn cushion.

"Oh, no," Lucy said, staying put and holding out her hand like a traffic cop. "You're disgusting. I'm not getting near you."

Eventually, after relaying the car crash part of his story, Jade was able to convince her to sit next to him.

"But don't touch me," she said. "I just took a shower, and you're still disgusting."

He told her about everything except Alice. He didn't like to talk to Lucy about Alice, especially about the mystical stuff, the visions, and religious rants. Lucy had never met Alice, and his mention of her had often sent their conversation on a tangent that could not find a direction among his evasions. But he told her the rest of his story, in graphic detail, which made Lucy squeamish at some parts and giddy at others. Lucy was unpredictable like that. After nearly two years with her, Jade was still surprised by her inconsistent reactions to events about which he had certain, obvious feelings. Sometimes she would laugh when it was inappropriate, cry when the situation didn't warrant tears, or remain mum when a reaction was expected. And in the very next moment, she'd reverse the reactions—garrulous when she should be quiet, crying when Jade thought she should be laughing, or laughing at something he considered serious.

This emotional roller coaster kept their relationship off-balance, their once-reliable bond now uncertain, unpredictable. Unable to anticipate Lucy's reactions or her moods, Jade was left guessing how to behave. He discovered he couldn't be natural around Lucy any longer. He couldn't remember what it felt like to be comfortable with her.

There was a time, early on, when he wallowed in the comfort of her. He was obsessed with her. He was a teenage boy under the spell of a girl he was uncontrollably attracted to, in a state of incessant priapic tremble. They were enveloped in each other's arms almost constantly, their fingers wound together, their hips always in contact. He couldn't wait to touch her, to feel her holding onto him. His mind would betray him at critical moments in school, as he smelled her on his clothes, and he had to quell the rush in his loins by digging his fingernails into his palms, by thinking of something painful, or even morbid, some eerie image Alice might have conjured.

Jade often dwelled on the first time he got horizontal and naked with Lucy. It was in The Highlands, at the parents' home of Free's girlfriend-of-the-moment. Jade couldn't remember the girl's name, but only how her father had padlocked the refrigerator and the kitchen cupboards, so the girl's older brother couldn't eat any of the family's food. This was a distraction for Jade on this special occasion. Lucy was willing, and Jade's body was certainly willing, but his mind kept wandering back to the weird dad and wondering when the guy was going to show up with a weapon and wipe out the three teenage couples, including his own daughter, who were shacking up in his house on a warm summer night. When the lights went out, Jade lay on the bed next to Lucy, still nervous about Padlock Dad. Lucy didn't say anything and didn't reach out to touch him, but he knew she was there, just inches away, naked. When he brushed up against her skin, he gasped, his heart pounding. Lucy laughed. Her voice sounded older and somehow tough. But her skin was silken. He didn't touch her with his hands at first, just felt all of her skin with his own. In the instant his touched hers, all the ideas he'd had about what this would feel like were erased. There was no idea that could have conjured this feeling. He lost all sense of himself and his own thoughts and felt airborne with her in the dark room. They floated together, time standing still. In a few more moments, or perhaps longer, he became focused, oddly, on the sound of his own trembling breath. And then, finally, as if they had descended back to the bed, his mind registered a conscious thought: He had never felt this high in his life. And so he held his breath. As if he could freeze this feeling forever. And for the next hour, Padlock Dad only entered his thoughts once, and he brushed it off as if he'd been crazy to worry about the guy.

There were other times, many times, when Jade and Lucy stayed together, seldom for the entire night, but often in the darkness of a strange room in the house of one of her friends or on the loveseat in Lucy's den where lying down with another person was challenging. But Jade didn't mind being squished against Lucy there or anywhere. There were nights when he wished he could stay that way until morning. And then through to the next morning.

When he wasn't with her, he was distracted by his obsessions about her. He would bump into people, stumble over his own feet, drift away in class at school—thinking about how different her body was from his. He couldn't stop dwelling on it, how remarkably opposite she was from him, and how delirious that made him, how feverish and unhinged. The parts of her that were always visible had set this notion in play—her delicate face, her luxurious hair, her smooth arms and legs, her long soft neck, her perfect ears, her exquisite hands, her gentle fingers—all of these parts were the opposite of his. These evident, public parts of her, these flawless gifts, were a revelation to him, leaving him helpless in a reverie of her beauty. But then, later, underneath her clothes, the revelations were overwhelming. It was as if he'd broken through to a new dimension and had found the place on that other side where he blended, melted perfectly into a body that not just fit his own, but made his disappear. He loved losing himself in her, for the first time and for each time he could go there afterward.

Often, in their early months together, he'd focus on a single part of Lucy's body and wallow in the sensation, the idea of that part, for a long time. When they were alone, he would keep his hand on Lucy's inner thigh, in the soft concave spot at the very top of her leg, at the very edge of oblivion, wallowing there in breathless anticipation, a whispering stroke away, wishing he could stay there all the time, even while they were watching TV or half-sleeping. He wouldn't know what they were watching, didn't care, as long as he could keep his hand and his mind there, lingering at the threshold. He did it so often, held her there, that she seemed to get used to it, as if she'd grown a third leg. She told him that one day.

"Wait," he said, removing his hand and looking into her eyes, smirking. "I'm the one with the third leg! And we share it. There is no other third leg."

"OK," she said. "Then how about this?" She unzipped his pants, reached down and gripped his erection. "Now, how would you like it if I just did this all the time?"

He could barely catch his breath. "OK. OK." He looked at her, his mouth open, trying to smile. "Sounds like a threat," he managed to gasp out. "But I hope it's a promise."

They laughed together at this, and they laughed often like this, silly and senseless and secret. Until he began to think about their laughter, how hers often came naturally, while his sometimes felt forced, even serious. This persistent difference finally awakened him from his boyish trance. He'd been so serious, so intense about sex, so obsessive, while Lucy seemed nonchalant, more physical, less constrained by thoughts. He made a conscious effort to be more like her, more natural, in touch with the moment. But his thoughts constantly intruded. He became aware of the necessity to step outside his own desires. While he still desperately craved to see and touch how different she was from him, he had to stop himself, to consider that each part of her was nothing in itself without the context of her, all of her. He needed to step out of himself and his own obsessions about their physical differences, his private world of wonder about her body. He got her message. This was not just about him.

While he couldn't be something that he wasn't—casual, more instinctive, more intuitive, like Lucy—he thought he could understand her better if he knew what she was thinking when he touched her, since she was no longer just the object of his own prurient fascination. While she was very physical and impulsive, there was another mind on alert here— a realization that made it far more fascinating for Jade. After that, when he touched her in a certain place and saw that her eyes had closed, he would ask her to open them and look at him. "Is that better or worse?" he'd say. And sometimes she'd say "better," sometimes, "it doesn't matter," and sometimes nothing, just her eyes daring him to figure it out. But she never said "worse."

Until then, his expectation of girls' roles in the sex game had been limited to their defensiveness—fending off the irrepressible aggression of boys. This notion, and other myths, had been embedded in his mind for two years at Pell Academy by the persistent conquest proclamations of upperclassmen and the increasingly noticeable absence of girls. Alice's female anatomy lessons had been instructive, but he had no one, no father or brother or older cousin, to guide him. He was the only son of a woman without a husband. Lucy was his only intimate source; but it didn't help that she was his only instructor in intimacy.

After a few months with Lucy, she finally told him, "I'm not letting you touch me, I'm wanting you to."

It finally sank in. The Pell boy was growing up. His sexual childhood was coming to an end. Her parts were not separate from her and touching them was not even pleasurable without the rest of her, without her mind, her voice, as reluctant as it sometimes was.

He could hear his mother's instructions. He tried to shun her words from his mind, annoyed that her prescient ideas had intruded, breaking this spell. But he knew she was right; Alice was his best guide all along. She had taught him about female anatomy and physiology, but somehow, without his knowing exactly when, Alice had been guiding him to understand that there was magic in intimate knowledge, not just about yourself, but especially about someone else.

It was an epiphany he tried to share with Lucy, but he stumbled and ultimately failed to articulate it. She didn't respond, or even attempt to understand what he was trying to say, other than to tease him about overthinking everything. He couldn't reach her. It was as if she was afraid of him saying too much, of her having to let go. When they touched each other, Lucy spoke with her eyes, her hands, and her body. Jade's responses were physical, too—in his touch, his breathing, his exploding heartbeat— but he couldn't stop his intruding mind, his blundering words. He tried to know what she wanted, but he could no longer tell; she wouldn't say. And he didn't know how to free her from herself. Still, he never wanted any of this to end.

But of course, it did. Eventually the passion, the obsession, the marvel, the loss of himself in her, the discovery of her urgency, her unspoken need for him, their struggle to define it all, her resistance to vulnerability—all of it was distracted by the world outside of them. That crude, intrusive, unwelcome other planet surrounding their secret life, exposing it to infection from without. It was inevitable—and that inevitability was an unacceptable notion to him, and one that she eventually felt doomed to be aware of, quietly resentful that she had to carry that burden. She was the practical one. When she said the guy in the green truck was trying to pick him up, she told Jade he was lost in his own world. She barked a forced laugh at him and feigned a groping move toward his groin and then she stepped back and leered at his body, up and down, making a hideous face. "How does it feel, pretty boy?" she snarled, with wary delight in her eyes. "You don't like it? Well, now you know what it's like being a girl. All day, every day."

Lucy got her buttery brown skin and dark hair and wide-set hazel eyes from her mother—a sullen, mostly silent woman who sorted peanut butter cups and chocolate drops in a candy factory in Ebonton. Her older brother had the pale pallor and pointed features of their very White father. The brother was a college dropout waiting for the draft to catch up with him. Both mother and son were glum and surly and barely cordial to Jade, even after they got to know him. Lucy's father, though, was the main distraction. A brawny, thick shouldered man with a bitterness he wore in his clenched jaw, he was a part-time resident at home—usually around the time of his wife's payday—and it was a rare occasion when he would be sober and civil to Jade, or even to his own family. Jade was used to drunk adults. He lived with one. And he knew who the other drunken parents were, even when they tried to disguise it. Living alone with Alice had given him an insight into adult behavior that he thought he would have been just fine without. He wasn't thrilled that he could pick out a drunk in a moment, no matter how clever their effort to camouflage.

But he had no experience handling belligerent, violent drunks. Alice could get rowdy and even rough, but she never beat him up or trashed furniture or blasted out in a rampage. Lucy's father was a routine practicer of those skills. He'd broken most of the family's furnishings at least once, and he'd spent as much time in remorse and apology as he had in creating mayhem. Fortunately for his family, he was a passable repairman, and he exorcised his guilt by patching and pasting and hammering back together the plasterboard and chairs and tables and lamps he'd smashed during his rages. As for the humans he'd broken, there was little he knew about fixing them, no matter how remorseful he got.

Jade learned how to steer around this truculent man, and he'd managed over nearly two years to avoid a direct confrontation with him. But he came close once when the old sot chased Lucy around their tiny house with a cat-o'-nine-tails he'd used on the children when they were too young to fight back. It was a Friday evening in early spring toward the end of his junior year, his first year at Ebonton High. Lucy was a sophomore. Her brother and mother were home, and Jade had stayed for pizza. The four of them were sitting silently in the den staring at *Hogan's Heroes* on the family's giant, unreliable black and white Zenith, not laughing. The old man stumbled through the front door. As he gazed bleary eyed around the small room, surveying each occupant with menacing but mute evaluations, he ended up at Lucy and decided he didn't like how short her miniskirt was.

"C'n see your *cunt!*" he slurred at her. "Whore!" His head bobbed, and he took a step toward Lucy and then grabbed the doorframe to steady himself.

Lucy's mother cried out, but Lucy overpowered her with a piercing screech of her own. "You filthy pig!" she wailed. "You goddamn animal! How dare you talk to me like that!" She was on her feet, tearing at his shirt and kicking his shins. The old man backed away and swung at Lucy with an open hand but missed her by two feet. He continued backward and fell into the dining room table, crunching one of the wobbly chairs he'd already broken and fixed many times.

Jade was up and rushing toward him, but Lucy's brother had already intervened. In what seemed like a single movement, he leaped at his father, picked him up and dragged him toward the stairs to the second floor without saying a word. The old man muttered curses to himself and let his son carry and push him up the narrow steps. Jade stood at the foot of the stairway, watching the struggle above him and listening—another "cunt" and then "useless bitch" and another "whore." He went to Lucy who was on the loveseat sobbing and pushing her mother away from her. Jade tried to console her, but she shoved him away, too. Then, in less than a minute from the time the old man had disappeared, he was bounding down the steps hollering "you ugly little slut!" and whirling another cat-o-nine tails over his head like a cowboy with his lasso.

Lucy heard the familiar crack of the whiptails and sprung for the dining room just ahead of her father. He chased her into the kitchen and whipped her once across her shoulder as she headed back through the dining room again and out the front door. The old man was stumbling in pursuit. Jade jumped toward the doorway ready to block him, but Lucy's brother got to him first, yet again. From the edge of Jade's vision, the brother flew horizontally at the old man and took him out with a body block that knocked him through a small fragile nightstand and into the wall just inside the vestibule.

When Jade found Lucy two blocks away sitting on the curb under a streetlight, he didn't say anything to her. She was crying without sobbing, just staring ahead, tears streaming down her cheeks. Jade noticed crimson stripes on her bare arm and tattered fabric at the side of her shirt over her breast. Later, she showed him the pink welts on the soft honey-colored skin of her breast, and he kissed them.

That was the worst that Jade had witnessed, but according to Lucy there'd been many more days and nights like that over the years. And worse. Like Jade, Lucy was hardened to the chaos of life with a drinker and had learned to ignore what she couldn't fix and seek solace in things she could control. But, unlike Jade, she was never in control of anyone else in her home. Where Jade had acted as parent to Alice on many occasions, Lucy had always been treated as a child by her mother, her brother, and especially by her father. She hated that her opinion was never taken seriously, and she resented the condescending tones that she'd grown up hearing. She desperately wanted to be in control of something, to be in charge of her own life, yet she was neither resourceful nor independent enough to do so. As she'd so often claimed, she was practical; but only when it came to others. For herself, she could not climb out of her fears. She was the baby of the family, whether she liked it or not, relying on others all her life.

When Jade finished the story of his harrowing day, Lucy stood up from the loveseat, pacing in front of him in the tiny den. During the recounting of his day, she'd been most curious about Wilson and had peppered Jade with questions about the former high school star. Everyone in school knew about Roland Wilson's prowess on the playing field, and Lucy was quick to assert that he had an outstanding record with the girls, as well. She was perplexed about Wilson's choice to work in the munitions factory, and she wanted to know more, but Jade wasn't much help. He'd told her everything he wanted her to know about Wilson. So she switched gears and focused on Jade.

"You have to go back to Wally's," she said. "It's the only way. You can't work in that place. You'll be killed."

This was the opening Jade had hoped for, but, impulsively, he began to argue the opposing view. He knew Lucy was trying to assert her control, to tell him what to do, so he simply opted to take the opposite track, even though he would like nothing more than to run from the factory job and return to Wally's.

"There's no way I'm going back to the diner," he heard himself say. "Not now. It's too late."

"It's not too late! Do you think Wally would turn you down?"

"No, he'd be thrilled that I proved him right. But I'm not going back there. I'm not going to make half of what I'm making now at the factory."

Lucy stopped pacing and flopped into a sofa chair across from him next to the television, her legs coming apart and revealing the crotch of her white cotton underpants. Jade's eyes instinctively gravitated to that spot, and he left them there. Lucy sat with her legs apart for another moment and then slowly leaned forward in the chair, closed her legs and pulled at her skirt. She sighed and gave him a look of exasperation.

"So tell me, James," she said in the tone of a friendly interviewer. "Are you going to work in this factory for the rest of your life? You haven't heard from the Army, and you're not going to college. So, is this it? You're gonna be a bomb maker your whole life?"

"And you'd prefer I wait on tables at a diner for the rest of my life?"

"I'd *prefer*, as you say, that you keep your job at Wally's and go to college." Her tone had moved from solicitous to condescending.

Jade jumped to his feet and marched into the dining room and back to the den, pounding the floor with his heavy boots.

"College!" he called out to the ceiling and waved his arms around. "College, she says! What college? And with what money?! It's a little late to try to get into a college, Lucy. And what exactly would I do there?"

"You could go to County Community—"

"Ha!" Jade shouted again at the ceiling. "Genius U! Thanks, honey. Send me to Genius U with all the other flunkies."

"Well at least those flunkies aren't working in a bomb factory for the rest of their lives!"

Jade stopped in front of her chair and put his hands on his hips, spread his feet wide and stared down at Lucy. He was starting to sweat again, perspiration on his chest seeping through his tee shirt. His face was flushed.

This was not going as he had hoped, and he had himself to blame. He had opted for his familiar role in their arguments rather than agreeing with Lucy and using her corroboration to justify quitting the Macson job. But this was the way conversations had gone for months between them. Cut off your nose to spite your face. Questions answered only by more questions. Frustrations heaped upon one another. Lucy persistently pointing out his shortcomings, and Jade tuning her out more and more each day. And now he'd lost his way in this latest argument. He'd had a chance in the beginning to take Lucy's lead and use it to bail out of Macson, but he'd blown it by taking the opposite tack, just so she wouldn't feel like she was in control.

They had been moving apart for some time, and Jade barely understood why. He no longer found Lucy exciting, except when his own body overwhelmed him with urges he could not ignore. Yet, even then, it was mechanical. He was saddened by the loss of something magical in his life. He once believed that a love as strong as theirs must have emanated from Lucy and that he had merely responded to it as one would a gift from the gods. He thought the powerful feelings he had for her had been somehow granted to him by her, that love had radiated from her, capturing him in its sweet grip.

But now, he concluded that the feeling had come from within himself, that his mind had generated what he had thought was "love," and that he had projected onto her what pleased him and then he craved it. In this self-induced state of "love," he began to assume responsibility for her happiness, just as he had always done with Alice. In the end, he decided that his passion for her had turned into an obligation of sorts, and he had overlooked for the longest time what he saw clearly now—a bellicose antagonist who took twisted solace in starting fights with him, in ridiculing his ideas, mocking his plans for the future, even mocking his clothing style, and belittling his physical frame. Tactics she'd learned well from her father.

"And you wonder why that guy, Wilson, picks on you?" she said, taking up the endless question loop again, and showing him she wasn't to be intimidated by him scowling over her in his big boots with his hands on his hips. "Don't you think it's because you're so scrawny?"

Jade moved away from her toward the dining room again. "And I'm supposed to build muscles at Wally's waiting on tables?" he said, waving his arms.

"What makes you think you'll get muscles at the factory, Jade? You can't put meat on those sticks no matter what you do! Chicken legs!" Lucy tried to hold back her laugh, but she let it go, a charitable white flag betraying her deeply hidden soft side.

Jade couldn't hold back his own smile. He shook his head and closed his eyes. He was grateful to let her disarm him. He was tired of the joust and relieved it was over. He'd come here for comfort and warmth and had gotten an empty reception and then a ridiculous argument, and ultimately, through his own stubbornness, had blown his chance to quit Macson.

His long day of surprise attacks and backfires had worn him down. He lay sideways on the loveseat and, like Ahab on his whale, he waved mechanically to Lucy to come to his side. She leaned into him on the loveseat, and they began to grapple almost reluctantly, pulling at each other's clothes in a routine their bodies had become accustomed to. It was as if this act were the only thing left between them. And yet it seemed to Jade that even this was becoming a struggle for control. Lucy was complying with his needs, after assuring herself that she had won the verbal battle. And, at the last possible moment, she pushed him out of her and let him rub himself against the outside of her until he finished. This had become their recent practice, their new method of birth control. Lucy had declared in early June that both rubbers and her intermittent use of The Pill were unreliable. It was the only part of her life over which she had complete command of someone else. And herself.

When Jade rolled off her, she pushed at him to get up.

"Shit! Get me a wet towel from the kitchen. Hurry! It's all over the loveseat."

22
Snitch

During the morning break in the factory yard, Jade explained to a disinterested Wilson his mother's reaction to his first day at work. Wilson sat with his head against the flagpole, eyes closed in the warm sun, tolerating Jade's tale. But when Jade got to the part about the falling shells and Wilson's rescue, and how Alice had screamed, then fell to her knees and started speaking in a strange voice, Wilson raised his hand and turned to Jade.

"Your mother speaks in tongues?!" Wilson said, his face twisting into a knot.

Jade realized he'd gone too far, that he'd revealed something he shouldn't have to a guy he'd just met.

"Sort of," he said in a low voice. "Sometimes."

"Speaks in tongues." Wilson was smiling now. "My aunt used to warn me about people who speak in tongues. Where she comes from, they're called Voodoo people." He widened his eyes and mocked a grimace at Jade.

"Well, I don't know if it's speaking in tongues, exactly," Jade said, stalling for a recovery. "She kind of gurgles and moans and makes strange sounds, sees things."

Wilson was now giving Jade his undivided attention. "Your *mother* does this."

"She's a little weird sometimes," Jade said. He bowed his head, ducking Wilson's piercing glare. "She probably worries too much."

"Sounds like *you* should be the one worrying, Skinny," Wilson said, chuckling. He turned away and resumed his position against the flagpole, closing his eyes. "You're living with some kind of witch."

Jade leaped to his feet, his face crimson with the heat of his blood. "Who the fuck do you think you are, asshole!" he shouted. Wilson's eyes popped open and his hands dropped to his sides, his shoulders back. His eyes moved back and forth as Jade danced in front of him in a rage. "Who are you callin' a witch? Who the FUCK are you callin' a witch, man!" He was flailing his arms and pacing in front of Wilson. He stopped and pointed his finger at Wilson's face. "Mother*fucker!*"

"Don't point that skinny finger at *me*, Irish boy," Wilson said, his voice deep and ominous. "If I get up off this block, you will be one very sorry skinny boy." Jade dropped his arm to his side and resumed pacing. "And if you don't sit your skinny ass down," Wilson said, "you won't make it to lunch time. And I will not pick up your slack today." He leaned forward, his eyes on Jade's. "Now, you were the one who volunteered all this information about your mother, so don't point your finger at *me* for telling *you* what you already told *me*."

Jade stopped and stared at Wilson's boots. Alice would have scolded him for his temper. Now, Wilson was taking on her role, but in the haughty tone of the stern Dr. Wilson. Last night, Alice had gone further off the deep end than ever before, and Jade had needed to tell someone, just to confirm that it wasn't a bad dream, that his mother had actually said those things, had made those eerie sounds. Wilson's reaction confirmed what Jade had learned long ago, but in the heat of the moment had forgotten—keep Alice's antics to himself.

"I'd sit my ass down if I were you," Wilson said. "Here comes the Commissioner."

Jade turned to watch a shiny black Fleetwood Cadillac roll to a stop ten feet away. It was the only car he'd seen in the vast concrete courtyard since he'd started the job. Points of sunlight reflected off the long hood and chrome fins of the sleek regal machine, the tinted windows creating an opposing void to the bright light, a vivid contrast that made the machine seem unearthly, an apparition from a future world. Jade thought of the moonshot and wondered if the astronauts would find life there.

The dark rear window popped and slid down with a hum. A thick pale hand reached out, a gold circle cufflink on a stark white shirt flashing in the sunlight. Jade recognized the huge ring on the third finger. A low voice boomed from the shadowy interior as the hand beckoned.

"Roland!"

It was Hafferty. Jade could see past the arm to the driver whose eyes were locked on his. Silver Head Stanley. Jade wondered what had happened to his greaseball sidekick, Zook. Hopefully dispensed with by now.

Wilson hoisted himself to his feet and sauntered to the open window, passing Jade without a glance. He put his forearm on the roof of the car and leaned his face into the open frame. Jade couldn't hear what Hafferty was saying, but he saw Wilson nod a few times, then back away. The cufflinked arm disappeared, and the tinted window filled the frame, with Stanley's glaring eyes the last to disappear. The Caddy drifted away toward Jensen's five-star office door.

"What was that all about?" Jade said, as Wilson strolled back to his seat, a smirk at the edge of his wide mouth. He sat down with a sigh and put his hands behind his head against the pole. He looked toward the main gate and the adjacent fences.

"That…was the Honorable Dennis Hafferty, County Commissioner for Life. He's your boss, Flynn."

"Yeah?"

"He's my boss, too." Wilson closed his eyes and tilted his face into the sun. "Look around you, Flynn. See anybody looking this way?"

Jade turned toward the front fence where yesterday's hecklers were lined up again. Instead of facing the street, some were watching the black Caddy glide toward the GM's office; others were staring at Jade and Wilson. Jade looked around at other clusters of men in the yard. All eyes were fixed on the scene at the flagpole.

"What's the matter, Flynn? Don't like being on center stage? Like I said before, you should sit somewhere else. Especially if you can't take 600 eyes on you at all times."

"He doesn't own this place," Jade said. "He's a politician. Jensen's the boss here."

Wilson chuckled. "Think about it, Flynn. This is an ordnance factory contracted to make Howitzer shells for the U.S. government. Hafferty is the most powerful politician in the valley. It's basic math. The man in the black Caddy? He's your boss, he's my boss, he's Jensen's boss, and he's the boss of all those guys who can't stop staring at you and me."

Jade looked around again. Most of the men were now huddled in small groups, chattering, but still staring at him and Wilson.

"Is that why you got union scale right away instead of having to wait like me? Because you have a special deal with the Commissioner? Because you're Black?"

Wilson's smile evaporated. He opened his eyes and looked at Jade. "You're rushing past basic math now, Skinny. Be careful."

"What'd he tell you just now?" Jade asked.

Wilson closed his eyes again and relaxed his head against his hands. "That's between the Commissioner and me."

"How do you know him?"

"Don't you mean, 'why would the Commissioner for Life, the boss of all of us, stop to talk with the only Negro out of 300 men in this yard?' Isn't that what you mean?"

"No," Jade said, his lips tensing. "What I mean is, how do you know him? Did he get you this job, or did you meet him after you started working here?"

"Stick with the basic math, Flynn," Wilson said as he stood up and stretched. "Time to get back to work. I can feel the whistle itching to blow." He started to saunter toward the entrance to the factory. As if on Wilson's cue, the whistle wound up from a halting whir to a full throttled wail, and Jade ducked his head, covering his ears. He'd never get used to that brain-piercing assault.

About a half-hour before lunch break, Wilson hung up his rod, jumped down from The Line, walked out into the courtyard, turned left and disappeared. Jade and another lineman pulled three more loads onto the floor over the next thirty minutes. When the lunch whistle blew,

Wilson still had not returned. Jade headed to the flagpole in the yard, and as he started to shovel in the peanut butter and jelly sandwiches he'd made, he shifted around toward Jensen's office to see if Wilson would emerge. Hafferty's black Caddy was still parked in front of the door.

Three workers approached Jade, stopping a few feet in front of him. The tallest of the three had an oily pink face rimmed in a bowl of jowl covered with a two-day beard. His blue short-sleeve shirt strained at the pillows of his body. A white oval patch over his pocket read "Cheese" in blue script.

"Where's your *part*ner?" he said to Jade. The voice was gravelly, the question dripping with sarcasm.

Jade squinted toward the sun and tried to find the man's eyes in a deep shadow under the bill of his cap. "Who'dya mean?"

"Bill Cosby." Cheese said, and his two sidekicks chuckled. "Who the fuck do you think I mean?"

The two other guys wore the same cap as Cheese—a greasy, blue-striped engineer's hat, easily ten years old. The thinner, smaller guy showed a few blackened teeth in his slack jaw as he swiveled his head in a little circle and let out bursts of air through his nose, as if he couldn't quite get his laugh started.

"I don't have a partner," Jade said, as he rolled up his lunch bag and packed it in his hands like a snowball. He inched closer to the edge of his seat and braced his legs.

"Don't play games with me, ass wipe," Cheese snarled, and the smaller guy sputtered closer to a full laugh, his head bobbing up and down. The third guy stood still, his thumbs hooked in his belt under a massive belly.

"We seen you holdin' hands with that spook, Wilson," Cheese said. "You two fags are like *I Spy* over here at the flagpole, gigglin' like a coupla pussies. There's a war goin' on, shithead, and we don't appreciate you sittin' here under our flag, jokin' around with that ass kisser coon partner of yours." Cheese stepped closer to Jade and leaned down into his face. "I don't care how many touchdowns that nigger scored," Cheese scowled, flakes of food in his beard, his onion breath searing Jade's eyes. "That boy's hero days are over. He's a management snitch now. Ain't no fuckin' way you're gonna get in our union the way he did, asshole. No *fuckin'* way. When day 28 comes for you, you're gonna be absent."

Up this close, Jade saw venom in the man's eyes, yellow bloodshot bulges in puffs of swollen pink skin. He tried to keep from swallowing but he failed, the fierceness he'd attempted slipping away. Cheese saw the change and smiled. A front tooth was missing, the other one in a silver frame, and the rest of them tobacco brown. "You won't make the 28-day cut, hippie boy. Don't even fuckin' think about it. Nigger lover." He turned and headed toward the group of men at the front fence, rolling on the outsides of his big feet in a bowlegged saunter while his sidekicks bobbed along at his flanks. About twenty men at the fence had been watching the flagpole scene, and one of them shouted as Cheese approached.

"D'ja get his first dues, Cheese?"

The men at the fence laughed in unison; then some of them turned away while a few others joined Cheese and his stooges. As the men converged, the little stooge with the slack jaw pointed a finger at Jade as if he were pointing a six-shooter. He pulled an imaginary trigger, his finger gun kicking backwards. Jade stared at him for a moment and then leaned back against the flagpole. With his eyes still fixed on his would-be assailant, Jade popped his balled-up lunch bag off the crook of his arm into the air. He caught the bag with the same hand, stood up, and then strolled toward the entrance just as the whistle blew. His heart was pounding, but he thought he looked Clint Eastwood cool.

23
Becoming Marte

Tuesday, June 24, 1969

She slipped the key into the lock, wrenched open the stubborn door, and slid into the driver's seat. She hesitated before touching the wheel. Whose hands will touch it now?

She felt exposed driving the rattly tin can by herself. The windshield was just inches from her nose, the road seemed a mere arm's length away. Hitting a rut felt like hitting a wall.

"People's car." That had made both of them laugh.

"What was wrong with those people?" she'd hollered over the roar of the road inches beneath them, the wind whisking them around like a piece of scrap metal.

The answer still rang in her head; she was embarrassed to recall it.

"To the people, it was a luxury. It still is. You are spoiled, my dear."

She could hear that voice over the blustering noises of this fragile little machine as if she were still here with her, as if they were riding side by side, smiling at the irony in that remark. But now she was alone, and somehow at the wheel. By mistake?

She was surprised the car had been there, still parked on a side street just off Reston. How long? A month? Two months? She couldn't begin to calculate. Weeks, days, hours, who knew how long? Had she even left the house in that time?

It was taking too long to get to Telford. She wondered if she'd taken the wrong road. She'd never paid attention when she rode shotgun, had never needed to navigate. She decided she was lost and started to panic. Then she remembered the breathing they'd practiced together. Start deep in the belly, focus on that point, imagine a bucket going down there, expanding your center, scooping up air, pulling it to the top as you push the air through your nose, and back again, the bucket dropping slowly then dipping.

At a fork in the road, the sun blinded her. She jerked the car onto the gravel and stopped right under a sign: "Telford 6."

She knew four spots in Telford—The Club, The Yankee Diner, the Fairhaven Hotel, and the Army Navy Store. That was it. Nothing else in this city of 50,000. There'd been no need to know. They'd had each other, and the music, and the nights had been long, and she'd been delirious with it all, beyond mere enchantment, this new life, this discovery.

In the Army Navy Store, she picked out everything she needed. Everything black, the smallest sizes they had. Used work boots, a new tee shirt, and a cotton collared shirt. A slightly used leather bomber jacket. A new pair of wool socks. A used belt and new dungarees. She didn't try on anything in the tiny curtained-off closet across from the cash register because she was alone. But, like everything in this store, the pants were men's, and she knew they'd be loose in the crotch. Nothing jamming up in there. What a concept!

She put forty dollars on the counter and asked, "Do you have scissors?"

The clerk was the only other person in the store. He was tall and heavy-set, probably younger than he looked, leaning against the back wall behind the counter, watching her with jaundiced eyes, a slack mouth. He had a deep five o'clock shadow. A rolled cigarette burned in the corner of his cracked lips. He looked toward the front door, shrugged, and reached for the cash, sliding it from the counter into his other hand.

"You can try on this stuff right over there," he said, with a nod toward the curtain.

"Don't need to. What about the scissors?"

He snorted and smiled sideways around the cigarette, showing off a sprinkling of brown teeth. "You gonna cut the pants to make 'em fit?"

"No. I need them for hair."

His eyes opened wide as he pulled a last drag from the cigarette and yanked it from his mouth. He let out a stream of smoke right at her, stepped back, and dropped the butt on the wooden floor, crushing it with his boot. "Cuttin' all that off?" He lifted his eyebrows and grinned. "It'd be a shame. Pretty little thing like you." He dropped his gaze to her breasts and held it there.

"Not mine. My boyfriend's."

He turned his head a notch, let his eyes graze over her body one more time, and sighed. He sauntered along behind his counter toward the front door, dropped the cash on the register and reached underneath, pulling out something shiny.

She held her breath and braced herself to run.

He ambled back along the counter toward her, holding the shiny object out of view. He stood in front of her and stared at her for a long moment. "The only pair I got," he said. He tossed an old pair of shears onto the counter. "They'll have to do. We're even, with the scissors."

She exhaled slowly through her nose, her entire body shaking as she watched him shove everything into two paper grocery bags. When he looked up, she nodded toward the cash register and gave him a quizzical look.

The man smirked and let out a sharp snuff from his nose. He looked her in the eyes. "You wanna try on those shirts and pants over there...and leave the curtain open...I'll give you all the change you need. Sweet stuff." He waited a beat, then shrugged and turned down his mouth. "Otherwise, we're even. Like I said."

The Yankee Diner had a separate restroom for women with a lock on the door. She pulled off her shirt and used the shears to cut her hair in front of the dingy mirror. The yellowed sink filled up with dark curls. When she was done, her hair was the same length it had been in the winter. A bit ragged, but very short.

She looked at her white floral pointed bra in the mirror and thought about the leering she had just endured. "God dammit," she said to her reflection. "This old thing." She brushed off the top of the sink and piled up her new clothes there. She reached back, unsnapped her bra, shrugged it off and tossed it into the trash can. She pulled on the new black tee shirt, then the collared shirt, changed into the rest of her new clothes, bought a coffee to go, and headed to The Club in the black VW Bug.

She stood for a moment in The Club parking lot, gathering her new self. It was too hot for the leather jacket, so she decided to leave it in the car. As she took it off, she changed her mind. The jacket was essential, emblematic of the image she had acquired, the person she'd become. She took off the shirt, tossed it in the back seat and as she put the jacket back on, she looked down at her tee shirt. It didn't matter now that, if she took off the jacket again, anyone could see her nipples through the thin black tee shirt. That's her real body, not the one bound and imprisoned by that old torpedo bra. She wasn't declaring her solidarity with braless rebels; she was shedding the shackles of her former life. Defying the rules that had defined her as just another target in a phallic world. She knew her transcendence was imminent. Even if more darkness lay beyond this darkness, she would bathe in the light this moment promised.

The band was warming up when she walked through the side entrance. Big Sam had his back to her, tuning his sax with Rolly who was nodding over his electric guitar. She looked over her shoulder as she approached the riser. The drummer and the bass player were at the bar, their backs to her. She sat on the stool in front of the mic stand, plucked the mic and held it in her lap as she spun around, waiting for Sam.

"You boys going to play," she said into the mic. "Or will you just pretend tonight?" She thought her Austrian accent sounded spot on.

Sam and Rolly halted their warmup, and Sam turned slowly, his big bear body moving in a rounded wave, the shoulders slumping, his eyes coming around first.

The room was quiet. The bar was on the side wall. Luke, the bartender, was staring at her, holding a towel in his suspended hand, his face blank. His skin looked waxy. A handful of guests, scattered at a few tables in the low-lit space, murmured among themselves.

She sang into the microphone, in German, the opening lines to *Falling in Love Again*. It had been their favorite Marlene Dietrich song. She closed her eyes and took a deep breath, straightening up on the stool, shoulders back. She felt the jacket fall open, the zipper edges rough against her nipples. She exhaled through her nose, opened her eyes, and laughed low into the mic, saying to no one in particular, "Warm up time." She turned to face Sam.

"What you doin' here?" he said to her, his deep voice low and somber, his frame draping over her like a giant willow tree, his big midnight features hovering over her face. His dark eyes were bloodshot, the lids at half-mast. He tilted his head to the side and frowned. He looked sadder than she'd ever seen him.

She set the mic in her lap again. "I'm going to do one set, Sam. And that is it. No more tonight. Do not even ask." She was on the accent with precision now; she knew it by the look on his face.

Sam's eyes lifted heavily from hers, and he looked toward the bar, to his bandmates who had turned toward him. Vic, the drummer, stood up, his hands at his sides. He showed his palms and shrugged ever so slightly. The murmuring guests grew quiet. One man cleared his throat.

"Baby, you can't do this," Sam said, his voice softer still, his big hands on her shoulders.

She'd seen him do the same thing once before, putting his hands on the shoulders of a leather jacket, his face low and grim. But never this sad. And this time, she could feel his hands.

"I am all ready to go, Sam," she said, looking up into his bloodshot eyes as he let his hands fall. "Tell the boys it's now or never." She smiled at him and then lifted the mic and tapped it twice, turning toward the bar. "Luke, get me the usual. Boys, let us play." She held her smile for them and tilted her head, coy and certain they couldn't resist her allure, her ambiguous manner, her mystery.

No one moved at the bar. Luke was still frozen there, holding his towel. Vic stood next to Rufus, the bass player, who had turned completely around on his stool, holding his drink. All three looked from her to Sam and back again, their faces blank as if stalled in time.

"What in hell are we waiting for?" she said into the mic, her accent perfect. "This place is at capacity." She laughed at her own joke, her amplified voice echoing in the near-empty room. She thought her laugh was spot on, too.

Sam moved between her and the bar, standing close to her. He held himself tall now, his head and body shrouding her in shadow. "Look at me, now," he said, stern, demanding. "Look in my eyes."

She looked up into the deep shadow where she thought his eyes would be.

"We all miss her," Sam said softly, and then he lowered his huge frame so that he was squatting in front of her, his eyes now at the level of hers and no longer in shadow. He held his palms out at the ends of his knees, pleading. "We got mad, too. For a long time. And we cried, too. But we can't bring her back. And neither can you. Honey, you just can't. It's not good for you. It's not good for us. She's gone. Forever. Let her go. Please. For me, and for the boys. But especially...for you."

Her mouth opened slowly as she prepared to say what was in her head, that she would carry on, that it was her duty to keep her spirit alive, that it was the only revenge, that it was what she would expect of her. But none of this came out of her mouth, only a pale whimper. Her lips moved again, her voice quavered, but no words, just a moan. She let the mic fall from her lap to the floor. The sound was like one loud clap of hands, and then a wheezing whistle, then dead. She felt her throat closing, her body shaking. She tried to speak again but it came out in a muzzy gurgle. She tried yet again, but it was just squeaks, little barks, helpless.

Sam caught her as she tipped backward on the stool. For such a big man, he moved in a flash. He lifted her into his arms, her shoulders and head on one giant limb, her knees bent over the other. A child lifted up into a great warm cradle. One of her boots was untied. She was trembling, barely conscious.

"Rolly," Sam said in a sharp command. "My keys are in my case. Follow me."

Sam walked toward the side door. Her legs were dangling, her head hidden in his chest, her voice tiny echoes of soft pleas.

A man at the tables protested. "Hey! Where's that big colored guy takin' her? Somebody call the cops!"

From another table, a different voice. "That ain't no "her," pal. That's a guy. He's a fag."

The first guy yelped a short laugh. "Those were tits, buddy. Nice ones. That's what *I* seen. Maybe you're on the wrong team."

Sputters of laughter scattered across the tables.

Luke slapped his towel on the bar with a crack and leaned forward, his finger pointing, his eyes on fire. "Someone should shut their fuckin' mouth!" he shouted. He stood up straight again, his finger still pointing. "You. And you. You're eighty-sixed. Now!"

24
Belly Bomb

Wednesday, June 25, 1969

At the morning break, Jade asked Wilson to confirm the union's probation rule—that a new employee needed to work 20 business days in the first 28 calendar days without an absence in order to qualify for union membership and pay scale. Wilson's response was vague and unhelpful. Jade assumed Wilson was reluctant to explain, because Wilson had bypassed the rule, compliments of Commissioner Hafferty. Jade wondered if Hafferty would trump Cheese and give Jade the same deferment. If so, what would Cheese do? Probably make membership in the union miserable for Jade. Still, he would talk with Hafferty. Jade needed his own meeting.

At lunch, Jade joined Wilson at the flagpole but, sensing Wilson's cold shoulder, he did not sit down. He decided to report the Cheese incident and then find a place to eat lunch alone. When he described the visit from the union crew, he left out the part about Wilson being a management snitch, but included the *I Spy* remark, hoping to get at least a rise out of Wilson.

"Like I told you, Skinny," Wilson said flatly, "you should sit somewhere else at break. These guys here, they don't like my kind. And they sure as hell don't like your kind either."

"What's my kind?"

Wilson sighed, turned slowly to Jade, and lifted his chin, like his father about to launch a lecture.

"Do you see anyone who looks like you, Flynn? Other than your skin color? You do not look like a vet; you look like a hippie. Smooth hands, no muscles, all that hair in your eyes and over your ears. These men do not like hippies. They think you're soft, lazy, and spoiled. They resent you taking a job from one of their own, so they'll make sure you won't be able to handle the work, that you'll quit real soon. The only ones they hate more than Blacks and hippies are college students. So, if you think you're going to college, don't think it out loud here."

Wilson scanned the yard and opened his lunch pail, keeping his eyes on his food while he talked.

"All those college protests all over the country last year and this spring—all about ending the war? To these guys, that means just one thing—taking away their jobs. In case you haven't noticed, there's not much protesting in this backwater town, just a few stragglers standing in the street with signs. But there's rumbling on the hill over there on the Dickson campus, especially after what happened in April at Cornell and Harvard. And these guys smell it coming their way. Just last week after work, a bunch of them saddled up their pickups and their rifles and rode over there and scared the life out of some of those college kids. Did not fire a shot, but they held their barrels on a few of them. Cops came late and asked the Macson boys very cordially to lower their weapons, like you would ask someone at the dinner table to pass the butter. Then they warned the college boys to keep off the city streets with their war protests, even the city streets that run through their campus. If they come over here to Macson, cops told them they'd be arrested. Probably worse. You've seen the news. Black guys with guns up at Cornell. That's getting too close to home for these guys. And the cops have their backs. They're loading up. Cops everywhere now have weapons of war, and they're ready to use them. Civil Rights peace parades are a thing of the past, Flynn. A word to the wise: we're surrounded by itchy trigger fingers."

Jade planned to grill Wilson about his Tuesday meeting with Hafferty in Jensen's office, but Wilson made it clear he'd said all he was going to say. So Jade walked down to Ralph's, bought a Nehi Orange, and ate his sandwiches by himself on the ground against the looming factory foundation wall where he'd dropped his soda bottle on Monday.

He was developing an appetite and felt stronger after just two days on the job. He convinced himself he was getting accustomed to the hard work and had put the first day's disasters behind him. At home, Alice had backed off after her wild reaction to his report after his first day at work. The next morning, she hadn't harassed him and had simply prayed out loud for him as he left their house to catch the Number 15. He hadn't seen her since, but this morning, he was surprised to find peanut butter and jelly sandwiches, an orange, and a box of Sunshine raisins in his lunch bag in the refrigerator. Jade could count on one hand the number of times Alice had made a meal for him or for herself in the last six years. From the time he was twelve, he was the cook, maid, bill payer, and resident social worker. Alice, when she was home, was the philosopher quoting literature, the hangover patient, the repairman (when she was sober), and now, the periodic Grotto supplicant. Jade's cooking skills were modest, but he'd kept both of them fed—when Alice was home. Her arrangement to have groceries delivered by Wally's friend had been, in her words, her "contribution to the cause."

Before they'd come to Pennsylvania, Jade had been unaware that Alice had a monthly source of income outside that of her various jobs. When she started with the library soon after their arrival on Reston Street, he wasn't sure she was getting paid, especially after his visit with Miss Filbert at the Sheldon library. If she was getting paid, she'd never shown him evidence of it, and likely wouldn't share it if she had. All of Jade's income from Wally's had been spent on utilities and basic household needs, as well as on his meager wardrobe, occasional 45 records, and little presents for Lucy. Alice had told him that they didn't have to pay rent, but she'd never explained why. When he finally learned about her alternative source of income, he confronted her, but she refused to let him know the amount or the source. It explained how Alice had afforded her booze, her cigarettes, her modest but occasionally imprudent wardrobe acquisitions, her transportation to who knows where over her many missing days and weeks, and, starting last fall, the increasing supply of her precious religious impedimenta—statues, candles, crucifixes, medals, holy water, framed photos of saints. In that same period, he'd witnessed her making cash donations to Catholic appeals—stuffing fives and tens into envelopes mailed to Pagan Baby funds, African and South American missions, various orders of nuns and priests, and a dozen other organizations that Jade had suspected were scams. Yet when Jade asked her about help from Welfare, Alice had ripped into him. She refused to subjugate herself or her son to the degradation of the state dole, she'd told him. She was not a beggar, she'd declared. How dare he even suggest such a thing! This, to her, was a matter of "personal integrity."

Thanks to Alice's personal integrity, Jade had worked most of his life since age eight. And now, with one of her peanut butter and jelly sandwiches in his hands, at the base of a towering concrete wall, he laughed out loud at her inept food preparation. The sandwiches were ball shaped—a giant wad of peanut butter between two flattened pieces of white bread saturated with grape jelly. He nearly choked on the first bite. But he was starving, and he figured the coagulated sandwich balls might just carry him through the hot afternoon. He began to wonder if Alice was on the threshold of a breakthrough. Perhaps her nurturing instincts were returning. Perhaps she was conscious of how hard he'd been working and had resolved to behave like a mother instead of a possessed oracle. Jade wasn't banking on these fragile hopes, but he made a resolution of his own after finishing his lunch. He decided that with his first paycheck he would take Alice out to dinner—not to Wally's, where she might expect him to take her—but to Illuzi's in downtown Ebonton, where you could get second helpings of spaghetti and where the owner gave his guests free rice pudding for dessert.

126

When the first whistle blew, Jade scrambled to his feet and hustled up the hill toward the gate. He envisioned his mother across the table from him at Illuzi's, her short mop of curls neatly trimmed and her skin glowing, her eyes bright and mischievous—the way he remembered them years ago. As he approached the gate, he imagined her smiling at him, a mother's smile, full of hope and promise. Maybe, he thought, she'd give him a lecture on literature.

Before the final lunch whistle, Jade was already on The Line flinging shells and dancing over the meshwork and the moving conveyor lines. When Wilson arrived after the whistle, he stood on the floor in front of The Line and gawked at Jade's performance as if it were an apparition. He didn't smile; he looked stunned.

By mid-afternoon, just before the break, the peanut butter bomb hit Jade's gut and he had to dash to "the head," as the men called the restroom. The head was more of an open latrine than a civilized relief station, fitting with the Macson military habitat. It was at the top of steep metal steps above the time clock. There was no door at the top of the steps and no doors on the toilet stalls. Jade discovered that if he sat on any of the three toilets, he could see the main floor below. And if anyone felt the urge to look up from the floor, he could see Jade sitting there in his compromised privacy.

Jade gave the flusher a kick just as the afternoon break whistle sounded. As he washed his hands, he turned to watch one of the Cheese sidekicks—the big, dark one with the tumescent overhang—stroll through the doorway.

"Hidin' out in the shitter, huh, kid?" the big guy growled, heading for a urinal. Jade dried his hands on an overused towel roll in a beat-up dispenser, watching the man's sweaty back in the cracked and grimy mirror. "No sense hidin' out up here, kid," the guy said over his shoulder. "If ya wanna jerk off, ya gotta come up with a better scheme than sneakin' to the head. No doors on them stalls for a reason, ya know."

Jade turned to leave but the doorway was blocked by Cheese and his little sidekick. Cheese curled his hairy tattooed arms, making fists of his big hands. He was gasping for breath, winded by the quick ascent, and his first words were lost in a heaving cough. Jade froze, waiting for the man to either catch his breath or keel over.

Cheese finally spoke in a wheezing growl. "Your nigger friend's still down on The Line doin' your work, hippie boy."

When Cheese started hacking again and holding his chest, his little sidekick recognized an opening. "Waitin' up here for the coon?" the little guy said. "So you can suck him off in one of them stalls? Faggot." He twitched his shoulders in a spasm and poked his head out the doorway. Jade turned to see the big guy at the urinal moving toward him.

"Nobody," the little guy reported in an excited gasp as Cheese recovered and then puffed out his chest. He spread his arms and stepped toward Jade. The other guy was at Jade's shoulder while the little one stood guard at the door. Cheese's head was inches from Jade's face.

"You wanna know somethin' about your jungle bunny friend, you hippy fag?" Cheese growled. "He ain't lookin' out for you. He ain't lookin' out for me. He ain't lookin' out for Moose, here, or Jacko over there. You know who he's lookin' out for, dick face? Besides his own ashy ass?!" His breath was gagging Jade. "He's a fuckin' snitch for Jensen and Hafferty. They got their own personal nigger in the woodshed."

Cheese growled and leaned closer. "Well now I'm tellin' you what you need to know about Hafferty, and about Jensen, our fuckin' slimeball General Manager. And about your jigaboo friend." He gasped for another pinch of air, his sewer breath wrenching Jade's aching stomach.

"Hafferty's a cunt, hippie boy. Plays it both ways, and the men here lose every time with that phony motherfucker. He's pro-union when it's election time, and he's no-union every other time. He gets Macson contracts because he's up Walsh's ass down in that fuckin' cesspool in Niggerville D.C. Contracts keep us workin', sure. Until little faggot worms like you and your spook friend come in and try to steal our jobs and shake down our union. And that's what your nigger pal is up to, and he's up to it with Hafferty and Jensen. Wilson's the inside guy, and Jensen is Hafferty's bagman, takin' payoffs for Hafferty from the company *and* the union. Jensen gets a cut, but Hafferty takes the lion's share. Wilson's here for the summer, then he goes back to college to play football and fuck White girls and spend our union money. It's a scam, hippie boy. And if we find out you're in on it, you won't have a dick left to piss with in that hole over there."

Jade had stopped shaking halfway through Cheese's little tirade. He felt the rage rise in his chest and neck. He'd had enough of the man's foul breath and crusty spittle. He pushed his chin up to Cheese's face and blurted out his first thought.

"Wilson's here to work and that's all, cheese breath. He says nothing about the union and nothing about Hafferty. To me or to anyone. And I'll work here as long as I want. So, fuck you!"

Jade saw the left hook coming and ducked aside. Cheese missed high and stumbled forward into Moose. Jade started for the door. But Jacko hit Jade in the gut with his head and they went down together. Cheese untangled himself from Moose, grabbed Jade by the hair and dragged him to his feet. He held Jade's mop of curls in his thick fist and screamed into his face.

"Don't fuck with me, faggot boy! Give this to your nigger friend. Tell him he's next!"

128

Jade's breath disappeared before he felt the pain. He doubled over and fell face first onto the concrete floor. He smelled onions and a faint scent of beer and somehow he wanted to laugh. He opened his mouth to breathe but no air came in. Then he felt another jolt of pain high on his hip. He knew it was the work of a steel-toed boot and that it had missed its mark. If it had been on target, he'd have a few broken ribs to remember the moment with.

As he struggled to regain his breath and find his feet, he heard Jacko's laugh in a fading echo. It had finally found release and had come out as a full howling cackle.

25
Squirrel

Wednesday, June 25, 1969

Jade was woozy on his feet, so he lay down again on the cold floor. Head pounding, cheek swollen, middle caved in, hip throbbing. He curled onto his side in a fetal ball, closed his eyes and convinced himself that if he did not move, he would not feel pain.

He wondered if he'd missed yet another warning from Alice. Was there something she'd said about this violent encounter that he'd misunderstood, or, more likely, ignored? She seemed to have predicted the car crash and the cascade of shells, and she often rambled on about things happening in threes, but she'd lost him completely on Monday evening after she'd heard his report about his first day at work. She launched into her worst rant ever. Wailing and keening, raw terror at the heart of her garbled words, she was nearly impossible to understand, to decipher details, much less meaning. In the end, he wasn't able to suss out another prediction, but he did understand, amid her rantings, that she was angry with him that he hadn't heeded her warnings, that he'd gone ahead and started work at Macson and had come to the edge of death twice, just as she had predicted, and that there had been dark faces involved in both incidents.

As he lay in his fetal ball on the cold gritty cement, he felt compelled, despite his own inner voice of resistance, to pay even closer attention to her next rants, to make a greater effort to listen, to try to make sense of them. He could not rely on her to predict his life's course, to warn him of every ensuing danger, but neither could he benefit from ignoring those hidden messages from her seer's eye, her connection to secrets beyond reason. He doubted her thoroughly, but he also wanted to have faith in her strange gift, to depend on her, to be somehow mothered by her, even if it was in her bizarre and confounding way. She was his only ally.

He unclutched his fetal curl and tried to stretch his legs out to stand, but the pain in his gut sent a shock to his head and he curled up again, trembling. He tried to think his way through what had just happened. His thoughts went first to how he'd been trying to warm up to Wilson after the falling shells rescue. Such an odd character, with his unusual accent, his insistence on deflecting attention, shunning Jade's appreciation for having saved him from the blunder that otherwise would have killed him. After all of Wilson's glory days on the playing field, he should be accustomed to such attention, such hero adulation for his instinctive physical prowess. And now, this accusation by Cheese, this money scheme, this idea that Wilson was in collusion with Jensen and, unbelievably, with Hafferty to bilk the union somehow. It seemed preposterous to Jade. Yet, Wilson's coolness toward him and his connection to Hafferty gave Jade pause. Perhaps Cheese and company were on to something.

"You gonna lie there all afternoon?"

The voice seemed far away. Jade took a deep breath before opening his eyes. He saw two boots with the steel toe exposed.

He turned his head, wincing at the effort. The man's aviator glasses were distinctive—too wide for his triangular face. The weak chin fading into a point. The mechanical edges of his crewcut. It was Gort, the bus stop robot.

Gort and Jade had ridden to work on the same bus for three days, but neither of them had spoken to the other and each had walked on different sides of the street every morning from the bus station to the factory, avoiding one another for no apparent reason.

Gort pulled Jade to his feet in a single motion. Jade's head spun and his knees wobbled as he struggled to find his balance. Gort held him by the shoulders until Jade groaned and bent over, holding his middle.

"You sick?" Gort asked, holding Jade's arm loosely now and backing away. "Gonna puke, better get to the bowl."

Jade opened his eyes and tried to straighten up. "I'm OK," he lied. "Just out of breath."

"Nasty cuts, kid. D'ja fall?" Something in his voice. He was playing dumb.

"Yeah," Jade said, going along with the game. He struggled to find words. "Felt a pain in my stomach...doubled over...lost balance. Hit my head on the sink." He looked up and met a blank stare on the other side of the oversized bug eyeglasses.

"Break's almost over," Gort said in a flat tone. "Better get back to work. Sure you're OK?"

130

"Yeah," Jade sighed. "Thanks." He turned to the mirror and grimaced at the blood streaming from his forehead and the swelling skin on his cheek and under his eye.

"Gotta watch out for them wash basins, kid," Gort deadpanned. "Damn things can sneak up on you when you least expect it." He disappeared through the doorway just as the break whistle sounded.

After Jade cleaned away the blood, his wounds appeared less severe, at least in the smeared cracked mirror over the sink. He could feel a lump forming under his eye, but when he returned to The Line, Wilson didn't seem to notice Jade's altered face or his slight limp, and Jade was relieved that he wouldn't have to explain.

His hip throbbed. He struggled with the shells, tentative in his lifting and uncertain with his rod and his footwork. Wilson didn't seem to notice this change either.

Just before quitting time, Jade felt his strength and concentration evaporating. As the shells seemed to run faster beneath him, his rod slipped out of the nose of one of them, and he stumbled onto his knee on the moving line. "Don't crap out on me, Skinny," Wilson shouted. Jade scrambled to right himself, and he had to concentrate to keep pace for what seemed like hours until the final whistle sounded.

In line at the punch clock, Jade was three guys behind Wilson. He caught up to him just before the gate, as the mob of workers split into three directions—some turning toward their cars parked on the street, others toward the downtown bus station, but most headed toward the sea of cars in a dirt parking lot across from the factory. Jade would usually follow the second group, but he walked alongside Wilson toward the lot.

"Where are *you* going?" Wilson said without looking at Jade.

Before Jade could answer, he heard someone call out to Wilson. A young guy with a blonde crew cut was seated cross-legged on the hood of a faded blue Corvair waving at them. Wilson chuckled to himself.

When they reached the car, the blonde guy stood up on the hood of the car and leaped into the air, landing on the dirt lot in a fighting stance.

"En guard, motherfuckers!" he said, his fists raised, his legs braced one behind the other. Wilson chuckled to himself, as if Jade weren't there. "Settle down, goofball," he said. "You'll scare someone."

Wilson's friend straightened up and shoved his open hand toward Jade. "They call me Squirrel. Betcha can't guess why." As he shook Jade's hand, he turned to show off his profile, his hook nose and his narrow grin of buck teeth over a weak chin. He let go of Jade's hand and faced him again. His close-set eyes were dark and beady. Jade failed to hold back his laughter.

"A special specimen of the species, I am," Squirrel announced, with a theatrical bow and then, standing tall, his shoulders back, his buck teeth in the air. He was at eye level with Jade. "You must be our latest victim here at Bombs Away."

Jade glanced at Wilson, but the big guy ignored him and stood tall with his arms crossed on his chest, his head cocked back, tolerating Squirrel. All across the parking lot, engines revved, and queues of pickups and sedans formed near the exits. Jade noticed a group of men standing in a cluster twenty feet away, staring at the scene Squirrel was creating, his voice clearly too loud for Wilson.

"You must be Jade the Fade!" Squirrel barked. He began shadow boxing, his feet dancing in place, his punches toward Jade landing harmlessly in mid-air. "Don't fade on me, Jade. Don't fade." Squirrel let out a cackle and jumped up on the hood of the Corvair and held out his arms toward the group of men watching.

"Holy Jesus shit!" Squirrel shouted, turning to Jade for a moment and then back to his audience of co-workers. "You're the guy everybody wants to kill! First, Harry Pellino tried it with his forklift full of shells, but Roland Wilson here, our legendary local hero—" Squirrel made a trumpet fanfare sound— "Roland saved the day!" He made a quick bow to Wilson. "Then, the ever subtle and clever Cheese and his gang of two tried to piss up your rain pipe right under Old Glory just yesterday, Jade, no doubt causing a brown stain to appear in your drawers. Did you check them at lunch, Mr. Fade?" He didn't wait for an answer. Squirrel pointed at Jade but continued to face the crowd. "And by Gawd, Jade, it looks like somebody *else* tried to kill you. Did you punch somebody in the fist with your face today?" He cackled, but the men just stared, grim-faced, hands in pockets, arms akimbo.

"Hey, Roland," Squirrel shouted, still looking toward the men. "I think we better get our Commissioner on the Bat Phone. Whaddya say? Got some real problems here in Bombs Away. This new kid's a magnet for trouble. Hell, the guy can't even take a shit in peace without some tough guy messing up his hair. I say we call in the National Guard. Oops! Can't do that! They all work here! Shit! How 'bout the FBI? No, dammit. They're all busy digging through backpacks of dangerous hippies looking for the tools of revolution. Abbie Hoffman says put a dead fish in a bank safe deposit box and throw away the key. Not a bad idea. I say, naked women are a much better solution. Can you see it? Fifty naked women walking around this yard at lunch every day? Hell, this place would shut down in the afternoon. Naked chicks for dessert for every man—*and* boy, thank you very much—in this factory yard and every other bomb yard like it throughout America. And you know what? Bomb production would come to a screeching halt! And this fiasco in Vet Nayim, as the news guys call it, would come to the same screeching halt!" He made a squealing noise that sounded exactly like tires skidding to a stop on macadam.

132

"Squirrel!" Wilson shouted. "Knock it off. Get down. Now!"

Squirrel froze in place, his arms still spread wide, his eyes glaring, his buck teeth bared in a silly smile. He stared at the men, then lowered his arms and raised one of them in his sweeping stage gesture, bowing again at the waist. He jumped to the ground next to Wilson. As the men began to spread out toward their cars, a few remained, staring at the trio.

"Get a hold of yourself, Squirrel" Wilson coaxed, a softness in his voice. "Take ten deep ones. Come on, sit on the hood, close your eyes. Breathe. C'mon." He filled his chest with wind and exhaled, prompting Squirrel to do the same. Squirrel looked at Wilson as if he didn't know him and then he slumped onto the Corvair fender, nodding his head dutifully and attempting to slow himself down by breathing along with Wilson.

Wilson sat next to Squirrel and turned to Jade. "So, you and Cheese and his boys had a little powwow in the head today. I don't know how he finds out about this stuff, but Squirrel heard that you tried to defend me in your little discussion with Cheese." He gave Jade a slanted smile and shook his head. "Let me tell you something, Flynn. I don't need you defending me. I can handle myself. And I'll remind you one more time. Sit somewhere else at the breaks. Otherwise, next time it won't be a little cut on your head. It'll be something you won't recover from."

"They think you're in on some money scam with Hafferty and Jensen," Jade said. "They think you're stealing or skimming union money. And that you're a snitch, a spy in the union."

"Ha!" Squirrel said, standing up and starting to pace between Jade and Wilson.

Wilson stood and grabbed Squirrel by the shoulders. "Keep your voice down. Sit!"

Squirrel sat on the hood and bent forward, whispering in a frantic tone. "I'll tell you who's skimming around here! It's the goons you punched in the fists with your face today, Flynn. I'm in that fuckin' union and do you know how much they take out of my pay every week? Been in this sewer for over a year now, and the goddamn union is into me for nearly a thousand bucks. And I only make three hundred a week!"

Wilson stood up. "Squirrel!" he said through gritted teeth. "Shut...the hell...up! Just sit here and shut up." Then he turned to Jade, and with a quick glance toward the remaining men who were talking among themselves, he raised his voice for their benefit. "You're here to work, that's all, got it, Flynn? Don't listen to *him*, just do your job."

Then, in a quieter voice, Wilson said, "And stay away from me. And stay away from this guy, too. You got it?"

Jade gave Wilson a long look, then glanced at the men.

"Hit the road, Flynn!" Wilson said, loud enough for the men to hear. "You're gonna miss your bus."

26
Keeper of the Sorrows

Wednesday, June 25, 1969

Her eyes popped open, and she sat up, startled. Dizzy. In her bedroom now, in her bed, still smelling the dream. Booze, cigarettes. The scent of someone's skin. Vague, yet familiar.

Her money. She pushed away the sheet and stood. Still dizzy. She took a deep breath and pulled the footstool into the closet and straightened up, exhaling. She shook her head to clear the dream. She climbed up and swept aside hat boxes crowding the closet shelf. She reached into the darkness and felt the metal.

Sitting on the bed, she counted the cash. The tally showed $2,260, but the count was $40 short. Two possibilities: she forgot to change the tally, or someone took the $40. Not Seamus. Or James. Or whatever he's calling himself now. Jade. He's so bold that he'd say it right out loud rather than steal some of it: Where did you get all this cash, Alice?

She looked down at herself. Black tee shirt, white underpants. On the floor, black dungarees and socks, black work boots. She got up and went to the full-length mirror. Her breath came in a sharp shock. It was real. Her hair. It was not a dream.

At the mirror over the sink in the bathroom, she ran her fingers through what was left of her hair. It looked hacked, not cut. There was a jacket, black leather. She went back into the bedroom. There. On the footboard. With zipper pockets, the leather broken in, not new.

In the bathtub, she washed the dream from her skin and hair, but it would not go away. She'd done it, she knew; it was real. She'd sung and no one had clapped. And Sam. Something about Sam. The scent was his.

In her red silk robe at the full-length mirror, she tried to focus. Her cheeks were blotchy, her eyes pink sores. She decided it was time. She'd make a call, deliver the key, share a plan. She was forgetting too much, too many black outs. It wasn't the booze. It was something else.

In The Grotto, she pulled the robe tight and glanced around at the statues and unlit candles, and then she met The Blessed Mother's gaze full on. She waited for the eyes to move, but they just stared at her. She let out a little laugh and gave the Virgin a snappy two-fingered salute. For the first time in a week, she felt clear, present in this moment. She wondered how long it would last this time. As she picked up the phone, she was relieved to hear a dial tone. The bill was paid. Thank God for her son. After maybe a dozen rings, finally, a connection.

"I'm so sorry to bother you, Wilma. No, everything's fine. He's OK, working hard. Yes, I'm sure you do. He misses you, too. I was wondering if I could speak with Wally, just for a moment."

At the First National Bank of Ebonton, in the private room, she added $2,000 to the neat stacks inside the safe deposit box, recounted the stacks, and changed her tally. She caught the 15 at the downtown bus station, got off at the stop near the diner, pressed the buzzer two longs and two shorts, and, at the click, she opened the door, letting a warm bath of June light into the dank windowless storage room. She winced at the sharp scent of fried onions as she stood next to Wally's office door waiting for him to emerge from the kitchen. She'd decided not to wear her new black outfit, to stay with a recognizable look for Wally's sake, just adding a black beret, in part to cover her hacked hair, but mainly she wore it in memoriam.

She smiled to herself as she thought about meeting Wally six years earlier in the Ebonton library four days after she'd arrived on Reston Street with Seamus. Wally had mistaken her for a librarian, asking her about books in English by Polish authors. She'd laughed at his question, then apologized for her impertinence and escorted him to the real librarian for help. They'd encountered each other again in the stacks a half hour later and had struck up a conversation. She'd learned a little about his past, his pride in his homeland, and hints of the suffering that he and Wilma had endured during the war, a family lost, his and Wilma's bizarre but serendipitous escape from a prison camp through Belgium to England and emigration to the U.S. And he, in turn, had learned a little about whatever Alice was willing to say about herself. They'd talked about her son, twelve years old at the time, and Wally had invited her to come to his diner to meet Wilma, to bring Seamus and perhaps Wally would find a "leetle job" at his diner for the boy. It was the first of her many visits with Wally, always through the diner back door, to help him with his English and, in turn, to rely on him to provide a father's guidance for her son. He became her confidante, the only person she could trust.

"I cannot embrace you, my dear. Wilma would be jealous." He smiled and touched her cheek with a brush of his thick fingers. "Plus, as usual, I smell bad. Onions, I know you hate." Wally raised his eyebrows at her beret as he wiped his hands on his apron and gestured for her to enter his office. He closed the door behind them.

She pushed a small key across the desk toward him. "Please keep this in a secure place," she said. "I will follow up with a letter in the mail which will explain the key."

"Are you going away to some place for a long time?" His eyes darkened, and he held out his hand to touch hers.

"No, not exactly. I'm just...very busy these days...and...I'm afraid I might miss the opportunity to...that I might forget about this. And if I do, well...Jade will be affected. I must do this now."

Wally turned his head sideways and sighed. "I'm sorry, my dear, but I do not understand. Is your Jimmy in trouble? His new job?"

"It's not that, no. But...then again, it might be." She reached across to lay her other hand on his. "I'm sorry, Wally, I'm confusing you. I'm having trouble, I'm...I can't seem to concentrate. I'm probably drinking too much. I can't remember things. Ever since...well, you know."

He held her hands in his. His mouth was a thin line, his eyes pinched for her.

"The letter will explain everything, Wally. I'll put it in the mail tomorrow. Should be here in a few days." She stood to go.

"And Jimmy?" Wally said, looking up at her, his eyes dark. "Oh I am sorry, I know it is Jade now."

She took in a deep breath and sighed. "Yes. I wish he'd leave that place. It's not safe there. I wish he'd come back here to work for you." Her lower lip quivered, and she blinked away tears. Wally stood up and came around the desk and reached out his hand, lifting her chin with a soft touch to meet his worried eyes and his uncertain smile.

"He can come back here any time he wants," he said. "I have a new boy, but there will always be room here for your son."

She shook her head, her voice starting to flutter. "He...he won't come back, Wally. I can't...I can't convince him of anything these days. I don't blame him, really, considering how I am, how I've been. But I warned him about Dennis, about taking a job from him, how taking a favor from him binds you to him forever. He wants everyone to owe him, so he can control you for the rest of your life. You know that, Wally. Look what he's done to me. And now, he wants to take Jade. He's already stolen so much from me. Think of James and—"

"No, you cannot say more," Wally urged. "You know it will come back to harm both you and Jade. You cannot say how you are connected to that man, you know that. You have made that commitment to yourself, and you have held onto it for years. You cannot let it go now. It will bring more harm to you and to your son."

"He's a de facto Republican now, Wally! Christ, he was elected a Democrat for years but he hated Bobby Kennedy for opposing the war— you know that and you know why—and now he's a goddamn closet Nixon man! Law and Order! What a joke. Of course, why should that surprise me? He'll go wherever the money is. His blood money, his weapons money. Just like my father. And people around here won't care one way or the other, as long as his favors keep coming. Their sons come home in boxes, and they don't make the connection to him. It's a sickness, and they're drinking his poison like it's—."

"Please stop! You're going to make it worse."

She turned and went to the door, talking to Wally, but facing the door. "I went to see him, Wally. On Monday. I wanted to demand that he let Jade go back here to the diner, but I didn't even get that far. I couldn't help myself! I shouted out what he needed to hear. That he is a murderer! That he had Marte killed, and that I know who did it for him! And do you know what he said to me, Wally?" She turned back to him.

Wally went to her and held her in his arms and let her sob. "Stop it. Stop it now," he whispered. "You will never do that again, do you hear? Promise me you will never go there to see him again, and that you will never say that to *anyone* again."

"Oh, no worries there," she said between gasps. "He told me if I ever came to his office again, or confronted him again, he'd have me committed to Valmore. For the rest of my life. I'm not afraid of him anymore, never again, Wally. But did you know he can do that, Wally? He can get away with that in this country. Men like him do it all the time to women who are inconvenient to them. Commit them to an insane asylum."

She was shaking in his arms. "Ok, ok," Wally said. "No more. No more visits to him, no more talk of this. Do you hear me?" He pulled away and lifted her chin. "Look at me. Do you hear me? You cannot say such things again. To anyone. Ever. Think of your son. You need to protect him."

There was a knock at the door and a muffled voice on the other side. "Wally?" It was Wilma. "I'm sorry, but we need you."

"OK, my love," Wally called to her. "One moment."

At the back exit, Wally hugged her one more time, apologizing with his fraught smile. "Now you smell like onions." She laughed softly, letting him go and wiping a handkerchief across her eyes. "Yes, thanks for that. Now, everyone on the bus will understand why I've been crying."

"No more," he said. "You must promise me. No more of this Dennis talk. You can tell me, but no one else. It is not safe."

She nodded and then opened the office door. As she pushed the outside door onto the alley, Wally called out to her, "I'll call a taxi for you." She shook her head and kept walking.

Sitting at her kitchen table with pen and paper, she stared for a long time at the cupboard over the refrigerator where she kept the Four Seasons. Then, in a mechanical trance, a focus that surprised her, she started the first of three letters: an authorization letter to the First National Bank, and then a letter to Jade, which she enclosed in a sealed envelope. She labeled the envelope in block printing: *James Dellworth Flynn, son of Alice Flynn*. She took out another sheet of paper.

Dear Wally,

For the last six years, your kindness and generosity have sustained me, especially in my darkest hours. You've been the father that my son never had and the keeper of many of my secret sorrows over these years. I especially enjoyed the time we spent together studying English (until I abandoned you last year, so sorry for that), and I am so proud of your persistence and success in learning this difficult language.

I trust you, Wally, more than anyone on earth. In the event of my death, or in the event of the legal or medical declaration of my incompetence, or in the event of my disappearance during which you cannot locate me within a reasonable period of time, please use the key I gave you and the attached authorization letter to access my safe deposit box at the First National Bank of Ebonton. Please place the letter to Jade and the contents of the box in a secure location, either at your business or at your home. I'm thinking the safe at the diner might be best. At the appropriate time, these should be given to my son, Jade. I leave it to you to decide what that appropriate time should be. His maturity at age 21 might be best, but it may help him sooner, if he's desperate. Whether he receives all the contents or partial allotments—that, again, I leave up to you.

If you cannot locate Jade at the time you determine suitable to begin distribution of the contents, please transfer the letter and the contents to James Lukas Wilson, Ph.D., along with this letter. If Dr. Wilson leaves Ebonton, his college should have his forwarding address. You know about him, but you've never met him. He may come across as unapproachable, and perhaps even mean-tempered, but, believe me, he is a good man, and once you explain why you've contacted him and shown him this letter, I trust he will endeavor to find Jade, no matter how long it takes him. In that case, I confer to Dr. Wilson the same discretion I've given you in terms of how and when to distribute to Jade the contents of the safe deposit box and the letter to him.

I know this letter may seem mysterious to you and may even imply that I am planning to leave this world of my own accord. I assure you that is not the case. While I have not been the best mother a boy could have, I would certainly not leave my son that way. And yet, my condition over the last year has deteriorated considerably. Due to my most recent loss, the details of which you are privy, I'm finding it increasingly difficult to maintain equilibrium, to recall important details in my daily life—a situation I feared would threaten the disposition of this important matter. I also remain in danger of harm from certain individuals, including possible involuntary confinement in an institution, or worse—a matter I hinted at with you, and one that may ultimately cause you to execute the wishes I have outlined herein.

I love you, Wally, and I love your dear Wilma. You have been the safe port in the storm of my life here in this lost valley. You have helped to raise my son in ways that I could never have achieved on my own. I know your dedication to Jade stems from the loss of your own children in the war so many years ago. So, I thank your children for the love that their father has extended to my son.

May the famous Wally's Diner live on forever!
With much love and eternal gratitude,
Alice Flynn

Part Three

27
The Deal

Wednesday, June 25, 1969

Jade hustled with a slight limp along Canton Avenue toward the bus station. He'd already missed the 3:45, and, if he missed the 4:15, he'd have to wait an hour. He considered walking the five miles home, but his hip was still aching, and he had nothing left in his tank. His strength was drained, his mind distracted. He'd been thinking about Wilson and his friend with the brain on fire—Squirrel, so funny and reckless, fearless. He cringed at the way Wilson had dismissed him in the parking lot, and he wondered why the guy was so determined to crush his will. It was a challenge Jade was not about to yield to, and he thought this new guy, Squirrel, might help him figure it out. Squirrel was flamboyant and skittish, possibly out of reach in the realm of common sense, but it was clear he and Wilson were close, so if the opening presented itself, Jade would take it up with Squirrel.

The sidewalks were jammed with commuters, and his body and head were throbbing from the men's room workover by Cheese and his sidekicks. He touched the gash over his eye and held out his hand. No more blood. But he could still feel the shock of it in the very center of his brain. It felt like he'd been hit by a hammer.

Jade checked the clock tower on the station just ahead. It was 4:15. He started to trot when he heard someone shout his name. The voice was coming from a black car just fifteen feet away. It was Hafferty's Fleetwood, and the voice belonged to Silver Head Stanley. He was sitting behind the wheel, his eyes drilling holes in Jade.

"Gotta catch a bus," Jade called out and kept walking toward the station.

"Get over here!" Stanley shouted, his voice like a foghorn. The crowd surrounding Jade collectively flinched and parted a path between him and the Fleetwood. Jade glanced skyward and then at Stanley's grim face. The guy was hardly Moses, but he had a voice that had the weight of authority in a town that was cowed by it.

As Jade approached the car, Stanley nodded toward the back door. "Get in. Somebody wants to see you."

Jade slid onto the gleaming black leather backseat and saw a face he hoped he'd never see again. "Shut the door, asswipe." It was Zook Zulkowski, riding shotgun and leaning into the opening between the front seats. As Jade pulled on the door, he was hit by the wall of Zook's breath, a mix of booze, cigarettes, and something foul he'd shoved in his moronic maw at his last meal.

Jade's stomach sank, and he gritted his teeth. "Zook," he snarled. "You loser." Heat was rising in his chest, revulsion at this man's hideous face. "I thought you'd be rotting in a cell by now."

Zook shoved his face between the front seats and smiled at Jade, a smear of carious teeth between wet puffy lips. "Looks like you've been the one in a cell, fuck face. Nice fuckin' shiner you got there. Heard Cheese used your head for a football today. It's what you get for giving blow jobs in the men's room on company time, sweetie pie. Like I said, you won't last a week in that joint."

Jade did what his mother had taught him to do a long time ago. He used the rage and smashed Zook's ugly mouth with a hard right. He wasn't going to lose another fight on this day. Zook's head snapped back, and he let out a wail that sounded like he'd been electrocuted. Stanley reached over and grabbed Zook by the hair and smashed the side of his face off the dashboard. Zook howled again, and Stanley pulled the man's head back and smashed the face again, nose first. Now there was blood spurting all over Zook and the front seat, and the wailing turned into a banshee's keen.

"What the fuck, Stanley!" Zook cried, his voice muffled by his hands covering his face. Stanley pulled on the gear shift, and the Cadillac lurched from the curb and shot across Canton Avenue in front of traffic that veered and screeched to avoid it. The car careened over a black steel bridge, roaring around slower traffic, and then pitched around a corner into an alley, the tires squealing and Zook falling into Stanley in the front seat.

The car skidded to a stop. "Get the fuck off me and get the fuck *out!*" Stanley used his right arm to lift Zook and hurl him at the shotgun door. Then he reached over Zook, pulled the door latch, pushed open the door, and leaned back to use his big wing tip to kick the stricken Zook out onto the alley pavement. Jade saw Zook's face twist at the impact, dark blood spraying. He'd hit the macadam teeth-first.

"Next time I see your ugly face," Stanley shouted, "it will be the last time you take a breath, you fuckin' scum of the earth." He pulled the passenger door closed and the Fleetwood took off like Apollo 10. Flush against the seat leather, Jade felt the car's g-force and thought for a moment it was going to lift off the ground.

140

When they pulled up to a large garage door along a dark street bordering the Macson plant, Stanley turned around to Jade. "Glad you took your shot, kid. Don't ever say I never did nothin' for you. That little fuckwad had it comin' for a long time."

He got out of the car and pressed a button next to the garage door. As Stanley returned to the driver's seat, a man stepped out of an adjacent metal door and nodded to him. The huge black wooden doors opened like a castle gate, and the Cadillac slid inside, took a sharp turn, and floated along a narrow passage between two brick walls. Jade realized they were somewhere in the backside of the munitions plant. "So, I guess the somebody who wants to see me wasn't Zook."

Stanley stopped the car near a blue door marked "Private" and tapped the horn twice. "No," he said to the windshield. "Zook was an opportunity. This one's an obligation. Let's go." As they got out of the car, a big man in grease-stained overalls opened the blue door and stepped outside. Stanley tossed the man his bloodied suit coat and the keys to the Caddy. "Get me a new jacket and get this interior cleaned. And I mean spit-shined. If I find a spot of blood in there, I'll break your fuckin' legs. Be back here in an hour."

Jade followed Stanley through the private entrance and around two turns in a long windowless hallway. When they came to another door marked "Private," Stanley rapped a coded knock, twisted the knob, and the door swung into a low-lit room. Jade recognized the small secretary's quarters outside Jensen's office—the spare, tiny room with the dirty porthole window overlooking a dull patch of the factory yard. This time, he'd entered from a back door he hadn't noticed earlier. And this time, the secretary was at her gunmetal gray desk, typing, as if no one else were there, including the men whose voices were coming from Jensen's office.

"I'll let you know when he's ready for him, Dorothy," Stanley said and disappeared into Jensen's office and closed the door, muffling the voices inside. Without looking up from her work, Dorothy took one hand off her keyboard and pointed to a wooden chair. Jade sat down as she continued to type. Dorothy was a big woman, hard to tell how old, but she wasn't young. Her dress and hair could not have been more plain, and her face could not have been more stoic.

After what seemed like an hour, but was only a few minutes, Jensen's door opened. "Send him in, Dorothy." It was Stanley. He stood to the side to let Jade enter. Jensen was leaning back in his desk chair with a slim ink-black cigar in his teeth, his pinpoint rat eyes beading on his new guest. Jade thought of Jensen's boot on his back and considered that the man's sadistic push-up routine was meant to toughen him up for the rough time he'd had at the plant over these first few days of his job. He wanted to thank him for his preparatory lesson in brutality, but Jensen cut him off with a bark. "Sit," he shouted, pointing at a chair against the wall. "Stanley, close that door on your way out."

Another door behind Jensen opened, and a man marched in with purpose, his eyes on Jade. He was average height, but thick from head to toe. He wore a cheap tan suit, no tie, the giant collar wings of a dull white shirt spilling onto the suit lapels. Jade smirked at the collar and thought if there was a fan blowing in this smoke-filled den, this guy would be airborne. The man's thin ash colored hair was arranged like a nest on his pale scalp. He picked up the chair next to Jensen's desk and turned it around to face Jade, but he didn't sit. As he leaned his meaty paws on the back of the chair, he gave Jade a slow, frowning assessment.

Jensen tossed a pack of Marlboros on the desk. The man used Jensen's desk lighter to fire one up. As he exhaled a cloud in Jade's direction, Jade thought that after living for six years in this valley choked with culm dump smoke, he should be immune to people greeting him by blowing smoke in his face. But he wasn't. So, he held his breath and returned the man's glare through the cloud.

"This is Detective Captain Marion of the city police department," Jensen growled. "He has a few questions for you, Flynn. Don't disappoint him."

Marion's face looked like it had been used as a punching bag. His eyes were blood-shot and swollen, his cheeks scraped and bruised, his lower lip puffed up with a fresh cut that extended nearly to the dimple in his stubbled chin. His mouth turned up on one side, and he let out a little huff.

"This is what your face will look like if you lie to me, kid," he said. "Only much worse. You should see the other guy. His face is the least of his worries." He took another drag on his Marlboro and began to pace back and forth in front of Jensen's desk. Jade felt like he was in a courtroom, which was clearly Marion's intent, but that would make Jensen the judge. Jade fought back a chuckle. Even if Jensen wore a clean shirt, a tie, and a black robe, and brushed his teeth, he couldn't pull off the judge act. Maybe a hanging judge in a back-alley courtroom. Or a cave.

"You were late for work on Monday—your first day on the job, according to the General Manager here." Marion kept his eyes on Jade as he pointed at Jensen. Jade's throat tightened. His stomach did a somersault.

"You were late because you were a witness to an automobile accident on Canton Avenue, in which a colored girl died. Isn't that right, Flynn? Don't look so dumb; I read the police report. And I know you were late because the foreman reported it to Mr. Jensen here. And because Mr. Jensen is a gentleman and a forgiving man, he didn't fire your lame ass for being late." Marion turned to Jensen. "Isn't that right, Mr. Jensen?"

142

"That's right, Detective Captain," Jensen muttered around his pencil stogie. "And the Detective Captain wants to know what you saw that morning that you didn't tell the cops."

Jade looked toward Marion and then back to Jensen.

"Since I'm the officer of the law in this room," Marion said, "I'll ask the question again." He stopped pacing, wrenched a smile on his cracked lips, and stooped over Jade's face. "What did you see that morning at the accident scene that you failed to report to the officers who questioned you in their squad car?"

Jade looked at Marion's bloodshot, swollen right eye. "I don't know what you mean." His voice was a hoarse whisper.

"I didn't hear you, son!" Marion shouted at Jade, his breath sour and hot. "You don't remember? Or you don't *want* to remember?"

"I saw a girl with her face smashed in the windshield," Jade said, his voice firm now, his heat rising. "She drove her car into a fire hydrant right in front of me."

"We know that, kid!" Jensen shouted, sitting forward now at his judge's bench and scowling. "And we know it was a red Mustang, too. The paper got the car wrong. That don't matter. What we wanna know is who else you saw there. Who else was in the car?"

"In the car?"

"Yeah, in the fuckin' car with the dead girl, asshole! Who was with her?" Jensen shouted.

Marion started to pace again, his Marlboro hanging from his lip and his shoulders crouched. He stopped in front of Jade again, fists on his hips. He looked like he wanted another shot at whoever had punched up his face, and Jade was the only one in range at the moment.

"I didn't see anyone else in the car," Jade said to Marion. He felt his chest fill up with rising anger, and he decided he wasn't going to give this idiot cop anything but salt. He stuck out his chin, and Marion stepped back. "The car was about to run me over. I was sure I was dead."

"Go on," Marion said, his hands on his hips, his face softening into a smirk.

Jade remembered the girl's face in the windshield, and his rage drained away. His voice faltered, and he swallowed hard. "The car was…it was flying. Really fast. I ducked my head down…and the next thing I saw was her face, all smashed up. Her hair was like…She was so…There was blood everywhere…And her mouth was open…"

"That's very moving, son," Marion slurred, mocking a sad face. "My heart breaks that you had to witness that. I'm about to cry." His face hardened again, and he leaned closer to Jade. "So, you're telling me you didn't see anybody else in the car when the ambulance came. You didn't notice the police or the ambulance driver attending to anyone else. You were blinded by the horror. Is that it, kid? Cuz that's fuckin' pathetic. And you..." His nose was an inch from Jade's. He poked him in the shoulder with his finger. "Are a fuckin' liar."

Jade winced, his blood rising again. He decided to give up nothing to these assholes. "I was sitting in the cop car. I didn't see anybody else. I heard the second whistle at Macson, and I knew I was late for work. On my first day on the job."

"You didn't *want* to see anybody else, is that what you're saying?" Marion stood over him now. "You didn't *want* to, but you know someone else was there. Let's start with the girl again. Did you see her get pulled from the car?"

"Yeah," Jade said. "I was in the cop car, and I saw the ambulance guy just yank her out onto a stretcher. She looked like a bloody doll, her arms and legs all loose and flopping."

Marion stuck his cigarette into his mouth and pushed his face close to Jade's again. Jade pulled back. Marion grabbed Jade hard by the shoulders. "*When* you remember who else you saw getting pulled from that car, and I'm saying *when* not *if,* because you *will* remember, and *when* that happens, Flynn, you will tell no one else but your boss, Mr. Jensen. *When* you remember. You got that? Jensen and no one else." He tapped an open hand twice on Jade's cheek, hard enough to show him more than a slap will come next time. "I said. No one else. You *got* that?"

Jade nodded at Marion just as the door behind Jensen opened again. Dennis Hafferty stepped into the room.

"Good afternoon, gentlemen," Hafferty announced. Jade recalled the man's entrance to the diner a few weeks earlier when it was just him and Dee and Stanley and Zook. Hafferty had acted like he owned the place. This time, it was no act.

He was wearing a pale gray summer suit, with the requisite red tie and gold embellishments to the expensive tailored fabric. He strode to the office front door and opened it. "Your car is waiting for you, Detective. Both of you. Stanley will take you."

Marion bolted out of the room with his head down but as Jensen rounded his desk, he stopped in front of Jade and leaned into his face. "If you don't come up with an answer, Flynn, you're done here at this plant." His rat eyes seemed even smaller at close range, and Jade wondered if they disappeared altogether when Jensen emerged into daylight.

"I'll take it from here, Jerry," Hafferty said. "Tell Dorothy to leave the keys on her desk. Stanley will lock up after us."

Hafferty closed the office door, took off his suit coat, and pointed at the chair Marion had leaned on. "Sit there, son. More comfortable." He hung his jacket on a hanger in a closet and tossed a gold box of Benson & Hedges on the desk as he took Jensen's seat. "Help yourself, son. Best cigarette in the world."

Jade hadn't smoked more than a few cigarettes in his life, but he considered reaching for the box. He thought this might be a moment to practice blowing smoke in someone else's face for a change, but he decided Hafferty might be the wrong target for now. "No thanks," he said.

"Don't worry about those two fellas," Hafferty said as he pulled a cigarette from the box. "They're just doing their jobs. Rest assured, son, *I'll* be the one who decides whether or not you keep your job here."

Jade met Hafferty's eyes. He thought about thanking Hafferty for shutting down the third-degree grilling, but he hesitated. Jade had wanted a meeting with Hafferty to ask for the same union scale pay that Wilson got, but Jade knew this was not that meeting. Hafferty's googly eyes told him the real agenda of the meeting was about to be revealed.

"I had a visitor in my office on Monday," Hafferty said as he leaned back in Jensen's chair, curled his lips, and leveled a long stream of smoke at the ceiling.

Jade was starting to understand the smoke signal code. This signal was a peace offering. As the fog descended around him, he blinked it away, and met Hafferty's eyes.

"A woman I used to know a long time ago," Hafferty said, offering a smile that, for once, looked genuine. No fluorescent flash this time. "She came to talk to me about you."

"Why me?"

"She's your mother."

Jade sat up in his chair and almost stood up. "How is that possible?"

Hafferty chuckled, genuine again. "It's possible because she's a constituent of mine, just like anybody else in this county. Just like you, Jade."

"I don't understand."

"She came to ask me to give your job here at Macson to someone else, to let you go back to Wally's Diner. She's worried about your safety. And by the looks of those cuts on your face, I can see why a mother would worry."

Jade checked his forehead for blood. Again, nothing.

"But I told her no. I told her you were a lot tougher than she thinks. I told her this job will benefit you in ways a mother could never understand. After your stint here, you will no longer be a boy. That's always difficult for a mother to hear."

Jade swallowed hard and tried to quell the rush of heat to his face. It wasn't rage this time, it was embarrassment. Alice had gone way over his head to keep him from executing his plan. She wasn't praying to her statues this time. She was playing Mommy. With the man who'd given him the job. He couldn't even look at Hafferty.

"You have nothing to be ashamed of, son. In fact, you should consider yourself lucky. There isn't another guy in this plant whose mother gives two shits about him. Yours pretty much thinks the sun rises and sets on you. She's just trying to protect you, son."

Jade met Hafferty's eyes again. Behind the thick lenses, the man's foggy blue orbs were weirdly exaggerated as before, but there was something soft about his gaze this time, even likable. Until now, Jade hadn't seen anything in those eyes but calculation.

"You said you knew her a long time ago."

Hafferty nodded while he took a long drag on his cigarette. "Yeah," he said, exhaling smoke at the ceiling again. "Haven't seen her in years." He smiled, as if to himself, and looked toward the office door. "She hasn't changed much, still one of a kind. When I knew her, she was different from other women. Girls, I should say. We were all kids—nineteen, twenty, twenty-one—just after the war. She was opinionated, smart. And she knew it. Very competitive, made the other girls look like kittens. Good looking, too. Still is. Back then, though, she had the will of a man. And the physical strength." He turned to look at Jade. "In her college years, she was the toast of the club set in New York. Not the booze club set; the suburban country club set. On the tennis court. And on horseback. She took all the women's medals in Westchester County and on The Island. Never lost a steeplechase, never lost a women's singles match or a mixed doubles match. And it wasn't because of her partner, no matter who he was. She was better than most men on the court."

Jade thought Hafferty was making up this stuff. It didn't sound at all like anything he'd ever heard from Alice, even in her most whimsical or delirious states.

"She ducked out of her debut in New York society, too. I could tell she hated that scene, wanted nothing to do with it. Disappointment to her family. Then she disappeared for some reason. I heard, a few years later, that she turned up in the Catskills at a Jewish family resort, taking the tennis crown from those spoiled JAPs from Westchester and The Island." He chuckled to himself. "I guess they were pretty pissed. They got one of their pros to press up on her. It got a little racy." He glanced at Jade and smirked. "The pro challenged her. If he wins, he gets to take her to bed. She countered. If she wins, she gets his car." Hafferty looked at Jade and let him stew for a moment. He took a drag on his smoke and smiled. "She drove away from that camp and all those pissed off JAPs with a new sky-blue Imperial convertible that day. Finest car ever made."

For Jade, a door seemed to open, light emerging from a long darkness. A point of clarity coming into focus. Yet still, there was something unreal about this story. He tried to see through this connection, to call on his instinct for doubt. But listening to this important man talking about Jade's mother cut through the suspicion, the apprehension, the lifetime of knowing only uncertainty. Somehow, this man whom Jade had thought was a complete fraud now felt like a close friend, a relative, maybe closer. He wasn't at all like Wally, all heart and soul; but there was something unguarded about this side of Hafferty that Jade was relieved to discover. Behind the plastic public face of this powerful man, Hafferty was giving him a glimpse of his private personality. Despite his theatrical performances, this man was no charlatan. Behind the curtain, he was real. He was a man Jade might actually trust.

"She ever teach you to play tennis?" Hafferty said, breaking into Jade's reverie. He looked at Jade as if he already knew the answer, as if he'd known him for his entire life.

Jade stared at him for a long moment and then looked away. "Yeah. She did. Sort of. Once. She got me a private lesson one day at The Shore. With a pro, I guess." It seemed like a dream, but he knew it was real. He could see her in her tennis whites, the only time he'd ever seen her like that. "I guess I was about, I don't know, six or seven years old. I could barely hold up the racket. Felt like a tree trunk." He chuckled to himself. "It was a long lesson, and I was glad when it was over. I think the guy was glad, too. But then she decided to step in to give me a few extra tips, and the next thing I know, I'm on the bench on the sideline watching her play against the teacher, the pro. I was pathetic on the court, but I'd learned how to keep score. I'm pretty sure it wasn't necessary, though. I don't think he won a single set. Maybe not even a point. I remember he was really mad. Threw his racket at the net. Wouldn't shake her hand, wouldn't take her money for my lesson. He cursed at her. I thought she'd be upset, maybe mad at me. But once he was gone, she just laughed and told me that some guys are sore losers. On the way home, she said that was my real lesson of the day. Don't be a sore loser."

"Sounds about right," Hafferty said. He grinned at Jade like a co-conspirator and reached for another cigarette.

"Did you know my father?" Jade asked, as Hafferty lit up. "Was he a tennis player, too?"

Hafferty blew his exhale in Jade's direction and chuckled. Jade was certain the question had caught him off-guard. The big man shifted in his chair, cleared his throat, and straightened his shoulders, sitting up tall. "Not sure, son. She always had a few suitors. I suppose I might have met him, but I can't be certain about it."

Hafferty stood up and stepped around the desk to face Jade. "Cover your mouth and your nose with your hand, son. Like this," and he showed him. "There. Your mother's eyes. No doubt about that. Dark eyebrows and those bright green eyes, always sparkling like a chandelier. She was hard to miss. The rest of your face, I guess it belongs to your father. No idea why your father—whoever he was—wouldn't want to stay with her."

He returned to his chair and sat back and gave Jade a long look. "I had my father until I was twenty-one years old. Greatest influence in my life. Made me what I am today, God bless that man. A boy needs a dad, you understand, and it's sad when he loses that wonderful guiding influence." He nodded at Jade, and their eyes met. That clear uncalculated look behind Hafferty's usual foggy lenses had returned. Then, in a blink, it was gone. Hafferty frowned and titled his head, his eyes calculating again. "She never told you about your dad?"

Jade looked down at his hands in his lap and shook his head. "No," he said. He thought of the old man on the bus, the guy he'd cursed. The guy who'd said Jade's father was a Jew. "No. He died...or left, I don't know...when I was a baby? Maybe even before I was born. She never talks about him, never answers my questions. She's pretty good at changing the subject."

"Yeah. I recall that talent," Hafferty said with a smirk, pulling himself up in the chair and dousing his cigarette in the crowded ashtray. "She employed it many times. Had a gift for argument when she was young. Could turn it around on you before you knew it. But like I said, son, I'd lost connection with her for quite a few years. Didn't hear much about her at all after that story about her Catskill performance. Didn't hear about a son for a long time. Years passed, and I was very busy here and in Washington, lots of clean up still to do around here after the mines closed. Homes and businesses closed, too, some of them literally falling into the earth, into the old mine voids. But we're bringing it back, I tell ya. Already, we've brought a lot of federal government money into this valley, you know. Getting it back on its feet. Still a long way to go, though.

"Then, after all those years passed, your mother...what was it, a few years ago? Maybe five years ago? I heard she showed up here with a kid in tow. I guess that would be you. Then I heard she and the kid had moved into a little bungalow in Mell Hollow. That was around the time I met you in Wally's Diner and shipped you off to Pell Academy. And now, the next thing I know, a couple years go by, and you and I are back in Wally's making a deal on your Macson job. A few weeks later, your mother shows up in my office. That was Monday. What a pleasant surprise." He chuckled for Jade's benefit. It seemed insincere.

"You said you knew her family," Jade said. "I don't know much about them. Her mother died when she was young, I think. Her father? Maybe died in the war? Does that sound right to you?"

A change came over Hafferty's face as he reached for the fancy gold cigarette box. Jade thought Hafferty could be the guy in the Benson & Hedges magazine ad—a silk smoking jacket in front of a fireplace, puffing on a cigarette in place of a pipe. Hafferty's face had looked like he wanted to continue to be Jade's uncle, but then it shifted, almost against his will, to his public facade. The uncle was gone. He stood up with the cigarette

148

box in his hand, went to the closet, and grabbed his suit jacket from the hanger.

"I didn't say I knew them, son. I said they must have been disappointed in her. For ditching out on the debutante thing. I just assumed it." He flashed the fluorescent smile as he stood over the desk and lit another cigarette.

"Mr. Hafferty," Jade said, turning to look up at him as he aimed his exhale over Jade's head. "I wanted to ask you something else." Hafferty nodded and took another drag. "Are you, by any chance, Jewish?"

Hafferty's laugh came out like a shotgun blast, and he pitched into a coughing fit, his hand waving away the smoke as he lurched toward the desk, his face a turnip. He teetered back and forth, coughing and laughing, and then stumbled back into Jensen's chair and nearly fell over backwards in it. As he caught himself and his breath, he looked at Jade and shouted, "Do I look like a Jew?! Look at this face! Do you see a Jew nose here?! For Chrissake, kid, this face is the goddamn map of Ireland!"

As Hafferty continued to choke on his laughter, Jade stood up and stepped toward him. "I'm sorry, Mr. Hafferty."

Hafferty shook his head, waved him away, and coughed. "Jesus, kid. Mother of Christ! What the hell made you ask that? I've been called lots of things in my life but never that! Do you even know what a Jew looks like? Do I act like a Jew? Jesus, Mary, and the Carpenter. That's a first." He coughed through more laughter, and then fell into a full fit of hacking, his face bursting red.

"I'm sorry, sir," Jade said, when the man finally caught his breath again. Jade's face felt hotter than Hafferty's looked. "I don't—"

"No, no, no, kid, it's alright." Hafferty pitched forward in his chair and reached for the ashtray. "Christ, you really are not from around here, are ya?" He held up his hand, took a pull on his cigarette, and talked while he exhaled a scattered cloud. "You got a lot to learn, son. Didn't your mother ever teach you anything about people? Christ almighty. Am I a Jew!"

He stood up and walked to the door, opened it, and turned back to face Jade. "That's a beauty, son. Let me tell you something. And I'm serious now. Don't ever say that again to anyone, no matter what. It's ok saying it to me. It was funny as hell. But you could get somebody in trouble by asking them that. And you could get yourself punched out if you ask the wrong guy. Jesus Christ!" He was shaking his head as he worked his tie back into place. "Whatever gave you that idea, son? I hope you were kidding me."

Jade shrugged and shook his head. "Yeah, I...I guess I was." He forced a smile. "I'm sorry."

Hafferty glanced into Dorothy's office and then turned back to Jade. "Listen, son. My flight to National leaves in an hour. It was nice chatting with you. Memorable, that's for sure. I'd like to do this again sometime soon. You're funny, and you don't even know it." He pointed his big right hand at Jade. "But listen to me. Seriously now. Before we meet again, I need to be sure I can count on you."

Jade stood up to leave. "Count on me?"

"Yes. First of all, I want you to help out Detective Captain Marion. Try to remember what you saw at the crash site, and follow up with your boss, Mr. Jensen, tomorrow or the next day, Monday at the latest. I know you're forgetting something. Yes, it was a scary event, God help that poor girl. But the memory is in your head somewhere. Dig it out. And tell Jensen. It's a good idea to have him on your side in this place."

"But—"

Hafferty held up his hand. "Just do as I ask." He looked at his wristwatch. "But listen now. There's something even more important I need from you." He straightened his tie again and shifted his jacket in place with a snap of his arms. "I have a deal for you. If you help me with a few things, I will help you. If you help me, I will make sure that you get through the summer here and then out of this hell hole of a factory and this...this crazy town, and into a good college. You're way too smart a kid to skip college. I know you didn't flunk out of Pell Academy. You quit. I know that. It wasn't for you. At the time. But now, you're older and wiser, and...and you're ready for college! Almost."

He turned toward the door and looked into the outer office again. "Thought I heard something out there." He turned back and stepped toward Jade. "Anyway, we're different, you and me. I skipped college and went right into politics, and it paid off for me. Youngest guy ever elected to a state rep office, I was. But I'm a people guy. You? Jesus Christ, you're smart, but holy hell, if you think I'm a Jew, you're not a very good people guy. You need to go to college. I'm telling you, put those brains to good use. Your mother's brains. You can*not* pass up this opportunity I'm about to give you. Your life depends on it."

"Yes, sir," Jade said, nodding, but his eyes were on Hafferty's shiny Italian loafers.

"Look at me, kid, when I talk to you. This is serious. I said your life depends on it. Here's why. I know you're eligible for the draft. You're out of high school, just turned 18, and you're One-A. Of course, you know that. But I can help you there." He lifted his chin and smiled, holding two thick fingers together in front of Jade's face. "I'm like this with the chairman of the local draft board. We're that tight." The Commissioner was back on stage.

"On the other hand," he said, shrugging his big shoulders, "if you don't want my help with college, I won't get in the way of the draft. The army needs a lot of good young soldiers to stop the wave of Communism sweeping out of Asia right past the Reds in California and into the heart of America. I can't stop the draft board if they think you'll be better off in a uniform. But!" He raised his finger in the air. "But! If you choose to help me, I *can* direct their attention away from you and toward other more appropriate candidates. A few eligible young guys in this joint could replace you in the draft, and no one would miss them. Not here, at least. That's for sure."

He stepped closer to Jade and put his meaty palm around the top of Jade's arm and squeezed, making an exaggerated face. "Jesus Christ, son. I hope this place puts some muscle on you. If you get drafted in your condition, Mother of God, you won't make it a week over there in Vietnam."

He stepped back from Jade but kept his eyes locked on him. "I could make this deal with any draft-eligible guy in this factory, Jade. But I chose you. You know why? I'll tell you why. I chose you, because your mother can't afford to lose you. She's a good person, and she has nobody else."

Hafferty's avuncular smile returned for a moment, and then, in a flash, he straightened his shoulders and his public face was back. "And I chose you because I knew you were too smart to let yourself get killed in a place like Vietnam. And you *would* die there, you know. Other guys will make it, but not you. You've seen the news on TV. Scary place. You heard of Hamburger Hill, right? Thick, confusing jungles, booby traps that rip your limbs off, mosquitoes the size of your fist, swamps with all kinds of vermin and killers lurking in them, an unending heat that you never get used to. You can't sleep at night 'cause you're too shittin' scared, and you can't stay awake in the day 'cause it's hotter than that furnace over there in the Forge next to The Line where you work. God help us, son, it's hell on earth over in that jungle. And the enemy is everywhere. They all look alike, you can't trust the ones who say they're your friends, and you can't tell them apart from your enemies! They're hiding in the goddamn grass and underground like rats, popping up everywhere, and even the women and children try to kill you over there. It's a helluva place to be for a young kid like you, son. A helluva terrible place."

Someone cleared his throat in the next room. Hafferty stepped into the doorway and looked into Dorothy's tiny office. "Jesus Christ, Stanley! You scared the shit out of us! Get some real leather on those shoes, will ya? Spookin' around like a cat burglar. How long have you been standing there?"

"Just got here, boss," Stanley said. "Sorry about that."

"Call the chief and get me an escort to the airport. We're out of time."

"Already did that, sir. Squad car is waiting outside."

"Good, good. Thank you, Stanley. Wait outside, too. I'll be there in a minute."

He waited for Stanley to leave and turned to Jade. "Let's take our time with this, son. You don't need to do anything right away, other than what I asked you to remember for Detective Marion. I'm giving you 'til Monday to tell Jensen what you know. Other than that, for now, I just need to be assured that you are on my team. The men out there in this factory are pretty tough. I can see by the shiner you got there that a few of those guys have already made a personal impression on you. They're mostly good men, all war vets—gotta have respect for them. Some of them have been through experiences you couldn't even imagine. But there are always a few hot heads around here, son. Blabber mouths, crybabies. But you have to learn to get along with them somehow. You're working with Wilson, but he's with me already. You probably noticed that. Anyway, you two working together is fine, but hanging around with each other, no. I can't have the others thinking you two are in it together. Mix it up with the other guys, get some flexibility in your game. You're too straight, too stiff." He stepped toward Jade and shook him by the shoulders, and then stepped back to look out the doorway again.

"Look, son, I just need you to listen to what they're grousing about, that's all. And we can take it from there. If you have anything you need to tell me, keep it to yourself and just give my secretary a call. You can tell her anything. She'll get it to me. Here's her name and phone number." He handed Jade a card. "Just don't call when your mother's around. I don't want her to get upset."

He held his chin high and smiled down at Jade. "Once it starts to work out, we can get together again soon, and maybe I can tell you a little more about your mother. If I can remember. It was a long time ago. But do me a favor. Don't tell her we met. She's not in a good state of mind, as you probably know. She's troubled. She was pretty mad at me on Monday. And I don't think she's ever liked me much, anyway."

He held out his hand for Jade to shake. The last time he shook this man's hand, Jade felt like his own hand was trapped in a vice. This time, he seized Hafferty's hand and squeezed it hard. Hafferty flinched for a moment and made a pained face. Then he offered his toothy smile and laughed.

"Atta boy," he said, as they held each other's grip. "And don't forget. If this works out, you have college in the fall. Name a place you'd like to go. Penn State? Someplace farther away? I can work that out for you. I can make that happen. If *you* can make it happen. Deal?"

Jade nodded and found himself smiling. He flashed on the words Cheese had used about Hafferty and Jensen—taking payoffs from the company *and* the union—but he shut down those thoughts. Too soon. He'd have to get past Jensen first, on Monday. He'd keep Cheese's remarks in his pocket for now. To his own surprise, he was already learning Hafferty's game.

"Good," Hafferty said, letting go of Jade's hand. "You've grown up already, son. You just made a deal with a very important man. You won't regret it. And I sure hope I won't."

He headed toward the outside door and then turned around. "Oh! I almost forgot the keys to this place." He grabbed them off Dorothy's desk. "Come on, I'll drop you at Diamond Taxi."

In the back seat of the Fleetwood, Hafferty pulled a fistful of cash out of his pocket and peeled off two twenties. "Take this for the cab, and a little extra spending money. I'd give you a ride home, but I'd miss my flight."

"Oh, no, that's ok, Mr. Hafferty." Jade held up his hands. "I can catch the bus."

"Nonsense, son. The money's yours. Take it. I insist. Take your girlfriend to the movies. Go see that one with Henry Fonda and that Bronson guy. Something about time in the West. It's pretty damn good. You'll see how real men win."

He turned his big face to Jade and leaned toward him, smiling his uncle smile, warm, real, almost familiar. "You're with *me* now, son. We wait for no one. Especially not a goddamn bus." He laughed in an unforced way—a way that made Jade laugh, too.

And for the rest of the two-minute ride, Jade sat back on the soft leather, floating in the Fleetwood, while Hafferty told Stanley the story of Jade asking if he was a Jew. They all laughed. Really loud. Gut laughs. Jade felt like a man and the Commissioner seemed like an uncle again. Maybe more than an uncle.

28
Colored Girl

Friday, June 27, 1969

Jade weaved through the rush of bodies exiting the main gates and headed toward the downtown bus station. The sense of relief was palpable among the Macson workers as their pace picked up, bumping into one another without complaint. It was Friday, payday, and a cool breeze washed over the mob, cleansing them after a week of toil amid the plant's poisoned fumes. Jade knew this late June gift of low humidity and sunshine would not last, but the prospect of a bright warm weekend and two days off from work gave him a fleeting sense of belonging among his co-workers, even as he joined their eager departure from one another.

He glanced toward the parking lot to see if he could spot Wilson and Squirrel, but the afternoon sun bounced off the car rooftops, blinding him. As he made his way up the hill toward Canton Avenue, he saw his bus comrade Gort. Jade was tempted to catch up to him but decided to stay back. These last two days had been quiet, and he didn't want to stir up the whirling madness that had been the first part of the week. He decided he wouldn't take the 15 bus home. He was in no rush to discover whatever drama Alice might present him. He'd walk to Wally's, maybe get a free dinner, witness his old family of coworkers and customers enjoying their Friday shenanigans, and then take a later bus home from there.

He let the mob of workers rush by him as he crested the hill into downtown. He followed the crowd left onto Canton Avenue, bustling with rush hour foot and car traffic. Just past the first intersection, he slowed his pace to look across the wide avenue at the site of the Monday car wreck. The fire hydrant still looked banged up, but there was no other evidence of the grisly scene he'd witnessed, the razor's edge of fate from which he'd been lucky to fall onto the living side. His stomach lurched as he recalled the impact of the car and the girl's mangled bloodied face against the windshield. He knew he'd have to tell Jensen on Monday about what else he'd seen after the accident. He couldn't remember everything he'd told the foreman that morning, but he was sure he'd mentioned the cops pulling something from the trunk of the wrecked Mustang. And he was certain that's how Jensen and Marion and Hafferty had found out.

As he passed the bus station, Jade searched furtively for the black Cadillac, for Stanley behind the wheel, watching him. But there was nothing. Still, he couldn't shake the feeling that his meeting with Hafferty on Wednesday had changed his life—not only complicating the plans he'd made for himself, but eliminating the independence he'd been accustomed to, the anonymity that, for the past six years in this dark valley, had kept him out of the path of danger. He'd noticed on Thursday and again on Friday that no one had bothered him at the plant—no Cheese gang harassment, no Wilson intimidation, no falling bomb shells, no surprise attacks in the men's room, not even a Squirrel sighting. But this sudden pause in unwanted attention wasn't the result of that detached feeling he'd projected for the past six years; rather, it was the opposite. It was as if he now had an invisible barrier around him, a transparent bubble, his anonymity now unmasked. He was being left alone on purpose; and he was being watched on all sides. Isolated. Under surveillance.

He'd spent his breaks and lunches alone, ignoring Hafferty's instructions to connect with other workers, but still, he was never really alone. If he turned his head in any direction, he could see that someone was watching from a distance. He sensed that his obligation to Hafferty, his deal, was somehow recognized by everyone around him. Hafferty surely wouldn't tell anyone else, but the men at the plant seemed to have a sixth sense, as if their collective experience, perhaps their shared military experience, gave them secret insight that he would never be part of. For him, he'd be just fine if he never experienced that shared insight. By agreeing to Hafferty's plan, he'd stay out of the draft and the war, and never have a chance to understand that soldier bond—a sacrifice he'd be more than willing to make. After all, as Hafferty had convinced him, he wouldn't live very long if he ended up in Vietnam.

These worries started to fade as Jade emerged from downtown, crossing over the Canton Avenue bridge and gathering momentum in his stride from the welcomed breeze at his back. When he saw Wally's Diner in the near distance, he forgot about everything, smiling to himself, returning home. Once a boy, now a man.

He pushed through the front door and stood in silence, a satisfied grin on his face. Wilma sat at the counter sorting through table checks. She didn't notice him, but Dee did and let out a squeal. Her order pad slipped through her hands and fell to her feet, and she flapped her arms like a teenage girl. Her voice took on the cadence of a Southern belle. The actress of her dreams was on stage again.

"He's bayack!" she hollered. "Oh, ma lordy, he's bayack!"

She minced around Wilma and rushed to Jade. She wrapped her arms around his shoulders and then, still holding him, she reached for a menu and started fanning herself.

"Ah declaya! A girl might need some smellin' sawlts hea," she called out to her captive audience. "Help me, Lawd, I'm about ta faint!"

It was an unusually sparse crowd for this Friday afternoon hour, but most of the diners chuckled at Dee's performance. Jade turned crimson as he tried to separate himself gently from the drama queen. But she held on tight, murmuring something about his shoulders. As he felt her push her breasts and hips against him in this center stage performance, Jade was panicked by his body's instinctive response, and he shot a desperate look for help to Wilma. He'd always known Dee had had a thing for him, and he often fantasized about something reckless and torrid happening between them, but not in public. Not on center stage in Wally's Diner.

"Jeemie!" Wilma called out in her Polish accent, smiling and peeling Dee off Jade and enveloping him in a smothering hug. Wilma was six inches shorter than Jade, but her breasts were giant pillows, and Jade drank in this motherly embrace like a man dying of thirst. He was even more grateful to hide his arousal behind Wilma's girth. He willed himself not to look at Dee until he calmed down.

"So, Flynn! Didja get wounded in battle over there or what?!" Dinty Connolly yelled from the far corner booth. "A coupla scratches on your face, and, by the way the girls are acting, you'd think the kid was in the war for the last five years." This brought just a chuckle or two from The Jury but Dinty, undaunted by the paltry response, took it up a notch, to his usual level of near-insult. "Dja bring back any souvenirs from the war, kid? Like a Honda 50 with your own slopehead driver?" The small crowd gave up a few more chuckles, and Dinty nodded and waved as if he were running for public office.

Jade noticed that Dinty was in the Judge's seat. No Red Larkin in sight. He got the feeling that Dinty had taken over, that Larkin's humiliation by Hafferty two weeks earlier had unseated Red from his throne for good. There was no sign of Red's son Timmy, Jade's replacement, and Jade surmised that father and son had departed Wally's together, permanently.

As he pulled away from Wilma's abundant clutch, Jade smirked at Dinty and nodded to a few of the diners, familiar faces all around, and he felt a surge of homesickness. He lifted a half-mast wave at the rest of The Jury—Bowl and a Roll Rondo, The Councilman, Big Gino Mecca, and even sullen Jerold Kent, the loneliest mailman on earth. Each Jury member nodded at Jade, and then he noticed the kitchen door swing open, with wall-eyed Gordon winking his good eye at him, while Brenda squeezed by Gordon to throw Jade a kiss from behind the counter. Jade was almost afraid to see Wally. He still felt he'd abandoned his own family, and, if Wally came in from the kitchen now, Jade might lose his composure altogether. But Dee saved him.

"Gimme a hand in the kitchen, will ya?" she said with sudden urgency in her voice. She grabbed his arm and pulled him through the swinging doors. For a moment, Jade thought she'd read his mind and was going to drag him into the back room with her. But she stopped near the grill and turned to him, looking conspiratorial.

"There's a colored girl in the office talking with Wally," Dee whispered, her face inches from Jade's. "Sent here by Hafferty! I think she's looking for a place to live. You know, one of Wally's apartments in the East End."

"So?" Jade said.

"So! If Wally puts her over there, those neighbors will kill him!"

"Wally can't control what the neighbors think."

"He can control what they do by what *he* does! And if he puts that girl in that neighborhood, what they'll do is burn down his house. Or worse." Dee was still inches from his face and breathless now. "You've got to talk him out of it, hon."

"I can't talk Wally out of renting his apartment to someone. That's Wally's decision."

Dee grabbed him by the shoulders. "Kid, you're the only one he listens to besides Wilma, and, right now, Wilma isn't talking to him."

"Why not?"

Dee waved her arm over her head. "Oh, it doesn't matter. One of their stupid fights. The point is that he's flyin' solo on this one, and I'm tellin' ya, kid, he's gonna get himself in deep over this decision. I know him. He's different from everybody else in this town."

156

"You mean he's not a bigot."

Dee smiled at him and pinched his cheek. "That's what I love about you, honey. You and Wally. You two think alike. And that's why you have to talk to him. You're the only one he'll listen to. You gotta get him to stall that girl and then talk to him later about what'll happen to him, to Wilma, to this place, everything. He can't rent to that colored girl in there. He'll have a race riot on his hands. Something this town never saw. But they watch the news, and they think it's comin' here sooner or later."

"I don't know, Dee."

Dee held his face in her hands and looked him in the eyes. Jade thought she was going to kiss him. "I'm scared, honey," she said. "And I'm right about this one."

"OK," Jade said. "But I'm not gonna tell him what to do. I'll just talk it over with him."

Dee kissed him on the mouth and pushed her hips against him, and Jade's body reacted instantly. Dee pulled away, startled. "Jesus, kid, I'm sorry." She glanced down at his pants and put her hand on her mouth, snorting a laugh. "I...I didn't mean to...I'm...I'm sorry. I guess I just...missed you this week."

"Yeah," he said, blushing and swallowing hard. He shifted back a step and covered the front of his pants with his hands, half-smiling. "I just came by to see how everybody was doing, and now I'm on a secret mission. *And* getting kissed by my favorite waitress."

She gave him a soft push on his chest. "Your favorite, huh? Thanks a lot. Between me and Brenda, that ain't sayin' much."

They both laughed, and then she hushed him, wiped her lipstick off his lips, and turned him toward the back room. He looked at her over his shoulder as he walked to Wally's office. She was standing at the swinging door and smiling at him and waving him on. He wished he'd said something more romantic to her, or at least more interesting. It was another one of his many missed moments.

At the office door, Jade heard voices inside and paused. He looked back again and saw Dee's face on the other side of the swinging door, peering through the tiny diamond-shaped window. Still watching her, he rapped on the office door. Wally opened it before Jade's hand fell to his side.

"Jimmy!" Wally called out, with a huge smile. "My boy!" He smothered Jade in a great bear hug, pounding his back with tender thumps.

"Easy, Wally," Jade laughed, "I'm getting stronger, but I'm still breakable!"

Wally released him, laughing, and patted Jade on the arms. "You look wonderful, my boy. And hey, you *are* getting stronger. Feel those muscles!"

Jade felt his face flush when he realized there were other eyes on them in this private moment.

"Ah, Jimmy—I mean, Jade. Jade, I want you to meet someone. Professor Chautier," he said nodding to the woman sitting in a folding chair in front of his desk, "This is Jade Flynn, my best employee—ah, former employee! Jade, meet Doctor Tamara Chautier."

Jade stepped toward the woman and offered his hand. As she smiled and took it, Wally laughed. "Ah, Jimmy, what did your mother tell you, always. Never offer your handshake to a lady until she offers hers to you."

Jade turned red again, and he smiled his apology to Professor Chautier.

"It's nice to meet you, Jade," she said. "Please call me Tamara." She held his hand a moment longer while she looked him in the eyes. Hers were a color he'd never seen, a deep brown with golden spokes around the pupils. And they were huge, almond-shaped, her pupils the size of shirt buttons. Her teeth were brilliant white against her pillowy lips, and Jade was struck by the shade of her skin. Prior to living here, he had been around kids and adults with dark skin many times, but he'd never met anyone like this. Her skin was golden black, as if the sun were rising beneath it. The sheen on her cheeks was silken and smooth. Jade wondered if she had pores.

"Jimmy, you're staring!" Wally said. "You're making our young lady here uncomfortable."

"No, not at all," Tamara said, smiling at Jade. "I'm getting used to people around here looking at me like that. I know he means no harm." Her voice was soft and deep and rhythmic, like a song. Jade was transfixed. He was staring at her again. She was smiling with her mouth closed and Jade was drawn to her eyes again. He felt locked, helpless in this trance.

"Doctor Chautier is from Dickson College," Wally said. "She is a professor of Music and English Literature. She could teach me maybe better English," he said to her, and she smiled at him. "She needs to rent an apartment from us. We have two nice places near the school that would be perfect for her—the one on New Haven Street that Mrs. Fetterman just left, and the third floor flat in our home on Hemlock—two flights up from Wilma and me."

Jade looked at Wally and then back at Tamara, and his secret mission returned to him. But it was already going awry. Everything had changed in the instant he had met this woman. He couldn't follow through with Dee's mission, not now. He did not want to discourage Wally from renting to Tamara; he wanted just the opposite.

"The Professor is a friend of Doctor James Wilson at the college," Wally said, his voice changing to a business tone. "And Doctor Wilson is a friend of Commissioner Hafferty." He turned to Tamara. "Doctor

Wilson mentioned Doctor Chautier was looking for an apartment, and, well, the Commissioner knows a lot of things." He smiled and nodded at Jade. "He knows that I have a few tenants, and he recommended me. Of course, I am flattered."

"You seem confused, Jade," Tamara said. She smiled at him, as if she understood his distracted thoughts and could read his calculations, as if she knew he was figuring out how Roland ended up at the Macson plant and could see his mind graphing the connections among Doctor Wilson and Hafferty and Roland—and now this Tamara—Doctor Chautier, as Wally called her.

"No, I'm ok." Jade said. "I just...I was trying to...I actually work with Doctor Wilson's son, Roland. He's my supervisor."

"Oh," Tamara said, her beaming smile fading slightly. "You work at the Macson plant."

"Yeah. Started there on Monday. Pretty hard work."

"I'll bet it is. Do you like it?"

"The money's good," Jade said, "but that's about it." He met her eyes and felt swallowed up by them.

Wally huffed a short laugh. "Money is never good, Jade. It is simply a necessity."

"Wally doesn't like that I left him for the factory," Jade said, forcing himself to look away from Tamara.

"Oy, it was his decision," Wally said, shaking his head and waving his hands in front of his face. He began shuffling papers on his desk. "I said to him, make your own decision. You are a man now, I said."

Jade felt his hands trembling, and he shoved them into his pockets. "Well, I better go," he said to Tamara. "It was nice to meet you, Professor...um, Doctor."

"It was my pleasure," she said, standing to offer her hand. "And please, I insist. Call me Tamara." Jade held on to her hand for what he knew was a moment too long, and he looked at her as if time had stopped to allow him to gaze at all of her—eyes at once warm and all-consuming, hair cut so close to her perfectly shaped head, giant gold hoop earrings, and long loose-fitting brocade dress, purple and green and gold. She wore two long gold necklaces offset by a turquoise shell hanging from a third woven necklace. He'd never seen anyone like her.

"You should take the place on Hemlock—at Wally's and Wilma's," Jade heard himself say to her, as if in a dream. "The view's great from the third floor, and the family on the second floor is really quiet."

Tamara showed her brilliant teeth again. "Thank you," she said, her voice like silk, her eyes dancing. Jade returned her smile and felt a rush of pleasure enveloping him.

As he pushed through the swinging door leading into the dining area, he was glowing inside. He walked right past Dee and Wilma and out the front door. The last thing he heard from inside the diner was Dinty's voice.

"Hey, gunner! Next time, bring back the heads of a few gooks, willya?"

Jade heard the sputter of laughter from the Jury, and then it was cut off as the door shushed behind him.

Out on the street, he took wide strides toward home. He had four miles to walk, but he felt as though he could be there in minutes. The pain in his hip had vanished. The Number 15 would roll by soon enough, but he wouldn't take it. He was not so much bound for home as simply headed that way. After all, what was there? Alice. Earlier, he had visions of a new Alice, but he couldn't fool himself any longer. She'd shown promise many times in the past and then had plunged back into the same abyss. Tonight, if she was home, she'd likely be lost in a séance of mystery and booze, swooning at him upon his arrival. Or, just as likely, she'd completely ignore him, as if no one had come through the door, as if just she and the Blessed Mother there in The Grotto were the only existences that mattered. A third possibility—she'd be gone until late at night or maybe all next week. And the week after that.

Jade felt driven, again, by the notion to get out. Move on. Find the road west. His plan had been altered by Hafferty's deal, but he could see now that if he could make it through the summer, he'd have not only money in his pocket, but possibly an exit strategy far more promising than simply going west. Hafferty had said Penn State, or possibly another college. Could that mean much farther west? Colorado? California?

He slowed his pace and let his arms swing in rhythm with his breathing. Reston Street rumbled with steady Friday traffic escaping Ebonton, but Jade barely noticed. He was distracted by the vision of Tamara. She'd invaded his thoughts of escape, and he became more conscious of his own body, his breathing, his slowing heartbeat. She had an aura about her, projecting patience and clarity and serenity, something he could almost feel on his skin. Her own skin was so dark and flawless, her smile, her mesmerizing voice a musical chord. Her eyes, too, hung in his mind, their soft luminescence piercing him, yet drinking him in at the same time. Her face was beautiful, a new revelation in his concept of beauty. This was not a face that could be measured by a standard he'd absorbed from this isolated valley. This was a face that defined beauty as truth—no pretenses, no expectations, a face that promised something he wasn't familiar with. She was hope incarnate.

He was adrift again. As suddenly as it had appeared, the image of Tamara's face vanished. But something of her remained with him, a new power that carried him forward. He heard his breath move faster in and out of his lungs, and he let thoughts slip through his mind until he no longer thought at all. He was his body alone now, marching and puffing

160

and swinging at a fevered pace. He was empty. Barely conscious. Yet somehow, fully aware.

His senses moved to high alert. He was absorbed by the sights and sounds and smells surrounding him. He saw an explosion of color across the deep lawns of upper Reston Street, as if for the first time. Summer's flowering trees were showing their glory to him. Brilliant lemon forsythia in full bloom, fiery red azalea, clusters of snow-white Daphne, emerging buds of pink and purple rhododendron, and then a magnolia's deeper shades of cream and magenta—a surreal tree with its comical tulips standing on branches, as if sketched by a winking cartoonist. And, up high, the stark white cones of chestnut blossoms swaying and the new lime leaves on old oaks and sugar maples and hickory trees, unfolding their collective umbrella over the rumbling street below.

The tree and flower scents were faint amid the acrid fumes of the passing traffic, but he was still drawn by the allure of their sweetness. Away from the row of storefronts now, Jade was focused on the soft white pear tree tufts all in a row in a vast yard that ran deeper away from Reston. And in the middle of this snowy swath, a Judas Tree hung heavily in the air, laden with its rootlike branches dusted lightly with a spray of purple wisps. A rambling four-story Victorian house sat at the far end of this yard, ice blue and slate and pale cream, a vestige from an era when it was prestigious to own a grand home on the main street. Jade's eye was drawn to a vibrant red rose bush near the front entrance and then a rope swing suspended from the branch of a great ash tree in the side yard. He imagined the scene as a painting: on the swing he would paint Tamara in her dazzling brocade dress, kicking her legs up to reach the highest arc.

He was startled from his reverie by the weak bleat of a car horn to his left. He turned at the sound of his name being called. It was coming from a face hanging out of the window of a small blue car pulled over at the curb. Jade was bemused by the pale visage and penetrating dark eyes, not recognizing what he was looking at.

"Ya look like Gomer Pyle marchin' in those big boots and skinny legs," the voice in the face shouted. "Where the hell are you goin'? Sheriff Andy's office?" The voice cackled with laughter. Squirrel.

"Home," Jade heard himself say, as he surveyed the beat up Corvair. The roof was sun-bleached, and the doors and wheel wells were pocked with rust. The wheels themselves likely hadn't worn hubcaps in years, and the lug nuts looked rusted enough to snap off at the next pothole. Squirrel was chuckling at Jade's appraisal of the odd little machine.

"C'mon, man! I'll give you a lift. Home's what? Three miles away?"

"Yeah," Jade said, tentatively. "How'd you know?"

"Just a guess." Squirrel slid across to the driver's side. When Jade plopped into the shotgun seat, he felt like he'd landed on the road. The seat was less a cushion than a piece of tattered material over the flimsy metal floor.

"Comfy, huh?" Squirrel laughed. He pulled down a small lever on the dashboard, and the car lurched forward, sputtering and then catching the road as Squirrel turned into the traffic lane. A horn blasted at them and Squirrel waved his hand out of his side window.

"Thank you!" he shouted over the heavy rumble of an engine in need of muffling. He glanced at Jade. "Welcome to one of the greatest acts of industrial irresponsibility in the present century."

"What?"

"Nader said that about my car. I'm not insulted, though. I'm honored. Modern Jesus, he is. Know what they did to him?"

"No."

"The guys at GM hired a bunch of spooks to poke into Ralphie's personal life, to see if he was a sex pervert or a Communist or a spy. Turns out the guy's a Harvard genius, and he sues GM, and the U.S. Senate forces an apology out of the GM brass, and Nader walks away in his construction boots with a pocket full of cash and starts a crusade against the very guys who had to pay him off. Modern Jesus, I say."

Squirrel held his weak chin over the wheel and fixed his buck-toothed mouth in a grimace. He projected his voice as if speaking to a vast audience. "'A great problem of contemporary life is how to control the power of economic interests, which ignore the harmful effects of their applied science and technology.'" He turned to Jade, smiling. "Nader said that, too. Same thing old Jesus was saying about Caesar and his thugs."

He reached in front of Jade, popped open the glove compartment and pushed a tape into an eight-track player. "Funny thing is, I love this great act of irresponsibility. Just like people love to say they follow Jesus, but then live their lives in defiance of his example." He turned a dial and music blared out of box speakers on the back seat. "You like Dylan?" he shouted.

Squirrel wasn't waiting for his answer. He wailed over Bob Dylan's voice, in a nearly perfect imitation whine, making *The Times They Are a-Changin'* sound like a duet.

"Dylan's saying the same thing as Nader, you know," Squirrel shouted, barely taking a breath after his nasal, twangy verse. "The guys in the suits, the guys in the halls of Congress—they don't understand what he's saying. They know he's singin' about them, though, and what's gonna happen to them, and they don't like it. Sort of like standing around a bunch of Puerto Ricans, and you know they're makin' fun of you, but you can't understand exactly what about you they find funny. You been to Puerto Rico?"

Jade shook his head. Squirrel's rapid-fire pace had Jade's head spinning.

162

"Neither have I," Squirrel laughed over the music. "But I've been to the Bronx!" He cackled sideways out his window. "Beautiful Brown girls there. All dolled up in crayon colors. I love it."

Squirrel lowered the volume and reached into the back seat. "Hey, ya hungry? I got tons of food back here. Melting popsicles, a jar of sweet pickles. You like pickles? I got Tastykakes, I got Milk Duds, I got Doctor Pepper, I got Jujubes, I got Good-N-Plentys. And somewhere back here, I have some Blackjack gum. Here it is."

Jade grabbed the wheel. "Watch out!" he shouted and pulled the Corvair out of the path of an oncoming truck.

"Hey!" Squirrel said. "Thanks. You wanna drive?"

"No, that's OK," Jade said. "I'll take some gum, though."

"Hey, Roland's cool, ya know," Squirrel said, holding the steering wheel with his knees while gripping a soda can and popping two triangular holes in it with a can opener. "Don't worry about that crap he said about you staying away from him and me. He just gets weird like that sometimes. He's a little uptight. His old man's kind of tough on him, doesn't give him any credit for his amazing sports achievements. Wants him to focus on the books. But Roland never paid much attention to that. He never had to. Always had sports to fall back on. He's the smartest guy I've ever known. Numbers and science. He's a natural. But he never had to put out in the classroom when he was so great on the field. But you know what? He likes you. He told me later, after you left. He thinks you work hard, and he said it's pretty cool that you stuck up for him in that men's room brawl with Cheese and his goons."

"Really wasn't much of a brawl," Jade offered. "More like a mugging."

Squirrel laughed again, this time in a high-pitched hyena howl. Then, he finished with an actual howl, eerily wolflike.

"Hey," he said in his next breath. "Let's go up to the rez tomorrow. The moon's supposed to come out in the day. I love when that happens. Might be the last time we see the lunar star in daylight before the spacemen land on it and fuck it up."

"What's 'the rez?'" Jade asked.

"A reservoir up on White Oak Ridge, high above the valley, away from all this mess. Water's so pure you can drink it while you swim. And it's colder than a witch's tit in a brass bra. Your dick'll do a turtle on ya and your nuts'll shrivel up like baby prunes. Especially now. It's barely thawed up there. Wolves aren't even awake yet."

"Sounds inviting," Jade said.

Squirrel burst into another hyena laugh. "You'll love it," he shouted, over Dylan's *With God on Our Side*. "We'll go around noon for a swim and wait for the moon to rise." He punched a button to silence Dylan, and then sang out the chorus line to Creedence Clearwater Revival's *Bad Moon Rising*, finishing with a wolf's howl.

"Supposed to be hot tomorrow," he shouted at Jade. "In the 80s. Finally! You with me?"

"Sure," Jade said, but he was paying only partial attention to the skittish Squirrel. They were stopped at a traffic signal just a few blocks from his house, and Jade spied a familiar face on a bench in front of Finn's Drug Store. It was the old wart-nosed cur who'd accosted him on the bus Monday morning. After he'd cursed the old man, he never expected to see him again. When the Corvair rolled by Finn's, the old guy looked up, his caved in black eyes coming alive, meeting Jade's with instant menace.

When they pulled up in front of his house, Jade looked through the back window, almost expecting to see the old man hobbling along Reston Street after them.

"See ya tomorrow then?" Squirrel asked. "Noonish?"

"Yeah, noon. But pick me up at my girlfriend's. I'll ask her to join us. She lives on Liberty Street, fourth door from the end of rowhouses at the bottom of Fireman's hill. You know the one, looks like a brick wall but it's really a road."

"Yeah, I know that one. The wall behind North Heights. Liberty is at the foot of the wall. No irony there, huh?"

Jade smiled and nodded. "Thanks for the ride."

"Can't wait to eat your girlfriend," Squirrel shouted. "I mean *meet* her!" He howled his hyena laugh as Jade smiled and nodded at the curb, offering a middle-finger salute.

The Corvair disappeared in a swirling cloud of gray exhaust, casting a haze over Jade's little brown house, giving it a dreamy, less tattered appearance. Cars and trucks rumbled in front of Jade as he stood at the curb. He hesitated before crossing the street. He had the odd sensation that something new would welcome him on the other side. Then, he stepped back, turned around, and walked to the top of the little knoll between the houses opposite his. He slipped into his alien mode, the visitor from a dream dropped here to question the existence of those who dwelled in this sad, sunken little structure. His gaze drifted up to the black mantis on the hill behind the neighborhood. It appeared to be leaning forward as if ready to stride. Or fall.

His eyes dropped to the woman in the front window holding back the curtain. Black beret, black shirt and pants, her eyes like lights in this golden hour. He could see her more clearly now than in weeks. As if she were about to give him another literature lecture. This time, though, the look on her face was not didactic. It was pleading.

29
Trance

It sounded like a screen door slamming over and over. Jade tuned out the rumble of Reston Street to identify the sound. Barking. He wasn't aware until now that he'd been hearing it for a while. The repetitive yelp of a dog in a trance. The certainty of no end to its Sisyphean mantra. Professor Alice might say that, handing him another obscure tome by Camus or Sartre. He missed her lectures.

The dog was in the near distance, maybe under the mantis on the smoldering hill across the river. When he'd come home earlier, he'd opened all the windows in the house. A southerly breeze had been pushing against the culm dump smoke, sparing them the usual suffocating stench. Now in his bedroom, he knew everyone's windows were open as lives were revealed in spurts between the rumble of trucks on Reston. Neighbors he'd never met shouting their intimate frustrations at one another. A mother cursing her wailing child. A teenage boy spewing his wordless guts out. A man close by grunting with the whump of a tool—his fist?—against an unyielding wall. The sounds of anger, toxic fear, occasional joy, abandon. And behind it all, the incessant, metronomic barking.

He lay on his bed, staring at the ceiling, still in his work clothes, too exhausted to remove anything but his boots. He knew he should call Lucy—it was Friday night—but he didn't have the will. She'd take plan B—carousing with meatheads Rocco and Free. He felt her disappearing from him. His gut, his loins, his chest—all empty. Hollowed out.

When he came home earlier, he'd found Alice sitting on the couch in the hot, stuffy Grotto, black beret on the cushion next to her, bare feet on the coffee table covered in books. She looked woozy in her long-sleeved black shirt and black dungarees, her face flushed and distant. No sight or smell of a drink or a cigarette. When he opened the windows, she seemed to have come alive.

"That feels good, thank you," she'd said, smiling at him, an open book in her lap.

"I'll get you some water," he'd said. When he returned, she was opening the buttons on her shirt, revealing a black tee shirt. He'd asked her what had happened to her hair, and she'd smiled and shrugged. "Dull shears?"

They'd talked as if nothing out of the ordinary had been occurring. Jade had felt the weight of their respective inner lives lurking in the shadows of the statues—his behind one of the saints, hers in the penumbra of the looming Blessed Mother. The candles had remained unlit, and some of the saints had been turned around, facing the walls. She'd offered him a few of her books, explaining their importance to him. Titles by authors she'd recommended in past impromptu lectures— Dorothy Parker, Herbert Marcuse, Doris Lessing, Mary McCarthy, Samuel Beckett, and a few others he hadn't heard of. She offered him Parker's *Enough Rope* in her left hand or Lessing's *The Golden Notebook* in her right. She smirked at him, her eyes alight, but he declined. Then she held out a book, *The Wretched of the Earth*, and said to him, her smirk now showing teeth, "Required reading for the coming fall of the American empire." He declined that one with a blank look. Then she had a little private chuckle with herself and handed him the book she said she'd been reading: *The Feminine Mystique*.

"As you'll discover from this one, your mother is more of a feminine *mistake*," she'd said, a gloating look on her face. "No housewife slave here. But failure to flower nonetheless." He declined that book, too, passing up the possible overture to a new lecture, going against his own wishes yet again. He thought of Lucy, wanting yet not wanting her.

"By the way, are you hungry?" Alice had said with a touch of sarcasm. "I'm not, but there must be something here to eat." She'd winked at him. He went up to bed. It was still light out.

The barking eventually drove Jade into his own trance. He focused on the repetitive sound, no longer hoping that each bark would be the last. He was losing his will altogether. He felt his body fading, limp from the week's work, slick with sweat, molded to the sheet, helpless. His arms and legs dead weight, vestigial extensions of his waning core.

Uncontrolled thought fragments floated between barks, a rhythmic slideshow of images, flickering one to the next, in cadence with the chronic cries of the beast out there in the heart of almost darkness. Squirrel at the wheel of his Corvair, but his head turned completely around, peering at something behind him, his buck teeth protruding, his skin looking much older. Then Lucy, looking much older too, but dressed in a private school uniform, her plaid pleated skirt too short, knee socks pushed to her ankles, her blouse askew. Next, she handed her torn sock to Wilson wearing a terry cloth white robe. Another bark. The figure of a man he did not at first recognize, but felt he knew. Business suit, red necktie, thick hand holding aloft Alice's red silk robe while laughing at Jade.

Still half-conscious, he understood somehow that Squirrel would never look like this, would not live to see his old age. And the other visions—Lucy, Wilson, Hafferty in the dark suit, and others clicking through his barking slide show—he understood that these were visitations to the underside of his mind, a mirror held up to his fears. Is this what Alice sees? Dreams that slip through the veil of reality? Visions that enter of their own accord and convert her emotions into electrical surges? Is this the beginning of her gift, her curse passing to him? Is Alice dying?

Early the next morning, he stood in the kitchen staring at the wall phone, head in a fog. No barking. Daylight and sulfuric haze poured through the open windows. Alice was gone from The Grotto. He fumbled with the receiver and heard it fall to the floor. As he reached for it, he heard a familiar voice.

"Are you there? Jade? Alice?"

"It's me," he managed feebly, the receiver against his cheek. "What time is it?"

"Seven," Wally told him.

"What day? Am I late for work?"

"What is the matter with you, son? It's Saturday morning. And you do not work here."

Jade started to hang up when he heard Wally's voice again. He was telling him Tamara would be moving into the apartment above the Mormons on Sunday and that he needed Jade to help her with the move. Wally said Tamara would get one or two more guys, but she wanted Jade there, too. "We're meeting there tomorrow at seven. In the morning. Top floor. Many steps. It will be a hot day, early start."

Tamara. Jade was fading again, and, for a moment, he saw Tamara in Lucy's schoolgirl uniform, and then he shook it off. His arm was leaden, his head in a deep fog. But he heard himself say, "Sure. I'll be there." And then he let the receiver fall to the floor.

Tamara.

30
To The Rez

Saturday June 28, 1969

Lucy was staring at late morning cartoons on the old Zenith when Jade pushed through the screen door. A Parliament burned in a cracked tea saucer on the coffee table. Her eyes were glazed over, and Jade knew she wasn't really watching the tube, the sound barely audible.

"I thought you quit," he said as he sat next to her on the worn loveseat.

Lucy shrugged and picked up the cigarette, took a deep drag, and exhaled a plume that tumbled around the TV. She shook her head slowly, her long smooth mane waving back and forth, her eyes somewhere beyond the screen.

"Where's your mother?"

"Where do you think?" she said, her voice flat.

On the TV, Daffy Duck had just been smashed by Bugs Bunny's giant hammer and lay flattened on the pavement in the middle of a road. Lucy took another drag on her cigarette, punched it out in the ashtray, blew another thick cloud, and stood up. She was wearing her Baby Doll pajamas, and Jade could see her pink bikini underpants through the sheer "shorty" bottom. It was an outfit that had never failed to make him tremble.

Lucy ran her index fingers under the bottom, tugging the elastic of her underpants and letting it snap over the edges of her buttocks. She leaned forward and pushed the button on the TV. The screen whistled dark, leaving a white pinhole at the center.

"Where were you last night?" she asked, turning around to look at him for the first time.

He told her he'd passed out after work and had slept until morning. In his work clothes. She put her hands on her hips, her feet apart. He could see her nipples and the curve of her breasts through the sheer top, and he felt the coil unraveling inside him. The stirring so familiar, like a magnet drawn helplessly to its polar opposite. Despite the fog enveloping his brain, the thought occurred to him that this was all mechanics, that his body and her body were never connected by fate, but by mere instincts. That all he had conjured for himself about his love for her was a fantasy, and that his body might have always been acting on its own.

She told him she'd gone drinking with Rocco and Free, that they'd had a blast, that he'd missed another good time. He told her a friend from work named Squirrel was picking him up in a half-hour and asked her to come with them to the Rez. She declined. She asked if Squirrel was a rodent or a person. He looked into her eyes and saw nothing. She asked him if Wilson would be joining them. He said no. He told her he would scope out the Rez for swimming, if she'd be interested next time.

It went on like that for a few more minutes. A monotone exchange. Her standing there staring at him with empty eyes, him sitting in front of her, matching her glare, his body betraying him, still wanting to touch her. His mouth felt dry, his heart speeding up. He knew she was slipping away, and he let it happen. His mind was numbed by it.

"We'll see," she said. "Right now, I'm getting a shower."

At the bottom of the steps to the second floor, she turned around to face him, and in a sweeping motion she lifted her pajama top over her head. Her bare breasts bounced once, and her black hair tumbled over them. She pulled her pajama bottom down to her knees and let it fall to the floor. She flicked it up in the air with her foot, caught it in one hand and stood there in her pink bikini underpants with her hands on her hips and her feet apart, her mouth in a pout, her eyes watching his.

"Be careful at that reservoir. Hope you two don't get snared in a rodent trap."

She turned and sashayed up the stairs, her Baby Doll bottom draped over her shoulder. Jade watched her pink backside until it disappeared. Then he got up, went to the foot of the stairs, picked up the Baby Doll top, tossed it onto the loveseat, and walked out the front door to wait for Squirrel. He stood under a tree, hand in his pocket pushing down on his erection. He ran through a list of sad thoughts to make it subside. It took a while.

As he lowered himself into the Corvair shotgun seat, Jade saw that Squirrel's ebullient spirit was absent. A new Squirrel was at the wheel, serious and foreboding, knots in his narrow forehead, his mouth in a curl. He didn't ask why Lucy wasn't joining them.

En route to the Rez, they drove through the Dickson campus, and Squirrel talked in the flat tones of a news reporter, pointing out the grassy knoll in front of the Student Union where the recent face-off between their Macson co-workers and the students had taken place. He talked in his same breathless patter, but there was no comedic cadence in his voice, only apprehension. He filled in Jade on details of the conflict and who, besides Cheese and his sidekicks, to watch out for at the factory. He told Jade that everyone at Macson owned weapons, and that some of them had declared they'd open fire on the students if they marched in front of the bomb factory gates. He rattled off a laundry list of coworkers' names, codifying them according to their roles in the Macson tribe—"soldier," "snitch," "sadist," "thief," "powder keg," "gofer," "girl-hater," "commander wannabe"—saving the most treacherous names for last— the leaders. Jade didn't recognize any of these surnames until Squirrel came to "Belden."

"The fat drone who sits up there on his pedestal in my building?!" he asked. "The guy with the Mona Lisa smile?"

"Yep. Ren Belden. That's our shop steward. Another Korean vet, mad as hell at the world, considers everyone who doesn't think or look like him a threat and a mortal enemy. He knows every move in the plant," Squirrel said. "He watches all from his perch, and, on break, he gathers information." Squirrel slowed down and turned to Jade. "And Mona Lisa ain't smilin', Jade. Check out his eyes next time. He'd cut old Mona's throat just for looking at him funny."

"How do you know all this stuff?" Jade said. "You've only been there a year."

"A year's a long time in a Hell hole like that," he said.

The two-lane road to the Rez wound through a forest misted with purple buds and hints of new green, the summer still spring at this higher elevation. Jade felt the coolness of the woods wash over him and took deep gulps of what seemed like impossibly fresh air.

As if energized by this gift of nature, a switch flipped in Squirrel, and his mood lifted; he was now the jaunty animated character Jade had met in the Macson parking lot. As he set into a satirical soliloquy that promised to be endless, Jade gazed into the trees whipping by, thousands of pickets in a deep three-dimensional fence, the sharp afternoon light popping through in a mesmerizing staccato, as if the sun were song. The Corvair barely broke thirty miles per hour on the steep grade, and every few minutes, a car rode up to their rear bumper, horn blaring, and then roared around them. The mountainside was new territory for Jade, so high up, a world away from the soot-choked valley. He could breathe.

Squirrel shoved a Jefferson Airplane tape into the eight-track and raised his voice to a shout over the music and the strained racket of the engine. In a hyper monologue, he pinballed from subject to subject, entertaining Jade with an imitation of John Lennon during his recent "Bed-In" with Yoko Ono, and then an imaginary news reporter declaring that Lennon was a doomed voice for peace in a world insatiable for blood and death. He imitated fast-talking Abbie Hoffman on the plan by six hundred hippies to elevate the Pentagon, and then he aped a soulful Romeo in Zeffirelli's film, pining for Juliet. "Did my heart love till now?" Squirrel mimicked, with one hand on his chest. "Forswear it sight, for ne'er saw true beauty till this night."

He went on to praise Satan's performance in *Rosemary's Baby* and shouted that the ghouls in *Night of the Living Dead* reminded him of his Macson coworkers. He waxed on about Hal taking over our lives in *2001: A Space Odyssey*. "What do you think we have Social Security cards for, Jade? They got your number, boy! They're watching you." Then he rambled on incoherently about the sex scenes in *Midnight Cowboy*, then switching to television and a rant about fucking his favorite TV goddesses, Elizabeth Montgomery, Mary Tyler Moore, Marlo Thomas, and Goldie Hawn, then back to movies for a rendition on taking Dustin Hoffman's place to have sex with Katharine Ross and then, "the ultimate switch: me taking Richard Benjamin's place, that dud, and getting to hump Ali McGraw!"

His spiel finally ended with a squealing laugh as he pulled off the road into a clearing with a view of the valley. He killed the engine. Squirrel's shouting and the blare of the music and rumble of the car were replaced by a silence so sudden it left a vacuum of ringing in Jade's ears. The view below and beyond them was surreal, the vast valley a colorless haze of shapes under a swarming sepia cloud, while above the valley, on the far side, the gentle rise and fall of a soft livid mountain range under an endless clear blue heaven. The mountains looked like a line of humpback whales heading south into the brilliance of another dimension. Jade realized by the smell and taste of the air that he and Squirrel were sitting in a clearing that mirrored the first of those endless mountains on the other side. Squirrel pointed above them, and there it was, as he'd promised, the orange edge of a daylight moon, its dark side visible against the bright crescent, awaiting the arrival of the Apollo 11 aliens from Earth. It was the clearest view of the orb Jade had seen since he was a kid in farmland New Jersey. He felt his breath taken away, a sensation he'd only read about in one of Alice's novels.

Below them, the valley was a dark chasm at the bottom of the vast cerulean dome, a swirling sewer of stagnant air, a choked pit. Jade could barely see through the haze, but Squirrel helped him get his bearings— the Macson smokestacks behind vague shadows of downtown buildings, and then to the east the steady rising black clouds from the burning culm dumps near Jade's little borough, Mell Hollow. Squirrel pointed to the gap in the dark landscape and told Jade to follow that crevice from Mell Hollow into Ebonton.

"That's The Filthy, the black snake of Ebonton," he said, whispering as if they were in a church. "Long ago, before the European invaders, it was probably a trout stream." Then he pointed east again. "See that gash in the mountain beyond the burning hill, next to the highway? They're taking the top off that hill for the valley's first mall. It's what they call progress. Looks like a landing strip now but in a year or so it'll be a big parking lot and bunch of boxy buildings that will drain what's left of the cozy life of downtown Ebonton. You'll need a car to get there, no more trolleys. But I doubt they'll allow my Nader-mobile in the new parking lot."

Just below the mall site, Jade could see the old coal breaker hovering above his neighborhood. From this distance, the praying mantis looked like a flimsy pile of charred twigs, its ominous presence now diminished to a mere whisper, a dying insect in its proper perspective. Jade wondered what his alien alter-ego would think of the great black beast now.

Squirrel made a crack about Ebonton's pathetic skyline and then asked Jade if he'd ever been to New York City. "That's the skyline you wanna see."

Jade said that when he lived in New Jersey, his mom had once taken him to New York to see a Broadway show. She had a thing about doing stuff just once. He'd never been back since then.

"Anytime you want to go, let me know," Squirrel said. "A New York train leaves Ebonton Station every Saturday morning and comes back at night. The scene in the Village is a circus. Freaks everywhere, hippies, bikers, girls with no bras, boys holding hands, girls making out with each other, music on the streets, even better music in the bars. And if you want to see a Broadway show your mom would *not* take you to, check out *O Calcutta.* Everybody's naked. It's amazing. *Hair!* Same thing. And just about every movie house in the Village has a film with naked people. New York is all nude, all the time!

"The city is too crowded and noisy for me," he said with a shrug, "but it's a human sideshow you should not miss. If you ever want to see how the world lives outside this time-stuck valley, just give me the nod."

"Saturday?" Jade said as his eyes drifted up toward the rolling mountains and clean sky and then up again to the curved orange sentinel. "I never had a Saturday off. Always worked at the diner."

"You can't live for work, man," Squirrel said, as he cranked the Corvair's stuttering starter. "You have Saturday's off now. Think about it. If you've never seen a braless girl walk down the street, you're living a sad life."

At the top of the mountain, Squirrel turned the Corvair onto a narrow path through the trees. Jade braced himself for impact, but the rattling little bucket of bolts bounced and thrashed through ruts and over rocks and roots and then lurched to a stop at a clearing at the edge of a lake. Squirrel killed the engine, and the music died. He fixed his eyes on a small flock of geese at the far end of the lake.

"My friends have returned," he said in a church whisper. "It's mating season."

He led Jade to the edge of the reservoir and then, still whispering, he began a lecture on the origins of the glacial reservoir and what seemed to Jade to be every living species in the water and surrounding woods— peepers, bats, tadpoles, bobcats, box turtles, beavers, ospreys, brown bears, copperheads. This place was a shrine for Squirrel, a resting place for his manic, peripatetic mind. He prompted Jade to listen in silence, as if Jade had a choice. Squirrel identified bird calls that for Jade had been just part of the wash of background chatter, woods noise. Squirrel named the familiar birds, but then he held up his hands and cocked his head.

"Listen!" He named the calls of an Oriel, a Purple Finch, a Cedar Waxwing, and the hammering of a Pileated Woodpecker. He whispered these names as if they were spirits. "These creatures deserve our deepest reverence," he whispered. They sat for a while listening to nature's music as Squirrel pointed and cocked his head at Jade, his eyeballs popping with each whistle and trill.

Squirrel's usual spontaneous outbursts had transformed into meditative dissertation. He was now a soft-spoken sage, a wizard beyond his years. He told Jade that his father had taken him to this spot many times when he was a child. They would camp out for days, and his father would test him on the sounds and sights of the lake and the woods. They weren't hunters or trappers, he said. For their visits to The Rez, they were simply part of the land and the water and the sky. Just another animal species.

He said his father had worked on the railroad that passed through the ridge at the foot of the mountain, not far from their home. He told Jade that the last and greatest thing his father did for him was to save his life a year earlier. Right after high school, Squirrel was about to sign up for the Marines when his dad was diagnosed with cancer and given less than a month to live. On his deathbed, the Korean War Marine vet had told his son to stay out of Vietnam at any cost. It had seemed not just an improbable but an impossible request for him to make. He was shaken to the core by his own words; but he was adamant. He'd told Squirrel that it was all wrong, that we don't belong there, that it was just another Korea, a war of politics that cannot be won. He begged Squirrel not to leave his mother alone. When Squirrel's father died, Squirrel learned about the deferment for sole surviving sons of war vets. He got a job at the munitions plant. "I'm not afraid of a fight," Squirrel said somberly, "and I was ready to take it to the jungle. But if it weren't for my dad, I'd be a piece of rotted meat by now with a bullet in my back and flies eating my skin. And for what? Nixon's ready to call it off. Millions dead for nothing."

The rustle of a black snake at the water's edge startled Jade to his feet. Squirrel told him Northern Watersnakes were harmless.

"Only a couple hundred in this lake," he said with a smile and pulled off his clothes and jumped in. When Jade followed his cue and dove into the water, he surfaced howling and swam back to the shore. "Holy shit! It's barely melted ice!"

As he checked the shallows for snakes, he heard the echo of Squirrel yodeling. He turned and watched in awe as the madman of the mountain backstroked toward the goose family, singing "When the Swallows Go Back to Capistrano," as if he were in a warm bath at a spa.

At the water's edge, they had a rock skipping contest. Jade was winning, so Squirrel tossed a small boulder into the water, declaring the game a bomb. He sat down in the grass and, without warning, started another monologue.

"Roland acts tough, you know, but he's a softie inside," Squirrel said. "He and I go back to sophomore year at Ebonton. He was the star, and I got to hold his sweaty towel. I was team manager for all the sports—baseball, basketball and football. And Roland was the best at every one of them, best in the valley, best in the state. The guys on the teams didn't like him. Said he was arrogant, a snob. Can you imagine? Just because he can speak English ten times better than they can, makes it sound like music. He's got that British flair, his dad's Bahamas accent. Hell, if he was a White guy from the Bahamas, his teammates would probably worship him. But the girls...Christ, they threw themselves at him. But he never took the bait. His father warned him about messing with White girls in this valley. No matter how much they come on to you, he told Roland, he would have to resist. Otherwise, he'd be dead before he got out of high school. So, he played it safe, dark girls only, even though there weren't too many to choose from. But the rumors persisted, and the guys on the teams were convinced he was banging White girls. So, while he had plenty of action, he had no friends, no steady girlfriend, and neither did I." Squirrel leaned his face toward Jade and smirked. "I offered to take his rejections off his hands many times, but somehow the dark girls weren't interested in this squirrely White boy. Can't imagine why, with this beautiful mug and manly physique." He grinned. His teeth were little white nuggets.

"We became friends by default, I guess. He was the only guy on any of the teams who thanked me for giving him water and a dry towel on the sidelines. The guy's a class act, but he keeps to himself mostly. Can't really blame him—Black guy in a completely White valley. I'm kind of the only one he can talk to. His dad's a prick, and he never knew his mom. His dad told him she died right after he was born. But he won't even tell Roland where she's buried or even what her name was. Hell, I think that's his main beef. I'm lucky I had a mom and a dad, but if I had to choose, I think I'd pick a mom. Roland really seems lost without one, and feels even worse not knowing who she was. He was really kind to my mom after my dad died. He still calls her once in a while. Now, he talks a lot these days about his dad's girlfriend. Finally has an older female in his life he can talk to. Not sure where he's going with that one, though. His eyes glaze over when he talks about her. Tamara says this, Tamara says that. Blah blah blah. I can't decide if she's his mom's replacement or someone he's falling for. She's older than us, but she's pretty young. And by Roland's account—which sounds like a song when he talks about her—she's beautiful. Teaches at Dickson, like Roland's dad."

Jade stood up and moved away from Squirrel, but the soliloquy continued. Jade listened from a distance.

"I started at Macson last summer after graduation, and Roland went on to Penn State. I felt like my big brother had abandoned me. But I flipped when I saw him last month in the Macson courtyard. We were high-fivin' and laughin' and hootin' it up. I could feel the goons staring at us, measuring us up. The factory boys have a thing about Black guys and a thing about anybody who hangs out with them, anybody who isn't what they are—ex-grunt rednecks. And you, my friend, they think you're a hippie with that crazy hair and those weird wide eyes, like everything is new to you, when it's the same-old same-old to them. And now that you're connected to Roland and me—well, get ready, man."

"If they think I'm a hippie, where does that put me with Commissioner Hafferty?" Jade asked, a bit startled by the sound of his own voice.

"Hafferty knows what they think, but he doesn't think like they think," Squirrel said. "And as for you, Hell, he doesn't even know who you are."

Jade looked toward the geese, a rush of heat on his neck and face. "He'll know soon enough if I keep hanging around with you and Roland."

"You'll be OK, man," Squirrel said.

"What about Hafferty and Wilson?" Jade asked. "What's the connection there?"

"Hafferty's like a godfather to Roland. He's a close friend of Roland's dad, James Wilson. *Doctor* Wilson, as he likes to be called. He's a biology professor at Dickson. Only colored professor there. Until Tamara got there, that is. Something about Hafferty getting Doc Wilson into medical school—that's how I think they're connected. Not sure why. But Hafferty's been around since Roland was a little kid."

"What's the deal with Hafferty and this union-busting thing that Cheese was talking about? Is Roland really part of that?"

Squirrel chuckled and shook his head. "Nah. Roland's tight with Hafferty, but he's not in on any union busting. I don't think Hafferty's up to that anyway. It's all a game to him. He greases our illustrious Congressman Walsh to get us Washington funding every year for Macson and for all the government jobs that are keeping people alive around here, and I figure he somehow lines his pockets with a piece of the millions from those deals. Kickbacks. You know the drill. It's a way of life in the valley."

"Yeah, I listened to the guys at Wally's talk about that crap for six years," Jade added. "Everybody's paying off somebody for a job or a favor. I just didn't think it would be the same at Macson."

"It's the same everywhere around Ebonton, my man. America's Great Depression started early here—in 1928—and it never left. We're stuck in a burning shithole of a polluted valley run by crooks and con men, the scavengers left behind by the great coal and railroad gods—those hallowed leaders who built this nightmare and then bolted just before it collapsed into rust and dust. And I'm sorry to burst your bubble about Macson, but that place is the black heart of this corrupt valley."

"How so?"

"It's the centerpiece of a partnership that rules over everybody. Jensen runs the joint, but we call him General Patton because he's a joke. The reality is that Papa G owns Macson, and our noble County Commissioner Hafferty runs the people who work there, as well as all the political hacks connected to it. He shows up at Macson twice a month or so and disappears into Patton's office for about an hour. I've seen Belden, the union steward, get called in when Hafferty's there, and a few other guys get called in from time to time, including Roland. But Hafferty's just trying to keep everyone off kilter. He's a backslapper, a big phony. He does you a favor and gets you to snitch on another guy. Then he does the other guy a favor and gets him to snitch on *you*. Nobody likes him, but somehow, he seems to get everyone to act as if they love him. He runs people—gets them jobs all over the valley, and his partner, Papa G, owns most of the abandoned rail and coal land and anything big related to construction and demolition. These two guys have their hands in every business in this county, but the jackpot is coming out of Washington these days. Walsh, their boy in Congress, is their main conduit. And Walsh is a Nixon suckup and a big war supporter, so that's what Hafferty's pushing. Always ginning up the locals about fighting for freedom against the Commies and all that horseshit. But it's all about the money and the power that comes from having it all. He's been County Commissioner forever, and he's been the asshole pal of Giallo for even longer than forever. They run it all."

"What about the union guys?"

"Hafferty and Giallo have their sway over the unions, too, because they supply the jobs. But Hafferty using Roland to bust the Macson union? Not a chance. Yeah, he got Roland into the union without Roland putting in the mandatory probation time, but that just proves he's got power over the union heads. So why would he want to bust them up? He controls management *and* the union. Plus, he needs the union guys to keep the local hippies and war protesters down. All those grunts need is a little provocation, and they're out there on the campus with their rifles locked and loaded and their teeth bared. Hafferty and Giallo need to keep those guys fired up. And I wouldn't be surprised if Hafferty and Papa G weren't in cahoots with the president of the college, keeping the students from turning Dickson into another Columbia or Harvard or Cornell shitstorm. Last thing Hafferty and Giallo want is an anti-war revolt in their secluded little fiefdom."

"Who's this Giallo you keep talking about?" Jade asked.

Squirrel's eyes bugged out and he smiled. "You for real? You been livin' here how long?

"Moved here when I was twelve, in '63. Why?"

"Jesus Christ, man. Are ya still twelve?! You never heard of Papa G?"

"Heard the name, but it never clicked. No reason to."

"Unbelievable," Squirrel said, shaking his head at Jade. "You live a sheltered life, my friend. Never been to New York, never got a Saturday off, never heard of Papa G. You ever hear of a band called The Beatles? What do you do with your life, man?"

Jade laughed. "I don't know. School work, diner work, I take care of my house, my mom. I read a lot. Listen to music sometimes. Movies. I have a girlfriend. At least for now."

"Sounds like a good life. But there's a big world out there, my man. And it will eat you up if you're not tuned in. And I'm not talkin' about tune in, turn on, and drop out. I'm talkin' about knowing what's going on around you. Let me give you a crash course on this valley where you've lived for the last six years. In your own little world. This rez, this crater lake here, this Shangri La of my dreams, this is one of the only sweet spots around the valley untouched by the filthy fingers of Papa G. He's Salvatore Giallo, known to his family as "Sallie G," which is pretty funny, because it's a girl's name. But then you meet him, and you're not laughin.' The guy's a mountain of meanness. That's why people outside his family call him "Papa G." If a guy's not family, and he calls him "Sallie G" behind his back, that guy is as good as dead. And Papa G, he owns everything. Owns every piece of acreage in the twenty-mile valley that was abandoned in the 30s and 40s by the railroads and the big coal companies, once they were broken up by the courts. Then, the mines started failing. It was a slow death, and everybody suffered, except the mine owners, of course. And the Giallo brothers. It's a long story, and I don't want to ruin our lovely moment here in Shangri La, Jade. But pay attention, man. You hear the name Papa G, or Sallie G, in a conversation, pay very close attention."

Jade sifted in the shoreline for another rock to skip. "So, what about Hafferty? He works for Papa G?"

"Not really," Squirrel said, knocking the rock out of Jade's hand and smiling. "They're longtime partners, sort of. G runs the business end, and Hafferty runs the people end. You don't see Papa G unless *he* wants to see *you*. Keeps a very low profile. Hafferty, on the other hand, wants to see everybody all the time. He wants to be inside your brain all day, every day. He loves to move people around like he's a chess master."

Jade flung a rock out onto the water and watched it skip three times before sinking. Squirrel kicked the soil and turned toward the car, letting out a shout that echoed across the water. He broke into a little dance, an awkward jig, his feet kicking out, his arms flailing. "Hey, man, don't worry, we'll get those motherfuckers! We're the fuckin' *Mod Squad!* You, me, and Wilson. We're the good guys. Roland's Link, you're Pete, and….and I'm Julie Barnes!" He broke into his high-pitched laugh, halted his jig, and threw his hands into the air, flapping his wrists. Then, he shoved one hand under his shirt and the other into the front of his pants. "Oh, Julie, oh Gawd, I love you! What a body!"

As they pulled out of the woods onto the main road, they heard a metallic squeal under the car and then a scraping sound.

"Fuckin' Julie Barnes, my evil twin, knocked off my tailpipe," Squirrel shouted over the engine's loud rumble. "Again!" He pulled the car onto the dirt shoulder, bounced out of the driver's seat, rummaged in the front trunk for tools and crawled under the car. Within a minute, he was standing next to Jade, brushing dirt off his clothes. "All fixed. Julie pulls on my pipe all the time, man." He laughed and twisted his face in a knot of rumpled Squirrel features, and they climbed back into the Corvair. Jade was still laughing as Squirrel started the car, but he stopped when he saw Squirrel staring into the rearview mirror. Jade heard the sound of a car on the gravel and turned to see a black Galaxy pulling in behind the Corvair. There were two men in the front seat.

"Let me do the talkin' here," Squirrel muttered under his breath as he killed the engine and pushed his shoulder against his door. Jade jumped out and joined him at the rear of the Corvair.

Another car passed by and then it was silent except for bird calls from the woods. For a moment, Jade had the idiotic notion that Squirrel might return the bird calls, but the look on Squirrel's face said otherwise. *Mod Squad* was over. The Galaxy engine shut off and the man behind the wheel took a drag on a cigarette, flicked it onto the road, and climbed out of the car. The second guy followed him.

"You girls havin' a little car trouble?" the first guy said with a crooked smile as he sauntered toward them and pulled at his crotch as if the little bump in his pants was too big to manage. His blonde hair was slicked back off a narrow forehead and his eyes were slits of suspicion, his lower jaw the bottom of a catcher's mitt. He was short, built like a bulldog, no neck, narrow hips, bowed legs, and huge shoulders stretching the seams of his work shirt. Jade saw mud caked on his boots, the pants above them wet to the knees. The second guy let out a pinched laugh and sauntered behind the bulldog. He was tall and gangly, his eyes dark shadows under a thick brow, his mouth a frowning thin line. He used the tip of his tongue to launch a stream of spit toward the boys.

"We got it, thanks, guys," Squirrel said, his voice steady and friendly. "Muffler came loose. It's tied up now."

The men stopped a few feet from Jade and Squirrel. The shorter guy reached into his pants pocket, pulled out a badge and held it next to his face, his crooked smile twisting down.

"Water's a little cold to be skinny dipping today, don't you think? Faggots? Musta been tricky tryin' to find each other's little dicks. All shriveled up like pussies."

The tall guy snorted and gave a tug on the side of his hip to reveal a holstered pistol.

"Reservoir's posted, you know," the shorter guy said. "We could haul your pansy asses in for trespassing. Not to mention public cock-sucking."

Squirrel cleared his throat and then tipped his head down to meet the man's eyes. "Been coming here for years with my dad, officer," he said, his tone even and calm, sincere as saccharine. Eddie Haskell, Jade thought. "No one's ever bothered us before, sir. My dad was a Marine, so if he thought it was trespassing, he would never have brought me here."

The short guy let out a fake laugh. "A Marine and a rule follower, huh? That's a first. I'll bet he'd be Marine proud to hear how sweet his son talks to an officer of the law. I wonder if he knows his boy's a dick sucker. Skinny dips with his boyfriend in the lake where daddy brings him."

Squirrel puffed up his chest as the man stepped closer to him. "With all due respect, officer, I don't think my dad would like to hear you say that about me. Especially since it's not true." Squirrel was six inches taller but the bulldog was twice as wide. He shoved his huge chin closer to Squirrel's neck.

"What's your name, rat face? I know I seen you around."

"Stephen Bozak, Junior, sir. I work at the Macson plant. I'm in the union there."

"That so, Junior? I'll check it out. If you're lyin' to me, Bozak, I'll find you. Meanwhile, stay away from the reservoir. That goes for your girlfriend here, too. It's private property. And tell your old man I said so. I don't give a shit if he's here in his fuckin' dress whites. It's off limits. I'm lettin' you little cunts go this time. But I'll be lookin' out for you two. And I won't be so generous next time. Now, get in that piece of junk and beat it. And don't come back here. Ever."

Jade was covered in sweat as they headed down the mountain, the Corvair rumbling like a truck. Squirrel was silent for the entire ride. When they stopped in front of Jade's house, Squirrel was still staring ahead, his jaw muscles working overtime.

"Who were those guys, Squirrel?"

Squirrel said nothing, just stared; but Jade wasn't going to get out without an answer. After a long silent standoff, Squirrel turned to him.

"Ebonton narcs. Undercover. Street guys call them Mutt 'n Jeff. Crooked as the day is long. We're lucky they didn't empty our wallets. Low-life scum bags. They have no right to bust anybody at The Rez or any other place outside the city. They were in old clothes, not their usual cheap suits and ties. They were dressed for cover of some kind. You notice their pants and boots were wet? They were up to something at the rez, and we probably surprised them when we went swimming."

"Narcs? At the rez? What's with that?"

Squirrel shook his head slowly and stared out the windshield. "Fuck. Them. We can go back there any time we want."

31

Bagman

In the cab, she was clear and focused. She felt calm despite the bumpy ride along Reston Street, the pavement still beat up from winter. She knew by now that it would be partly repaired by October, only to fall apart again by next spring. The patterns of decay in a valley on a circular descending cycle. She couldn't decide if this was *Purgatorio* or *Inferno*.

"Your name isn't Virgil, is it?" she asked the cab driver, smirking to herself.

He gave her a blank look in the rear-view mirror. A few minutes later, she got out and showed him a twenty-dollar bill. She ripped it through and gave him half. "Wait for me," she said.

As she opened the heavy wooden door at the top of the marble steps, she hesitated when she saw the tiny form at the desk in the center of the great vault of books. Helen Filbert. Perched in perfect posture at her Seat of All Knowledge, as she had privately nicknamed Helen's assumed position of royalty. It was a benign mockery of the prim, humorless, but kind little woman who had indulged in Alice the fantasy of an independent worldly woman—inflamed it, actually, in a vicarious and thrilling projection of an ambition the little woman would never allow herself to pursue.

"Hello, Helen," she said, with a wistful smile.

Helen Filbert looked up, distracted as always, and put on her required dimpled smile. "Yes, how may I—." Her mouth froze, her face fell.

"Sorry about the disappearance, Helen. I've had some distractions."

Helen stood up and used the tips of her unadorned fingers to guide her teetering body around to the front of the desk, finding her footing at last and standing as tall as her stubby heels would permit.

"I...I barely recognized you!" Helen said in an elevated departure from her always measured tone. She looked up and down as if at an apparition. "My God, you've transformed yourself!"

"Pretty magical, huh?" Alice touched her beret with her fingertips, giving it a jaunty tilt.

"Are you...are you an artist now?" Helen touched her lips with two fingers, her look wide-eyed, her smile inverted. "My goodness, no, you're a...you're a beatnik! That's it! All the black. The men's boots. And no makeup, for the love of God. And where's your hair? Good Lord, who *are* you, woman?"

Alice sputtered a burst of laughter and swept forward in a single movement, pulling Helen into her arms. The older woman felt like a small

180

wooden totem, her arms fastened to her sides, her head rigid against Alice's chest. She let her go, and Helen came alive with a brisk backward step.

"My, you're strong!" Helen said, stricken by the contact.

Alice smiled down at her. "Part of the beatnik thing, I suppose. Tough world out there, Helen."

Helen looked perplexed and said nothing.

"Well, as I was saying, I've been distracted over these last few—"

Helen held up her hand and closed her eyes, still settling herself from the bear hug. "No need. No need. You live your life, I live mine. No explanation required." She shuddered and then turned and walked toward her desk. "We appreciate all you've done here, my dear, and you are most welcome back anytime. Your things are still here. I have them locked in the desk up in the workroom. Others have used the desk, but no one can open the locked drawer, I assure you. Let me get the key."

"I'm so grateful, Helen. I really do appreciate your—"

"No, no," Helen said. "No need, no need." She held up the key, and then said in a low voice, "We single girls must stick together." Her dimples lit up, and she set the key on the desk. "Take what you need, dear, and leave whatever you want to, and I'll continue to store your work here if you like. Your memoir is safe with me, as always. The desk drawer is your spot, whenever you need it. Safe and sound. And locked up." She gave Alice a heavy-lidded slow wink.

Alice waited at the desk in the balcony workroom until two other guests left. In the drawer, she pushed aside the notebooks and the framed photos, and picked up the memoir in the black binder, opened it to the last page, then put it back. She reached deep into the drawer and pulled out a paper bag. She checked inside, shoved the bag in her hip pocket, and locked the drawer.

When Alice went to return the key, Helen was busy with guests, but she held up her stubby index finger, signaling Alice to wait. Saturday was the library's busiest day, as Alice knew. She recognized a few of the guests but was relieved they hadn't recognized her.

Helen finally pulled her aside into a nook in the stacks. "I assume you took what you needed," she whispered, glancing at the bulge in the pocket of Alice's black dungarees. "I'm not one to pry, as you know, but I think it's dangerous for you to have that."

"I appreciate your concern, Helen. And I'm relieved you're not one to pry." Helen flushed and lowered her eyes. "I should have kept this out of the library, I apologize for that. It was reckless of me. Thank you for keeping the desk locked."

"But why would you need that...that *thing*...now? Or ever?" She glanced sidelong at the bulge as if it were about to explode.

"All my life," Alice said in a low voice, "I've known that certain types of men need to be stopped. I lost the nerve to do so a long time ago. But now it's back. As you said, Helen, we single girls need to stick together." She handed Helen a bulky white envelope. "Thank you for taking care of my things."

As she pushed through the great wooden door, she turned to see Helen wiping her eye with a pink hanky, her chin quivering. Out front, the cab was still waiting.

In her kitchen, Alice pulled the silver .38 from the paper bag, loaded it, rolled the barrel, snapped it back into place, and let the weight of the pistol settle in her hand. She checked the clock over the back door and practiced her balance while swinging the gun from position to position, taking aim at the door, the clock, and the mirror over the sink, recalling the basics of her lessons from many years ago, her practice sessions with rifles and pistols on her father's range. In the mirror, she caught her reflection, and it stopped her, the barrel of the snub nose looking like a third eye on her face. She didn't recognize this person at all. That's good, she thought. The element of surprise. She pulled out a chair from the wobbly table and waited.

At four o'clock, as scheduled, there was a loud knock at the back door. She saw the shadow of a large man behind the checkered curtain, and she waited a beat. Then she stood up abruptly and opened the door.

"Well, look at you," the man said behind the screen door, unhidden mockery in his gravelly voice. "If I wasn't following you for months, I'd think I was at the wrong place. Haven't seen the new look up close, though. I think it suits you. Hair's a little fucked up, but the outfit, yes. Bad ass. Looks about right, now that you're on the other team." He chuckled at his own words. Alice did not.

"Just set the bag at the base of the door and move along, Stanley," she said. "You must have errands to run, now that your boss has flown away. Left you with lots of bags to deliver. Errand boy. Maybe a body bag or two to bury?"

"Aren't you gonna invite me in for a drink, Alice?" He smirked down his long nose at her. "Or don't you drink with men anymore? Just guys with cunts."

"You know the rules. No drinks, no chatter. Drop the bag at your feet and leave the property. Now."

Stanley pulled open the screen door and held out the brown bag. "Don't you want to count it?"

Alice stepped back and balanced her legs, her left hand on the gun sheltered beneath the counter. She fixed her eyes on his. "It's always wrong, Stanley. You slimeballs always take your cut, *and* some. That's the only thing I can count on. Now, leave the bag at your feet, step out of the doorway, and let the screen close. You don't want me to call your daddy, now, do you?"

"If you're referring to the Commissioner, bitch, he doesn't want to talk to you, ever again. Told me you already got a drop on Monday, and he said he won't be takin' your calls no more, either. *Ever.* Gave you a pile of cash to make you go away, and now you're gettin' another one? What'd he do, make you suck his cock to get another payday in the same week?"

"No room under his desk with you in the way, Errand Boy." She grinned up at him, then scowled. "One more time, Stanley: Drop the bag. And leave."

Stanley's nostrils flared, and his chest heaved. He squeezed the bag in his fist, the paper crunching as he held it just out of her reach. He wrenched his frown into a stricken smile, his gray eyes lighting up with fire.

"You got a new girlfriend in there with you now, Alice? Hey, I don't mind two chicks goin' at it, ya know. I enjoy watchin'. Are you the boy or the girl this time, Alice? Or do you switch hit? She wears the bat, then you wear it."

Alice raised the pistol and aimed it at his face. "You know what I would enjoy watching right now, dimwit? Your little brain scattering all over my backyard. It's a tiny yard, granted. But it's a tiny brain."

Stanley glanced at the gun and then locked his eyes on hers as he slowly raised his hands, the right hand still squeezing the bag. "Ooo. Alice. I thought that was a bulge in your pants, but I guess you're just happy to see me."

Alice cocked the hammer on the pistol. "You're so stupid, Stanley, you even screw up a good old joke. Now, drop the bag. Or I drop you."

She saw it in his eyes. She aimed the barrel at his ear and squeezed. He was already coming at her, his head down. His shoulder met her chest, and they fell onto the floor, the top of her head hitting the refrigerator as she landed. He had her pinned in a flash and was sitting up, spit flying from his mouth as he screamed at her face.

"You crazy fuckin' cunt! You ugly dyke! I'm gonna fuckin' kill you! You worthless whore."

He was sitting on her legs, his hands pinning her arms. He had her by a hundred pounds.

Alice was stunned, her head numb, her body smothered, her breath caught in her throat. She saw a line of blood running down Stanley's ear and realized her shot had grazed him. He was wild eyed above her. He let go of her arm to raise his fist just as she saw a black mass clonk him in the side of the head.

He tumbled sideways off her, his fist still cocked. He hit the floor with a heavy thud and lay lifeless, his bottom half on top of her, the top half sprawled next to her.

Jade was standing over Stanley with an iron frying pan held high above his head with both hands.

Alice found her breath at last and pushed out a scream that filled the house.

"Noooooo!"

32

Confession

Saturday, June 28, 1969

After the men had dragged a groggy Stanley out the back door, Jade drew a hot bubble bath for Alice, at her request. He carried her upstairs to her bed, but she sat up right away and said she was fine, that she'd feel better once she'd cleaned the foul scent of that man from her skin.

Jade had done this before—drawn a bubble bath for her. He'd even helped her bathe on more than one occasion during her worst binges. Cleaned the vomit from her bed, from her hair, scrubbed her skin raw, washed her soiled clothes by hand. It was embarrassing at first, but he'd gotten used to it, and so, it seemed, had she. The cover of the bubbles had helped to maintain a semblance of modesty, but she'd always needed assistance getting into the tub and sometimes out of it. These were the awkward illusory moments when Jade had begun to learn how to compartmentalize.

This time, she wasn't drunk, but dazed by Stanley's assault, and Jade helped her from her bed to the bathroom, an arm around her waist, her hand in his. When he pulled the bathroom door closed, she told him to leave it open. She steadied herself at the sink, took off her shirt, and looked into the mirror.

"That's going to be a nice bruise," she said and turned to show Jade the red mark where Stanley's shoulder had landed between her clavicle and the top of the black shirt she was holding over her breasts. "You can turn around now, just don't go away. I have to talk to you."

He heard her get out of the rest of her clothes and then sink into the bubbles with a satisfied sigh.

Jade looked down the stairs and rested his hand on his pocket where he'd shoved Alice's pistol after he pulled Stanley's legs off her. Laying on the kitchen floor stunned, she'd stared at the ceiling and had pleaded with him over and over not to hit him again. Jade had made sure Stanley was alive but still unconscious and then carried Alice to the couch in The Grotto. She muttered something about Stanley's gun. Left side, she'd said.

Holster. Jade struggled to turn Stanley but found his .38 and held it up for Alice to see. She'd told him how to empty the chamber and to put the gun back in the holster. Then he grabbed the phone and dialed a number. From the couch, Alice had protested softly, too shaken to raise her voice again. Within fifteen minutes, two men had arrived and, without looking at either Jade or Alice, they lifted Stanley to his feet, slapped his face to no avail, and struggled to haul the big man out the back door. The side of his face and neck had been covered in blood.

"I have to clean up the mess in the kitchen," Jade called out to her, but she begged him to leave the bathroom door open and listen to her.

"I'll clean that later," she said from the bath, her voice clearer now. "You saved my life, my son. It's the least I can do for you."

Jade stood in the open doorway and watched the mirror over the sink fog up with bathwater steam. "What was Stanley Selczyk doing here, Alice?" he asked, his voice cold and flat. He stepped closer to the tub and looked at her, the face floating in the bubbles as if that was all she was, big eyes and a bodiless face with a halo of sudsy hair. "And don't tell me you don't know him."

She frowned and turned away from him, slumping further into the bubbles, her knees and thighs popping out of the foamy mirage, her hair underwater. Her legs seemed far away, like the towers of a distant bridge poking through fog, her face an island suspended in the froth. He watched her eyes meet his and her mouth move. "He's a small-time swindler who owed me money, and he came here to deliver. But he wanted something else I wasn't willing to give him." She sat up again, breaking the dreamy spell as her knees disappeared. She stretched her face closer to him, bubbles popping on her chin and neck and the tops of her breasts. "How do *you* know him, Shay?"

Jade turned his head, his gaze falling on the foggy mirror. "He's Commissioner Hafferty's driver, his bodyguard. I think you know that, Alice."

There was a pause as she sank back into the bubbles, then responded in a girlish voice, sweet and naive. "Are you pals now, Shay, with the great Commissioner? Was that his secretary on the phone? Louise?"

Jade sighed and turned to leave. "Get cleaned up, Alice. I'll take care of the kitchen. You need rest."

"No!" she called out, but he'd already started down the steps to mop up the blood and pick up the cash scattered on the floor, the cash that Hafferty's men had stepped over like it was broken glass as they hauled the unconscious Stanley through the kitchen and into the fading dusk.

Later, in The Grotto, Alice lit two candles and stood before the Blessed Virgin, closing her eyes and murmuring a prayer, her head bowed and her hands folded in a collapsed tent. Jade watched her in silence as she draped a small blanket over the head of the Virgin and turned the saints around so the backs of the statues faced him on the couch.

"I'm uncomfortable with what I want to say to you," she said, avoiding Jade's eyes. "I can't have them staring at us." She gathered the loose material of her red silk robe, tightened it with the cincture, and sat next to him on the couch. She lay her head on his shoulder and sighed. He was ready to push her away if she asked him for a drink.

"What did you do with the money and the gun, honey?"

"Money's in the cupboard over the kitchen sink, next to your Four Roses. The gun is in my pocket."

She chuckled and lifted her head, turning to him. "Very clever spot for the money, Shay. Did you count it?"

"No. But some of it has blood on it. I guess we'd have to call that blood money if this were one of your favorite Highsmith novels. But this is real, Alice. And so is Stanley. He's injured, but he's not going to die. I don't know how I feel about that. I suppose I should be glad that I didn't kill him, but, in a way, I wish I did. He was on top of you, and he was going to murder you, I knew it. And now, he'll want to kill us both. I wish this really were one of your books, and we could just put it down and walk away."

Jade set his elbows on his knees and lowered his face into his hands. Alice ran her fingers through his hair, gently tousling it. "Honey, it's going to be ok. That man will never bother us again, I promise you. The Commissioner knows what you told Louise about what happened here. Stanley will disappear. That's the way Hafferty operates, as you may have noticed."

Jade pulled away from her on the couch. "No, I haven't noticed that, Alice. And how exactly will he operate when he hears Stanley's side of the story? That you fired a gun at him! How is he going to hear your side of the story? From you? I know you've been to his office. He told me so. How do you know him, Alice? Were you close with him, once, a long time ago? Before I was born?"

"Close? Ha!" She stood up suddenly and headed for the kitchen. "Don't worry," she called back to him, "I'm not going for a bottle. I just need water. Do you want some?"

She told him she knew Hafferty when she was younger but had lost touch with him. She said that years later, when they'd lived in New Jersey, she'd heard he'd become a power politician in this part of Pennsylvania— a man who ran things, had influence, controlled jobs in a place with a shortage of them. When things weren't working out in New Jersey, she said, she contacted him, and he offered her a job and a place to live. She said the place was this one, but the job didn't come through, so she found her own way after that.

Jade had too many questions and didn't know where to start. Alice and Hafferty had given him conflicting versions of her arrival with him in the Black Diamond Valley six years ago, but Jade knew that if he started challenging Alice on minor points, he'd never get to ask the one question he most needed an answer to. They were sitting side by side on the couch now, water glasses on the coffee table, their bodies leaning forward, eyes on the floor, hands folded in front of them as if they were at a wake. He broke the silence by asking about her gun. Before she could answer, he said he knew the blood money in the kitchen wasn't Stanley's debt repayment, that it was yet another in a long string of cash payments she'd received over the years. He told her he'd met with Hafferty more than once, and that he knew that Stanley did Hafferty's dirty work. Jade said he was "in good" with Hafferty now, that the Commissioner was the real boss of the Macson factory. He said he'd promised to help Hafferty at the Macson plant in exchange for getting him into a college. Wherever he wanted to go. As far away as possible. He said what he wanted most now was for Alice to give him a straight answer, for once in her life.

"Is Dennis Hafferty my father?"

33
Servants' Quarters

Sunday, June 29, 1969

When Jade arrived at Wally's home, Wally and Tamara were standing at the curb next to a small U-Haul van watching the Mormon family from the second floor apartment parade down the front porch steps in their pastel Sunday best. Father in his tan suit and fuchsia tie, mother in her primrose and lavender dress and modest cream heels, two pre-teen girls in plain white blouses and long flouncy pink and yellow skirts, and a sturdy young boy in a soft blue dress shirt, white suspenders, creased short pants, pale knee socks, and shiny white shoes. The father had light brown hair, the mother and children were blonde. Their skin was the color of pastry flour.

No one was willing to make eye contact until it almost seemed too late. Wally, Tamara, and Jade watched in silence as the family marched with heads down to their white Falcon station wagon parked in front of the U-Haul. The father opened the back door for his kids and then the front passenger door for his wife. All slid soundlessly into the interior; but just before she ducked her head, the wife looked up and met Jade's eyes. Her mouth turned up at one corner, and she nodded. After her husband closed his wife's door with gentle firmness, he strode to his side of the car and said cheerfully to the threesome at the curb, "Take care now," as if they'd just spent the weekend together with this scrubbed and tidy family.

When the little station wagon disappeared around the corner, Tamara looked wide-eyed at Wally and Jade and said with a shrug, "There goes the neighborhood."

Tamara's laugh was deep and rich, and she closed her eyes to enjoy the feeling, her shoulders jouncing, her teeth peeking through her compressed grin. Wally studied his shuffling feet while Jade forced a weak laugh. It was all he could muster after his sleepless night. The heart-to-heart with Alice had devolved into a shouting match. At first, she'd seemed stunned by his question about Hafferty, but it had taken only moments for her to laugh at the idea and then to divert the conversation, claiming exhaustion and pain from her kitchen battle with Stanley. "I've had enough drama for one day," she'd said. When he'd pushed for a plan to thwart Stanley's inevitable retaliation, she turned the tables on him by flicking a switch in her bifurcated brain and suddenly shouting at him. "Why don't you figure it out, Jade?! Why don't you just fix it with your new pal, The Commissioner?" After she'd gone to bed, Jade had hidden the pistol and the bottle of Four Roses but had left the money in the kitchen cupboard. He'd spent the rest of the night worrying about Stanley. As early morning approached, he started to drift off on the couch and, in a half-dream state, he saw what he'd witnessed after the Mustang accident. He stood up next to the couch sweating, the memory vivid. He had one day to figure out whether he'd tell Jensen everything he'd witnessed, or just part of it. As he stood trembling, his six-a.m. alarm jangled like a school bell upstairs in his bedroom. He changed his clothes, then checked on Alice. She was in a deep sleep, her forehead quite warm but not feverish. He looked out her open bedroom window onto Reston Street, silenced by Sunday morning. He opened her other window and felt a soft cross breeze, surprising him with its freshness. He stood in the kitchen in a trance, making a peanut butter and jelly sandwich for his bus ride. He closed and locked all the first-floor windows and rummaged for house keys they'd never used, and he finally found a front door key. He closed the curtains on the backdoor window and wedged a chair under the doorknob. He left Alice a note, telling her he'd be home at noon, to wait for him, stay put, don't answer the door. On the front stoop, he struggled with the unfamiliar front door key, and it finally caught. He waited a long time for the 15, half-asleep on his feet. He got off at the Ebonton terminal and walked to Tamara's new apartment in Wally's and Wilma's house.

He couldn't help staring now at Tamara as she laughed about her own joke. Her lustrous skin shimmering in the morning light, her hands floating like wings from her sides to her shoulders and back in some kind of secret signal of simple joy. She opened her eyes, parted her teeth to let her pink tongue touch her dark lips, and then smiled at Jade, her eyes luminous, cutting through him and soothing him at the same time. He felt his belly flip, and he held his breath to stop his body from betraying him. In her loose-fitting, rainbow tunic, Tamara floated before him like a Nile queen in a time warp, dropped there amid the unwashed by some cosmic error. He felt his blood rush under her gaze, and he was revived, suddenly, by its energy, grateful for the gods' mistake. He so desperately wanted to please her. But as he smiled back at her, he couldn't shake Dee's warning echoing in his head. "If Wally puts her up over there, the neighbors will kill him!"

The apartment came modestly furnished. In their first hour of work, they unloaded light boxes, wall decor, small lamps, and a few extra chairs. Tamara and Jade moved quickly, while Wally negotiated the narrow, steep climb to the third floor with practiced patience. It was hotter here in the city than in Mell Hollow, and the rooms were stuffy. Wally and Jade labored at the windows, managing to budge just two from their swollen frames. At the end of the first hour, Jade encouraged Wally to stay put in the apartment, but Wally wouldn't hear of it. He was a bull, and despite his labored breathing up and down the stairs, he provided the backbone for the heavy stuff they had unwittingly saved for last—a small refrigerator, a large desk and chair, and five boxes of books. Wally didn't pause once, just pushed through the work until it was done.

The house was Victorian—a tall, lean, monotone gray wooden building whose prime had passed decades earlier. Long slender windows on the first two floors were topped by shorter, narrower versions on the third floor, where broken layers of wood shingles and carved cornices gave the place the appearance of a neglected masterpiece, a weary relic of a time when artisans had worked their craft with great care. It was a place among many like it in this section of town, where architectural grace and social privilege had emerged in abundance from black diamond money, where inordinate wealth and comfort just a half century earlier had been created literally from the found bounty of the earth.

"These were servants' quarters," Wally told Tamara and Jade as they sat in a row on the low couch in the front room, gulping iced tea and wiping sweat from their faces. It was only eight-thirty in the morning, but the persistent summer sun blazed through the open front windows, giving them little reprieve from the heavy air. "Wilma and I lived in these quarters for five years before we bought this house. But we were no one's servants. That era had passed long before us. Still, those who had lived in these quarters over the years were probably our people—Polish, maybe Hungarian, Slovaks. Housekeepers, laborers, cooks, caretakers, raising children not their own. The people who built this place owned coal mines and even part of a railroad. They were English. They lived here only a short time before they built a larger home up on The North Heights."

Tamara let her head fall back against the cushion and closed her eyes. "If you listen, you can hear the children playing on the stairway," she whispered. "You can smell onions and potatoes—pierogies, Wally?—wafting from the kitchen up to these quarters." She was smiling now. "Can you smell them?"

Jade gave Wally a quizzical look, but Wally just smiled at him, put his head back, closed his eyes and nodded his assent.

"And music," Tamara whispered. "Someone's playing a piano. It's coming from the first floor. It's Rachmaninov. Can you hear it, Wally? So regal. And so subtly shielding pain and sorrow."

Jade, seated between them, turned to see Tamara nodding to herself, her eyes closed, and then he turned toward Wally who seemed lost in Tamara's dream. Jade's heart pounded at the unwelcome thought that Tamara was somehow connected to Alice and that she was falling into one of Alice's trances. Then he looked at Wally again, and his heartbeat slowed. Tamara was simply imagining for them the sounds and scents of this house so long ago. Like a shaman, she was calling on the soul of this place, awakening them to a consciousness greater than their own. Tamara wasn't like Alice at all, Jade assured himself. Tamara wasn't a seer lost in her private, frightened religious fervor; she was simply a guide to the possibilities of the imagination, to the magic of time and timelessness, to the common links of human experience.

To Jade, Tamara was in some ways more mysterious than his mother. He knew so little about her, yet he was mesmerized by her, hanging on to her every word as if it were the first truth he'd ever learned. He felt himself being pulled toward this mystery, this exotic force. She was not just a girl, like Lucy; she was wise and self-assured, emanating knowledge and genuine warmth, someone who'd been here before, an old soul. And yet there was something else about her that had only been hinted at, a playful and carefree spirit, as if an impulsive teenager still lingered beneath her skin waiting to be re-invited to the heated game.

He looked at her body while her eyes were still closed. She remained hidden in her loose colorful clothing, but even seated in relaxation, her posture seemed perfect—her neck long and straight, her wiry shoulders taut yet somehow relaxed, her arms at ease but ready to wave again like swift-moving clouds. He could see she was strong; he'd watched her move with grace, even while struggling on the steps with her boxes of books. Jade wanted to reach over and touch her skin. And as she opened her eyes and turned, looking directly at him, he was drawn like a fallen leaf into a whirlpool. Brown and golden eyes with soft pupils pulling him inward, even against his will. She still held a smile on her wide mouth, but it had curled into a cheshire grin, and she seemed on the brink of laughing about her vision of this home; but, to Jade, there was no room for humor amid his lofty feelings for this ethereal beauty.

190

They turned in unison at the sound of heavy footfalls on the stairway. Jade looked to Wally and then back to Tamara, but she was already on her feet. The footsteps stopped, and a shadow filled the doorway to the apartment. Roland Wilson.

"You didn't save me anything to do," Roland said to Tamara, smiling slightly. "I guess I can just turn around and go home."

Wally scrambled to his feet. "Roland Wilson?! What is this? What are you doing here?! So good to see you! Welcome, welcome!" He shook Wilson's hand up and down, too long for Wilson's evident discomfort. Wally was still breathing heavily from the heat and the exertion, and his words were coming out in excited gasps. "But how do…? What are you doing here?" He turned to Tamara. She smiled at him. "Ah, you said you would get some help, but oy, Roland Wilson?!" He turned back to Wilson, then to Jade. "This is a great honor! Jimmy, you know who this is, don't you? My God, this is the greatest athlete this valley has ever known!"

Roland backed into the shadow of the doorway.

"Don't go yet," Tamara said to him. "Please. We'll need your help setting up here. We can't get more than two windows open." Her smile had disappeared. For the first time, Jade heard uncertainty in her voice. She faced Roland in the doorway, her shoulders back, her arms at her side, but there was a reserve about her that hadn't been there before, a reluctance. Jade could see the outline of her breasts pushing against the thin cotton tunic. Her eyes were fixed on Wilson, but the soft, self-assured look in them was gone. Even their golden hue seemed darker. He thought he saw fear there.

Jade scrambled to his feet and moved toward the front window. "Hey, Wilson, check out this view! The sky is actually clear this morning. You can see the freighter coming around the West Mountain. Hear the horn? And you can see the Macson stacks. No smoke today. Sunday. Probably why it's so clear."

Wilson stepped into the room but didn't join Jade at the window. "I hope you haven't burned yourself out here, Flynn," he said flatly. "We have a long week ahead of us. The boss tells me a heavy push is on. You made it through one week. But you're barely out of the dugout."

"The big boss?"

"The only boss."

Jade held Wilson's look for much longer than he could in the Macson yard. It was becoming clear now: Hafferty was at the center of all of this. Hafferty had known Roland since he was a child and his father even longer; he'd put Tamara in touch with Wally, perhaps at the request of Dr. Wilson. Now, Jade was part of this circle, an acolyte of Hafferty, already in a deal with the man that hinged in part on what he had to tell Jensen the next morning.

Wally shuffled to the center of the room between Jade and Wilson. "You work together? How could this be? Jimmy, you did not tell me!? Roland Wilson, what are you doing at Macson Munitions? Jimmy?"

"It's Jade, Wally. And he's my supervisor," Jade said, looking at Wilson instead of Wally. "He's a head lineman. Working there for the summer. He's in college. Penn State."

"I asked Roland to help today," Tamara said, smiling at Wally. "I am a friend of his family."

Wally turned now to Tamara, speechless, shaking his head in bewilderment.

"I normally speak for myself," Roland said to Wally, and then gave a long look at Tamara and a glance at Jade. He crossed his arms in front of his big chest. "I don't think I caught your name."

Wally turned to Roland, laughing to himself and shaking his head. "I guess I'm the stupid old man here. Everyone knows everyone. But me? I know nothing. Jimmy…er I mean Jade. This boy Jade, now a man. I don't even know if I know him any longer."

"He's Wally Wolczynski," Jade interjected. He returned Wilson's hard look. "He owns this house, lives on the first floor with his wife, Wilma. And he owns Wally's Diner near the stadium. And he's my godfather."

Wally gave Jade a surprised smile, and then winked at him. He held out his right hand to Wilson.

"OK," Roland said with a sigh, as he shook Wally's hand. "Now everybody knows everybody."

"I met Tamara on Friday for the first time," Wally said, his voice still shaking. "A friend called me and asked me to help her out. He knew I had a few apartments, and…well, I did not know she knew the great Roland Wilson!" He was smiling again at Wilson and chuckling to himself.

"The great Mr. Wilson missed all the heavy lifting," Tamara said, "so we're hoping he can put his greatness to use with the windows and moving some of this furniture." She spoke with an edge in her voice, but she was smiling at Wilson just the same. Wilson let his arms fall to his side and offered her a smile as if in surrender.

"I'm all yours," he said, holding her look. "For an hour."

The men opened boxes and rearranged furniture, and Roland managed to open four windows while Tamara floated among them, giving instructions and repeatedly thanking each of them. Soft tones had returned to her voice, and twice Jade observed Tamara and Wilson laughing quietly together. After an hour, the apartment was taking form, with furniture rearranged and curtains on the windows. Jade got a lesson in Jamaican and African art from Tamara each time he reached into a box or hung a decoration on the wall. In short order, the place was transformed from a sparsely furnished Victorian garret to an exotic pad, with beads hanging in doorways, Kenyan masks on the walls, a yellow sacco chair and handcrafted Turkish carpets. Jade felt like he was on a Hollywood set.

Wally sat heavily on the couch near the front window, letting out a sigh and dropping his head onto the cushion. Jade thought it was odd that Wally hadn't pressed Wilson for more information, or at least recounted one of his Roland Wilson high school hero tales for all to enjoy. But he knew how aloof Wilson could be, and he knew this coolness must have come as a surprise to Wally. Jade wondered if Wally felt disappointed, if he believed he would have been better off never having met the great Mr. Wilson.

"Roland, how many bombs do you make in a day at Macson?" Wally called out. He had caught his breath and now seemed to be coming out of his distance, his pensiveness. The sycophantic thrill in his voice was gone. He was not disappointed, Jade realized; he was boiling with suppressed urgency, his Polish nature, for impulsively speaking his mind without a social filter. Jade knew they were about to encounter the Wally that he knew well—a man who could charge the atmosphere with one comment, and who could draw out an answer to a difficult question by surrounding it with lesser questions, a dance around the elephant in the room.

Roland was hanging a framed poster of Malcolm X, and he took a moment to straighten it on the wall before turning to Wally. Jade and Tamara were a few feet away unloading books from boxes onto low shelving.

"I'm not sure," Wilson said, glancing toward Wally. "I guess it depends on the day." He picked up a box and started toward the kitchen.

"I was just wondering," Wally said, holding up his hand. "Is it in the hundreds? Or in the thousands? I mean, if it is in the thousands, how many thousands of bombs are made in, say, a month? Fifty thousand? One hundred thousand?

Wilson stood over Wally holding the box and glaring at the older man. "I couldn't tell you."

"But you're a head lineman," Wally persisted. "You must have an idea of the count. My assistant knows how many eggs we need on a weekday as opposed to a Saturday, for example. He needs to know this."

Wilson forced his mouth into a grin. "I have no idea. Maybe you could ask your assistant to come by and count them one day." He turned and made his escape to the kitchen.

Wally shifted in his seat and called out to Jade in a voice Wilson could hear. "Jade! Do you know? How many bombs you make in a day?"

"What difference does it make, Wally?" Jade muttered, trying to disarm the conversation. He continued to hand books to Tamara, and she placed them in a certain order on the shelves.

"Well," Wally continued, "it makes a difference to the Army, or to the Marines, or whoever uses the bombs. It makes a difference to the government paying for them. It makes a difference to the people who make the profits from making the bombs. And most of all...it makes a difference to the people on the ground who are on the receiving end of the bombs. You know, the people who get killed by the bombs."

Jade stopped handing books to Tamara. She looked at him and then at Wilson, who was now standing in the doorway of the front room with his arms crossed again.

"Wally's still mad that I left the diner for Macson," Jade said to Wilson. "I worked at Wally's for six years. Since I was twelve."

"It is a job, Wally," Wilson said, his eyebrows raised, his voice flat, pedantic, a hint of his father's island accent slipping through. "*That* is all it is. When I finish the job at the end of August, I will go back to school. I don't count the munitions. I just do the job."

Wally held Wilson's glare and then turned slowly to Jade. "I am not angry with you, Jade," he said. His eyes were heavy, and, to Jade, he looked exhausted. "I am very proud of you.

As I told you before—you are a man now. You make a choice? You must live with the responsibilities...*and* the consequences."

34
Retaliation

Sunday June 29, 1969

She was sitting in a corner booth, her back to the door, when a new pack of Luckys came spinning across the table and into her lap. She was pissed that she'd flinched.

"Tennis anyone?"

"Quit," she said, not looking up at him. She stole a look at his lower half. A belly now, a pretty big one. Why should that surprise her? Once a hedonist, always a hedonist. She put the pack on the table and pushed it toward him.

"The nails? Or the tennis?"

"Both," she said, lying about the smoking. "But I could still kick your ass, especially with that gut on you."

His laugh was still the same, a baritone bark. He slid into the seat across from her. "If she comes in here, she won't be happy, you know."

She met his eyes, finally. "She won't recognize me. You did because your horns stood up. Your acute sense of smell betrayed you, Lenny. Yet again."

He was grinning now, his eyes soft and yielding. She could see a dim and distant light there, a faded trace of hope, craving energy, drawing light from her look, drifting willingly out of his own control and into hers. "What are you doing here, Alice? Disappear for fourteen years and show up like a dark ghost. The haircut, the black dye job, the beret, the get-up. Jesus, Allie, you look like a dyke."

She grinned back at him, giving him nothing. "Town is dead, Lenny. Heard you've had nothing but rain since May. Too bad. I was hoping you'd be closed, and then I'd have to pound on the back door upstairs and tell whoever lives there to get out of my apartment." He chuckled and lit a Marlboro and tossed the pack on the table next to the Luckys. "It's Sunday, Lenny. Why aren't you at church with your family, praying for redemption?"

He shook his head and held his sheepish grin. He blew a cloud over her head and looked at his watch. "Times have changed, Allie. Money to be made on a Sunday, even in a slow season. Church crowd should be shuffling in pretty soon for the buffet brunch. Better make this fast if you don't want a scene."

"I didn't want a scene back then either, Lenny. Things just happened. You know that. I'm not here for a replay, I just needed to get away, see the ocean again. My car drove me here. A trade-in, '63 gold Impala, black spongy interior. I feel like an insurance salesman in the damn thing, but it beats the hell out of the VW bug I was in. Felt like I was driving a rickshaw."

She reached for the Luckys and started peeling off the wrapper. "Barely made it across the causeway with my new Chevy hiccupping like an old sot. It's either the carburetor or the timing chain or the fuel pump. Is your buddy Zeke still fleecing the tourists? Can you get him out of bed on a Sunday for me?"

Lenny finally let go of his stifled laugh, filling the empty dining room, his booming voice bouncing off the huge mirror behind the bar.

"You laugh like you own the place," she deadpanned with a smirk, setting her pale eyes on his.

He got her a room in a bed and breakfast on the square at the center of town and had his busboy drive her there. If she was lucky, Zeke would look at the Impala Monday morning. If he wasn't still drunk. Zeke was enjoying an unexpected extension of his seven-month hibernation celebration.

She spent Sunday evening walking the beach, fighting off the memories. Fewer tourists meant more space to wander undistracted. As dusk fell, she sauntered off the cooling sand and headed for the bandstand, her favorite old spot, back in the beginning when no one knew her. She figured she was invisible once again. And she liked it.

She'd lost her nerve back there after Lenny showed up at the booth. She'd had him in her palm, as always, and she let him go. She'd told him she missed the ocean, maybe leading him to believe she missed him, but it wasn't that at all. She'd driven here in a haze, but she did have a plan. She needed a favor. The kind she knew Lenny could deliver, for the right amount. She'd brought three thousand in cash, figuring he could lure one of his lowlife pals out of the shadows, the guys he'd known from his darker days, before he'd met Gail and took on her family's failing beach bar, married her, had a few kids with her. Before he met Alice a couple years later, hired her to wait tables, put her up in the rooms above the bar with her little kid, then let her talk him into turning the place into a tourist trap—a restaurant-bar with Atlantic City kitsch. Before he put her in charge of the day-to-day operation and watched the place turn its first profit in years. Before Alice had become irresistible to him. Before she let him seduce her, out of indifference, out of the numbness that she'd endured since Vermont—even earlier. Since that first confinement on this very oceanfront, ninety minutes south. Sister Saint Joe and her saintly mob of tormentors. Her first baby. Taken from her.

She sat on the top step of the bandstand in the waning golden light, clutching the strap of her shoulder bag stuffed with cash under the false bottom. She turned her head slowly each way and then behind her, a lighthouse beacon searching for movement in this island village. There was nothing. It was late June, but the eerie silence felt like the town was holding its breath—the empty square of patchy lawn before her, the vacant streets on all sides, the familiar bed and breakfast joints with fresh paint and deserted porch rockers, the silent sentry of the white clapboard church steeple on the next block, even the surf just over the dunes—all of it hushed by anxious anticipation, stunned by Sunday's evening pall—a shroud over time itself.

For a long moment, she considered that she had somehow caused this pause in time. She felt her pulse surge when she couldn't remember who she was now, why she was here, dropped into this familiar spot in a dimension void of movement. She was startled by the vivid memory of an eerie black and white TV show she'd watched with Seamus once, in which a man and a woman found themselves trapped alone on a life-size model train set, a town just like this with no one in it. The squirrel on a low branch was fake. All the homes were empty, the food on the shelves painted props. She remembered Seamus having nightmares about that show and then her having nightmares, too. The memory spilled a cold wave down her spine, and she felt the hair on the back of her neck rising.

A siren blared in the distance, and she stood up and pitched herself forward, nearly falling down the old wooden steps to the spongy cold lawn. She hurried from the bandstand and the square, drawn to the beach, her chin in the air, craving the sound of surf crashing. Nearing the top of the dunes that were still encased in eerie silence, she saw a couple strolling on the sand, and then a fisherman on a jetty and another couple further down the shoreline, and then, at last, there it was—the tumble of soft waves, the caress of a calm sea washing her back from the edge of that vacant silent dimension.

She closed her eyes and listened to the ocean, took gulps of the salt air and shook off the onset of terror that had seized her. At the water's edge, she steadied herself and pulled off her shoes. The surf was ice cold, the sand wet and sharply pitched, and she began to walk south in an awkward barefoot march along its hardened edge, a purpose to her pace, as if she were in a city, late for an appointment. The last wash of light on the horizon reminded her of Seamus here at this beach, the child pointing to the colors in the sky, calling out their names to her. She knew he was called Jade now and she was relieved by the awareness of her feet—cold, wet, and splashing in her urgent hobbling stride—and by the cries of terns and shouts from kids in the distance rushing toward the water. By the welcome worry that their parents should be watching them at this darkening hour.

She wondered what Jade was doing at this moment. Nuzzling with his girlfriend, no doubt. Nurturing in preparation for another week in that Macson hell hole. The kind of nurture Alice could never provide. She felt reluctant gratitude that he was loved by the girl. Assuming that's what it was at their age. But what did he really know about love? Had he learned anything at all from his mother? She'd given him rules and parameters and had shown him some of her tricks, how to fight, how to be mannered, even kind, how to read with discretion, how to learn sports she knew he would never be good at. But it wasn't enough. She knew that. The long absences, the dark passages of time lost to hiding in shadows, to salving her pain. Those literature rants she'd entertained him with, those movies she'd taken him to see, those attempts to make up time, to lure him away from their life stuck in an endless kaleidoscope of confusion, panic, and lost time. Was any of that love? Or were those exercises just another set of Alice performances? Pantomimes of her imagined self. Ways to distract her son from the numbness of her soul, the life she'd hidden from him. Had he ever known her?

She hadn't had a drink in a week, and she'd made a decision within that window of clarity that frightened her with its certainty, as if it were a foregone conclusion. She'd driven hundreds of silent miles in the rain, letting the decision direct her, letting her new car sail toward an old outpost. In this drift toward her past, toward the sea, she was on a two-lane road in the flatlands of central Jersey when she thought of Updike's Rabbit Angstrom on the run from his mistaken life, and she laughed out loud, the first sound inside the car in hours. Had she always been hiding inside a story? Someone else's contrivance?

This time, she decided, this version would be her own. This plan, this retaliation for a stolen life, for *four* stolen lives, for years of slow and relentless anguish, punishment for something she'd long ago lost sight of and had been running from without knowing why.

She had been certain of this plan, this persuasive performance. And she had told herself she would not be distracted from it. And then, when the curtain rose and she looked up from the cigarette pack on the table into Lenny's eyes, into the glimmer of his hope for fire, she smiled at him, because she knew he could resurrect his own past and get it done for her. But then the lights went down, and the second-guessing set in, and her performance froze. If he got the job done, then what? Would he pay for her sins yet again? They'd catch up to him surely, they always did. Trace the deed to his doorstep, as they so often had done before. Lenny had his own shadows to dodge. Now she would bring him hers, yet again.

She'd sleep this night by the sea, turn off her stage lights, empty her fears, and focus on the last act. She'd find her nerve in the morning, set her course. Deconstruct Lenny's life again, follow through on the plan, her version of her story, resurrect her talent for nailing the final act. After Zeke fixed the Impala, she'd see Lenny one more time and settle the deal. She might even put on a little fake up for the performance.

Part Four

35
Out Sick

Monday, June 30, 1969

Jade stood on the back stoop staring at the old oil drum in the center of the little dirt yard. The blind sentinel. Asleep on the job, as always, having missed both Stanley the intruder and Alice the escapee. The old colorless drum in silent shadow, never exposed to direct sunlight even now at the height of the brightest season. Jade lifted his gaze to the outlines of the slouching rooftops behind Reston Street and then beyond into the pale dawn light, where he could see just part of the upper tower under the pointed peak of the old breaker on the hill—the great mantis, the charcoal hide stark against a chalky sky. The omniscient breaker, the exhausted soldier of the great coal winning, waiting to exhale and fall someday soon. He wondered if the mantis had witnessed what the sentinel had not.

The dawn air was moving, crisp and clean, another rare gift of a steady breeze carrying toward the city the ever-present culm cloud enshrouding these homes. He knew he would later pay for this reprieve by choking on the transplanted stench from his neighborhood as it mixed with the noisome gag of the Macson plant in center city. But now, as he cleansed his lungs in desperate breaths, he felt his eyes being tugged upward from the mantis to the faint circle above him, the dawn moon, a whisper of itself, a fading shadow of light left over from a long nighttime voyage. He wondered if the moon was relieved that the Apollo 10 crew had come close but had not landed there in May. It had been a test run, the F Mission, so the papers had said, a dress rehearsal for the real landing to come. Had the ascent module landed on the moon, the crew would never have gotten off; there wasn't enough fuel. They'd have been trapped there. Forever.

He knew he would need to make his own test run this week toward his ultimate escape, his own far-away landing—Hafferty's college deal. In the promised meeting later on this day, he would need to tell just enough of what he knew about the accident to stay on Hafferty's good side, but not everything. He wanted to hold something back until he was satisfied that Stanley's attack on Alice was not connected to Hafferty, at least not directed by him. It would be a tightrope walk, especially since he was certain that Jensen would not be alone in the meeting, that Detective Marion would be there, maybe Hafferty, and perhaps even Stanley, a death glare in his eyes, a bloody bandage on the side of his leathery face. Jade needed to seal Hafferty's college offer, not so much to attend school, but simply to secure a paid opportunity to get away from here, from his torturous and endlessly conflicted life with Alice; from his unraveling love for Lucy, now descending headlong into bickering bitterness; and from this fallow and mephitic valley of poisoned earth, peevish men, and broken souls. And now, he saw clearly that he could no longer pretend he'd be immune from the draft, a predicament that, if triggered, would end, as Hafferty had predicted, in certain death in a faraway jungle. He needed that part of the deal more than anything else, in order to take hold of his own destiny.

But could he just leave Alice to whatever plans Hafferty or Stanley were hatching for her? Why had Hafferty been so solicitous with him about Alice, while Stanley, seemingly out of nowhere, had been so enraged by her that he'd tried to kill her? He wanted to believe that Hafferty would not have orchestrated such an attack.

And what about Tamara? After spending more time with her at Wally's flat after the move, he knew he must see her again, as often as he could. Leaving right now was not possible; he needed to stay at Macson through the summer to seal his deal with Hafferty. But, if he grew closer to Tamara, how would he ever break away from her by summer's end? He was drawn to her, against his reason, lured by her eyes and voice and the mere wave of her hands, the way she held herself, her gentle power, her otherworldly essence. Against the logic of his plan, which now, more than ever, felt real and achievable, he was pulled by an unknown need, even stronger than physical desire, to be in the company of Tamara, in the center of that essence.

He'd stayed too long at Wally's and Wilma's flat on Sunday. But Tamara had been there; he had to have stayed. After the move, Wally had insisted they join him and Wilma for brunch—Wally's "perfect poached eggs and salmon," by his own report, and Wilma's blintzes smothered in a fresh cherry sauce—tastes and textures Jade had never experienced. A Jewish feast where he'd felt instantly and inexplicably at home. Wilson had declined the invitation at the front door of the first-floor flat, telling Wally and Wilma he had a meeting with his former high school football coach. After he'd gone, Tamara had become visibly more relaxed, and Jade, too, had felt relief. He'd sensed in Wilson not only a competitor for Tamara's attention, but someone who'd known her well, perhaps too well. Wilson's departure had been an opening for Jade, and he'd leaped into it headfirst. By mid-meal, he'd lost track of time and worry and had let himself fall completely under Tamara's spell, his mind unfolding, his eyes on her every move, his thoughts consumed by her ideas, his heart pounding just to be across the table from her.

By the time he'd returned home an hour and a half later than he'd promised Alice, her bed was empty, the house abandoned. He'd checked the cupboard over the sink. The money was gone. There was a note on the kitchen table: "Seamus, Do Not Stay Here." She'd signed it with an "A" encircled in a heart. Over the years, she had often disappeared for days without warning; this was the first time she had ever left him a note.

He'd tried to stay up all night waiting for her but he'd fallen asleep on the couch in The Grotto. He'd locked the front door but had left the back door unbarred in case she might return. He'd forced himself to stop fearing another appearance by Stanley; he'd just wanted Alice to come home.

Now standing on the back stoop, the kitchen door wide open behind him, he wanted to let this rare early morning breeze freshen the house, in case she returned while he was at work. It was the first day of his second week on the job. The five workdays behind him had felt like years. His body and his armor were veterans now—his fingers calloused, his biceps and back no longer aching, his work gloves nearly worn through, his feet numb and settled into notched ridges in the soles of his steel toed boots which were already torn at the front. Just standing there in the doorway, he could feel the strength in his legs, his middle and upper body a tight coil. He puffed up his chest and ran his hand over a solid pectoral muscle. He wondered if he had gotten taller. That made him think of Alice again, and it allowed him to laugh, just a little.

In the distance, the morning bells tolled at Saint John the Divine Church, and Jade knew he had just twenty minutes to eat something and pack a lunch before catching the 15. He'd been waiting at the curb every workday with the same people—the three silent women and Gort, his robot-like coworker and rescuer after the Cheese gang assault. But neither Jade nor Gort had exchanged a word since then. Each morning, Gort had stood at the front of the bus stop queue and had fixed his aviator gaze toward the north—as if he could use his robot powers to will the arrival of the bus. Jade wanted to thank him for his help, but he sensed the man preferred to be left alone, that he had his guard up and would remain that way. It was the same wall of resistance he faced with all of his co-workers. Despite his directive from Hafferty to mix it up with the Macson men, Jade found them not just unapproachable, but hostile. They were union, and he was not. And if Cheese was their de facto leader, it would remain that way.

When he arrived at The Line five minutes early, Jade was approached by a short wiry man with "Dimmock" on his pocket patch. He told Jade that Wilson was "out sick" and that he would be Jade's boss until Wilson returned. "*If* he returns," Dimmock said. The man's look wasn't fierce like some of the other men; it was fearless—the vacant look of a man without a soul, a look Jade had witnessed among some of the biker guys at school, who had seemed older than their years. Alice had warned him about men with these eyes. She'd said they were not just dangerous; they were lethal. A man with this dead look would tear limbs from an innocent animal without flinching, she'd said. The image hung with Jade over the years, a portent he could expect but never truly prepare for. When he looked at Dimmock's pinpoint pupils, his leathery face, his mouth in a permanent scowl, he knew this man would relish bringing harm to him.

Dimmock gripped his iron rod with both hands and held it across his hips like a weapon. "You better be ready to work, asshole," he said. "The Forge is on double-time today, and your nigger union buster boyfriend ain't here to hold your dick for you." He brushed past Jade and used the base of his rod to push the start button. Jade stumbled as the conveyor kicked into gear beneath his feet. Over the rumble of The Line and the roar of machines starting up all over the building, Jade's new boss hollered an ultimatum. "You fall today, Flynn, you're outta here."

All morning, Jade managed to concentrate on keeping up with the rush of shells toward The Forge and to stay out of the path of deadeye Dimmock. Still, he couldn't keep his mind from drifting to Sunday's brunch at Wally's, to thinking about Tamara. At the table, before lifting her fork, she had closed her eyes for a long moment, seeming to pray silently to herself. When she'd opened them, she looked directly into Jade's and smiled, her teeth brilliant in their dark frame, her eyes liquid light reflecting the mid-day sun through Wally's tall front windows. He couldn't remember if he smiled back; he could only recall the feeling that had washed over him. He'd been awe-struck, barely able to breathe.

He hadn't known how long he'd been caught in her gaze when Wally tapped his arm with a plate of cherry blintzes. Throughout the brunch, Tamara's hands glided across her meal, delicate gestures in tasting small portions and then resting at ease to offer her hosts a warm compliment. Jade noticed the trace of an accent for the first time—her diction and command of the language more refined than any teacher he'd ever had, but Tamara had just a hint of an inflection that sounded exotic to Jade's untrained ear. While he and Wally had dived into their meal as if it were their last, he slowed down when he noticed how Tamara addressed her plate, seeming to study each flavor, savor each morsel. When she spoke, everything else stopped, forks held in mid-air, all eyes upon her. She told them stories about her brilliant piano and violin teachers and then about the gift of her own students in her first full year of teaching and how *they* had taught *her*. Her voice was lyrical, mesmerizing, inclusive, her eyes meeting everyone's and drawing them in, the soft power of her force irresistible. They learned that she held a B.A. in English and an MFA in music theory and had been a graduate teaching assistant at the University of Chicago while studying for her Ph.D. in English Literature, and that she later taught for a year at Howard University in Washington, D.C. She'd come to this town, she said, after she had met Roland's father at a conference at Howard, his alma mater.

"So, Roland Wilson's father works with you here at Dickson College?" Wally had asked.

"Yes," Tamara had replied. "He's a biology professor and chairman of the Science Department, as well as a recognized research scientist—well published," she'd said. Jade noticed a slight hitch in Tamara's soothing voice, and she glanced at him as if she were reading his thoughts. She smiled then and, with a shyness Jade had not yet seen, she said, "He's not much of a fan of English Lit. Or music, for that matter."

Jade had counted five bracelets on her golden-brown forearms—woven hemp, copper, pewter, ornately carved wood, and a thick silver band encasing a large onyx that changed colors in the dance of light and shadows. She wore large hoop earrings and rings on all four fingers of her left hand and one on the index finger of her right hand—a huge topaz that seemed to sparkle at Jade with each cloudlike movement of her hand.

Jade had finally found his voice. "So, you knew Roland Wilson when he was in high school?"

"Yes," she'd said, "briefly, and not well. I had met him once while visiting James to consider a faculty opening at Dickson. Roland was a high school senior. After he went to Penn State, I accepted the faculty position and moved here and got to know him better over semester break. But I had heard a great deal about him before that from his father."

"So, you lived at their house, with James and Roland? That's where you're moving from now?"

She nodded and put her fork down, touching her napkin to her soft lips.

"Must have been tough hearing about football all the time," Jade suggested, imagining the men bellowing about sports over a serene and politely silent Tamara.

Tamara's mouth stretched into a strained grin. "Well, not exactly," she said, her eyes falling to her plate. "James never boasted about his son's athletic prowess, and Roland, during his visits from school, was rather quiet about all that. Prior to Roland's first visit, James had mentioned to me once that he felt Roland had not applied himself in school and had relied on his sports achievements to get by." She lifted her eyes to meet Jade's. "James is a scholar. A man who lives the life of the mind. He loves his son sincerely, but he's not prone to boasting about anyone's athletic prowess, least of all his son's."

"He is the greatest athlete Pennsylvania ever saw!" Wally exclaimed, as if in Roland's unsolicited defense. In his excitement, Wally shook the table with his thick forearms, water glasses wobbling, silverware clattering. He quickly apologized, making an exaggerated effort to steady the table with his big hands. "But he must have changed since he went away to college," he said, his voice humbled by his own outburst. "Something is not right with that young man."

"He is likely in a better mood when he is away at school," Tamara offered. "He and his father look at the sea of life from opposite shores."

On The Line, while he was daydreaming about Tamara, Jade had let a few extra shells pass by him. Dimmock bellowed in his direction. "Flynn, you worthless cunt! Pay attention! Move those shells offline *now* or we're gonna have a fuckin' mess on the other end. And if we do, I will rip your fuckin' head off and shove it down your goddamn neck!"

Jade scrambled, his heart pounding, Alice's words about limbless animals roaring in his head. He pulled a dozen shells offline in the next minute and then worked his way forward on The Line until the logjam abated. No more words were exchanged between Jade and Dimmock for the rest of the morning. But at the noon whistle, Dimmock stepped in front of Jade and stared at him. He was inches shorter than Jade but the look in his eyes—of cold malice, of imminent violence—made him seem ten feet taller.

Jade rushed out into the yard and gasped for air, immediately regretting it. His breath burned in his throat, and he bent forward choking. He'd forgotten what he'd known just hours ago—that the air here would be doubly noxious, a mix of culm soot and factory spew. He nearly fell to his knees, gagging.

He shuffled toward the flagpole with his lunch bag in hand, and for a moment, he imagined Wilson sitting on the concrete base waiting for him. As men filed passed him into the far reaches of the yard, Jade slumped onto the base, closed his eyes, and rested his head on the flagpole.

He felt someone brush up behind him and grab his upper arm, nearly lifting him to his feet.

It was Squirrel. "We have to talk," he said in a hasty whisper as he sat on the adjacent side of the base. Jade expected Squirrel to start a performance but when he turned to look at his face, there was no wild-eyed expression there.

Squirrel glanced around furtively as if he expected someone to attack them from a blind side. "Just start eating and listen," he said, as he opened his lunch pail and pulled out a sandwich and a soda bottle.

Jade felt his throat tighten. He was starving but Dimmock's eyes and Squirrel's urgency had stolen his appetite. His belly—the barometer of his anxiety—twisted in the grip of an inner fist.

"Roland's not sick," Squirrel said, tearing into his sandwich and continuing to talk while he chewed. "Don't look at me, and don't act surprised," he said. Jade lowered his face and began reluctant work on his lunch.

"He spent the night in jail," Squirrel continued. Jade turned to him, and Squirrel snapped, "Don't look at me, I said!"

"After he left you at Wally's house yesterday, he went to the VFW in Marvin Gap on the East Side. His high school coach wanted to talk about football at Penn State or some such shit. Roland doesn't flinch at going into places like that, even though no Black guy has set foot in that joint, ever! He figured it was OK since his coach had invited him."

"Did Wilson tell you this?"

"Just shut up and listen, will ya?" Squirrel said. He took a slug of his soda. "It turns out there are five or six other guys in the bar, it's quiet. At least two of them are Macson guys. The coach is pretty cool about Roland showing up, introducing him to the guys and to the bartender, and everything is going along fine. They talk sports, and everybody starts going on about Roland Wilson and what a great star he was. Roland doesn't want a drink, but the bartender sets a beer in front of him anyway. Bottle of Schlitz." Squirrel took another quick look around before he continued.

"So, a few minutes into the friendly chat, one of the guys starts talking about that colored girl who got killed on Canton Avenue last Monday morning."

Jade stopped chewing and put down his sandwich.

"The guys at the bar start asking Roland if he knows the girl, and Roland says, 'No!' Tells them he does not know all the Black people in this town. The guys laugh at that, but Roland's not laughing. Then one of the Macson guys says the article in Tuesday's paper said the colored girl was driving a stolen car. The story called her a prostitute from New York, the guy said. Mister Know-it-all, Roland called him. I think Mr. Know-it-all works in the Forge. So anyway, Know-it-all says the paper got it all wrong. He says he knows whose car the girl was driving, and she was not a New Yorker, but a local hooker. Roland keeps quiet, but Know-it-all wants to tell them more. He says the girl was a regular whore the cops liked to play around with and that the car she was driving was one of the cops' own cars. A new '69 red Mustang."

Jade put his partially eaten sandwich in the bag and looked sideways at Squirrel.

"The newspaper, Know-it-all says, reported the car as a stolen black Firebird, but Know-it-all insists it was a red Mustang, and it was owned by a cop named Belden and that the girl was high on something Belden gave her. Know-it-all says the newspaper said nothing about who gave her what, because the paper is in on it with the cops, and then he says isn't it funny that the accident happened a block away from the TV station and two blocks from the radio station, and nothing showed up on either one of them."

"Squirrel," Jade said.

"Don't interrupt," Squirrel said, holding up his hand. "There's more, and we don't have much time left for lunch. It gets uglier." Flecks of his sandwich flew off his lips as Squirrel's chatter ramped up to top speed. "Roland told me he did, in fact, know who the girl was, that not many things happen in the small Black world around here that they all don't know about. He said the girl was about ten years older than us, and that he didn't really know her, but he remembered her when he was a kid. Said his father knew the girl's mother. Mister Know-it-all at the bar was right—she's not from New York, she's from here.

"Anyway, Know-it-all is going on with his newspaper and cops cover-up theory, and the guy next to him—also a Macson guy—interrupts and starts yammering about who gives a shit about some nigger hooker getting killed, and all of a sudden Roland's paying very close attention. The coach puts his hand on Roland's arm, and Roland shakes it off and reaches for the bottle of Schlitz like he's gonna chug it. The second Macson guy continues mouthing off and says he doesn't give a shit about cops or newspapers covering up the story, and that newspapers shouldn't waste any ink on dead niggers, and that a dead nigger girl is good news, because they just reproduce like bunnies, and what we don't need in this world is any more jungle bunnies."

Squirrel stopped to have another look around while he took a quick chug on his soda.

"And that just about does it for Roland Wilson. He takes the full bottle of Schlitz and leaps down the five stools to the Macson guy and cracks him over the head with the Schlitz. Blood and beer spray all over the place, the Macson guy goes down instantly, and Mister Know-it-all takes a swing at Roland, but Roland decks him, and then two more guys jump on his back and the coach tries to get in the middle, and he gets slugged, and, all of a sudden, Roland slams one of the guys down on the floor and pins the last guy up against a wall, and then a gunshot goes off. The bartender yells for Roland to let go, and Roland turns around, and the bartender has a thirty-eight pointed at Wilson's face."

"Holy shit."

"Holy shit is right," Squirrel said. "The bartender holds everybody in place and calls the cops, and guess who gets dragged in? Not the assholes who started it all, but Wilson. Big surprise there, huh?"

"Squirrel, I gotta tell you something," Jade said, but Squirrel cut him off.

"It gets worse. While Roland gets cuffed and dragged out of the VFW, his old coach acts like he doesn't even know him. Then, they get to the station and toss Roland in a cell, and, about an hour later, a cop comes into his cell and takes a couple gut-shots at Roland and starts asking him what he knows about the dead hooker. Roland doesn't give him anything, but that doesn't stop the cop from taking a few more free shots at him. Another hour goes by, and another cop comes into the cell and starts talking nicey-nice and tells him he remembers the great Roland Wilson from his glory days on the football field. All of a sudden, everybody's nice to Roland, and about a half hour later, his father, Doctor Wilson, shows up with one of Hafferty's goons, and Roland goes home with dad. But not before Roland lets the cops have a few of his favorite sarcastic expressions, and that really pisses off Doc Wilson, and when they get home, the dad takes the cops' side, and Roland goes berserk and runs out of the house."

Squirrel stood up at the flagpole and started pacing. Jade glanced around the yard and noticed a few of the men near the fence watching them.

"Roland's old man can't catch his son, so he calls Hafferty's goon squad for help. The goons find him and drag him home. They're up all night arguing and at some point, Hafferty himself shows up and finally gets Roland to calm down. Now it's getting light outside, so everybody leaves, and Roland goes to bed, but he can't sleep, so he calls me. He says Hafferty was grilling him about someone at Macson knowing more about the hooker's accident. Roland isn't too clear on this, but he says Hafferty seemed really interested in talking to whoever at the plant might have witnessed the accident. Roland thinks Hafferty is talking about Mister Know-it-all at the bar, who works in The Forge, but Hafferty says it was somebody else. Somebody who works on The Line."

Squirrel stopped his pacing and looked at Jade. "Do you know who that 'somebody' is, Jade?"

Jade looked toward the men at the fence. More of them were gathering, huddling in small clusters. Jade felt his throat tighten.

"It was a new red Mustang," he said. "Know-it-all was right."

"What?"

"I was trying to tell you. It wasn't a black Firebird; it was a new red Mustang."

"How the hell do you know?"

"I saw the whole thing!" Jade blurted out, a bit too loud. He looked toward the men at the fence, and Squirrel gave him the hairy eyeball. "The girl almost killed me with her goddamn car. It was my first day on the job. I was heading here on Canton, and this red Mustang jumped the curb twenty feet away, barreled right at me, and all of a sudden, it crashed into a fire hydrant right in front of me! It felt like a bomb blowing up in my face. I wasn't even sure I was alive."

"You saw this?!" Squirrel whispered.

"Saw it? I almost ate it!" Jade said. "The cops came and pulled me aside, and I watched that girl get yanked out of the wreck, then die right in front of me on the stretcher, and nobody flinched. They just hauled her body away like it was the carcass of an old dog. The cops made me wait in their squad car, and I heard the plant whistle, and I knew I was late for my first day, but my head was pounding, and I was shaking like I was freezing to death. In June."

"Did you tell Roland any of this?" Squirrel was leaning into Jade's face.

Jade hissed. "Are you kidding? Wilson wasn't exactly the Macson welcome wagon on my first day. And then I almost got killed again at the end of the day by the forklift loaded with shells."

Squirrel straightened up and smiled. "Oh, yeah. That was a good one. Great start on the new job. Roland saved your life, didn't he?"

"Yeah. He probably regrets that move. But I never told him anything about the accident. Hafferty must have been fishing when he quizzed Roland, because Hafferty definitely knows I'm a witness. I'll bet he's checking to see if I'm telling anybody else about it."

"How does Hafferty know it was you?

"I told the foreman, the guy who met me at the gate that morning."

"Kranick? OK, no wonder Hafferty knows. Kranick's Jensen's tool. Was he quizzing you?"

"No. I thought he was going to fire me right there on the spot, so I just told him the truth, why I was almost an hour late. But when I started to talk about the accident, he shut me down. Said they'd look into it. Then he took me to The Line where I met my supervisor, Mr. Happy Wilson."

"What about the cops? They had you in their car. What did they ask you?"

Jade looked away, toward the men along the fence. He just shook his head. "Usual stuff, I guess. I was a witness."

"You didn't see any reporters or people other than the cops and the ambulance guys?"

"It was seven o'clock on a Monday morning, Squirrel. Not many people around. But lots of cop cars, lots of cops. I don't know any reporters, but the cops showed up so fast, it was like they were waiting around the corner. Their cars made a circle around the scene, some of them unmarked, and the cops pushed a few people away, kept the scene closed off. Some cops were rushing into the buildings around the scene."

"But you were right in the middle of it, a perfect view from the back seat of the squad car. Did you see anything happen inside that circle?"

Jade leaned forward, resting his forearms on his knees, his head down. He thought Squirrel was acting like a lawyer, seeming to know the answers to his questions before he asked them. Sometime after lunch, Jensen and possibly Hafferty would be grilling Jade with these same questions. He wanted to trust Squirrel, but he had too much to lose. He had to hear Jensen's and Hafferty's questions first. But Squirrel always had good inside info, something that could help Jade in the meeting. The tightrope he'd expected to walk in that meeting was already under his feet.

"Listen, man," he said to Squirrel, his head still down. "I never saw someone get killed before. That girl's face smashed against the windshield, her head twisted all wrong. And then she takes her last breath right in front of me. And the way they hauled her away like she was not even human. I didn't want to see much more. Even if I did, there was a big cop standing right next to my window, his fat ass blocking most of what I could see."

"OK, Jademan," Squirrel said, as he stood up. "That's cool. There's just one thing. Mister Know-it-all at the VFW said the Mustang was owned by a cop named Belden. That would be Joey Belden. Guess who his brother is?"

Jade lifted his head and stared at Squirrel. "No."

"That's right. Our own shop steward, Ren Belden. Sleaze runs deep in that family. Whole bunch of bad brothers. Grew up on the West End, most of them spent time in juvie, one of them's in jail now, and another one of them killed a grade school mate and got away with it. Couple of them are cops—Joey's a detective, one of them's a fireman, one's a County political hack, and our boy, Ren, is the union boss—all of them bought their jobs from politicians, and every one of them is on the take. Joey was one of the narcs in the black Galaxy who hassled us on Saturday near the Rez. Mutt 'n Jeff. He was Mutt, the short punk who did all the talking. Flashed his badge like it was his wannabe big dick. Napoleon narc. Has a rep for shaking down whores, pimps, and dealers, and gets a City paycheck on top of it all for saving us ever-so-grateful citizens from all those bad, bad people. And the tall guy? Just found this out today: he's Billy Jensen. Our own General Patton's kid brother."

He watched Jade's reaction and then pushed his rodent nose toward him.

"You know their faces, Jademan. Were they at the Mustang scene? Was the black Galaxy one of those unmarked cars you saw?"

Jade swallowed hard and shook his head and lowered it into his hands. "I don't know, man. Maybe. All I could think of was the dead girl. And, like I said, I couldn't see much around that fat cop."

Squirrel was silent for a long moment. "Cool, man," he said, finally. "Finish your lunch. The whistle's gonna blow in about two minutes. And don't look so glum. Pull your head up and stand tall. That asshole, Dimmock, is watching us right now in the doorway to The Line. Just to let you know, he's one of Ren Belden's lackeys, his German Shepherd. Your good buddy Cheese is putting heat on Ren, starting a war inside the union, so he can take Ren's shop steward post, among other things. Like getting his hands on the money he thinks Ren is getting from Hafferty to keep the union in check. If Dimmock thinks you know something about Ren's brother that could hurt Ren, he won't hesitate to pull the info out of you the hard way. If you know what I mean."

Jade grabbed his lunch bag and stood up. "Is Wilson coming back?"

Squirrel smiled and pushed back his shoulders. "Roland Wilson always gets back up. And when he does, he's always stronger."

Just before the mid-afternoon break, Kranick, the foreman, appeared at The Line and signaled to Dimmock. Jade continued to flip shells on The Line but kept an eye on the two men. They were looking in his direction while the foreman did the talking, and then Dimmock signaled to Jade to join them.

"Jensen wants to see you," Kranick shouted. "Follow me."

Jade glanced at Dimmock and was met with the dead-eye stare. Dimmock stepped toward Jade and brushed him with his shoulder and then sauntered toward The Line.

The trek through the building felt like a long, slow perp walk. Kranick strode ahead of Jade as they headed toward the huge doorway to the courtyard. All around him, Jade heard the machines pause, including The Line, and the men stood at their stations, watching. Jade glanced at a few of them but made direct eye contact with just one—Ren Beldon, the dumpy little bald man who sat above the floor on his honing platform like the rooster of the hen house. Jade watched a slow grin creep across the thin line of Belden's tight little mouth, followed by a barely discernible head nod. Message sent.

In the tiny room outside Jensen's office, Jade sat on a metal chair watching Dorothy bang away on her typewriter, her heavy gray face scowling at the hand-written page on her desk. He'd greeted her when Kranick had left him there, but she'd ignored him, her head bowed to her work. He could hear Jensen and Marion arguing behind the office door, their voices loud enough for Jade to hear Jensen say something about Joey Belden and his hookers, and Marion saying whores were one thing, but Billy breaking Papa G's rules on drugs was going too far. His voice lowered, and he said something about melons and lasagna, and then a commanding third voice shouted him down and all went silent. Jade leaned in to listen for more when the office door sprung open. He nearly jumped out of his chair.

"Come right in, son, we've been waiting for you!"

It was Hafferty in Jensen's doorway, with his dayglow smile on, his thick glasses reflecting the sallow ceiling light in Dorothy's little chamber. He stuck out his big paw, and Jade grasped the hand without looking at Hafferty and stepped into Jensen's office, casting a glance at Marion and Jensen.

"How's my boy today? Second week on the job, huh?" Hafferty was beaming at him in full politician mode. "The Forge is cranking 'em out this week, so I hope those big muscles you've got are up to the challenge." He gave Jade's shoulder a soft punch as Jade started to move slowly toward the chair against the wall.

All three men had their shirt sleeves rolled up and cigarettes in their fingers. A rattling fan on a stand in the far corner tossed the smoke around the room, and the windows next to Jensen's desk were all the way up. "A little stuffy in here," Hafferty said, "so we'll make this quick."

Jensen lounged with his feet on his desk and his hands behind his small round head, while Marion slumped in the captain's chair alongside it, as they watched Hafferty stride back and forth on his stage. He looked more disheveled than usual. His pressed white shirt was wrinkled, with sweat stains under the arms, his red suspenders pulled taut against his bulging girth, the bottom of his shirt coming loose from his pants.

"I decided to stop by today, because I wanted to hear your report firsthand, son," Hafferty said in a tumid tone, as if he were launching his opening statement in a courtroom. Jade thought he was in for another pompous oration, but Hafferty stopped and turned his big body to face him, letting his hands fall to his sides. Then he nearly whispered. "It's not that I don't trust Mr. Jensen or Detective Marion. But I wanted to see your face when you reported what you saw last Monday. I wanted to watch you remember exactly what you witnessed while you were sitting there in the back of the squad car. Do tell us, Jade." He stepped toward the wall and pulled out another chair and sat across from Jade, his arms crossed on his vast belly, his legs splayed and a half-smile on his closed mouth.

Hafferty's odd antics gave Jade pause. He wondered if it was more than a report that Hafferty wanted. After hearing pieces of the argument from the other room, he thought that Hafferty might be giving him a cue, that he was asking him to play the part of an actor in an audition and that Hafferty was the director. Jade gave Jensen and Marion a blank look and then looked at Hafferty for another sign. When the big man's mouth turned up at the corner and one eyebrow arched, Jade took a deep breath and looked at Hafferty's coke bottle glasses, trying to find the center of his eyes in the fog of blue. He saw movement in one of the watery lenses and realized it was a wink.

"Like I told you before, Mr. Hafferty, I was pretty out of it," Jade said, "pretty shocked by what had just happened, the car almost killing me, and then the girl." He shook his head and lowered his gaze. "The ambulance guys, they just hauled her off, one guy lost his grip, and her head hit the ground, a sound I never heard before. And then they just…"

"We know that part, Jade," Hafferty said, coaxing, gentle, leaning forward so Jade could see his nodding face, his theater director's smile of encouragement. "Pretty awful stuff. But what else did you see, son? Who else was there? You recognize anybody?"

There was a supplicating tone to Hafferty's voice now, as if he were more priest than director, and Jade was the penitent. Jade licked his lips and glanced at the others before he returned to Hafferty's softened face. He opened his eyes wide, trying to look vulnerable, hoping this was what Hafferty was after. "There was a fat cop standing in front of my window, but I sat forward, and I could see a little of the action outside through the driver's window. It was chaos, Mr. Hafferty. Sirens, lights flashing, cops shouting, police cars moving in fast and skidding to a stop. After the ambulance took the girl away, I saw cops running into the buildings on Canton, and others chasing away people on the sidewalk. Lots of cops." Jade shifted his wide eyes to Jensen and then Marion. "It was a new red Mustang, not a Firebird like the paper reported. And the girl, they said in the paper she was from New York, but she wasn't. She's from here."

Marion stood up and pointed a finger at Jade. "We know about the fuckin' car, kid, and we don't wanna hear what you heard on the street about that whore! We wanna know what you saw, asshole."

Hafferty held up his hand without turning around, and Marion sat down. "Go ahead, son." The priest was now the good cop, and Jade almost smirked at him.

"I saw a black car; it was not a cop car. It pulled up next to the Mustang, and two guys got out," Jade said to Hafferty and then glanced at Marion and Jensen. Both leaned forward in their chairs. "They wore white shirts and ties, and the one guy, the shorter one with blond hair, he talked to two cops, and then the cops called over a bunch of other cops, and they made a blue wall around the back ends of the two cars. I couldn't see what was going on, but the two guys in ties were moving around back there, behind the wall of cops."

"Doing what, shithead?!" Jensen shouted. "Havin' a circle jerk?" He'd pitched himself from his chair and was standing behind his desk, his stogie clenched in a fist pointing at Jade.

Hafferty stood up and turned casually to Jensen and Marion. "We need to talk, gentlemen. The three of us. But first, I'd like a private moment with our witness here. So, take five, boys. Go have a piss and a smoke. I'm taking Mr. Flynn here for a short ride. It's too hot in this office for all of us. I'll be back." He held out his hand as if to show the men the way out, and Jensen and Marion shuffled to their feet, sulking like scolded children. As he walked behind Jensen, Marion kept his head down until he got to the doorway. Then he paused and shot Jade a baleful look. Jade tried to appear frightened; but he wanted to laugh in the man's face.

Hafferty drove and didn't say anything until the air conditioning had cooled the Fleetwood interior.

"You put on quite a show in there, son. You've come a long way in a short time. I think you're coming out of your shell. You're growing up fast in that nuthouse."

Jade smiled and glanced over at Hafferty, but the Commissioner looked straight ahead as he swung the car onto the street behind the plant and headed away from downtown. When he came to a stop sign, he turned to Jade.

"My boy Stanley," he said, pausing to catch Jade's eye. "He has a fractured skull, son. Still in critical care, in and out of consciousness. Whoever hit him on Saturday got him good. Must have used a tire iron or, Jesus, I don't know, maybe a hammer. Got a full swing at him. From behind. Stanley didn't have a chance. I sure hope he makes it. Sure don't want to have a homicide on our hands." He leaned his head back and froze Jade with that foggy look behind his glasses. "Do we?" His smile had no teeth.

Jade felt his neck heat up. He turned toward the windshield, and Hafferty pushed the pedal hard, and the Fleetwood sailed through the bumpy city streets, horns and sirens muffled outside the sealed womb of the Cadillac's interior.

"My mother is missing," Jade said. "Did you know that?" His voice almost squeaked. "Do you know where she is? Did you have somebody take her somewhere?"

Hafferty laid on the horn as a truck caused him to swerve the Fleetwood through an intersection. "Fuckin' idiot! Stupid asshole! I know that guy. He's never driven a sober moment in his life. Gonna kill somebody someday."

Jade sat up in his seat and turned to Hafferty. "The red Mustang wasn't stolen. A cop owns it. Ren Belden's brother."

Hafferty swung the car to the curb, put it in park, and left the engine running. They were under a tree in front of a block of row houses. He turned his big body in the seat, the leather squeaking underneath him. He pushed in the lighter on the dashboard and offered Jade a Benson & Hedges from the open box. Jade shook his head. The lighter popped, and Hafferty lit his cigarette and let out a stream of smoke that shrouded the windshield.

Jade looked out the side window toward the row homes. A porch light flicked on, and he saw a woman standing in the doorway in curlers and a housecoat staring at their car.

"I'm not telling you what I really saw at the back of that Mustang," Jade said, his voice steady, "until you tell me where my mother is and why Stanley tried to kill her."

Hafferty pushed a button, and the air conditioner kicked up a notch. When Jade turned, the Commissioner gave him his full fluorescent smile, his googly eyes softening to a blur behind the lenses. He wasn't the director or the priest now. He was the politician.

"You know what, son? I'm starting to like you more and more each time we meet. I think you've lived a sheltered life, under your mother's skirt. I'll bet you read too many books. Just like she used to. Gotta get out of your head, son. Live in *this* world. Yes, you got a little education working at the diner, all that chatter from those boneheads. But you were just an observer, no stake in the game. In fact, I don't think you've ever had a stake in *any* game. You really know nothing about people. You're self-contained, living in your own world. And you're no card player, that's for sure. But I'll tell you this: you're a quick study, son. I like the way you played along with me in that meeting just now, and I really like the way you just tried to leverage me. Let's just say you've learned all that from me. Like I said, you're quick. So here's your next lesson, kid. Don't ever tip your hand. Because now, I not only know every card you have, but I know every card you need. Now, I can play you however I want."

Jade forced himself to ignore the politician. He didn't want the priest or the director, either. He glared through Hafferty's thick lenses, through those foggy blue eyes, until he found what he was looking for. "I know you're more than who you say you are to me. And to my mother. Stanley's your bodyguard, your muscle, the guy you call when bad things need to happen. I've seen what he does to people. He was about to kill my mother. Why? Did you tell him to?"

Hafferty's smile disappeared. His shoulders softened. He turned toward the windshield and put his hands on the wheel. He was looking beyond the front of the car into the deep shadows of the gritty streets. His voice came out flat, remote, as if from another body. "Why do you think I gave you that full scholarship to Pell Academy, Jade? Why do you think I gave you the Macson job and a chance to go to college? For free. Who do you think gave you and your mother a place to live out there in Mell Hollow? For nothing. No obligations. Who do you think has kept your mother and you alive all these years?"

In a single move, Hafferty squelched his cigarette in the ashtray, pulled the gear lever into drive, and gunned the accelerator. The Fleetwood took off, and the car caromed around corners and bolted up side streets, coming to a screeching stop at the back garage doors of the Macson plant.

Hafferty put the gear shift in park, shoved in the lighter, and grabbed another cigarette from the box on the seat between them. He talked to the dashboard, the car still running, the air conditioning blasting. "I have no idea where your mother is. I can find her, if you'd like. But I don't think she wants to be found. And Stanley? He'll live. But when he recovers, he'll move away. Somewhere far away." The lighter popped, and he lit the cigarette and pulled a long drag, the coals at the end throwing a red cast on his big face. He turned and stared at Jade, his exhale cloud gliding an inch over Jade's head. "As for what you know, I already know it all. I'm not just the other card player here, son. I'm the dealer. Joey Belden and his partner unloaded grocery bags filled with pills, marijuana, and heroin from that Mustang, surrounded by cops, and they stowed them into the trunk of Joey's unmarked detective car, a black Galaxy. There's a crackdown in Mexico, and everybody's trying to make a killing on rising pot prices, including those two idiots. Now they're messing with heroin, speed, everything. And people like that colored girl are starting to die."

He took another drag on his cigarette and looked out his side window. "They pulled something else from that Mustang trunk, son. Something cumbersome. It took both guys to make the transfer to their car. It's what everybody's so worried about." He sucked on his cigarette and then punched it out in the ashtray and glanced at Jade through the side of his thick lenses. "And you forgot to mention the tarp the cops held over the backs of the Mustang and the Galaxy, in case someone was watching from one of the buildings above."

He shifted his big body to face Jade full on, his eyes visible now and soft, his smile real, just a thin line, no teeth. "Remember what I told you in the back room of Wally's the day I came to put out the Red Larkin fire? About eyes and ears? Those cops giving Joey and Billy cover behind the Galaxy and the Mustang? Those are trained eyes and ears. But our GM, Jerry Jensen, or even Marion, our fine Detective Captain, don't hear what I hear from those cops. Or see what I see. Jensen and Marion know about the drugs. But the body? They'll only know about it if it shows up somewhere. Right now, they smell a bad scent, and they were counting on you to tell them what it was. But you played it right, Jade. And by the time they find out, maybe it'll be too late for them."

Jade's heart was pounding, but he felt a calmness in his gut—the harbor of his fears. There was a loosening there, as if someone had pulled on a string that set free a suffocating cincture.

"We have a deal, you and I," Hafferty said, his business voice returning. He turned off the motor, and the cabin of the car seemed to shut down, leaving the trapped pressure of silence in Jade's ears. He could see a sliver of light emerging as the smaller door in the factory wall opened slowly. He expected to see the big guy in the greasy coveralls, but the door opened only enough to let out a narrow column of interior light. Hafferty turned his full bulky frame to face Jade again. "You're my eyes and ears inside this place. I need to know what's being said, who says it, when, and who they say it to. You have to mix it up, son. You've got crappy people moves, but you're gonna have to step it up anyway. Open up a little. Learn how to make somebody laugh, for Chrissake, get 'em to let their guard down. Let them talk. Guys here, they love to sound off. All you have to do is give them an ear."

Jade nodded and looked toward the door as more light emerged, framing the figure of a large man. Hafferty held up his index finger and the door slid closed, snuffing the light.

"You need to know this," he continued, his eyes on the door where the man's feet cast shadows at the bottom. "Ren Belden is losing his grip on the union, and now his brother is making another mess. Meanwhile, that idiot, Cheese Mulgrew, might just muscle Belden aside. But he's a brainless bully. The union needs new leadership, but don't get yourself in the middle of all that. It'll work itself out. Just keep your ears open, and for cryin' out loud, don't be so goddamned standoffish. Mix it up with these guys. They're not all idiots, even though they act like they are."

He punched out his cigarette in the ashtray, turned once more to Jade and put his meaty hand on Jade's forearm, engulfing it in a solid grip. "Behavior," he said, his eyes meeting Jade's. "That's my commodity, son. Not money, not coal in the ground, not real estate, or even banks or fancy mansions. All those things disappear over time, some sooner than you expect. But people, they'll always be around. Hell, there are two billion people on this planet, and billions more coming. How they behave and what they want—those are commodities that will never go away. That's what I deal in. People's behavior. The more you know about them—what they do, what they want, and what they think they want—the more you can predict what they'll do for it. And the more you can predict that, the more power you have. The guy with the most information about people—individuals, tribes, nations—is the guy who will have the world in his grip.

"Mark my words, son. People's behavior will be the commodity of the future. And it will be a gold mine for those who know how to use it."

He unloosed his grip on Jade's arm and tapped on the horn. The garage doors parted. "Just go back to your post, Jade. I'll handle Jensen and Marion. And one more thing. Roland Wilson. You already know he's on our team. But keep your distance, like I told you. Think of yourselves as separate agents in the field. Gathering information. Eyes and ears." He turned to Jade, pointed his thick finger at him, and flashed his fluorescent smile. "You're gathering information about behavior. It's the ultimate commodity. Enjoy the power, son. You'll know it when you get it."

As the Fleetwood glided along the tunnel inside the Macson walls and pulled to stop at Jensen's back entrance, Hafferty lit another cigarette and pressed his shoulders back, sitting up tall. "You can probably guess that Roland's absence today was not due to illness. He's never been sick a day in his life. He needed a little detention for bad behavior, that's all. He'll be back tomorrow. But I want you to know this about our good pal, Roland Wilson. He didn't win a scholarship to Penn State a year ago. He was One-A, just like you, draft eligible, Vietnam ready. Unlike you, the Army would not need to spend time getting him ready. He's a physical specimen. A warrior in waiting. No college wanted him, because he never completed his high school degree. Even the idiot colleges that look the other way just to grab a colored guy who can put up the sports numbers for them. His academic record was that bad."

Hafferty exhaled a bank of smoke at the windshield, the spew billowing around Jade's head like a culm dump cloud. He turned to Jade and offered his luminescent smile. Jade met it with a stunned frown.

"I was the one who got him into Penn State, son, and it wasn't on scholarship. He probably didn't tell you he spent his freshman year red-shirted, and, if it wasn't for me, he'd be booted out of there. He works out with the football team, but he works even harder with the girls. He doesn't drink or do drugs. But the girls, Christ Almighty. They line up at his dorm room door like they're in a fuck factory—White girls, colored girls, spics, chinks—all kinds and all of them young and beautiful. I've warned him a thousand times about his schoolwork, but he can barely show up for class. He's majoring in pussy and minoring in football practice. Meanwhile, this summer, he's on a short leash. And, yesterday, he almost fucked himself entirely. If he doesn't stay out of trouble here this summer and then shape up at Penn State this fall, I'll have no choice. He'll be drafted. And both he and his father know it. He's a very bright young man, but he's got a hair up his ass about school. It's almost as if he's trying to fail just to piss off his father—the professor, the amazing scientist, the man who hates to play a stereotype and hates it even more when his son fulfills it. Dr. Wilson is one of my oldest friends, and I've been a godfather to Roland since he was a child. I cannot stand to see Roland do this to himself, but perhaps he needs to learn the hard way. It's entirely up to him. In a world where behavior predicts patterns, I don't need to tell you where he's headed."

Jade was shaking his head. "He doesn't date White girls."

Hafferty barked out a laugh. "Date? We're not talking *dates* here, son. His pal Bozak might have told you Roland never did White girls around here, because it was the only rule his father gave him that he ever followed. This isn't Jersey, where you came from. This valley is snowy white, in case you haven't noticed. Couple hundred thousand Caucasian people spread along a twenty-mile river valley, but it's really a small town. And prejudice here? Well, no one knows about it better than a man like Dr. Wilson, and that's why he enforced that rule with his son. People around here hate the coloreds, especially with all this Black Power madness coming on now. But out at Penn State, middle of nowhere, fifteen thousand college kids, it's a free-for-all. No one threatens to kill a colored guy walking across campus holding hands with a White girl. Provided he stays on campus. And Penn State has an endless supply of free-minded girls. That's college life in 1969, son. Something you should keep in mind for yourself."

The fluorescent smile lit up the interior of the car. And this time, there was no doubt about the wink.

36
Invitation

She crumpled the empty pack, dropped it on the porch floor, and watched a gust from the bay toss it into a corner, jamming it under the rail of a white wicker rocking chair, one of three empty rockers. She tilted back in hers, feeling old, tasting the first sweet drag of her last Lucky, and watching a growing flock of terns pick at a small black mound near the bandstand. The town was still abandoned, the sun still absent, and a bay breeze brought swarms of green biting flies, keeping her off the beach.

Her breakfast had been cold again, the bath water lukewarm. There was no one else staying in the place, and yet the owner, Mrs. Schwartz, had treated her like a leper. When she had paid up front, the old lady's nose pinched up, her mouth puckering, her eyes scouring her like a bristle brush from head to toe. She could feel the old lady's contempt, not just for her appearance, but for her independence, a bitter disdain for any woman who didn't look like a shiny housewife with kids in tow in the shadow of a solid husband.

She told Mrs. Schwartz that the bath water was cold again, but the old lady just shrugged and asked how many more nights she'd intended to stay, as if the haunted Vacancy sign squeaking in the wind on the front porch was just a prop.

She knew by now it wasn't going to happen. More than twenty-four hours had gone by and still no Lenny. She knew the lights would not come up for her final act. Lenny had stage fright. She wondered who had put it into him.

On Monday evening, she'd used the pay phone across the street in front of Thompson Drugs to call him. He said Zeke needed another day; it was the carburetor. She asked him to come to the B&B, but he said no, all tied up. So she went right at it and asked him for the favor. There was a long silence; she thought the line had gone dead. Finally, he said he would make some calls, then come by the B&B.

After Lenny had hung up, she called home, but Jade hadn't answered, so she called the diner and asked Wally to pass a message to Jade if he stopped by. Wally told her she was in luck; Jade was there having dinner after work. "Before I put him on," Wally said in a low voice, "I must tell you something very important. Jade's supervisor at Macson is someone you know."

After a long drag on her Lucky, she said casually, "And who would that be, Wally?"

"Roland Wilson."

The smoke burst from her lungs, and she pitched forward in a coughing fit. Wally apologized, but, when she caught her breath, he apologized again and asked her if she was OK.

"Of course," she said. "That makes perfect sense. For Dennis. Put my son on the phone please, Wally."

When Jade came to the phone, she told him she was safe and that he should not go back to their house. He told her Mr. Hafferty had informed him Stanley was in the hospital in critical condition and unlikely to get back on his feet for a while, and that, if and when he does, he would go away. He would disappear. She sniffed at that, reminding Jade that she'd warned him about that Hafferty trait—he makes people disappear. Still, she said she couldn't trust Hafferty, and that she would not come back to their house, insisting that Jade stay elsewhere—at Lucy's or at another friend's home. Jade let out a sigh of exasperation and said all those options were impossible, that he'd stay at home, and that he had her gun for protection. She corrected him. She had the pistol. She'd found it easily before she left home. She told him to stay at a hotel in Ebonton, that he'd find money to pay for it in her closet, more than enough for a few days at the hotel until she could return. He declined, complaining that she'd found her gun. She asked him to take the money to Wally, that it wasn't safe leaving it at home, that Stanley's people would come to search the house. Jade said the money belonged to them, so let them take it back. When he said, "I won't touch that money," his voice had a hollow sound she recognized as her own.

After rewinding that conversation in her head a few times, she pulled one last drag on her Lucky, flicked it over the railing, and stood up to head to Thompsons for a new pack. She paused at the edge of the porch and looked over to the corner of Third Street. The Thunderbird was just a block away on Atlantic. She figured Stevie was behind the bar, probably still looking like a kid, and she pictured herself nursing a whiskey and soda, a new pack of Luckys in front of her on the bar while she waited for Lenny, for the hundredth time. Seemed like yesterday.

She decided to skip the bar and started down the steps, heading for Thompsons. At the bottom, she glanced once more at the terns pecking at their dark feast and then found herself turning toward Third Street, a voiceless urge pulling her toward The Thunderbird.

At the corner, Lenny's truck pulled up in front of her. His thick hairy arm was wedged in the window frame, and he was smiling at her as if it were the first time.

"Headin' to The Bird, young lady? Come on, I'll give you a lift." He had that distant look of hope in his eyes, but he knew he'd already disappointed her. It was all over his face.

She started for the other side of the truck but changed her mind and walked to his window. He pulled his arm in, a sheepish grin struggling to stay in place on his thick jaw.

"Come up to my room," she said without smiling back. "We have things to go over."

Mrs. Schwartz's scowl evaporated when she saw Lenny striding through the front door. As they started for the steps, the old lady stood up, beaming at him. "Good to see you, Lenny. You take good care of that girl now, hear?"

In the room, she pointed to a chair and took off her boots and sprawled on the bed, holding herself up by her elbows. Lenny pulled out a pack of Luckys and held them out for her to catch. She held up a stop sign with her palm.

"I quit. Remember?"

He shrugged, tossed the Luckys on the bed, and lit a Marlboro for himself. "Got anything to drink in here?"

She shook her head. "Old Mrs. Schwartz treats you like a regular. Is this where you take your quickies?"

Lenny gasped out a cloud of smoke and coughed into his fist. His face flushed as he pulled his hand away from his mouth and shrugged at her.

She sniffed at him. "You still taking instructions on how to please a woman?"

He smiled, his face lighting up. "You want me to lock that door?"

She huffed out a laugh, the first in a long time. "You were a good trainee back then, Lenny. A rarity in a man, someone who would listen and actually try to please. Seems like you've forgotten how to do that. You already screwed me on this visit, Lenny. But not the way you used to, and not the way you'd hoped to."

He slumped back in the chair and took another drag on his cigarette. He blew a cloud at the cracked ceiling. His eyes widened. "Your target is too hot, Allie. Can't find anyone who'll touch it. Can't even ask. People up there are connected to people down here. You know how it is, one big family. If one of my guys steps into that arena, the blowback on me would be…" He shook his head and dropped his gaze to the floor.

He leaned forward, his arms on his knees, and looked up at her. "But listen. I can still help you. I talked with a guy who can put things straight for you."

She sat up on the bed and slid to her feet. She took a few steps toward him and pointed her finger at him. "I'm not gonna let you put your wandering cock in me, Lenny, so don't try to sweeten your sour copout with a line of bullshit. I didn't come here to get your rocks off for old time's sake. You owe me, and you know it. I wore the scarlet letter for you. I played the homewrecker so your kids would grow up with a daddy.

I was the seducer; you were the poor victim—the opposite of what really happened. I let you make it look like I pulled your cock out of your pants. I took the fall. Evil woman, banished from this town. The same woman who set up your family business and made you tons of money, made you the hero your wife couldn't kick out. You owe me, Lenny. I had a kid, too. Remember?"

She took two more steps toward him, and Lenny sat up straight. She put her hands on her hips and locked her eyes on him. "That man intends to kill my son and then kill me," she said, her teeth gritted. "I need him taken out. Now!"

Lenny held up a hand. "I talked to the man up there, a guy they call Papa G," he said, his voice shaky. "Stanley will disappear. Papa G guaranteed it. He knows you're here. And Stanley won't get close to your boy or to you ever again."

"You told Giallo I was here!" she hissed. "You fucking coward!"

Lenny got up and brushed by her. He turned to her with his hand on the doorknob. "You're smart enough to know how these things work, Allie. I made one phone call about this guy, Stanley, and the next thing I know, I'm talking to fucking Papa G, king of the hill where you live. It's a closed circuit. I could never talk to a guy like that in the old days, and now he's calling *me*. These people hear things before you even say them out loud."

"Get out." She turned and walked toward the window. "Get out!" she shouted.

"He knows where your girlfriend is, Allie. Stanley did not kill her."

She spun toward him and rushed at him in a flash, grabbing him by the shirt, her eyes on fire inches from his face. She shoved him into the door. "What the hell are you saying? What does that even mean? Are you trying to Sweet Charlotte me, Lenny? Play some sick game to make me think I'm out of my mind?"

Lenny didn't move. "Stanley got her, for sure. He was the one who grabbed her out of her place, and he probably roughed her up, maybe more than that. But he did not kill her. She was transported somewhere else."

She let go of his shirt and then grabbed it again. "You're a pathetic liar!"

Her fists were knotted at his throat, and he gently tugged at them, his eyes contrite, pleading with her. "He's willing to see you, Allie, if you want to know more. One visit, that's all you get. Ask him whatever you want. There's this guy named Hafferty, he said you'd know who he was. He said Hafferty won't know about your visit if you follow Papa G's instructions."

She let go of his shirt and sat on the bed. She lowered her head into her hands and ran her fingers through her hair, her heart punching at her chest. Her breaths came in gulps and gasps.

Lenny stepped toward her, and she sat up and shoved her palm at him, shaking her head. "Don't come near me."

"He knows where your boy's dad is, too," Lenny said. "Both of them are alive, Allie. Marte. Jake Levin. They were made to disappear. But they're not dead."

She shook her head slowly and stared into an empty space between them. "You're lying."

"Zeke's bringing your car here in an hour. Here's the number for Giallo." He dropped a matchbook on the bed next to her and went to the door.

"If you do go see him, Allie, know that he's old school. He won't tell you anything if you dress like you are now. And even if you change your look to suit him, there's no guarantee he'll say anything to cross Hafferty. Whoever Hafferty is, and no matter what you think about him, Giallo might hide stuff from him, but he will not go against him."

He opened the door a few inches and then closed it softly, waiting for her to stop sobbing. When she picked her head up to look at him, her cheeks were wet, her eyes puffy and bloodshot, lost. She knew he wanted to hold her, but he stood still.

She looked down at his shoes, shiny new Italian loafers. "Just go, will you? Please get out," she said, her voice cracking.

"One more thing, Allie. If Giallo gives you information, you must do what he says about it. If you cross him…"

She let out a squeal, a broken laugh. "What could he do to me that hasn't already been done?"

Lenny stepped close to her and put his hand on her cheek, rubbing at her tears with his thick thumb. "I'm sorry, Allie. I always loved you, always will. More than anyone. I know that sounds stupid, especially now. But I'm telling you about Giallo, because I know if you try to get rid of that Stanley guy on your own, you won't survive. The wrong people will make sure of that. He's the scum of the earth. His life will never be worth yours. No life will ever be worth yours."

She removed his hand from her face and wiped her cheeks with her palms. She looked up at him, cold and empty. "You're right, Lenny. That does sound stupid. All of it. Especially now."

37
Love It or Leave It

Tuesday, July 1, 1969

A soiled blanket of heat hung over the valley, fouling moods and bringing the burden of August to the beginning of July. The air had weight and a pervasive stench of rotten eggs, a poisonous swarm that clogged the lungs and sinuses of even the most benumbed natives of the old coal valley. Monday's cool start was a fleeting moment of spring that had expired by midday when the air turned moist, hot, and foul. By Tuesday at Macson, the burden was inescapable. Inside the sweltering bomb factory, the men moved in slow-motion. Blood was boiling, the mood cantankerous.

Jade was relieved that Wilson was back on the job, but they ignored each other and everyone else on The Line. Jade knew now that it was more than skin color that had kept Roland ostracized. Everyone in the plant knew about his allegiance to Hafferty, and now, all would assume the same about Jade. He felt connected to and yet further distanced from Wilson; they had something in common, but it wasn't something to brag about, or even to share. Hafferty had each of them in a different corner, alone. And both had the rest of the plant surrounding them. Just before the break, Jade caught the eye of Dimmock at the near end of the conveyor, the man's lethal glare smoldering in the suffocating air like a branding iron over a flame.

At the morning break, Jade and Roland chose to rest in separate slips of shadow along the factory wall, while their perch at the foot of the flagpole remained empty; above it, Old Glory hung limply, almost lost in the haze. Other men lingered along the wall, out of the sun, but Cheese and his sycophants clustered near the main entrance, smoking and casting wanton glances toward Jade and Roland and shouting angry taunts to passersby on the sidewalks beyond the fence.

Just before the end of the break, Squirrel dropped down next to Jade, as if out of mid-air. Jade was startled but had to chuckle when he saw Squirrel's expression—wide-eyed, shifting his head around like a cat, his face lurching back and forth in mock desperation.

"They're after me!" he stage-whispered to Jade out of the side of his mouth. They're after my soul, Mr. Flynn! Call me Faustus, if you will, but my real name is Dr. Faucet, as in devil-dealing sperm spewer. But this time, there's no deal making, no choice. My soul is doomed, like it or not." He pushed his vermin nose closer to Jade. "And what do I get in exchange, you ask? What's my gain for a lost soul in a one-sided bargain? Well, I'll tell you. I get to have a bigger dick! Sold my soul and got a twelve-inch snake in my trousers! Ladies of the night, behold! Women of the world, lay down your asses! Faucet's massive reptile is on the move!"

Squirrel fell onto his side, cackling. Jade chuckled at him, marveling at his energy in such heat. He glanced around the yard to measure the reaction to Squirrel's outburst. Cheese and his men glared at them, and other workers along the walls stopped their grumbling conversations, held their cigarettes in mid-motion, and gawked at this odd burst of theater. Jade glanced over at Roland and saw that his eyes were closed and his head against the wall, and he knew the unflappable Wilson was tuned in but immune to his friend's antics.

Squirrel leaned toward Jade with his silly grin still in place. But now, he spoke in a serious tone, using his smile as a cover, speed-talking in a single breath while barely moving his lips. "Everyone knows you talked to Hafferty, but Jensen's not saying what was said. He's got his boys in the mix, and they're not with Cheese. They're with Belden. They know Cheese is planning a surprise strike on Monday, but no one's sure how many guys will walk with him. And while Jensen was mysterious about your conversation, he did say something to Ren Belden. It had to do with his brother, Joey. And Jensen's brother, Billy. Our pals Mutt and Jeff from the Rez. Narcs Incorporated. They're in some kind of trouble about that car wreck. And you are the star witness."

Squirrel wiped the fake smile off his face and jumped to his feet. He bent over to adjust his shoes and muttered to Jade before walking away. "Cheese's boys are hot about Wilson's bar brawl. They want him dead. We need to talk. You, me, Wilson. After work. We'll meet at Wally's at six. I know you can arrange that with Wally."

Jade watched Squirrel head for the entrance to his wing of the plant. A moment later, he was startled to his feet by the piercing wail of the whistle.

The heat inside was so oppressive that no one had the energy to do more than the very minimum, trudging heavily through the motions of their jobs like a chain gang on a forced march. At lunch, the men were listless and silent, shuffling to the shadows, heads down, feet dragging. The air was choked with soot from The Forge, trapped by the valley's heavy gray drape of cloud and culm smoke. This unrelenting turn in the weather soured Jade's expectations for the summer of liberation he'd been counting on. For his freedom, he realized now, he would have to pay some painful dues.

The plant whistle at the end of the day was met with a collective sigh of relief, and the machines came to a halt in unison for the first time since Jade had started the job. The line at the punch clock moved swiftly, the mass exit solemn, the workers stricken by the notion that the Friday holiday was still a long way off, and that weather like this so early in the summer promised little to look forward to.

Jade was barely around the corner on Canton Avenue heading toward the bus station when a shiny red pickup pulled alongside him at the curb. He looked over at the driver. Ren Belden.

"Hop in, kid, I'll give you a lift," Belden said, attempting a genuine smile. His pickup rolled along at Jade's walking pace.

"Thanks," Jade said, "but I'll catch the bus." He kept his pace, looking ahead. He wiped a river of sweat from his brow and shook his dripping hand out to his side. His boots were dead weights. He glanced at Belden's truck tracking him. He looked ahead for his bus stop co-worker, Gort, hoping he could catch up to him, maybe break the ice with him. But Belden persisted.

"Suit yourself, Flynn. Catch the bus," Belden called. "But if you were smart, you'd stop for a second and listen to what I have to tell you. It's about you and Hafferty. I know what he said to you yesterday."

Jade slowed and looked over at the little man behind the wheel of his sparkling F-150. Even before Saturday at the rez, when Squirrel had warned Jade about Belden, Jade had been leery of the little man. He'd often looked up at him and sensed something off about the peculiar man, up there on his elevated platform—hairless and smug, a human dumpling on a pedestal. Belden acted like a god but seemed more like a blubbery ball of flesh with mechanical parts, shifting his arms and legs in unison with the levers and pedals, his head and eyes swiveling back and forth like a robot's as he surveyed The Line and the floor beneath his throne. Watching everyone. Jade stopped walking and peered into the cab of the truck.

Belden waved him to the shotgun door. Jade took one more look for Gort, but the guy was nowhere in sight. He poked his head into the window frame, looked at Belden's face and then down toward the seat at what Belden was holding. It was a long-barreled pistol pointed at Jade's face. Belden barked at him.

"Get in the fuckin' truck, asshole!" He moved the gun closer to Jade. "I could either shoot you right here on the street or hunt you down if you don't get in the goddamn truck right now! I know where you live, and I know your mommy ain't home to hide you under her skirt. If you don't get in the fuckin' truck, you'll find a very unpleasant surprise waiting for you at your little brown shack in Mell Hollow."

As Jade opened the door, he saw Belden put the gun under the seat between his knees. He noticed a rifle on a gun rack over the cab's back window, and two bumper stickers on the window. He made a crinkling sound as he sat down. The seat was covered in clear, thick plastic. The dashboard sparkled and the red floor carpet looked brand new. The little man gripped the shiny steering wheel and slipped the truck into traffic.

"Just shut your fuckin' trap and listen to me," he said without looking at Jade. "This ride won't cost you nothin'. You can spend your bus fare on a pack of rubbers. You might not have this job for long, so you don't wanna knock up that pretty little half-breed cunt of yours, Lucy Melburn." He leered at Jade and watched him swallow hard. "Juicy Lucy."

Belden glided the truck at a crawl past the bus station. Jade spied Gort waiting in line for the 15.

"Don't worry about him," Belden said. "He don't know much, and he can't help you. He wasn't tryin' to be your friend when he picked you up in the shitter after Cheese worked you over."

He looked at Belden and, this time, a genuine smirk appeared at the corner of the man's stingy mouth. He shifted the truck into third gear too soon, and the cab bounced a few times before coming to a smooth glide.

"There ain't much I don't know, kid," Belden gushed. "I know every move in that plant. That's why this ride'll be a lucky stroke for you if you pay attention. Macson ain't just a good place to work; it's the only place in this fuckin' valley worth the time you put in. Nobody gets the scale we get, and if you're smart and keep your little asshole clean, you'll get into the union and get some of the gettin', too."

"Cheese told me there was no way I was ever gonna get into the union," Jade said.

"You listen to me, kid," Belden said, weaving his slow-moving truck carefully around potholes and broken glass along Reston Street. "You'll get in the union if I say you get in. I'm shop steward, not Cheese. He'd like to be, but Hafferty and Jensen don't want that to happen. And, as long as I'm around, it never will."

Belden popped the gear lever into neutral and coasted to a stop at a traffic signal near Wally's Diner. "That nigger pal of yours? Wilson? He's got himself in a nice jam with Cheese and his boys. I did Hafferty a favor by lettin' Wilson in the union, but now our football star has really fucked it up. Cheese and his boys want Wilson's jig ass in cement at the bottom of The Filthy after what he done at the VFW Sunday night. Stupid coon. He goddamn almost killed one of our boys. You don't fuck with us like that. If Hafferty didn't step in, Cheese would have strangled that nigger as soon as he stepped out of the pokey Sunday night."

"How did Hafferty stop Cheese?" Jade said.

Belden chuckled. The light flicked green, and Belden slowly let out the clutch, drifting into the intersection to check both ways for red light runners.

"For now, all you need to know is this. You want in the union, you do what I tell you. Hafferty and Jensen and me, we'll protect you from Cheese as long as you do what we say. Wilson has our protection for the time being, not because we like his black ass, but because Hafferty wants us to lay off."

Jade could see the roofline of Wally's Diner among the litter of retail signs along Reston.

"And I know what your deal is with Hafferty," Belden said, glancing over at Jade, his close-set dark eyes following Jade's toward the diner.

"Did Jensen tell you about our meeting?" Jade said. "Or do you have listening devices all over the plant?"

"Don't get smart with me, you skinny fuck," Belden snarled. "You get out of line with me, and you won't make it through the rest of this week, never mind gettin' into our union." He reached under the seat and put the pistol in his lap. "You see this weapon, boy? Don't think for one second I won't use it. On you, on your nigger friend, on your mother, or on your Juicy Lucy cunt! Or on that scumbag Bozak—that pain-in-the-ass, rat-faced friend of you and Wilson. That slime sticks his wet nose in places where it don't belong, and one day he's gonna get it shot off. And you can tell him I said so."

They passed Wally's at a slow coast. Jade slid low in his seat and peered at the diner windows.

"Miss your old job, boy?" Belden growled. "Miss that sassy little waitress? What's her name? Dee? Mmm. Some hummer she gives. All the boys like Dee. Great legs. Nice tits. Great ass. Great lips." He forced a chuckle, and Jade turned to see him run his stubby fingers over the barrel of his gun.

Jade gripped the door handle and stared straight ahead, his jaw tightening. They drove in silence until they crossed the line into Mell Hollow.

"I'll tell you what, Flynn. I know Hafferty thinks you're his, but if you think he'll protect you at all times, think again. Same goes for your nigger partner. Hafferty can't hang over that boy like a guardian fuckin' angel twenty-four hours a day. You tell that Black Power boon to watch his ass. I'll do my best to keep Cheese and his boys away from you two, but we can't guarantee nothin'. And, as for that deal you got with Hafferty? Keepin' you outta the army is one thing, but you gotta deliver on the other side. When Hafferty wants something, you gotta give it to him."

Jade turned to Belden. "How'd you know about that?"

The little man just smiled as he pulled the truck along the curb a block from Jade's house. He turned his head slowly toward Jade and mimed a solicitous look. "If you have somethin' you wanna tell Hafferty about that accident, son, you don't have to wait for him to show up at the plant. You can tell me. Those two guys in shirts and ties you saw at the wreck? You recognize them? Cuz they recognized you. They saw you watchin' from the squad car. And they know who you are, and they know your rat-faced friend, too." He raised his pudgy fist and pointed a finger at Jade's face. "If you ID them to anyone—*any*one—you won't just get eighty-sixed from your job. They know where you live, they know when your mommy disappears for a week or two, and they know where Juicy

Lucy lives, over there on Liberty Street in the Backend. Pretty girl. Hate to see what could happen to her."

He looked toward the road again. "You see that house right there? The gray one with the broken fence. That's your pal Smitty's, your bus riding partner, the guy who picked you up off the shitter floor last week. Like I said, Smitty don't know nothin', but he'll be watchin' you. He can see your house from here, and he'll know your every move. He knows somethin' else, too. He knows who butters his bread."

Belden pulled the shift lever into first gear and put the gun under his seat again. "Remember. You tell me, not nobody else." He shoved his pug nose at Jade and raised his eyebrows. "You can walk from here, boy."

Jade watched Belden's truck slip away from the curb. The window stickers were red, white and blue. *Wallace for President* and *America: Love It or Leave It*. He thought he heard a little toot from the truck's horn.

On the sidewalk, the air felt cool against his sopping shirt and dungarees. He looked up at the gray house and shook his head, deciding Gort was a much better name than Smitty. Then he looked down the street to his own house. The tilted chimney seemed closer than ever to tumbling sideways.

38
Squirrel's Plot

Tuesday, July 1, 1969

Jade started to tell Louise the story when she cut him off and put him on hold. A minute later, Hafferty came on the line.

"So how's my new agent in the field doing? Got something worthwhile for me?"

Jade's heart was pounding. After his ride with Belden, he had hoped to find Alice home, but the house had been empty, closed up, and stuffy. After a cool bath, he'd called Wally to arrange the meeting in the diner office at six with Squirrel and Roland. Then he put his story in order and called Hafferty's number. But now, Hafferty's voice rattled him, and he blurted out the first thing he thought Hafferty would want to hear.

"Cheese is planning a walk-out on Monday."

Hafferty snorted on the other end. "Did he ask you to strike with him?"

"No. I didn't talk to him. I just heard."

"I know all about our boy, Cheese. He's in for a surprise. Do you read the newspapers, kid?"

"Sometimes. I used to every day at Wally's, but not lately."

228

"Read the morning paper tomorrow before you go to work. Front page article will be about that *Life* magazine story with all those soldiers who died in Vietnam. Cover of the goddam magazine was filled with their pictures. The story had two hundred and some names and photos. You might have heard about it."

"No, I—"

"Well, you will. Seven of those guys, we know they were from here, our county. The goddamn peaceniks in Washington and New York are raising hell over the story, and I happen to know that a local reporter has talked with our Congressman Walsh about it. He asked Walsh what impact this story would have on Macson jobs, and our dear Congressman said it would have none. But the reporter called back a few hours later and said he was holding a copy of the Macson contract with the Defense Department and that it expires at the end of this year. Of course, we don't know how the reporter got hold of that copy, but the Congressman, being well-informed himself, assured the reporter that the contract would be renewed, and no jobs would be lost at Macson. So, we know what the reporter will lead with—jobs will be lost at Macson. I'm surprised you didn't hear about that *Life* story at the plant. The boys must be talking about it by now."

"No. Just the strike by Cheese and his guys. Starts Monday."

"There will be no strike, son. After our boys at the plant read tomorrow's paper, they will be shit-scared about the war ending and their jobs disappearing. Nobody, especially that lug, Cheese, is gonna convince union guys to strike when their jobs are about to disappear. Problem solved. Big Cheese will melt, and Belden will remain shop steward. At least until I can get a man with half a brain to take his place."

"So what about that contract? If it ends in December, won't a lot of guys lose their jobs?"

"Listen, kid. You and Roland don't have to worry about that. You'll be in college in September. You let me and the Congressman worry about that contract. There's no way the United States of America is going to just fold its tent and walk away from that war. Believe me, I know our President. Personally. He's playing games with the peaceniks. His troop drawdown announced on Sunday? That's a decoy. He wants to win that goddamn war. And he will. He already has a counter move under way, a secret surprise for those gooks. No matter what some of those limp-wristed girly boys on The Hill say, we *will* stop Communism right there. And Macson will keep supplying the ordnance to do it."

Hafferty's voice became muffled, and Jade realized he was holding his hand over the mouthpiece, talking with someone in his office. He came back on with a bark. "You keep that to yourself, son! Don't say a thing on the job. Just wait for the reactions from the morning paper. Wait, watch, listen. Eyes and ears, kid. Eyes and ears."

"There's something else," Jade said.

"Make it fast, son," Hafferty muttered. "I'm on the run."

"Ren Belden knows everything we talked about. He gave me a ride home from work today. Even though I said no. He held a gun on me."

Hafferty's laugh sounded like an explosion on the other end. "Jesus Christ! Did he pull his Colt .45 on you, kid? You know why a guy like him carries around a cannon like that? Well, the answer is on his wife's face. He provides her with a good living, but she's the most miserable woman on the planet. What does that tell you? The man has a little problem in his pants. Very little. He loves waving that cowboy cannon around, but he wouldn't know what to do with it. Whatever he told you, pay no attention. He's crapping in his panties about Cheese, and he's scrambling for cover."

"But he told me he knew the deal you offered me, about the draft and college. And he told me Cheese was aiming to kill Roland Wilson. And that if I said anything to anyone about the two guys at the car wreck, his brother Joey would do something to me and my mother and my girlfriend."

There was a pause at the other end. Jade could hear Hafferty breathing. "You tell anybody else about this? Wilson? Bozak? Your girlfriend?"

"No."

"Your mother there with you? You tell her?"

"No. I thought you might know where she is."

"Listen, wise guy. I told you before. I don't follow her around. So you listen to me. The Macson plant is like a goddamn leaky faucet. Can't keep a conversation private anywhere on the site. I have a good idea about how Belden heard what you and I discussed, but it doesn't matter. I will deal with him. He'll have his little steward job secured come tomorrow, at least for the time being. Don't worry about his threats. He's from a nutcase family, but he's all talk and no action. Just like his tiny dick, his balls are useless."

"What about Roland? Belden told me Cheese and the guys are gunning for him over that fight at the VFW—the Macson guy Roland hit over the head with a beer bottle."

"Roland's a big boy. He can take care of himself. He's been a colored kid in this white bread valley for most of his life, for Chrissake. You think this is the first time he's been threatened? Think again, kid. He took down three guys at once in that bar brawl, so he can certainly handle a broken old grunt like Cheese. Roland will be fine. You just keep your mouth shut, your ear to the ground, and your eyes on all the doors. I gotta go."

Jade was ten minutes late for the meeting at Wally's. When he pushed through the front door, he waved to Wilma, nodded a thanks to Wally, and rushed into the kitchen. A few steps from Wally's office door, Dee intercepted him and pushed him against the walk-in cooler, her face close to his, her finger on her lips. He could hear Squirrel and Roland arguing in the office.

"Look," Dee said, gritting her teeth up at Jade and holding him by the shoulder. "Last week, you let Wally rent to that colored girl, and now we have another one—the colored football player. He came through the back door with a friend of yours. Wally said it was OK for them to be here with you, but I don't like it. If any of those people out there in the diner finds out, Wally's gonna have to close this place down!"

"Why, Dee?" Jade said, affronted and disappointed. "Because a Black guy is in the building?"

"No, Jade. It's because Wally keeps offering them protection, and it doesn't sit right with our clientele. You know what I mean."

"Protection! He's not protecting anyone, Dee. He's doing people favors. Like me, using his office. Wally makes his own choices, and he lives with them, Dee. That's his code. You know that. If he wants to help people, he's gonna do it, no matter what color they are or where they come from. And the thing he's taught me? He lives with the consequences, no matter what. If you're worried about losing business over this, maybe you're working for the wrong guy."

Dee let go of his shoulder and stepped back. She stared at him, her eyes swelling. "I love Wally as much as you do, kid. And I don't want to see him ruined over this, that's all." She put her hand on his face and stroked his cheek. "I don't know what you're getting yourself into with all these people, honey. I'm not just worried for Wally; I'm worried about you."

The lines on Dee's face were more exaggerated than ever, a streak of mascara spilling over the edge of her eye, her pancake make-up thick in all the wrong places. He thought about what Belden had said about Dee, and his stomach churned. He reached his arms out and pulled Dee to him. She folded into his chest and lifted her hips up against him. He fought off the sudden charge in his loins and tightened his arms around her, whispering, "It's OK, Dee. It's no big deal. I promise. And if anything goes wrong, you can blame me. Not Wally. I mean it."

Inside Wally's office, Jade found a role reversal. Roland was pacing back and forth while Squirrel was trying to calm him down.

"You're right," Squirrel said. "Everyone knows that asshole deserved a bottle over his head. But everyone at Macson also wants your black ass in a coffin over it. I'll bet half the guys right out there in the diner know about it and would look the other way if someone shot you dead at Wally's counter. You know how these guys are around here!"

Roland glared at Squirrel, then shifted his venom toward Jade. "What's this meeting about, Flynn? Why'd you drag me here? I don't need this."

Jade held up his palms. "Wait a minute—"

"It was my idea," Squirrel said. "I asked Jade to set it up. Everybody calm down for a minute and listen. Take a seat, Roland. Please."

"I'll stand," Roland said, crossing his arms over his chest. Jade picked a corner to lean into.

"No one's saying you can't look out for yourself, Ro," Squirrel said, waving his hands. "But the situation is bigger than that. You've got Cheese after you for the bar brawl, yeah, but you have Hafferty and Jensen and Belden as a wedge against Cheese. Let's use that to our advantage. And now, they have Jade here dragged into their net, too. But we can use that, too. Combine forces here. The three of us. Stick together. Cheese and his gang already think you and Jade are management snitches, and they hate my guts just because they hate my guts. Everybody hates my guts. I have the most hated guts in North America!"

Squirrel made a face, and Wilson's laugh came out in a snort. Jade chuckled, unable to hold back. The tension in the room lifted.

"So," Squirrel said, searching the others' faces. "We take the protection Hafferty, Jensen, and Belden give us for now, and we keep them hanging on, waiting for Jade to remember whatever they want him to remember from that accident."

"And what exactly is that?" Wilson said. "Skinny, you have some secret you're holding back?"

Jade scowled at Roland. "Jade," he said in a lifeless tone. "I'll tell you one more time. The name's 'Jade.' Get it straight." Wilson stared back at him and then turned to Squirrel, who opened his palms in a mollifying gesture.

"Peace, brothers," he said, turning his head on a pivot. Then he crossed his eyes and stuck out his tongue.

"You're an idiot, Squirrel." Roland said, smirking and shaking his head.

Jade left his corner and started his own pacing. He told them about the accident, about his meeting with Hafferty, Jensen, and Marion, and about his ride with Ren Belden.

"I didn't tell Jensen and Marion anything new, but Hafferty took me for a ride alone and told me everything before I got a chance to talk. He knows more than I do. I don't know what he told the others later, but Belden knows I saw his brother and his partner moving stuff from that Mustang trunk. Pretty sure he got that info from our General Manager. And he threatened to do serious harm to me, my mother, and my girlfriend if I ever ID those two guys to anyone. And he said to tell you the same thing, Squirrel.

"Mutt and Jeff," Squirrel said, nodding his head and looking at Roland. "I told you about those guys, Ro. Narcs who showed up out of the blue at the rez last weekend and tried to shake us down. Joey Belden and Billy Jensen. Brothers of Ren and our great leader, General Patton."

"Let me guess," Roland said, with a smirk at Jade. "The narcs were at the rez to stash drugs they stole from their dealer perps, and they were afraid you saw them. And our fearless leader and our union boss are scared to death they'll be sunk by their stupid brothers."

"Bingo," Squirrel said. "And Hafferty knows all about it. But he's giving our General Manager and our union steward only part of the story and letting them scramble to cover their brothers' lame asses. And, if Hafferty already knows everything, then Papa G knows, too. And everybody knows Papa G looks the other way on everything but drugs. That's where he draws the line, and it looks like our narc buddies have crossed it."

"So, there goes our protection from our G.M. and our union steward," Roland said, puffing up his chest and crossing his arms again. "Cheese and his small army can kill me on Friday and lead a walkout on Monday at Macson, and no one can stop them."

"Not so fast," Jade said. "I don't know if anyone can keep you safe in this town, Wilson, but there will be no strike. Hafferty's throwing a blocker at Cheese tomorrow that will disable his strike and keep him from getting Belden's steward job. Once that happens, I don't think Cheese will be laying a hand on you or anyone else."

"How the hell do you know all that?" Roland said.

"Same way you would. Hafferty. Give him a call."

Roland sputtered a laugh and shook his head. "I don't call him; he calls me. Looks like he tells you more than he tells me. After all these years."

"I don't know about that. I think he tells something different to everybody. Keeps us all in check that way."

"Listen guys," Squirrel said, suddenly sweeping around the office, his head crouched, his voice low, ramping up for one of his speed raps. "Listen up. Hafferty has you both covered, and we all know how he works. One guy against the other, all day long. Look at what he has you guys doing right now—bickering at each other. I say we put a stop to Hafferty altogether, once and for all. Expose him for the crook he is. I know he's on the take from Macson. And I mean big time cash. I got it from more than one source there. He gets Walsh to push through his inflated contracts in Washington, and then he skims the difference. He keeps the lion's share and hands out his scraps to Jensen and Belden, and then it's on them to keep everybody in line. And you gotta wonder if Papa G knows about it. Or maybe he gets a cut, too. Anyway, I can prove that cash money is exchanged in Jensen's office. Trust me. There's a big catwalk in the rafters above Jensen's drop ceiling where we can listen to everything they say. I know a guy who's been in that factory forever, and he was up there running wires and air ducts a few years ago when they were renovating. Hafferty's going there again on Thursday after our shift, and the three of us can get up there and listen, maybe even watch, as he doles out Fourth of July government cash to Jensen and Belden."

Roland held up his hands and shouted. "Stop!"

Squirrel froze and looked at him.

"You are not going anywhere near that office! Nobody is. I don't care if Hafferty is pulling a million dollars a day out of that place. No one, especially not us, will be eavesdropping on him or anyone else."

Roland stepped to the desk and rested his big hands there, leaning in toward Squirrel, keeping his voice low. "What is the matter with you? Do you think you're in a movie? You think you're going to bust the most powerful man in this valley and get a medal for it on the steps of City Hall? Hafferty *owns* City Hall! And every job in this valley. And if you try to rat him out, you rat out Papa G, too. You really want that on your head? Don't be so damn stupid! This is not a Hardy Boys story, Squirrel. This is real.

"You listen to me now," he said, standing up tall again and glowering at Squirrel. "You are my best friend, so if you get caught, I get dragged into it too, even if you do this idiotic mission all by yourself, or with Flynn here, if he's dumb enough to go along with you. I'm already up against the wall in that factory, as you just pointed out, and Hafferty is not too happy with me right now. If you pull something stupid like this on him, the three of us will not only get fired, we'll end up in a place we'll never get out of."

He stepped away from the desk and held out his hands. "Slow down and use your head for a minute, Squirrel. These guys you're talking about—these narcs, these brothers of Jensen and Belden—they're in a swirl of their own making right now. Let that play out. If I know Hafferty—and I've known him a lot longer than either of you—he will enlist Papa G's boys to shut down Joey Belden and Billy Jensen and make them disappear. And Hafferty will handle their brothers on his own. He'll have our General Manager and our union steward shipped out to who knows where for the rest of their lives. Vanished. Never heard from again. I've seen it happen. I can assure you Hafferty has already got the wheels in motion.

"Meanwhile, you and I and Flynn—we stay under the radar. And we keep our mouths shut. We let Hafferty do his thing. I'll bet when he visits Macson on Thursday, he'll put the hammer down on all of them. And if Flynn is right about Cheese getting iced out of his walkout, that fat load will be out the door with the rest of them."

Jade watched Squirrel lower his head as if he'd been scolded by a parent. "You're right, Ro," Squirrel said. "As always, you're right. I'll just shut up and stay in my corner."

Roland put his hand on Squirrel's shoulder. "You're getting ahead of yourself, Squirrel, that's all. Have patience. You have a steady job at that place. No sense messing it up over something you can't control. And you sure as hell don't want to drag me into another disaster right now, do you? If Hafferty comes down on me for some sneak attack on him, I'll be out of a job, out of school, and picking shrapnel out of my backside in Southeast Asia. Flynn, too. You, meanwhile, have your Sole Survivor deferment. You're safe, if you stay out of trouble. But if you screw with Hafferty, he can make that deferment go away, and then all three of us would be in the jungle, and probably not together. Is that what you want?"

This was the first time Jade had heard Roland say much more than a snide remark or two. It was the first time he'd heard him strategize. The otherwise vague edges of his British-tinted accent had sharpened, and his delivery reminded Jade of Dr. Wilson's Biology lectures. Roland was convincing and confident. But there was something else about Roland's voice. And the way he held his head high and looked down his nose at Jade. He remembered him now. Finally.

"Flynn, I need to hear it from you," Roland said. "You're in agreement?"

Jade stared at him for a long moment. "Yeah," he said. "I'm on board. Keep our heads down at Macson, and we might make it to September. Whaddya say, Squirrel?"

Squirrel lifted his head and looked at his friends' faces. The light in his eyes had dulled. His voice came out in a whisper. "Yeah. I'm on board. Fuck it."

39
Papa G

Wednesday, July 2, 1969

She woke up in a strange bed. Nothing unusual in that; but she couldn't place this one. Her dreams had been sweet for once, and her first waking feeling was that of a child, some other child, not the one she'd been. But the room shattered that sweet spell with its stale aura of cigarettes and mold, soiled chintz on the walls, stains of cold reality on the ceiling. She turned to the other single bed with relief. Empty. When she pulled aside the dusty, faded curtain and saw the front end of her Impala, she remembered. She'd nearly passed out at the wheel after crossing into Pennsylvania and had pulled over to a motel. She looked down at her body. Still in her clothes, her Army Navy boots.

She pulled out of the motel lot, the Impala chugging again. Goddamn Zeke. She punched the steering wheel with the soft edge of her fist and was startled by a shrieking sound. A flashing red light in the mirror.

"License and owner's card, ma'am." The cop leaned his face into the open window. The brim of his hat was too big to let him get closer. She backed away from his stale breath.

"I wasn't speeding, officer. Is there a problem?"

When she couldn't find the owner's card, he ordered her out of her car and into the back seat of the patrol car. He tossed her keys to his partner in the shotgun seat, an older cop who turned to look her over. "You look like a boy with tits," he said, shaking his head. "Jesus Christ. This world..." He hoisted his wide girth out of the car as the first cop settled in behind the wheel, setting his wide-brimmed hat on his partner's empty seat. Cowboy? Or Canadian Mountie? No, she couldn't see this automaton riding a horse. This was Pennsylvania. They call them "Stateys" here. She watched the older, wide-assed Statey get into her Impala. The car sank with the new weight.

"What's going on?" she said, trying to sound unphased.

As he pulled out ahead of the Impala, he told her she'd been driving a stolen car.

"That's not possible. Am I under arrest?"

"Not yet."

He didn't speak for the next hour, and out of self-protection, she went along with the silence game, checking every few minutes for the Impala behind them. They turned off the highway at Ebonton and drove to the South End, pulling to a stop behind a church at the top of a hilly neighborhood of silent streets and humble homes with tiny lawns. The Impala slid alongside them, and the older cop leered at her again. She saw it in his eyes. Dangerous perv. Preys on the weak.

"What is this?" she said, breaking the long silence.

"Someone wants to see you," the younger cop said, as he secured the chin strap of his hat.

"Who?"

The older cop used the top of the doorframe to pull himself out of the Impala. He put on his hat, letting the strap hang to one side, and handed the keys to his partner. His jodhpurs and black boots made her think of her filly, Lucky Girl. She turned away so the perv couldn't see her thin smile. Lucky had been fast, and she remembered breathing in time with her rhythm. The new thrill in her loins.

The younger cop escorted her to the back entrance of a large brick home next to the church. A priest opened the door to let them in, but the cop just handed him the Impala keys, tipped his hat, and disappeared down the back porch steps. Inside, the priest led her down a quiet dim hallway to a large office and closed the door behind them. She winced at the acrid odor.

"Have a seat, my dear." The priest—sallow skin, big ears, fleshy wet mouth—gathered his cassock and sank with a grunt into a black leather swivel chair behind a grand oak desk covered in papers. A gold-trimmed onyx lighter sat next to a large glass ashtray strewn with cigar butts. She tried to blink away the sharp stench.

Standing next to the green leather armchair he'd pointed to, she looked around the room. It had the familiar opulence of the innermost sanctum of a Catholic rectory, but even more lavish than the few she'd seen. The furnishings reminded her of her father's home—luxury without comfort. Fine fabrics, hand-carved wood, gold embellishments—bounty crafted and acquired in some foreign land. The high, expansive walls were a matrix of dark wood panels in neat squares and triangles and hexagons, topped by a gold cornice that accentuated the ornate globe overhead. Icons everywhere—crucifixes, small statues, a large loud painting of The Sacred Heart of Jesus, framed prints of saints she recognized, and, in a corner behind his desk, a life-size Blessed Virgin that rivaled her own in her Grotto. Her feet were cushioned by a thick red and beige hand-hewn Turkish rug with gold fringe. She faced a wide window covered in heavy purple drapes under a gilded valance.

"Go ahead, sit down, Mrs. Flynn. Make yourself comfortable," the priest said, his gray bloodshot eyes sweeping past her face, his mouth watery and loose. "I'm Father Russo. Sister Santa Maria will bring us coffee momentarily while we wait for Mr. Giallo. I just said a private family mass for his mother, God bless her soul, may she rest in peace." He blessed himself and nodded to her, prompting her, but she just stared at him, stunned.

He spread a practiced yellow smile across his leathery cheeks and told her they would start the conversation with a prayer, once Mr. Giallo joined them in a few minutes. He said he understood that she had been a member of Saint John the Divine parish until recently. He said he could fix that problem for her.

"Interesting police station you have here, Father," she said, still standing. "I'm flattered by my holding cell. It looks like it was built for Marie Antionette." She held out her palm and met his dull eyes. "Hand over my car keys. I need to leave."

"That won't be necessary, Mrs. Flynn." Russo opened his desk drawer and she held her breath, bracing for an unwanted surprise. He watched her with a knowing smile, as he dropped her keys into the drawer and then picked up something else and held it out of her sight. He waited for her eyes to meet his, and then he lifted his hand above the drawer and turned it to show her a short cigar in his thick palm. She let out an involuntary sigh as he reached for the desk lighter and stoked his cigar over the flame. He exhaled a cloud in her direction as the door opened, and a nun entered pushing a wooden cart with a silver tray of Lenox coffee cups and small plates, two silver pots, and a cake plate teeming with biscotti.

"Ah, Sister, *grazie, grazie!*" Russo barked through the haze. "Look at this, Mrs. Flynn. *Cantucci! Amaretto! Meraviglioso,* Sister. Please, Mrs. Flynn, sit and enjoy. You've had a long ride." He waved his right hand toward the nun while she moved papers aside and set the tray on his desk. "This is Sister Santa Maria."

The nun ignored Alice and bowed her head to Russo, then pointed a trembling gnarled hand at the silver coffee pots. "*Americano,* and this is *macchiato.*" Her face, squeezed inside her wimple, was pale and wrinkled, her eyes downcast, her voice a wheezy whisper.

Another voice boomed in the doorway. "Ah, you're here! *Buona!* Taking care of her, are you, Father? Thank you, thank you. Sister, *grazie.* I had to have a last prayer with my family, you understand." The man strode toward the desk without making eye contact. He was tall and broad and slightly stooped, his large head hanging forward as if under a yoke. He looked uncomfortable in his black double-breasted suit and gold tie, his shoulders flexing as if trapped. He waved a huge hand at the nun, and she disappeared.

"Yes! Mr. Giallo, welcome," Russo said as he rose to his feet in a jerky reflex, plucking his cigar from the ashtray. He stepped aside and gestured in deference as Giallo filled the leather chair with a sigh.

"Thank you, Father. I think we can skip the prayer for now. I'm all prayed out today." Giallo guffawed while the priest, his head bobbing and eyes on the floor, made an unctuous squeal and shuffled toward the exit. "But do come back later, Father. I think you and Mrs. Flynn need to straighten out her little parish problem. Perhaps she could join our parish here!" At this, he winked at her and the priest, his cassock whisking behind him, quietly closed the door.

"Please. Sit, sit," Giallo said, waving at her while reaching across the desk with a long arm and pouring coffee into two cups. "I'm assuming *Americano,* of course," he said as he placed a steaming cup in front of her. "But please, you look tired. Perhaps your second could be the *macchiato.* It picks you up a little more at this hour." He piled a handful of biscotti onto a small plate for himself. "Grab a plate. I'm partial to the *amaretto,* but, please, everything is fresh. The sisters—all of this made by their dedicated hands right next door in the convent kitchen. Miraculous, eh?" He waved his beefy workman's hand at the tray and glanced at her. "Now, sit. Eat. Relax. We'll talk." He set to the biscotti like a stallion at the trough.

She was relieved to feel soft leather underneath her, surprised by its comfort. The hot coffee tasted so good that she had to resist chugging it. She placed two cookies on a plate and set it on the desk in front of her, sampling the *amaretto.*

Giallo's smile matched his eyes, wide and warm. Hints of silver streaks peeked through his thick black hair, slicked straight back from his shallow forehead. He was much more handsome than she had expected.

His tanned face had seen far more sun than this opulent chamber would ever allow. He handled the delicate cookies with concentration, perhaps trying not to crush them.

"I apologize for the special escort," he said, wiping his wrist across his mouth. He looked at the tray. "Jesus, didn't she bring us napkins?" He shrugged with a sheepish grin and she couldn't resist smiling back at him. "I'm so sorry, Mrs. Flynn. Would you like me to call Sister—"

"It doesn't matter," she said, as if someone else had taken over her voice, someone much more polite than she had wanted to be. She nibbled at her cookie and set it on her plate.

"Can I call you that? Mrs. Flynn?"

"Alice," she said, with a feathery sweep of her fingertips to clear imagined crumbs from her mouth.

She was startled when he stood and picked up the ashtray, dropped it into a wastebasket with a great thud, placed the basket outside the door, yanked it shut with a bang, and returned to his chair. He moved with the quickness of a smaller man. She tried to place his age.

"I don't smoke those things anymore. Can't taste food with all that acid on your tongue. The smell, it gets in my clothes. It's terrible. He knows that and still he leaves them here. I apologize." He caught her eye and said, with his bold smile and a shrug, "That's two apologies. Sounds like I'm in the confessional, doesn't it? I don't usually apologize to anyone but God...and to my devoted wife, of course."

"I guess I bring it out in some men," she said. It was silky, someone else's voice coming out of her again. Someone she was a long time ago.

He was smiling and nodding as he inhaled two more cookies and gulped his coffee. His movements were all-encompassing, urgent, like thunderstorms. He wiped his wrist on his mouth again and sat back, the leather squeaking. "You know, ah. Alice. We met a long time ago. You don't remember. They didn't call you Alice back then."

She swallowed a mouthful of coffee and set her cup on the desk, staring at him. She couldn't find that voice, the one she'd been channeling.

"I wanted to see you because I knew your father. He was a good man. And he was much much more than a good friend to me." Giallo tented his huge coarse hands in front of him as he rocked ever so slightly in the chair, waiting for his words to sink in.

She blinked. "No. I don't remember you," but she knew this wasn't entirely true. His face did seem familiar, his gestures, his voice, his presence. His eyes, the color of the *Americano*, irresistible and bracing. Foreboding. As if his pleasantries were lures to be followed by an ambush, perhaps pain.

"Several times at your father's homes—*your* homes," he said, the tent breaking up so he could point at her, his smile spreading, his eyes on hers. "And a few times out there on the Gold Coast. Oyster Bay. What a palace.

Magnifica!" He nodded at her, pausing for her concurrence, which didn't come. His darkening eyes registered disappointment, but he seemed otherwise unphased. "You were just a child, maybe seven or eight. Your father loved to show you off in front of his guests. He was so proud of you. So poised you were, doing his bidding. At home on his estate, in that big drawing room, you'd play the piano, sing. I remember once he made you sing in Italian for me, something from an Opera."

He stood up to pace behind the desk, his eyes still fixed on hers, his hands in motion, the purple drapes behind him a royal stage. "You'd answer his complicated math problems. Made it seem easy. Best man with numbers I've ever known, before or since. But you had the answers. And then at the villa in Oyster Bay, he really brought out the show. We would stand on his grand balcony talking business and watch you practice riding and jumping, watch you play tennis. You were his pride and joy. He said you would be a steeplechase champion and that no one could ever beat you at tennis. Not even him."

She broke the trance and stood up, pouring *macchiato* into her cup. She pointed the silver pot at him, but he held up his hand.

"No, no. *You* enjoy. Feel better." He waved her back to her seat and flopped into his leather chair, flashing his smile. Big and shiny white, a small chip in one of his front teeth. She felt trapped by his charm. She wanted to remember the younger version of him, but she'd blocked out so much of that time that only vague images remained. Many men passing through, businessmen, always talking in hushed huddles, and then putting on loud social faces when required. She could see him being one of those.

He leaned forward onto his elbows and watched her sip the hot coffee. She lowered her gaze to his giant hands, feeling his eyes on her mouth, seeming to touch her lips with them. His voice softened, nearly a whisper. "When I heard what you were up to, Alice, I was very surprised." He waited for her to look up and then pushed back into his chair and stood up. "No! I take that back," his voice raised, his thick finger in the air. He stepped around the desk and stood facing her, his hand gesturing toward her body, her boots. "I was *not* surprised. Considering how you dress, and what—how should I say? Considering your peculiar *interests...*" He spread his hands by his side, shook his huge head with a frown, his eyes in a dark cloud. "No, I was not surprised. I'll tell you what I was. I was disappointed. That's what I was. I was disappointed that the favorite child of my good friend—a man I admired, a man I *respected*, a man of class and dignity—your father, the brilliant businessman—I was disappointed that his favorite girl would resort to such a scheme. So, I decided to intervene before it was too late."

She looked up at him, towering there, palms out, feigning supplication in this holy room. Who was the crucified one in this place? Hardly him. This was the ambush she'd expected.

240

She guessed now that he was sixty, maybe sixty-five, but still, the vigor of youth. In three strides, he moved to the window and held aside a heavy purple drape for a moment before turning back to face her. He seemed taller. She thought the coffee may have straightened out his stoop. It definitely made him more focused. He began to talk faster, to look for her to respond to him. He used his big hands to prompt her.

"I don't ever do this," he said. "I leave this kind of thing to others. But out of respect for the memory of your father, God bless his soul, I must break my own rule. This man, this, this...Stanley Selczyk? Ach!" He shook his head in disgust. "*Schifoso.*" His mouth curled up in a broken smile as he looked at her and shrugged. "*Capisce?*"

"Disgusting person. Nasty louse. But much worse than that. *Stupratore. Assassino.*"

His smile collapsed. "Those are strong words, Alice. Be careful." Then he smiled again, his eyes lighting up. "Did they teach you Italian in debutante school?"

"No. French. I learned Italian names for car parts when I was a child. From a mechanic. The curse words came later, in New Jersey. Swarming with Italians. Lots of shouting."

"Ah ha! Yes, of course." He held his finger aloft as if he could see a face. "That was Emilio. Your father's all-around man, much more than a mechanic. Emilio went on to work for me! Imagine that! Now why would Emilio teach a young girl about cars? Was he so close to you? You know...hands and everything." His dark eyes danced and he held out his own prodding fingers, exploring like tentacles.

"I wanted to know how things work," she said, her flat tone freezing his lurid pantomime. "And he taught me. He was kind to me. When I was nine, I could diagnose every wrong sound an engine made. In Italian."

Giallo shook his head, held out his arms, and laughed at the ceiling. "Of course you could! You were the child prodigy! And now? You're still a smart girl."

"I'm thirty-nine years old," she said, lifting her chin.

"Yes," he said, smiling wide, his teeth flashing. "So you're still a very *young* smart girl. And despite whatever you're trying to do to yourself," he said, waving his hand at her clothes and boots, "you're still very beautiful. Just like you were as a child."

He started pacing the office, and she followed him with her eyes, turning in her chair, watching his shoulders flexing like impatient wings, the stoop returning. He peeled off his suit coat and tossed it onto a small settee, ripped off his tie with one pull, and struggled impatiently to open his shirt collar. When he rolled up his sleeves, she saw thick forearms covered in dark fur. He was a bear.

"This Stanley," he said, turning, waiting for her eyes to meet his. "He will never bother you again. You have my word. *Capisce?*" He smiled and nodded at her. "And Dennis Hafferty? I will deal with him. You know Dennis, of course. Or you did. A long time ago. He is a close business associate, I respect his talents, his contributions. He is not the man your father was but...this Selczyk, he goes too far, too often. He will be contained. Dennis will guarantee it. I promise you this."

"I don't care if Selczyk is bound and gagged in a dark cell. He will get out," she said, her voice returning, the voice from the past, the one that, when provoked, demurred, seething. "He killed someone I love..." Her breath coming in two sharp bursts, then controlled again. "Loved. He tried to rape me more than once. Tried to kill me in my own house. And now, he'll kill my son, no matter what anyone tells him to do or not to do. There are no guarantees with that man. He needs to be put down. Like a rabid dog."

Giallo stepped to the desk and stood over her. He lingered there like a storm cloud. She looked up at him. She was boiling.

"I can see how you disappointed your father all those years ago," he said, his voice suddenly low, his tone restrained pique. "You have his will; you have his fight. If you had been a son, you would have disappointed him by being just like him. Instead, you disappointed him by doing what only a daughter can do to bring shame to her father."

She stood up, shoving her chair away with a flick of her leg. She lifted her chin to him and fixed her raging eyes on his.

"I did what I wanted to do, because he had tossed me aside. He wanted me to be his show girl long after the show was over. He wanted invisibility everywhere except in New York society. Only among the gilded elite. There, he wanted status, his daughter a debutante. Laying out my wares to snare some rich Ivy narcissist, to become his ornament, spread my legs, and bear his progeny. A line of show pieces for my father's mantle. No, thank you. He'd been proud of me, not just because I was his showcase, but because he knew I was good at everything he was good at, and more. Until it dawned on him that his favorite, his next-in-line, could not possibly be a lower form of himself—a female. So he found a replacement for me. And I was to become another over-educated Manhattan society hostess, a highbrowed breeder. His alternative to me? An intruder in our family. An arrival out of nowhere, the smug and permanently adolescent son of my father's new wife. A bumbling fool my father at first dismissed for his many inadequacies, but then decided he could mold him to his liking. He passed over me for a charlatan for one reason and one reason only: I had the wrong genitalia! Imagine that, Mr. Giallo. The great businessman, your mentor, your respected man of vision! Choosing mediocrity over brilliance because of a tiny set of testes."

Giallo grinned down at her. He turned his back and moved to the window, drawing aside the drape. "Your replacement, Mrs. Flynn, has done more for you than you deserve." He let go of the drape and returned to the desk and leaned over the coffee tray, his thick fingers gripping the edge of the desk. He glared at her, his mouth in a scowl.

"You betrayed your father when you fell in with the *melanzane. Capisce?* The Bahama man. You knew your father's rules. And you defied him. I was there when he gave the order to your brother to get *rid* of them! Send them back, father and son, to where they belonged. Give them to Roland Snowcroft, the benefactor of that Bahama man. It was the right thing to do. But your brother had his own ideas."

"Stepbrother." She glared back at him. "We do not share blood. Yet he's quite generous about shedding the blood of anyone I care for. Isn't that what he's really done for me, Mr. Giallo? Taken away the ones I love. Even murdered one of them. Such a gift I should be grateful for?" She glowered at him, her nostrils flaring. "And now, my son is next."

Giallo hoisted his big frame higher across the desk and looked down into her furious face. His eyes softened along with his voice. "Your brother defied your father, took care of the *melanzane*, got him into an American medical school. A foreign Negro. In 1950. But do you know what your brother told your father? He said the Bahama Negro and his infant son had been returned to Snowcroft where they belonged. Your father knew he'd lied to him, but he was getting ill, just had his first stroke, a mild one, but he knew he was in trouble. So he let your brother's disobedience pass. He began to depend on your brother. You were absent, Mrs. Flynn—not there to help your father. Your brother was present. I disagreed with him about the *melanzane,* but I respected his courage, and he gave that man and his son a chance—in 1950—that no one else ever would." He leaned closer to her face.

"Could you have done that? Alice? No. Of course not. You had to rebel yet again. The child prodigy gone mad. You had to have revenge. Get with your new Jew boy and try to bring down your father's business, *all* of our businesses. Then, your brother stepped in and took care of it before your father was destroyed, on his deathbed. Destroyed by you and your vengeance and your Jew. Then, your brother provided for your next son, the white one, and you, too. For years. And now he is there for your boy, again, offering him a chance for college."

"And sending his goon, Stanley, to kill me!" she shouted. "Why? Out of the goodness of his heart? Get rid of the drunken mother, so he can take my child under his wing and raise him to be a charlatan and a grifter like he is? A con man who hustles sick, old, rich men and crushes women and tells them he's saving them. Not my son. Not again will he take a son from me."

Giallo sat back in his chair and held up his massive hands. "I have already promised you, Stanley will not harm you or your son. And neither will Dennis. If you know my reputation, you will know that I keep my promises." He nodded toward the coffee tray. "Now, please. Alice. Sit.

Have another coffee, a biscotti. I have something to tell you about your father and me, and why I brought you here to help you."

"I'll stand. Tell me what you want, and then give me my keys. I've had enough of this charade."

He reached into a drawer and dropped the Impala keys in front of him on the desk. "I'm not holding you here against your will, Mrs. Flynn. You can leave when you want to, but let me first explain something that you may know nothing about. Something important to you."

His face and eyes softened, but his tone was aggrieved. "Some people think I'm a bad man, Mrs. Flynn. An ignorant immigrant, an uneducated brute, a man given to violence when he does not get his way. And maybe I was like that when I was a young man, working like an animal, and fighting like one, just to feed my family in a place where people thought I was just that—an animal.

"But one man was kind to me, and I changed because of him. I grew up quickly under his guidance. And he gave me an education I could not buy. That man was your father. He appreciated not only my hard work, but my ability to turn, as they say, lemons into lemonade. I took coal mine wastelands and created new enterprises from land others had abandoned as useless. Your father taught me, in his own special way, how to make the numbers work. He was a genius in the mechanics of capital. And he taught me how to speak in the language of businessmen, how to think like a man with long-range vision, someone who could help fulfill this country's promise as a way of repaying America for taking me in.

"But there was another side to him that was more complicated—a political and social side, focused on the future and based on the wisdom of the founders of this nation. His father, your grandfather, was a pioneer in coal and railroading and the manufacture of ordnance in support of this country's defense, and he provided your father with the means to build on that success. He also handed down to your father his abolitionist convictions. That's right, Mrs. Flynn. Abolition. He knew slavery was wrong, but he also knew there would be no place in America for the freed slave. He was a member of The American Colonization Society. Their abolitionist goal was to return freed slaves to their homeland of Africa. Even Abraham Lincoln agreed. But there were other abolitionists who wanted not just to free the slaves, but to make them American citizens. Your grandfather, and your father, were certain these other abolitionists and their theory would fail.

"By the time your grandfather died in the 1930s, your father was one of the few remaining members of The Society, but he was steadfast in his and his father's belief that there was no good future for Negroes in this country. And, because the liberal elite politicians in our government disagreed, here we are today. But your grandfather and your father were right. The Negroes are a lost people without a homeland. They have their

Civil Rights now, but their men abandon their families, leaving them in poverty. They sell drugs to their own people and let them die in addiction. They riot now in cities across America, destroying their own homes and businesses. And it's getting worse. This Black Power thing, disgracing America in front of the world at the Olympics? It's too much. And now, those Black Panthers with their weapons and their plans to destroy the foundation of our country—it's all coming true. Your father was right. And it was why he was so angry with you so long ago for your fling with the Bahama man, when you were still a child, a teenager, a girl who couldn't understand the burden your father was under, his legacy, his own father's strongest beliefs in what was best for this country—all destroyed by your weak knees for a *melanzane*."

She was seated now, her hands in her lap, her heart still. "My father introduced me to him—the Black Bahama man, as you call him. Isn't that ironic, Mr. Giallo? I'll bet you did not know that. And I was not an ignorant little girl. I was a thriving student at Barnard. But I was entrapped by my father's self-serving plans for my debut in New York society. And I was there in 1949 at my father's villa on Grand Bahama, at a small dinner party he threw for his rich White Bahamian pal, Roland Snowcroft, and his young Black protege, a brilliant Bahamian student at Howard University, sponsored, of course, by Snowcroft. Dennis was there, too.

"My father had devised a ridiculous scheme, similar to Snowcroft's. He wanted to educate bright young Black men at American colleges and then have them lead their people back to Africa. An absurd notion for a man you call brilliant with numbers. A similar repatriation scheme had failed miserably in the late 1800s. But, by 1949, there were more than *ten million* Black people in the U.S. What was he going to do, put them all on boats and hope they find their way?

"My Bahama man, as you say, was Snowcroft's protege, James Wilson, introduced to me by my father. Surely, you know him. *Doctor* Wilson. Snowcroft's prototype for the fulfillment of *his* version of the repatriation scheme. James actually believed Snowcroft loved him like a father. He even went so far as to give our child a middle name, after Roland Snowcroft.

"My own father had no such candidate. He was still wallowing in the theoretical, many steps behind Snowcroft and clearly envious of him. So, a month after that dinner party, Dennis, in his bootlicking zeal to please my father, decided to steal James from Snowcroft and set him up as my father's prototype. Dennis invited James to Oyster Bay for a visit, and soon Snowcroft was pushed aside when the rising politician, Dennis, got American citizenship for James. His intention was to place James in an American medical school, a key step that Snowcroft had been struggling with. But I got in the way. That is, James and I got in the way.

"When my father was dying, Dennis promised him that he would fulfill my father's absurd repatriation plan, and my father—your brilliant business mentor—then decided to replace me, the Scarlet Letter daughter, with Dennis as executor of his will. Punishment for my defiance of his anti-miscegenation rule.

"When Dennis learned I was pregnant, he panicked. His political career would be destroyed if anyone found out. So, he kidnapped me and shuttled me off to a remote convent on the Jersey shore, a locked-down nuthouse for unwed mothers-to-be. He told the nuns my name was Alison Isobel Flynn—my mother's maiden name. He did it out of spite, I'm sure, to diminish my mother somehow in his demented mind. He told the nuns to call me Alice. I told them my name was Issa. They told me I was insane. They called me Alice.

"Then, he convinced James that I did not want him or the baby in my life. He told him that if he tried to find me, Dennis would withdraw his promise of medical school. A Faustian deal for James, but what choice did he have? When the baby was born, Dennis arranged for him to be raised in Maryland by relatives of James. I held my baby once, escaped with him on the beach. They found us, and took him, and I never saw him again. Then my father died. And my life completely unraveled. All because of your genius mentor and his slimy grifter stepson, your partner, Dennis Hafferty.

"So, tell me, Mr. Giallo, how did you end up owning the Macson ordnance plant? Why did Dennis give it up, along with the four munitions operations my father had built in other states before the war? Aside from the fact that Dennis could not count to ten without getting lost.

"What was the deal, Mr. Giallo? You and his other cronies would own the munitions factories, and Dennis would get you the military contracts, and you'd funnel his share to him? If you're his partner, Mr. Giallo, why are you one of Dennis's toadies instead of your own man? Why are you doing the bidding today of a small-time dirty politician twenty years your junior, when you could rule your own kingdom here? Who are you really saving today? Me? Or yourself? Protecting yourself from having to order another hit on behalf of your boss?"

Giallo smiled and nodded. He leaned forward on his desk, set his elbows in place, and made another tent with his massive hands. His dark eyes softened. Those charming eyes. She knew he was letting her enjoy her little Pyrrhic victory. Another ambush would come.

"We are business partners, your...*step*brother and I. We share some common goals, but we are very different men. He loves politics; I hate it. I love the business, the numbers, the way your father taught me. And yes, Dennis is not a numbers man, but you sell him short. He has a way with everyday people that I do not have. He has an instinct for opportunity and a gift for persuasion on the public stage. An Irish politician like his

246

real father, but much more successful at it. Born Catholic, like his real father, but he and his mother dropped the faith when they joined your family. Then he picked it up again after your father died, when he needed it for his first campaign. The opportunist in action. Not a truly religious man. Myself? I am a humble man. I stick to my traditions. We complement each other, Dennis and me. And I thank God for what I have."

She snorted a stifled laugh. "Well, you certainly play the role well here in the name of God. In this holy cell of opulence. Did you know that my father hated Catholics?"

Giallo spread his hands wide and shrugged his shoulders. "He married a Catholic girl from Ireland and their children were educated in Catholic schools. He was a Protestant, but he was a very generous Catholic donor. After all, he gave his oldest daughter to the Church. She's still a nun today."

"Yes, my half-sister Dierdre, the oldest." She took a deep breath and leaned forward onto the desk, lifting her face closer to Giallo. "In cloister for nearly forty years now. Locked up in a convent in Newark since she was 15. That's quite a life, isn't it, Mr. Giallo? You could visit her if you'd like. I did. Several times. Let me tell *you* something, Mr. Giallo, that you do not know about my father. Your great mentor gave his first daughter to the Church, not out of generosity to Catholics, but because he wanted to hide his crime. He was very skilled at that, too. I worshiped him when I was a child and even after I fell out of his graces. But I never knew what he'd done to his own family until after he died."

She stood up and stepped around the desk and moved toward the statue of the Blessed Mother. Giallo leaned back in his chair and watched her, his darkened eyes on hers.

"Jake Levin knew. He was the one who found Dierdre. I met him here in this town after giving birth to my baby in New Jersey. My stolen baby. I came here to take down Dennis, the newly elected state rep, the rising political star. Jake was working for a New York newspaper, looking into cozy relationships between New York businessmen and Pennsylvania politicians in the coal regions—something you might have known about, Mr. Giallo. Jake dug up a lot about my late father's business affairs, as well as his back-to-Africa lunacy, but he stumbled onto a secret that led him to me, and when I said everything he was telling me was a lie, he offered to take me to Dierdre."

She touched the hand of the Blessed Mother statue and turned to face Giallo.

"Sister Saint George," she said, offering him a forced grin. "A man's name! Imagine that! A man's name for a meek, crushed mouse of a girl, even in adulthood, shielded behind a screen. We could talk, but I never saw her face. She said she had letters from our brother, Tormud, in the years leading up to his death. And she wanted me to have them. Tormud had been banished by my father when I was a child, and I never knew why. Until I met Jake. It took a while for Dierdre to mail the letters to me, but, in the meantime, Jake told me about what happened to my baby, how Dennis had arranged it all. And what had happened to Tormud, his unexplained death in a mine accident. Jake and I became close, as you clearly know."

Giallo grinned and nodded. "Yes. Of course I do. Your Jew. He taught you how to drink. Heavily, I'm told. Newspaper men are drunks. They must drown their many shortcomings somehow. But do go on. You've come up with quite a fable."

She lost her smirk and stepped back to the front of the desk, where she stood and watched Giallo's face. "Tormud's letters were like knives driven ever so slowly into my heart. I didn't believe them. But when we returned to Dierdre, she quietly confirmed everything. Over the years, she'd heard the same stories from her sisters, Frances and Tara.

"Their mother, Bridget, was 17 years old when my father took her from the west of Ireland as his bride. She died in childbirth eight years later. She was 25. The child, Tormud, of course, lived. He was her sixth in eight years. A short time later, my father married Alison Isobel Flynn, an Ulster Scot Protestant like himself. I was her third child, and my father's last *real* child. He named me Cairstine—Scottish Gaelic for "Flower of Christ"—after his mother, Cairstine Morgan. But he called me Carrie, as you must know. He gave me a middle name, same as my mother's middle name—Isobel. Mother called me Issa. When I was in college, and free from my father, that's the name I used. Issa.

"After I was born, my mother took to her bed, where she remained for the last nine years of her life. It was shortly after my birth that my father first raped Dierdre. She was 14. Within a year, she was in cloister.

"I was six years old when he clarified for our family a long-repressed frustration about living in a house filled with Catholics. He declared at our 1936 Christmas dinner that, after the death of his Irish Catholic wife, Bridget, he'd been freed from the burden of the greedy dark-cloaked beggars of the Roman papacy. Those were his words. Sister Saint George recited them to me—words emblazoned on her memory.

"He then told all his children they were to be transferred out of their Catholic schools immediately. Our sister, Tara, was devastated. She was a devout Catholic student and completely fell apart after that. She was unable to do anything, least of all attend her new Presbyterian boarding school. So, she returned home and became my best friend for the next three years. Beautiful Tara. My secret, impassioned, Catholic religious teacher, my literary scholar, my sweet and gentle and sad Tara. Terrified of something I never knew. I was the one who found her in her bed, my mother's medicine bottles on the table. I was not allowed to attend her funeral. Two years later, right after my mother died, my father brought home his new wife, his third. Mhairi Hafferty, widow of his enemy, Michael Dennis Hafferty, another Irish Catholic, whose death in a New York hotel remained a mystery, until I read those letters. It was rumored he'd hanged himself, but the letters prove otherwise."

She saw Giallo flinch and then regain his placid look. She raised her eyebrows to let him know she saw, and then continued.

"But the new wife Mhairi—Scottish, of course, for Mary—had been raised, conveniently, an Ulster Scot Protestant. Which must have momentarily warmed my father's cold heart. But, along with Mhairi came her only child, Michael Dennis, Jr., the interloper. Loath to acknowledge the boy's real father in any way, my father insisted the boy drop the name, Michael Junior, and use his middle name, Dennis. And thus was born the menace we know today."

She reached for her coffee, took a sip, and then gave Giallo a flat smile, her eyes cold.

"I can tell by the look on your face, Mr. Giallo, that you knew very little of what I just revealed, especially about how he hated your Roman church so much that he must have loved using it as a shield for his crimes. While he was tutoring you, my father surely did what he had done with his wife and children—hid all that venom he had held for your Catholic Church and its followers—the Papists, he had called them, according to Dierdre. He held all that back from you while he taught you the soulless ways of English businessmen, whom he worshiped."

Giallo folded his tented hands and sat back in his leather chair. His face was solemn, his eyes heavy in shadow. He waited in silence for her to sit down, and, when she finally did, he leaned forward on his long arms, softening his eyes, his mouth stretching into a turned down grin.

"I brought you here to help you, not to argue with you," he said in a solicitous tone, soft and low. "You are not well, Mrs. Flynn. You drink too much. You do perverted things with sick people who will only bring harm to you. And you see things, you imagine things, you make things up—stories no one can believe." He raised himself up and sat back in his chair, his hands held palms up, as if in communion with her. "But you have a good soul, I know you do. And, like me, you are devoted to God and to his Blessed Mother, Mrs. Flynn. I am a very religious man. No one can take that away from me. Your father never tried to. And I know you are a religious woman, a recent Catholic convert, thank God. And no one can take that away from you either, no matter what their sickness is, no matter what they make you do. They don't love you, Mrs. Flynn. They just use you."

He turned his big body in the chair and, still looking at her, pointed to the statue behind him. He sounded almost desperate, his eyes wide now with conviction, his mouth a fully inverted smile. "*She* loves you, Mrs.

Flynn." He raised his voice. "She. Loves. You." He swung his thick arm from the statue to Alice's face and back again. "The Blessed Virgin, Mrs. Flynn. *She* is watching over us right now. *She* is with us, Our Mother, as always. And I know she is with you. I know you pray to her, too, right there in your parlor. I know that, and I respect that. You are a holy woman, Mrs. Flynn, in your heart and in your soul. And you want to make peace with God, I know you do. And I can help you." He stretched his inverted smile into a frozen grin and extended his arms toward her.

"I will ask Father Russo to bring you into our parish here. We have people who help women like you to become fully committed again to God and to the Blessed Mother. In my own family, I have witnessed women nearly destroy their lives with drink, and then they heal those lives through God and his Holy Blessed Mother. We have good people who've been through what you—"

"I was told you have proof that Marte is still alive," she said, standing up suddenly, cold and unmoved by his solicitation, his performance, his real purpose, his final ambush. She pushed her chin out. "I don't believe it. I know Stanley killed her. If she were alive, she would have contacted me. But you had her killed. On orders from Dennis."

Giallo flinched and took in a quick breath, as if he'd been slapped. His face hardened, his eyes narrowing, his jaw twitching, his mouth a pinched line. He sighed heavily and then pushed the keys toward her on the desk. He held up his wrist to check his watch and then reached down and opened a desk drawer. He tossed a manilla envelope onto Russo's litter of papers. "She's not dead, Carrie. Or Issa. Or Alice. Or whoever you are today. No one killed her. And neither is your Jew, Jake Levin."

She opened the envelope. Steadying her feet, she pushed her coffee and plate aside and spread news clippings and black and white prints on the desk in front of her. Her face went cold, then her body. Her knees buckled, and she stumbled backward, finding her chair and collapsing there. She pulled her chair closer to the desk and looked at them again.

"These are fake," she said, her head lolling back and forth and her eyes filling up. "You had these made up."

"I don't own a newspaper," Giallo said in a glib tone. "And, if I did, it would be in English, maybe Italian. But never German. I hate the Germans. They gave us the Jews. And I don't own a real estate agency in California. Or anywhere. That's not the way I deal with land."

He reached over the desk and picked up one of the clippings for her to see. "This was last month. May 1969. See? She's standing in front of a nightclub in West Berlin." He shuffled through the photos. "Here she is on stage. And here...that's her new interest. Hard to say, but I think it's a man. Who knows? Europe is already gone to hell with these young people and their drugs and their perversions. Their Communism. America is next, you know. Unless we stop them."

He pulled another clipping from the pile, pointing. "And this ad, here? *San Francisco Chronicle*. November of last year. That's Jerry Valentine. Real Estate man. Does quite well. He had to quit drinking, part of the arrangement. But it turned out that that joke was on us. He was never a drinker. He just played one to win you over, to get what he wanted— information on your father, and a little something on the side. Lives in Marin County with his wife and three children. Expensive private schools. Nice clean life he pretends to have." He pulled a photo from the pile. "Except he's a pervert, like all Jews. Here he is in the city. At The Cliff House bar. From the window, you could see seals in the wild waters of the Golden Gate. Beautiful place, San Francisco. Reminds me sometimes of Italy. But I would not go there now. It's a mess. Hippies and queers and perverts everywhere. By the way, that woman with Jerry? Or should I say Jake? She is not his wife. He does this swapping thing now, popular in California. I suppose we'll start hearing about more illegitimate children sired by Jake Levin. Bastard children like your second son, the white one, the son of the Jew."

He leaned back in his chair again and waited while she sobbed, his ambush under way, the pain delivered. He reached into his back pocket and held out a handkerchief to her. She grabbed it and pressed it to her face.

"I'm sorry to say this to you, Mrs. Flynn, but she will never return. Her American papers have been revoked. Forever. I don't believe she wants to anyway. Found someone new, a man, a woman, I don't know. No offense to you, of course. It's just the way these people are these days. Free love? Huh. *Devianti*.

"As for him, he's been Jerry Valentine for almost twenty years. Your Jake Levin, your newspaper man from New York. His real name? Yakub Lewanowicz. Born in Poland. Yakub means James. Pretty ironic, as you would say, Mrs. Flynn. Seems you were attracted to men with that name. Gave it to your son, too. *His* son. Lewanowicz was a lucky Jew boy, thanks to his father. Brought him here in '28—just in time. They settled somewhere in Jersey, but, years later, what happens? Turns out the father was a Communist. That did not work out so well for Jake in 1950 when you knew him."

She let the soaked hanky slip from her hands into her lap. Her chest was heaving, but she couldn't find air. Through her tears the room warped. She scratched at the clippings and photos, scattering them. She looked up at Giallo. His smug face swirled, his teeth flickering like a flashlight in a dim tunnel.

She sucked in air at last and felt a surge of anger, strength in her center. She made a ball out of the wet handkerchief and threw it at his face. He caught it with a sweep of his huge right paw, the motion strobing in the air before her.

She blinked away the strange image and stood up and leaned across his desk, breathing fire, the scream already echoing in her head. "You didn't drag me here to help me! You did it to finish me off!" Her lips foaming, spit spraying. "You're in on it with him! You took away *everything* I loved! You're *worse* than he is! Tutored by my rapist father. You pig! You lying, cheating bigot. *Melanzane? Melanzane?* Really? *You* are *schifoso. Capisce?!* Eh? *Capisce?! Diavolo! DIAVOLO!"*

She was drowning, her chest filling up. She looked over at the Blessed Virgin in the corner and was startled to see the Virgin looking back at her, alive as she once was in The Grotto. She wanted to move, to go to her. But her legs would not respond. She heard the clatter of dishes, smelled the sharp essence of coffee, felt her hand sweep papers away from her like leaves floating in an updraft. As she started to crumble, she grabbed the edge of the desk and righted herself, found her footing. She pushed herself tall, closed her eyes, and breathed in through her nose. The bucket dropping into her belly. Exhaling. Breathing in again.

He was a blur in her vision now. She grabbed her keys and some of the photos and went to the door. She didn't look back as she pulled it closed behind her with a bang.

In the Impala, she clutched the steering wheel and glanced back at the rectory. She slid across the front seat, shoved open the shotgun door, and vomited onto the pavement, her throat scorched from the fiery bile of coffee and sweets, the lure of *il diavolo.*

On the floor in the back, she found her leather shoulder bag. It had been rifled through, but her wallet seemed undisturbed. She used the keys to pry open the false bottom of the bag. The cash and her pistol were still there. She checked the chamber and looked up at the rectory, imagining herself in that room again, her feet and arms and body in perfect balance, her aim steady, the barrel lined up with his face. She blinked and gasped when she saw the purple drape parting, the baseball mitt of a hand on the royal cloth.

She turned the key, and the Impala coughed into a rumbling start. As she pulled away, the car backfired, and she gasped again and glanced into the rear-view mirror, her heart pounding, her breath coming in gulps. She punched the steering wheel twice with the soft part of her fist.

"Goddamn you, Zeke! God*damn* you!"

40
Chaos on Camera

Wednesday, July 2, 1969

The atmosphere at Macson was doubly oppressive under the swelter of low, damp clouds and the weight of the news in the morning paper. The Line halted moments after it had jolted to its usual start, and The Forge sent one more blast of black soot up its stack before shutting down. All machinery in the building was silenced. Even Ren Belden sat still on his power perch, his honing machine stalled, his small round head with its double chin swiveling from side to side like Jell-O unbound. As more men abandoned their posts and headed into the open yard, Jade stood a few feet from Roland, waiting for his cue to move outside. They'd been leaning up against The Line's platform next to a stack of shells, arms folded, saying nothing to each other, just watching. Roland didn't acknowledge it when Jade said Hafferty was right. The newspaper had offered a subhead on its coverage of the *Life* story: "Macson Jobs Threatened?" Even the men who could barely read had known five minutes after their arrival at work that their lives were about to change.

Wilson was stoic when Jade asked him about the bruises and cuts on his face. He shrugged at first and then revealed he'd been mugged the day before in front of his father's house just before dark by three Macson men. Still enough daylight out, he said, but no one called the cops. Not that he'd expected anyone would. He'd beaten back all three of them, but they'd gotten their licks in. He said he'd expected worse, but figured it was just a warning. Jade told him the assault would be the last of it once Cheese got waxed, but Roland said nothing to that. He told Jade that Squirrel also got a warning, but with a much lighter touch. They'd merely slashed all four of his Corvair's tires. He had to take the bus to work.

"Looks like you might be next if you keep hanging around with us outsiders," Roland said. Then he shifted his body forward and said, "Let's get out of this building, find some shade, wait it out. With the news story sinking in, these guys are going to start picking sides and fighting among themselves. I can just feel it."

As they started a slow walk toward the exit, they noticed Belden had climbed down from his roost and was shuffling toward the metal stairs, headed for the head. Jade and Roland waited until he disappeared into the men's room and then exited to the yard, sheltering along the wall. Roland's prediction unfolded as if on his command. At each end of the yard, two groups of men started pushing and shoving in separate scuffles. Roland turned to Jade and smirked.

"Dissension in the ranks," he said. "The pecking order is...out of order. Who will come out to settle the hens first, Belden or Cheese?"

Men shouted inside each scuffling group, and the fighting stopped. But immediately, more pushing erupted in both circles and the fighting resumed. Then it subsided again.

"I finally remembered who you are," Jade said during a lull in the action. Roland tilted his head toward him, but kept his eyes on the yard, his face wrinkling into a scowl. "You're Junior. That's what they called you. It was the summer we moved here. Six years ago. At Lola's house not far from here. All the kids called you Junior, and so did Lola. She was so nice to me that I wanted her to be my grandma. You were the biggest, but you were much younger looking, much smaller than you are now. A few years later, I learned about Roland Wilson, the superstar from my high school. Who didn't? But I never knew Junior's real name. If it weren't for your voice, I might not have figured it out. That accent, just like your father's. Only much more subtle. But, most of all, it's the look you give me. Brings me right back to Lola's that summer. My mother took me there just a few times. She called Lola by her full name—Dolores. Maybe Lola was *your* grandmother, I never knew. Every time you showed up while I was playing with the other kids, you pulled me from the game and made me sit. You were a prick. I was the only white kid there. You must remember me."

Roland turned and looked down at Jade and shook his head, his scowl now a smirk. "Your mother, huh? The same mother who talks in tongues and sees things? Flynn, you are definitely her son, I can tell you that. You're living in some kind of dream world."

Another fight broke out, this time closer to Jade and Roland. Then, at the gate, men gathered to watch a van pull up. Two men got out and started pulling equipment from the back of the van. As they mounted a film camera on a tripod, another fight erupted near the flagpole. The sides in all of these fights seemed even, giving Jade the idea that Cheese had as many backers in the union as Belden.

Roland got to his feet and started toward the entrance to their building. "Let's go, Flynn. Here comes the cavalry."

Jade turned toward Jensen's office and saw a phalanx of cops in helmets with batons in hand marching toward the flagpole scrum. The lead cop blew a whistle, and a moment later, the air shrieked with vibration as the factory version screamed a penetrating wail across the yard. Jade ducked and put his hands over his ears; he knew if he didn't, the ringing would never end.

The men near the flagpole began dispersing as the police unit approached them. There were at least twenty cops. Jade saw Jensen at the rear of the phalanx. He was holding a bullhorn.

"Flynn!" Roland shouted from the huge doorway. "Let's go! Now!"

Jade looked at him and then took one more glance at the approaching cops. He started to walk fast toward Roland when he heard Jensen's voice on the bullhorn.

"Get back to work! Everyone. Now! If you fight, you will be arrested. And you will lose your job! Your union prohibits fighting on the premises. The punishment is termination. Now get back to your posts. That's an order!"

Roland was standing in the shadow of the doorway when Jade reached him. They watched as the police formed a sweep in two directions, forcing the men to move back inside the buildings.

"Now, where did all those cops come from so fast?" Roland said. "Looks like someone anticipated this. Who do you suppose that was?" He looked down at Jade and forced a smile. "This story just got bigger than a newspaper article, Flynn. We just might see it in living color tonight on TV. Unless our boss decides that wouldn't work for him."

"He can't stop it once it's on TV," Jade said.

"Uh huh. Right." Roland sauntered toward The Line and called over his shoulder. "Don't bet on it, Flynn. Maybe you should give him a call and find out if he plans to block the story. The man still takes your calls, doesn't he?"

Jade started toward The Line when the factory whistle ripped through the air again, cutting right to the middle of his skull. He would never, ever get used to it.

At home after work, there was no sign of a break-in. No sign of Alice, either. Stanley's bag of cash in the kitchen cupboard was gone, and all the money she'd said was stashed in her closet was gone, too. A note she left in the strongbox showed scratched out numbers and $3,200 as the last entry. He searched the rest of the closet. Her suitcase was missing.

He called Lucy's number after supper, but her mother said she wasn't home. He asked her if she knew where Lucy had gone and when she'd be back, and she said no. He asked her if Lucy was OK, and her mother said, "What's OK? Miserable? If that's OK, then she's OK." Same conversation as always with the mother. Few words, rarely a kind one.

He asked if anything unusual had happened to them, like someone trying to bother them. The mother said no. "Should I expect something unusual? Did you do something to bring trouble here? Because if you did, you'll have hell to pay. We don't need no more trouble around here. I don't want you bothering with her if you're gonna bring trouble. Do you hear me? My husband won't have it. And he'll let you know about it himself if you show up here."

Squirrel called a half hour later to tell him the Macson story had not run on the six o'clock news and that he would call later to let him know if it showed up on the news at eleven.

"Time to get your goddamn TV fixed, man," Squirrel had said, cackling.

Around ten, Lucy called, sounding tipsy. "Uh, yes, officer?" she blurted out in her signature drunk voice: clear, but megaphone loud. "This is Lucy Melburn, and I'd like to report a missing person. Name's J. D. Flynn. Jade, to his close friends, like his former girlfriend." Jade hissed a laugh at her, holding the phone away from his ear. "He's about six feet tall, light brown wavy hair, over his ears and down his neck. Starting to look like a hippie. Got dark eyebrows, light green eyes. Like an alien. Yeah! The look on his face? It's like he's living in outer space."

"Lucy, listen, I have to ask you—"

"I'm not finished, officer!" she shouted. "He's got long skinny arms. Looks like they belong on someone else, maybe an ape. Legs long, too, but chicken skinny. Big feet, long fingers. He's got something else that's long, too. And pretty thick. But I can't say it over the phone. You'll find it in his pants. Or maybe not. Maybe it fell off, who knows? Certainly not me, I'm just the forgotten girlfriend. How would I know? But if he wants to find me, tell him to look for a new Camaro. I'll be behind the wheel. I got a new boyfriend who cares about me."

"Lucy, I wanted to—"

"Not done yet! This guy? This Jade? He has kind of a big nose, too. Like a Wop or a Jew. So, if you see him, officer, don't call me. Just arrest him. For being selfish, self-centered, ignorant, and lost in his own world. Cares only about himself. Me me me me me me! If you ask me, he should be in jail."

"Lucy—"

The line went dead. He tried calling her back, but her mother answered. "Not here!" she barked, and slammed down the phone.

Squirrel called just before midnight to tell him the story showed up on the eleven o'clock news, buried at the end. But it was there. He asked Jade if he'd been visited by the Cheese boys like he and Roland had been.

"No. And no one's been here. I checked with Lucy, too. Nothing."

Squirrel tried to revive his theory about Hafferty being on the take, claiming Hafferty had orchestrated the entire fiasco at Macson to stop Cheese from exposing Hafferty's graft and corruption, but Jade didn't take the bait.

"All bets are off now, Squirrel," he said. "Even if Cheese fed his boys your same theory, those boys are scared shitless about losing their jobs. If the theory is true, they'll have to live with it, because their leader is as good as gone. Just like we'll have to live with it, Squirrel. Roland's right. You can't bring down Hafferty by spying on him at the plant. Not now. Not ever."

256

41
Tea on Nob Hill

Thursday, July 3, 1969

When the doorbell buzzed, she held up a finger to Sam. When it rang again, she nodded. Sam opened the door and paused, as she'd requested, filling the doorway with his massive tuxedoed frame. The man on the other side was visibly startled.

"Who is calling, please?" Sam said, his baritone filling the room, his chin held high, eyes cold and half-mast and bearing down on the man below him.

"Jerry Valentine," the man replied, a trill in his tenor voice.

Sam glared at him for another beat and then smiled and lowered his gaze, bluffing obeisance. "Mr. Valentine. Of course. Please come in, sir." He stepped back, pulling the door wide as Valentine lifted his jutting chin and stepped into the room.

She stood at the full-length mirror in the bedroom and listened while Sam directed Valentine to a sitting area near the windows of the suite. When she heard Valentine sigh as he sat down, she gave herself one more appraisal and then made her entrance, turning first to Sam and then to Valentine. "Thank you, Sam," she said, a wry smirk at the corner of her mouth. "Ah, Mr. Valentine. So kind of you to visit with me on such short notice."

Valentine stood and started to offer his hand, but she held hers by her side, so he lifted his to brush a phantom loose hair from his collar. "Mrs. Kinley," he said, bowing his head slightly. "A pleasure." He started to sit again, until he noticed her still standing, and he straightened up, pushing back his broad shoulders and offering a frozen smile while grazing his eyes too slowly over her body. She noticed he'd fixed the dead tooth at the edge of his smile.

She grinned at him, restraining a laugh as she saw how he fell for her costume—a tight-fitting rose-pink dress cut just above her knees, no stockings, and blood red high heels. Her fake string of pearls rested neatly at the neckline of the high-cut dress. Her hair was blonde and crop-cut like Twiggy's. Her makeup was casual but had been carefully applied to distract without revealing.

When she sat, Valentine followed suit, and she gave a quick glance at his eyes to read his reaction. As expected, he was watching her legs as she crossed them, missing his first opportunity to look into her eyes. Then his look fell to her ring, an obscenely huge diamond-studded emerald Sam had borrowed from his pawn broker pal.

"May I offer you a drink, Mr. Valentine? I'm having tea, but Sam will bring you whatever you like. The Top of The Mark was kind enough to stock our bar appropriately. I would have met you up there in the restaurant, but I think our privacy is better suited here."

Valentine glanced at her eyes, but missed them yet again as he turned to Sam. "Just tea for me as well, Sam. Thanks." He turned toward the balcony and gazed out at the view of the bay and nodded as she talked.

"I appreciate your visit, Mr. Valentine, as I know too well how busy a man you are. Certainly in high demand, I am told. And I assume your assistant informed you about what I'm looking for. She said you had several opportunities in Pacific Heights and in Sea Cliff, among others. I hope it was appropriate for me to ask her directly. It seemed you were too tied up with important matters to speak with me at the time."

Valentine's California tan darkened a shade as he turned back to her, shifted in his chair and crossed his own legs, glancing again at hers. His smile turned up a notch as he told her he was happy to accommodate her needs in person and that, yes, he could show her properties in those areas, but he had come up with a better idea—a fantastic opportunity that had just opened up in Tiburon. "Much more suitable for you and your husband," Valentine said, his voice lifting into selling mode. "More privacy, more land. More of everything!" he said. "Marin is on fire these days."

Sam entered holding a silver tray filled with teacups, a silver pot, a collection of sweets, two Depression Glass plates, and two pale pink linen napkins. He set them on a table to her left, filled their cups, bowed to her, and then moved to the door where he stood with his big hands folded low in front of him, his eyes on Valentine's twitching fingers. Valentine glanced at Sam standing there, huge and expressionless, and then he turned to the sweets and tea.

"My husband and I are not looking for a fire, Mr. Valentine," she said, reaching for her teacup. "And we prefer to stay in the city, so why don't we just focus there."

"Of course," Valentine said. He sipped at his cup, and, as he set it down, he looked at her face for the first time. She looked right back at him; he blinked and looked away. "Your husband, uh, will he be joining us some time this weekend for a tour of what I have to show you?" He took a sip of his tea and blinked again, this time glancing at her face and then fixing his eyes on her pearls.

"No," she said. "Once I narrow the options to a property I'm impressed with, he'll make arrangements to see it. He doesn't have time to waste on choosing. He trusts me."

Valentine recrossed his legs and looked at hers yet again. "Of course," he said, reaching for a napkin and wiping his palms with it. "Um, did my assistant mention the fee? That you should have it today?"

She recrossed her legs, slowly this time, and watched his eyes. She left her knees apart for a beat before lifting her leg to settle in place. "I have the fee, Mr. Valentine," she said, smirking at his slack jaw. "Did you bring the contract?"

Valentine swallowed and took a breath. As he exhaled, he glanced at her face and then fumbled in his suit jacket pocket. He stood to hand her the folded paper. "All the terms are there, Mrs. Kinley," he said, his chilly smile returning. "I hope my assistant spelled your first names correctly. It's Deirdre and Francis, right? With an e before the i. And his with an i."

"Yes, mine is tricky, but his name is fairly standard. I see here you've got it right. Have a seat, Mr. Valentine, and I'll get the fee. You said cash, correct?"

Valentine remained standing and licked his lips. "Yes," he said, with a nervous nod. "Seems to work best that way."

"And will you produce a receipt, Mr. Valentine?" She stood and met his eyes. In her heels, she was his height. She smiled for the first time and watched his smile waver. He studied her eyes for a long moment and then glanced over at Sam and then back to her.

"Do I...do I know you, Mrs. Kinley?" he said, his eyes and head shifting in opposite directions. He held his swiveling head in place at last and fixed his eyes on hers. He swallowed, and his mouth collapsed at the edges.

"You certainly do," she said, holding him with her gaze. She'd trimmed her eyebrows but had left them dark. Her eyes were still the same pale green, difficult to forget. "Jake. Or should I call you Yakub? Jake Levin? Yakub Lewanowicz? Jerry Valentine? The man with so many names."

He shifted on his feet and stepped toward the door, but stopped when Sam lifted his eyes and having abandoned his passive gaze, froze Valentine in place.

"What the hell is this?" he said, looking back at her, then to Sam. "Who *are* you?"

She laughed, her smile breaking open for the first time, and she saw that he recognized her, finally.

He denied everything at first, telling her she had the wrong guy, that he could have her arrested if he wanted to. But when Sam moved closer to them, Valentine backed away from his blustery attack. She told him to sit, and she presented him with her terms. She didn't want money for herself or for her son. She wanted information. In exchange, she would not disclose his identity to his wife, his children, his wife-swapping partners, or to the *San Francisco Chronicle*. As a former newsman, she said, he would understand how that would work—a trusted high-end real estate salesman, but with oh-so-many names. She told him he was still being watched, just in case he thought that part of his deal with Giallo and Hafferty was over, given that it was made oh so long ago.

It took more than an hour, but he gave her everything she wanted, and then some. He remembered more than she expected he would. He expressed no regret or concern for her or her son, claiming he'd been given no choice. Still, she'd anticipated at least the courtesy of pretense, that he might feign remorse. But he was a businessman now, he said, and this was a transaction, just as their past relationship had been. He had no feelings where that deal was concerned. He said he never really loved her, if that mattered to her. She said the feeling was always mutual. She wasn't here to cry over a lost love. She was here to settle a score. He owed her, she said, and the information he gave her was all she wanted. After all, she told him, it was information she had helped him uncover, but he'd kept what he'd found out to himself, for a story he never wrote.

He said it was the story that almost got him killed, thanks to her family. He said that if she or her ape man, Sam, ever bothered him again, he'd have them both taken care of. She laughed at his empty bravado. She told him he had nothing to worry about from her, that she'd gotten what she came for. But, as for Sam, she said, he doesn't appreciate being referred to as a beast. She told him Sam was a talented artist and more of a man than he could ever hope to be. Sam stepped closer to him and did not smile.

At the door, she said he'd be best advised to grow some eyes on the back of his head. She described the photos she'd seen, and Sam stepped toward the door and tossed them at Valentine's feet. His eyes widened, and he reached for them just as Sam rested his foot on the photos. "Those do not belong to you," Sam said in his deepest bass baritone.

She said he should know that he would never be free of their surveillance. Ever. And that if she discovered he'd held back some information, or that if any of it turned out to be false, well, it was just a matter of a few phone calls, and his family life and his business would be in ruins.

As he left the suite, he paused to curse her. He said he hoped she would use the information he gave her to bring about her own demise.

"That's the only outcome you should expect," he scowled. "And the only one you deserve. Cunt!"

42
Holiday Fireworks

Thursday, July 3, 1969

Jade used Gort's real name when he tried to talk with him at the morning bus stop. He knew Smitty was on Belden's side and figured he might know what was going to happen next. He was even ready to ask him if he was still watching his house. Watching whom? Alice? Watching who was making the cash drops? Was that his job? For whom?

But he only got as far as "Smitty." The taller man glared at him behind his aviator glasses, his thin lips tight. He turned his back and leaned his upper body into the road, summoning the 15. Gort was back.

Jade shrugged and moved to his spot at the end of the queue. He didn't have the energy to persist with Gort. He was barely awake after a sleepless night. He'd kept the front door locked and had barricaded the back door with Alice's statues and had stood guard in the kitchen for as long as he could stay on his feet. He woke up on the couch at dawn. No sign of a breach.

A pall hung over Macson. The weather still hadn't lifted, and the men moved as if mired in quicksand; but there was a different kind of suppression in the air. Ten workers had been fired—all lieutenants of Cheese. And Cheese himself was absent from work. "General Patton" Jensen and Shop Steward Belden conducted a walking tour of the entire facility, pitching unity among the workers. The unspoken threat of termination hung over their pitch. There'd been many more than ten fighters in the melee, and Jensen and Belden knew who they were. By the end of the day, the Cheese faction, now leaderless and cornered, would back away into the ranks. Belden's position was secure.

There was no TV news van parked out front, but the news of the morning paper was stark. This time, the men did not stop working to read the newspaper and convene in the courtyard; instead, they made sure they'd read it before work and had clocked in on time and remained busy at their jobs, mindful of their supervisors. Or of an invisible eye. A half-hour after start time, there was no chatter among them, and, at the breaks, the yard was as silent as an empty church. No one knew who was next on the list, and now the possibilities had expanded to everyone.

"Leaders Reject Rumors; Give Nod to Moonshot." It was the lead story, a bold double headline. Hafferty had been interviewed, along with Congressman Walsh, for the follow-up story on the Macson plant's fate in a waning war effort, the fights there on Wednesday, and the national mood swing toward bringing the war to an end. Walsh was quoted giving reassurances about the Macson contract, and he added some vague references to a new upcoming contract; but it was Hafferty who made the story a redirect for the readers of the newspaper and then a stunner for the men at Macson.

He was quoted at length about how proud he and Walsh were of the Macson family of workers, toiling in the wicked heat to keep production going on the ordnance for America's fight against Communism. He said the disruption at the plant on Wednesday was caused by the heat wave, not by any dissension in the ranks, and he declared that the story was blown out of proportion by the clips shown on TV news.

"Making villains of our Macson family," he was quoted as saying, "is just as bad as those peacenik criminals making villains out of our returning soldiers—men who sacrifice life and limb for all Americans. Using the news to incite people against their own is a crime, in my view, and in the view of most Americans who love their country. Constant negative news turns a nation into cynics, always expecting the next story to be negative. Pretty soon, that's all people will want—negative news. And what does that leave us with? America at war with itself."

And then there was the redirect. "What we need to focus on now is the race to the moon! America has taken a back seat to the Soviets for the last decade or more, but that era is over. In just two weeks, we will be the first to put a man on the moon, taking our rightful position at the front of the race to reach new frontiers. The news our local TV stations seem to be missing is the excitement our region has for the moonshot."

And then, the stunner. When the story concluded with a recap about the Macson disruption on Wednesday, it used a quote from Hafferty that hadn't been used in the opening paragraphs. "I've been in discussions with the ownership of Macson Munitions," he was quoted as saying, "and I've learned there will be changes in personnel there." That quote was the callout in the middle of the front page, and it held every man at Macson in a frozen state of unspoken speculation.

At lunch break, Jade found Squirrel alone in a shaded corner of the yard. "You could hear a fart in China around here," he said, as Jade sat on the concrete next to him. "I thought I was finally deaf after a year with these goddamn machines, but I know that's not it. Everybody's holding their breath."

"Still no sign of Cheese?" Jade asked.

"That's one thing you shouldn't hold your breath for, brother," Squirrel replied. "That fat ugly douche bag shipped out with his family last night to who knows where. That's the scuttle, anyway. And you'll get a kick out of this one. Our good buddies Mutt and Jeff? They're on leave until further notice. Word at City Hall is that they'll show up next week in uniform walking separate beats. Big demotion. That doesn't make it safe for us to walk those streets while they're on leave, though. In fact, it makes it worse. Those two on nobody's chain in this town is like unleashing two rabid dogs in a schoolyard. The unsuspecting among us will be the most vulnerable. Better watch your back, Mr. Flynn."

"How are their big brothers taking the news?"

"How do you think? They're caught in the middle. Gripe about it, and they lose their rank and privileges. Take action on it, and they lose their jobs. I have a funny feeling those personnel changes Hafferty mentioned will start with those two assholes. The question is, who will replace them? And when?"

Squirrel closed his lunch pail and stood up to stretch. "Now, I guess we'll just have to wait and see who Hafferty's new payoff pals are gonna be. Today was the day I wanted to execute my spy mission. Guess I'll have to put it off until the dust settles."

"That's never gonna happen around here, Squirrel. It's a constant dust storm. You should get that crazy scheme out of your head, my friend."

Squirrel looked down at Jade and frowned. "You're starting to sound like your boss, Mr. Roland Wilson. Pretty soon you'll be picking up his fancy accent." He shuffled away muttering to himself.

At the final whistle, the workers cleared the plant in minutes. Roland vanished before Jade could catch him, and there was no sign of Squirrel. At the gate, a TV news reporter shouted questions in vain to the passing mob, sticking his microphone in a few faces until it got swatted from his hand by one of the bigger workers. The reporter and his cameraman scrambled to their van for cover.

Jade watched all of this from the side of the gate, wondering why he was there at all. He didn't belong at Macson. He wasn't one of these guys, and he never would be. He'd be out by early September, but that was two months away. At this rate, he wouldn't make it. Every choice he'd made about this job seemed to lead to turmoil. He wondered if Hafferty had finally made the wrong move. If the news story backfired on him, his whole empire could crumble. And, if so, Jade's deal with him would disappear. No chance for college. Even if he didn't lose his job in all this mess, without Hafferty's protection the Army was certain to give him the call that would end everything for him.

And, while he was relieved that Cheese was no longer a threat, Jade still wasn't sure about Ren Belden. Hafferty knew about the other Belden and Jensen—Joey and Billy. But did Ren think Jade had identified them to Hafferty? And, if so, it wasn't just Ren Belden he'd be threatened by; it would be his brother and his partner. They seemed a lot more dangerous than Ren. What would they do to him? Or worse, to Alice or Lucy?

As he neared the downtown bus station, Jade saw a Black woman in a long colorful dress getting on the 37 bus to Dickson College, and he hustled to get closer. At the door, the bus driver barked, "On or off, pal." Jade took one step up, just as the woman turned to sit down. She wasn't

Tamara. He turned and jumped off, and the doors clattered shut behind him.

On the 15 bus, he watched a blur of familiar territory glide by and wished he could talk with Tamara, wondering what she would think of his predicament. He closed his eyes and saw her face, her look of self-containment, of calm and welcome embrace. She couldn't protect him, but she could give him solace, peace, maybe a way out. He made a plan to get her phone number from Wally. But first, he had to check again on Lucy, to be sure she was safe. At least she now had the protection of Rocco, for what that was worth. As for Alice? He hoped, for once, she would not be home. There, she was a sitting duck.

As he got off at his stop near Smitty's house, Jade was startled by a red pickup pulling over and skidding to a stop in the gravel. He heard the familiar nasal yelp of Ren Belden and jumped back from the curb.

"Giving you fair warning, kid," Belden hollered from behind the wheel, beckoning Jade closer with his pudgy finger. As Jade ducked into the shotgun window, Belden's voice lowered to a snarl, his pudgy hands gripping the wheel, his cold vacant eyes drilling a hole into Jade. "Hafferty told me you didn't rat out my brother, but Joey don't believe it. He's gettin' hung out to dry over that colored girl's accident, and he needs somebody to blame. Looks like that might be you, kid. Better find your mother before he does. And that Juicy Lucy half-breed girlfriend of yours? Joey likes young girls, ya know." His thin lips pinched into a pucker, and his eyes bulged. "She's a slim one, tight little ass. But as Joey always says, the meat is sweeter closer to the bone, especially the dark meat." Belden pulled on the gear shift, and Jade stepped back as the pickup made a sudden lurch away from the curb, the tires spitting gravel around Jade's feet.

At home, there was still no Alice. The house looked undisturbed, no sign of unwelcome visitors. He barricaded the back door and called Lucy. No answer. He tried her later, and her mother said she was out. He didn't hear from Squirrel about a TV news follow up, so he called Hafferty's office to ask him about Ren Belden, but Louise said Hafferty would not be available through the holiday weekend. Jade urged her to have her boss call him, but she said she doubted he would. Jade took one more desperate stab at rousing her boss from his possum game. He told her Cheese had spread word at Macson that Hafferty was stealing federal government money from the munitions operation and that Jensen and Belden were getting cuts. He said he wasn't sure how many workers Cheese had told, but it was making the rounds fast.

"Are you still there?" he asked when Louise fell silent.

"Yes," she said, her voice low. "I wrote it down. He'll get the message."

264

Jade wondered if his bait would backfire. He knew he'd stepped on Squirrel's toes by sharing his suspicions, but it was worth the gambit. Squirrel's plan was hairbrained at best; but the information would surely arouse alarm in Hafferty.

While Jade waited for Hafferty's call back, he took a chance at tying up the line and called Lucy again. Her mother hung up on him. Since he still hadn't heard from Squirrel about a TV news follow up, he tried to relax on the couch. He pulled a book from Alice's stack of suggested titles on the coffee table. *The Price of Salt.* Patricia Highsmith. He hoped it wasn't another one of her psychological thrillers.

He was startled awake in the dark house by a blaring horn that brought him to his feet trembling. He didn't know where he was until another horn blast filled the house. He stumbled in the shadows to the front window and moved the curtain an inch, the faded fabric trembling in his fist. The knot in his gut tightened. A dark coupe was parked in front of the house just a few feet away, the engine running and the lights on. He could make out the shadow of a guy at shotgun, but he couldn't see the driver. It wasn't the black Galaxy, but it could have been Billy Jensen's car, which would mean the guy at shotgun was Joey.

The horn blasted again, the shotgun window opened, and a man's voice shouted from the shadow, "Flynn! Jade Flynn! Your number's up, boy." He saw the shadow's arm cocking in the frame. The arm hurled something at the house, and it thudded against the front door. Jade hit the floor and held his arms over his head.

But there was no explosion. The horn blasted yet again, and then the engine revved with a roar. As Jade crept to his knees to peek out the window, the coupe jumped from the curb in a squeal of tires and a cloud of smoke. Jade saw a flash of color under a streetlight as the car sped away. He opened the door a crack, waiting for his eyes to adjust, then pulled the door wider and stepped outside. Something was sizzling at the curb. He ducked back toward the door, but then caught himself. It wasn't a fuse; it was a spume of foam spraying from a pierced beer can, leaking suds into the street.

"Rocco's Camaro," Jade muttered to himself, his heart pounding. He jumped when a porch light next door flicked on. He ducked inside, sucking in air, trying to slow the hammering in his chest. The knot tightened deeper in his belly.

That was Lucy behind the wheel, no doubt. Two drunks on the night before July Fourth, out on another one of Rocco's pathetic hunts. This time, Jade was the prey.

Part Five

43
The Wall

Saturday, July 5, 1969

She slipped inside the door, a sliver of daylight piercing the dark room with a flash of summer. In the dim light, she took off her sunglasses and tried to focus. Sam and the boys were busy setting up for a session. He looked tired as he lumbered over his instrument cases and microphone stands, wires unfurling at his huge feet. She waited.

Luke poked his head around the bar wall, a towel on his shoulder. He looked her over slowly and smirked. "We open at six, miss," he said, surveying her again. He stepped into the open and cocked his head, trying to figure out who he was looking at. She nodded once, then lifted her chin toward Sam. Luke gave her another quizzical look, and then turned toward the band members. "Hey, Sam. You got a visitor."

She'd considered dying her hair again, but she'd been too exhausted. Long-distance travel, her Nob Hill gambit, and the effects of her abstinence had worn her down. She felt dull and had tried to use the old trick of dressing nice to push down the emptiness, but it wasn't working. The happy summer look she'd picked up in cold San Francisco—red boat-neck top, beige clam diggers, a big pink beach bag, and low-cut white tennies she bought at City of Paris on Union Square—made her feel more like a fraud than a cheerful blonde out for a summer afternoon frolic. Who was she kidding? Last time here, she was in all-black, her mind lost in a dreamscape. Now, she was trying out the flip side of that look, but it felt as meaningless as it probably appeared.

"Well, check you out, all dressed for the beach," Sam said, his tired eyes smiling down at her. That baritone laugh made her chuckle in spite of herself.

"Ridiculous, huh?" she shrugged. "I can't stay here, Sam. The stale smell of cigarettes and booze makes me want to camp out at that bar for a week. But I'm on a mission. Gotta stay straight. I must give you this and go." She held out an envelope filled with cash.

"Oh no, no," Sam said, holding up his massive palms and frowning. "You owe me nothin', honey. Hell, I flew first class. Both ways. First time ever. Stayed in a fancy hotel with clean sheets. Got to see my favorite city, even though it doesn't look like it did in the fifties—hell they even closed The Tin Angel. Anyway, you keep that. You already went through a bundle. You need it, now."

"You lost three nights of work for me, Sam. And you must be exhausted. This is the least I can do for what you've done for me." She held the envelope up toward his face.

He stepped back and shook his head, grinning. "First class. The looks we got? Worth ten nights' work to me," he said, a chuckle bubbling up in his huge frame. "The story of this entire nation was written on those faces. Big Black man riding first class with a beautiful White woman? I thought their eyeballs were gonna pop out of their heads. 'Specially the chubby White guys in their stiff shirts and red ties with their first-class martinis. Hell, even the stewardess, who gets paid to smile, looked at us like we were a damn house on fire."

She laughed with him as she stuffed the envelope back into her bag, shaking her head.

"We had a good time, didn't we, Sam?" she said. "We pulled off a great show. You're a natural actor."

"Been on stage most of my life, honey," he said, nodding his giant head, his grin savoring the memory.

"Why are you so good to me, Sam?" she said, her eyes welling up.

He glanced over his shoulder for Luke, then tipped his face down to hers. "That first night she brought you in here? I could tell you were on your own, been that way for a long time. People on their own don't ask nobody for help. But when our Marte disappeared and then you come back here lookin' lost? I figured it was the last I'd ever see you. Then you come back again and ask for my help?" Sam shook his great head and gave her a sad smile, his eyes growing wider. "I don't make a practice of playin' bodyguard for nobody, 'specially a White woman who's got what you got." His eyes danced as they swept over her hair and her face and her body, and then he frowned. "A man my size and color attracts enough trouble on my own, so I don't need to go lookin' for it. But I knew you been through real tough times, 'specially with her gone and all. I knew it musta meant you were at the end of your rope. I just couldn't stand by and watch you slam into whatever wall you were comin' up on."

She nodded, then lowered her head and swiped the back of her hand across her moist eyes.

"And one other thing, honey. All that stuff you and that fella talked about, and all the stuff you told me later?" He threw his hands up like wings taking off. "Poof. It's all gone. I don't remember a word of it. 'Specially if somebody nosey comes askin'."

268

She set her bag on the floor and wrapped her arms around his thick middle and lay her head on his massive chest. It felt like she was hugging a redwood. He left her there against him for a moment and then set his hands on her shoulders and gently tugged her away from his big body. His eyes turned serious as he looked down into her face again.

"You tell me, honey. Tell me you're gonna forget all that, too. You need to put it behind you. Walk away. That's what Marte would do. Hell, we thought we lost her, but she got taken from us. And the way you told me, I think she knew there was nothin' she could do about it. So she just moved on. Which is exactly what you need to do. You can't bring a pea shooter to a gunfight, honey. Those two guys you told me about? They got big guns, and no sheriff watchin' over 'em. They make people disappear, honey. You told me so."

She wanted to hug him again, but she just tried to grin at him. She failed. "They make everyone I love disappear, Sam." She blinked away tears and looked up at his face again. "But not me. They just keep me on their leash, on the very edge of sanity."

She shook her head and put the strap of her pink bag on her shoulder. "You're right about that wall, Sam. It's still there; we just moved it back a little, that's all. I have to get over it. Or through it somehow. And now, I finally have a way to do that. Thanks to you."

She turned toward the door, put her hand on the knob and looked back at Sam. He was a mountain in the shadows. And she could see his big head moving from side to side.

"Just walk away, honey. It's too dangerous. You don't need to go over or through that wall. Just walk in another direction. Fast as you can go."

She opened the door, letting a wash of daylight fill the club. Sam held his hand over his eyes to block the sudden brilliance. He looked like a giant soldier saluting.

"Thank you, Sam," she said, and then slipped out, into the blinding light.

44

Rescue at the Rez

Saturday, July 5, 1969

Jade stood on the dirt patch between the sidewalk and the narrow front porch. Lucy's bare feet were perched on the banister in the sun, the calf muscles of her long honey-colored legs flexing in rhythm as she rocked mechanically in a metal lawn chair. Her white cut-offs were hiked to the tops of her legs, the fringe making a feathery penumbra there. Her face was in the shadow of the awning, and Jade saw it light up bronze as she sucked on a Parliament, her eyes wide on him.

He could tell she was trying to hide her surprise at his sudden appearance, pursing her lips and then narrowing her eyes to roll out her unwelcome mat. He'd taken the 15 into town and had hiked at a slow pace through the steep North Heights and down into the moat of her shabby neighborhood. He thought the rowhouses here seemed only slightly less exhausted than those in Mell Hollow. But just like his neighborhood on this weekend, American flags gave color to nearly every porch along Lucy's street. It was expected that neighborhoods like his and hers—the ones that supplied most of the region's young men for Vietnam—would display their continued allegiance to the war effort, some perhaps in response to Hafferty's jingoistic exhortation in the newspaper, others in appreciation of the freebies handed out in Friday's annual Independence Day parade by Hafferty's smiling girls in tri-colored bikinis perched on the rear seats of his fleet of Cadillac convertibles. Lucy's porch was among the few that wasn't adorned with the Stars and Stripes.

"You gonna stand there all day and stare at me?" Lucy chided without a smile. Her silky black hair was pulled back in a ponytail, the peroxided fringe setting off her chestnut brown face. She was wearing that white eye shadow he hated. Her breasts pushed at the thin cotton fabric of her white tank top, bouncing softly in her rocking motion. Jade could see her nipples through the shirt. She was braless.

He shifted his Converse high tops in the dirt, nodded his head, and struggled to smile.

"You gonna invite me up on the porch?"

"Invitation's in the mail," she snapped, as she increased the rhythm of her rocking and took another drag on her cigarette.

"Writing me hate mail now?"

"Who said I hate you?" she said as she exhaled, her voice shrouded in smoke. "You're the one who never calls."

Now Jade's smile was genuine. He sighed and shook his head. "Here we go. Barely see each other for a week, and we're at it right away."

Lucy rocked steadily and took another drag. She blew a cloud into the air, then wedged the cigarette expertly on her thumb and middle finger and flicked it into the yard a few feet from Jade.

"I'm not the one who forgets to call," she said.

Jade one-hopped the short steps and perched himself on the banister to face her. "I called you a half-dozen times in the last two days. According to your mother, you're never home. Out in Rocco's Camaro harassing neighbors, I suppose. Tossing loaded beer cans at front doors?"

Lucy continued to rock and looked toward the street, pretending to watch a passing car. "Don't know what you're talking about."

"Don't know? Or don't remember? Last night around midnight. You were driving, he rode shotgun. He tossed a loaded beer at my front door, and you peeled out like you were in the Pocono quarter mile."

She spurted a laugh she couldn't hold in and stood up. She pulled her ponytail out and shook her hair loose, her breasts swaying. "Must've been a bad dream," she said behind the veil of her hair, her voice innocent as a child's. "Having lots of those lately?" She emerged from the veil and pouted at him. "Poor baby." She turned her body to face him and offered a deadpan face.

Jade hopped off the banister and stood at the top of the steps, his hands on his hips. Lucy asked him if he were leaving. He wanted to say, "Yes," but instead he looked out onto the street, watched another passing car in silence, and wondered why he was denying his instinct—just walk away from this dead end. He stood there staring at nothing, certain of just one thing: this relationship was the only remaining string of attachment he had left in the frayed rope of his life. If it snapped, he'd be in a freefall.

He was distracted from this impasse by the sudden appearance of a long shiny new black car that seemed to have materialized at the curb in front of them. It was so out of place in a neighborhood where the cars were mostly beat up bombs that Jade doubted for a moment what he was staring at. When he recognized the Fleetwood Caddy, his stomach flipped. Stanley. He looked quickly to his left to identify an escape path. The driver's tinted window opened with a pop, and Jade stiffened as he struggled with the instinct to dive out of the way of gunfire.

The face in the open window confused him. If it wasn't Stanley, the best Jade could have expected was Dennis Hafferty's neon smile of capped teeth filling the frame. Instead, he saw a dark-faced man in black sunglasses wearing a black beret. The man smiled. His teeth were not capped; they were perfect.

"At your service, sir," the man called out over a hard-driving bass guitar coming from the car stereo. When the song's vocals started with a man imploring a woman to get into his big, black car, Jade knew the song: it was Cream's *Politician*. The driver nodded his head to the rhythm of the music, leaned back and turned up the volume. A deep, grinding guitar riff and heavy bass notes thumped through the ground, rumbling the porch beneath Jade's feet.

The music stopped, and the driver stepped out of the car, still smiling. He was wearing a black shirt and black pants, and he removed his beret and made a deep bow toward the porch. "I am here to cool you off," the driver announced, his voice hitting Jade like a wave of light. "To liberate you from your sweltering surroundings." The accent was unmistakable.

Jade's jaw hung open. He turned to Lucy, half-expecting her to see nothing, unaware of what surely must be Jade's own daydream. But she was on the top step next to him, smiling and then laughing. "Oh, my God," she squealed. "Roland Wilson? I must be dreaming. What a car!" Then she turned to Jade. "A big, black one!"

Lucy laughed and scrambled onto the sidewalk, and then halted halfway toward Roland. His smile waned for a moment as his eyes ran over her. The smile returned.

"At your service, madam," Roland said, nodding his head, his beret held to his chest. Then he stepped back and pulled open the rear door. The interior was dark but Jade could see the sheen of the familiar leather seat. "You heard the man sing it, honey." Roland said to Lucy, his smile beaming. "Be my guest."

Lucy squealed again and turned around to look at Jade. He could see an excitement in her eyes that he hadn't witnessed in a long time. "Aren't you going to introduce me?" she said, offering the coquettish smile he'd almost forgotten.

Roland interrupted. "No need," he said to her. "You must be Lucy."

Lucy turned around to him and held out an imaginary skirt and curtsied. Roland bowed his head again, beret still at his chest.

Jade was perplexed by Roland's sudden change in attitude, as if someone had switched off his mordant personality and flipped on a new, outgoing, cordial one, with a less than subtle touch of sarcasm to it. Could this guy actually have a sense of humor?

"How did you know about Lucy and where she lives?" Jade asked, as Lucy minced around the Caddy in her bare feet, running her thin hands along the gleaming black fenders and polished chrome, shaking her head, her mouth hanging open.

"How do you think I knew?" Roland said with that smile Jade hadn't recognized. "Who would you ask if you wanted to know such things?"

Jade smirked and nodded with a huff. The omniscient Squirrel, of course.

Jade rode shotgun, Lucy in the back. Roland turned on the music again, as Lucy lay on the wide leather seat and crooned about it being her "royal bed." She announced she was being fanned and fed grapes by naked, royal servants—men, she said, who longed for her, but could only look and want. Roland laughed heartily at Lucy's lusty drama, accompanied by Cream wailing on the stereo speakers about a white room with black curtains. Suddenly done with this playacting, Lucy scrambled into the front seat between Roland and Jade.

"I really *am* dreaming!" she bleated, holding the sides of her face. Then she ran her long fingers over the gleaming wood veneer dashboard.

The car seemed to float through Lucy's neighborhood. Jade felt like they were in a movie. He couldn't feel the road, and the music was so clear it seemed to be coming from inside his head. When Roland switched the tape and sang out the opening lyrics of "Crosstown Traffic" along with Hendrix, Jade wasn't sure if the selection was intentional, but, by the end of the first verse, he was certain that Roland was more than just surprisingly funny. He was ironic. Was this sudden transformation from somber bitterness to playful levity an act or a revelation? Was this performance for Lucy, whom Roland had never met, or for Jade? If it was for him, why? Had Hafferty put Roland up to this game?

Roland turned onto Cobalt Avenue and announced he was heading for the hills. Jade reached in front of Lucy and turned down the volume.

"What the hell are you doing with Hafferty's car?" he said. Lucy frowned at Jade and reached for the dial, but he held her wrist. He glared at her, and she pulled away and stuck out her tongue at him.

Roland frowned and looked over the top of his sunglasses. "You're bringing me down, Flynn," he said, his smile now at half-mast." He shut off the music and looked at Jade again, but this time through the dark lenses. "He asked me to get it washed for him," Roland said. "He's visiting with the professor. Time for little boys to run along."

Jade was about to ask him if he'd talked to Hafferty about Ren and Joey Belden, but he held back when Roland's eyes met his above the dark lenses again, and he shook his head, as if he knew what Jade was thinking. Roland reached in front of Lucy and turned on the music again.

"Let's hit the rez!" he shouted, leaning toward Lucy, his perfect smile rebounding.

She nodded to him, smiling back, and then turned to Jade, raising her voice over the music. "Isn't that where you and that rodent guy went last weekend?"

"You know about the rez?" Jade asked Roland, shouting over Lucy's head.

"Of course I do," he said. "Been hanging around with Squirrel for years. That's his sanctuary. Been there plenty of times. I almost have his nature lecture memorized." He looked over at Jade and smiled. "You must have had your first lesson last week."

"The guy is nuts," Jade said. "That water's cold enough to frost your balls, and that loony bastard spends a half hour in it flopping around like it's a bathtub."

"I'm not goin' in if it's that cold," Lucy said, "balls or no balls."

"Nobody's gonna force you in, Lucy," Roland assured her. "If you can't swim, it doesn't matter how cold it is."

"I didn't say I couldn't swim," Lucy retorted. "I just don't want to swim in ice water."

Halfway up the mountain, Jade noticed that the trees had filled in since the previous Saturday. In just one week, the rows of scrub oaks and ash and maples along the winding road had thickened with new lime green leaves, camouflaging the depth of the forest and eliminating the hypnotic picket-fence effect that Jade had been entranced by on his trip with Squirrel. In the Corvair shotgun seat, Jade had felt every crack in the road. This time, he was soaring above it, Hafferty's Fleetwood flying around turns at rocket ship speed and providing a cushion from both nature and reality that seemed surreal to Jade.

"That was one thing I couldn't do when I was a kid," Roland said as he lowered the music volume.

"What are you talking about?" Lucy asked.

"Swim," Roland said. "I couldn't swim when I was a kid."

"No one just swims automatically," Lucy said. "I didn't learn until my brother threw me in the Lincoln Park pool. What a sewer. Worse than The Filthy." She reached back and retied her ponytail, her braless breasts wobbling with the effort, her nipples erect. Jade saw Roland glance down at them. "I had to learn fast so I wouldn't swallow any turds!" she said, squealing out a laugh.

"My father pushed me in, too," Roland said. "It was at the Y; I was eleven. I excelled at every other sport, and he was determined, I swear, to find one I could not do. And he sure did. 'Black boys can't swim,' he said to me, as he shoved me into the pool. 'That's what they say,' he told me, 'Negroes can't swim.' So I flopped around gasping for air, and then trying my ass off for the next two weeks to do exactly what he wanted me to do—prove everybody wrong."

"So how long did it take you?"

"About a year," Roland laughed. "I ended up joining the swim team, but I couldn't finish better than third place in anything. That was new to me, and I think that's what my father wanted ultimately—to show me I can't be the best in everything. He wanted to disprove the myth about Black swimmers, but even more so, he wanted to let me know I wasn't invincible."

At the top of the mountain, Roland swerved off the winding road, launching a dust cloud around the Caddy and eliciting a screech from Lucy. He gave a sharp tug at the wheel, and the big machine floated sideways for a moment and then straightened out onto a dirt road. Jade and Lucy were flung toward Roland, all three in a crush in the driver's seat.

"Jesus Christ, man!" Jade hollered. "I hope you swim better than you drive!"

Roland just laughed, managing the wheel with one hand as the car careened and fishtailed along the road. Jade pushed himself away from Lucy and slid across to shotgun, but Lucy stayed in place, holding onto Roland's unoccupied arm, laughing. "Oh, my God!" she shrieked. "You're insane!"

Roland seemed as familiar with the road to the reservoir as Squirrel had been. He swerved around fallen branches and deep ruts as if the Caddy were a slalom racer. They reached the reservoir in half the time it had taken the Corvair. Roland plunged the big machine up the final knoll and slid the car to a stop ten yards from the water's edge.

"Jesus!" Lucy screamed. "I thought you were gonna plunge this thing right in!" She flopped back against the seat with a sigh and laughed. "My God, I'm exhausted and we haven't even done anything."

Jade was the first one to the water's edge. He peered along the shoreline to the dam, looking for geese. He surveyed the knotted bushes and timothy grass along the shoreline for signs of other creatures from Squirrel's nature lecture, but he came up empty. He shoved the toe of his Converse into the rocky soil, hoping to stir something, even a snail or a worm. Nothing.

"Hear the woodpecker?" Roland said, sidling up next to Jade. "My favorite creature," he said, chuckling. "Squirrel describe him to you?"

Jade nodded.

"But you didn't see him, did you?"

"I didn't see ninety-nine percent of the creatures he was pointing out," Jade said. "I didn't know if they were really here, or he was just making it all up." He looked at Roland for an answer but got a poker face and smirk.

"Ouch!" Lucy called out, as she inched down the knoll toward the shoreline, tentatively stepping between reeds and rocks. "Why didn't you tell me I needed shoes?"

Roland chuckled at her. "You need to toughen up those feet," he said.

"These feet are plenty tough," she shot back without taking her eyes from her path. "But there's broken glass here."

"And snakes!" Jade chided. "A big black snake chased me out of the water last week just over there."

"Goddamn it, Jade!" Lucy scolded. "I'll kill you if I get bitten by a black snake."

Roland smiled to himself as he picked up a handful of slate stones and started skipping them across the water's surface. His wrist flicked, and the stones sailed like flying saucers, skimming the surface only to find air again and again. Jade held his ammo at his side as he marveled at

Roland's little spaceships skipping all the way to the opposite shore. He leaned over and started to fire away with a few of his own when Lucy complained loudly. "Go ahead, you two. Have a nice old time while a girl gets stabbed by glass and bitten by snakes."

The sun felt warmer at this elevation, the air so fresh, so liberating to Jade, compared to the clogged, sodden mass that choked the valley. Bugs danced over the water and in the high grass at the reservoir edge. The sweet scents of the wild, the heavy aroma of the earth coming alive again. He took a deep breath of this fresh stuff and exhaled. He closed his eyes and tried to renew his acquaintance with the finer sounds, his ears numbed now after two weeks of assault at the Macson plant. He wanted desperately to reawaken his lost senses, his self-sacrifice to the god of lucre.

But Lucy wouldn't let him revel in his renewal. She persisted with her noisy mincing toward the shoreline, squealing and yelping with every step among the tall reeds and broken shale. "Goddamn it, Jade, at least you could help me! You're just standing there! This is painful."

Jade opened his eyes and turned to watch Roland move away from the water toward Lucy. When he reached her side, she clung heavily to his outstretched arm and hopped alongside Roland toward the water.

"So, there *is* a gentleman here after all!" Lucy exclaimed.

Jade caught her irritated look and then turned back toward the water. In the distance, on the far shore, he spied five geese descending from the tall grasses into the murky ford near the dam. Squirrel's family of friends all settled in now.

Roland left Lucy at the water's edge and walked into a copse of hickory and maple trees. As he disappeared into the shadows, Jade assumed he was responding to nature's call. He was surprised when nature took an unexpected turn.

Roland came running from the trees, naked except for his black sneakers. "I can't swim! I can't swim! I can't swim!" he yelled as he headed pell-mell toward the reservoir edge. His body gleamed in the high sun, his dark muscles etched by the contrast of shadow and light as he ran toward the water, his arms flailing with exaggeration. "Black boys can't swim!" he hollered as his legs cut into the dark water, and he pitched himself headfirst into the rez.

Jade turned to Lucy who had stopped in the grass ten feet from the water's edge to witness Roland's mad dash. She wasn't smiling; she was gaping, her eyes like saucers. Jade turned back to watch Roland's head and shoulders emerge at the surface of the water.

"Yeeeeoww! It's fucking freezing!" Roland shouted. "My balls just fell off!"

He plunged back toward the shoreline and hoisted himself from the water, trudging through the muddy edge and emerging onto the shore with heavy footfalls and an exaggerated shiver. He turned around toward the water and bent over to look at himself. "They're gone! My balls are gone!"

Lucy erupted into laughter, nearly doubling over but keeping her eyes on Roland. Jade felt suddenly unsteady on his feet, even though he wasn't moving.

Roland turned around to face them. "They're gone!" he shouted, smiling at Lucy, and holding out his hands. "My frozen balls have fallen off."

Jade could see that this was not the case. Roland's genitals were intact, even if his testicles did seem to have disappeared up high behind his dark pendulous penis. As Roland stood up straight in the mud and held out his arms wider, Jade could see that Roland was a perfect specimen. His thighs were thick and his calves sharply defined—a running back's legs. His shoulders and chest were masses of cut muscle.

"Come on, you two," Roland called. "Get your clothes off and help me find my lost balls!" He was laughing now and waving his arms at Lucy and Jade. She looked over at Jade. He could see that she wanted to follow Roland's lead, but that she wanted Jade's consent. He needed to make the first move.

Jade pulled his tee shirt over his head and flung it into the reeds. Roland let out a howl, and, in response, Lucy crisscrossed her hands and lifted her tank top over her head and tossed it aside. Her breasts bounced lazily on her ribs, and she reached up and liberated her ponytail. Black and blonde-streaked hair tumbled over her shoulders onto her breasts. She looked over to Jade and then to Roland, smiling, her eyes on fire. She let her head fall back to her shoulders and shouted into the blue expanse above.

"I'm gonna freeze my balls off!"

Roland yelped his approval, and then Lucy twisted and swayed her body in a dance to silent music, her undulating breasts creating the beat. She pulled at the top of her cutoffs. She ran her thumbs around the front of her waistband, and then unsnapped the button with a dramatic flick of her hand.

Jade moved his hands to his own belt but left them there. He felt a cold wave of air on his back and shivered just a little. He took his eyes off Lucy for a moment to watch Roland staring and smiling at her. Roland started to clap his hands in time with her as if he, too, heard the music she was dancing to.

Lucy's breasts started a new rhythm as she shifted her hips back and forth and ran her hands up her sides and into the air. Her body was now moving at Roland's clapping beat. She pushed her knees together and unzipped her shorts and pulled them open, revealing the lacy top of her white bikini underpants. As she shifted her hips from side to side, she held her chin in the air and closed her eyes.

Jade could see that she was smirking more than smiling now. He swallowed hard as he watched her tug at the top of her shorts and yank them down below her hips. She twisted her body again, letting the moment of revelation sink in, the white panties now in full view.

"Oh, yeah!" Roland yelled out, his rhythmic clapping picking up the pace.

Lucy kept her eyes closed and continued to sway back and forth for another long moment, her breasts shifting under her long hair, the nipples dark against her light brown skin. Then, she opened her knees and the shorts fell to her feet. She gave one more shift of the hips and then stepped out of her shorts. She pushed her hair up in a sweep of her hands and then turned her back to Roland and sashayed her panty-clad rear at him, looking over her shoulder for his reaction.

"Yeah, baby!" Wilson shouted, still clapping. "Mmm hmmm, you're a foxy lady, Lucy!"

Jade's stomach was starting to betray him. He felt a wave of nausea pass through him and push up toward his throat. This was an act Lucy had performed for him often enough, but it was altogether different now. He wasn't sure theirs was even a relationship at this point, and he wondered if he had the right to feel jealous about what was happening. But his stomach—his trusty barometer—was telling him he wasn't ready for this. As distant as he'd felt from Lucy in recent weeks, it was too soon for her to simply throw herself at someone else—Roland Wilson, no less—right in front of him. Jade felt his throat close. He wanted to shout out but his voice was trapped.

Lucy wiggled her rear end a few more times and then tugged slowly at the seat of her panties until they slipped below her buttocks. Then she wiggled again, opened her legs and let the panties parachute to the ground.

Roland let out a cheer and turned his rhythmic clapping into applause. Lucy turned around slowly and faced him, fully naked now. Although Roland and Lucy were twenty feet apart, Jade could see they were carefully inspecting each other's bodies. Jade was close enough to her that he could see Lucy's face change, her carefree stripper's smirk melting into a stunned line, her eyes glowing. She stood as she did a week ago in her living room, her legs slightly apart, hands on her hips, her long hair strewn over her breasts. But this time, she wasn't wearing panties, and this time, she wasn't looking at Jade. He watched her eyes for a moment longer and then looked down at her full breasts, her flat tummy and the neat slit her belly button made. Her body was so familiar to him, and yet he was looking at it now as if he'd never before seen it. Finally, he let his eyes fall to the place at the top of her open legs, the small tuft of soft curls and then below, the gash of silky folds and the slightly parted pink lips—her secret, as she had called it. A secret no longer.

"C'mon, Flynn, take off your pants!" Roland called out. "Everybody's naked!"

Lucy started to walk through the remaining few feet of brush toward the water. Jade noticed that she moved with purpose, no longer tentative. He pulled at his own clothing in a mechanical way as he watched her approach the water's edge. As she passed without looking at him, he let his pants fall to the ground. He stood in his boxers, socks and sneakers and watched her test the water with her toes, as Roland gazed at her body up close.

"Time for a dip!" Roland shouted. He plunged into the dark water, swam a few strong strokes and then dove headlong. His backside appeared above the surface in a showy maneuver, and his legs and feet followed as he disappeared. Lucy's back was to Jade now, but he could see her shoulders shaking with laughter. Her own backside looked sexier to him now than he'd ever thought before.

Suddenly, Roland's head and shoulders burst out of the water, and he let out a blood-curdling gasping cry. "Aaaggghhh!"

He was twenty feet from the shore and flailing his arms in the water and hollering words Jade couldn't make out.

Lucy bent forward, laughing, and then turned to look at Jade. He could see she thought Roland was toying with them, pretending to be drowning, pretending to carry on with his earlier ruse, mocking the myth about Black swimmers. But Jade sensed that Roland wasn't playacting at all. His motions were too frantic to be intentional. And when Roland turned his head to look at Lucy and Jade, his eyes looked angry. He wasn't treading water so much as fighting it.

"He's in trouble!" Jade shouted, finally finding his voice. Lucy was still smiling as she turned around completely toward him. She was startled as he rushed past her into the water, diving headfirst.

By the time he reached Roland, the flailing had subsided to a few splashes and Roland's shoulders and neck had sunk beneath the water's surface. He was working hard at treading water. Jade stopped swimming a few feet from Roland and looked at his face. His eyes were wide with terror. He was choking and gasping for air.

"Roland!" Jade called to him. "Give me your hand." He reached out, but Roland just continued to thrash at the water and gasp. Jade moved closer, and Roland pushed a wave of water at his face.

"Nah!" was all that Roland could utter. Jade moved closer. He reached out again, this time touching Roland's shoulder under the water. Suddenly, Jade was stung in the nose with a backhand from Roland. Jade paddled backward to a safe distance, and then he dove under and surfaced just a foot in front of Roland's face and punched him squarely in the nose.

Wilson was startled for a moment, and then Jade felt something hit him hard in the middle. As he ducked under water, he saw Roland's leg withdrawing. The kick packed more surprise than wallop, and Jade resurfaced behind Roland. He grabbed the big man under the chin and tried to pull him toward the shore. Roland thrashed and tried to punch and claw at Jade. In the struggle, they'd moved closer to the shoreline; but then Roland landed a solid punch to Jade's face, and he went under. The punch penetrated to the core of Jade's brain. He was still conscious, but he was stunned and felt himself sinking.

Suddenly, he felt something tugging at his hair. He was being pulled to the surface by the top of his head. Jade clenched his fist and came up swinging but hit nothing but air. He looked to his left and saw the top of Roland's head. He wasn't moving.

"Hey!" Lucy yelled to him. She was right behind him. It had been her hand in his hair. "Get his head out of the water. I'll get a hip under him. Let's go!"

They pulled and pushed Roland, grappling with his resistance. His strength was drained, but still formidable. Just as exhaustion started to overcome them, Jade felt land underfoot. They dragged Roland into the shallow water and collapsed next to him on their knees. He lay on his back, sinking in the reeds. Jade pushed himself to his feet and grabbed Roland under the arms. He was dead weight.

"Get up!" he yelled to Lucy. "Help!"

Lucy struggled to her feet. Water and mud sloughed off her knees and calves. She shook the wet strings of hair out of her face and helped Jade drag Roland to dry land.

On the shore, they took turns trying to revive Roland. Finally, he choked and gasped and vomited a stream of water and then struggled to his knees. He tried to stand. Jade marveled for a moment at the man's strength, but Roland quickly fell to his knees and then onto all fours, choking and spitting up more water.

"Jesus Christ, we all nearly drowned!" Lucy gasped at Roland, coughing. "What the hell were you doing out there?" She was breathing heavily, on all fours facing Roland, the front of her body covered in mud. She sat on her heels and pulled her hair back and twisted it into a knot on her neck, her breasts heaving, her face hot with anger. "I thought you were kidding around! Goddamn it, Roland, you really *can't* swim! Why the hell did you dive in like that?"

Roland continued to cough and choke up water. He tried to talk but his words were muffled, so he just lowered his head and hacked away.

"I'll go find his clothes," Jade said. "Don't let him stand yet."

When Jade returned to the shore, Roland had stopped hacking and was sitting back on his heels a few feet from Lucy, facing the water. Jade thought they looked like shipwreck victims. They were exhausted, staring at the ground in front of them. Roland pushed himself up on his knees and attempted to stand but his stomach was still convulsing, his lungs barking out more water, and he sat back on his heels and sagged. Jade looked down at Roland's penis contracted into a lump amid wiry black hair and chuckled to himself. He couldn't tell if his balls were still there.

Roland suddenly found his feet and stumbled to his pile of clothes. "We have to go," he croaked and then coughed in a fit again. As he started to dress, he found his voice. "Get your clothes, we have to leave."

"What's the rush," Lucy said. "Jesus, I'm barely alive here." She knelt in the shallow water and washed the mud from the front of her body.

Jade looked out onto the reservoir and thought he saw something on the surface of the water. He stood up and stepped toward the water's edge, shielding his eyes from the sharp reflection of the sun.

"I have to get the car back," Wilson said, his voice stronger. He pulled his pants over his jockey briefs and grappled with his shirt until he was able to tug it down over his trunk. He coughed a few more times and then raised his voice again. "Let's go! Everyone. Get your clothes on."

"Hold on. I thought I saw something in the water," Jade said. He waded a few more feet into the surf and squinted into the sun.

"I don't give a shit," Wilson shot back. "I have to get that car back right now. Find your clothes, and let's get the hell out of here."

"Aye aye, captain," Lucy mocked as she slowly found her feet and shuffled into the tall grass. "You're welcome, by the way. For saving your life!"

Roland re-tied his black sneakers in silence and then started toward the car. Jade squinted one more time toward the reflecting water and then found his pile of clothes and began dressing.

Lucy shuffled through the tall grass nearby. She was still naked, her hair dripping and tangled, her body blotched with mud.

"Anybody see a pair of white panties?"

45

In Her Arms, On the Dunes

Saturday, July 5, 1969

The ride down the mountain was fast, but quiet, except on the sharp turns in the road when the tires squealed underneath them. Lucy asked Roland to turn on some music, but he just stared straight ahead as if she hadn't spoken. She was alone in the cavernous back seat; Jade was at shotgun. The Caddy soared over the road, a living room on the loose, floating and fishtailing down the steep decline. Roland wove the big swaying machine through tight curves as if he were driving a sports car. Jade was certain they would end up in the woods.

At the foot of the mountain, back on the grid of the valley streets, Jade finally broke the silence.

"What happened to you up there?"

His words sounded more accusatory than he'd intended. But, aside from the muscle twitching in Roland's jaw, the big man seemed unfazed. Still, Jade thought he looked more vulnerable without his beret and sunglasses.

After a long pause, Roland glanced at Jade and then at Lucy in the rear-view mirror. "Swallowed some water, that's all," he said.

"Jesus," Lucy quipped. "You acted like you were trying to kill us for saving your life. Remind me not to give you a drink of water any time soon. I wouldn't want you to choke on it and turn into Mr. Hyde again."

Roland let out a sigh and stretched his neck to offer a weak smile in the mirror to Lucy, his jaw relaxing.

Jade wasn't about to let him off the hook with Lucy's sweetened reprieve.

"I saw something floating on the surface when we were on the shoreline," Jade said. "But you were so hyped to get out of there, I couldn't stop to get a better look. Did you see something when you were out there?"

Roland's grin disappeared, and the twitch returned to his jaw. "Nothin'," he muttered. Then he announced that he'd drop Jade off first, since his house was closer.

When they pulled up to the curb, Jade stepped out of the car and looked back at Lucy, but she just stared past him, at his house, or at nothing. "See you Monday," he said to Roland, but got no response. As he closed the door, he heard Lucy say to Roland in a playful tone, "Home, James." The Caddy pulled away, kicking up dusty debris from the Reston Street gutter.

Jade found Alice in the grotto in new summer clothes, her short hair dyed blonde. She was on her knees at the Blessed Mother statue, rosary in hand, eyes closed. The house was stuffy and hot, cigarette smoke hanging in the air, the windows shut tight. She did not acknowledge her son. She was moaning something he couldn't decipher. He didn't smell booze in the dankness, but he suspected she'd been drinking.

"Nice to see you, Alice," he announced. "Where've you been?" She kept her head bowed, her lips whispering prayers. He knew the rule about waiting for her to finish but he wasn't having it. "Oh really? That's interesting. Want to hear about *my* week?"

He opened all the windows on the first floor, but the air did not move. Sulfury soot from the culm dump lay thick in the smoldering heat. Jade pined for the fresh air of the mountain he'd just left behind. After all the windows were open, he stood in the small kitchen and wished he had left them shut. So did Alice.

"I keep them closed for a reason," she called out, startling him. He thought she might be in one of her distant, incoherent trances, but her voice sounded normal, even focused. She was standing in The Grotto, the rosary gone. She looked at him as if she'd just awakened from a deep sleep, her eyes unfocused, lids heavy and half-open.

"Would you like something to drink?" she asked, her voice changing yet again—raspy, almost sultry. He winced at the suggestion. He couldn't tell if her eyes wore the weight of the noxious air or some provocative memory from her week out there, wherever she'd gone. He was used to Alice's sudden mood changes, but he still struggled with how to respond. He had to select his words and tone carefully to avoid setting her off.

"I can get it, mom," he said, choosing a soothing, passive approach. It seemed to be the right one; she gave him her coquettish smile. "You look nice," he said, straining to smile back at her—a rookie salesman with a reluctant buyer. "Like you just came from the beach." Then he took a chance. "Can we sit at the table? I want to ask you something."

Alice frowned, and Jade thought she was going to sulk or throw a tantrum, go dark on him. But she quickly recovered and smiled, as if a switch had been flicked inside her. "Of course, honey." Her eyes widened, picking up the light from the open windows. Jade saw her eyes change, at once weary and innocent, tired, yet uncluttered. It was her little girl lost look. But there was no hiding the hard lines of fear and turmoil etched at the edges.

At the kitchen table, he started the conversation slowly, hoping patience would serve him, perhaps luring Alice into telling him more than she wanted to say. She seemed buzzed but not drunk—loose, yet still coherent. He slid a glass of iced water in front of her and held his breath. If she drank more booze, Jade would lose her quickly. He had to move with caution through her minefield of triggers.

"I was thinking we could go on a little vacation later this summer, if I can get a Thursday and Friday off," he said as she pondered the water glass, her eyes expanding as if it were a rare stone. "Maybe mid-August. I'm making money now, and we could take the train and then a bus and get a room at the shore. It doesn't have to be fancy. We could spend the days at the beach."

Alice's eyes lit up, her mouth grinning and then opening to let her perfect teeth join the transformation. She tilted her head slightly and nodded to her son. Jade had never bought the blonde hair myth, but he saw that she did look younger now.

"Just you and me, mom. We could go to Atlantic City, hit the boardwalk at night. Have dinner in a nice restaurant overlooking the ocean."

Alice continued to smile, but the glow in her eyes waned.

"Or some other shore town you like. I'm sure you know more about where we could go than I do."

Alice blinked a few times and then sat up, straightening her shoulders and pushing her chest out. She cleared her throat. "I do," she said, almost in a whisper.

Jade nodded and smiled, waiting.

Alice cleared her throat again. "I prefer Beach Haven, actually," she said. "Much cleaner, quieter, not as crowded. The beach is pristine, and there are homes right on the dunes we could walk along. Beautiful homes. I used to lay up against those dunes, away from the wind, and let my eyes drift, and just listen to the ocean, nothing more." She closed her eyes, and her thick, soft lips parted in a tired smile. She hummed, drifting into the image she was seeing. Then her smile hardened and curved down at the edges.

"It wasn't there, though," she said, opening her eyes and looking past Jade. "It was further south, another town. Another life." Her voice was drifting. "It was the soothing sea, my salvation, my refuge, my private paradise. Even in that awful fall and winter. If the air was too cold, I would just huddle there at the dunes, the winter sun sharing all the warmth it could spare. Birds, even in winter, played in the dune grasses around me. They spoke to me kindly." She paused, her mouth in a pout. "They were the only ones who would."

"Was I there with you?" Jade asked tentatively. "At the shore?"

Her gaze was on something behind Jade, her eyes unfocused. "You?" she said dreamily, almost a whisper. "You? Yes. You were there. Brand new. I bundled you up once. Brought you to the dunes with me. We just lay there in the sun. It was late spring, cool at the beach, but sunny. No one was there. You were so new. And I wasn't supposed to have you. I carried you to the surf, high tide, and I lowered your toes into the rush at my feet, and you squealed with delight." She laughed softly and closed her eyes again, muttering quietly. "So tiny, so sweet. Skin was light then. Just tiny dark curls on top. Precious." She hummed a sweet lullaby, smiling.

They sat at the kitchen table, Jade silent, watching Alice alone and far away with her child's tune, her eyes closed under heavy lids, her blonde head nodding and swaying. She muttered something he didn't catch, but he didn't pursue it. He hadn't seen her so peaceful in a long, long time. He'd intended the conversation to go in a different direction, but he was glad it hadn't. He knew if he tried to steer Alice back to his vacation plan, he would lose her altogether. He wanted her to stay where she was, wherever that was, in peace, inside her warm memories, momentarily free of her demons.

When she finally stopped nodding and humming, she caught her breath as if awakening, and her eyes met his; she let out a girlish giggle. Then, suddenly, her face clouded over, her chin jutting out, her brow creasing. She pushed a fierce breath out of her nose.

"They took him away," she said to him, though she seemed to be talking to someone else. Her anger turned to sadness in a moment. "So sweet," she whispered. "So sweet. And they took him away from me." Her lower lip quivered, and her eyes filled.

"But I'm here now, mom," Jade said, reaching across the table and touching her hand. "I'm here with you."

Her face changed yet again, grief now replaced by a distant, weary expression. She looked at him as if she didn't know him. "You?" she said dreamily. Then her eyes focused, and she looked at Jade as if she just recognized him for the first time as part of this conversation. She smiled at him. "No, honey. I wouldn't let them take you away."

Jade pulled his hand from hers. He still tried to speak softly, but his voice emerged anxious and edgy. "I....I don't understand. I thought we lived at the shore. Wasn't I there in the dunes with you?"

"No," she said, curtly, as if he should have understood. "No. That was another place. The mountains. A long winter. God, it was long, and so cold! And you brought the spring with you, finally. But I wouldn't let them take you away. I'd learned my lesson."

Jade sighed. He couldn't follow her wandering mind. He wanted to shake her, but he felt closer to getting answers than ever before. He was tempted to offer her a whiskey, just to keep her going, but he was afraid she'd melt down, turn on a tirade.

"Was my father there in the mountains with us?" he finally said, his heart pounding. He sat up straight, gripping the edge of the table, preparing for Alice to explode.

Alice glared at him and frowned. Then she snorted a terse laugh and blurted out a stream of thoughts he could barely follow. "With us? Ho," she chuckled. "With *us*? He was never with us. He was gone. Who knows where, I don't care anymore." She grimaced. "It was the interloper; he was the one. He made everyone disappear. He got rid of Jake. Got rid of him just like he got rid of James. We got too close to the truth, Jake and I, and the interloper knew it. Jake was clever, smart, nervy. Knew exactly what questions to ask, and who had the answers. He wasn't afraid. But they got rid of him. He never came to the mountains to see me, never called me, no letter, no money in the mail, nothing. Just silence. Years later, I learned he was made to disappear."

Jade waited for more, but Alice just stared at him. Finally, he broke a long silence.

"So was his name Jake Flynn?" he asked, repressing the urge to scream it out. When Alice remained silent, he relaxed enough to ask, "So who was Jake?"

"Jake?" Alice replied, again drifting, her eyes distant and filmy. "He had a nose for secrets. He could sniff them out. Took me to see the sister. But that was the beginning of the end. He knew too much by then. And so did I. But he knew more. And now I know what he knew. Now I know what I must do. It's just, I... just can't...I can't...I know I have to, but...he will actually kill me this time. I know it."

"Who will kill you, Alice?" Jade said, his eyes on fire. "Jake?"

"Ha!" She spewed out a laugh. "That wimp. Screw somebody, yes. Especially if she's pretty. But kill somebody? No. Not him." She sighed and pushed away from the table, standing up wearily. "Where are my cigarettes? I need a drink."

"I need to know who Jake Flynn was!" Jade exploded, his voice cracking. He was on his feet, inches from her face, his own face crimson, his breath in spurts, his eyes demanding hers.

Alice didn't wince. She met her son's angry glare with a lifeless look, her mouth a flat line.

"Who was my father?!" Jade bawled. "Did you make him up?!"

Alice smirked and blinked. She looked down at his chest, and then back into his eyes. "Yes," she whispered. "My fantasy of hope. Vanished."

Jade felt himself shrink, pierced by her simple word, a lesion burning in his gut. He leaned closer to her, looking straight at her fuzzy green eyes. "What did you say?" he whispered, his voice now hoarse and grainy. His mouth hung open.

Alice held her smirk. "You heard me," she said, smooth and direct, returning now from her ethereal drift.

Jade backed away, stumbling against the sink and knocking two glasses into it. One of them smashed into pieces against the far side of the oily porcelain. He braced himself with both hands against the sink and stared at his mother, now on her feet coming at him.

"You're in my way," she said, her teeth gritted. She pushed him aside with one hand and he yielded easily. She opened the stained cabinet above the sink and retrieved a bottle of Four Roses, nearly empty. She poured the remains into a juice glass, filling it halfway. She dumped most of it down her throat and turned to her son. The look in her eyes had changed yet again. It was familiar to Jade, yet frightening. He'd seen this metamorphosis for years, but each time he was never prepared for what would follow the look. She cleared her throat with a low moan.

"I did it for you," she finally said, her eyes wide and filling up, her lips quivering. "He was a scorned man, tarred and feathered and hurled over the castle wall. You could not bear his name. You needed a clean slate. I couldn't give you mine because...my name...." She looked past her son into a fog. Then she blinked it away and sighed at him, her breath sharp with booze, her eyes softening. "I was given a new name," she said, shrugging. "And I went with it. A new start, a new identity. And you got one, too." She turned away from Jade and poured the rest of the whiskey into her mouth.

Jade stood in the doorway, moving only his eyes to follow his mother as she rummaged through small cupboards and under a stool in the corner, where old newspapers and cleaning rags were rumpled together in a heap. She pitched herself into The Grotto, up the stairs, and returned a minute later holding another Four Roses, this one nearly full. She sat at the table and worked awkwardly at the bottle top until it twisted off. She looked at it in her hand as if she'd never seen one until that moment. Jade found his voice.

"Alice," he said through gritted teeth. "Is that your real name? Alice?" He didn't pause long enough for her to answer. "What. The. Hell...is *my* real name? What the FUCK, Alice! Is James Dellworth Flynn something you made up out of the blue?! Am I really your son? Or did you pick me up at the beach, hold me to your heart on the dunes, pretending to be my mother? What the fuck, Alice? Who are we?! Who are *you*? And who the hell am *I*?"

He was hollering now and waving his arms and swooping around the tiny kitchen like a bat trapped in a cage. He stopped inches from her face, as she held her glass of brown whiskey to her full lips.

She took a quick drink and looked up at her son. "You have no idea what I went through," she said, her acrid breath swirling under Jade's nose. "You have no idea, and you have no RIGHT!" Now it was her turn to scream. "You have no RIGHT to chastise me, you have no RIGHT to blame me, you have no idea what I endured for you! You ungrateful bastard!" She punched him in the chest with a solid fist, and he backed away, looking at his mother with a mixture of pity and revulsion. He stood still and watched her toss down the rest of her glass of Four Roses and pour herself another.

Alice settled at the wobbly kitchen table with her bottle and glass, and, eventually, her head began to nod. Jade stood in the corner of the kitchen, watching her drink in silence. He was stunned. His stomach churned and twisted, a steady ache throbbing there. Eventually, he found himself standing in The Grotto holding the telephone receiver. Lucy's mother told him she wasn't home. She didn't sound concerned and said she'd tell Lucy he called. For the next half hour, Jade stared at the receiver in its cradle, expecting it to ring.

He was getting out of the tub when he heard the wailing. He stood at the top of the steps wrapped in a thin gray towel and listened to the moans escalating in pitch. He felt the hair on the back of his neck tickling with electricity. He stepped into his room, ditched the towel, pulled on clean boxers, and descended the narrow stairway in his bare feet, tiptoeing up to his mother at the kitchen table.

She was moaning about someone dying. She was in one of her trances, chanting religious incantations again. "Be not afraid, be not afraid," he heard her say. Then her tone changed, the sounds becoming more guttural. He couldn't make out the words, but he heard something horrible in what she was saying, as if she were speaking in someone else's frightened voice, someone's terrified wheezing. Gasps. As if they were her last.

46
James

Sunday, July 6, 1969

She rose early, at first light, in response to a calling. She stood at the couch where she'd fallen asleep, the vague memory of a horror dream. She faced The Grotto of silent saints and unlit candles, sensing yet another expectant plea rising within her, knowing that forgiveness would be granted. But she was distracted by the light from the windows. In the warm glow of dawn, she felt her self-inflicted fog lifting, a purpose resurfacing, almost lost, but now coming into focus again. As she stepped closer to the front window, she sensed the height of the season upon her, an urgency, as if the sun at its apex were giving her instruction now, taking over for the stone saints and the taciturn Virgin. Outside, in the brilliant new light, there was clarity; inside, in this musty cave of stale human air and empty icons, there was the dying fog of time. She touched her face, the skin moist and swollen.

At the window, she pushed aside the curtains and sheers and was startled to see brilliant blue in the southern sky above the sunken rooftops of her silent Mell Hollow neighborhood. Cirrus clouds raced high along the cerulean frontier, another urgent message. Awake, with eyes wide now, she remembered the voice, the last sounds of the night before, like so many previous voices, unbidden but arising there at the edge of her consciousness, imposing, asserting knowledge that wasn't hers, and she not knowing who these sounds belonged to until later, if at all. It was a crease in time in which she had fallen too often since Marte disappeared, and she had begged The Blessed Mother over and over again for release. But on this morning, at this dawn, she didn't beg. This time, it came to her in the light of the high season; now she recognized the guttural voice at the end of last night. It had been her own. There was no more putting it off. It was time. Her release was upon her.

She held the Four Roses bottle upside down over the drain and emptied the last inches, washing away the sour scent with a full blast from the faucet. She'd done this before, and she knew there would be enough money to replenish the supply, to renew the curse. He'd always made sure of that with an easy envelope, a sure bet that she'd fall again into a muddy swoon, unraveling whatever intentions she might have mustered, her memory and her declarations a hodgepodge of nonsense, so that anyone who encountered her would run the other way. But not this time. This would be the last time. She knew what she must do, closing her eyes and banishing fear.

She tiptoed in her bare feet past Jade's door and shut herself in the bathroom. She risked waking him with the whistle and rush of bathwater, but, as she lowered herself into the steam, she listened against the wall for him and there was nothing. She dunked her head and dug shampoo into her scalp, massaging the throbs inside, dispersing the persistent haze. With a rough washcloth, she skimmed layers of her foulness from her face and body. She emptied the tub and began filling it again, kneeling to rinse her hair under the faucet as it poured the last of warmth from their ancient water heater. She sank her body into the new pool of coolness, a full rinsing of her final fall.

At the mirror, she hesitated, but then went ahead with the application. She needed to cover the evidence of last night, to add sharpness where there was none, to erase the creases at the edges of her mouth and bury the dark evidence under her eyes, the eyes of someone who'd become unlucky, a wight, a lost soul. She needed a face that matched the clarity of her intentions. For this man, after so many years, she needed to be what she once was.

She'd gotten rid of the Impala, had traded it for a two-toned '57 Chevy, the steering wheel as loose as a sailboat's, but otherwise proof that the quality of American cars had peaked in the previous decade. She loved this machine, the rumble and power of its engine, the crisp lines of its chrome accents, its sleek air-bound fins. Still, she knew the switch would not throw Giallo off her tail. But she wasn't worried; she could pick out his shadows with ease—wannabe dicks with their dated wide-brimmed fedoras and B-movie newspaper tropes. You'd have to be blind to miss illiterate men pretending to read the paper while sitting at the wheel of a parked sedan. When she drove toward the Dickson campus, she watched in her rearview mirror as the dope in the black Pontiac tacked along behind her, at first two blocks back, then closer. She veered away from the campus toward center city and then cut back through alleys and side streets of the crumbling neighborhood wedged between downtown and the college.

The Ebonton neighborhood streets were draped in the new spring leaves of stately elms, oaks, hemlocks and ash, canopies of lime and rose hues casting a deceiving glow of hope over the collection of slouching homes that once, in a prosperous time, may have been as majestic as the natural wonders that gave them cover. The bones of these old homes were tired from neglect and perhaps regret. A life once grand, then lost, even stolen. The idea sunk into her chest, her breath, her heart.

As she passed through these silent streets, daylight poking through the canopy, she was struck by the notion that the spirit of this place, this town, this entire valley, had given up, in part from abandonment by the powers of wealth, and in part from a lifetime of lost chances to retain glory, of neglect and even mistreatment beyond their resistance. In these weary streets, she saw her own life drifting by the windshield, once so promising, and then so suddenly diverted, cast aside, left adrift, cut off at every hopeful turn, the very essence of her self wrestled from her grasp. She would not deny her own role in the battle, her own weaknesses. But, like these homes, once radiant with assurance and filled with occupants confident and hopeful, she knew that the true center of her life had been torn from her. Yet, unlike these sad relics of a time gone by, she would not let her spirit wither in defeat. She was finished with self-pity. She was nobody's victim. She felt the old competitor rising in her now, the rush of certainty she once found in her strong and agile body, the gift of concentration that looked through and beyond an opponent and gave clarity and purpose to her intention. She would win this long struggle. But she wouldn't just take him down; she'd rise above him, leave him foundering in her wake.

The black Pontiac was right behind her now, their little parade of two cars the only moving vehicles in these early morning streets. As she turned onto a wide avenue in the direction of center city, she saw the steeples of two churches and then the gaggle of people in their Sunday best crowding the sidewalks in front of the churches, one on the near end and the other on the far end of the block ahead. It was not uncommon, she'd learned, that two or three Catholic churches would cluster in the same block in this town, a vestige of European tribes clinging to their parochial past. The Polish church was a hundred feet from the Italian church, which was a block away from the Irish church. All the same religion but segregated from each other by habit and by fear.

She cranked open her window and aimed her Chevy toward the nearest crowd spilling into the street—Italians dressed in summer colors, arms waving, voices rising with increasing certainty to overcome each other. She slowed the Chevy to a steady crawl and eyed Giallo's man in her mirror. She could see him gaping at faces he recognized. The churchgoers seemed oblivious to the approaching cars as they pushed each other into a tighter swoon toward the center of the street. She kept her pace, slow but certain, and began tapping the horn. She took one more glance at her tail in the Pontiac and then glided through the mob, nearly bumping into a man with her left fender and then another with her right, both shouting at her in Italian. She laughed to herself, recognizing their soft curses, and smiling at them, knowing that, away from the church, such indignation would be expressed with much more vitriol, lewd and depraved, disappointing in its predictably limited vocabulary. As she pushed through to the far edge of the crowd, she saw in her mirror that the Pontiac had stopped in the middle of the gathering, and the driver was leaning out his side window engaged with three men in a friendly banter. Several more crowded onto the other side of his car and in a moment the Pontiac was engulfed in the boisterous crowd.

As her Chevy emerged from the gaggle, she picked up speed and sailed through the Irish gathering, nodding her thanks to two self-appointed traffic cops in jackets and ties who held back their more compliant comrades to make way for the pretty woman in the fine Chevy. She tooted her horn and waved, then headed straight for two more blocks, and glanced in her mirror at the trapped Pontiac in the distance before turning onto a side street and wending her way back to the Dickson campus. She parked the Chevy behind a large team van in a secluded corner of the gymnasium lot and used a back entrance to the adjacent faculty building.

She guessed he'd be there, the dedicated scholar taking advantage of a Sunday morning in summer session to concentrate on his research, while the rest of the college slept off Saturday night. She was dressed in seaside tans—a simple cotton blouse and pleated skirt, bare legs, white tennis shoes. Her hair would throw him for a moment, but she counted on that to give herself an advantage. He was observant, but he was a born academic, often adrift from this mortal coil, a reliable step behind reality.

She hadn't seen him in nearly six years, since the day he yelled across the street from his doorstep, warning her to come no closer, that if she didn't stop following him, sneaking up on him, bothering his family and his neighbors, that if she didn't stay away from them for the rest of her life, he'd have her hauled away. That had made her laugh at him, but he'd just shouted one more time, and then turned and slammed his front door behind him. She'd gotten close several times before that, coming around when he wasn't there, getting to know his aunt, Dolores, who knew who she was, but pretended she didn't. She'd taken Seamus with her, hoping to make a connection for him, and, after a few visits, she saw that Dolores had a soft heart for Seamus and that the rest of the kids let him play with them, all except the oldest, the one she most wanted him to play with. Then, on the fifth or sixth visit, this time without Seamus, she was shut out, banished by the mandate from the top of the front steps. There was no sign of Dolores or the children or the oldest one. It was just him, his fist in the air. Stay away. Never come back here. Never. Forever.

Now she needed him, not his heart, but his judgment—his cold, distant logic, his solid rock of reason, impenetrable by emotion. She knew he'd long ago shut down his locked-up feelings for her, for the sake of his own survival, his own career. But not for his soul, which he'd sold. By now, for her, all of that was sealed in the past, locked in its tomb of lost hope. Now, she simply needed his cold analysis of her chances for success with this, her last act of resistance, her final restoration of justice, her desperate bold act to save at least one of her sons and, with the help of this man, the other son, too. She had all the facts now, information he'd never have known about. He'd told her once that only through knowledge could you find freedom. Now, here it was. She had the knowledge. She knew he'd long ago sold his own opportunity for freedom, but this was *her* chance, her final crusade. And, despite his edict six years earlier, there was even a possibility he could buy back a slice of his own freedom, if he was willing to listen to her. She needed assurance from the brightest analytical mind she'd ever known that this time she would, beyond a doubt, prevail.

Behind the closed door, he hollered that whoever had been knocking so persistently must stop, must go away, that office hours were Wednesdays between one and three. And, when he finally yanked open the office door, and his head snapped back at the sight of her, his reading glasses flipped off his face and skittered on the shiny tile toward her tennis shoes.

She'd guessed correctly. His eyes were lost in the life of his mind; the shock of her face hadn't yet registered. It was as if his heart knew who this was, but his mind wouldn't allow it. Then he began to see her, his eyes blinking toward clarity; but the blonde hair gave him pause, so she took her advantage.

"No worries, doctor," she said, smiling, sealing his memory of her. "I'm not here to ask you to change my failed grade from way back in the early classroom of your life. In fact, I won't ask you anything that approximates an assumption that you have feelings. I'm here to tap your enormous brain. And to provide a fair warning to you." She saw him bring his eyes into focus. His nostrils ballooned, and his chin tilted up as he looked down at her, all of her, collecting her parts and matching them up in his memory, calculating the answer before he could speak it. She didn't let him.

"I've been to see Salvatore Giallo, and I've spent time with Jake Levin in California. I have all of it now, James. Everything I need to bring an end to this long masquerade. And I'm here to warn you that you'd best get far away from this place, and bring Roland with you, because, in the next few weeks, Dennis Hafferty's empire of deceit will crumble, and you won't want to be inside the castle when that happens."

He glanced up and down the hallway.

"No one is here, James. No colleagues, no students, no campus rent-a-cop. It's Sunday morning, summer session. It's why you're here, right where I knew I'd find you."

His face settled into a deadpan glare at her, his shoulders slumping. "What do you want?"

"I'll give you fifteen minutes of summary, doctor, and then you can decide what you want to do with it. I don't need your participation. I just need you to know that I *will* act on this information, and that I'm giving you a chance to dodge the bullets before they fly. Not for your sake, but for Roland's. He's in danger, and you know it. But it's worse than you might think."

His eyes softened, and his mouth fell open, but no words emerged. He turned around and walked into his office, leaving the door open for her.

She tossed a photo onto his desk. There was a note clipped to it. "They're following him," she reported. "That's him on the curbside, there in the rear, looking over the heads of the crowd toward the marching men in black berets and raised fists. Look at the date. April 11. The Black Panthers march in New York City. Roland appraising the marchers with his eyes on fire, his anger and righteousness stirring."

James grabbed the photo and sat at his desk. His hand trembled as he glared at the image. "Where did this come from? This note. It says he's part of a faction at Penn State. A radical faction? Is that what it means? Who gave this to you?"

"It's not a love note, James. The sender doesn't need to sign his name. Perhaps you recognize the handwriting. The colleague of your colleague? The partner of your sponsor? He's my new pen pal, James, only it's a one-way communication. After my visit with him, I've received two of these. The other one shows Roland in Washington at a community center near Howard University, emerging from a Panther presentation. It seems Roland does some traveling while he's at college, and this summer, on weekends, he takes the train to New York and to who knows where else. My pen pal assured me that your sponsor knows nothing about this, but it's a warning that if Roland continues to explore these political leanings, your sponsor will find out. And Roland will be swept from his bomb factory job and shipped off like one of his ancestors to a place from which he will never return."

James dropped the photo on the desk and lifted himself up in his chair, glaring down at her. "What do you want from me?"

She stood up and leaned over his desk, pushing her face closer to his. "It's no secret that he spent a few hours in jail after a bar fight last week, and then he was attacked right in front of your house by Macson goons. Hafferty will only stick his nose out so far, even for Roland. And if he learns about this? You can see it coming, James. Hafferty will betray him, and you. He no longer needs either of you. He's a closet Nixon man, hiding in a Democrat's sheepskin. He doesn't need token Black props to get favors from his majority colleagues in Washington any longer. The Black Power movement and all the other protests are wearing down the idealists on the Hill, even the liberal Democrats, and emboldening the Nixon crowd. The tide is shifting in D.C., James. And Hafferty will go wherever opportunity leads him. You know this. He has no principles; his only credo is to serve himself, and he'll abandon past allegiances in an instant to save his own skin. If Hafferty gets wind of Roland's new interests, he'll unplug him from college and send him away to that hideous war, where he will die, leaving you with nothing but your microscopes to justify your devil's bargain with Hafferty."

James pushed himself away from his desk and stood up, stepping toward the window, glancing through the blinds. "I will ask you just once more: what do you want from me?"

"I want you to listen to me, James. Analyze the logic of and the potential for my plan. I have information that I am about to share with someone in New York who can change everything, take Roland out of the line of fire, and maybe my son, Jade, too. Roland is Jade's supervisor now at Macson, I'm sure you know that. And Jade is now ensnared by Dennis, just as Roland has been for years. Let's just call Jade a new recruit. And he's in danger, too."

"Who is this miracle worker in New York who can stop Dennis Hafferty from doing anything he wants to do?"

"He's an old associate of mine. One of your former rivals, James. A Columbia man. Can you remember that far back? Or have you blotted out your past entirely? Self-imposed amnesia."

He pulled the blinds shut and stepped toward her. "I do not forget *anything*." He put his hands on the edge of the desk and leaned his big shoulders forward to level his eyes with hers. "I make choices, and I stick to them. For better or for worse. And I know exactly who you are referring to. He's *The Washington Post* New York bureau chief. Has had quite a career. His advantages, of course, played a monumental role in his path to success. Advantages I did not have. Looks like you made the wrong choice back then."

She froze, her jaw set, her eyes wide on him. Then she turned abruptly and sat down in a leather chair facing his desk. Repressing the urge to stand and shout and connect with a hundred punches to his arrogant face, she instead offered a clenched smile. "That's so rich of you, James. Avoiding me for twenty years, shunning me whenever I got close, letting me wither away in the locked vault of your steely mind. And now, *that's* what you come up with? I made the wrong choice?"

She could hold back no longer. She stood up and clenched her fists and shoulders. She felt the competitor rising, and her own nostrils flared, matching his. "I let my heart make my choice, and I chose you. Was that a mistake? Not at the time. Choices in that state of mind and heart are never wrong at the time. But in hindsight? In the academic's view? For you, of course they were. Clearly wrong. What esteemed scholar would ever let the flitty whimsy of a heart's desire overcome the brilliant brace of his steel skull? Certainly not the would-be Doctor James Wilson. You let my heart's choice destroy me, while you made your hard-headed choice, your self-preserving deal with the man who would ruin us all."

She leaned across the desk, her face level with his, her rage expended, her control returning, steely.

"And as for the Columbia man? He's with *The Times* now," she said in deadpan, as if reporting on the weather. "And, for what it's worth, I was very, very fond of him. But he would never have been my choice."

She sat down again and watched his face, certain she'd detected a softening in his eyes. "He's offered to listen to me. He's a rising editor, highly regarded for his political reporting, and now he has his own stable of reporters, and he's interested in my story," she said, tilting her head and pursing her mouth in a half smile. "And the least that you can do now, Dr. Wilson—the very least you would ever have to do for me in my entire life—is to listen now to what I plan to tell him. I need to be assured that my approach will work. I'm not asking for your support, or your approval, or even your cooperation. I'm on my own here. Always have been. What I need from you now is what you're best at. Cold, composed, dispassionate analysis, and a clear path. For better or for worse, as you say."

After fifteen minutes of listening to her, he broke his silence. He did not look into her eyes, but at the papers in her hands, the ream of typed notes shaking in her grasp, her adrenaline rushing. She saw that he noticed, so she set the notes on his desk and folded her hands.

He pursed his lips, concentrating on his thoughts, and then stared into her eyes for a long moment. "There are elements of your story that I did not know about," he said in a flat tone. "Your family, for example. I knew some of that, but not all that your sister had revealed. Certainly not about the abuse of her and your other sister and your brother, Tormud. Of course, I never heard their names from you or from anyone else. So

I'm taking your word for it, that they existed and that what had happened to them was true, since, as you say, it was confirmed by the nun, your sister." As his dark eyes softened, she saw a look she'd erased from her memory.

"And the transfer of property—the munitions plants," he continued. "There is no way I would have known about that, but it does seem to explain a great deal of what I've witnessed since then." His voice was calm, no longer defensive, revealing more of the song-like Bahamian accent that he'd evidently spent years trying to suppress.

He lowered his eyes and stared at the papers on the desk in front of her. She saw his face drop off into that aloof place, the life of his mind, the locked world of his memory. "What I do know, and perhaps you do not know, is that Dennis Hafferty made a single payment of indemnity to my former benefactor, Roland Snowcroft, in order to make him feel as though he'd won the battle between them for my…my hide." He lifted his eyes to hers, and she saw a hint of the man she once knew, a young Black man caught dreaming in a world that would not allow it.

"Snowcroft," he continued, with a sneer, "was never one to be fooled by another man's pretense. He told me he'd been paid fifty thousand dollars in cash, assuring Hafferty, as part of the deal, that he would not interfere with Hafferty's plans for me—a guaranteed spot in a U.S. medical school. But Snowcroft knew he hadn't won at all, that he had been forced by Hafferty's upper hand to give up his many years of educational investment in me and his goal for making millions on my return to the Bahamas to be a pawn in his labor management scheme. He never communicated again with Hafferty, but he did with me." He lowered his eyes again, as if to close her out of his shame. "He warned me, in our final conversation, on a suffocating afternoon in August 1949, at the heart of the Howard campus. He threatened my life. Ironic, I suppose, that right there on the steps of Founders Library, the palace of books, the seat of the knowledge he had encouraged me to pursue, he warned me that if I ever returned to the Bahamas, I would be killed. He called me a traitor, and he belittled me, saying I was nothing more than a piece of property. He did not use the word 'slave,' probably because he believed the absurd notion that he was an abolitionist. But that's what I was—then and now. A body whose transfer from one rich White man to another simply locked me up in a continued life of bondage."

James lifted his eyes from the papers and met hers. She felt her guard falling, her jaw unclenching. She saw his defensiveness subsiding as well, his eyes pleading with her, his rigid chin relaxing the way it once had so many years ago. It was as if his face had begun to thaw after twenty years in ice.

"Hafferty knew nothing of that conversation, as far as I could tell," James said, holding her now with a look of certainty, returning with resignation to the real world, his voice flattening into a report, a testimony under oath. "Once the money changed hands, he considered Snowcroft a threat no longer. But he did not know, and I would never tell him, that Snowcroft continued to send messages to me through surrogates. He let me know that I was being monitored. He let me know that he would follow me wherever I went and with whomever I associated."

He took a breath and pushed back into his chair and looked at her hands folded on his desk. "Snowcroft finally died of cancer just six months ago, and I'm still not sure whether I should expect to continue to receive messages from his replacement, his inheritor, whoever that might be. I've become so accustomed to watching over my shoulder that I know I will never be assured that he is gone from my life."

He lifted his gaze to her again and returned to his professor's monotone. "So, you see, it was not Hafferty's medical school offer that made me, as you call it, sell my soul. I had no soul to sell. I would always be owned by one rich White man or another, obliged to do their will against my own. Or, if not, lose my life. It was not my opportunity to study medicine in the U.S. that had forced me to abandon you. If that were my choice, I would have turned it down. There was no choice. I was owned by your brother—or whatever you call him. He had already bought me at the behest of your father—the man who taught Dennis everything he knows about controlling people. But your father lost control of you when you and I were together, and then he directed Dennis to regain that control. And yes, Dennis held the medical school threat over my head, but it wasn't just Dennis who sealed my fate. It was Snowcroft, as well. Together, they held me in a virtual lockdown, a life in a glass classroom, a cell, always monitored, always under threat from one slaveholder or the other."

He stood up suddenly and turned away from her and stood at the window, bending a venetian blind as if to monitor someone outside.

"After the child was born, Dennis appeared to have lost his nerve to act on your father's directive to do away with me and the child. Ship us off somewhere, maybe Africa, perhaps even murder us. It took me years to realize that Dennis hadn't lost his nerve at all. He'd simply taken advantage of your father's weakened health condition in order to set up a scheme to improve his own political opportunities in the future. Dennis is nothing if not a schemer for his own aggrandizement, as I am sure you must know by now. So, when he allowed me to send the child to my Aunt Dolores in Maryland, I was fooled into thinking he was being magnanimous. Indeed, after your father died, he told me that he'd defied the old man's command to make the boy and me disappear, because he cared for us, as human beings, he had said."

He let go of the blind and turned back to her. "For that favor, he sealed my fate. I actually believed—or convinced myself to believe—that he defied your father out of pure generosity of spirit, a belief in a promising future for me, as he so often repeated over and over and over in the decades to come. He even declared he respected me and my gifts as he would his own brother's. I believed all of that, along with what he told me about you. I believed it for years, despite what I felt inside, in a compartment I kept closed and locked. I believed it, and I believed him. Right up until you showed up in Ebonton six years ago."

He turned back to the window and held open the blind again, and she remained silent in her chair, staring into the white light slipping through the slat under his hand. This was the first time she'd been alone with him in twenty years, and yet, except for the few moments they'd just shared at his desk, he seemed as far away from her now as he'd always been over those years. She could see a glimpse of the man she once knew, just a few feet away; yet he seemed to be standing on the opposite side of a bottomless chasm, a collapse of time and memory that left her wondering if they ever had anything at all between them.

"Of course, you know what he told me back then," he said, still staring into the slant of light. "Dennis, I mean. What he told me about you."

Her heart pounded in her chest, and she wanted to tell him to be still, that she did not want to relive the past. But she knew he had to say it. "I can imagine it," she said, trying to sound light-hearted. "Lies, no doubt."

He laughed at that, but it wasn't a laugh of humor. He let go of the blind and stood in front of the window facing her, the shaded light of day surrounding his shoulders and head. She could not see his eyes, and his voice seemed to be coming from another room, another dimension.

"He told me you were in the process of getting it fixed, when he stepped in and convinced you to let the pregnancy persist. He said he found you proper care during the necessary time, and that he convinced you to let him make adoption arrangements. He told me you were in disgrace and ashamed for what you had done. With me. And that you wanted him to do something to me, send me away. Perhaps worse."

"And you believed him," she whispered, the air rushing from her voice.

"Not at first, of course. I insisted on seeing you, but he told me if I attempted to find you, I would be...well, as he put it, my life would be in danger, given that your father had put a mark out on me. Imagine that. The great abolitionist had put a price on my head—an idea that I could not fathom until Dennis explained to me that what your father believed in was a final solution to the Negro Problem—the expatriation of all Black people to Africa—and that mixing the races was precisely why expatriation was needed. Not the liberation of Blacks, mind you, but the guarantee that miscegenation would be prevented." He turned away again toward the blinds and the light seeping between them.

"It was preposterous, of course, and I countered that it was far too late to stop racial mixing, but Dennis said your father was beyond reason on that notion, and that he, in fact, wanted me dead. Dennis then promised me he would protect me from your father and keep me in school at Howard. I was undone by all of this, of course, especially when your father and Dennis began to spread the word among your college and social friends in New York that you had been institutionalized for a nervous breakdown due to academic pressures at Barnard." He turned back to her. She could see his eyes now.

"I was forbidden to derail those rumors," he said, his voice deepening. "And I was sent by Dennis into hiding in an apartment near Howard to protect me from—in Dennis's words—your father's assassins. Dennis even went so far as to provide me with a bodyguard, so I could attend classes and continue to pursue my studies toward graduation and then medical school. Little did I know that the only real threats to me were Snowcroft's people. When your father took ill, Dennis assured me that the old man was too sick to continue his pursuit of me for the time being, and I was free to come out of hiding and resume my schoolwork. But I was forbidden to try to find or reach you again, because your father would recover soon and would have me killed if I persisted with you."

He took a deep breath and sighed and turned back to the window.

"My dear Issa," he said, staring into the staggered light. His voice sounded as if he were smiling, but she couldn't tell. "What have we wrought?"

He turned to her, daylight disappearing behind him. He wasn't smiling, she could see. "I don't expect you to answer that, Issa. You must know that rhetorical questions have no place in the real world. That is why I have been using them for so long in the classroom." She might have laughed at that, but his tone was humorless. He started to pace behind his desk, his lecture voice indicating a conclusion to a theory.

"I have no quarrel with the plan you wish to undertake. Indeed, in a laboratory, I'd find that your evidence is solid, and your hypothesis would stand. But that's my world, of course. Isolated, uninhabited by lawless unruly humans. Whereas the world in which you wish to assert your claim, your plan, is swarming with the very antithesis of truth. Your discoveries may be provable, but I expect your truth will be abrogated by the very forces you wish to undo. As you literary people would say, your victory, at best, would be Pyrrhic."

He approached the desk, and her. He leaned over and put his hands there, just inches in front of her. His voice remained professorial, but his eyes softened. "Yes, the plan has merit, Issa. But your adversaries have the power to turn your truth against you."

He straightened up and raised his hand, as if in debate with himself. "That said, there is another human element that needs to be considered.

Your former suitor. He certainly has equal or greater power and influence than our dear Dennis and his partner, Mr. Giallo. But does he have the willingness to exert it? That's on you, Issa. You certainly held sway over Dell Cranstone way back when. And while I would not suggest anything inappropriate, you certainly know you have the strength of your personality and the power of your intelligence; but you also have the artfulness of your gender in your favor." He cleared his throat and gave her a sheepish look.

"For starters, may I suggest that if you wish to exert your power of persuasion, you might start with changing your appearance, returning to your original *look*, as they say now. Blonde hair on women is used to attract attention, which you need not do, given the characters you say who are following you. It also does not suit you, especially if you are trying to persuade a man who remembers you best with your natural auburn hair color and, dare I say, a rather more sophisticated clothing style." He tilted his head and shrugged, his large hands opening and his eyes wide with exaggeration. "Of course, I'm the egghead, not the fashion stylist."

She almost laughed, but she was softened by his sudden turn from confident pedagogue to cultural naïf. She let her smile emerge, but it was restrained; she did not want to let herself go too soft.

"I'll certainly keep that in mind," she said as their eyes met and then, as quickly, averted. She cleared her throat and steadied her voice. "What about Roland?"

His face fell, and he looked at her as if she'd slapped him. Then he started pacing again, reasserting his control of the turf on which she had encroached. He stopped mid-step and looked toward the window and then turned to her. "You knew about his street fight and his arrest. Did Giallo tell you that? In addition to supplying those photos and his commentary? What else has he told you?"

She wanted to stare at him, to make him wither with guilt, but she relented. "He knows, of course, that Roland and Jade work together, under Dennis's thumb, at the Macson plant. Making bombs for this idiotic war we've dug ourselves into. Did you approve of him taking that job?"

"Ha!" James said, feigning a laugh and collapsing, finally, into his leather chair. "No more than you approved when it was your turn to hand over your second son to Hafferty," he bellowed, his nostrils flaring under fierce eyes. Then his eyes softened again, and he sighed and sat back. His face looked much older in the bright light, tired, dispossessed.

"I lost control of Roland a long time ago," he said, with a frown. "And, if you think I can talk him out of something, like that job, or out of whatever he's gotten himself into with these political radicals, you are mistaken. He would not listen to me if I begged him on my knees." He snorted at the image. "Although he'd love to see that."

She stiffened in the chair and started gathering her papers. "I think we're finished here," she said. She stood and stepped toward the door. "Thank you for—"

"I'm sorry," he said. He held up his hands. He met her surprised look and attempted a conciliatory smile. "It's just...It's complicated with Roland. I feel as though I've lost him altogether. But," he said, holding up his finger as if to make one more didactic point before the conclusion of his class. "I do know someone to whom he listens." He took a breath and finally let go of his posturing. He looked at his papers as if reading something there. "She lives in an apartment above her landlord—he's someone you know, the man who owns the diner. Perhaps you could go see her. She will not speak to me, but if you meet with her, you may learn something important before you go to New York. And you may, although not directly I suppose...but you may be able to help *him*. Through her."

He looked up at her, and she saw the softness return to his eyes, a trace of the lost heart he'd long ago buried. "Her name is Tamara Chautier. She's a professor here at Dickson. She knows Roland very well. And she may even be able to get him to talk to you. If you wish to do that."

47
Professor Chautier

Sunday, July 6, 1969

Jade awoke with a start at the clanging of a bell. He'd finally fallen asleep just before dawn, and now his sheet was soaked in sweat. A weak fan rotated on his dresser, pushing acrid air around the tiny room. He was drained; his arms and legs were dead weight. But the clanging persisted, and he dropped his feet to the wooden floor and then stumbled down the steps to the kitchen. Squirrel was on the phone.

"Why are you calling here so goddamn early?" Jade scowled.

"Early! This is early? I've been up since five, Jademan." Squirrel replied, chuckling. "It's after ten. Are you hung-over or what?"

Jade flopped onto a kitchen chair and slowly lowered his forehead onto the table. The mention of drinking turned his stomach, and he breathed through his mouth to avoid the stench of stale booze Alice had left in the kitchen.

"Not me, man." he muttered. "Don't touch the stuff. But what the hell's so urgent that you have to get me out of bed. I hope you didn't wake my mother. I can't handle her right now."

"Got something you need to know, Jademan" Squirrel said, shifting to his clandestine whisper. "The cops dragged a dead body out of the rez early this morning. Some kids discovered the floater late yesterday, crapped their pants, and then told their parents. It's all over town. It'll probably come on as a special news bulletin, if they can find a sober reporter on a Sunday morning. Turns out it's a young guy, about fifteen. No name yet, but word is he was in the rez for a couple days or even a week or more. Coulda been there when you and I were up there last Saturday."

Jade sat upright in his chair, his heart thumping, his voice caught in his throat. He managed a croaking sound and struggled to hold onto the receiver.

"I know what you're thinking," Squirrel said. "I thought it, too. That kid could've been floating right under me while I swam over to visit my goose family. Can you imagine what he looked like? Probably scared that snake right out of the water—the one you were running from like a girl." Squirrel forced out a laugh, but Jade was silent.

"Hey, I was pretty freaked out, too, Jademan," Squirrel said, "but don't take it so hard. At least we didn't have to discover it. Those kids'll have nightmares for the rest of their lives."

Jade was wide awake now and found his voice. "You talk to Wilson last night?"

"No. Last time I saw him was Friday after work. I dropped him at his house. Why?"

"You didn't talk to him this morning?"

"Roland doesn't get his ass out of the sack til noon on Sundays. If he's even home at all. He disappears most weekends. Probably a new girlfriend."

"I have to talk to him," Jade muttered, staring at the steps to the second floor, wondering if the phone woke Alice.

"You have to talk to him about what?" Squirrel said.

"We were there yesterday. At the rez," Jade said, his trembling fingers picking at the chipped linoleum tabletop. "Me, Lucy, and him. He had Hafferty's Caddy."

"Roland? You and Lucy? What the hell were you doing at the rez? Hafferty's Fleetwood! Jesus, man! And you didn't call me? I'm the tour guide of the fucking rez, man, and you guys left me out?"

"I think I saw the body," Jade said. "And I think Wilson saw it, too. Up close."

"Woah, woah, woah! What the hell do you mean, you *think* you saw the body? You either saw it or you didn't. It's not exactly something you think you saw. It's a fucking dead body, Jademan. Doesn't look much like anything else."

"I saw it from the shoreline," Jade said, his eyes narrowing as if he were still squinting into the sun's reflection on the water. "I couldn't make out what it was, but I definitely saw something white floating on the surface. Something big. About twenty yards out. And Wilson didn't want me to see it for some reason. He was in a panic to get out of there. He almost drowned. I thought he just got a big mouthful and freaked out. I swam out to help him, but he punched the shit out of me. If it wasn't for Lucy, both of us would've drowned."

"I don't follow you, Jademan," Squirrel said. "Why would Roland want to ditch out on a dead body? Are you saying he had something to do with the dead kid?"

"I don't know what I'm saying," Jade stammered. "All I know is...Wilson freaked out in the water for no good reason. And we had to rescue him. And we all nearly drowned. Then he wouldn't talk, and he forced us to bolt out of there. Never thanked us, not a word. And he practically dragged me away from the shoreline, so I wouldn't get a good look at what was floating out there. I thought it was weird at the time, but now it's starting to make sense."

"Doesn't make much sense to me, Jademan," Squirrel said. "But I will tell you something that did make sense to me after I heard the story this morning. Remember Mutt 'n Jeff in the black Galaxy last Saturday? Those guys were tailing us up on that mountain for a reason. And I'll give you ten to one odds it had something to do with that dead kid. Roland might've freaked on you up there, but I know him. He didn't have anything to do with a dead body other than coming across it at the wrong time."

"I gotta go," Jade said. "Gotta check on something."

"Don't leave me out this time, Jademan," Squirrel shouted as Jade hung up.

Jade took the steps two at a time and found Alice's bed empty and cold. A Lucky Strike stub lay on the floor next to her bed, the wood singed black under the end of the butt.

"Goddamn it, Alice. You'll burn us down yet." He checked her closet and found her empty suitcase jammed in the back. He wondered if she was still drunk when she left.

He took a quick bath, made eggs and toast, and called Wally at the diner. When he asked him for Tamara's number, Wally said she was still waiting for the phone company to hook up her line. When Wally asked him why he wanted to speak with her, Jade lied. He muttered something about a book she promised to give him. He was pretty sure Wally didn't believe him.

He told the driver to drop him at the corner; he didn't want Tamara to see him get out of a cab in front of her house. In case Wilma wasn't working at the diner, he rang the first-floor doorbell. There was no answer. Staring at the entrance to the upper floors, he decided against going up there. He was sure he'd just make a fool of himself. As he started down the front steps to the sidewalk, he heard the click of a door behind him and turned to see the little girl from the Mormon family standing in the doorway to the upper floors.

"They're not home," she said. "They work on Sunday. My father says that's sinful."

Jade smiled at her. "Well, Wally and Wilma have to work to live. So I guess you could say they're doing the Lord's work."

The little girl turned her head at an angle and frowned at him. "You worked on a Sunday. I saw you with Wally and the colored lady the day she moved in. Are you a sinner, too?"

Jade held back a laugh and returned her stern gaze with a soft one. "That was really hard work on a very hot day. So I think that was definitely the Lord's work."

The girl straightened her head and smiled at him. "Did you want to visit the colored lady? She's home. I heard her walking around. She plays records a lot. The piano, too."

He followed her up the first flight and learned that she loved the music she would hear from the third floor and that her father said it was too loud. At her apartment door, she pointed up the steps.

"Her name is Tamara," she said. "I think she's nice."

"Can I tell her you said so?"

The girl nodded once and slipped into her apartment, closing the door with barely a sound. Jade climbed the last flight and stood still, staring at Tamara's door, gathering his courage. The music on the other side of the door wasn't at all loud; it was music Alice used to listen to when their parlor record player worked, the soothing sad faraway voice of a woman alone on a stage.

Jade couldn't recall any of what he'd rehearsed during the cab ride, and he felt his brain go blank as he watched his hand, as if it were attached to another body, reach up and knock softly on the door. He thought he saw movement through the peephole and then he heard Tamara say his name as she unlatched the lock and opened the door.

"What a pleasant surprise," she said, her brilliant smile and her deep brown and gold-flecked eyes lifting Jade from his timid slump. He squared his shoulders and smiled back, but he couldn't find his voice. "So what brings you to this part of town? Surely you know Wally and Wilma work on Sunday."

She was wearing tight white shorts and a bright lemon tee shirt and stood barefoot in her doorway. Her gaze moved over his body, his snug red tee shirt and tight dungarees and down to his black Converse All Stars and then quickly back to his eyes. He was in his second, more careful survey of her body, and his heart was pounding. He hadn't seen her in anything but a long loose-fitting dress, and he had to fight off the warm rush coming over him as he took in her unveiled form. She was still tall, but her body was slimmer than he'd expected, her dark legs long and lean and separated at the top where the cotton of her shorts was tight at her crotch and her hip bones formed taut wings in the white fabric. He resisted the urge to look again at her tee shirt. She was braless.

"Come in, come in," she said, stepping back and opening her door. The sorrowful voice of the jazz singer floated past him like a warm cloud, and Jade finally choked out a "Thanks," as he stepped into the familiar living room with its ceiling angled by the dormers and its furnishing still feeling like a Hollywood set. There were more decorations on the walls now and he smelled coffee and, underneath it, a sweet aroma of summer. Jade felt as though he'd stepped into a dream.

"Please sit down, Jade," she said, gesturing toward the couch. "Can I get you something to drink? Iced tea? Or coffee? I know it's hot but sometimes…well, I just made a fresh pot, so I can stay awake correcting essays. Seems I'm in the barrel of the classic English faculty hazing routine of sticking the new Ph.D. with all the summer Composition courses while the tenures vacation in Europe."

Jade stood at the couch, hesitating to sit. She looked at him with her hands on her hips, smiling, waiting for his response. He noticed her hoop earrings and bracelets and rings were missing, and then he weakened his resolve by glancing once more at her breasts, the clear outline of her nipples pushing through the soft bright cotton. When she shifted her hips and tilted her head with feigned impatience, he saw her breasts waver and then settle inside the thin shirt. It was hot in the apartment.

He swallowed hard and made eye contact again. "I'm a…not a coffee drinker," he said, alarmed by how loud his voice came out. "Sorry, I…I love the way it smells, but it's…just the taste, it's too bitter. Bothers my stomach." He could tell she'd seen him ogling her breasts, and he suddenly felt the need to leave. "I'm interrupting your work, I'm sorry. I shouldn't have knocked on your door out of the blue. Wally told me you don't have a phone hooked up yet."

She crossed her arms over her breasts and smiled at him. "I'll get you some iced chamomile tea. Good for the stomach. Have a seat, Jade. Turn up that fan if you'd like. And you're not intruding at all. On the contrary, you're saving me from ruining a peaceful Sunday morning with freshman essays." She rolled her big eyes and smiled at him, pointing to the couch. She set the other hand back on her hip and tilted her head, her smile lighting up, her perfect teeth brilliant in the morning glow from the tall bay windows. "And I have delicious fresh blueberries and a few cherry tarts Wilma made for me. How that woman bakes in this weather is beyond me. Especially after spending her long days in the diner. Now, you sit down, Jade. Please." She nodded at the couch. "Relax. Listen to Billie. You'll learn to love her in no time."

She turned and disappeared through the dining room into the back of the apartment and, a moment later, Jade heard a door close. A bouquet of red gardenias in a porcelain vase filled the center of the polished mahogany dining room table, and, on the side wall, an upright piano stood under a stained-glass window. He wondered who had moved the piano all the way up here for her.

He couldn't sit, not while his body was still surging with the tumescent rush of blood. So he stepped to the bay window and looked out at the city below. It was bathed in the sharp light of the morning sun, the air clear enough to make him wonder again if he'd entered a dream. Tamara had been so much a part of both his daydreams and night dreams that it was possible this visit wasn't real, that he'd simply entered another dream. But, when he focused his gaze and saw the dormant concrete smokestacks of the Macson plant, the reality of work erased his dreamy thoughts and drained his body's blood rush response to Tamara, and, for once, he was grateful for that horrid bomb factory.

"So," she said, this time smiling with her lips closed, her eyebrows raised in a professor's prompt. "You didn't just stumble upon my doorstep, did you, Jade?" She was sitting across from him in a low-backed chair, the bay windows behind her bathing her in soft light. He saw that she'd not only changed her outfit, but that her breasts were bundled now inside a bra and loose shirt, the nipples discretely shrouded. He was relieved by her modesty. And embarrassed by her discernment. She wasn't a girl.

"No, uh...I...um. Well, the little girl downstairs, she uh...she said she likes you. Likes your music."

"Little Patsy, yes." Tamara said, smirking now. "She's a cute one. Doesn't miss a trick, that girl. Somehow, she must have known just where you wanted to go, I suppose." She raised her eyebrows at him. "Smart kid."

She wasn't going to let it go, so Jade just gave in. "Yeah," he nodded, spilling out a laugh of relief, then meeting her eyes. "I...I needed to talk to someone. And I...uh..." His voice caught and he swallowed hard. "I thought of you. I wanted to call you but—"

"Yes, I know. Wally told you I don't have a connected phone. The telephone company keeps promising, but nothing yet. So. What did you need to talk about, Jade?"

He stumbled through a series of false starts, rambling about the war and Macson and being an outsider there, then shifting to the diner and how he missed the cranky old Judge and Jury guys, and then wandering into an open field of disconnected references to Alice, Lucy, Hafferty and Stanley, and then some vague comments about walking to his new job on

306

that first day and having his cinematic daydream shattered by a car nearly killing him, but actually killing the driver, a Black girl. He told her about the rez, a place that seemed like heaven and how he's always felt like an alien in this valley, how he missed the farmlands of New Jersey, which he could barely remember, and he started to tell her about the real threat of Ren and Joey Belden and Stanley, but he stopped talking when he uttered the name he'd wanted to say from the start.

"Ah," she said, raising her pencil thin eyebrows and setting her cup and saucer on the coffee table between them. "So you think I can help you solve the Roland Wilson conundrum."

"I don't know," Jade said, his eyes on her coffee cup. "I guess so. He's not easy to get along with. He's my supervisor at work, and he's the best friend of another guy I work with, who seems to like me, but every time I try to be friends with Roland, he treats me like dirt." He looked up and met Tamara's eyes. "And now, he's with Lucy. At least I'm pretty sure he is. Which makes everything even more complicated. I mean, she's not really my girlfriend anymore." He shifted his eyes to her coffee cup again. "I mean, we kind of broke up...or at least it seems like we did...before Roland showed up anyway. I mean, I don't want to hate the guy's guts, but how can I not?"

He looked up at her, but she just nodded her head ever so slightly and looked right at him.

"I thought it was getting better between him and me," he said, dropping his eyes to his clenched hands, trying to control the trembling. "It seemed like he was getting more friendly, but now it looks like he was just planning to move in on my girlfriend. And I told him the other day that I finally realized that I knew him from a long time ago, when we were much younger, when my mother took me to visit an older woman she knew, a few times in our first summer here, and Roland was there. I think he lived there; the woman must have been his grandmother. Really nice to me. I wished at the time that she was *my* grandmother. But Roland— they called him Junior back then—he let me know I wasn't wanted there. Just like now, he treated me like dirt.

"And, when I told him all this last week at work, he acted like he had no idea what I was talking about, like I was making it all up. But it seems like he *does* know me, and that maybe he thinks I did something to him way back then, and he won't forget it; but I know I didn't, because he couldn't stand to be in my presence, even for a minute, back then. And we were just kids. Although he was much bigger than all of us."

Jade looked at her again for a cue, and she nodded for him to continue. He looked down at his hands again.

"I know it must be crazy being the only Black guy at Macson. But the three of us—Roland, Squirrel and me—we're allies against an army of angry workers who hate us. And The Line where Roland and I work? It has three sections—ours has two workers, Roland and me, but the other two sections have four workers each. He doesn't seem to care; he just works twice as hard and expects me to do the same. And he's mixed up with Hafferty, and I am, too, but he seems pissed at me, because I'm in on the Hafferty connection. And now, with Roland taking Lucy, it looks like our three-man alliance is over. And I know you know him pretty well, so..." He met her eyes again. "Yeah, like you said, I thought you could...well, tell me what I'm missing. The guy's supposed to be my boss, and maybe my ally along with Squirrel, but he just stole my girlfriend. And something else happened at the rez yesterday that I think is gonna need us to remain allies, not enemies. Some trouble Roland's gonna need my help with. To stand up for him."

Tamara nodded, her face in deep reflection. She reached for her coffee and took a sip and looked up at him. "Your mother. She was a friend of the older Black woman you'd visited that summer. Roland's grandmother, you said."

"Yes."

She looked past him and then reached for her coffee again. "Hmm." She seemed lost in thought as she turned her face up to him again, her eyes on him but also somewhere else.

Jade sat back and watched her ponder what he had said. Her look was soft and open, and he tried to send her a message without saying it. He thought she could read his mind. He thought she could see in his desperate face everything he was feeling but not saying: that he was finished with his girlfriend, that if Wilson was Tamara's boyfriend, she should be done with him now, because he's with Lucy. He wanted to declare to Tamara that he loved being around her, that he dreamed about her, that she made him feel free from himself to be someone he could never be without her. She was so much older than he was, out of his league, he knew that; but this overwhelming attraction to her was far more complex, more alluring and irresistible, than the kind of blissful obsession he'd had for Lucy, that long-ago insanity of new passion, that uncontrollable heat that he now realized was mere mechanics, a chemical reaction, not a connection of real love. He wasn't sure that Tamara would offer him love of any kind at all, or even allow him a single step closer to her life. But he'd been unable to stop thinking of her, wondering about her, how if she let him into her life, he would give her everything of himself, all that he knew and all that he did not yet know. He wanted to shout it out that he'd never met anyone like her. And that he never would ever again. And that she was perfect. And that he just loved her, that's all.

"Jade?" She leaned forward and put both hands on the coffee table, searching his unfocused eyes. "Are you still with me?"

He felt his breath catching as he met her eyes, and he tried to blink away the desperation of his musings. He stood up abruptly and stepped past her chair toward the bay windows and reached for the dial on the fan. "Yeah" he said, his back to her, "I'm definitely with you." He flicked the dial to High and stared out the windows beyond the sharp shadows of the city and toward the blue-gray mountains he could only imagine were still there. "This is exactly where I want to be." He said it loud enough over the pitch of the fan so that he knew she could hear him.

They talked until the living room began to bake in the rising sun of another blistering August day in July. They moved from the soft furniture to stand together at the bay windows, the fan on them, and then back to the couch and low-backed chair. They ate the blueberries and the tarts, and she drank more coffee and he tasted some of it but switched back to the iced chamomile.

She assured him Roland would not steal his girlfriend, that Roland was anything but impulsive, that he was the opposite, in fact; that he was careful, mindful of his actions and words, and his impact on others. She said he was nothing at all like the guy some assumed he was—a stuck-up self-indulgent jock hero, out for kicks, and a user of other people. She said Roland seemed stoic, but he was just cautious; that he was thoughtful and very aware of his impact on people in this community, given his reputation as an athlete. That it had become something of a burden to him, especially in a city where everyone else was White. She said that, while he had a charming and alluring effect on girls and women, he'd always abided by his father's warnings about personal relationships in this city—a place where certain situations could be very dangerous for him. She said he'd recently become even more restrained, and very particular about who he allowed himself to get close to. She said he'd been going through some life-changing experiences since he went away to college, and that he's starting to expand his awareness far beyond football and girls, and that he's working and staying here in Ebonton because he needs to save money. She said he's conflicted about making bombs for Vietnam at Macson, that he walked around this apartment just last week quoting Mohammed Ali about having no quarrel with the Viet Cong and about not wanting to put on a uniform and drop bombs on Brown people, when Black people here in the U.S. are treated like dogs.

"In college," she said, "he learned, mainly from his new friends, that there was a war not just in that far away country, but right here in the U.S.—a long-time war, renewed yet again by the Civil Rights movement, a war between the established powers and the Black underclass, a battle that is now enjoined and bolstered by White middle class students against the war and against that establishment."

She said Roland now believes that this town where he grew up is emblematic of all that is wrong in America, and, while he won't come right out and say it, it's clear he's conflicted by his connection to Hafferty, which he can't seem to let go of, because of both the privileges and the protections it has provided him and his distinguished professor father, Doctor James Wilson. Still, Roland won't tell Hafferty or James that he's decided not to return to Penn State. He's already set up his transfer to Howard University, without their knowledge or approval, not to play sports, but to study history under noted Black scholars there.

"He's becoming a man," she said, "no longer a child lost in a facile world of sports heroics, false idolatry, and a reliance on men he does not, in his heart, agree with. Including Dennis Hafferty. And, unfortunately, his father."

She sat down again in the low-backed chair, facing him on the couch, the softer light from the now murky sky seeping through the bay windows and forming a surreal halo around her short cropped dark hair and chiseled face, her high cheekbones in shadow under piercing dark eyes. She looked both intense and tired, despite the coffee, and he realized that what she had been telling him was draining her energy. It was perhaps more than she'd wanted to say, but by then it was too late. The conversation was now about Roland, not Jade. His unspoken feelings for her had been transmitted, but either not received, or worse, rebuffed and replaced by an explanation that left him feeling foolish, childish, and embarrassed. But he wasn't crushed. When he looked at her and watched her start to speak again, he was still awed by her beauty and the light in her eyes and the song in her voice. He knew this was what he wanted from her. Enlightenment, knowledge. The route for his escape from this valley of darkness was through Tamara. His love for her would not be thwarted but enhanced now.

"You talk of feeling like an alien in this town, Jade, and I understand that. Believe me," she said, pursing her soft pillowy lips and holding his eyes with hers. "My students look at me like I'm from outer space, all those untroubled White faces not wanting to be there, not willing to listen to a Black woman, not trusting me, even though I know their mother language far better than they do, and even though I have mastered the theories behind the music of their European culture, dating back well beyond even their grandparents' lives.

"And Roland? If you want to hear what I know about Roland," she said, her voice flattening as she took a sip from her cup, "I'll tell you. But be prepared. Some of it may surprise you, perhaps even more so than what I just told you about him. But I can see that you need to know this. For many reasons, including some that neither you nor I yet understand."

She cleared her throat, and with a delicate touch she set her cup in its saucer and looked once more at him, before standing up and walking to the bay windows. She nodded for him to join her. They stood side by side watching the heat rising over the small city, the familiar haze now seeping its poison into the sky, leaving the edges of the buildings muddy where they'd been in sharp relief in the earlier clear light.

"Roland Wilson has lived in this culturally cloistered White valley since he arrived here in the mid-Fifties at the age of six. So, he's been here roughly thirteen years, coming of age in a place still stuck in the post-war Forties, becoming a reluctant hero among strangers, a lone Black gladiator in a Coliseum filled pillar to pillar with White faces." She turned to Jade with a curt smile, her wide nose flaring and her eyes becoming full circles inside the aura of daylight on her face. "No one in this valley, Jade, no one...feels more alien than James Roland Wilson. Not even you."

Jade held her look and watched the gold flares in her eyes catch the light and whirl it inside the perfect circle of each dark iris. He wished at that moment that she could be his teacher. He'd be the exception, the White kid in her class in the front row, rapt in awe at her every word and gesture. "Tell me more," he said, his voice a whisper.

She turned her gaze back to the now miasmic city view, took a shallow breath and sighed. "Roland lived with his father's aunt in rural Maryland for his first six years. Like you, he remembers those early years only vaguely, but he holds them in his mind as an ideal life he was wrenched from by his father, who took him here to live with him. He imagines those years in Maryland as the best times in his life, when he was with cousins and real friends, running free through the rural villages and the woods and marshes and streams in a world he thinks of as someone else's dream.

"When he came here, he was immediately recognized by the adults in school as a gifted athlete. He lived with his father, James, and his aunt in the only all-Black community in Ebonton, several blocks of old homes at the edge of the commercial and governmental center of the city—some of them owned by Blacks, like James, but most owned by absentee White landlords. It was considered a slum." She turned to Jade and locked her eyes on his. "Sounds like you may have been there. That grandmother you mentioned? She was Roland's great aunt, Dolores. She'd moved here with him from Maryland, to help his father raise Roland."

Jade felt he was hearing the straight truth for the first time in his life. She turned her gaze away from him and back to the hazy skyline, resuming her history lesson. Professor Tamara.

"In those days," she continued, "the commercial centers of cities like this one were bustling with people, workers and shoppers, visitors and entertainers. But this one, according to Roland's father, was already dying. The deep coal mines were no longer extant, and the strip mines were dying out as well, and employment across the valley was in rapid decline, neighborhoods emptying out to the suburbs and to other cities. And, of course, the Black workers here were among the first to lose their jobs—in the entertainment, restaurant and hotel businesses that were collapsing, some literally into the mine voids. Black men had never been permitted to work in the mines, which was work that was considered desirable, and therefore remained the exclusive domain of the White European immigrants.

"Early in this decade, the federal government began to infuse money into these declining cities, and a place like Ebonton, hopeless as it seemed to be, received enormous influxes of federal dollars to begin the cleanup of the coal industry waste—a monumental and, at the time, seemingly impossible task, according to James. It's still going on today, and, as James says, it still seems Sisyphean.

"One of the most infamous federal programs is called Urban Renewal—you might have heard of it. A euphemism for dismantling Black communities. Calling them slums makes it much easier. Calling them "blight" compels the theory. Language, Jade, is the weapon of justification for the ruling class in this and every colonized society.

"James and Roland and his great aunt, Dolores—along with hundreds of other Black people—families, church groups, friends—were put out of their homes, and entire blocks were bulldozed. They'd been promised a slot in the new apartments that the government would build to replace the so-called slum, but, in the meantime, they had no place to go. The community was broken up, the people dispersed, scattered to wherever they could land. Some were determined to hang on, living at the fringes until the new buildings were erected. But you've seen that tract of land, Jade; there's still nothing there. And the people from that community, that slum? Most simply moved away, to other bigger cities, some back to the South, some back home to the Caribbean. Families, friends, church congregations—all dispersed. In the name of progress.

"James found a home in the city among the blue-collar Whites. I suppose the joke on the White realtor who allowed him to buy there was that the realtor had told the neighbors that James was a doctor, not knowing he was a Ph.D., not an M.D. If they'd known, they'd never have let him in.

"So, that's where Roland spent his high school years—living in the stunted low end of the middle class, attending a private school for the first year, and then finishing at the city's public school, and his only pass among the Whites was his status as a sports hero. As you've likely come to understand, there is nothing in this valley more important than high school sports, especially football, and he excelled at it, as well as the other sports.

"James hated that stereotype for his son, but he'd already accepted the ruse of his own role as a "medical doctor" among the Whites, so he was compromised all around. His solution? To shelter himself from it all. He burrowed into his research and his teaching, and at home, he stayed inside, hiding from his neighbors, never attending his son's athletic performances, and driving a deep emotional wedge between himself and Roland. Dolores never made the move to the new home with them. She wanted nothing to do with hiding among White people. She went back to Maryland, and Roland was left with no female influence in his home life. That did not have a good impact on him."

Tamara turned away from the windows and stepped behind Jade. "It's too hot here in this spot," she said. "Let's go out to my back porch. It should be in shadow by now. Are you hungry, Jade? I can make us some sandwiches." He shook his head. His stomach had been in a knot, but it was just now starting to unravel; he was hungry, but food was not what he needed most. She led the way through the apartment to the back porch, stopping at the refrigerator for more iced tea. "I have to hold off on the coffee now, or I won't ever stop talking," she said, smiling and raising her eyebrows at him and holding up the cold container of chamomile.

Jade felt the dream rise suddenly again, imagining that they lived here together. He saw himself showing her how to be a short order cook and her showing him how to make secret recipes handed down from her family, and they would have long discussions about books, and she would teach him how to play that upright piano and open his mind further about the whirling world around him that he'd been hiding from until now. And they would spend lots of time in her bedroom. *Their* bedroom. It was a thrilling moment that made him laugh to himself, a release from the weight of her story.

"What's so funny?" she said, smiling as she set the tea on a small metal table and arranged the back porch chairs. "I haven't said anything funny, have I? Sometimes people say I'm funny, but I never know why. I certainly don't try to be."

Jade knew that his blushing face would vitiate his attempt to lie about his laughing, so he fessed up. "I...uh...I just feel better, that's all. You don't need to say anything funny. I just like listening to you. It makes me happy. My mother does that for me sometimes. She talks like a teacher, but also like someone sharing a special secret with me. She's charming, I guess. Her imagination is contagious."

Tamara tipped the iced tea pitcher toward his glass and softened her smile. "You're lucky, Jade. She sounds interesting. And fun."

"Oh, yeah," he said. "Interesting is a good word for her." He reached for the glass of tea and gulped it so he wouldn't say anything more about Alice. It was too soon for Alice to enter the stage; she'd likely take over the show completely.

"This is much cooler back here, don't you think?" Tamara said, fanning herself with a linen napkin and handing one to Jade. "Anything more about your mother? Or should I finish my story?"

Jade nodded as he drank the last of his tea and poured more. "Please finish."

"All right. I think you get the picture about Roland's high school experience. College, on the other hand, has been quite different for him, as it often is for many students who go away from home for the first time, ostensibly to study. But for the first few months of Roland's college life, there was little studying going on. He discovered a freedom he'd never known, but he chose the familiar, immature ways of experiencing it— carousing with football pals, staying up all night, sleeping all day, often with random girls. He was reveling in the hedonism of the new sexual permissiveness, and he nearly got carried away completely by it.

"But, in winter, in the middle of the football season, he woke up. He quit the team and started attending classes. Ironically, it all began with a girl—not one of the random playgirls but one with charisma and vision— a Black girl from Pittsburgh. She told him she saw something in him that he was blind to and that he would only see it if he got off the runaway train of his thoughtless lifestyle and started paying attention to the world around him. And participating in it. He attended classes consistently for the first time and learned that his college professors, unlike many of his high school teachers, had interesting, often important ideas for him to consider.

"He soon met other young Black students from Pittsburgh and Philadelphia, who were asking the tough questions about history in America, who knew first-hand about the Civil Rights movement, and who were seeking new ways of understanding themselves. They gave him what he hadn't had since he was a child in Maryland—a community of Black people and the enlightenment that comes with seeing yourself in others all around you.

"He began reading in earnest, for the first time, tuning into ideas he'd once considered outlandish, only because he'd had no experience living in a place where Black voices are heard. He's been testing these new feelings of rebelling against his accepted self, taking chances he'd never have taken before, risks he'd always considered reckless, even dangerous—especially by the strict standards of his father. He's still a high school kid in many ways, still posing as a tough guy, still taking some foolish and thoughtless chances, still resorting to the easy comforts of sarcasm to disguise his real feelings. But he's finally taking seriously the world outside himself, and the changes he's made so far portend a struggle he'll likely carry with him for the rest of his life. But, if he keeps learning, he'll have a life worth living, I'm sure of it."

Jade felt as though she was talking about someone altogether different from the Roland Wilson she knew, some mythical figure from her own version of one of Alice's literary lectures. But he realized that was Tamara's point, her purpose. To unravel the mystery of Roland Wilson, a guy Jade was drawn to, but repelled by. He hadn't known anything about Roland. But then, how could he? The guy had built a wall around himself and had barely let Jade get a glimpse of who he might be. The sex dance between Roland and Lucy at the rez had been just a game, he decided.

Another jab at Jade, another dose of the resentment Roland felt toward him, even though Jade still couldn't understand why. It was a way, he figured, for Roland to keep him on the other side of his wall.

"Roland's relationship with girls and women has been strained," Tamara continued, as if reading Jade's mind. "In part because his father has had so little time for women in his closed academic world, and, in part, because Roland never knew his mother. And that troubles him deeply. He had strong women in his Maryland family, and his father was wise enough to include one of them to be part of Roland's young life after he moved here. But he feels like he's missed a key part of growing up—the special bond between mother and son."

"Dolores," Jade said, and she nodded and smiled. "Lola, the kids called her. She was so nice to me, and to my mother. And he was such a bastard."

Tamara flattened her smile and fixed her big eyes on him. "Perhaps he was jealous, Jade. You had a mother."

"But no father," Jade said, nodding and letting her eyes read his, focused at last. "So, we're like fraternal twins, I guess," he said, smiling at her. "We have little in common physically, but we're somehow connected by our absences. He has light black skin; I have dark white skin. He's strong and athletic; I'm skinny and weird. He gets a father; I get a mother."

Tamara's eyes widened and she nodded, grinning with approval. She seemed enlightened by this observation, as if Jade were on to something, as if he'd followed her lead without her expecting it, her teacher's natural prompts toward understanding, toward generating new ideas from empirical lessons. She took a sip of her iced tea.

"Roland's father is a brilliant, troubled man," Tamara said. Her eyes softened and seemed to disappear from Jade as she drifted among her thoughts. "I know him, but only as well as he would allow me to know him. He's very self-contained. A man who spends a lot of his energy denying his feelings. It's almost as if he were guilty of something and got away with it; but, like all guilt, it continues to haunt him. I don't know what it is, but I do know that his son has suffered from his father's emotional absence, and the son is struggling to learn how *not* to imitate the father's life—the life that's locked inside the prison of Roland's memory."

"He was my teacher," Jade said, and Tamara's eyes came back into focus; she blinked, startled. "But only for three classes. It was at Pell Academy. He was the Bio teacher, but he quit after a week and returned to teaching only at the college. Some kids said he taught Bio at Pell just to keep an eye on Roland, and that, when Roland left after freshman year, Doctor Wilson had no reason to stay. I remember him as stern, and, for some weird reason, very obvious in his dislike for me. It was the same treatment I've gotten from his son—back when we were kids and now when we're workers together."

"Huh," Tamara uttered, her eyes fogging up again. "Perhaps you remind one or both of them of something they want to forget."

"But I never really knew either of them before. What is it that I could remind them of?"

"Your guess is as good as mine," Tamara said, her eyes sharp on him. "And as of now, I don't think a guess would help anyone. But I do know that Roland, and to a certain degree, James, live with what every Black person lives with in this society, this country."

"What do you mean?"

She took a drink of her tea and looked at him with her professor eyes. "You talked of your daydream walk to work on that first day of your new job. Roland can never walk in a daydream. He needs to be at the ready, his fists prepared, whenever and wherever he goes. He cannot casually walk alone in these streets like you can. He's heard the threats from dark corners and public places alike; he's suffered the assaults, defending not just his body, but his life, more often than you can imagine. He's been in the jail cells of this town more than once. He's a hero to many, but only in a sports uniform.

"His father, too. A Doctor of Philosophy, a Doctor of Biology. A learned man. Respected by his peers. But liked? No. He's stern and cold, and seemingly superior. But just like his son, he's a Black person who made it to a status in White society that sets him apart from his people, not for his own benefit, but for the benefit of those who need him as their emblem of racial tolerance. Singled out, made an example of, held up as a token of the great benevolence of the White society. He's a smart man, they'd say, for a Black man. Same for Roland. He's such a great ballplayer, they'd say. He doesn't even talk like a colored boy."

She sat up tall in her chair and looked at Jade, as if he were a juror in a courtroom and she was the prosecutor. "Roland has a wonderful, strong, beautiful body," she declared, her voice rising. "But he does not own it. His body has been on loan to the sports-worshiping community of this valley for nearly his whole life. And that body? It's never felt safe. It's always looking over its shoulder, always wary, always ready to be attacked. Even by people who say they love him because he's a star on their field.

"And James, he has a superior mind, so yes, it's right for him to seem superior. But his mind is on loan to that same society. He does not own it. He does not use it to teach young Black students about the wonders of Biology. He uses it at the behest of the wealthy Whites, whose children need to check off a science course in their idle trek toward graduation and guaranteed employment."

She saw something in Jade's face that made her stop. She gave him one of her curt smiles. "Still smitten by me, Jade?"

His response came in a rush of heat to his face, and he disconnected from her eyes and reached for his tea.

"I'm sorry if that offends you, Jade," she said. "I'm a bit more complicated than some Beatrice you admire from a distance."

"Bay-ah-TREE-che?" He felt the color drop from his face, and he began to see something in her that he'd not noticed before. A certain haughtiness, a barrier he was not welcome to cross.

"Dante Alighieri," she said. "*La Vita Nuova.* You'll study The Italian Renaissance in college, perhaps. Me? I'm a bit saturated, frankly, with European literature, music, and history. It seems to ooze out of me of its own accord. It's what happens when you immerse yourself for years in study. The agony of it is that I know more about White culture than I know about my own. Roland is not the only one who is waking up to the reality of who he has been and what he needs to do to become who he actually is. All that I just told you about being a Black man in this town? Take it up a notch for a Black woman. She has two strikes against her before she even wakes up in the morning in a place like this."

The first silent moment in hours fell between them as Tamara stood up and started to clear the iced tea container and the napkins and glasses.

Jade lost patience with the silence just as she started toward the kitchen. "What did you mean by Baya—" he started to say, swallowing the word he did not understand.

She smiled down at him and tried to open the screen door with her foot. He jumped up and pulled open the door. Their faces were closer together than they'd ever been.

"So are you in love with him?" Jade said, nearly choking on the words. "Roland?"

Tamara stared at him for a moment, her expression unreadable. Then she turned and set everything down again, and sat in her chair at the metal table, waiting for him. He sat down.

"Jade. Listen," she said, lowering her eyes for a moment and then looking at him with the soft eyes that had turned sharp with the growing intensity of her dissertation on the evolution of Roland Wilson. Jade felt foolish, ashamed of his raw feelings, of what must have looked pathetic to her, his long morning of puppy dog eyes and his first moments in her apartment—his obvious arousal at the sight of her barefoot in the doorway in tiny shorts and a revealing tee shirt. He had the odd thought that if he hadn't chosen to wear boxer undershorts, his raw desire for her would not have been so evident. She must think he's just a kid, interested only in her body. And now he knew what was coming and he braced himself to hear it.

"I'm not a teenage girl you can fall in love with," she said, with tenderness in her voice. "And I'm certainly not blind to the way you look at me or unaware of the feelings you might have for me. I like you, Jade. I do. Very much. You're smart, and very sensitive, and you're attractive. But you're—"

"Too young?" he asserted, his tone harsh, but resigned. "Too dazed and confused?" He pulled himself up from a slouch and sat up straight to face her, feeling clever about his pop music reference, but doubtful she got it. "Tamara, I know that you're older than I am. And I know that you probably see me as one of your students—not the ones who don't pay attention to you, but the one guy who pays too much attention to you."

"Oh, Jade," she said with a sigh. Then, she held up her hand. "Please don't," she said. "Don't take this out on yourself. I can see that you have too many conflicts in your life for someone your age. And you don't need another one, especially with someone like me. I have my own complications, and I don't want to make them yours. I'm trying to be reasonable."

He pushed his chair back, and it scraped heavily against the damp wood deck. As he stood up, he felt sweat rolling down his sides and back. He forced a smile and nodded his head, but she stopped him before he could dismiss her.

"Don't just walk out and never talk to me again, Jade," she said, with a firmness that surprised him as she rose quickly and stood in his path. "I know you need help, and I know you came here with both a complicated heart and a desperate spirit, reaching out for someone who might be on your side, when it seems there's no one else. I can do that. I can help you get through all of this. But I cannot be your lifesaver, and I cannot be your lover, as much as that might be wonderful. I can feel how much you have to give. But I won't go there. Not just because I have others in my life, but because it's not right for me, and it's not right for you either. And, what's most important, is that it's not safe for either of us.

"Look around you, Jade. All of these threats in your life? Imagine how many more would come at you if you were seen walking down the street holding the hand of your Black lover. Not in this town, Jade. Not anywhere in this cheerless valley. If you've been listening to me, you'll know that I don't feel safe here on my own, much less on the arm of a young White man a dozen years younger than I. If you care about me, you must think about that. You do not belong here. And neither do I."

She wrapped her hand firmly around his bicep. He was at once startled by the strength of her grip and disappointed that the first time she'd ever reached out to touch him was not for the reasons he'd dreamed about.

"Jade," she said, "I've been telling you about Roland, because I know how much he has affected your life, in ways you don't yet understand.

318

And I can help you get there, help you to figure out that connection between you and him. It's not just that you share an inside track with Dennis Hafferty and that you share space on The Line at work, and you share some common enemies, and...and now you share a connection with me. It's more than all that. You two seem to have more in common than either of you knows. I'm not yet certain what it is, but I have some ideas, because I know his father. He's told me a lot about his past and his son, but he hasn't told me the whole story. Yet. There's a conspicuous void around Roland's mother." Tamara let go of Jade's arm. "He was about to tell me something important about her when he discovered...he discovered this spring that...that I was having an affair with Roland."

Her voice seemed to fade away on that last thought. Jade's own voice was stuck in his throat. He wasn't sure he'd ever hear it again.

"It was over quickly," Tamara said, still looking at him. "But not without pain, a great deal of pain. James helped me get this apartment—through Dennis Hafferty, of course—but he wouldn't help me move out of his home. He's still angry with me, and I don't blame him. But I still love him, and he knows that. I am not in love with his son. I made a terrible mistake."

Jade looked down at where she'd held him and then up at her eyes. He felt like he was about to double over. His stomach was on fire.

"James will tell me soon enough what he's been hiding inside for so long and what it has to do with Roland, and perhaps why you remind him and Roland of something that upsets them. I need more time with James, if he'll see me. You must tell me something, Jade, so I can relay it to him, since Roland may need his help. I need to know what trouble Roland is in, what it was that you said happened yesterday at...what was it called? The rez?"

Jade's shoulders sunk, and he reached down to the table to steady himself. The gut punch of her revelations left him reeling. She grabbed his arm again, this time to keep him from falling, but he shrugged away from her. He heard her start to say something in her softer, more intimate voice about misjudging him and about how her feelings for Roland and James had come before knowing him and had nothing to do with him, but it was all too late.

He brushed past her, saying he had to go. As he opened the screen door, he turned and apologized to her for dropping in like this, and then he walked quickly toward the front door. She called out to him, asking him to wait, saying she was sorry she told him too much too soon, that she hadn't meant to hurt him. She took a few steps toward him, but she stopped at the piano.

When he put his hand on the doorknob, she implored him. "I want to help you, Jade."

He opened the door and looked back at her.

"You're hurt, I know," she said, one hand resting on the keyboard and the other reaching toward him. "I'm so sorry you are hurting. Please don't stay away. When you heal from this, just know that my door will always be open to you. I can help you. I *want* to help you."

He spent a long time on the streets before he realized he'd been walking in the wrong direction. He was somewhere in the South End. Home was the other way. Completely the other way.

Part Six

48
Lost

Monday, July 7, 1969

Jade had found his way home on Sunday and had collapsed on the couch. He'd slept at the bottom of an ancient sea, a dreamless loss of consciousness that, when he awoke, could have meant he was either another being altogether, or that he was dead.

It was early, according to the Big Ben clock on the coffee table, the clock a weird knockoff from a time and place he may have lived in another life. The hands of Ben indicated five o'clock, but he wasn't sure it was telling the truth. There was light coming in his window, an eerie rinse of shades that could mean it was either dusk or dawn, or simply the color of air in a dream. He smelled nothing, and that told him that he'd expected to be assaulted by his first breath of air, making him feel detached from himself. He couldn't remember what that assault might consist of, but its absence gave him a sense of lost time and place, an expectation of familiar order that had failed to materialize.

He put his feet on the floor and felt his memory pouring into him in electrified jolts—his clay feet stirring, his permanence here forming in the hands held before him, his senses startled by sulfur in the air and grit in his eyes. His life in the soot-bound valley. He looked around the room and rediscovered his old reality in the statues of the saints and in the blank, frozen, pallid face and empty eyes of the Virgin—the eyes a blue that matched her clay robe. He felt the urge to mock her. And her creator.

He remembered that before he'd hovered over the couch with an empty mind, he had searched the house for Alice and discovered nothing had changed, that she was still absent, out there, probably on another bender. He'd also telephoned Lucy and Squirrel and then Wally and even Hafferty's office. No answers anywhere. With the caution of a lost child, he'd stepped gingerly around the statues and parted the front window curtain and peered out there into the dark, holding his breath, searching for signs of Joey Belden or Stanley or even Roland Wilson, who he'd both wanted and had not wanted to see. Then, he'd turned and saluted the

Blessed Mother and made his way to the edge of the couch where he had let himself fall face first into the emptiness of oblivion.

He blinked hard now, shook his foggy head, stood up, and looked to the Virgin's eyes again, willing her to send a message to Alice. But the Virgin rebuffed him with an icy stare. He thought he should try praying sometime, just to see if those painted eyes would move, just to check on the progress of Alice's gift to him.

He looked down at his rumpled tee shirt, his dungarees, and his sneakers, and he registered the need to go through familiar motions while not knowing why. He changed into work clothes and boots and prepared lunch and ate breakfast, and he knew he had a destination, but he was still too lost in the emptiness of forgotten thoughts to remember exactly what it was. His brain, he knew, had exhausted itself—its capacity for emotional chaos had hit the red zone and had canceled out everything else—which was when he remembered Tamara.

An hour later, he heard the 15 trundling by and squealing to a stop to pick up his comrades standing in the morning queue—Gort and the three women. Without him. He'd missed it. The next bus would be thirty minutes later. He'd be late for work.

He sauntered into the maw of the massive building with its mechanical pulses in full throttle and picked his timecard out of the rack and slid it into the punch clock. Ka-chunk. He felt the sound in his feet, his ears already plugged and dull. He turned toward the chaos of the factory floor, glancing up to Ren Belden on his throne staring, as expected, directly at Jade. He shuffled to The Line where Dimmock was bending over a stack of shells on the floor, lifting them slowly one by one up to the platform and then pushing them onto the nearest moving conveyors. Jade thought he might just stand there and watch this procedure for a while, Dimmock looking like a gravedigger picking up hardened cadavers from the concrete earth. Jade chuckled at the conjured image. Dimmock stopped his picking and turned to Jade and his mouth fell open. Words sprayed out under the man's demonic glare as he shifted his full frame to face Jade. Something about "late" and "fucking kill." Something that roared from the flaming windows of his Hell.

In the yard at the break, Squirrel descended on him like a hawk on prey, his talons digging into Jade's nape, his squawk scratching at Jade's ear. Screeching something about Roland, his father saying he didn't know where he was, the men saying it had to do with the kid they found at the Rez, and did he know where Roland was. He showed Jade the newspaper. The frontpage headline. "Teen's Body Found at Reservoir." Squirrel pointing to copy on the front page. Detective Captain Marion. Patrolmen and former detectives Joseph Belden and William Jensen reinstated and charged with investigating the cause of death. He was shaking Jade's shoulder.

322

"Where's Roland? Why isn't he here? Did you check with Lucy?"

Jade turned to Squirrel and stared at his rodent face, the small black pupils centered in sky blue, his blonde eyebrows twisted in swirls on his wrinkled forehead, too old for such a young guy. Jade stood up at the flagpole and heard himself say, "I'll go get him," and then he walked toward the gate, Squirrel shouting something behind him that sounded like "filed." Fined. Fired.

On the walk toward Dickson College, he stayed in the street, along the curb, cars veering around him honking their horns, men hollering at him, curses, the screech of brakes, the jolt of horns, more horns.

He leaned on the trunk of a tree across from Wally's house waiting for the door to the upper floors to open. When he felt the bark of the tree leaving an impression on his shoulder, he started to mark time. He later counted three levels of numbness since he'd started to lean there.

The girl's blonde hair sashayed in the doorway. Patsy. She stepped onto the porch and pirouetted to the railing and coasted down the wooden steps to the sidewalk. He pulled himself from the warmth of the bark and felt his shoulder reforming to its shape, the one he thought he should know. He heard traffic noise from the adjacent avenue and saw the girl come clearly into focus. She was calling to him from the curb across the street.

He started toward her, and she screamed at him, her hands in the air, her face frozen in terror. He stopped. A car horn blared inside his head as the machine whooshed by inches from him, the sound of the motor following it, horn echoing. Did he remember to take out his ear plugs?

"I can't tell you," the girl said. "It's a secret."

"Is he a Black man with curly hair, a short Afro?" he asked.

"No," she said and flicked her hair to the side. She smiled with her inside knowledge. "Sort of brownish, I'd say. He's tall."

"How long has he been there?"

"It's a secret," she said, her chin wrinkling with her squinting eyes. "It's not a sin to have secrets, you know."

He went back to his tree and sat on its exposed roots, his forehead aimed toward the house, waiting, watching the third-floor windows so high up that there was no need for curtains. The girl played hopscotch on the sidewalk, her skirt flipping, her bobby sox poking out of her smart shoes. A man's voice at his shoulder asked him if he was OK, and he said without looking at the man, "Fine. Waiting for a friend."

The girl had disappeared behind the door sometime earlier, and he wasn't sure how long he'd sat there, staring at the house. He pulled himself to his feet by grasping the bark of his tree. He patted the bark like it was a pelt and walked back to center city and took the 15 home and collapsed on the couch again. He dreamed of Tamara.

49
Dellworth Cranstone IV

I f this were California, we could hug in public and no one would blink."
The tall man stood erect, grinning down at her, his face flush.

She let go of his handshake and felt a surge of warmth in her loins.
"We don't do that sort of thing in New York, do we, Dell?" She held his
look for another moment and then sat down at the table. She heard the
debutante in her own voice, the supercilious inflection, the mix of
assertiveness and acquiescence that gives off certain coded signals he
would recognize. "And I don't care how long you stand there, darling. I'm
not going to get up and hug you, no matter where we are."

She smiled at him without effort. She'd always liked him, even at his
most pompous and arrogant as a Boston-bred Columbia brain boy in
relentless, but unsuccessful, pursuit of her favor. She'd liked his
persistence and his incisive mind, his keen observation skills and his
understated wit. She'd even been attracted to his occasional sullen moods,
so like her own that she'd identified with him in both his darkness as well
as in his self-driven recovery. She saw him back then as a model for
overcoming doubt through large doses of willful self-confidence—a
master over his emotions. She doubted now whether he'd ever cheated
on his wife or intentionally lied to anyone, notwithstanding his inbred
Brahmin tendency to season the truth with a subtle sprinkling of self-
promotion. But Dellworth Cranstone the Fourth was nothing if not a
gentleman.

He looked nearly the same now, his patrician face wrinkle free and
still elevated above the fray, a dusting of gray around the temples barely
discernible in the full head of ash blonde hair, his signature military
posture—the Walking Erection, as her girlfriends used to say—and an
agonized look in his eyes at the very sight of her. He was a martyr of
unrequited lust, and she still seemed to bring that out in him, all these
years later.

As he wavered there on his feet for a moment too long, she
wondered if he might just turn around and walk out on her—payback for
disappearing on him so long ago. If he did walk out, she'd chase him into
the street and hug him for dear life, New York be damned. She had to
play a cool hand, though, to keep him coming; but if she overplayed it,
she'd have no one else to turn to. She wondered if he could read the
desperation behind her cool resistance to his transparent ploy to put his
arms around her.

He signaled a waiter as he sat across from her. The lighting in the restaurant was low and soft, as she had requested of him, and their table was a curtained booth, not for romantic purposes, but for whatever privacy could be mustered in Midtown in midday and midweek in the company of a *New York Times* editor and political analyst. Giallo's tail was easy to shake in Ebonton, but, if he had one on her here in New York, the guy would probably have a fully operating brain. She still wasn't sure if her San Francisco masquerade went undetected, but she was more concerned about this meeting, given Giallo's east coast web of influence she'd witnessed in Beach Haven with Lenny, and his well-known sensitivity to press coverage.

She made a quick sweep of the room and saw no one who might fit the role. Heavy wine-colored drapes on the front windows held back the bright afternoon sunlight, and the voices at the tables around them were low, silverware clinking in the near silence. She was tempted to ask Dell to close the curtain on their booth, but she didn't want to encourage him any further in his resurrected ardor for her. She would have to remind herself not to sweeten her tone, no matter where this conversation would lead.

"Well, if you won't hug me, at least let me buy you a drink," Dell said, his long neck seeming to extend another few inches as he looked down his nose at her and smirked. "Maybe you'll loosen up and let me hug you California-style after lunch, at which point you'll think to yourself, 'What a fool I was to turn him down twenty years ago.'" He winked at her and smiled, and ordered a Manhattan, up.

"Just an iced tea for me, thank you," she said to the waiter.

Dell's neck shrunk, his chin receding. He frowned. "Iced tea? Good Lord, woman, you're freezing me out worse than you did at Barnard. My old broken heart is cracking yet again. Soon it will be in permanently shattered pieces on the floor right here in this tomb of a place you wanted to meet in." His frown turned into a smile, and he nodded at her. "But, darling, I don't blame you. Look at you. Whatever horrible things you say might have happened to you, you're still beautiful, and those eyes are still the most intriguing I've ever looked into."

"Dangerous flattery coming from a twenty-year married man," she said, her deb voice still in play. "And a daddy, to boot. Lordy, what they would *say!*" She tilted her head and turned the eyes he professed to love into hard question marks. "If I didn't know better, I'd never guess by your boyish approach that you're a hardened newsman at the top of your game at the topmost paper in the nation."

He leaned back and pulled a pack of Raleighs from his breast pocket and tapped open the end until several cigarettes popped up. His fingernails were manicured, and the backs of his hands were dusted in soft blonde hair. His mouth was now a frown within a smile. He held the pack out to her.

"No thanks," she said.

"My goodness," he said, laying on the sarcasm. "No hugging, no drinking, no smoking. Next, you'll be telling me 'No talking, no looking at me.' I know from what you told me on the phone that you did not spend the last twenty years in a convent, so what's with the ban on vices? This is the last year in a decade of tumult, after all. Don't tell me you haven't indulged in any of the decadent delights of the decline of civilized society." He lit his Raleigh with a gold Zippo and flicked it closed with a practiced twitch of the wrist. As he exhaled toward the ceiling, she could hear a slight tremor in the sound of his breath. Self-doubt was peeking out from under the veil of his performance.

She'd asked him on the phone why a man of his standing and education would go into the newspaper business, and he'd told her he didn't want to be part of his family business back in Boston, that he'd considered getting into politics, but his family had refused to support him, so he decided to get into it on his own terms, from under the hood of politics—the news business. Ultimately, he said, he's headed for the editors' suite. He wants to write opinions, perhaps even a column of his own.

"So, either you invited me to lunch to try to seduce me for old times' sake, or you truly believe you can help me. Which is it, Dell? Because even if it's the former, just lie to me and tell me you think my story is worth pursuing. I need your help."

He took a deep drink from his Manhattan and then a deeper draught from his Raleigh, and as the stream of smoke streaked from his pursed lips toward the ceiling, he looked at her sidelong and then let out a laugh with the final cloud. "What if I said it was both. Where would we be then?"

She swirled the glass stir stick twice in her iced tea and then looked up at him with a blank expression. "I'd prefer the lie," she said. "Even though you're lousy at it."

Dell sighed and then lifted his shoulders, recovering his military posture. "All right, we'll start with the story. But I'll give you fair warning. I'm not giving up on my, shall we say, personal interest in you. I still need to know why you disappeared so suddenly twenty years ago. I was in love with you, Issa, for Chrissake. And I know the feeling wasn't mutual, but I do know you felt *something* for me. We dated dozens of times, for nearly a year. We had something swell going, even if it wasn't mutual love. But it might have blossomed into that over time. Instead, you just vanished. No warning, no letter, no nothing. The rumors were flying everywhere, of course. Some had you eloping to Europe with a married man, others had you living in squalor in the Village with a Jewish poet or a Negro jazz man. Still others had you dead in some freak accident, lost at sea in Devil's Triangle or under an avalanche in the Swiss Alps. Most of those rather dramatic conjectures came from your former classmates and society sisters, all of whom, by the way, were jealous of the way you had dodged the entire debut set-up—the ballroom and classical dancing and etiquette lessons and the side courses in French and all the classes about rules for social life—all because you'd already had all of that as a child. And you'd already driven home the final nail into their resentful little hearts when they learned you'd snubbed your own debut after all. It was all jealousy, Issa, and I didn't believe any of those stories after you'd vanished, but I do know that your disappearance was followed less than a year later by the disappearance of your father from New York society. The following year, his North Shore estate was sold, and then the rumors started swirling that he'd died, but no one could confirm anything. He was mysteriously and simply gone. I was in grad school at the time, not yet a news reporter, but I had my ear to the ground and connections at *The Times* and *The Herald*, and, well, after a while, by the mid-fifties, your name and that of your father simply disappeared from the planet. I'll be quite surprised if the story you started to share with me over the phone doesn't begin somewhere around the time you disappeared from Barnard, and New York, and me."

She reached across the table and plucked a cigarette from his Raleigh pack. As she leaned over to take the flame he offered, she looked at his sky-blue eyes, warm in the light of the flame, but heavily burdened. She wondered if he was still the master of his emotions, with the power of his calculated confidence to overcome doubt. Or lost love.

"This story is not about me, Dell," she said, fighting the dizzy effect of her first cigarette in a week. She took another quick drag and exhaled, feeling charged now. "It's about politics, which is why it should interest you. It's about how the political ambition of one man began in deceit and betrayal, and how that pattern continues to this day, destroying lives all around him, while he remains untouched, unscathed. He's a criminal, and so is his partner. And they've been getting away with it for decades. It needs to be exposed. He needs to be taken down."

Dell reached for his Raleighs just as the waiter appeared. They ordered lunch, and he asked for two iced teas this time. When the waiter left, he lit his cigarette and leaned back in his seat. She saw his face change—harden, his chin lifting, his eyes glazing over. He sighed.

"Issa," he said, in his professorial Brahmin tone, sounding the consonants as "sh" as if to hush her while he prepared to expatiate. "If *The New York Times* were to cover every incident of politics joining hands with organized crime in the United States, we'd have to have the resources of the federal budget to fund the reporters and researchers and lawyers and time and expenses that it would take. I don't have the tiniest fraction of such a budget under my direction. And, even if we had the resources to chase, say, regional stories of corruption in politics, we don't have to go all the way to Pennsylvania to do so. We have our fill of them right here in the city. And, if we run out of stories here—which we won't—all we'd need to do is cross over the Hudson, and there are literally hundreds, if not thousands, of such stories crawling all over New Jersey, from Jersey City to the PA border, from Newark to Philadelphia. And don't even get me started on that one—Philadelphia. The fact is that *every* state and *every* city in this country has such stories. It's American capitalism in motion, Issa. We call our brand of capitalism a democracy to give it legitimacy, but it's still capitalism. Wherever there's public money and private enterprise, there will be corruption. Your story, Issa, is one of millions, I'm sorry to say."

She stared at him for the few moments it took him to deflate and slouch toward the table and take another Raleigh from his pack. "You met him, Dell," she said, tipping her head and opening her eyes wide. She gave him an enigmatic smirk, knowing he'd start rolling his vast memory reel.

"Who?" he said at last, giving in to the mystery.

"Dennis Hafferty."

"What?" He shook his head and set down his cigarette. "Where?"

"He used to appear, uninvited, at Columbia parties, telling everyone I was his little sister. He maneuvered briefly into my life at Barnard, pretending to be part of our social scene. You must recall, Dell. Thick eyeglasses, small head, large body, not nearly your height, but meaty, loud, crude, and craven. Always showed up in an out-of-date tuxedo that looked like he'd retrieved it from a rental shop's trash can. But that never held him back. He was much too bumptious to be missed."

Dell's eyes widened, and he reached for his cigarette. He took a drag and looked at her. "You don't mean that buffoon who pushed you into your pool at your father's Oyster Bay dinner party for Governor Dewey?"

She let out a soft laugh, closed her eyes, and nodded.

"Good God, what a lout. The governor's men gave him the bum's rush, if I remember correctly, and he certainly deserved it. I wanted to kick him in the pants as they dragged him out. Must have embarrassed your father to no end."

"It wasn't the first time," she said, "but it prompted him to finally decide to send Dennis to a sanatorium to dry out."

"I just don't recall meeting him otherwise, Issa. You say I did. He wasn't a Columbia man, was he?"

This time, her laugh burst out of her. "He barely made it out of secondary school. My father sent him to three colleges—I can't even remember where—and he washed out of all of them inside of a year. Academics were not his calling, shall we say. But he was evidently quite popular on the party circuit. A laundry list of disciplinary actions at each school. Ultimately, my father decided, I suppose, that Dennis was well-suited for politics, but certainly not at a New York level. So, with father's help, Dennis wormed his way into a place where the brand of politics matched his personality. And eventually, with significant help from the money that he stole from my family and continues to earn millions from, he clawed and bamboozled and bought his way to the top of a small hill he now calls his own. That's our man, Dell. Dennis Hafferty, an American man's man."

She took a drag on her cigarette and reached into her handbag. She pushed a thick envelope across the table to Dell. "These are my notes from my meeting with Jake Levin. I even typed them up for you. All the names, places, dates, deals, and transactions that he uncovered in 1950 are right here. At least three, if not more, of the people named here are still alive. With the exception of one, whom I won't identify, all of these people can be made to talk, since all of them have something to lose if they don't. I know this story will work for you, Dell, no matter what your reservations are. I've had someone else look at it, someone with, shall we say, less emotional connection to the story—someone who was there for most of these events and has an inside track on Hafferty. That person, who has something to lose by the publication of the story but even more to lose by not having it published—that person studied every possible angle and inspired me to develop a course of action that I've outlined here for you, which is not only logical and exacting, but airtight. All I'm asking you to do is to read it. You'll see for yourself that it's worth the effort. And the expense. Your readers will love it, and your ad sales guys will love *you*. And you'll be saving lives in the process."

He held the envelope and nodded at her, his eyes returning to their earlier luster. His voice was softer, and he let his shoulders sag as he leaned further toward her.

"I'll read it, Issa. I can't promise you anything other than that. I'll read it, and I'll even ask around to see if any of these names ring a bell. I already struck out with Jake Levin. Seems nobody who worked the newspaper circuit back then remembers him. Hell, there were so many New York dailies and weeklies in those days, it's a needle in a haystack, even worse now that more than half are defunct. That said, it's unlikely any paper outside of the bigs would spend resources on a Pennsylvania wild goose chase. Maybe you have his editor's name or someone else's name in here that connects Levin to reporting in New York, but so far, he's an unknown. I'm not even sure he was a reporter at all. But I'll find out. For you."

She felt her stomach flip and her heartbeat speed up, and she thought about ordering a drink. A whiskey straight up would be just right. Dell surely wouldn't mind. It would serve his ulterior motive. Get her lubed up with a drink, get her guard down.

"You know what I think I'd like, Dell?" she said, managing a soft smile for him.

"What's that, Issa?"

She saw his face light up. He was such a puppy. A big bright White man with two degrees from Columbia, a man with a prominent post in New York journalism, a Midtown man with a wife and kid in Westchester, no doubt a member of the downtown Union Club and a golf club in Westchester, a summer place on the Island, probably the Hamptons. But he was a puppy for her attention. Still desperate for her love.

"Never mind," she said, reaching for the cigarette pack. "Just give me a light, would you?"

As he extended the lighter toward her with his long arm, she looked at his hand again. It was delicate. He was a delicate man. So out of place in the rough and gritty newspaper business. He should have been a teacher, perhaps a college professor. She smiled at that thought, imagining him fawning over young coeds who looked like she did in 1949. He'd be much happier doing that. Finding his Issa in other, younger women.

"Here's lunch," Dell said with a lightness in his voice as the waiter placed their plates in front of them. "Perhaps we can take a walk after we dine. Grab a cab to the park, get some fresh air."

"That might be nice," she said, although she had no intention of walking in public with Dell. She took another look around the restaurant and spotted a man dining alone at a table near the door. He looked like a businessman, but the missing tie gave her a start. That and the day-old growth on his tan face. Papa G's man?

As the waiter cleared the table and Dell asked for the check, she told him she couldn't go for that walk, that she had to get back to her hotel, pack up, and head for The Tubes. Dell's face fell for a moment, and then he recovered, still reliable in his ability to overcome rejection, yet again. Then, she saw his business face come on and braced herself.

"Listen, Issa. I...ehm...I'll go ahead and read what you have here and give it serious consideration, but what I need in order to pursue anything remotely like this—an evidently complicated historical story that would require a serious investment of time and resources—is a link to national politics that has current value to our readership. That is to say, local corruption that interplays with national politics. And I'm not talking about back door deals between U.S. congressmen or administration officials that involve local politicians and indiscreet payoffs. Again, that's a somewhat common story. What I need is a link to prominent national political figures. Your man—Hafferty? I've already had one of my fellows do a little legwork on him. He's a typical local tribal boss. A bully. He uses a congressman to funnel federal funds to his associates, yes; but again, it's a common story. He's not well known beyond your valley. And as for his partner, Salvatore Giallo, he's part of the mid-Atlantic syndicate, but he's strictly a local player. We're *The New York Times*, Issa. Your story is a local newspaper's story. And yes, I know, your man Hafferty pulls strings there, in your local newsrooms and board rooms. They all do, everywhere in this country."

He took another drag on his cigarette and punched it out in the ashtray. "I'm sorry, Issa. I'm sorry for whatever happened to you. I truly am. But you need to move on, get beyond it. Get the hell out of that godforsaken place, for starters."

She'd smoked another cigarette down to the filter listening to him. Her hand was trembling as she shoved the butt into the ashtray.

"I'm forty years old," Dell continued, in his all-business tone. "And you're right behind me, Issa. We both look young for our age, thank God, especially you. You're going to live a long time, my dear. You have many more lives ahead of you, much joy, I can assure you. Is this what you really want now? Your family's dirty laundry dragged out into the public square? Your father's legacy unfurled in some seedy tale of greed and corruption, and who knows what else we'll find?"

He picked up his iced tea and then set it down again. He leaned forward to find her face, to will her eyes to lift up and meet his own.

"You and I, Issa, we come from privileged families fraught with ugly histories, most of them kept secret for a reason—the protection of the family, including its best and worst members. In the short time since we spoke by phone, I've confirmed at least the basics of your story, and the direction it could go might very easily backfire on you. Certainly, you've been mistreated—I'm not sure I want to know exactly how. But, at least now, you have your privacy and a future of your own determining. What you're asking for is one thing—the end of your stepbrother's reign of terror over you. But what you'll get may be far worse. According to my researcher, Hafferty is a seasoned manipulator of the press. He has a gift for turning negative news stories about him into far worse stories about his accusers. And, while our reporters are the best in the country, even they cannot control how a man like Hafferty could use our reporting to his advantage, and to your distinct and devastating disadvantage. And, if the story fell to the local reporters after we broke it, believe me, you'd be destroyed." He reached his open hand to her, but she didn't respond. "Issa, I couldn't live with myself if I put in motion a story that would end up destroying you."

She stopped looking at his eyes, letting her own go blurry, the edges of his face disappearing. "You're wrong," she said, not seeing him, not wanting to. "I don't have a future." Her own voice sounded distant, as if she were falling away from the table. "This...pretty face," the voice said in a slow cadence, "the shell you see, the preserved body...it's simple heredity. A gift from my father who was robust and youthful right up to his stroke. But *inside* this good body and face, a soul is crushed, a mind barely able to function, a spirit already dead. I drink to drown the pain, you know...and to find my way into the darkness where I can rest, and be alone...away from the endless weight, the pushing down into a bottomless pit."

She sighed, and then took a deep breath and felt herself coming back. She refocused her eyes onto his. "I have a son. Two of them, in fact, although I barely know one of them. I have nothing else. Nothing. Those boys are under his thumb now, and I'm losing them. Rapidly. Their survival of him is the only force keeping me alive. And, if he either captures them for good or dispenses with them in whatever cruel and horrifying way he chooses, I will be done. Finished. I feel it coming at me, like a wave out on the ocean you cannot yet see, but you know it is coming. Very soon. My only hope is a slim one. But I will try. With or without you. I know two other big city newsmen, but you're my best bet. All odds against me notwithstanding, I will stop him from taking my sons from the promise of their own lives. One way or another."

He reached across the table and took her hand. His touch was gentle; she let him. He held it there until he heard the waiter clearing his throat in order to discreetly deposit the check on the table. The leather tablet landed with a muted thud.

50
Fall Guy

Thursday, July 10, 1969

On Tuesday, Jade called off sick and lay on the couch with his eyes half-open, expecting nothing.

On Wednesday, he called off again. Jensen's secretary, Dorothy, warned him he'd lose his job if he called off one more day. In the evening, the phone rang four separate times, but each time, the familiar clanging felt distant, not worth responding to. Alice would never call, and he didn't want to listen to anyone else. In the kitchen, he stared into the barren refrigerator and then made himself a peanut butter sandwich. He tried a few bites; his knotted gut refused entry.

The weather had broken sometime early in the day, but instead of going outside, he opened all the windows and let the cool breeze wash through the house. It came from the south, so there was no sulfur in the air, and he felt his brain awakening, startled by the subtle scent of the mountains. He saw the picket fence of trees whooshing by on that first ride up the twisting road in Squirrel's Corvair; the geese family squawking and stirring ripples at the far end of the rez. He smelled the air filled with sweetness and earth, and he heard whistles and trills, the steady buzz of life. Actual life. An awakening.

At dusk, he went up to his bedroom and collapsed face down on his bed. The rez. Lucy's white panties floating beneath her thighs as she swayed to Roland's clapping, her secret in full view; Roland's own nakedness, his chiseled chest, his hips swaying, the dangling dark penis the pendulum of her beat; the rear-end high above the water in a jack-knife surface dive; then, dark arms thrashing up close, Roland gasping; the sudden thud all the way to the core of the brain and the force of water, sinking, knowing suddenly that Roland had delivered the punch with a purpose.

In a single movement, he pushed himself up from his bed and leaped to his feet, gasping. He stood there in a tremor, his heart thrumming, his breath pumping, his lungs lusting for air. His eyes alight. His brain was burning.

On Thursday, when Jade reported early for work, the plant was at a standstill, transformed into an outdoor reading room for the second time in a week. Men sat outside in the yard against the wall and the fence and inside on racks and forklifts and honing machines, on The Line and even on the floor, heads buried behind the paper wings of *The Clarion*. The vastness of the silence was a void, a deadness, an absence conspicuous in this place. He plucked out his ear plugs and smiled, looking around the yard and into the silent maw of his workplace. This was his dream job—reading for a living in the silent open air.

Near the timeclock, his fantasy evaporated in the rising heat as he picked up a discarded newspaper from the floor and read the banner headline. "Ebonton Man Held in Teen Death." When he saw the photo of the suspect, Jade felt his knees buckling and he grabbed onto the timeclock, the back section of the paper fluttering to his feet as he struggled to find his balance.

The face in the photo stared back at Jade as if it were alive right there on the page, glaring at him, only at him. Jade felt sweat rolling down his sides and yet another knot forming in his belly. He was stunned, frozen at the time clock, staring at the face staring at him from the front page. The anxious narrow dark eyes, the nervous sweaty face, the mouth in a twisted frown, half-smiling, half-weeping. The photo had captured the man's face at a self-conscious moment that seemed an exact replica of the face Jade had seen in the window of the green pickup truck. The little man's trembling voice, his obsequious compliments, his persistence. His desperate, hungry eyes. It all came to Jade in a visceral wave, and he looked up to the men's room doorway. If his stomach lurched once more, he'd have to take those steps three at a time to make it to a stall. He closed his eyes and held his breath, willing the burn to subside. An hour earlier, he'd finished his first meal in days, and he knew if he threw it up, he'd be too weary to work. He'd be fired.

He took a few more deep breaths and looked down at the newspaper again. The caption under the photo read, "Ralph Ismeltz, murder suspect." He picked up the paper and scanned the article. Arresting officers Joseph Belden and William Jensen said they found evidence in the suspect's apartment and pickup truck that directly linked him to the Raines boy. No motive was cited, but Belden was quoted as saying Ismeltz was known for his homosexual activity. An autopsy had revealed that Raines had been dead for over a week when he was found, and that the toxicology report indicated he had cocaine and heroin in his blood.

Jade felt another set of eyes on him, and he looked up. Across the vast dirty cement floor, he met Dimmock's frowning glare. He was standing on the edge of The Line, the conveyors idle behind him, clusters of shells waiting to be shuttled to the Forge. Dimmock pointed to his watch and his frown deepened. Jade scanned The Line. No sign of Roland. A moment later, the 7:30 whistle pierced the air, and all around him, workers put down their newspapers and sauntered to their posts, forklift engines coughing, machines whirring to life, and The Line clacking and rumbling to a start.

At the flagpole at lunch, Jade sat on the concrete base and watched a harried Squirrel pace back and forth in front of him. All along the fence and walls, small groups of workers clustered together under the veil of the morning news, but the tone had changed. Some were shouting, some even laughing. The somber library atmosphere of the morning had transformed into something else, something less reflective, more sinister. As Jade listened to the call outs, he recognized the energy shift, the thrill that people manifest when they realize that a horrible tragedy did not happen to them or to anyone they cared about. For them, it was no longer a tragedy. It was a comedy.

"Listen to them," Squirrel snarled. "They're celebrating!" His head was bowed, and his shoulders hunched as he paced like a caged animal. "I heard the buzz get started in my building, and now it's all over the yard. These fuckers are eating up the bullshit laid out for the press by Mutt and Jeff. They're scarfing down the rotten meat like dogs and turning rabid. Those two scums will be made full detectives again, just you wait. They picked off the weakest guy on the street—this poor sap, Ismeltz—and they're pinning a fucking murder on him. And the newspaper creeps are feeding the beast, not even questioning the crap Belden handed them. Pinning the job on a queer. Now, these assholes here are celebrating that a queer will be thrown in jail. Next thing you know, he'll be killed there. And no one's gonna give a shit. What's another dead queer. That's what they're saying now in my building about the dead kid—that he's a queer too, so he deserved to die. They're fucking celebrating, and Mutt and Jeff are gonna keep it up until they get their old jobs back. What a goddamn farce."

As if on Squirrel's cue, two men at the front fence started mincing toward the gate, hands flopping at their sides. They shouted in lispy high voices to a passerby on the sidewalk below, "Hey, it's another Izzy Ismeltz. Look at the swish on him. Or is it a *her*? Izzy, Izzy, what is ya? Is you a him? Or a her?" The men around these taunters burst into laughter. Jade watched others around the yard join the fun and noticed a few more bad imitators of a woman's walk as they shouted out their standard fag taunts.

"Look at these fucking lemmings," Squirrel scowled, his hands on hips as he surveyed the yard. "They're playing right into the hands of our noble Ebonton police. Two crooked cops commit a heinous crime, arrest a fall guy, and get a promotion. Makes me sick."

He stepped closer to Jade. "And I think you're holding out on me about what you saw at that car wreck. I think Mutt and Jeff are the murderers, Jademan. They're running drugs, and that kid was their victim, just like the Black girl. I think they dumped the kid's body in the rez, and, a few days later, they found us there and ordered us to stay away, so we wouldn't discover their dirty work. And then they went looking for a fall guy.

"That's why Roland stayed out of work this week. He called me Monday night and told me Lucy called him late Sunday to tell him Mutt and Jeff stopped by her house that afternoon to talk to her about riding around in a black Caddy with a colored guy on Saturday. Of course, they used a different word for him. Said the two of them were seen up on the mountain near the rez, and they wanted to know if the colored guy had his way with her in the woods. Using different words, of course. The slimes that they are. Then they wanted to know if the colored guy showed her his favorite swimming spot—the rez."

"What the hell?" Jade blurted out. "Lucy? How…how the hell did they know? What did she tell them?"

Squirrel sat down on the slab and turned to Jade, his mouth in a grimace that looked like suspicion to Jade. "Don't worry, lover boy. She didn't dime you out. Roland told me they didn't ask her about you. Not sure why. Maybe their witnesses only saw Roland and Lucy. Who knows? But Lucy kept her mouth shut. Denied everything. Her mother was in the kitchen, listening to the whole thing, so Roland figured the story would be out soon enough—two cops visiting their little house in the Backend as part of a murder investigation. Hot news for the gossip circuit. So Roland went into hiding. That's where he was when he called me, but he wouldn't say where he was hiding. The cops probably visited his father, but Roland didn't let Doc Wilson know where he was, so whatever the good doctor told them was probably the truth—he didn't know where his son was hiding."

"I know where he was," Jade said. "And I bet his father figured it out, even if Roland didn't tell him."

Squirrel eyed him again with misgiving. "Who the hell are you, Robert Culp? Mister *I Spy*? Were you with your partner, Bill Cosby, all that time you were off? You two have been off work three days. Are ya plotting a takeover without me?"

Jade smirked and stood up. "It doesn't matter," he said, grabbing his uneaten lunch and stepping away from the flagpole. He looked toward the fence again and then toward the entrance to his building. Dimmock was standing in the doorway, arms folded, staring at him. "I'm sure Roland is safe."

"Well, he's not with Lucy, I can tell you that," Squirrel said. "And he's never been with her, if you get my drift. I know what you think, but it never happened. He told me he was so shittin' scared after his dive in the rez that he couldn't get rid of Lucy fast enough. He said she was trying to play nicey-nice with him, but he got her home in a flash and took off. He was pretty sure the neighbors saw her get out of his car. He thinks like that, Jademan. He's way more of an *I Spy* than you are. He has to be. Eyes on the back of his head at all times. Wrong skin tone in this valley."

Jade nodded and met Squirrel's eyes. "I'm no *I Spy*, Squirrel. I wasn't with Roland. And I'm not his pal. You are. I don't know what it's like to be Roland, and I don't want to be him—standing out like a sore thumb, all eyes on him all the time. I'm just the opposite. Invisible. At least I was, until I started working here."

Jade looked around once more and stepped closer to Squirrel. "And I gotta tell you something else, but you gotta keep it to yourself. Can you do that for me? I gotta tell this to someone."

"Shoot, Jademan. I'm a collector of good info, and I use it wisely. No gossip allowed here."

Jade took a deep breath and looked at the men at the fence, some of whom were looking at him.

"That guy, Ismeltz? The guy they picked up for the kid's murder? He tried to pick me up in his truck two weeks ago. It was the end of my first day at Macson, and I was on my way to Lucy's house, and he kept harassing me. I told him to fuck off, and eventually he did.

"I thought about it all morning, whenever Dimmock wasn't howling at me like a lunatic. Anyway, I started to feel sorry for Ismeltz. I don't know why. I guess deadeye Dimmock would make you feel sorry for most other humans who get beaten down by sadists like him.

"I don't think Ismeltz could have killed that kid or anyone else. When I saw him, he looked scared, that's all. Scared and lonely, not crazy or dangerous. So, yeah, you're right. He's getting pinned for something he didn't do. But he's really getting punished for something he wants to do—pick up other guys. I think that's what Mutt and Jeff and all these guys around us are pinning on him. That he's a fag, and that he should die for it."

The whistle wailed, sucking the air out of the sky, and Jade ducked, covering his ears.

"Gotta stop doing that, Jademan," Squirrel said as the whistle wound down. He stood up to leave. "Makes ya look weak. And you don't want to look weak in a place swarming with jackals.

Jade flinched as Squirrel stepped closer to him.

"You better grow eyes in the back of your head, man. Mutt and Jeff might have left you out of their little chat with Lucy, but they know you're the only one who saw what they were up to at that car wreck. If it was what I think it was, they'll be gunning for you. You're the only one who can put a hole in their Ralph Ismeltz story."

51
The Rumor

Thursday, July 10, 1969

The sound of a rattling bell ejected her from a bizarre dream, and she shot up into a seated position on the bed, expecting to be attacked. She held both fists in front of her and braced herself, her eyes wild with terror.

The phone rang again. She gasped for breath and turned to the clanging on the bedside table. It rang again. She slowly inhaled a bucket of air into her gut and reached for the receiver.

"Yes, who is it?" She let out the air in a controlled stream, the bucket rising up.

A woman's voice was on the other end, a British accent. "Good morning, ma'am, this is your eleven-a.m. wake-up call, as requested."

"What?" Her own voice felt strained as if she'd been shouting. Or singing too much.

"Your wake-up call, ma'am. It's eleven a.m."

"Yes, you said that. What day is it?"

"It's Thursday, ma'am."

"What's the date?"

"It's the tenth day of July, ma'am."

She felt her face for bruises, or maybe blood. The dream still lingered. Someone had chased her, set his hands on her, she'd gotten away. She checked the back of her head, where she was sure she'd been struck by something. She looked at her hand. Nothing. In the dream, she'd looked down in her bed and had seen a bloody erection at first seeming to penetrate her and then seeming to be growing out of her, unclear where the head of the thing was. Then she was running again. No, she was walking very fast. It was Manhattan. Then it was Reston Street. She had the strongest sense yet of her impending death. Imminent. Closing in. Then the phone rang.

"What's the year?" she asked the Brit voice, still struggling for her breath.

"The year, ma'am? The year is nineteen sixty-nine."

"Oh," she sighed. Her breathing leveled. "I know that, yes. I'm sorry, I'm...your accent, it threw me a bit, that's all."

"Not a concern, ma'am. It happens all the time, what with people traveling about and so forth."

"Yes, thank you." She searched the room with a sweep of her head and then gasped another question.

"Wait! Where...what hotel is this?"

She heard the answer, and, without pausing, asked for an extension on check out to two o'clock. She asked for a reservation for lunch in the dining room, but the operator informed her that construction for the new Empire Room had forced the temporary closure of the dining room. She offered to secure a reservation for her at a suitable alternative just steps from the hotel.

"No, no. Thank you. That won't be necessary. Just extend my check out time, please. In fact, I may stay the extra night, I'm not sure yet. Just hold the room for me, please."

She pulled herself out of bed and started to undress when the phone rang again.

"I'm sorry for the bother again, ma'am, but a call for you has just now come through. A Mister Dellworth Cranstone. Would you like to take it?"

She sighed and sat down on the bed. "I suppose so. Yes, go ahead. Put him through."

Before she heard more than "Hello, Issa," she set into him about having her followed. The man she'd seen in the restaurant with the two-day growth wasn't Giallo's man at all. He was Dell's. She assumed the man had followed her to the Waldorf, and then, later, downtown to the Village, since she ran into him coming out of the men's room as she was leaving Arthur's Tavern sometime after midnight. She said the man had been weirdly polite, for a stalker, and he ended up getting her a cab, which she'd appreciated at that hour, but hadn't told him so at the risk of sounding acquiescent, which would have given him the wrong idea, as men like him seldom need encouragement to pursue their salacious objectives.

338

Dell, by this point, was clearly restraining his laughter. He offered an apology couched as an explanation that he was merely looking out for her, a beautiful woman on her own in the city, a city that had changed for the worse, very much so, since 1949. She was on her feet pacing now, the base of the phone in her hand, yanking on the cord and retorting that she knew this goddamn city better than he did, and that she'd been here more often in the last twenty years than he'd been in his entire life, and that she did not need his protection, she could handle herself just fine, and that if he did not stop bothering her, she'd call his wife and tell her that her husband is stalking a woman in a Manhattan hotel.

Dell finally let go, but it was his old self-protective laugh, the one she remembered well, the offensive initial burst that softened to an apologetic murmur within seconds, revealing his brittle emotions hiding behind his royal demeanor. Then he took charge in his passive aggressive way and told her he had new information that he'd like to share with her over lunch. If she'd like to hear it.

She was silent for a long moment. She'd been out late, had had fun for the first time in months, and had fallen for the lure of her old ways and was disappointed in herself, although she was pleased she hadn't gotten out of hand. When she'd walked into Arthur's, old Helen, the street singer, was up on the small stage in the back. At Arthur's, anyone could take the stage, provided the assemblage of drunks and self-appointed critics would allow it. Helen was a regular and a favorite, and, as Alice found a small table against the wall, Helen transitioned into "Backwater Blues" in the midst of her Bessie Smith routine. She accompanied herself on the old black, pre-war Blüthner upright that Ralph the bartender had sworn repeatedly over the years was once concert quality, and would be again, if he could get the goddamn owner to have it tuned. When Helen spotted Alice at the end of the song, she nodded and sang out to her, "my long-lost friend" and then set right into "Nobody Knows You When You're Down and Out," which brought out a smattering of applause from the artfully restrained audience, and a shout from Alice. "Bessie!" she'd cried, and Helen nodded in appreciation, her ivory smile filling up her beaming ebony face, skin so smooth that she looked half her age. They laughed later when they compared their blonde hair, and Helen picked at Alice's curls looking for her roots, and Alice attempted to touch the rim of Helen's wig, only to have her hand slapped away. Later, in the middle of her Billie Holiday set, Helen begged Alice to come up and accompany her for "All of Me," which was a struggle at first for Alice, but Helen covered her, and Alice found the groove on the old Blüthner after she let Helen buy her a whiskey and soda, which was followed by Helen's perfect Billie on "Blue Moon," with Alice on piano and Kenny, another street player she hadn't seen in a few years, playing trumpet, which picked up the sleepy audience. Still later, Alice let Helen talk her into a solo on the keys, for which she'd needed another drink. After turning down Helen's pleas for the "Moonlight song from that German guy" or "Show-pain's" sonata—Alice telling her both songs would put the crowd into an even deeper slumber—she acquiesced to Helen at last with a jazzed-up version of "Ave Maria," after which Alice had to have another drink, while she pondered for a long moment what the Blessed Mother would think of her rearranged Schubert.

"Issa? Are you still there?" Dell asked.

"Yes…yes, I'm here. Sorry," she said, sitting on the bed with the handset to her ear and gently placing the phone box back on the bedside table. "I'll meet you there at one."

"I can pick you up in my cab," he insisted.

"Not necessary, Dell," she said and hung up.

As she showered, she gave herself a mental pat on the back for having stopped the drinking at her third, but she remembered now that the man Dell had hired had put his hand on her waist and then slid it down onto her rear end and held it there as she stooped into the cab. "It's sad, Dell," she said to herself, practicing her droll deb voice while rubbing the suds into her scalp. "You've lost the gentlemanly touch. Hiring a low-class lech. But oh, that certainly mustn't be _your_ fault, but rather that of the changed city, as you call it."

She stood in the lobby for a few minutes fighting off a wave of nausea rising into her chest. She bit her lip, tasting the new lipstick she'd bought in the hotel shop along with a pair of saucer-size sunglasses. She was disappointed in herself for having fallen off the wagon, risking the possibility of losing her momentum and her focus. But she'd had a good time, and she convinced herself that she'd needed a good time, and she congratulated herself that she had not ended up sharing a bed with a stranger.

It was a sunny afternoon, so she walked to the restaurant off Park near Grand Central, and, as expected, Dell was waiting for her at the door, offering his cheery Brahmin smile, helplessly looking down his nose at her, still playing the role of the fine gentleman, which she quickly told him under her breath at the doorway that he was not. "Your sleuth grabbed my ass last night. Your surrogate hand. Very classy, Dell." She frowned, not at him but at herself. She was disappointed that she hadn't used the debutante schtick she'd practiced. It was the damn brain fog of booze. She gave herself an ultimatum: no more; otherwise you fail.

At her request, they took a table in the darkest corner of the restaurant, whose name she didn't recognize, and he proceeded to apologize too much for his man's uncalled for behavior. He'd been hired with explicit instructions to look out for her, Dell said, to protect her if necessary, and he'd been told in no uncertain terms to keep it clean. He pushed out his jaw and announced in a firm tone that he would withhold the man's final payment.

"You're just going to make him worse, Dell, if you don't pay him," she countered, noticing his high horse had already been dismounted. "Give him his thirty silver coins. Otherwise, he'll take it out on someone else, probably a woman." She expanded her smile theatrically, satisfied now that she'd recovered her debutante tone. "And let this be a lesson to you on another front as well. When you hire someone to do your dirty work, Dell," she said as he lit her cigarette, "you get a dirty man. It's sad to see how far you've fallen from grace." She batted her pale green eyes at him as she sucked on her Raleigh and watched him fumble for his own cigarette.

After stuttering through a few more apologies, Dell dove into his report for her. He told her, with veiled excitement in his voice, that an interesting development had emerged. She fought the urge to show too much hope, but her heart was pounding in her chest. He said the development is a rumor he'd heard—that Dennis Hafferty is on the short list to run against the long-standing Pennsylvania Republican, Congressman Henry Walsh, and that Ted Kennedy, anticipating his Presidential run in '72, wants that seat back. It's a blue-collar valley, long owned by the Democrats, but with a Republican in the seat for two decades. It's an embarrassment. That was the way Ted had put it, according to the source.

"The rumor," said Dell as he leaned closer to her in a low voice, "presents the possibility that if Hafferty is the chosen candidate, some elements of your story could be part of that larger national political story which, as I'd explained to you, we would need." He said he wouldn't know for sure, however, until he confirmed the rumor.

She leaned in, just inches from his face, and she saw resilient hope rise yet again in Dell's eyes. She told him Walsh had been funded and managed by Hafferty for as long as he'd held the seat in Washington, according to her local sources, which was actually Wally, but she couldn't tell him that. She said it would be fitting that Hafferty would double cross his man on The Hill for his own aggrandizement. Then she leaned closer still.

"Could this take a direction that exposes Hafferty without tying me to the story as the source?"

Dell was watching her mouth, as if in a sudden trance. It was so close to his own. Then he lifted his eyes to meet hers. Hope for the hopeless one more time. Dell, the puppy. She smiled, wondering if he could smell the sourness from last night lingering on the back of her tongue.

"That remains to be seen," Dell said, almost in a whisper. "We'll have to confirm, as I said, and then take it one step at a time."

She pulled back and took a drag on her cigarette, and, as she exhaled over his head, she saw the waiter moving in with their menus. Dell was still hunched over the table, oblivious of the waiter, hoping she would come in close again. The waiter slid the menus under Dell's chin, and he sat back, smiling awkwardly. The waiter apologized and then took their orders.

She was relieved that Dell had asked for an iced tea instead of whiskey. When the drinks arrived, she took a sip of her tea and leaned forward again, her voice soft but urgent. "Did you read my notes?"

"Yes," Dell replied. He remained sitting tall, surprising her with his sudden restraint. "I heard the rumor right after I returned from lunch with you, and then I dove into your report. It's compelling, no doubt. But, as I've said, we need to see if the rumor holds up."

She asked him if he found a record of Jake Levin as a New York newspaper reporter. He said he hadn't followed up further on that yet, but he did have questions about a few other people in her report.

"Your half-sister, the nun," he said. "Is she still alive?"

"Deirdre?" Alice said. "Yes. At least as of late last fall. I stop in to see her from time to time on my occasional New York trips, but I haven't heard anything to indicate she's not well. They have my address as her next of kin, so I would know. She's in her early fifties, and she gets three squares and presumably regular exercise, and, of course, endless prayers. She always seems healthy, at least physically. She doesn't like to talk about the past much. I think she believes that by having passed on Tormud's letters, she has absolved herself of having to further share family history. So, it might take some encouragement. Which, of course, I could provide. She's certainly credible. I think she'd have a breakdown if she attempted a lie."

Dell chuckled and dove into his lunch, nodding to her, his smile persisting as he chewed. Alice joined him, hungry from her evening without nutrients. She thought about Deirdre in the cloister—a glorified asylum that looked like a castle, surrounded by a Newark neighborhood that had deteriorated in the last decade. The castle was well-maintained, presumably by donations from wealthy Catholic men whose unwanted daughters were hidden there, withering away for sins committed against them, not by them. She thought of her own father and suddenly lost her appetite, setting down her fork and pulling a Raleigh from Dell's pack.

He looked up from his lunch and stopped his chewing when he saw the look on her face. He swallowed, dabbed his lips with a napkin, and reached for the lighter. "What about your father's lawyer? MacInnes. You write that he took a hefty pay off from Hafferty to adjust your father's will while your father was incapacitated. An adjustment that left your share, and that of your surviving siblings, in trust with Hafferty. And you say MacInnes wrote the deals for Hafferty's sale of the munitions plants, including the terms for Hafferty's lifetime revenue shares in those facilities as well as the sale of the Macson plant to Giallo. You say MacInnes included a lifetime cut of those deals for himself, as well. Is he still alive?"

She doused her cigarette and closed her eyes. She didn't want him to see evidence of her nausea. "Yes," she said with a perfunctory nod. She swallowed the lump in her throat and looked up at him. "At least I hope he is. Although death can't come soon enough for him. I believe he was a partner in a firm in Boston for a number of years, and then he retired to Virginia. One of those remote estates where men hide from their crimes inside their vaults of money."

Dell nodded. "Hmmm. Speaking of estates, I gather from my researcher that Hafferty lives in your father's former estate mansion, does he not? You don't mention that in your notes."

She gave Dell a blank stare and then reached for the cigarette pack again. He was quick to the flame for her. She exhaled a smoke stream over his head and forced a smile.

"Pretty good researcher you have there, Dell. Few people know who owned the place before Dennis. He erased my family from history. It wasn't all that difficult to do, actually. My father was extremely private, especially there. He wanted no one to know who lived there, kept armed guards around the place for years. And Dennis managed to make that anonymity permanent. I'm assuming my father was buried in the family plot at the estate, but Dennis had all the markers and stones removed and paved it over with a heliport."

"Actually, I was just assuming that was your family estate," Dell said. "My researcher stumbled on an old article about your father, linking him to that remote region by way of his influence in having the railroad build a small depot on the New York line just a few miles from the estate. In a little town called Ulster. He learned Hafferty now lives on an estate near Ulster and, well, we, meaning I, just put two and two together…"

She nodded and smirked at him. "I've not been there in twenty years, but I understand that there is no evidence of my father or my family. Dennis made sure of it. I'm told he let the small farm there go fallow, fired everyone, sold the horses, and he destroyed most of the facilities he hated, including the stable and steeplechase course, the indoor and outdoor tennis courts, the homes where the help had lived, the dance hall my father had built for them.

"It was clear to me that he got rid of all the people and places that had meant the most to my father. And to me.

"Of course, he kept the house and the support facilities—the garages and storage buildings, the golf range, and he's added a few amenities. And the idiot rebuilt our natatorium, changing it from the training facility it once was into some kind of entertainment space. Pathetic. He'd drown if he tried to swim so much as a single length." She took a drag and exhaled over Dell's head. "Perhaps I'll send him a swimsuit. If I can find a large enough parachute from which it can be hewn." She smiled at Dell, but the corners of her mouth were turned down.

"He has a staff that maintains the estate, some living there, others in little Ulster," she continued. "He lives there on weekends, evidently. Otherwise, he has a penthouse suite in the Sheeley Hotel in Ebonton, near his office, and I'm told he has an apartment off Connecticut Avenue in D.C., just a few stumbles down Mass Ave to Capitol Hill." She waved her hand absently, her cigarette perched there. "Oh, and he apparently has a place in Florida—Naples, I think it is." She took another drag on her cigarette and huffed a sarcastic laugh. "Posh life, huh? For an insignificant County Commissioner in a dead-end old coal valley?"

Dell nodded, pushed away his plate, and lit up a Raleigh. "On a salary of what? Thirty thousand?"

She laughed one note and doused her cigarette. "I know it looks like he's grabbing cash from every till in the valley, and I believe everyone else there thinks the same thing. But he doesn't need to get dirty at that level. In fact, he gives away much of his locally sourced money. He makes a spectacle of it—his generosity and selfless devotion to his people—by giving quietly but making sure everyone knows about it. He gives away his annual salary every year at Christmas in a stunt he claims no one knows about, but it gets covered in the local newspapers, on TV, and on radio stations. The newspapers call him Santa Hafferty for a couple weeks in December. It's obnoxious."

She reached for another cigarette but dropped the pack, held out her shaking fingers, and sat back, smirking at Dell's startled look. "The Catholics worship him, of course, for smothering them in donations—since they're winning the population race there—and I understand he even throws a few bones to the Jews and the various Protestant churches. And Dickson College gets a ton of backdoor cash from him, as do judges, lawyers, prominent business owners, hospital chiefs, you name it. But he doesn't need the nickel-and-dime kickbacks from local government contracts. He's sitting on hundreds of millions he stole from my family through my father's altered will and millions more that comes in every year from his revenue shares at the five munitions factories—the deal MacInnes and he struck back in the early fifties with Giallo for Macson Munitions and the owners of the other four facilities. Throughout that decade, the Cold War build-up kept the munitions plants—and Dennis—flush with cash, and then Vietnam blew up, and he's been wallowing in bloody bounty like a gluttonous pig in a mud bath.

"He gets Walsh and four other congressmen to push the sweetest federal munitions contracts to the five facilities, and he swims in his guaranteed chunk of their sales revenue. Not their profits, but their revenue. Before any expenses. So, technically, he's not stealing from the government, although he certainly greases Walsh and the other four guys on The Hill. But who *doesn't* do that?"

Dell lit another cigarette without offering her one. "He clearly has extraordinary wealth," he said, exhaling over her head. "Yet he spends, according to my research man, most of his time and energy in that old coal valley—a place where wealth is largely absent. Where poverty and marginal income is predominant."

"Unlike my father," Alice said flatly, "Dennis does not like to cavort with his financial peers. He never goes to New York City or The Caribbean or Europe or Asia. Obviously, he visits D.C. regularly for a specific purpose, and he spends a week in Naples twice a year. But, essentially, he's a cultural buffoon. He never reads, has no interest in art, music, or theater, and manifests the narrowest of world views—if it's not happening to him, it's simply not happening. He's uncomfortable in places where he's not familiar with every business and leisure spot and in complete control of the entire population. And he's found the perfect spot for that limited proclivity."

"Did you write all that in your report?" Dell asked, tapping his cigarette on the ashtray. "I don't recall seeing much more than a few references to this sort of thing."

"Sort of thing, Dell? I'd say it's more of a sordid thing. And if I wrote down everything, I'd still be writing. Your reporters must do at least *some* legwork, don't you think?"

Dell sat back and gave her a quizzical look. She fumbled with the pack of Raleighs, dropping them on the table and reaching for her tea.

"You've named several possible sources," Dell said, "including your half-sister and MacInnes, and even Giallo, although I'm not sure how that would work. So, I assume you have others who can confirm what you've written and what you've just told me."

She smiled and lifted her chin. "Again, that's what reporters do, isn't it, Dell?" She finally relented and pulled out one of Dell's Raleighs and helped herself to his lighter. She handed the pack to him and held out her flame. "When you've run a regime like Hafferty has for twenty years, in a place where people have few options for getting work or accumulating power, you can't avoid making enemies eventually. They call him Santa, but Dennis has stepped on the toes of many brittle egos in his path toward local sainthood. Giallo will talk if your team uses the right leverage on him, Dell. You know how it's done better than I do. You guys are basically prosecutors without the law license. You deal in virtual plea bargains all the time. Giallo is covered in so much dirt, you'd have to be blind and deaf not to find something with which to leverage him. And, if he sees Hafferty getting cornered, he'll turn on him in a flash. Those two aren't partners in a business marriage, Dell. They're criminals in a wary alliance.

"And, if the rumor you told me turns out to be true—Kennedy wanting Hafferty to run for Walsh's seat—you have another crooked partner to play with. Walsh will not lie down after Hafferty double crosses him. And then there are the other four congressmen—Walsh's counterparts in the other states where the munitions plants lie. If the heat's on Walsh, he'll start talking, and then you press his congressional colleagues. It becomes part of your national story, Dell."

Dell nodded but didn't allow the smile she'd expected from him. She leaned forward on the table and held out her open palms to him.

"On the local front, Dell, there are more than just a few who would be champing at the bit to dime out Hafferty on any of the matters I've mentioned, as well as others I haven't heard about. There's a guy named Red Larkin, for instance. Once a devotee of Hafferty for giving him a county job that doesn't tax Larkin's small brain, he's been publicly humiliated by Dennis and is now a sworn enemy of the Commissioner, and very vocal about it. Then, there's Robert Freeman, an insurance salesman who's getting richer by the hour and has positioned himself as the Republican alternative to Hafferty for the Commissioner's seat. He's no threat to Dennis, but if bad news starts coming out about Hafferty on the national level, Freeman will jump at the chance to tell you everything he's dug up about the sitting Commissioner."

Dell glanced at his watch and doused his cigarette. "You must be fairly active in that valley, Alice. You seem to know a lot about the players."

Alice sputtered a half-laugh. "I'm a ghost in that valley, Dell. I spend as little time there as possible. I have contacts elsewhere, good ones, even in *your* business, Dell, but not in the Diamond Valley—which by the way used to be known as the *Black* Diamond Valley until Hafferty dropped the Black—such a surprise. Anyway, in that hovel of a place, you could count my contacts on one hand and still have fingers left. I have two, maybe three reliable sources, and I'm not dragging any of them into this. But, as I said, you boys are the pros; you can easily confirm or refute anything I've told you."

Dell smiled, genuinely this time. "I must leave in a few moments, Issa. But there's one thing I'm curious about that you only vaguely hint at in your report. Hafferty's love life. He's not married, correct? Never has been?"

"That's right," she said, nodding, her smile turning into a frown. "He's always had a woman by his side when it was politically or socially necessary, but no one permanent or even superficially so. Rumors have it that he cavorts with prostitutes, but I don't believe that. I think he's simply in love with himself. Either that or he's afraid of something else in his blood."

"Such as?" Dell asked and waved at the waiter to clear the table. Alice stubbed out her cigarette and glanced around the restaurant, expecting to see Dell's unshaven sleuth nearby, but he was not in sight. She spied someone who might be a Giallo man, but she shook it off. She told herself to stop looking for spies; if Giallo was having her followed, she could do nothing about it.

"You were going to say something," Dell said, leaning over the cleared table and offering her another cigarette.

"No thanks. I've smoked a hundred of those things in the last two days." She coughed lightly and gave him a sheepish smile, wondering how he'd respond to the answer she was about to give him, hoping it wouldn't undermine her story.

"His real father, Michael Hafferty," she said, looking down at the tremor in her hands, "was County Commissioner in the twenties, for nearly the entire decade. My father, having his own motives both political and personal, lured Michael away from his seat of power with a job as head of the growing munitions company. Lots more money for Michael, no doubt. A few years later, Michael was found hanging by the neck in a hotel room in New York. A note was left. It said he was homosexual. My father took Michael's widow, Mhairi, for his third wife. Dennis tagged along."

Dell's response gave Alice pause. He said nothing, and stared at her with raised eyebrows and a turned down mouth. She was afraid she'd blown it.

But Dell was gentle, his voice soft and no longer probing. "That information did not make it to your notes, Issa," he said, almost whispering.

She nodded and stared at him, her eyes in a haze; then she snapped out of it. She lifted her chin, feigning control. "You won't get anyone to talk about that, Dell," she said. "Not even Deirdre. Everything I wrote down for you, and most of what I've told you, can be corroborated through named sources. I did not write down what I just told you, because only two people can corroborate it. And they will lie to you. Their partnership depends on it."

52
Ben Hur

Jade arrived at work early again and was surprised, but relieved, to see Roland Wilson on The Line instead of Dimmock. Wilson was standing on the floor against the base of the platform with his arms folded, a blank look on his face as he watched Jade approach.

"Man, am I glad to see you," Jade said, as he glanced to his right to see Dimmock standing on The Line thirty feet away watching them. "Another day with that sadist would have been my last, man."

"There you go with that 'man' thing, again," Wilson said, his face still blank. "Don't worry about Dimmock. He's the least of your concerns. Squirrel's meeting me at the flagpole at lunch break, and for once, I'm inviting you to be there instead of you inviting yourself."

"Okay," Jade said. He thought he detected the sliver of a smirk on Wilson's stony face. It was the first time they'd seen each other since their trip to the rez, and Jade sensed that Wilson the cavalier Caddy driver was lurking somewhere behind his workplace face. Either that, or what Squirrel had told him about Wilson and Lucy wasn't true. It might not have been a cavalier look on Wilson's face; it might have been a guilty one.

"Let's get to work," Wilson said as he turned and hoisted himself up on The Line, effortless as ever. The 7:30 whistle pierced the air as Jade climbed up to the platform. He didn't cover his ears this time.

At the first break, they went their separate ways to rest against the factory wall, out of the searing sun. But, at lunch, they walked silently together to the flagpole and started at their lunches. The air was thinner than usual, but the heat was rising. The summer sun flamed above them, stalled at its apex. The other workers had already clustered in small groups in their usual spots, and Jade felt their six hundred eyes on him and Roland. More like six thousand.

"They're disappointed, no doubt, that I am not in jail for the murder of that boy," Wilson said, without looking up from his sandwich. His father's intonement was more evident than usual. "I know they were hoping to don their white hoods for my lynching, but they will have to wait for another day. The guy they arrested was the next best thing to a Black man, so they're satisfied. For now. Soon enough, they'll try to pin something else on me. The hatred here is thicker than the smog we breathe."

Jade looked toward Squirrel's building but didn't see him yet. "Listen, Roland," he said, "I gotta tell you something before Squirrel gets here. It's not about the rez on Saturday, it's about the car wreck—the one where that Black girl got killed."

"Save it," Wilson said. "I know all about it. You'd be dead if it weren't for a fire hydrant, and you saw them drag her body out of the car, and you got grilled by the cops, and now they think you saw something else happen at the wreck, but you cannot remember, conveniently, and they want an answer. Squirrel told me all about it."

Jade glanced toward Squirrel's building again. Still no sign of him.

"Yeah, but I have to tell you that I do remember what I saw," Jade said. "I've been holding back for a reason. I haven't told anybody yet, but I think Squirrel has figured it out, and I'm pretty sure Hafferty has, too, but he's just letting me hang out to dry until I decide to confirm it with him. He's the one who wants to hear me say it more than anyone else, but I'm holding out because it gives me something I can exchange with him. For something I want. Meanwhile, those two narcs, Joey Belden and Billy Jensen, are gunning for me, because they want me to keep my mouth shut. I'm pretty sure their visit with Lucy on Sunday was as much about me as it was about you. They're sending me a message. Ren Belden told me they'd do something to Lucy and my mother if I told anyone what I saw."

"Uh huh," Wilson said, still not looking at Jade. "Because if you talk, you'll blow the narcs' phony story about the Ismeltz guy killing the kid. So why tell me? What makes you think I won't tell anyone else. Like Hafferty."

"You won't have to," Jade said. "I'll tell him. Just hear me out. I stayed away from here for most of this week, just like you did, and I figured you were lying low because you knew word would get out that you were at the rez on Saturday, and the boys here would think you had something to do with the Raines kid's death." He looked over at Wilson who continued to stare at his own feet while he finished his sandwich.

"You're a prick to me, Wilson—or you were until Saturday, when you became another person in the Caddy and at the rez—and now you're back to being your hardass self here at work. And I'm still not sure what happened between you and Lucy—not that I should care, because she's not my girlfriend anymore. But prick or no prick, Lucy or no Lucy, I sure as hell don't want you to get set up for a murder you didn't commit. Same with Ismeltz. He didn't kill the kid, I'm certain of it. And, if I tell you what I saw, and something happens to me, you'll have the information, in case the Ismeltz arrest gets thrown out and they come after you for the murder."

Wilson pushed his lunch tin aside and stood up and stretched. "So now you suddenly know what you saw? And, if you tell me, what do I do with it after the narcs rub you out? Tell the cops my deceased co-worker, Flynn, told me he saw the narcs pull that dead kid's body from the trunk of the Black girl's car and dump it into *their* trunk? The cops would laugh at me, and then give me a beating, and then they'd get the noose ready and tell the mob here where the lynching would take place."

Jade looked up at Wilson, standing with his back to the sun, a blinding glow around the silhouette of his head and face, an eclipse. "That's exactly what I saw, Roland," Jade said. "Except the Mustang wasn't hers, it was Joey Belden's. Which means the body in Joey's Mustang trunk was moved by him and Jensen to their undercover cop car, and then to the rez, where they dumped it. But I wouldn't tell that to the cops, because a dozen of them were there at the wrecked Mustang helping to cover for Belden and Jensen while they moved the body. *And* while they moved the grocery bags filled with heroin and who knows what else. That girl died because of Joey Belden and his drugs. And Joey wouldn't think twice about making sure you died, too, if the Ismeltz charges don't stick."

Wilson's face was still in the shadow of his eclipse. "So again, you're telling me...why? So I can tell it to the cops when they haul me in for murder after Joey and Billy murder *you?*" He shrugged his big shoulders and shook his head at Jade.

"No, of course not. I want you to get me in front of Hafferty. All three of us. You, me, Hafferty. I want him to hear it from me. With you as a witness. He's your insurance policy against being the alternate fall guy."

"Hey, it's the *I Spy* duo together again!" It was Squirrel, approaching the flagpole in a jaunty walk, his buck teeth preceding him. He was in one of his hijinks moods.

"What's the buzz, ladies?" he bayed as he plunked down his lunch pail on the flagpole base and spread his arms wide. Jade knew Squirrel was making a scene for the audience of three hundred.

Squirrel's face fell as he suddenly switched gears and sat down, fumbling with his lunch pail and speaking in a deliberate monotone. "Word has it there's a big summer party tomorrow at the honorable Commissioner's manse in the woods. Big secret everybody knows about. Except not everybody's invited. Just the guys Hafferty owns. You guys get your invitations yet?" He looked up at Wilson, then at Jade. He switched to his manic look again and stood up.

"Dear Mr. Cosby and Mr. Culp," he announced, pacing in front of them, holding an imaginary invitation. "Please join me, as I honor myself in yet another show of my generosity and your obedience to my command. Yours in Christ and Bombs, Your Loving Commissioner." He put his long nose in the air and opened his buck-toothed smile and let out a howl.

"Sit down, Squirrel," Wilson said, his voice deep and threatening. "If that's all you have to tell us, this meeting is over."

"Okay, okay," Squirrel said, looking plaintively toward Wilson. "Stay here for a moment, Ro. I got something else for you."

"Here comes Hafferty," Jade said, straightening up in his seat at the flagpole and rumpling his lunch bag into a ball. Squirrel spun on the concrete seat and froze. Wilson folded his arms and turned his head toward the approaching car.

The black Fleetwood floated slowly across the concrete like a cabin cruiser about to be moored, the sunlight gleaming off its chrome ornaments. Jade glanced around at the men in the yard. All eyes were on the SS Commissioner ship.

When the Fleetwood came to a stop at the flagpole, Jade felt his stomach tighten. The sun's heat suddenly intensified, the air thickening. A musty low cloud passed between them and the massive car.

The Commissioner's thick bejeweled paw jutted out of the back window, and he beckoned Wilson with a flick of his fingers.

Wilson leaned into the window, Hafferty's voice muffled behind him. Jade could see a familiar shaped head behind the wheel, but he couldn't make out the face in the shadowy interior.

The hair was slicked back and silver. Jade's stomach tightened another notch, and he felt the blood draining from his head.

Wilson stepped away from the car and stood in front of Jade. He was still in sharp shadow. "You look like you just saw a ghost, Flynn. You gonna make it?"

Jade tried to focus on Wilson's face. "I'm fine," he said, gritting his teeth.

"Good. Because it looks like you're gonna get that meeting sooner than you'd hoped. Be careful what you wish for. He wants you to come with us. Get in the back on the other side."

"Us?" Squirrel said, standing up. "Does that mean what I think it does?"

"Not this time, Squirrel," Wilson said. He gave a slight shrug of his shoulders for his best friend and climbed into the shotgun seat and closed the door.

In the back seat, Jade looked across the vast leather bench at Hafferty and then at the silver haired head in front of him. He swallowed a dry knot.

"Something wrong, Jade?" Hafferty said, grinning. "No one's gonna bite you in here."

Jade turned to Hafferty. He couldn't find his voice.

"Looks like my request to have you two keep your distance from each other has fallen on deaf ears, gentlemen," Hafferty said, his voice thick with sarcasm. "That's okay. Things have changed. I understand. After all, two guys backed into a corner is a little more comforting than one. I assume you've got each other's backs now, is that right?"

Wilson turned around to answer, but he was cut off by Hafferty raising a finger at him. "Not now, Roland. Ronnie," he said to the driver, "take us to the five-star doorway straight ahead. We'll get out there. Leave the car and the air conditioning running, but move it twenty feet down along the wall. It's hot enough in Jensen's office without car exhaust pouring in the windows, choking us to death in there."

As the car pulled away, Jade looked out at Squirrel standing at the flagpole, watching them depart. Jade was sure a message was being sent to Squirrel, and he felt he and Wilson had abandoned him.

"Ronnie is Stanley's brother, Mr. Flynn," Hafferty said, with a cordial lilt as if they were at an afternoon baseball game. "I bet you realized that. They look a lot alike, don't they? You probably want to ask Ronnie how Stanley's feeling. Don't you, son?"

Jade glanced at the back of Ronnie's head and turned to Hafferty, swallowing another knot. "Yeah," he said flatly. "I do."

"Ronnie, did you hear that?" Hafferty said with a toothy smile toward Jade. "The kid wants to know how your big brother's doing. Probably wonders if we caught the guy yet—the guy who hit him in the side of the head, from behind, with…I don't know what. A woman's steam iron? A frying pan? Some kind of mom's housewifey tool, don't you think, Ronnie?"

Ronnie said nothing. His silver head just nodded twice.

Inside the General Manager's office suite, Hafferty dismissed Dorothy with a wave of his hand and asked her where Jensen was.

"He's at lunch," she said as she stood and, with quick movements, gathered her purse and started toward the back door. She moved with her head down, her feet shuffling with urgency.

"All by himself?" Hafferty asked her. "Or is it a lunch meeting? Who's he meeting with, Dorothy? Somebody I know?"

Dorothy fumbled with the strap of her purse and then looked up at Hafferty, her eyes wide, her voice shaking. "He's with Ren…uh…Mister Belden, Commissioner. The shop steward."

"Ah," Hafferty said, turning to Wilson and Jade. "Jensen and Belden. Belden and Jensen. What a combo. I wonder what they're meeting about. Probably union negotiations, don't you think, boys?" He smirked and winked at them and raised his eyebrows above his thick lenses.

Jade and Wilson watched Dorothy shamble through the back doorway.

"Lock it behind you, Dorothy," Hafferty called out. "That way, I'll hear him when he comes back."

In Jensen's office, Hafferty directed Jade and Roland to the side chairs as he hung up his suit jacket in the closet, loosened his tie, and sauntered toward Jensen's seat. The corner fan was rattling away but providing little relief from the stultifying air.

"Jesus Christ," Hafferty said, as he wrenched open his top shirt button and then lit up a Benson & Hedges. "No wonder Jensen's so miserable. This place is hotter than a Hong Kong sweatshop." He blew a stream of smoke over the heads of Jade and Roland.

He sat back in Jensen's chair, the spring squeaking under his girth. Jade remembered that first meeting, when Hafferty almost fell over backwards in that chair when Jade asked him if he was Jewish. Now, Hafferty was in full control. His face was unreadable, his swollen eyeballs flat behind the thick lenses—opaque windows to his capricious moods.

"You fellas might be wondering why we're here—just the three of us," Hafferty said, his voice flat, unenhanced by his vocal undulations—adjustments that could set a somber tone or put a room on edge or lift it up lighter than air. Such was the mastery of his gift. Despite all that had happened, Jade was still in awe of this man of performance.

"I rolled through the front gates of this plant just after noon on this beautiful, if a bit hot, early summer day," he said, his voice rising, "because I wanted to send a message to the men here, and I knew all of them would be gathered outside, like a blood-thirsty mob at the Roman Colosseum." He sprang from the chair and stepped around the desk, facing them with his arms out. "And lo and behold, I found you two gladiators right there in the center of the arena, waiting for the lions to come at you." His fluorescent smile flashed as he held up his hands and shrugged. "So…I guess that makes me Ben Hur, riding up in my shiny black chariot, whisking away the doomed gladiators just in time."

He sucked on his cigarette and let out a plume toward the ceiling. "I like that image, don't you, fellas?" He nodded, the smile still frozen on his face—his giant eyes making an exaggerated entreaty to join in his drama. Jade stiffened in his chair. He thought Hafferty would be better suited as Caesar standing in his guarded balcony above the Colosseum mob, holding out his fist, the gladiators' fate a mere thumb flick away.

"I came here today with a single intention," Hafferty said, now pacing in front of the boys, his voice elevating, enunciating with intent. He held his cigarette aloft, as if it were a teacher's pointer. "I came here because I learned that you two were back on the job after your…illnesses…your simul*taneo*us illnesses. Such a curious coincidence." He sucked on his cigarette and exhaled a cloud at the ceiling as he paced.

"And I thought it was appropriate to come at the lunch hour, when all would be gathered in the courtyard, just as they are now. My purpose was to send a message to the Macson men—these wonderful, dedicated American patriots who have been greatly stressed by the threat to their jobs as reported by the press. A message for these same men who have been just as greatly distracted by the news of the Raines boy's death—as if it had something to do with the goddamn work they're paid to do here.

As if it were up to them, and not to the police, or the District Attorney, to conjure up the most likely perpetrator of this heinous crime. But, just like old women in some medieval village, they seem all excited by the witchcraft of their speculation, and, prior to today's news story, the leading flap-jaws among them had arrived at a conclusion whipped up from thin air that the perpetrator of this horrific crime is none other than the outlier in their midst. The one who doesn't look like them, the young man they so recently loved for his prowess on the playing fields, but who now, somehow, as if by hypnosis or magic, has turned murderous."

He stopped in front of Roland and held his hands by his hips, palms out. "Why? Because a rumor got around to the usual handful of gossips that Mr. Wilson was at the Scrub Oak Reservoir on the same day that the Raines boy was dragged dead from the water. A situation that immediately set fire to the limited imaginations of our otherwise excellent workforce, and all of a sudden, Roland Wilson was their prime suspect in the murder of the 15-year-old boy. Until they read otherwise in this morning's paper." He took a drag on his cigarette and resumed pacing.

"Seems like a good reason for Roland to call in sick from Monday until today, wouldn't you say, Mr. Flynn?" Hafferty glared at him, but Jade said nothing. "So, I decided that, since the matter of the boy's death has been more or less resolved with the apprehension of a prime suspect, I would make an entrance and a gesture at high noon today that would reassure the handful of medieval gossip mongers—and now the entire Colosseum mob of blood-hungry hyenas that follow them—that Roland Wilson was still in my good graces and that, blood-hungry or not, the biddies of Macson Munitions should shut their fucking flap traps about Roland Wilson once and for all."

He stopped in front of both boys and spread his hands by his side again, his palms red with perspiration and his stiff white shirt growing sweat stains under his arms. "And why, you might ask, would I make such a gesture on behalf of Roland Wilson?" He pivoted his big body away for a moment and then pitched it closer to them, leaning his red face into theirs. "Because I am *loyal* to him!" he declared, his voice rising. "As he is to me! And because I've watched over Roland Wilson since he was six years old! I've looked out for him and encouraged him, and I gave him every opportunity to succeed, and I took him under my wing when he most needed help." He stood up straight and puffed up his chest, holding his hand there without touching his shirt. "And I knew in my heart...in my *heart*...that Roland Wilson, the son of my dear friend, Doctor James Wilson, would *never ever* have anything to do with the death of that boy, or the death of anyone. And that everyone in this goddamn place...*Every*one...needed to know that. And needs to know that going forward. *Everyone!*"

He began to pace again. "Yes, I'd heard the rumor about Roland at the reservoir with the girl—" He turned to Jade and pointed at him. "Your girl, Jade, that little beauty from the row houses on Liberty Street—the Melburn kid. What's her first name? I *know* who she is. I know her old man, Cal Melburn—that pathetic sot, who brags he's descended from the Puritans on the Mayflower. Sweet Jesus, the man hasn't a single drop of Puritan work ethic, for Chrissake. He hasn't held a job for more than a few weeks at a time in his entire life, but he thinks, because he's descended from the fucking Mayflower, he's entitled to royal benefits from the county. A job under my watch. A guy like that is a miserable excuse for a human being. How he produced a beauty like your girl...what's her first name—"

"Lucy," Jade said.

"Lucy! That's right. Lucy Melburn. She should have taken her mother's last name, whatever that is. Spanish name, I think. That woman is a saint. Works in a candy factory making slave wages. What is she, Jade? Mexican?"

"She's from the Philippines," Jade said.

"That's right!" Hafferty snapped, his thick finger in the air. "Old Cal was banging native girls there, while his army mates were dying in Korea. Not sure how he pulled that off, but he brought home one of those island girls, and he treats her like his slave." He nodded to Jade. "I remember her when old Calvin, the drunk from the goddamn Mayflower, got dragged in for beating up his Mexican wife. Or whatever she is. The girl, Lucy, came to the police station with her mother. I happened to be there, and it was a shame. Turned my stomach. The wife wouldn't say a damn thing against him. The kid was angry as hell at the old man. I used to see the girl around town after that. In the winter, she's almost White—I guess that's the old man's English blood—and then, in summer, she's brown as a chestnut. That's the mother coming through. Gorgeous girl! Stands out in any crowd." He pointed his thick finger at Jade. "But she is a sad girl, I can see it. And God knows, she has reason to be sad, very sad. She's at Ebonton High now, isn't she, Jade? She's a real looker, but she's an outcast, like you two were at that school. Half-breed, I heard they call her. Kids are tough at that school."

He suddenly broke into a grin and held his arms out, looking from Jade to Wilson and back again. "I betcha thought you were all alone—just the three of you up on that mountain last Saturday. Sorry to disappoint, fellas, but I happened to know that our lovely Lucy did a helluva hoochie-coochie dance at the reservoir waterfront for you, Roland. And that you, Jade, were right there, too. What the hell, guys, did you do a threesome with her?"

Jade and Roland glanced at each other, and Roland pushed out his chin to Hafferty to speak.

Hafferty held up his hands and lowered his head. "No, no, no, no. Don't answer that. I don't want to know. What I *do* want to know, however, is why you—Roland—took my Cadillac to get it washed, as I requested, while I met with your father, but instead, you picked up this guy here and Lucy Melburn and took them up the mountain, ran my Fleetwood through the woods like you were in a movie car chase, the bottom all muddy and the sides all scratched, and then you brought it back and left the keys on the visor and you *did not even call me!*" He leaned toward Roland's face. His cheeks were flushed and his googly eyes alive with fire. "At all! I never heard from you. Until now. A week later! And I had to come *here* to find you! Your father was scared out of his mind, thinking you were going to get pinned for that murder, and I had every guy I could muster—a goddamn posse looking for you. Where the hell were you? Did you leave town? One of my guys said he thought he saw you get on the train for New York. Is that where you were?"

Wilson wore his stone face. He was staring at Hafferty. Jade could see him measuring his thoughts, his chin out, his eyes alight. But his voice came out calm, reserved, a quiet version of his father's. "I stayed with a friend," he said. "Like you just said, I was scared. Scared I was going to take the fall, but even more scared by what I had seen. When I dove into the water, the dead boy's face was floating up at mine, and I almost swallowed the entire reservoir. Jade and Lucy dragged me out. Saved my life. But I didn't tell them what I saw. I just hustled them out of there. My mind was in two places—I couldn't stop thinking of that face, rising up fast at me and hitting me right in my forehead, and then, after I got out, I knew immediately that I could not tell Jade or Lucy or anyone." He turned toward Jade, his eyes wide, and then back to Hafferty. "Just imagine it, if you possibly can," he said through gritted teeth. "A Black man finds the body of a White boy in the reservoir. Who do you think would be the primary suspect? When you found out I was up there swimming on Saturday, you had the same thought. And so did everyone here at Macson."

Hafferty took off his glasses and used a handkerchief to wipe his forehead and eyes. He looked smaller, less puffed up; without his thick eyeglasses, his eyes were shrunken dots on his jowled face. He sighed and put his glasses on and walked to the desk and sat down. "Jesus Christ. Of course you'd think that. No matter who you reported it to, you'd be the suspect. Jesus Christ, son." He closed his eyes, shaking his head.

The fan filled up the silence in the room, rattling and humming uselessly in the corner, its harsh hot breeze wafting over them. Jade decided to fill the void.

"Commissioner, I have something to tell you," he said, glancing at Wilson and then turning towards Jensen's desk. Hafferty sat slumped over the ashtray, his cigarette in his hand, his mind somewhere else.

"I saw what you thought I might have seen at that car wreck," Jade said, his voice firm, committed. "I didn't have trouble remembering it, I just held it back, so I could get you to tell me what happened to my mother, why Stanley came to our house and attacked her. I thought you might have ordered him to do it. And I still don't know whether you did, but I'm giving up my hand, as you would say, before I get what I want. You might say I'm a fool, but I have my reasons."

Jade stood up and walked to the desk. Hafferty straightened up, wiped off his glasses again and put them on. His googly eyes looked focused for the first time in the meeting.

"I definitely saw Joey Belden and Billy Jensen, with the help of two uniformed cops, pull all those brown bags out of the Mustang trunk and put them into the black Galaxy trunk. I was no more than fifteen feet away in that squad car. Then I saw them pull a body from the Mustang trunk. It wasn't that big. I thought it might be another girl, like the one at the wheel, but White. White arms and hands. Then I saw his face. It was the Raines kid, the same face I saw in the newspaper, only whiter than white…like his blood was drained. They almost dropped him, and Belden yelled at Jensen to help the cops. I could see it all, because the two cops who helped them were part of the wall of cops around them, and, when they moved forward to help, the gap they left didn't close. I saw it all. At the Galaxy trunk, they almost dropped the body again. When it hit the trunk, I saw the Galaxy bounce a little, and then Belden slammed it shut."

Jade looked at Hafferty for a response, but the man just stared straight at him.

"I saw Belden's face and Jensen's, too. I could tell you exactly what they were wearing. I've seen them in my dreams ever since.

"And there's something else. I had a…an encounter with Ralph Ismeltz. He tried to pick me up in his green truck on my way through the North Heights toward Lucy's house after work on my first day at Macson. He failed to get me to come near him, but I can tell you, he was more scared than aggressive. That guy was terrified about what he was trying to do. If I ran at him, he'd probably have a heart attack. He's no killer, Mr. Hafferty. He got set up.

"It's pretty clear to me who killed that kid. It was the same guy who killed the Black girl driving his car. He killed both of them with his drugs. The newspaper said the autopsy of the Raines boy showed he had heroin and cocaine in his blood. They must have known how much and whether it could have killed him, and that he didn't die from drowning. But the paper didn't say anything like that. So something must be available to the cops to check the trunks of both cars for matching—"

"Stop!" Hafferty shouted and stood up at the desk, raising a pointed finger at Jade. "That's enough!" He came around the desk and pointed at Jade's chair. "Sit down."

He stood in front of them as before, his hands on his hips this time, his voice cold and steady.

"You're not a detective, kid. What you've said is all conjecture. You have no evidence, no proof, no motive," he said, waving his hand like an ax at each word. "You can*not* accuse two policemen of murder based on what you say you saw. You can only speculate. You have nothing. You have your opinion, that's all. Hell, after all this time, these delays you've created…hell, I don't even know if *I* believe you saw what you say you saw. And in a courtroom, even a rookie lawyer could punch holes in your story."

He took a deep breath and exhaled. "Look, fellas," he said with a burst of his fluorescent smile, his tone friendly. "They have a suspect. But they only have circumstantial evidence on him, so they might not get a conviction." He held out his arms, shrugging his big shoulders, still smiling. "And if they do get one, he won't do much time. Ten years, maybe. Hell, he's a queer anyway. What he does with other guys, boys even—it's illegal. He could get a helluva lot more jail time for that alone. He could be put into an institution. For the rest of his life.

"Boys, listen to me. We're all getting ahead of ourselves here. Including me. Hell, I don't know what they're gonna do with that homo." He started his pacing again, nodding his head as he talked. "But I will tell you this. From now on, we take this one step at a time. We'll let the D.A. do his job, and we'll play our hand as new information comes forward. I know what you say you saw, Jade, and now Roland knows, too." He stopped in front of them. "And I assume you told your friend—what's his name—Bozak. With the rat face. Am I right? You told him?"

Jade shook his head. "No, but he's already figured it out without me saying so."

"So, you need to put a clamp on his mouth about this, because it's not only you who will have to worry; it's Bozak himself. If he starts rattling his trap about what you saw, he'll have no one to protect him. Not even you, Roland."

"You mean, protect him from the cops—Joey and Billy," Jade said.

Hafferty raised his hands. "Let's stop the speculating, boys. Let's just agree that your pal must keep his mouth shut. And I'm leaving that job up to you two."

He moved toward the desk, sat down with a sigh and lit a cigarette.

"Now, listen to me," he said through a cloud of exhale. "I will handle everything about this going forward. I will take care of Joey and Billy, and I will deal with their two brothers, our General Manager and our union steward. Those two stand to lose a great deal if their idiot brothers don't back off. And I don't just mean back off from threatening you, Jade, or your mother or your girlfriend. Or Roland's girlfriend, or whoever the hell's girl she is now.

"What I mean is, backing off from their crooked drug enforcement practice. Bring it to a close. Cut it off completely. Shut down their operation and let the Chief of Police direct a new way to apprehend dealers and destroy the drugs they try to bring into this county. I know a certain powerful man who will not stand for any more drugs, I can assure you. And I will back him up one thousand percent. My county will *not* become a drug-infested haven for low-lifers. Mark my words."

He stood up and headed for the closet. He pulled on his suit jacket, sucked in his gut, and buttoned the jacket. "That's enough for now. I will take care of *every*thing we talked about and more. Rest assured, gentlemen. You two guys go about your business, get back to work. Get focused on your future. You're working here to pay your way through college, both of you. And that's it. Do not lose sight of that goal. Keep me informed about what you see and hear, but otherwise, keep your noses out of the politics around this place. The self-appointed union stooges of Macson will back off from you two, and so will the gossipers, and all the other troublemakers. I guarantee it. And I will have our GM and our union steward guarantee it with me, or they'll be out on the street with their asses in a sling, begging for handouts." He brushed cigarette ashes off his jacket lapels and pulled his cufflinked sleeves out of the jacket arms.

"Now that all that nonsense is settled," he said, his politician's smile popping onto his cheeks, a magic flash of light, "I have a little surprise for you two. A *good* surprise. Something special you're gonna like. A chance to get your minds off all of this, to have a little fun, get a little education about how things in society work, see how the other side lives and plays." He paused and opened his palms and raised his eyes to the ceiling. "*And* a one-time opportunity to make a ton of extra money. Just one day. Long hours, but the work will be rewarding. Two-hundred fifty apiece, plus all the tips you can charm out of a bunch of rich guys, who are sometimes a little tipsy. Generous gentlemen, most of them."

There was a rattling at the back door in Dorothy's office, and Hafferty stepped out of the room to call out, just as the door opened. "Hang in there a moment, Jerry. I need a little more time in your office. Take a stroll to the men's, have a smoke. And when you come back, we need to talk about your lunch meeting with our union steward. Gimme ten minutes."

He stepped back into Jensen's office and closed the office door quietly and held up his hands.

"Here's the deal, boys," he said in a low tone. "Every couple years, I have a summer party at my place in the country. My way of showing appreciation for the best men in the county, and men from beyond, too— up and down the valley, some even from New York. Give 'em a chance to let their hair down, if you know what I mean. The big party happens tomorrow. And the weatherman is calling for a perfect afternoon and evening.

"It starts with cocktails, conversation, and then a fabulous five-course dinner, with gorgeous waitresses and one of New York's top chefs running the kitchen. After dinner, the guys will enjoy a little outdoor recreation in the late afternoon sun—bocce ball, golf range, putting green, plenty of space for everyone. Some of us will break up into small groups for a few private meetings, the rest will do whatever they want. Some guys play cards, swing the golf clubs, lots of conversation, deal-making and…other amenities, according to taste." His eyes lit up and his fluorescent smile expanded to its limits.

"It's the biggest affair of its kind between here and New York, and it's all on me. These are the most important men in this region and in this state. And I have a little surprise for a select few of them. A special announcement—something you boys will remember for the rest of your lives. Something that will set the stage for your own personal success. *If* …" He held up his finger. "*If* you stay by my side, loyal to me. Boys, you are going to be eyewitnesses to history.

"All you two need to do is get cleaned up after work today and stop by my tailor's in the Sheeley Hotel—Harold Wise. His shop is on the first floor, he'll be waiting for you. He'll put you in a crisp white shirt and black slacks, decent black shoes. You'll be mixing it up with some of the most gorgeous waitresses on the east coast, so you'll want to look your best."

"We're waiters?" Roland asked, his look both incredulous and irritated.

"You're whatever the chef tells you to be," Hafferty said, still smiling. "The girls will bring out the food, but you two, you will be the face of the kitchen *and* the handsome young representatives of my estate. So, be ready to take drink orders, clear away tables, give direction, solve any problems, make the guests happy, whatever the chef tells you to do. A good job could make you upwards of two hundred bucks in tips, maybe more—and that's on top of the two-fifty base. These men—they get a little loose, and they start throwing around cash. You'll see. It's unbelievable."

He stepped toward Roland and Jade and put a hand on each of their shoulders. "Now, listen, boys, there's a caveat. This is a private, highly confidential event. You can*not*, under any circumstances, tell anyone you're going to this event. You cannot tell anyone afterward that you went to this event. You cannot tell anyone, *ever*, who you saw there and what they were doing. All the helpers I've hired know these rules, and I will know if you break them. I don't think you will, because you are my boys. But, if you do, I promise you, the consequences will be dire. Do you understand?"

Roland and Jade nodded.

"Good!" He waved them toward Dorothy's little office, his sales voice back in full swing. "This is an exclusive opportunity for you boys to mingle with men of power. It's an experience that could change your life, if you know how to work it. Plus, you could make more money in one day than you do in two weeks in this factory. College money. Remember your goal, boys."

He steered them toward the exit to the factory yard, just as Jensen unlocked the back door and stepped inside. "Hang on there, Jerry," Hafferty shouted to him. "Wait outside for another minute while I finish up with these boys." Jensen stared at them for a long moment, anger and fear in his beady eyes. When he closed the door, Hafferty turned to Jade and Roland, his voice low.

"Jade, tell Ronnie I said for him to get the Fleetwood washed right now and then come back for me. Half hour, tops. Roland, I'm giving you the Caddy tomorrow to get Jade and yourself out to my place. I'll be using different transportation. And don't fuck it up this time, Roland. I'm giving you a second chance to earn this privilege. Harold Wise will give you the keys and the directions to my estate. Be at my place in the country by ten tomorrow morning, but wear your casual clothes. The chef is gonna have some running around for you to do at the estate and maybe some lifting for you guys to help him out with. You'll need to shower and change before three. That's when the guests start arriving."

He pointed to the exit, and Roland opened the door. Jade hesitated. Hafferty put his hand on Jade's back and started to give him a firm push.

"Mr. Hafferty," Jade said. He felt his voice tighten in his throat, as Hafferty dropped his hand. "It's about Ronnie. I...I can tell him what you said about the car, no problem. But...I thought you told me Stanley would go away once he gets better. If Ronnie takes his place—"

"Just do what I told you to do, kid," Hafferty said. "Ronnie is just another German Shepherd, son. Don't worry about him. Or about Stanley. Your mom is gonna be safe, guaranteed. *If* she ever returns home, that is."

"Let's go, Flynn," Roland said. "Lunch break is over, and we're behind. We've got work to do."

Jade nodded to him and turned to Hafferty. "What do you mean, ever?" Jade said.

Hafferty smirked at him and waved his hand. "Get a move on now, son. 'Ever' is just a manner of speaking. Don't forget to tell Ronnie about the car wash. He won't bite you."

He disappeared behind the closing door as Jade heard him calling out to Jensen. "Jerry! What's with the love-in between you and Ren? Did he ask you to marry him or just join the union?"

Jade heard Jensen's odd laugh. That he even had a laugh was a revelation; still, it wasn't a happy one.

53

Muse

She liked the authoritative sound her heels made on the hallway floor as she approached the office. But she didn't like the way they felt—squished toes, pinched heels, and legs precariously balanced on what felt like two needlepoint awls. Designed, no doubt, by the same bozo who came up with the torpedo bra.

After she had left Dell, she'd spent the afternoon in Manhattan getting her hair dyed and shopping for a new outfit, and she had buyer's remorse on the morning train home. She'd become accustomed to wearing her comfortable casual shoes and clothes and wondered why she'd acted on James's advice, even though he was right about Dell, who had clearly appreciated the dress and heels she'd worn for their luncheon. As for the hair, she'd decided after her second Dell meeting that she'd get rid of the blonde look before returning home. She'd asked for black, but it turned out auburn, close to her original color, so many years ago.

Now, she was feeling self-conscious in the new pencil skirt and tight-fitting sleeveless   silk blouse and teetering heels. It was the opposite of the confidence she'd felt after speaking with Tamara Gauthier on the phone from her room in The Waldorf. In her plan for their meeting at Dickson College, she'd envisioned presenting herself to Dr. Gauthier as a woman who'd tossed aside these fashion trappings for a life of independence. But now, she felt she'd betrayed herself, abandoning her new identity to the old standby of being a woman in a skirt and heels and a perfect pearl necklace. It was a false sense of security, and she felt defensive, having abandoned a cause she thought the college professor might respect, even admire. Now, despite her stylish New York attire and haircut, Alice had the sinking sense that she would be considered just another middle-aged woman, trying to look like New York, but obviously hailing from Nowhere USA. At least she'd gone light on the make-up.

A tall Black woman with short-cropped hair appeared in the office doorway. "Hello," the woman said, her eyes warm, her smile bright and welcoming. "You must be Alice," she said. She had large gold hoop earrings. Her loose-fitting sateen dress fell to her ankles in an explosion of color. "Please come in. You're in the right place, no worries."

Alice couldn't find her words. It was the woman's face, her eyes, even the tone of her voice. She'd seen and heard her before, often. She was the face in her visions, the one with encouragement and promise—the sole voice of hope amid sorrow. For a long moment, Alice wondered if she'd fallen back into one of her reveries, her daytime trances. Perhaps it was triggered by the night out with Helen in the Village, the drinking, the late hours. Had she drifted somehow into one of those other worlds, those waking dreams?

"Alice?" the woman said. "Are you okay?" She reached out to touch Alice's elbow, a gentle hand grounding Alice in the warmth of reality. Skin on skin.

"Yes. Oh ye…yes, I'm fine," Alice heard herself say, further grounded by the sound of her own voice. But she could not explain, would not want to try, not now, if ever. She took a deep breath and lifted her chin and smiled, her soft voice surprising herself. "I've been traveling. And the train, it…it sometimes does that to me. I'm… so sorry."

Tamara had her elbow in a firmer grip now and led her through the office doorway. "Here, please sit down, you'll feel better if you get off your feet," she said as she pulled a cushioned office chair from her deskside and guided Alice into it. "I'll get you a cup of cold water." She stepped behind Alice and closed the office door.

"Thank you," Alice said, turning to watch Tamara at a small corner kitchenette, pouring water from a silver pitcher into a glass. Alice cleared her throat and looked around the large office. Crowded bookshelves almost to the ceiling lined the wall behind the desk, and an upright black Steinway stood gleaming against the far wall, its keyboard glistening. The remaining two walls were filled with musically themed paintings and sketches, some small sculptures on stands, and dozens of photos of people in academic attire holding plaques, shaking hands, straining to smile. Tamara had told Alice to come to the office of the Dean of Arts and Humanities, whom Tamara had indicated was traveling abroad for the summer. She'd told Alice that her own office was so small that two people could barely fit inside it standing up. Alice remembered laughing at that along with Tamara and feeling an immediate sense of comfort with her, something she wished now she could regain, but she was still distracted by the woman's limpid eyes and by her musical voice, so familiar, so comforting, and she felt the ambush of her own self-consciousness fading. She looked down at her hands clutching the arms of the chair and her bare knees emerging from her tight skirt, as if these body parts could provide assurances to her that all of this was real.

Her drink arrived in a crystal Waterford tumbler. "The Dean has exquisite taste in material things," Tamara said as she settled into the black leather chair behind the dark cherry desk and smiled at Alice.

"Indeed," Alice said, as she raised the water to her lips and took a deep drink. She found her bearings then and gestured toward the piano. "That Steinway looks brand new. Must be nice to be Dean." She raised her eyebrows to Tamara, and they chuckled at each other. Tamara's smile was even more brilliant than it had been in Alice's daydreams.

"I must say, she's earned it," Tamara said. "She's been here for twelve years, made her own way through perseverance, the odds stacked up against her at every turn. The usual boys club, you know? The Dean's musical talent, her credentials, her pedagogy, and, not the least, of course, her ability to hold sway with both town and gown—all of this put her logically in the path of the President's office. But she's quite sure Dean is her limit."

"Why is that?" Alice said, taking another sip from the heavy cut glass, and settling on the notion that Tamara was, indeed, a real person.

"She's a woman, first of all. And she's South American, born in Columbia, and, while her relatively fair complexion and her marriage to a prominent local White physician afford her certain advantages, most of those at the top here at the college know she's merely passing."

"Passing," Alice said, nodding, remembering a classmate at Barnard whose race had been gossiped about. "And you know this because…"

Tamara looked surprised at first; then she grinned, seeing that Alice understood. "She's been nice to me, and very open with me," Tamara said. "One of the few. She encourages me to stick it out here, follow her lead. But, in the next breath she admits it's fruitless. At least she's honest."

"Passing doesn't qualify as dishonest?" Alice asserted, at once regretting the remark.

Tamara shook her head. "For the Dean, in her generation, it's been a choice between survival and succeeding. What I meant to say is that she's honest about *my* chances here. Look at me. I'm not exactly the passing type. I was born in Jamaica. My mother was descended from one of the Maroon tribes there who escaped the European slavers. My father was half-Creole—a Caribbean Arawak, really. His other half was White French Canadian—hence the surname. But my color runs deep. Even if I had a chance to pass, I would not take it. Times are changing, Alice. And so am I, finally. I've been awakened by this experience and by changes I've witnessed in others close to me. I'm grateful for the Dean's counsel, but she knows now that I am determined to succeed on my own merits and credentials and experience—bigotry notwithstanding. And I won't waste any more time here pushing the boulder up the hill, alongside the Dean. I plan to leave this college before fall semester, if my application goes through in Chicago. If not, I'll be gone by December, for sure. Perhaps California, or back to Toronto. I want to live in an intentional community, with people from all over the world—many languages, races, practices, histories, art, literature, and beliefs. I refuse to be stuck here in a single dimensional reality."

"What about James?" Alice said. "I assume you came here for him, or at least at his behest."

Tamara's tongue settled between her lips, and she lowered her gaze, her eyes darkening. Suddenly, her face lost softness and warmth.

364

"That remains to be seen," she said, lifting her shadowed eyes to meet Alice's. The confidence in her voice had wavered. "He knows I'm unsatisfied here, at this irrelevant institution—a hiding place for academics who've lost their perspective, if not their motivation. I am an island here. And not just because I'm one of two Black professors on a campus with literally a handful of students who are not White. I'm accustomed to the absurd color imbalance in higher education—in all of American education for that matter. But here, even my younger colleagues seem stuck in a time gone by, and their complacency is deflating. I came here with fire in my belly, and now my core is drowning in the backwater of this disappointing campus, and this valley stuck in a time warp. And James needs to be released as well. From his isolation, his entrapment, his fealty to certain forces here, his stalled progress as a human. A Black man with a great mind in need of new inspiration."

Alice nodded, her dark eyebrows lifting in a semi-circle over the pale green eyes. "You didn't see all that—the backward culture, the complacent faculty, the trapped man—when you first visited here, first interviewed at this college?" she asked, prodding for something she knew she should leave alone, but could not resist.

Tamara smiled knowingly, recognizing the bait. "I was blind," she said with a wide-eyed smirk. "Shot with an arrow." Then she frowned and leaned forward on the desk again and peered at Alice. "You know the feeling, Alice." She turned her head but kept her eyes on Alice's. "Or you did know it. A long time ago."

Tamara stood up and headed toward the piano. Alice noticed her posture and bearing—erect but graceful, her arms floating at her sides, her long, colorful dress sailing softly in her wake, a flutter of mystical rainbows. Her shoes were flat. And did not make a sound.

"Do you play?" Tamara said casually as she sat at the piano and began tinkering with the keys and then sampling chords and accompanying melodies. The sound filled Alice, elevating her from her plunge into peevishness. Tamara played with ease, and the music was an elixir to Alice, a salve, and she relaxed into the security of the comfortable chair. She felt her shoulders give way and her breath come in soft waves. This woman from her dreams was a gift. She was real.

When Tamara stopped her warmup and turned around on the bench, Alice smiled at her. "Yes, I do play," she said, calmly, surprised by her contented tone. "Quite rusty these days, I'm afraid, but I was well-trained as a child. It's something that doesn't leave you. I have a piano at home, but it's in such bad shape that I only play it when I'm desperate for a way to drown out the racket in my brain."

Tamara let out a full laugh as she stood up from the keyboard. Her bright smile returned, her fiery eyes lighting up the room. Alice couldn't resist laughing back.

"I know the feeling," Tamara said. "My piano in the apartment sounds like it has twenty flat tires. It's a rough ride. Not a shiny new Steinway, needless to say."

Alice stood up and approached the piano, and, as Tamara stepped aside, Alice sat at the keyboard and began to play. She was startled at first by the Steinway's muscular sound, but she let her fingers go and closed her eyes, relishing the rich tones and supple responses to her touch and letting her thoughts drift to another time. After a few minutes of warm up, she found herself falling into the old reliable sonata she used to play for her father and his associates. It was easy, like swimming in the pool again, leaning into Lucky over the jumps, reaching up for a high backhand volley. She stopped suddenly when the face of Salvatore Giallo surfaced in her mind.

"Oh Alice, keep going! Please," Tamara said, smiling. "That was a lovely Beethoven. Sonata fourteen, if I'm not mistaken?"

Alice turned to her and then pushed herself away from the piano. "Yes. Opus thirteen, The Adagio. It's called *Pathetique*. Which is apropos of my playing, I suppose."

"Oh my, no. It was wonderful. You're nowhere nearly as rusty as I am."

"You must have something you'd like to play," Alice said in a bubbly tone, as she stood up. But she saw by Tamara's reaction that her own voice did not match her eyes. She was still blinking away the face of *El Diavolo*. His transition from charmer to man of malice and hostility. She shook her head to chase it away, and then she was embarrassed, certain Tamara had observed her mental battle.

"Why don't we get back to our conversation," Tamara said, gesturing toward the desk. "Maybe we can try a duet a little later. We have much to discuss."

Alice asked if she could help herself to another glass of water. When they returned to their seats, Tamara leaned forward on the desk and gave Alice a level look. "James called me this morning to let me know you might want to meet with me. I told him we'd already spoken by phone and that we would be meeting today."

"Always a beat late, that James," Alice said, reacting without thinking.

Tamara raised her eyebrows and offered a thin smile. "Yes, the scientist often has to ponder carefully before he allows himself to act."

Alice forced a grin, attempting to shift from her blunder. "Did he tell you why I might contact you?"

"He said it would be about Roland," Tamara said, "but that's all he would offer. He's very curt with me these days."

Alice was tempted to further dissect this relationship, but she decided to wait. "I assume he's told you what you need to know about me and why I would have interest in Roland."

Tamara's eyes flattened and her smile softened to a puffy line, her face an enigma. "He hasn't told me anything in detail about you, but he's told me enough, which, when added to what your son, Jade, told me last weekend, allows me to at least arrive at a reasonable hypothesis."

"Jade?" Alice asked, her hackles raised, her throat tightening, her heartbeat punching at her chest.

"Yes," Tamara said coolly, "I met Jade at Wally's Diner, and, two weeks ago, he helped me—and Wally and Roland—move my furniture into my apartment on the third floor of Wally's and Wilma's house. I assume you know them, the diner owners. Then, Jade dropped by my place last Sunday to speak with me about Roland, who happens to be his supervisor at work. At one point, he mentioned having visited a woman named Dolores in the now-dispersed Black section of Ebonton. He said you'd taken him there several times just after you'd moved here six years ago, and that there was a boy named Junior, the oldest of the Black children in Dolores's care."

"I see," Alice said as she sipped at the water glass. "And what did you say to that?"

Tamara held her enigmatic look and paused a long moment before speaking. "Why don't we just move right to my hypothesis," she said, with certain authority.

Alice straightened her shoulders and sat back in the chair. "All right, Professor," she said levelly. "Make your case."

Tamara's flat look softened, and she folded her hands on the desk and leaned forward, her golden-brown irises focused and certain.

"In my short time here, I've come to know two young men, who I believe to be brothers," she said. "But they themselves do not know this. Your sons, Alice." Her eyes widened. "And I'm probably among a very small group of people who either know this or suspect it. Those in the know would be you, of course, as well as James and Commissioner Hafferty; and those who suspect would be Wally, and maybe Wilma. And now me. And I'm postulating that Jade's father may know, but it's likely he has not been in the picture at all for many years. If he's still living."

Alice held Tamara's look for a prolonged beat, and then broke eye contact and looked down at herself. Reality had sufficient weight now, her high-heeled feet planted on the floor. Her tight skirt had risen a few inches, exposing more skin than just her bare knees. Her legs were pinkish, in need of color, especially against the deep tan fabric of the skirt. She closed her eyes for a moment and found her breath, lowering the bucket into her belly and back out again, the processed air seeping from her nose like warm cigarette smoke. In her ears, she felt her pulse slowing from a throb to a soft beat. She looked up to meet Tamara's eyes again.

"So, I assume you shared your theory with Jade," Alice said. There was a challenge in her tone she did not intend.

Tamara kept her cool poise, her eyes still warm. "No, of course not. It's a theory, as you say. And it is certainly not my place to pose it to him."

Alice smirked and let a little huff slip out of her nose. "I could see why Jade might want to confide in you. Older woman, but not old enough to be his mother. Perhaps a sister. Perhaps something more. Bright, articulate, educated, sophisticated, and certainly very attractive—arrestingly so, actually—in a way that my son would be drawn to." She smiled as she noticed Tamara's skin tone deepen; then she settled back and looked away, toward the piano.

"His name is Seamus, actually, but I switched it to the Anglo version, James, when we first moved here. But he seems to have forsaken that moniker for love, or deep lust, or whatever. Now he's Jade—a play on the initials of his first and middle names, evidently created by the girlfriend. He doesn't have many friends—a couple of idiot boys from high school, and the girl, of course. But he's mainly introverted, a reader and a ponderer like me, I guess. No father to teach him how to be crude in this heartless place, so I tried to do my best in that category. Failing miserably, I certainly hope." She laughed and glanced toward Tamara, who nodded and smiled, her professorial composure returning.

"When it comes to females," Alice continued, "he seems drawn to those who, like himself, do not fit in." She grinned and lifted her face, looking directly at Tamara for a moment and then shifting her unfocused gaze to the bookshelves. "I remember his first little girlfriend. We were in New Jersey. She was a sweet, sassy, beautiful Brown girl—a precocious child of migrant farm workers I was working with as their liaison with a few local farmers. The girl could speak English very well, and Seamus was enthralled by her, tried to get her to teach him Spanish, but she would only speak to him in English. It was so cute. He begged me to teach him some Spanish, and I knew why, so I did. A little bit, anyway. I saw them holding hands often in the fields, by themselves. They were about ten years old. He was crushed when her family didn't come back to Jersey the next spring." She sighed and returned her focus to Tamara. "And now, he's been with a girl from his high school. Lucy something. I've never met her but I'm sure she's an outcast like he is. She seems to put him into a general gloom, from what I can tell. But then again, I'm not always around, so…"

Alice looked to Tamara, as if to say it was her turn, but Tamara just smiled and nodded her head again, her eyes wide open. She was a listener.

"Seamus has always been an outsider," Alice continued. "A misfit, I suppose. Thanks to me. We've wandered, he and I, from place to place for his entire childhood, and now, we're here in this gloomy valley for longer than we've put down anywhere else, which is ironic, since this is the worst of the places I've dragged him to. I haven't really been a reliable mother, that's for sure. And certainly not one he could confide in at this vulnerable stage of his life. I suppose I should be grateful to you."

Tamara sat back into the Dean's leather chair, and it swayed with her weight. When she rocked forward, she settled her arms on the desk and folded her hands. Alice noticed her rings for the first time—an array of large stones and gleaming metals covering most of her long dark fingers. Her many bracelets clicked against the rich wood of the desk as she leaned forward to get closer to Alice.

"I don't have children, Alice, and I never will," Tamara said, her large eyes suddenly moist and emitting a fiery light from their dark base. "It's a physical condition I have. I don't know what kind of mother I would have been, but I do know that your son thinks…well, if I recall his words correctly, I believe he said that you make him happy, and that you are *charming*—which was an interesting adjective, considering his age. And he said that your imagination is contagious. You were mentioned only briefly in our conversation, but it was clear to me, Alice. Not just from the words, but from the look on his face when he talked about you. If he has a hero, she is you. I think he worships you."

The words struck Alice like a punch—an unexpected jolt, taking her breath away. She opened her mouth to say something, but she couldn't form the words. Instead, she made a quiet croaking sound as she tried to catch her breath. She reached for the water. The glass was shaking in her hand as she put it to her lips.

It took her a long moment to find her voice. "I'm nobody's hero," she said, in a raspy whisper. She cleared her throat and turned her hands in front of herself and looked at her palms and trembling fingers. "Certainly not his. I think the only thing I've given him is a rudimentary blueprint for survival. On his own. And the first rule is: Don't do as I have done." She put her hands in her lap and looked up at Tamara, clearing her throat again. "I am not his hero, Doctor Gauthier. And I'm not much of a mother, that's for sure. I'm not there enough, and when I am, well, I'm not really there." She forced a smile at Tamara, her eyes coming to life. Then, suddenly, her full voice returned as if a spotlight shone on her. "I think the bard described me best: I'm the inconstant moon."

Tamara grinned and raised her eyebrows. She lifted her chest and took a deep breath and looked into Alice's eyes. "Oh, swear not by the moon, the inconstant moon, that monthly changes in her circled orb," she said, her voice almost in song. "Lest that thy love prove likewise variable."

Alice sighed a little laugh and nodded, smiling. "Touché!" she said, imitating Tamara's wide eyes. "Your students must be in awe of you, Doctor Gauthier."

Tamara's face fell from her moment on the stage, and she let out a guffaw that startled Alice. "Oh please!" she exclaimed, shaking her head.

"It's exactly the opposite. I have a student in my three hundred level lit course who asked me if I thought the play was based on Zeffirelli's film! *Three hundred* level, Alice!" She raised her arms at her side as if on a crucifix. Her eyes were bulging, her mouth agape. "I tried to use the film to get them to explore the text, but the boys could only get as far as chattering about how beautiful Juliet looked naked in bed. One boy even asked why the protagonists killed themselves! Of course, he hadn't read the play, but he'd watched the film! And still didn't get it. Three hundred level!"

They laughed together, sharing Tamara's exasperation. Alice shook her head, commiserating as she watched Tamara shrug and throw up her hands. Something yielded between them. A wall starting to give way, parts of it crumbling, a fissure of light peeking through. Tamara seemed to recognize this and spoke first.

"So, Alice. Please call me Tamara. And now it's my turn to ask you about this place," she said, her tone collusive, sisterly. "If this is the worst of all the places you and Jade have lived, why have you stayed here the longest? As you say, it's ironic. But what's driving the irony? What's the lure? What's the glue that keeps you stuck in such a place? As with myself, and James, and your son...*both* of your sons...you do not seem to belong here."

Alice gazed at this woman. This stunning Black woman, this face and voice now fully realized, anticipated in those many visions, those unsolicited daydreams. Had she imagined or dreamed this muse into life? It was not surprising that she looked unlike anyone else in this valley, but, to Alice, she was as familiar as her own sister, her own blood. And yet, at the same time, she could see clearly that Tamara was very uniquely her own self. Her slight hint of an island accent suggested her faraway roots, but her bearing was her own—the way she held herself, even when seated—so steady, so self-assured, relaxed, and, at the same, time ready. Her eyes calmly on alert, her jaw both lax and poised. She was a lioness reclining in a golden field, saving her energy for the inevitable—an attack at her back. Or an opportunity at her flank.

"There were two reasons I came here," Alice said, slightly wary of the lioness, but trusting the apparition from her visions now come to life, the only hopeful voice of her dreams. "Two *people*, actually."

"James?" Tamara asked, prompting not threatening.

"No," Alice said, glancing away from Tamara. "That flame was doused years ago."

"Hafferty," Tamara said. "He's the first reason."

Alice nodded, her eyes meeting Tamara's. Candor, at last. She was more than an apparition; she was the vision and the voice incarnate.

"He was the one who doused the flame," Alice said. "He turned James against me, imprisoned me in a convent, stole my child. He cut me off from my family and my inheritance, and, for the next twenty years, he interfered with every effort I made to live independently—as a single mother without a husband."

She gave Tamara a half-smile and leaned toward her. "Did you know, Tamara, that in post-World War Two in the U.S.—the late forties through this decade, a single mother without a husband is simply a non-person? Over those years, I couldn't get a legitimate job, could not open a bank account, could not buy a car or a home, could only *rent* a decent place to live at the discretion of a landlord, and often one with salacious expectations. I could barely get so much as cash credit at a local grocery store. Without a husband, a man who governed me, I was invisible. And, for the most part, I still am. And I'm not Black, as you can see. Just female, unmarried, with a child."

Tamara smirked and nodded.

"But he made sure I survived," Alice continued, looking behind Tamara toward the fog of bookshelves. "He who giveth, and he who taketh away. He tore me from whatever menial job and relationship I tried to develop in every bus stop town I moved to with my son in tow. But he kept us in cash—like a pimp with his hooker—but only after we suffered indignities far worse than a woman on her back. His thugs would come to the town where we lived and start the rumors in the local shops and bars. She's a prostitute, she's a Communist sympathizer, she's a homewrecker, she's a union organizer for the migrants, she's a thief, she's an escaped convict.

"It was the whisper campaign all over again, just as he'd done in New York when I disappeared from college. His campaign got to every classmate, every friend I'd had in the city. She's had a nervous breakdown. She's been committed to an institution. That part was true, of course. That convent he put me in. It was a prison. An asylum.

"A man can do that, Tamara. Did you know that? A man can institutionalize a female relative for any reason at all. Hysteria, adultery, being pregnant with my lover's baby—whatever he wants to say. A man can do that in this country. Legally.

"And when I tried to fight back, with the help of a newspaper reporter, he made the reporter disappear. And he shipped me off, pregnant again, to another Catholic institution—a home for unwed mothers. The cursed of society.

"He told everyone I had another nervous breakdown. He told my family and the people who worked on our estate—the people who raised me and whom I loved. And, when I finally got out on my own, with my Seamus, he had me followed, tracked me down like prey, interfered with whatever life I tried to build, got me fired, and then dropped a packet of cash on me, a couple hundred dollars, enough to get me to the next town and find someone off the legal circuit who would offer me and my son a place to live, maybe a menial job, if we were lucky. And it would go well for a while, sometimes a year or even two, and then the whispering would begin again, and I'd be kicked out, ostracized, beaten up even, twice nearly raped, my child taken from me once. It went on for years. And then we came here."

"Why?" Tamara asked, her eyes wider than ever now. "Why take your child into the nest of your tormentor?"

Alice looked up into those startled eyes. "The closer we got to this place along our path, the more cash he'd give me. Cash he'd stolen from my inheritance. Giving me my own money in nibbles, bags of dirt delivered by seedy men with ugly motives, always taking their cut, and often trying to take a piece of me, as well. So, as we moved ever closer to his lair, the allowance—the pimp payout—would increase.

"But I had my own motive for seeming to give in to his game. And that was the second reason—the second *person* who compelled me to come here. It wasn't the additional money, although the bagmen who dropped it off certainly let me know that their boss considered my decision a victory, that he said he knew all I wanted was more money."

"Roland," Tamara said. "Your main reason."

Alice nodded. "He was called James, originally, as I came to understand it, and then James Junior. And then just Junior. But yes, he was the second reason. Actually, you're right: he was the primary reason. All I wanted was to see my son. The one they took from me. That's all I wanted. Just to touch and kiss his face, to look into his eyes, to tell him I did not abandon him.

"When I came here, I did not make plans to take him away with me; I just wanted to see him, to talk with him, to become part of his life. But his father...he was given his orders. And this time, it was more than a whisper. It was a shout! I was a pariah. A danger to James's family. A fallen woman, a prostitute even, with a second illegitimate son. That's what James was told. But he knew none of that was true, and he knew how wrong all of it was. Just as he knew it was wrong the first time he listened to Dennis more than a decade earlier.

"But James was in a trap he'd grown accustomed to. When he was young in The Bahamas, he was beguiled by his self-appointed sponsor, a rich White man named Roland Snowcroft, and he was still devoted to him when he came to college in Washington, so much so that he gave his son—*our* son—that man's name along with his own. But he told me just last week that when he came under the control of Dennis, he'd been merely exchanged as a piece of property from one overlord to the next. And now what irony! His son goes by his middle name—Snowcroft's *first* name. That must haunt James."

Alice reached down and slipped off her high-heeled shoes and sighed. "These damn shoes were made to torture women," she said, standing and stretching her arms and her neck, massaging her lower back.

She walked toward the piano, her toes spreading and gripping the carpet. "Oh, that's good," she said, smiling at Tamara. "I feel like I'm walking on the beach."

When she reached the piano, she considered getting lost in a melody, but instead, she closed the fallboard gently and turned to Tamara.

"Did James tell you about the photos of Roland?"

Tamara looked confused. "Photos? No."

Alice told her about the men who follow her and follow Roland as well, and the notes and photographs she'd received from Giallo. "I cannot tell from the photos or the cryptic notes just how involved he is in Panther politics, but I urge you to speed up your departure plans and to take James and Roland with you. To Chicago or to California or to Canada or wherever you can get to. Within the next week."

"That's not possible," Tamara said, shaking her head, her eyes narrowing. "James barely speaks to me. And Roland...he has his own plans, and he's hardly in a position to just up and move away with me and his father. Our relationships are on tenterhooks, all three of us. I couldn't convince either of them to have *lunch* with me, much less move away with me in a week. Why would you propose such a thing?"

Alice returned to her chair and sat down with a sigh. "I have good reason to believe that our beloved Commissioner is about to be ensnared in a public scandal that will set him off on a campaign of rage and retribution, and that Roland and James will be caught up in the whirlwind."

She put her hands on the desk and leaned toward the wide-eyed Tamara. "You must know by now that Hafferty and Giallo run this valley in every aspect—politically, socially, economically, and even morally, if you believe that their black-robed pals are the valley's guardians of morality. All that power and control—all of it—is about to come crashing down."

Tamara frowned and her eyes darkened. "How?"

"An investigation is about to be launched that will expose those two and their long history of corruption, racketeering, government influence peddling, profiteering on war, abuse of innocent people, and more. And, as he discovers the traps surrounding him, Hafferty will turn on anyone and everyone to divert blame away from himself. He's a master at that trick. As for Giallo, his reaction may be much more direct—even deadly. I am at risk of fallout from both men, but I'll take care of Jade and myself. I've already warned James, and now I'm asking you to advise Roland and to make a plan to act quickly—all three of you—before it's too late."

"How do you know about this investigation?" Tamara asked. "And why would Roland and James be in danger?"

"I can't tell you how I know, but I can tell you how Dennis behaves when he's in a corner. Everyone in close proximity to him will be subject to his narcissistic and vindictive instincts—incriminate everyone he's done favors for in order to protect himself. And James and Roland have been closer to him and in his favor more often than anyone else over the last two decades. Hafferty stands to spend many years in jail if he's convicted, but he won't go down without first dragging down everyone under his influence. As for Giallo, I know two salient characteristics about him: he has connections to people who make others disappear, in one way or another; and he has deep-seated resentment and hatred for Black people."

Tamara's face did not seem to correspond with what Alice had just said. Her eyes were soft, her aura serene. She gave Alice an equivocal smile and nodded.

"I will speak with James and Roland," she said. "But please don't hold much hope that they will act, at least not until they see the handwriting on the wall. At that point, maybe. And if you'd like, I will ask Roland to meet with you. Again, no guarantees there. But I know the life of his mother has been a mystery he's wanted to solve for a long, long time. Whether or not the time is now will be up to him."

When Tamara escorted Alice to the door, she put her hand on the doorknob and held it there. She looked at Alice's face and then into her eyes, and she gave her a full and warm smile, her eyes glowing golden brown.

"You have a great deal of forgiving to do, Alice," she said. "You might find some peace by starting to forgive in small doses. It will restore you. Retributive justice is this nation's greatest social failure. You will not find satisfaction by trying to bring down a malicious and powerful man. Extraordinary wealth breeds impunity, and all the pain shifts to the accuser. Leave him to his own devices; he will fall on his own sword in due time. Forgive him in your mind and heart, and then move on with your life. You are a bright and talented young woman, with many wonderful years ahead of you…*if* you can forgive. Living with vengeance is not living; but living with forgiveness frees you to live with hope and promise. Think of your sons and how you can help them grow into the good men they can become. Set yourself free, Alice."

Alice moved closer to Tamara and reached out her arms. The sateen fabric felt like baby skin and the woman's cheek was cool against Alice's own. She smelled a sweetness on Tamara's skin that brought her back to her childhood, to spring afternoons, when Tara walked with her through poppy fields, and they sang French nursery songs and the air was fresh and the sky soared above them, a cerulean wave that went on forever.

54
Troubadours

Jade had never flown in an airplane, but he thought riding in the Fleetwood was what it must feel like. The big black machine soared over the road, never seeming to come in contact with ruts or potholes—the pavement ordinary folks ride on. With the windows sealed and the air conditioning purring, this hovercraft from the future floated above the gritty streets of Mell Hollow, separated from all earthly sensations. The feeling of weightlessness in motion sent Jade drifting into his alien daydream. In his alternate consciousness, and now defying gravitational forces, he wondered again how people could live in such ruin. In this soaring bubble, he was invisible, propelled further into dissociation from the soot-bound earth of his neighborhood. Behind the tinted windows, he was gliding now, undetected, past the familiar slouching little homes and the scattering of dim storefronts covered in layers of culm dust, their faded and broken signs unreadable. Weary people, mostly old, shuffled along the bumpy and broken slate sidewalks, and Jade knew he should recognize some of them, but in his alien persona and at the removed distance and speed at which he now traveled, he let himself see them as beings from a bygone existence—humans, as they were once known, now already dead, just bodies twitching through their last nervous impulses before they collapse and turn to dust. He glanced up at the charcoal mantis on the smoky culm dump, teetering on spindly legs, leaning toward its own final collapse—a falling false god amid the ruins of its makers.

He was thrilled about this elevated escape from all his trappings, and he mused that perhaps this alien craft would tilt upward at any moment and, with a rocket thrust, head at warp speed toward the next stop on this separating cruise—the surface of the moon. And when he arrived and settled in there, would he welcome the Apollo 11 crew next week? Or would he zap them from the black atmosphere like annoying mosquitos, unworthy of entry into the sacred and endless frontier of stars and spheres beyond the doomed Earth? Banishing, even vaporizing, the heedless invading humans, lest they threaten the rest of the untouched universe with their ruinous ideas, their belief that taking without replenishing is a promise for more life instead of what it actually is—a formula for demise.

"Where are you, Flynn? What do you wanna hear?"

Jade blinked away his brooding alien self and let out a soft laugh, embarrassed that Roland might have read his thoughts.

"Here?" Jade said, still foggy. "What do you mean, here?"

"Hear, Flynn. As in listen. Music. Know what that is?" Roland let out a laugh like a bark, sounding a bit like Squirrel. "Are you in outer space or something?"

Jade turned to Roland, astonished.

"We're gonna hear Aretha whether you like it or not," Roland said as he shoved an eight track into the slot below the radio dial.

The voice that filled the cabin was not alien at all, but quite human, a pitch perfect cry of passion, a plea for respect in tones that stirred Jade's blood and returned him fully to his senses, his own fragile body. He nodded in spontaneous agreement with the sound and smiled at Roland, but the man behind the wheel was looking straight ahead, the car sailing, the scene outside blurred, the somber gray sky whisking past the panoramic windshield.

Jade watched Roland out of the corner of his eye, the big Black man cruising at the helm of the Caddy, aloof in his thoughts. His silhouette reminded Jade of the last time they rode in this car together, with Roland in his beret and sunglasses and Lucy in the backseat. He thought about the sudden apparition of Roland behind the wheel of this car in front of Lucy's house, and the odd revelation that Roland had a personality behind the wall he'd built against Jade. As he remembered all that had transpired on that day at the rez and afterward, he couldn't help saying out loud his next thought.

"So I guess you and Lucy are, like, a thing now." He saw Roland flinch and stiffen his jaw. Aretha wailed, and Roland turned her down a few notches.

"A thing?" He smirked sideways at Jade and turned down the sound another notch.

Jade was fully human now, his heart pounding at his ribs and thumping in his ears, drowning out Aretha. "Yeah," he said, swallowing. "I thought you were together—I mean, after last weekend and everything, after her big striptease at the rez. And then you took her home, and then I couldn't get her to answer my phone calls. Squirrel told me you weren't together, but I'm not sure I believe him. Especially after the strip show. I mean, how could you resist that?"

Roland pushed a button on the dash, and Aretha fell silent. He steered the Caddy toward the curb, and the cruiser made a soft landing on gritty earth. He put the car in Park, left the engine running, and turned to Jade. He didn't elevate his chin, as he usually did, and he didn't glare at him; he just tilted his head and looked at Jade as if for the first time.

Jade listened to the purr of the air conditioning and studied Roland's face. He looked like his father, the stern teacher, but there was something softer in his features. His eyes were lighter brown than his father's, a hint of green, like new grass around the pupils, and his mouth was softer too, almost feminine. He had his father's broad nose but his skin wasn't as dark, more the color of coffee with a splash of cream. Jade remembered what Tamara had said about Roland never knowing his mother, and he wondered if Roland had ever looked in the mirror to find something of what she might have looked like.

"You have a nice girlfriend, Flynn," Roland said, his voice soft and, for once, nonthreatening. "She's very pretty, too. Beautiful body. And she certainly knows how to show it off. But I don't think that performance at the rez was for me. I think it was for you. It's what happens when two people get tired of each other. They don't know what to do to start it up again, so one of them does something outrageous, risking everything, just to get the spark going again. I've been there a few times. And I'm always the one to do something stupid to set off that spark in someone I wanted back. And, for me, it always blows up in my face. I just lost someone I really cared for because I was stupid, just like Lucy was. I was trying too hard to get her attention, but, in the process, I drove the wedge deeper. You should give Lucy another chance. She might be just trying to get your attention, make you want her back." He held up the palms of his hands like white flags and slowly shook his head. "Hey, I'm no psychologist; I'm just telling you what I know from experience. But I can assure you, I am not *together*, as you say, with Lucy. In fact, we barely spoke after I dropped you off at your house. She tried to talk, but I wasn't having it. I was thinking about something a lot more important than her exotic dance." He smirked at Jade. "Even though it was a very, very sexy dance."

Jade's laugh was more of an exhale, a release of something fragile he'd been hanging onto—the final snap of that frail string in the frayed rope that connected him to Lucy. He'd felt it weaken with each conversation they'd had since early spring, and now the last string had given way. Not because of what Roland had said, but because Jade knew he could let it break, and it was ok to fall. He wasn't depending any longer on someone else to hold him up. He'd lost Lucy long ago, and the connection he'd been hanging onto was an illusion, much less real than even the thinnest of threads. It was more of a skin they both had shed, but he had felt naked without it. With her sexy lakeside dance, she made him face her nakedness, not to get his attention, as Roland had thought, but to tell him she was free from their old life. She was willing to be naked in the world, and she invited him to try it out. After all, she was always the one with the clay feet; he was the one lost in his head, in the sky and stars of his ruminations. She'd made the first move, and he'd clung to the slim hope that she wasn't finished with it all, with him. Now, he realized, it was over for good. He'd lost Lucy, not to Roland, but to herself and to her freedom from first love.

And then there was the epiphany of Tamara, real love, not just lust, but a love of mind, body, and soul. An idea absorbed somehow along his inchoate literary journey inspired by Alice, an idea only partly learned and not yet realized, until he'd found Tamara. But he lost her before he even got a chance to know her, to reach so much as the foot of the pedestal where he'd placed her, out of his own reach.

And Alice? As much as he might want to lose her, he knew she was too much a part of him to just walk away from her. As capricious and unreliable as she was, he knew now that Alice, and no one else, would be the one who would stay with him always, in his heart and in his mind and forever in the flighty but curious intellect that she'd inspired in him. No matter who his father was, it was Alice who'd given him life, and it was Alice who would always be with him, even when she was gone.

"The body in the water," he said, acknowledging the more important matter that Roland had referred to. Roland just nodded back and seemed to look right through him.

"I drove home, looking for my father," Roland said. "I was late, so I figured Hafferty had already left our house, and I was right. He'd probably called one of his lackeys to pick him up in one of his other cars, probably his Lincoln or his Mercedes. I didn't get the Cadillac washed like I'd promised him, I just wanted to get home, I wanted to know what I should do. My father would be angry and would probably want to throw me out, but I hoped he'd see what kind of trouble I might be in and use his big brain to help me. I was never so scared in my entire life. That face was the mask of a ghost rising up in the water. It rushed up to meet mine as I was diving down, and it struck me right in the forehead. Smacked me so hard that I took a fast breath and choked and closed my eyes and...I don't remember what happened after that, until I was on land, throwing up water and then trying to get away from that mask out there, get us all out of there. But I can still see it, that pale wrinkled skin and cold blue eyes. Even now, I see it every time I close my own eyes. Until yesterday, I couldn't sleep. I could barely function."

"What did your father say?"

"My father? He wasn't home. He was where he always is when he's not sleeping—in his office at the college. So I called him, and I told him what had happened. He didn't yell, but he also didn't tell me what to do. He just said call Dennis Hafferty, and he hung up. Good old Doctor Wilson with the brilliant mind. When it comes to me, he can't even muster a suggestion without deferring to his sponsor, the great Dennis Hafferty. My father can't be a father when he passes that job off to another man."

"So what did the Commissioner say?"

Roland chuckled and smirked like a big brother at Jade. "The Commissioner. Yeah. Well, I haven't been following my father's advice about the Commissioner lately. And you heard the scolding I got from Hafferty yesterday about his car. I just dropped off the muddy Cadillac at his office and left the keys over the visor and didn't even call him. I couldn't. I just walked to the only place where I knew I'd be safe."

"Tamara's," Jade said.

Roland let out a soft laugh and turned up that familiar competitor's chin. "I know you visited her early on Sunday, Flynn. And I know you like her. A lot." He let that cavalier smirk grow on his wide mouth, and Jade felt a rush of heat in his own face—not rage this time, but embarrassment.

"I could see it in your eyes on that day you helped her move in," Wilson said, holding Jade's eyes with his and starting to chuckle. "You were like a puppy dog at her feet. Sitting next to her on the floor, taking her books from her like they were sacred objects and putting them in the bookcase so carefully, like they were made of porcelain. It was all over you, Flynn. You were stunned by her light. And I don't blame you one bit. How could you not see what she has? She's magnificent, beyond beautiful. She's brilliant and she's kind." He lost his smirk and turned his eyes away from Jade, into the distance.

"I grew up with the first half of that combination, but I never knew the second half existed until I met Tamara." He refocused on Jade's face, his voice softening. "And I know you must have seen it right away. Your eyes followed her wherever she went on that hot day in that stuffy apartment. But you didn't even notice the heat. That look on your face, like you were some kind of outer space explorer, discovering the brightest star in the sky."

His smile relaxed and he looked past Jade again, his eyes lost in his own thoughts. "She's unlike anyone else in this world. No other girl or woman—or human, for that matter—comes close." He returned his gaze to Jade's face and nodded, as if looking to Jade for affirmation of his vision of her.

"She has a gift, Flynn," Roland continued. "She sees you. You know what I mean? She listens. And she watches. And she feels and sees you. She's centered on the earth, but her voice and her heart fill the sky, the entire universe."

Jade was stunned into silence—not just by what Roland was saying, but that he was saying it at all. This stoic, distant, self-possessed, intimidating man was rendering poetry in his worship of the woman both he and Jade loved. It was out of place, out of character for this tough guy, this lone Black guy in a perpetually threatening world. That Tamara could induce in Roland the kind of reverence and passion that he'd just expressed was proof to Jade that she was, indeed, magic; she was the essence of what life should be, and what was so far out of reach for him that it crushed his will to speak.

"You surprised me, though, Flynn," Roland said, with a look of approval, grounded now after his musing. "You really did surprise me. You're a skinny young White boy in this whiter than snow valley, and, somehow, you broke through the idea that Tamara was a Black woman. I grew up here, for the most part anyway, and I never knew a White guy around here who wanted to be in love with anyone other than a pretty blonde or an Irish redhead or one of those curvy Italian girls who have the darkest skin a White boy could tolerate. I mean, Tamara is beyond special, but she told me, in her selfless way of course, that in the six months she's lived here, she hasn't turned the head of one White guy, of any age. So, how did you do it, Flynn. Get beyond the skin to see the beauty?"

Jade was flummoxed by the question; but then he found his voice. "Her skin?" He shook his head and turned away from Wilson's glare. "I saw her skin as the beginning of her beauty, not something to get past. Tamara's skin is the window to her self. It glows. There are no pores in her skin. She's perfect. And when she smiles, the world stands still."

Roland let out a man's laugh, deep and resonant. "Wow. Flynn. You're a poet."

Jade smiled at his comrade in love. "Just like you, Wilson. Did you hear yourself just now? You sounded like a Shakespearean sonnet." Jade shrugged. "OK, maybe not that great, but you spoke like you were inspired. Hell, I haven't heard you say a positive word since I met you. But today, when you talk about Tamara, you sound like a troubadour."

"A what?"

Jade shrugged again. "That's what Alice would say, anyway. My mother. She talks that way all the time. She's my literary guide. Always shoving books in my face and giving lectures on Western Literature, the Italian Renaissance, Shakespeare, and lately, the writers today who are breaking all the rules. I don't get those ideas from Ebonton High School, you know."

"Uh huh," Roland uttered. "Is this the same mother who speaks in tong—"

"Don't even say it, Wilson," Jade said, pointing his finger at Roland. "You've never met her, so you can't judge her. I've met Tamara. I know your muse. When you meet mine, we'll decide who speaks in tongues and who speaks the truth. Just let me know when you want to meet Alice."

Roland started up the Caddy. "Muse, huh?" he said looking in the rear-view mirror. "Troubadour. Muse. I've heard Tamara talk like that, too. Shakespeare, Dante, Boccaccio, like I'm supposed to know who those guys were. Or care. I try to tell her about Eldridge Cleaver and H. Rap Brown, but she looks at me like I'm crazy. She knows more about European history and literature and music than she does about what's going on right now in front of her and in front of all of us. She's perfect, but sometimes she seems disconnected from the real world. Like your Alice. Your mother. People around here seem lost in time. You grew up here, so you know what I mean. Did Alice grow up here, too?"

"No. And neither did I. We've been here for six years, but it's felt like a hundred. Until now. I feel all of a sudden like this time tunnel town might catch up to reality sooner than it wants to."

Roland looked Jade in the eye and held it there for a moment. "Actually, I did meet your mother. Long time ago. And I remember you, too. Although you look completely different now. She kept coming around, bothering my father. Very persistent. He gave me and my Aunt Lola strict instructions to keep her away from our home and our neighborhood, but she kept coming back when he wasn't around. She was very pretty, I remember that, and very charming. Lola fell for the charm, but I didn't. My father told us she was a danger to us, and he put me in charge of keeping her away when he wasn't around. When she started to bring you along with her, my father went off the deep end. He dealt with her himself, and, when she continued to bother him, he got help. I'm pretty sure it was from Dennis Hafferty."

Jade was surprised by this revelation and by the sound of his own voice in reply. "So you knew me on my first day of work, didn't you? And all along you've pretended not to."

"I did not know you at Macson in the beginning," Roland said, his eyes steady on Jade's. "It was when you started to recall visiting Lola that the memory was triggered, but I kept it down where it belonged. It was Tamara who pulled it out of me, just this week, at her apartment, when I was having a meltdown. I'm pretty closed off to the world, Flynn. It's a survival thing you wouldn't understand, being White in this valley. I've had so many bad experiences here that I've trained my mind to keep them all locked up, never let them out. But Tamara…" His eyes drifted away from Jade's, and he shook his head. "She's the only one who can unlock them. Probably because I let her. No one knows me better than she does."

Jade wanted to speak but he couldn't focus. He wished Tamara knew him that well.

"Tamara didn't tell me what you two talked about when you were at her place on Sunday, but she told me you spent a couple hours there," Roland said, his eyes refocusing on Jade's. "She asked me to lighten up on you. She said you were not my enemy. I knew that, but I didn't want you as a friend, either. But she said there's something between us—you and me—that we need to discover. And she means to get underneath what it is. Hafferty's our main connection, but I'm not sure why he singled you out. I've known him for years. What's he to you?"

Jade turned away from Roland and looked out his side window at the empty storefront of an abandoned candy store just ten feet away. On the front door, a White woman's smiling face was imposed on a faded red background, and her hand held up a full bottle of Coca-Cola. Her fingernails on the bottle matched her bright red lipstick, but someone had blackened one of her white teeth, and one of her eyes had been scratched away to the metal underneath. On the front stoop below her, a crow was pecking at a bloodied mass—the remains of something that might have been alive when he and Roland had set out on this adventure a half hour earlier.

He turned away from the grisly scene and shrugged at Roland. "Still trying to figure that one out myself," he said. "He knows my mother. Or at least he said he knew her a long time ago. But he knows everybody around here. That's his thing—knowing everybody and their personal business. So why me and not some other guy? I don't know for sure. He said he's looking out for me because of my mother, but she's...I don't know. She was mad when I told her he'd offered me the job at Macson, and she said Hafferty was a user of people, that I would always owe him. And she thinks I'm gonna die there or something. She went to his office right after I started, and she tried to get him to let me go. But I'm glad he didn't. If I go back to Wally's, I'll never get out of this valley."

Roland was silent, and Jade turned to look at him. He was studying Jade's face. "You look like her, especially around the eyes," Roland said. "And you don't look at all like Hafferty. But do you think he might be related to you?"

"You mean, is he my father?" Jade asked, with a crooked smile. "No, I already went down that road. It's a dead end. As far as I know, Hafferty is nobody to me—he's just the key to my exit plan. So, I'm going along for the ride as long as I can, until I step through that Macson gate and on to college. Or wherever. I don't care either way. Just take my cash and get the hell out of this place."

Roland let out a huff. "I guess that's what we have in common, then. I'll have to tell Tamara we figured it out." He put the car in gear and checked the side and rear-view mirrors.

"Enough of this heavy stuff, Flynn," he said. "We're supposed to have a good time today at this big party." He reached across to Jade and shook his shoulder and smiled. "C'mon, ma-a-a-n! Let's go suck up to some fat cat White guys and, with our sincerest gratitude and deepest humility, accept the large piles of cash they throw at us." He laughed and revved the engine and held down the horn. "Hell, Flynn," he shouted over the din, a wide grin on his face, "we might make enough money to quit Macson before August. I don't know about you, but I'm up to my neck with making cannon shells for killing dark-skinned people."

He gunned the gas, and the Fleetwood spit stones and kicked up dust into a swirling cloud behind them. Jade watched in his side mirror as the crow flew above the dust cloud, then circled back and dove toward its victim.

55
Farewell Tour

After she left Tamara on Friday, she took a cab to her '57 Chevy parked a block off Reston Street. The carburetor was acting up, reminding her of Zeke's botched job on her Impala, but she persisted through the Chevy's coughs and drove to The Fairhaven Hotel in Telford, where she had spent some of her best evenings with Marte. She had an early dinner in her room and started to read *The Price of Salt* yet again, hoping to revive the dreamlike memories of those times gone by just months earlier, nights and days that seemed like another life altogether—the only such life in her entire existence.

She opened the story to a dogeared favorite chapter, but she couldn't concentrate. She tossed the book onto the bag of new clothes she'd bought in New York. Tamara's advice had haunted the corners of her mind, and now it was in the forefront, nudging aside not only her hope for a sweet momentary distraction, but interfering with the certainty of her plans, her strategy with Dell, her fixation on finishing off this madness. How could she forgive a man who'd been determined not just to destroy her life, but to make her suffer endlessly in the process and then take both of her sons away from her in his final rapacious act of acrimony and predation?

This wasn't a matter of forgiveness. It was a matter of life and death. Forgiveness would have to wait. Her muse had materialized—that, indeed, had been stunning. Tamara the real person was extraordinary. But it wasn't up to Tamara the muse to decide what to do with the advice she had to offer. It wasn't even advice, really; it was a kind of philosophy, one that did not fit well with what needed to be done. If a meeting with Roland came out of her visit with Tamara, that would be enough. But forgiving Dennis, and his partner, *El Diavolo*? That would never happen. Yes, as Tamara had said, the justice system was driven by retribution, but that system served Dennis and the Devil, not her. She didn't have the time to waste on coaxing blood from that stone and failing in the end; what she wanted was to derail Hafferty long enough to provide liberation from him. For her sons, and for herself.

She sensed from her visions and dreams that her time was coming to an end; and, since her muse had materialized, the impending finish to her life would materialize as well, possibly very soon. Perhaps that would be her liberation. To shuffle off her mortal coil, to emerge free finally from the burden of her earthly life. But first, her sons' freedom—their liberation from Hafferty's control—was paramount.

On Saturday, around mid-morning, she called home, but the phone just rang and rang. She waited thirty minutes and tried again. Same result. Forty minutes later, she passed by the house, took the first right, made a U-turn, and pulled over to the curb. She killed the engine and sat in her Chevy twenty feet from the corner of Reston Street, in the protective shadow of a massive ash tree. It was noon in the height of the season of light, and the sky was somehow smoke-free and bright, but the little brown house looked sadder than ever, a whimper away from expiring in a heap. It was as if the end of this day might well bring the end of time for the exhausted old place, its windows sagging, the front door now tilted to match the chimney's perilous pitch, the peeled siding looking like the pelt of mortally ill prey, so mottled and scabrous that even the hungriest predator would pass it up. She'd always hated this place.

After ten minutes of watching for human movement, she locked the Chevy and stood for a moment at the curb, still in the shadow of the looming ash. Traffic was light, and, if someone were watching, they might not recognize her with her new hair color and styling, her huge sunglasses and her hip New York casual outfit—peasant girl top and flared jeans. The flat shoes felt like sweet slippers compared with the hideous heels she'd worn for the visit with Tamara, and she felt nimble enough in them to move quickly, if necessary. She reached back to feel the pistol in her belt, spreading the loose-fitting blouse over the grip.

In the tiny barren backyard, she stared at the old oil drum for a moment, shaking off a flash of memory from an altered state. She looked around at the backs and sides of neighboring houses for peering eyes, figures in the sharp shadows; but there was no one. It occurred to her that she and Jade had known not a single neighbor in this weary collection of wilting homes along the polluted Filthy, perhaps because no one here wanted to be known. Perhaps it was a last stop for all of them.

Inside, she reached back for her pistol and listened for Jade, whose radar was always on. He'd wake up from a dead sleep with the squeak of the back door. But there wasn't a sound. He wasn't there.

She made a careful tour of the house, checking the closets and under the beds, and then, with even more caution and trepidation, she grabbed a flashlight and descended, step by creaking step, to the dimly lit basement with its low ceiling and dangling cobwebs and shadowed corners—all perfect hiding places for Stanley or his thugs. When she gathered her strength to check the laundry room and then the coal bin and found them empty, she felt a heavy weight lifting from her shoulders and a heavier one from her heart. Still, she kept the pistol at her shoulder, ready for an ambush.

On the first floor, she took note of how clean the house was, relieved, but not surprised, that Jade had kept the place in good order. She wondered if Jade had hosted guests while she was gone. "I hope so," she whispered. Then with a sad smirk, she said more softly, "but I doubt it."

The air in the house was stuffy, but there was nothing to be done about that. She didn't plan to stay long. The kitchen sink was empty, and the table and floor as clean as their dull and careworn surfaces would allow. She opened the refrigerator and was pleased to see that Wally and his grocer pal, Abe Lever, had kept Jade in sufficient food supply. She put her finger into a cherry pie and tasted the filling. "Wilma," she whispered, smiling with the memory of the woman who had, in many ways, replaced her as a mother to Jade. He was lucky, at least, for that.

She stared at the closed cupboard over the sink, waiting for a sensation, a weakness, a certain longing. She felt nothing.

Upstairs, she shoved the pistol in her back waistband and pulled her suitcase out of her closet and filled it with clothes. In the bathroom, she filled a small travel case with tubes and tinctures and toiletries.

At the top of the stairs, she paused to look into Jade's room, a rush of heat rising in her chest and neck and face. She swallowed a lump of dryness.

"I don't feel like a hero," she said aloud, frowning at Tamara's attempt to lift her up.

She stepped into his room and smelled his scent, his teenage musk. Lost forever was the sweet scent of his childhood, such as it was. She bowed her head and closed her eyes, imagining the forgiveness from Jade that she refused to grant to Dennis Hafferty. Perhaps Tamara could help her son move on once she was gone.

She went to a small table in the corner near Jade's closet, where his old mono record player sat, and, underneath it, a small box of forty-fives and a handful of long-play albums. Among the forty-fives were the expected hits from The Beatles, Dylan, Hendrix, The Temptations, The Everly Brothers, The Stones, as well as other pop musicians she'd never heard of. But she was taken aback when she looked at the forty-five sitting on the record player—*White Rabbit* by The Jefferson Airplane. She'd heard it often enough on the car radio and chuckled to herself about the girl lost in wonderland, but she was uncertain if resigned levity was the right reaction.

When she leafed through the small album collection, she grimaced at Pink Floyd and Cream, but was surprised to find that the collection had more of her old albums than his newer ones—Ella Fitzgerald, Tommy Dorsey, Nat King Cole, The Platters, and even a Bessie Smith recording. As she switched on the machine to listen to the lyrics of *White Rabbit*, it occurred to her that she hadn't heard music from Jade's bedroom in a year or more. Perhaps he played it in her absence. Plenty of opportunity there.

She turned to his neatly made bed and smiled, a wave of self-congratulations coming over her. He was disciplined—a good sign that he'd listened instead of imitating. She scanned the book spines on his bedside table and on the floor next to his bed. From the spot closest to his bed, she picked up *Sons and Lovers,* his all-time favorite. How he had struggled with it when he was so young, but how he'd persevered and then read it again and again. It was the faded green leather-bound gilt-edged copy from her father's collection, and she'd given it to Seamus when he was ten, saying he'd read it some day when he was older; but he dove right into it immediately. It took him months. Now and always since then, it was on his bedside, its dog-eared pages and penciled notes assuring her the book was a reliable reflection of a life with which he identified.

She stepped to his desk, where school textbooks had been replaced by novels in a neat row. She smiled at *The Maltese Falcon* and frowned at *Slaughterhouse Five,* and her eyes opened wide at *Lolita* and *Tropic of Cancer* and *Lady Chatterley's Lover*—strange bedfellows, indeed. And then she smiled again at *Gatsby* and *Pride and Prejudice,* but wrinkled her brow at *A Fan's Notes* by an author she hadn't read but had heard about. And, when she picked up *The Fire Next Time* and turned to dog eared pages and found underscores and margin notes, she nodded and grinned. "Oh my, he's been paying attention," she said in a whisper.

There was a handful of titles near the front of the desk that he appeared to be reading now: *Siddhartha, On the Road,* and, on top, *Rabbit Run,* open in the middle, spine up. She flushed, thinking of her road trip to see Lenny when she felt like Rabbit Angstrom on the run. Was it possible that she'd sensed her son reading this novel? That he'd transmitted unconscious thoughts to her across the ether world, that he had the same access to another dimension that she so often fell into?

On the floor next to the desk, she found the new copy of *Slouching Toward Bethlehem* she'd given him, but the spine was not yet cracked. She began to skim it, realizing that the other three titles were evidence of his recent vague ruminations about hitting the trail, as he'd put it, especially to dreamy California. *California Dreamin'.* She could hear the repetitive chorus of that song—four-part harmony, with the big woman on top. An anthem for Jade's age. She looked down at *Slouching Toward Bethlehem* and was surprised to see the book trembling in her hand. His escape plans were not just brewing; they were imminent.

She found a pen and underscored a few paragraphs in Didion's book, placed a ripped paper at the top of each annotated page, and then, on a blank sheet torn from a school tablet, she scribbled a message encouraging him to read those sections. *"Please note, Seamus: The Summer of Love is over. Just ask Joan. And if you don't believe her, go ask Alice."*

It's too late, she thought, as she set the note on the book. You can leave a warning, even a glib attempt to understand his generation, but it's too late. Jade will be what he can be, without her. All she can do now is free him from the grasp of The Interloper, the jaws of that piranha who devoured her vibrant young life and would do the same to Jade—unless she stopped the predator cold.

Down in The Grotto, she looked around at her shrine and wondered if Tamara would reappear in her daydreams now that she knew her in the real world. Perhaps Tamara had cured her of those daydreams altogether. Had she also cured her of her supplication, her erstwhile devotion to the painted clay replicas of people from a distant time and place that now, in the bright sober light of a high summer day, seemed fanciful, if not farcical?

Still, the power of prayer in her weakened states lurked in the stale air, and she forced herself to turn away from its beckoning. Averting her eyes from the faces of the Blessed Mother and her gallery of saintly onlookers, she tossed bedsheets over the Virgin and a few of the larger statues, and turned the smaller ones to face the walls.

She glanced at the piano, sighing at the soiled caved-in keys. She sat heavily on the bench and held her hands over the keyboard. But she couldn't do it. The pure sound and feel of the Steinway, still so richly redolent in the fine nerves of her fingers, would be erased.

At the Chevy, she placed her New York shopping bags in the trunk and grabbed her shoulder purse and a leather satchel. In the front seat, she stashed the pistol in the false bottom of the purse alongside her remaining stacks of cash. She headed up to the Sheldon library to clear out her desk and visit with Helen one more time.

At four-thirty, she sat on the bed in her room at the hotel in Telford and called Wally to ask him if she could use his office in the diner to meet Jade the next day, sometime after closing time, suggesting two o'clock. Wally was excited to hear from her. "Oh, I cannot wait to see you—*both* of you," he exclaimed, palpable joy in his voice. "But, of course, I will give you your privacy, my dear," he promised. "I will only stay a few minutes. You stay as long as you like. With your son."

Alice ordered a sandwich and salad from room service and then called Dell. She was surprised not only to find him in the office, but to hear his voice right away.

"Why are you answering your own phone, Dell? Have you been demoted? And what are you doing at work on a Saturday in mid-July? New York is dead! Look out your window, the streets are empty! Executives like you are out on the Island or in Cannes, or golfing in Scotland or sipping mint juleps with their mistresses on yachts in The Caribbean. Did they can you, Dell? Is that why you're there? Collecting all your stuff in a cardboard box and using Saturday to avoid the march of shame?"

Dell laughed his Brahmin haw-haw. She could imagine his jaw jutting, his bottom lip curling over his lower teeth.

"It's the moon shot," he explained, an unexpected lift in his voice. "We're all here, building background for the Wednesday launch and the landing three or four days later, God willing. It's a world event, Issa! Especially for *my* team. *The Times* is planning a special section, and we're driving it. It's the big break we've all been waiting for—all of us as a nation, I mean. An about face in the long dark trudge for America over these last few years. We're going to kick the Soviets' backsides, Issa! They've had us in their space race rearview mirror since '57, for God's sake."

"My goodness, Dellworth," Alice said, kicking in her debutante tone, "are you wearing stars and stripes boxer shorts? Such an enthusiast you are. I thought of you as the steely journalist type, but who knew the gung-ho prep boy was lurking beneath your suit of armor." Then, she said in as flat a British tone as she could muster without laughing, "Hip hip hooray."

Dell chuckled a little at Alice, and at himself, and his tone deflated a bit. "Yes, I suppose I'm a little excited," he said. "And of course, it's always exciting to hear *your* voice, Issa."

"Oh please, Dell," Alice deadpanned. "I'm hardly a match for a giant flying phallus, all pumped up with exploding fuel and anti-commie hyperbole. Here's hoping it stays erect all the way up there."

This time Dell couldn't restrain himself. His laughter erupted in a roar.

Alice let him calm down. "OK, enough dirty talk for now," she said, her tone icy. "Listen. I've turned up that elusive source we talked about. I just got back from a visit to my hiding place in this dark valley—The Cairstine Morgan Library and Art Gallery in the little borough of Sheldon, just up the road from Ebonton. It's been a great source of new reading material for me here in this heart of darkness, since the librarian and I have become pals, and she orders whatever books I need. Plus, she's been providing me with an office for my writing, such as it is, for the past few years. The library's name was my initial draw to the place. Cairstine Morgan was my grandmother, although she died before I was born. My father built it in honor of his art collector mother, who visited here when she first came to the U.S. with my grandfather and was evidently smitten by that little burg and its once-lovely view of the river and mountains. That was before it was turned into a coal wasteland and the river into an open sewer. Hail, industrialism! Hail, America! Next stop, Dell? The moon, for Chrissake!"

"Go on," he said, chuckling. "You have a point, I presume."

"The place is immaculately kept and has a collection of literature and art that fits with neither little Sheldon nor its inhabitants. So, right from my first visit, I was certain it was privately funded. The librarian resisted my inquiries about the funding source, and so I bided my time, waiting for the right moment, which was today. Helen, the librarian who became my friend, was stunned when I made my lineage claim but, long story short, I went on to prove that I am who I said I was, and she was convinced. She showed me the deed and legal documents. The place is funded by a trust administered by a law firm in Alexandria, Virginia, whose principal is Neal MacInnes. As you will recall, he was my father's ambitious attorney who, at Hafferty's behest, adjusted papa's will in favor of Dennis while the old man lay incapacitated by his second stroke. Papa was barely cool in the ground when MacInnes arranged the sale of my father's five munitions plants, one of which is Macson Munitions in Ebonton. Salvatore Giallo, as you might recall, was the lucky winner in that lottery. MacInnes also set up the legal work to assure the distribution of a percentage of revenue shares from all five operations to Dennis Hafferty as well as to MacInnes himself. In perpetuity.

"The Morgan Library deed and documents revealed my father's intention for the facility to be open to the public, but it specified that Cairstine Morgan would only be identified as a European scholar of the arts who preferred to remain private. Morgan was her maiden name, and her married name—my grandfather's and my father's last name—was not to be associated with the library. Just like grandpa, my father was obsessive about his privacy, and likely didn't want other nonprofits hounding him for donations.

"Evidently, MacInnes and Hafferty decided to keep the trust alive. Who knows why? Guilt? Probably not. They likely didn't want the attention that closing it down might bring, and what's a few thousand a year in expenses to guys hauling in tens of millions?

"MacInnes lives on a gated horsey estate near Manassas, Virginia, but he has an office in downtown Alexandria. I'll give you the address and phone number. He will likely stonewall you until he learns what you've got on him, but how you play your hand is your business, Dell."

There was silence on the other end of the line.

"Dell? Are you still there?"

"Yes, yes, I'm here," Dell said. "Just jotting down a few things. It's quite busy here, Issa. Give me MacInnes's information, and I'll follow up. In fact, why don't you bring it here? Come early next week. Tuesday. We'll have dinner. And we'll watch the launch together on television here with my team on Wednesday morning."

There was a knock at her door. Room service. She made no promises to Dell, but neither did she say no to his invitation. Before she hung up the phone, he'd said, "It will be one of the most important moments in all of history, Issa. And you'll be right here in New York, at the news center of the nation. With me."

At the desk in her room, she pushed aside her partially eaten meal and opened the new hardcover book Helen had presented to her as a special gift: Lillian Helman's memoir, *An Unfinished Woman*. "A parting irony," Helen had said, so proud of her stab at wit and wisdom for the woman she'd believed Alice was—a woman of the world. "It came out in June and was nearly impossible to get," she'd said, looking up at Alice with her face slightly turned away and tears welling in her eyes. "But nothing's impossible for a woman like you, my dear."

At seven o'clock, she went to the Club to see Sam. The Fairhaven room had her thinking too much about Marte, and she needed to vent some of it. And she wanted to see Sam, to thank him one last time for introducing her to Marte, and to tell him that it saved her life at a time when she was about to close the door on it.

The band looked ready to go, but the place was nearly empty; it was too early. Sam was standing with the other guys in the back; he didn't see her come in. The boys were listening to a woman warm up at the microphone. She was tall and lean and young, her voice low and gravelly, but very sexy. Her skin was chalky brown, a mixed-race girl with the entire world's collection of features on her face. Her eyes were huge, and they settled on Alice. The woman turned down her mouth and winked at her, and then she started a jazzy vocal exercise that covered three octaves.

Sam was watching the singer with intensity as his guitarist, Rolly, whispered something to him. Sam nodded and smiled but kept his eyes on the singer. Alice moved to the back of the bar and sat at a table in the corner. He still hadn't noticed her; perhaps it was her changed appearance. But, as she watched the band warm up and then start right in with their set, she noticed Sam's sax was better than she'd ever heard it. His eyes were on fire. His sound was pure joy.

She decided to keep her thoughts to herself and to look for an opening to slip out the side door unseen. Sam wouldn't want to hear her sad song, not now. He'd been so kind to her, but he did not deserve to serve as her giant wailing wall yet again. He needed to be free, and it was clear he'd found out how.

"You didn't fool me this time." It was Luke the bartender, leaning over her table and setting a scotch and soda in front of her. "But I gotta hand it to ya, honey. You're a real chameleon."

She took off her sunglasses and smiled up at him. "You're a detective now, huh, Luke?"

"Yes, ma'am," he said, slumping over and squinting his right eye at her. "Columbo's got nothin' on me."

She forced a smile and pushed the drink away. "Thanks, Luke. You're way too clever for me. But I'm dry now. I'd appreciate a club soda, if you'd be so kind."

She sat back and watched the singer and noticed that the tables had started to fill, and she wondered how she had missed seeing everyone arrive. It was a new crowd, very different from Marte's followers, less like music lovers, more like curious locals. She thought about the times she sat up front, at her own table, just feet from the band, watching Marte, and feeling like she was in a city, not in this small town, maybe even in Paris or Barcelona. Far away from prying eyes, men shadowing her, taking notes for her keeper.

She was watching the singer when she decided, without knowing why, that she'd come to terms with Marte, that she was actually happy for her, back in her own part of the world, safe from this place and its furtive intentions, its unavoidable traps. She knew she could not relive the way they had been together, so natural and comfortable with each other, absent the tension and judgment and competition she'd so often felt with her other companions and lovers, all men.

That's what she'd wanted to tell Sam—that Marte had loved her in a way that was so completely new and different from anyone before her, not just because Marte was not a man, but because the love was mutual, the feelings were shared and listened to, the terrors embraced, the hopelessness forgiven, the music meaningful at last. With men over the years, even with James—the man who'd meant the most to her—the love had been a one-way street—from her to him—and rarely a mutual exchange. With Marte, she felt loved like never before; it was a shared love, not always equal, but always open, the deepest secrets and fears and joys unveiled without shame, without the fear of disparagement or diminution.

She'd wanted to say all that to Sam, but now she knew it was more than he would want to hear. It was obvious to her that he was swept off his feet by his new young talent, and so she smiled at him from afar, pleased that he was in love.

Back in the Chevy, she sat for a while in the parking lot trying to decide whether to go home. How odd it was to think of that place as home. That place where she'd fallen again and again into her darkest self. That house of ambush, that slice of Hell engulfed by suffocating air from those burning hills of culm, the festering darkness even in daylight, the feeling of being endlessly trapped there. It was the prison where The Interloper had captured her and her son—not at all the Purgatory she'd assumed when she'd first arrived. Not a temporary stop for cleansing before being released, but a destiny, a permanent fate, a forever nightmare of punishment for sins she'd been accused of and, over time, had come to believe she was guilty of having committed. It was her fault, all of it.

That's what she'd come to believe after years of the slow but persistent draining of her strength, and then the capture there in Mell Hollow, where the relentless heavy foot of The Interloper pressed on the neck of her soul.

In that place, she saw and heard things she could not reconcile, but only feel her way through. And, in her desperation, she trusted many of those visions and apparitions, some of them terrifying. And she drank and prayed as a way to survive the confinement, as a salve for the ceaseless striping wounds of oppression, a means to numb the guilt she held for making her son stay there with her. But why did she leave him alone there so often? She should have taken him away from there, not abandoned him. She was a bad mother, she knew that.

And then it struck her: Seamus was in charge there. Under his new moniker, Jade. How clean the place was just a few hours ago, and how he had done all the cooking and housework since they'd arrived on Reston Street, and how it must have been peaceful with her gone, and perhaps that's when he would play his records and even try out the piano. And then she'd return, and the place would become a nightmare again for him. It was there and in no other place that she'd had the visions, as if the spirits of her haunted soul were trapped there waiting for her. And she had stayed away from her son and that place so often, because she could be clear and safe elsewhere, even in the least safe places, like the Village in New York or hotels in small cities, where she could heal herself by meeting strangers, sometimes sleeping with them, creating a story about who she could have been. She would drink, but not always, and never too much, and in such places with strangers, she would always try to be her real self, the one she knew deep inside, the one she'd buried. And then she'd return home—not home, but to that wretched little house, where the drinking went far beyond too much and where her son had to witness her madness. She was a bad mother.

She would not return there this night. But she would have to go there soon. That was where she saw it all unravel to the end of the tether. And she could not escape it now.

56
A Kennedy Man

Saturday, July 12, 1969

As the Fleetwood climbed into the mountains east of the valley, the woods thickened along the roadway. A slate gray sky was breaking up above the pines and hemlocks, slips of blue peeking through.

The route to the party took them along winding two-lane roads, sometimes narrowing to a single lane. Hafferty's rules about keeping everything a secret raised a question that baffled Jade. Hafferty had implied that dozens of distinguished men would be in attendance, and that this event happened every few years. With so many participants, along with a group of serving people, a secret like that would be hard to keep. Jade couldn't imagine Hafferty having that much control over who talked about the event.

"I wish Squirrel was invited to this thing," Roland said, as he took a left fork in the road, and the Caddy climbed yet another steep serpentine road. Through the towering treetops, shards of sunlight and flashes of dazzling blue splashed onto the windshield. "We could use his help navigating these guests. Squirrel seems to know everybody on the Who's Who list—something I don't pay attention to at all."

"I don't either," Jade said. "But I think we'll be alright if we just do our jobs and keep out of the way. We're here to make lots of money. Remember?"

"I remember," Roland said. "But that announcement Hafferty called historic makes me think some pretty big hitters will be on hand, not just from Pennsylvania and New York City, but possibly Washington. And as Squirrel used to say to me all the time, knowledge is not only power, it's the key to advantage on unfamiliar turf. He has his wild ups and downs, you know, but the Squirrel also has a special gift. I mean, aside from his sudden rants and sarcastic performances, which are part of his ups. The downs, you don't get to see too often, lucky for you. But his real talents are persistence and strategy. When he wants to find out something, nothing gets in his way. He was my eyes and ears over our four years in high school together. My strategist, my recon guy."

"Reconnaissance? Like a spy?"

Roland glanced at Jade and smirked. "More of a personal advisor," he said, smiling to himself. "He just took on the role all by himself freshman year and kept it up through senior year. He'd actually scout the competition in every sport—baseball, basketball, and football. Kept books on them, drove all over the place by himself, at night, missing school, which didn't bother him, because he still got passing grades. He had a green VW bug back then. For the state championship games, he spent days away from home, all over the state, sleeping in his little car, scouting the potential teams and key players. And the night before every game, he'd spend an hour, sometimes two, going over strategy with me. I'm a pretty good athlete, but I was the best at winning because of the Squirrel. My body was reliable, but he was the one who taught me strategy in competition. Thanks to Squirrel, I could anticipate every good player's strengths and weaknesses. I would not have scored all those points or lead my teams to all those championships without him."

"So, if Squirrel's your close advisor," Jade said, "why won't you heed his advice about Hafferty? He keeps telling you Hafferty can't be trusted, but you just push back on that advice."

Roland hit the brakes and pulled to the side of the road. "We missed a turn." He pulled out the paper Hafferty's tailor had given him and handed it to Jade. "I hope you can read this chicken scratch. Once I turn this thing around, we'll go left at the sign for the train station. After that, let me know if I make a wrong turn." He pulled a U-turn and made a sharp left at the sign for the Ulster Train Station. "Like I said, Squirrel is a great strategist. But when it comes to Hafferty, he lets his emotions get in the way. And that's how Hafferty always wins. He gets you in a lather, and then he owns you. I've known him for a lot longer than I've known Squirrel."

"Bear right up here," Jade said, pointing at another fork in the road.

After a few more turns, they passed a sign that read "Ulster, Founded 1907," just as a train whistle pierced the silence inside the floating Fleetwood. The road pitched downward, winding through two S-curves and past a smattering of small homes and rural shops and then a sprawling stately building high on a hill above the town. As they made the last descent into Ulster, they had a panoramic view—a tiny village nestled among lofty blue mountains. Jade felt like they were descending on a movie set, somewhere in Europe.

When they leveled off on the main street, they saw smoke seeping from the stack of a steam engine on their right. Above the cluster of storefronts on the main street, the Ulster station's upward sweeping roofline and cupola were dwarfed by the behemoth black steam engine. At a crossroads stop sign with a full view of the station platform, Roland pointed to a large group of well-dressed men heading toward several shiny new vans at the end of the platform.

"Early arrivals from New York," he said. "Probably headed to the big hotel and a round of golf before the party."

About twenty more people emerged from the last two cars of the short passenger train.

"There's our caste system in full view, Mr. Flynn. First class gets out first, and the commoners last—out the ass end of the train. Those folks right there? They're headed to the same place we are. Our fellow servants. Lots of Brown and Black faces, mostly young, some very pretty White girls, all with their little day bags." He pointed to a school bus at the far end of the small station. "No fancy vans for them." He gave Jade a toothy smile. "Looks like you might be the only White boy in our group, Flynn. Welcome to my world, mister odd man out."

As they left the station behind, they passed the Ulster General Store, a tiny clapboard church with an equally tiny steeple, and then a two-story hotel, The Ulster Inn. More movie set pieces, Jade thought. "Is that where they'll stay tonight?" he asked.

"Maybe," Roland said. "Looks small and shabby enough for them. Probably a dozen of them will stay there—the ones on clean up duty. They sure won't be staying at that big place we passed back there on the hill. That's where those vans are headed. The Starlight Inn and Resort, rich White people only, except for the help, of course. Fancy guest quarters for friends of the guys who own the handful of hidden estates around here. This whole town and train station were built by the man who used to own Hafferty's estate, the biggest of all at more than a thousand acres, including three reservoirs. I guess the guy needed his own town to keep his help close by and the train station to get himself and his friends back and forth to New York.

"That short train we saw will pull off to the side track, and the engine will decouple and turn around at the roundhouse behind those trees. It'll hook on to the other end of the train for the trip back to the city tonight after the party's over." He turned to Jade. "Dennis Hafferty pulls that kind of weight."

"Pays for a private New York train just for this party?" Jade asked.

"Uh-huh," Roland said, smiling. "He has a helipad up on the estate, too. For super special guests."

As Roland guided the Caddy up a steep road away from the picturesque little village, Jade watched Ulster get smaller until it looked more like an H-O train set. "Who owned Hafferty's estate before he did?" he asked.

"Don't know," Roland said. "Hafferty told me the town and the station were built by his predecessor, but he never mentioned his name and neither did my father. And I was only there twice, for short visits. Last year, I was a guest with my father and the Penn State coach, right before I got the offer to play football there. We had dinner at The Starlight, and Hafferty ran the entire conversation, talking about how great I was on the field, while the maître d', the waiters, the other guests, and even the Black busboy kept staring at me as if I were a giant turd in their midst. Pretty awkward."

Along a high ridge, the Caddy hit a straightaway and picked up speed. "The first time I was at the estate was seven years ago," he said. "I competed in the National Punt Pass and Kick contest in Washington, and, afterward, Hafferty hosted a bunch of politicians at a hotel near the White House. My father and I were the showpiece Negroes on display in our suits and ties and submissive smiles—perfect for a President who wanted to show his support for the *good* Negro, but not the uppity kind causing trouble in the South." He turned to Jade with a smirk, as the car sailed along the ridge. "And no, I did not win the contest. Came in second after a late entry by a big White farm boy from Alabama. Age limit was twelve, but he sure looked twenty-five to me." He chuckled and slowed the car as he negotiated two sharp curves. Then, he picked up speed on another mountaintop straightaway, as Jade looked out over the forest below and the brilliant blue sky soaring above it. He had a flash of absurd wonder that Hafferty pulled enough weight to order perfect weather for this day.

"The politicians," Roland continued, "were all amped up about my father meeting President Kennedy that weekend, thanks to Hafferty, of course. He made sure the photo got published—the brilliant Negro scientist sandwiched by Hafferty and The President. The next day, we took the train from D.C. to New York, where Hafferty put us up at a hotel and hosted a dinner for us and a few New York politicians. More awkward posing for my father and me. Next afternoon, we took the train up here to the mountains, to Hafferty's estate. Another staged dinner for more politicians—local ones, I guess. I noticed that the chauffeur and the butler and all the serving people and the cook—all of them were Black. I was a twelve-year-old kid, and I'd seen *Gone with the Wind*, just like everybody else, so, at dinner, I asked Hafferty, in front of all the men, if this gigantic place of his was a plantation. It was an innocent question, but it caused a big uproar, the men laughing at first, and then Hafferty seeming mad, but he laughed anyway, and then he changed the subject with one of his loud jokey stories, which is what he does when he's in a tight spot.

"The next night, when my father and I were at home, I went to bed early, but before I fell asleep, my father burst into the room and started walloping me with his belt. I'd been half asleep and didn't know what was happening, but he kept screaming how I humiliated him in front of everyone, and he kept hitting me until he made me cry. The next day, he moved me to the other half of our house where Lola lived. I stayed there for six months. He wouldn't talk to me. It was around the time I moved back in with him that your mother started showing up, and then you came along. I'd learned to follow my father's orders by that time, not to speak my mind without his permission."

Jade was silent. He stole a glance at Roland just as the big guy turned to him, smiling. "And that, Mr. Flynn, is my fondest memory of the Hafferty estate. That's when I learned to keep my thoughts to myself, which is what we should do today at the party."

He pointed ahead of them. "There's the estate road." At a wide opening in the trees, a large sign marked the entrance to a passageway through the trees. *"PRIVATE. Security Surveillance. Trespassers Will Be Prosecuted."*

They traveled about a mile over a smooth gravel lane surrounded by a pine forest. At a T at the end of the road, two police cars with their flashers on faced each other, blocking both ways. As the Caddy pulled to a stop, a uniformed cop emerged from each car and in unison they put on their wide-brimmed Mounty style hats and approached the Fleetwood.

"Stateys," Roland said. "I'll do the talking." He pushed the power buttons to lower his and Jade's windows.

The cop at the shotgun window stood with his hands on his hips and stared at Jade. The guy at Roland's window put a hand on his holstered gun and stooped low to look inside the car. "Where d'you think you're goin', boy? And who the fuck did you steal this brand-new Caddy from?"

Roland slowly reached up to the visor for two cards and handed them to the cop. "This is Commissioner Hafferty's car, officer," he said, his voice subdued. "He hired us to work the event at his estate today and he asked me to bring his car here, sir. This is Jade Flynn, my co-worker at the Macson Munitions plant in Ebonton. My name is James Roland Wilson, sir."

"I can read, boy," the cop said, handing the cards back to Roland. "Take the left-hand road here for the servants parking area. You can hike it from there to the house."

"Mr. Hafferty wants his car near the main entrance, officer," Roland said, his tone more supplicating. "So, should I take the right-hand road for that?"

The cop leaned his face into the window frame, his mouth turned down, his yellow teeth in a vice grip. "You take the road I tell you to take," he snarled. "Nigger." He stood up straight, hoisted his gun belt higher onto his vast belly and strolled toward his squad car. It took him five minutes to move it aside, opening access to the left road.

At the end of the gravel road, Roland defied the cop by driving through the area marked "Service and Bus Parking," a grassy clearing where a dozen beat up cars were scattered in loose rows, and then along another tree-lined gravel drive that emerged onto a paved road alongside a massive manicured garden. Around a bend, about a hundred yards ahead of them, the mansion appeared. A castle in the forest. To Jade, it was yet another Hollywood set. Surreal.

"Fuck that fat cracker," Roland snarled, as he pulled within a hundred feet of the mansion and parked the Fleetwood along a stone wall under a huge red maple tree. "I'm leaving it here."

Jade had seen mansions in movies, but he had not expected to feel so small in the presence of a real one. Up close, it was massive, both in scale and in grandeur—more like a museum in a major city than a big house in the woods. Its enormous fieldstone walls stood four stories high, each story twice the normal height. Jade tipped his head back to look at the four stone chimneys rising from a soaring slate roof, surrounded by eight white wooden gables with six tall windows per gable facing the front.

"Almost fifty windows on the top floor alone, and probably more on the back side" he said to himself in quiet awe. He walked toward the front entrance of the mansion and turned around to look at the curved driveway under its long, pillared portico. He was standing on a red carpet stretched over a marble walkway between the covered driveway and the broad stone steps leading to the front porch, which extended across the entire face of the building. The massive carved porch balustrade ran between huge white pillars supporting a roof so high it touched the sky. The windows along the porch extended from the floor to the porch ceiling with gold-trimmed casements, enabling the lower sections to be opened like French doors. In the heart of the lofty main entrance was a fifteen-foot-high carved mahogany double door, its gold fixtures gleaming as if in complement to the soaring sun above.

Jade heard someone yell out, and he turned to see Roland ten feet away on the cobblestone driveway and then a man behind him waving from a distance.

"You two! The Chef's lookin' for you." It was a uniformed guard with a holster, but he wasn't a state cop. "Go around back through the garden," the guard shouted. "You'll see the other workers. But you can't leave that car there. Gotta move it back to the service parking lot."

Roland waved at him and smiled. "It's Mr. Hafferty's car," he called out. "That's where he told me to park it." He turned to Jade and said, "Let's go," and he led the way around the building through the garden. In the back, dozens of young men and women were scurrying about in black shirts and pants, setting up tables with huge centerpieces on a vast lawn under three massive white tents.

"Ah, now here are the rest of my people," Roland said, as he held Jade by the arm to take in the scene. "The early shift." Most of the attendants were dark-skinned. A tall, broad shouldered, bearded, greasy-haired White man wrapped in a dirty apron stood in a ground level doorway and beckoned them with his thick hairy arm.

"You two are on pig duty," the man bellowed as they approached him. His red face was in a scowl, but he seemed to be trying to smile at them. "You ever set up a pig roast?" When Roland and Jade didn't respond, the man opened his big mouth with a sarcastic bark of a laugh. "We're gonna have two of them tonight, ladies, so you're gonna learn fast.

Throw your gear in the gang shower on the left behind the kitchen. The one on the right's for the girls. I'll be at the loading dock waiting for you."

After more than three hours of hauling cases of champagne and booze, and crates of kitchen supplies and sides of beef, setting up the pig roasts, chopping wood for outdoor fireplaces, and dozens of other tasks ordered by the chef, Jade and Roland were told to hit the showers and get dressed in their black and whites. When Roland learned he and Jade were going to be busboys, not waiters, he challenged the chef with a protest. The burly man was as tall as Roland and fifty pounds heavier. He stepped up to meet Roland chin to chin and smiled at him, but his eyes didn't sparkle.

"I'm your payday, son," he said in a deep growl. "Two-fifty a piece. That's a lot of money. Commissioner's special rate for his special boys, I guess. But I'm the one holdin' your cash. And you're gonna work for it. You two do as I say, or there ain't no payday."

Roland took a deep breath, sighed, smirked at the chef, and headed to the gang showers with Jade in tow. "Only girls wait on tables here," the chef shouted after them. "Commissioner's rule. You wanna cut off your dicks and put on black skirts, be my guest. I got a real sharp knife that can make that happen for ya."

In a corner of the cavernous foyer, dressed in their starched white shirts, pressed black pants, and gleaming, uncomfortable patent leather shoes, Jade and Roland watched the girls in black and white open all the porch French doors and start setting up serving stations. The girls were their age, some a little older, and each one more attractive than the next.

"I don't think I'd look quite that good in a mini," Roland said, scratching his chin.

Jade stepped back and gave Roland a once-over. "I don't know about that. You've got a big ass, but I bet you would look pretty good in a pair of those red stilettos."

Roland sputtered a laugh. "Fuck you, Flynn."

They helped the girls with the setup, and then decided to take a quick tour of the mansion, but the place was so huge they only got as far as the main rooms on the first floor. Twenty-foot high intricately painted ceilings, enormous gleaming chandeliers, a field of marble floors in the foyer, and massive oriental rugs over parquet floors in the other rooms. Throughout, there were prodigious paintings of battle scenes and uniformed men in regal poses, gilded molding on walls bordering scenes made of woven tapestry, wood furniture that must have taken years to craft, Romanesque statues on marble pedestals, and even a knight in a coat of arms guarding the foot of the curving sweep of double granite staircases to the upper floors. They wandered in awe from room to room, until they heard the bark of the chef booming through the doors to the upper kitchen. They shrugged at each other as if they were volunteering for the gallows and headed toward the swinging doors.

The kitchen was an orchestra gone mad, a cacophony of chaos. Pots and pans clanging, voices hollering, some singing, others wailing in what sounded like agony. The bombastic voice of the sweaty chef rose above it all, as he stood in the center ring, barking orders and browbeating his kitchen help, throwing pots and pans and utensils at them and anyone else who came within his line of sight. He had transformed from a bossy but sarcastic director into a raging commandant. With a sadistic flair.

But, somehow, he'd missed Roland and Jade standing in the doorway. Roland spun quickly on his heels and bolted, and Jade was right behind him. "Man's insane," Roland said as he headed for the front of the mansion, where the parade of arrivals was commencing. They found an empty drawing room looking out to the front entrance, where they could watch the grand parade. Shiny, dark, secretive cars—Cadillacs, Lincolns, Imperials, and Benzes—drifted up, one by one, under the driveway portico, where uniformed, white-gloved valets opened car doors for tuxedoed middle-aged White men. They looked identical to Jade— confident, well fed, an unmistakable air of self-importance. As more guests arrived, the huge porch bulged with these lookalike, pink-skinned, round-faced men in their funny penguin outfits. And, as each car delivered a new guest, he was greeted by a rising wave of noisy voices that, to Jade, sounded like a cheer. These men were delighted with themselves and each other, and with their exclusive lives.

Within ten minutes, the front porch was rumbling with male voices—sudden shouts and bursts of laughter rising into the bright summer afternoon, as the guests swilled champagne, smoked cigars, and one-upped each other with tall tales. Jade and Roland weaved through the crowd, clearing away empty glasses and maneuvering deftly to avoid distracting the men or jostling the serving girls with their trays of champagne.

As if on cue, the raucous, discordant din came to a sudden halt. Shushing sounds filtered through the crowd like sparks on a wire.

Two small American flags fluttered on opposing front fenders of a silver Rolls Royce as its white-walled tires crunched gravel in a delicate popping sound and then cruised over the cobblestone drive to a soft landing under the portico. The crowd murmured in anticipation, and, when the valet opened the rear door, Jade could see a familiar ringed hand and cufflinked wrist reach out to grab the doorframe. The valet moved toward the opening, but he was chased away by a sharp reprimand from within the car. In a moment, Dennis Hafferty stepped from the limo into the sunlight, held his arms wide, and offered up his signature fluorescent smile to the crowded porch. His dark brown hair was slicked straight back against his small round head, and his cheeks were pinched under the pressure of his grin, his thick horn-rimmed eyeglasses popping in the glare of the summer sun. He wore a gold cummerbund and matching bow tie under his midnight blue tuxedo jacket, a green carnation in his lapel. The crowd of men erupted into a spontaneous cheer. Several of them rushed to the car and, in a moment, a dark-suited mob surrounded Hafferty, and the noisy conversation on the porch renewed with excited energy.

By five in the afternoon, the men began moving out of the dining rooms, through the library and the drawing room and into the ante chambers, where valets assisted the men in changing into casual clothes for outdoor activities. Jade and Roland had gathered discarded plates and drinks for two hours and had listened to bits and pieces of speeches some of the men had given at the formal afternoon dinner. Hafferty had made the final and longest speech, peppered with jokes and clever jabs at the best-known men in the room. He'd provided rhetorical cues for rousing applause for his positions on the war, the economy, jobs, and, especially, references to his influence in Washington that provided financial benefit to every tuxedoed man in the house.

Jade and Roland had stood together in the back of the second dining room as Hafferty brought his oration to a close. His volume had increased with each line as he carried on about patriotism, the fight against Communism, the war on the home front against the corruption of American youth, sexual depravity among the young, drugs infesting major cities.

"We will not have it here, I tell you," he said to chants of approval from the men. "We will not tolerate the anti-war, anti-American heathens and the drug pushers and the morally corrupt at our gates. We will not let them poison our lives, our great valley, our young children, our women— our Christian nation! We will not tolerate their disrespect for the President of the United States of America, their disdain for our American way of life. If they don't like it here in the land of God-given freedom, if they'd prefer to live in huts and eat rice with the Commies in Asia, or freeze to death over cold borscht with the Commies in Russia, well then, we will invite them to do so. *This is America!* Love it or leave it!"

The men leapt to their feet, cheering, pounding the tables, rushing toward Hafferty. He stepped away from the podium and got swallowed up in a sea of disciples and adherents, devotees and admirers, hangers-on and friends-for-the-moment.

But there'd been nothing in his speech that appeared to be a crucial announcement, much less an historic one, and Roland and Jade agreed that they had either missed it somehow, or that Hafferty had changed his mind.

After escaping from their tuxedos, the men gathered outside, some under the huge tents, others on the bocce courts and further out on the driving range, where attendants dressed in white assisted the men with golfing gear. Drinks flowed throughout, sweets and delicacies and cigars and cigarettes were proffered by the young serving women. Poker games formed at some of the tables under the tents, and soon cigars were alight everywhere. As a group of musicians began playing Big Band sounds under the far edge of the last tent, Jade looked up at the cloudless sky and shrugged in awe. Just a few weeks past summer solstice, the day was promising to stay bright for several more hours, a fitting endorsement of this event that Hafferty had described in his speech as a day designed by Almighty God especially for them.

Jade couldn't help noticing that the dinner waitresses now serving under the tents had changed from black and white to tank tops and miniskirts, but still in high heels. He saw one of them stumble as she struggled to walk in the grass with her drink tray. As he worked through the tables picking up empties and lighting a few cigars for the men, he made his way to the perimeter of the tents and looked out at the rolling blue-green mountain tops and, below them, the men at the golf range and the bocce courts, and, in the foreground, a massive manicured lawn and a huge fountain with stone cupids spewing water streams and surrounded by dozens of blooming floral arrangements. For a moment, he lost awareness of himself and felt he was drifting through a dream. The sounds around him were dissonant and then muffled.

Holding a tray on his shoulder, he turned to look at the back side of the mansion. Among the countless windows, his eyes were drawn to the top floor, where a lone figure stood in the light of the sun, the room behind her in darkness. It was a young girl, perhaps ten years old, with light skin and auburn pigtails falling over her chest to her waist. In the floor to ceiling window, Jade could see that she was wearing tennis whites and clutching something white in her hands at her waist. At first, she seemed to be watching the crowd, but suddenly Jade felt her eyes falling on him, pale and piercing under dark brows.

A hand fell on his shoulder, startling him, and he turned to see Roland at his side. "If Chef sees you spacing out like that, Flynn, he'll cut off your dick and put a skirt on you," Roland said. "What's with you? You look like you've seen a ghost."

Jade blinked at him and turned back toward the fourth-floor window. A man and woman stood there now, the man in a dark suit and red necktie and the woman in a red silk robe to her knees. The colors of their clothing were faded, as were their features, as if the sun were suddenly absent from just that window alone.

"What?" Jade said, turning back to Roland. "Sorry, yeah. I just...I thought I saw—"

"Squirrel's here," Roland said with wide eyes and a big grin. "He's in black and white, just like us. And he told me he's already been upstairs to all floors."

402

"What!" Jade said. "Why? How? I mean...how the hell did he get in?"

Roland spurted a laugh. "He's the Squirrel. Nothing stops him. I told you so. I was pissed when I first saw him, but, like I said before, I wanted him to be here, so...he's here. Like magic. He's already cased the entire mansion, almost slammed into the chef charging out of the kitchen. Upstairs, he saw some of these girls out here when they were getting changed out of their black and whites with the bedroom doors wide open. Said they saw him looking at them, and they just laughed. I think he had to spend some private time in the bathroom after that."

Roland chuckled, and Jade winced and shook away the image. "Where is he now?"

"He's out there at the driving range and the bocce courts, sizing up the more active guests, the gamers and jokers and big dicks who like to wager and toss their money around. And he's already filled me in on some of the big players he's spotted. A federal judge, a few corporate guys, a state senator, two county judges, a D.A., some local business owners, a bunch of lawyers, some doctors, a few mayors, county commissioners, of course, and even the President of Dickson College." He smiled and winked at Jade. "I'll have to tell my father I saw his boss."

A thumping and whirring sound filled the sky above them, and they turned to watch a helicopter descend behind the trees to the south of the driving range. The action at the range and the bocce courts stopped, and the men turned in unison toward the landing scene behind the trees, as if they were witnessing a miracle. As the roar of the helicopter settled to a distant whistling, Roland turned to Jade and nodded.

"Here come the heavies," he said. "I don't think we missed Hafferty's historic announcement."

They made their way to their spot in the drawing room, just as Hafferty's Rolls pulled up under the front portico. When the valets opened the rear doors, three men in casual attire emerged. They were highly polished versions of the rest of the guests—tan faces, Hollywood haircuts, tailored dress shirts, slacks with razor sharp creases, shoes of shining soft leather. The tallest had a rose-red face, a nose like a lightbulb, and a huge wave of white hair rising from his forehead. Each of the men stood with his chin and chest out, casually assessing the mansion as if he were measuring its features against his own.

"Who's dick is bigger?"

Jade and Roland turned around at the familiar voice and the looks on their faces set off a cackle from Squirrel that drew a quick hush from Roland.

"Keep it down!" he hissed. "You *trying* to get caught?"

"Don't worry about me," Squirrel said, as he jostled between Roland and Jade to watch the three special guests make their way toward the front door. "The only guys who could recognize me are Hafferty and Jensen. And I know right where they are at all times, believe me. Everyone else? I know who a lot of them are, but they wouldn't know me or even look at me if they had a gun to their fat heads. I'm invisible to them, just like you two. Or at least you, Jade. Roland, you're famous, so yes, you'd better steer clear of us two lower beings."

Roland sneered at him, and then held up his hand. "Wait, you said Jensen's here? Talk about a lower being. He's out of place here."

"I don't think he's here for the entire evening," Squirrel said, as he moved to another window to get a better look at the arrivals shaking hands with Hafferty on the vast front porch. "Hafferty's got him and Detective Marion and a few of his other local tools upstairs in one of the suites waiting for his return. They'll have a meeting, I'm sure of it, and then Hafferty will dispense with them. And I plan on observing that meeting."

Roland raised two hands this time. "No way, Squirrel. You cannot screw this up for us."

"Relax, Ro," Squirrel said as he pulled a curtain aside. "I'm a special agent, remember? I'm an information gatherer. Did a lot of that for you for four years, and no one got hurt. In fact, it worked out pretty well for you. Have a little faith, my brother."

He stepped closer to the window. "Hey, one of those guys is a U.S. Congressman," he said, excitement in his voice. "I've seen his photo in the paper. He's from Boston. Big deal with the Dems." He tapped his finger against his temple. "His name is right at the edge of my scrambled brain."

"Listen, Squirrel," Roland said, grabbing Squirrel's arm and pulling him away from the window. "I'm glad you're here, I really am. But you can't get caught eavesdropping on private meetings. We're here to make money, that's it. If you get caught, we get caught. And everything Hafferty's done to protect us will be out the window."

"Easy, Ro," Squirrel said, prying the big guy's hand from his arm. "I have it all staked out. I won't get caught, I promise you. And I will find out everything we all want to know, rest assured. My hunch is that money will be handed out. Dirty money. But even if that doesn't go down, I know I will witness something important to all of us. If Jensen and Marion are in that meeting, then you know it's about Jensen's brother and Joey Belden, and the fate of that guy, Ismeltz. We need to know if Mutt and Jeff will be getting off or not. And Ismeltz? We know he didn't kill that Raines kid. My gut tells me this is the meeting that will settle it all. And I will be there." He looked back at the window. "They're comin' inside now. Let's get outta here. I'll find you guys later and give you the scoop." He held up his finger, his eyes wild. "And then...I will be attending, in secret, the next meeting. Hafferty and his helicopter pals. That will be the supernova meeting, believe me."

He slipped out of the drawing room before Roland could say another word.

For the next hour, Jade shuffled through the outdoor crowd with his head down, crossing Roland's path a few times, but staying busy. Roland was barely working. A recognizable face among the men, he'd been held up at nearly every table to talk sports. Dressed as a servant, he was in his place; but he was still a local sports hero.

In the kitchen, Jade was snared by the chef and ordered to bus the second and third floors. "But you have to be out of there by six-thirty, asshole," he snarled. "And, if a door is closed, you knock. If no one answers, open it slowly and announce yourself, you understand? And remember: nobody goes upstairs after six-thirty unless I say so. And pick up your pace. This isn't a fucking funeral."

Jade ran into Squirrel on his first pass through the upper floors. He was in one of the suites on the third floor.

"It's goin' down in the sitting room next door in thirty minutes," Squirrel said excitedly. He asked Jade to help him test the sound by talking out loud in the sitting room. Squirrel had cut a small hole in the back wall of a hallway utility closet. "It's perfect," he said to Jade when he returned. "You should join me."

"Not on your fucking insane life," Jade said, and Squirrel laughed.

On his second round of the upper floors, Jade entered a bedroom after knocking and then announcing himself. Music and shouting from the party carried into the room through the open windows. He didn't hear the water running until he was standing in the bathroom doorway. Sudden high-pitched laughter startled him, and he struggled to keep the empty glasses and bottles from falling off his tray.

He saw two young women standing naked in a huge, claw-foot tub. A broad-shouldered man with a thick white mustache and bushy black eyebrows sat between them, up to his middle in bubbly water, his hairy flattened breasts resting lazily on top of a massive swollen pink belly. Water ran heavily from the bathtub spout. The woman facing Jade had a hand on her hip and used the other hand to rub suds over the man's mostly bald head while he sat with his eyes closed, an unlit cigar jutting from his thick mouth, and his soapy right hand roaming blindly over the woman's body—her breast, hip, and back side. She was streaked with suds but Jade could see that her pubic area was shaved clean. The other woman had her back to Jade and appeared to be looking at the ceiling, her hands clasped behind her head. She was standing with her legs apart, and Jade could see the man's thick left arm moving up and down between them.

The first woman saw Jade fumbling with the tray and called out to him. "Hey, cutey, nothin' for you to do," she said with a laugh. "We're doin' all the cleaning up here."

"Wha?" the man blurted out and opened his eyes. His cigar fell onto his belly and rolled into the bubbles. He looked directly at Jade. His thorny black eyebrows arched into his soapy forehead and his dark eyes attempted to blink into focus. "What the fuck?!" he hollered as he yanked his hands away from the women's bodies and grabbed the edge of the tub. Jade turned and headed for the bedroom door. "Hey, you!" the man shouted. "Get the hell back here! Hey!"

At six-thirty, Jade went to the kitchen, but the chef wasn't there, so he wandered out to the tents. Many of the men had disappeared indoors, spreading out over the mansion, but a dozen still lingered under the tents, playing cards, shouting at each other, and drinking heavily. The sun had a lot of light left, and a handful of Bocce players persisted on the elevated lawn. The band continued to set a playful mood, moving closer to the Sixties in song selection. When they started on an instrumental version of "Rock Around the Clock," Jade watched as one of the drunken guests grabbed a waitress and tossed her around the small dance floor in what looked more like a wrestling match than a two-step. The young woman was laughing, but twice she nearly fell off her high heels, so violent was her besotted partner.

As Jade bused the card players' tables, he saw more cash than he'd ever seen in one place—twenties, fifties, and hundreds littered each table in careless piles, the men groping their way through the cash and the cards, barking at each other, swilling liquor straight from the bottle, and puffing endlessly on pungent cigars. He recognized one of them. It was Free's father—an older version of the son—tall, broad shoulders, reddish gray hair, freckly skin, bull in a china closet attitude. He was very drunk and shouting something about Commissioner Hafferty. His tone was not convivial.

Jade made another attempt to check in with the chef, and, this time, the big man yelled to him across the kitchen. "Hey, you! Up to the second floor with that trolley of supplies—right over there in front of the service elevator. Just wait at the end of the main corridor on the second floor, and the girls will come to you for supplies. And don't touch them. Don't even look at them. And where the hell is your colored pal?"

Jade shrugged and entered the elevator with his trolley of booze bottles, ice buckets, cocktail tumblers, and linen supplies. He hadn't seen Roland in over an hour. On the second floor, he stepped out of the elevator and was startled by a transformation among the women servers. They were carrying trays of drinks along the corridors, in and out of the conference rooms, bedrooms, and suites, and they were still wearing their miniskirts and heels, but they were nude from the waist up. He rolled his trolley to the end of the second-floor corridor and waited.

As the cocktail waitresses walked up to him one by one and transferred bottles and supplies to their trays, Jade couldn't keep his eyes off their bodies, so close to him. The women were beyond beautiful, and so casual. Their bodies were at ease, but his was not. His breath came in short huffs, and he felt his throat tightening and his loins boiling up. When the trolley was empty, he rolled it back near the elevator and just watched them smiling at him as they minced by, his mouth agape.

"You'll catch flies that way!"

He turned to see one of the women standing in a bedroom doorway a few feet away, holding an empty tray at her side. He recognized her as one of the girls he'd helped earlier with the porch set-ups, but now she was smiling at him, her bare breasts fuller than he'd imagined, her nipples aimed at him like a pair of eyes.

She laughed and shook her breasts at him and then looked down at the front of his pants. She smirked and her eyes widened.

"These are for the big boys, honey," she said, giving her breasts another little shake. "But you'd better get to a *little* boys room and work that thing off before you stain yourself." She turned and sashayed down the hall, lifting her skirt to show him her bare buttocks. "Look all you want, sweet boy," she called out over her shoulder. "But no touching!"

Just before seven, Jade ran into Roland on the terrace floor, at the entrance to the indoor pool. He nodded at the glass door, and Jade peeked in. Girls in bikinis, some of them topless, others completely nude, were dancing to recorded music poolside in a Rockette lineup, while a handful of men watched and hooted from an elevated bar.

"Where the hell have you been?" Jade asked.

Roland looked around and beckoned Jade to follow him. In an empty weight room, he shut the door and pulled his fists out of his pockets and held them up.

"Holy shit," Jade gasped. "You got a couple heads of lettuce there, man."

Roland's smirk grew into a broad smile. "Yeah. *Man,*" he said, dripping with sarcasm. "I gave up busing an hour and a half ago. Just got back from the kitchen. I asked the chef for my money, and he told me I'm getting half because I disappeared, so I told him to keep his lousy two-fifty. I've been out in the golf cottage, back by the helipad. It's more like a golf museum. Place is huge. I was holding court with a bunch of drunken ex-jocks. Damn fools wanted to hear war stories from my glory days. They threw piles of cash on the table and asked me for details. 'Strategy,' they said. How I figured out how to play the big guys from Philly and Pittsburgh in all the championship series. I sure as hell didn't tell them about Squirrel's recon work, so I just made up some bullshit.

And they ate it up. And kept paying for it, chapter by chapter, game by game. There's eight hundred dollars here. These idiots are dripping in cash and don't know what the hell to do with it."

Jade stared at the money and shrugged. "I think they'll have their hands full if they go up to the second floor," he said. "Lots of half-naked girls floating around up there. Good thing you got your money off the table. Beautiful, willing girls probably command a bit more cash than high school sports stories."

Roland just laughed. "You make any tips?"

"Yeah," Jade said, "but nowhere near eight hundred bucks. I'm not giving up my two-fifty."

Roland nodded and smiled. "Let's get upstairs and find Squirrel. I'm bailing out of here as soon as I find out he hasn't been busted. I'll wait for you to get paid by the chef, and we'll meet at the car. You let me know if he holds out on you. I'd love to slam his fat head off a couple cooler doors just for the exercise."

They headed up the backstairs, where they met Squirrel rumbling down from the upper floors. He whooped when he saw them.

"Let's go in the library," he said with a Cheshire grin. "Nobody's reading on a day like today."

They gathered in a corner of the quietest room on the first floor. Jade marveled at the number of shelves along the wall, filled to the ceiling with books. "I'm surprised," he declared. "I never took Hafferty for much of a reader."

"Don't be fooled," Squirrel said. "These books are collecting dust in here. It's all for show, believe me. Hafferty must have bought somebody else's collection."

"No," Roland said. "All these and more belonged to the guy he bought the estate from. I've been told there's another library up in the Presidential Suite."

Jade pulled a thick book from one of the shelves. "*History of the Decline and Fall of the Roman Empire*, Volume One" he announced. "This might be one that Hafferty should study very carefully."

"Nah," Squirrel quipped. "I see six volumes in that tome. He'd have to get somebody to read him the *Cliff Notes*."

He gathered them at a reading table and delivered the updates in a fast-paced whispering voice. He told them he got faked out—the meetings had been switched. The one with Jensen and the others on the third floor was moved to seven-thirty. The helicopter guys' meeting took place in the fourth floor Presidential Suite, and he didn't know about it until it was almost over, but he managed to sneak into a hall closet and listen with a cup against the wall. The men were taking turns talking to someone on the phone, and Hafferty was the last one up.

"He sounded so different from his usual bluster," Squirrel whispered, "saying 'yes sir this and yes sir that.' He was talking with somebody real important. I think it was a Senator."

Squirrel said Hafferty told the caller, "'I accept your challenge, sir, and I'm honored by your request, and I'm ready to get to work.' He said they'd announce it soon after the moon landing, but they'd wait for the green light from the Senator first. He sounded almost like a boy scout. As soon as the meeting ended, I heard Hafferty walking with his guests toward the back elevator in the corridor outside the Presidential Suite. He told one guy to send the advertising contract to his lawyer in Alexandria, a guy named Neal MacInnes.

"And he addressed the other two guys as 'Congressman,' but neither one was Congressman Walsh, our long-time representative and asshole buddy of Hafferty. In fact, I heard lots of muttering today at the golf range and bocce courts about Walsh's conspicuous absence from this event. They said he's never missed one of these parties."

Roland held up his finger. "Listen," he said. There was a muffled rumble in the distance, and then the distinctive sound of the helicopter lifting into the air. "The big boys are out of here. Now, the local knuckleheads can really let their hair down."

Squirrel nodded and held up his own finger. "Yeah, but first some of them have to meet with Hafferty in the third-floor conference room in twenty minutes, and I'm headed there. Ro, I know you want no part of this, but, Jade, if I were you, I'd come along and listen. I already have small holes cut in the closet wall for us to see who's there and hear what they say. You're gonna want to witness this. Don't just take my word for it. You need to hear it all for yourself. Especially the part about Mutt and Jeff. *Your* life and the lives of your mother and your…um…*former* girlfriend are at stake."

Jade looked over at Roland, and the big man sighed and shook his head. "Hafferty told Roland and me he'd take care of those two," Jade said, "and that we don't have to worry about them or anybody else."

Squirrel held up his hands. "Listen. What I just witnessed changes the stakes for Hafferty, and for everybody else, including us. He's in with somebody big on the national stage, and now he has to clean up the messes in his own backyard before he announces whatever he's going to announce. My bet is he'll be running for Walsh's seat. Walsh is a Republican. And the big Dem with the white hair and the senator on the phone? I'm guessing they're after that seat to flip it to the Dems. Hafferty is technically a Democrat, and he has more money than God. And more power, too. At least around here.

"So, I think we're gonna hear just how Hafferty plans to clean up his act, so he can run for Congress, and my hunch is that there will be a purge at Macson, and maybe even City Hall, and City Police, too, and maybe the

County. That means General Patton, Ren Belden, Detective Marion, and the police chief—all of them could be jettisoned. A total purge. Hafferty's up to his eyeballs in stupid underlings taking side deals, and now he's got drugs, prostitution, and murder to deal with in the shadow of a campaign for a seat in the U.S. Congress. Between him and Papa G, they can make all the dopes and grifters disappear fast. We've seen them do that before."

"Joey Belden and Billy Jensen are low men on that totem pole," Jade said. "So what if Hafferty just sets them loose—fires them and then they're out there on their own? Looking for guys like us for payback."

"Could happen," Squirrel said. "That's why we need to witness this meeting, so we'll know how to prepare for what could be big trouble for us. And for your mom and your old girlfriend." He turned to Roland. "What do you say, Ro?"

Roland looked at Squirrel, and then Jade, and then beyond them to the vast shelves of books. His silence seemed an eternity to Jade. Finally, Roland sighed and looked at each of them. "All right," he said. "I know this is a mistake, but I'll go along. We all have our reasons for wanting to know what they have in store for us. Even though I'm not a target for those two punks, you two skinny shits could use the help if those assholes are set free. I guess it comes down to the three of us against everybody else. I know I don't seem like one, but I'm a team player."

Squirrel smiled and stood up, his energy suddenly amped. "My man, Roland!" he said, a bit too loudly. "*Mod Squad* is back!" he said, his wild eyes skittering between his pals, his finger pointing first at Roland and then at Jade. "Linc! Pete! We're on! And I'm still ok with being Julie Barnes." He closed his eyes and rubbed his hands on his chest. "Oh, Julie, I still love your mind as much as your body. Honest to gawd I do."

Jade made another trip with the liquor trolley, but this time he just left it in the middle of the second floor and turned back toward the elevator to head up to Squirrel's third floor rendezvous point. As he passed one of the bedroom doors, he heard two women moaning and he stopped. He thought they might be hurt, but then he listened carefully at the door and felt foolish. He was startled by a familiar voice behind him.

"No touching, no listening!"

It was the same girl he'd encountered earlier, but this time she was completely nude, leaning against the frame of an open bedroom door, her hand on a hip, her legs apart, a narrow strip of brown hair on her mons offsetting the pink folds beneath it. "Christ, kid. You keep this up, and your balls are gonna be so blue, they'll either blow up or fall off before the night's over."

Jade took a last look at her body and headed toward the elevator, her laughter echoing down the corridor. He closed the elevator door, took some deep breaths, and conjured a few sad thoughts.

As he got off at the third floor, he looked down the corridor to see three men step into the conference room. Detective Marion, the mayor of Ebonton, and the fat guy with the white mustache and dark eyebrows he'd seen earlier in the bathtub with the naked women. The guy wore thick eyeglasses, but he looked much better with his clothes on.

The three spies were jammed together in a dark hallway supplies closet adjacent to the conference room. They could hear the men talking and laughing as Squirrel held a tiny flashlight on six holes at eye level in the closet wall. Roland had to bend over to look through his set, but Jade's view was nearly perfect. There were eight men plus Hafferty sitting around a huge oblong conference table. He could see Jensen, the fat guy from the bathtub, Marion, the Ebonton mayor, one of Hafferty's fellow Commissioners, and a guy he thought he recognized from newspaper photos as the District Attorney. He couldn't see the faces of the other two.

There were liquor bottles on the table, drinks scattered around, and everyone was smoking a cigar or a cigarette. Evidently, some had been waiting for Hafferty for a while. Hafferty was settling into the biggest chair at the far end, cigarette in hand as he tossed his Benson & Hedges pack and gold lighter in front of him onto the table. Two young women, dark-skinned and naked, started rubbing his shoulders while he talked to the man next to him. A naked White woman accompanied each of the other men at the table, some sitting in their laps, others standing behind them, touching them casually. One woman was perched on the table in front of the fattest man in the group—the bathtub guy. The woman sat back on her elbows, smiling at the fat man, her knees up and apart. Bathtub man had his hands on her calves and was staring at her body. Under his thick mustache, his patchy pink and white tongue wriggled and twitched.

"Fat guy with the drool is a county judge," Squirrel whispered in Jade's ear.

Hafferty was finishing a joke, his booming voice carrying above the others. "And the White guy says, 'First thing I'd do is pull down my pants and take a look at how long my dick was!'"

The room erupted with laughter. Hafferty glowed, his red face bouncing on his excess chin. His neon white teeth filled his round cheeks as he nodded at each of the men. Then, he reached back and put his hand behind the neck of one of the women and yanked her around to sit in his lap. She stumbled on her high heels and fell against him, landing sideways on his legs.

"Jesus Christ, bitch!" he yelled. "Are you drunk?!" He pushed her off him and brushed his hand on his pants, as if she'd left an unwanted imprint. She fell to the floor with a thud. "Great tits, but can't hold her booze," he said to the men nearest to him, and they laughed. The woman stood up and resumed rubbing Hafferty's shoulders, a strain in her smile.

"All right, boys," he announced, his fist hitting the table. "Let's get the business out of the way, and then we'll carry on downstairs with a little more entertainment." He clapped his hands and his voice boomed. "Girls! Get out! Scoot! Make it snappy." The women scurried toward the exit.

He pushed his chair back, stood up, and leaned forward onto the table, putting his weight onto his thick hands, his googly eyes scanning the faces before him.

"I'll get right to the point, gentlemen. Less than an hour ago, I had a meeting with four distinguished men from Washington and agreed to make a change in my life that will affect each and every one of you. You'll find out what that is in a week or so, after the moon landing, but suffice it to say that things will be getting even better in this county and in this entire region, for all of you, and for many more people, as a result of my decision."

The men at the table sat still. All eyes were on Hafferty.

He pushed on his hands and stood up tall, his thick thumbs in his waistband under his bulging belly. "In the meantime, there are certain things that need to change in this valley. Immediately. I'm starting at the county level, and I'll be recommending changes at the city level, as well. A few of you will be affected directly; others will not. All of you will participate.

"I've been in touch with Mr. Giallo, and he's aware of these changes, and he will be conducting some personnel adjustments of his own. He may be contacting some of you. Take his call. I recommend it."

Squirrel's whisper startled Jade. "Take the call, Jade. Take the call." He snorted a muffled laugh and quickly returned to his peepholes.

"As I said," Hafferty continued, "the decision I made will benefit all of you and this region in ways that we've never before enjoyed. More support from Washington, more resources to continue doing the great work we've been doing. But..." He held up his thick bejeweled left hand. "But in order to reap the benefits that I promise will come your way, we need to work together to adjust some of the enterprises in this valley so that we will benefit from the change without hampering our way forward."

He shifted his weight and started walking behind the men at the table. "Specific enterprises will need to come to an end, and other matters will need to be settled. Immediately." He stopped behind the judge's seat and put his hands on the man's large shoulders.

"Judge Albert Lewis. You, my friend, will need to assist me with a few of these operational adjustments. The drug trade in this valley will come to an end. It is threatening our lives and our livelihood by opening our doors to the worst kind of human slime and the heinous crimes that come with them. We cannot end up like the goddamn Bronx or the sewer once known as Philadelphia. Illegal drugs are ruining our cities across the nation, and we will not allow them to fester here any longer. No more!"

He reached in front of the judge and pounded the table, startling Lewis so that the pink jowls under his thick white mustache jiggled like Jell-O.

"The judge will commence *immediately* with a purging of dealers at the street level, as well as those involved in law enforcement, who either look the other way or benefit themselves by dealing seized drugs. Mr. Mayor and Police Chief Haney will assist Judge Lewis in the immediate eradication of both types of drug criminals in our midst."

He pointed at the police chief and Detective Captain Marion and shouted. "It's over! Dirty cops, detectives on the drug take—they're done here! Finished! And if you two cannot make that happen in the next week, I will find replacements for you who can."

He walked around the table and stopped behind Jensen and the man Jade thought was the D.A. "We have another problem that requires immediate action," Hafferty said, his voice calmer now. "We have the very serious matter of a boy found dead in a county reservoir just a few weeks ago. This crime—and it is a crime—is the direct result of what I just talked about. Drugs invading our valley. Cheap marijuana out of Mexico, heroin out of New York, and now cocaine out of wherever the hell it comes from—South America, the Caribbean, whatever."

He put his hands on the D.A.'s shoulders. "And we have a pathetic suspect in custody charged with murdering that boy. But, gentlemen, you know and I know that the guy in jail is innocent of that murder. Just because he's a fag does not mean he's a murderer. I want that man released, Mr. District Attorney. We have the flimsiest of evidence against him—all circumstantial—and you know goddamn well we cannot pin this horrible killing on that man, no matter how perverted he is otherwise." He leaned over next to the D.A. and pointed to the judge. "Fix it, gentlemen. Make it right. Handle it. The newspapers and the television assholes will try to make you look like idiots, but you will persevere. Set that man free."

He lifted his hands from the D.A.'s shoulders and raised them into the air as if he were a preacher reaching for the heavens. "*I know* what killed that boy! And everyone in this room knows it, too! It's the fucking, goddamn drugs being peddled by back door cops that caused this entire mess."

Jade pulled away from the viewing holes and met Squirrel's enlarged eyes inches from his own.

Hafferty's hands were now on Jerry Jensen's shoulders. When Hafferty applied added pressure to his grip, Jensen jumped in his chair. "Mr. Jensen and I will take care of making sure that the men responsible for that boy's death—and there are two of them, in case you all have forgotten—are sent away to a place from which they will never return. And we will put that action into play *tonight*. The boy's death will remain unsolved, but his killers will be banished to a place where they will *never* be heard from again." He patted Jensen's shoulders heavily. "And, Jerry, you really need to do nothing—which is something you're accustomed to doing, of course." Jensen attempted to turn his head, but Hafferty lowered his face next to Jensen's ear. "It will be handled by a much more capable individual. You will just need to keep your goddamn mouth shut and watch from the sidelines. And, if you can't do that, Jerry, because one of those killers is your brother, then let me know now. Because God help you if you try to interfere."

He pushed away from Jensen's frozen face and walked back toward his seat at the head of the table. "Two more matters, gentlemen. And then you can go. Some of you will be invited to rejoin the party. Others will be escorted to your cars so that you can get back to the city and get to the work of solving these matters before the weekend is out."

He stood at his spot and gazed around the table. No one looked back at him. "I need your attention!" He pounded the table with his fist. "Right here! Look in my eyes, goddammit!" he shouted. Everyone at the table looked up at him.

"First matter: war protesters. We will continue to keep them in their places, Mr. Police Chief, and we will be merciless with those who break our laws and harass our citizens and our Macson workers who are giving their lives to support our nation's efforts to keep us safe from Communism." He pounded the table again. "Enforcement! Those limp-wristed college punks will be hounded out of town if they so much as peep about our effort to save southeast Asia and the rest of the world from the fucking Communists. And I've received assurances from the President of Dickson College that his administration will welcome the enforcement of public order by our city police and county sheriffs and their associates—should that be necessary. Those college brats will get plenty of advanced warning from their President's office, and we will spare no offenders, no matter how well connected their daddies are.

"And so, I entreat each of you in positions of enforcing the law to keep your goddamn foot on the necks of these college boy traitors and the outsiders influencing them. No street protests will be tolerated, and no anti-war rhetoric will be uttered without severe consequences. I've got people everywhere, watching and listening. And so should you."

He took a deep breath and suddenly his face erupted with his fluorescent smile. "I have just one more matter, and it is a personal one."

He started to pace again behind the men. "There was much speculation—indeed, some of it outright accusation—about the supposed involvement of a young man I know well—his supposed involvement in the murder of that boy. You all know who I am talking about. His father

414

is a dear friend of mine and a great contributor to science and education in our community."

Hafferty picked up his stride, drawing the men out of their comfortable spots as they strained to see who he would choose to descend on next. Jade took his eyes off the scene for a moment to look at Roland who was staring through his viewing holes, crouched over, his hands on the wall. The light of the room through the peepholes reflected in his eyes and Jade saw them widen in anticipation.

"Because he is a colored boy, it was assumed this young man was bringing drugs into our community. It was assumed he was a Black Power guy because he wore a black beret one Saturday recently. It was assumed he was a car thief because he was a teenage colored boy behind the wheel of a new Cadillac. He was with a White girl, so the rumors went, in that very same Cadillac on that Saturday, which according to some in this room is against the law. He was seen with her in that Caddy coming out of the road to the very same reservoir where the dead body of that boy was found. And so, the rumors mounted while the police were searching for the boy's killer."

He stopped behind the judge and held out his arms and looked at each of the solemn faces around him.

"Roland Wilson was the killer, they said. Druggie. Black Panther. Daring to mix it up with a White girl. Driving a stolen Caddy. Running from the scene of the murder. A killer, they said."

Hafferty marched back to his own chair and held out his arms again. "Do you have any idea what that young man went through just for *living his life*?!" He pounded his fist on the table and the men recoiled. "Do you?!" he shouted.

"Well, I will tell you what I know about Roland Wilson. He hates drugs, never uses them, never sold them. He's a rising star on the Penn State University football team, and he's an excellent student. He drives my black Cadillac because I *ask* him to do so. One of my drivers is injured, and Roland stands in from time to time. The so-called White girl? She's a mulatto! Part islander of some kind. The incident at the reservoir? He went there with the girl and another friend to enjoy nature, for Chrissake. Not to dump a body in the lake. That seedy task was already done nearly a week earlier by our two killers."

As Hafferty glared at Jensen's lowered head, he leaned forward on the table and shouted. "And he's the best goddam worker at Macson Munitions! *Despite* being discriminated against by Mr. Jensen over here and his union pal, Ren Belden, by giving Mr. Wilson just one other worker while other Line supervisors have three!"

He stood over Jensen and waived a pointed finger at the faces around him. "I'll tell you men, once and for all. If I hear *any*body trashing Roland Wilson *or* his father, the consequences will be dire. If any one of you here wants to take issue with either of the Wilsons, you should take it up with me first—right here, right now. Put up or shut up. And, if I hear any more chatter about it coming from this crew or any of the people you're responsible for, *all* of you will be replaced. And *dis*placed. Shipped out! For good!"

He sat down heavily and blew out a long breath, while the men looked at the table or the floor or the wall or the ceiling.

"I didn't want it to get personal here," he said, his voice subdued, "but goddamn it, your people made it personal for me."

Then he shot to his feet and raised his voice even louder. "That kid spent a *week* missing work, *hiding* out, because he thought he was going to be *lynched*, for Chrissake! Your people are *fucking* animals!" He pounded his fist once more. "I'm trying to give this young man a chance at a life and your people—the same goddam people who cheered for him on the football field—*your* people suddenly wanted him arrested for something he *did not do*! And your people wanted it *because he is colored*!"

The room was so silent that Jade thought he could hear one of the men breathing—a wheezy, strained sound. He was sure it was the fat judge.

Hafferty sat down and then broke the silence with a calmer, more matter-of-fact tone. "One more thing," he said, his finger in the air. "In just a few days, we'll begin witnessing the greatest human technological achievement in world history. Our nation, The United States of America, the greatest nation on earth, is launching Apollo 11 on Wednesday, and we will have a man on the moon by this time next weekend."

He stood up again and leaned forward on the table, raising his voice again. "It's about goddam fucking time we celebrate America! Enough of the anti-war *shit*. As Jesus Christ is my witness, there will *always* be a war somewhere, goddammit! We will *always* be at war protecting our sacred democracy, our destiny as designed by God himself! Enough of the anti-war *bull*shit! Enough of the whining and complaining about rights this and rights that. Enough of the drugs and the hippies and the college protesters and the degradation of our American values. Thanks to Almighty God, we're about to beat the sneaky, conniving bastard Soviets in a race they've been winning for too long!"

He pushed his shoulders back and flashed his fluorescent smile and held his arms out wide. "Let's celebrate America for a change, gentlemen!"

The men raised their voices in assent, but Hafferty held up a finger to silence them.

"Starting next Wednesday, I'm sponsoring an ongoing celebration in the County Civic Center, and everyone in the valley is invited to stop by. Food, drinks, games for the kids, entertainment, and I've arranged for fifty televisions to be set up around the center where members of our community can witness history in the making. From Wednesday through Sunday, or whatever day our men land on the moon. We'll be open from nine in the morning through midnight every day, until our American astronauts are standing on the surface of the goddamn *moon*! And *claiming* it for these United States of America!"

He smiled at each of the men and nodded and shrugged his big shoulders at them, holding out his hands. Hesitantly at first, with a few claps, but then in unison the men broke into applause and then cheers. They turned to each other as much in relief as in feigned excitement over the promised event.

"Tell your people, tell your friends, tell your families. We're celebrating America in this county. America is back!"

He raised his hands, and the applause from the eight men increased and they stood up at the table, smiling at Hafferty. Amid the excitement, he shouted, "Meeting adjourned!" and pointed his finger at four men. "Lewis, Haney, Marion, Mitchell—you stay here. The rest of you, go downstairs and outside and enjoy the festivities. And keep your hands off those women!" He let out a burst of laughter, and it caught fire among the men.

"Let's go!" Squirrel said over the mayhem. He turned and opened the closet door a notch to peek out and then pushed it wide and stepped into the hallway. As Roland moved to follow him, Squirrel stopped, and Roland bumped into him, pushing him forward. When Jade emerged, he saw Squirrel fall into the hands of Ronnie. Another man's arm grabbed Roland's shoulder, and Jade turned.

Stanley had Roland's arm twisted up his back as Ronnie grabbed Jade by the collar. In a moment, all three were ushered through a backdoor into a small room adjacent to the conference room. The boys were tossed onto cushioned chairs, and Stanley and Ronnie stood over them.

"Not a fucking word out of any of you," Stanley snarled. "You wait here with Ronnie." He handed Ronnie a pistol. "Wait until Mr. Hafferty is ready for you." He smirked at Jade. "Could be a few days."

As Stanley disappeared through a door to the conference room, Jade got a good look at the side of his face. A red scar ran from his hairline down his temple to his lower jaw. It looked like the wound was repaired by a blind shoemaker.

Five minutes later, Stanley came back and took the pistol from his brother and nodded toward Squirrel. Ronnie picked up Squirrel by an arm and pulled him to the hallway door.

"What the hell, man!" Squirrel hollered. "What are you doing?"

Roland jumped to his feet, took a step and stopped. Stanley held the barrel of the gun to Roland's jaw. Ronnie yanked Squirrel through the hallway exit, muttering, "Say one more word, and I'll break your fuckin' arm."

By the time Hafferty entered the room twenty minutes later, Jade had given up his stare-down contest with Stanley. Not a word had been exchanged, but Jade could taste the venom in the charged air between them.

Hafferty stood in the middle of the small room for half a minute, grinning at Jade and Roland. "Boys," he said finally. "I can't really call you 'men', given your amateurish tactics, so I'll just call you 'boys.'" He turned to Stanley. "Put the weapon away, Stan." He nodded toward the hallway door, and Stanley disappeared.

Hafferty opened the door to his conference room and nodded for Roland and Jade to follow him. They walked through the conference room and a drawing room and then a library. It was the one Roland had referred to, with hundreds more books lining the walls. Finally, they reached a large room with a bar and kitchenette, a baby grand piano and several seating arrangements of furniture. Hafferty gestured to the large leather club chairs adjacent to the bar and kitchenette.

"Can I offer you an adult beverage, boys?" he asked, his hands open at his sides. "Oh, wait, neither of you is an adult yet, am I right?" He smiled at them and reached into the refrigerator. "Let's have a few soda pops, then, boys. Shall we?" He handed them Coca-Cola bottles and settled in the largest chair with his own Coke, gesturing for them to sit.

"Did you really think you were going to get away with spying on my meeting, boys?" he said, flashing his politician's smile. "Or should I reserve that question for your spymaster pal, Mr. Bozak? I don't know what you see in that idiot, Roland. He's so transparent. We had him tracked from the moment he hit the outskirts of Ebonton, up until the moment Ronnie escorted him to his little blue bomb down in the servants' lot. No, I correct myself. We're still tracking him, and we will continue to do so until he reaches that little home up in Sheldon that he shares with his widowed mama." He took a drink from his soda. "Seriously, Roland. There's something wrong with that guy. Couple screws loose, don't you think?"

Roland raised his eyes for the first time since Stanley held the gun to his head. "He has a condition called manic depression," he said, his eyes hard on Hafferty's, his voice sounding more like his professor father's than ever before. "Extreme ups and downs. His father had the same thing. Ended up killing himself. Squirrel tells the story that his father died of cancer, but it's his way of avoiding the subject. Squirrel happens to be my best friend in this valley. Has been for five years. He is excitable, something he cannot help. And he's easily depressed. Often suddenly. But he's very smart and very funny, sometimes silly, and I would trust him with my life more than anyone I know."

Hafferty looked alarmed, even a little hurt. But he recovered quickly, popping his politician smile. "Well, well, Mr. Wilson. Or should I call you

Doctor Wilson *Junior.* My goodness, that's quite a professional analysis, doctor, and what an endorsement," Hafferty exclaimed with an oblique look through his googly lenses. "But it looks like your best friend has put your life in jeopardy today, wouldn't you say, doctor? You joined him in his espionage adventure, and you ended up with Stanley holding a gun in your face."

Roland just stared at Hafferty in silence.

Hafferty stood up abruptly and headed for the bar, reaching to grab a bottle from an upper cabinet. "I'm having a Scotch, gentlemen. And I'll pour one for each of you. Single malt. Straight from my cellar here at my estate. This one's from the late thirties," he said as he held out the bottle for their disinterested inspection. "Never been opened. Drink it if you want to, fellas. Or leave it. Up to you."

In a moment, he set two cut glass tumblers of Scotch on ice on a small table between Jade and Roland and remained standing next to the bar.

"Behavior," Hafferty announced, as if addressing a classroom. "I've given that lecture to each of you on separate occasions." He held up his glass for a toast but neither Jade nor Roland picked up their drinks. "People are predictable, gentlemen, and if you have reliable information on them, your chances of knowing what their next move is…well, your chances are pretty high." He set his drink on the bar and lit up a Benson & Hedges and tossed the cigarette box on the small table.

"Take you two, for instance. Today, Roland spent half of his time using his experience and his wits to make a lot of money from a bunch of drunken wealthy men, telling them what they wanted to hear. That's smart. But it's also a very predictable behavior pattern. My eyes on the party—my guys and my girls—they had no trouble keeping track of you, Roland, starting with your bold entrance, then with your confrontation with the chef, then the flattery of recognition you received when you bussed the tables under the tents, which pattern you then parlayed into a bankroll of dough out in the golf hut."

Roland took a sip from the Scotch and sat back in the soft chair, his eyes on the bar behind Hafferty.

"Then there's you, Mr. Flynn," Hafferty said. "More dedicated to doing the job you were asked to do today, but predictably spacy in the execution. Still lost in your head half the time. And so flummoxed by the girls. My God, boy. You must have some serious seminal back up. You need to get laid more. My girls here—they're just partly naked girls, Mr. Flynn. That's all they are. A few of them are completely naked, yes, but they're just girls. Playthings, really. You can't take them so seriously. If you spend the rest of your life taking women so seriously, son, you'll end up insane." He flashed his smile when Jade looked up at him with caution.

Hafferty forced a laugh and sat down heavily in a third soft leather chair, sighing and reaching for his drink while taking a drag on his cigarette. "Actually," he said, exhaling toward the ceiling, "I'm glad you two heard what I had to say today in those meetings," He waited for Roland to look at him, and he flashed his fluorescent smile. "I promised you I'd take care of those two lame detectives, and you heard what will be happening to them. Just a few minutes ago, I finalized all that in person with the judge, the D.A., the police chief, and our esteemed head detective, Mr. Marion. I've also alerted Mr. Giallo by phone that the terms have been laid out."

He turned to Jade. "You two have nothing to worry about, just as I promised you. And that poor fag, Ismeltz. He'll be back on the street trying to pick up young boys, and maybe he'll get arrested for that in the future, but, right now, I just couldn't see us pinning that murder on him. That was the lazy, sleazy work of Joey and Billy, which I have officially ended today. I think your mother and your mulatto girl, Lucy Melburn, can rest at ease, Jade."

He winked at Jade, but Jade shot back a fierce look, his heart pounding. "That's fine, but Stanley's back, which is even worse," Jade said. "You assured me he would go away. Now he's here. Does that mean the two killers won't really disappear either? No one's safe with them and Stanley on the loose again."

Hafferty held up his thick hand. "Hold on, there, son. Joey Belden and Billy Jensen are not convicted killers, so let's back off using that term. I know I used it in the meeting, but that was part of the moment, a little theater for obvious purposes." He offered his paternal smile to Jade, a rare appearance. "Those two slimes will never be heard from in this valley again, I can assure you. As for Stanley, he's made only a partial recovery. His memory is cloudy at best, most times completely gone. Seems whoever hit him in the head really knocked out a key part of his brain. He doesn't even know who you are."

Jade blanched. "He most definitely does! He wanted to kill me in that little room while we waited for you. I could feel his hate."

Hafferty let out a one-note punch of a laugh. "Stanley hates everyone, son. He gives me that same look when I ask him to pass the salt. But he remembers no one in his past. Barely knows Ronnie, his own brother. Did he say your name? No. Did he say *any*thing other than a few grunted threats? No. Because he's only half there. He can follow directions, but he can barely communicate in more than a few snorts and curses." He paused and took a drag on his Benson & Hedges. "Whoever hit him, Jade, really did some damage. Someday we'll find that guy."

Jade couldn't tell for sure, but he thought he saw a wink in the smoky blue haze behind Hafferty's foggy lens.

420

"And Roland," Hafferty said, turning away from Jade, "I meant every word I said about you in that meeting. You're like a son to me, you know that, don't you?"

Roland gave Hafferty a long look, his eyes stern, his mouth sealed tight.

"And I know I probably made you a little nervous," Hafferty said calmly, "when I said you were a great student and a rising football star at Penn State, since you have no intention of returning there."

Roland's eyes widened. Hafferty drained his Scotch in a huge gulp and stood up and headed to the bar. "I spend a lot of time in Washington, as you know, Roland," he said, switching to his booming voice as he scooped ice into a fresh glass and made a new drink for himself. He looked up at Roland and gave him the high-beam smile. "I even know where the Howard University campus is, believe it or not. And, as for that black beret incident I mentioned in the meeting? Well, I sounded pretty adamant about the absurdity of you as a Black Power guy, but I also know about your interest in the Black Panthers, since you've been to their rallies in the city and in upstate New York, and you've been to their meetings in D.C. But that's entirely your business, Roland."

He sank into his chair with a sigh and stared at Roland. "I will defend you, Roland, until I cannot. And that's the God's honest truth." His smile turned warm for a moment, and then he took another drink. "But I meant what I said about those people taking shots at you and your father. That kind of harassment—whether physical or psychological, whether it's gossip or in your face—will not be tolerated. I've known you all your life, son. You're still family to me, no matter what meetings you attend." He stood up and patted Roland on his knee as he headed back to the bar. "Let's just call you curious, that's all. Roland. Nothing wrong with being curious, is there? So, let's just leave it at that. No harm, no foul."

Roland took another sip from his Scotch and then stared at Hafferty, his full lips in a narrow grip.

Hafferty leaned forward on the bar and looked at both of them. "Boys, I have something I want to tell you that is very exciting for me and presents a tremendous opportunity for you two. I haven't told anyone else, but I need to tell you because, like I said about Roland—you, Jade, are *family* to me. Roland has a great father, but you got left out in that department. A tough hand to be dealt. But I believe we've gotten pretty close, you and I, and I want to make sure you get on the right path. You have great potential. If you can keep your head out of the clouds." He smirked at Jade. "*And* your pecker in your pants!" He let out a burst of laughter, and Jade forced a chuckle.

Hafferty moved to the front of the bar, put down his drink, and settled his thumbs behind the suspenders that were straining to hold back his tumescent middle. He took an exaggerated breath and held it. Jade sensed an oratorical swoon about to burst forth.

"Today, boys…" he announced, his voice filling the huge room. "I mean, gentlemen," he declared, grinning. "Today, gentlemen, I accepted the encouragement, endorsement, and support of Senator Edward 'Ted' Kennedy to run for the United States Congress, representing our fine district. Our good friend, Congressman Walsh has done a fine job for us in Washington, but Senator Kennedy frankly wants *me* in that spot. In part, because I am a Democrat. The Senator wants a Democrat in this seat, not only to strengthen the party, but…and this is just a guess, he didn't say this…but I'm guessing he expects to run for President in '72, and he wants a Democratic Congress on his side.

"The other part is that Congressman Walsh—my dear friend—is a Republican in a district dominated by Democratic voters. That gets in the Senator's craw, I'll tell you. And the other thing is that Walsh is sixty-seven years old, while I'm just forty-one. He has about two good years left in him, while I have at least thirty. Maybe fifty." He smirked and winked at Jade.

"I'm telling you two this, because I want you to join my campaign when it launches in a few weeks. You can quit your Macson jobs immediately, if you want to, and I'll put you on my campaign payroll right away. I need young men like you—smart, capable, hard workers. *Family*.

"We have a lot of organizing to do, and quickly; but I want you two to be a key part of it. I know you both have college plans, but this is an opportunity of a lifetime for you—an experience that will give you a focus for when you do go to college, Jade, and back to college for you, Roland. You'll both be political science guys with a resume and world-class experience to prove it.

"As for the draft, I've got you covered, no worries there. And you'll still get your 2S deferment for college whenever you do go there."

He held out his arms, his drink in one hand, his cigarette in the other. "I know it's a lot to think about, fellas, but I want you to know this: you two men will have your pick of where you want to work and live. You could stay here in my Congressional district and work the home front. Or you could move to Washington with me. We'd have separate apartments, of course, but you'd be close by. Either way, you'd have a first-rate apartment in the Nation's Capital, all expenses paid, and a great start on your own careers."

Jade was stunned. He turned to Roland, who looked lost in thought.

"You don't have to give me your answers now, fellas," Hafferty said. "Just sleep on it and let me know by the middle of the week, Thursday at the latest. I'm moving fast, and once we make the announcement in a week or so, I want to be ready with a core team of players—young guys like you, as well as some other more experienced political people. We already have a New York ad agency lined up and a D.C. communications team. And we have very deep pockets. You'll be operating in a first-class organization."

He moved toward his chair between Roland and Jade and stood, looking from one to the other, smiling at their befuddlement.

"Listen, boys, this part is very important. Look at me." He waved his hands toward his face as he turned to each of them. "No matter what you decide, it is of *paramount* importance that you keep this information to yourselves, especially about Senator Kennedy. He's insisting on hitting hard and fast with a surprise announcement, and I can't afford to disappoint him, if you know what I mean. So, please. Lips are sealed. You were *not* at this event today, you know *nothing* about it, and you have *no* idea what *any*one is talking about, if they ask you about me and my intentions." He made eye contact with each of them. "You got it? You got it?"

Jade turned to Roland again, and, this time, he saw the big guy take in a deep breath and then nod his head. "Got it," he said, but his eyes were elsewhere.

"I got it, too," Jade said. A knot formed instantly in his stomach and tightened with each breath.

Hafferty gestured at the door and led the way, stopping at a desk and picking up two envelopes. He shook his head in apparent disbelief, turned to the boys, handed each of them an envelope and then said, almost to himself, "Who would ever have guessed I'd be a Kennedy man?" He let out a half laugh and held his arms out, his large round face aimed at the ceiling.

"Thanks, fellas, for a good day," he said as he grabbed each of their right hands in turn and shook them. "You worked hard. I told the chef I'd take care of your wages today, so you don't have to go down there to see him. There's two-fifty for each of you in those envelopes, as promised, plus an extra fifty just for the hell of it."

He gave them his fluorescent smile and opened the door to the corridor outside the Presidential Suite. "See ya Thursday, fellas."

Stanley stood opposite the door with his arms crossed. He glared at Roland and Hafferty with the same empty eyes. Then he settled on Jade, and his eyes widened, his nostrils flared, his jaw twitched, and his stingy mouth disappeared into a pucker.

Part Seven

57
Goodbye, Mother

Sunday, July 13, 1969

Jade woke up at the phone ringing down in the kitchen. It was Roland.

"Squirrel never made it home," he said. "His mother told me he's been out late most Saturdays, and sometimes not home until Sunday night. But I didn't tell her he was with us at the estate party. I have a bad feeling about this."

Jade was still in dreamland. He muttered a few "um's" and walked around the kitchen to get his blood flowing. When he turned at the doorway to The Grotto, he was startled by the sheet-covered statues. The Blessed Virgin looked especially haunting, larger than she'd seemed uncovered. Alice had been home, and she must have done something she didn't want her spectral friends to observe.

He finally found his voice. "Didn't Hafferty say someone would follow Squirrel home?"

"Yeah, I tried Hafferty's office and his suite at the Sheeley, but there was no answer," Roland said. "Probably hungover at the mansion."

"Maybe it's like his mother said. He'll come home later today."

Roland sighed heavily. "Yeah. Maybe."

Jade thought of their ride home from the estate. Silence for the entire hour.

"So, what do you make of Hafferty's offer?"

"I don't know, Flynn," Roland said. "Sounds too good to be true. But then…I know Hafferty. He usually gets what he wants."

"Meaning what? That he'll kidnap us and make us work for him in bondage while he's flitting around Washington playing Congressman?"

"Pretty funny, Flynn. What I mean is, he will get elected, and the jobs he's offering us will go to *some*body. I'm just not sure I want it to be me. Wouldn't mind living in D.C., in a rent-free apartment, all expenses covered. But the place would probably be bugged. He knows everything everybody does. Has spies everywhere. His damn behavior monitoring is getting under my skin."

"Same here. But he does seem to have your back. Plus, the deal sounds pretty sweet. Getting out of Macson, for starters, and then getting paid right off the bat before the campaign even begins. To me, D.C. sounds as good as any place at this point."

"I don't know. It messes with my plans but, yeah, it does put me in Washington. And it gives me a shot at Howard. For free. But I still don't know. We have a couple days, and I'm not quitting Macson until I'm absolutely sure about Dennis. Right now, I need to know what happened to Squirrel. I'll keep in touch. Let me know if you hear from him."

In the kitchen, Jade started making breakfast, when he remembered seeing something out of place in his bedroom. He went upstairs and discovered Alice's cryptic note about California. He glanced at the paragraphs she'd underscored in Didion's book. Scathing commentary about delusional young people squandering the Summer of Love's confectionary dream. He thought the last highlighted quote could have been written by Alice. *'Their only proficient vocabulary is in the society's platitudes.'*

He checked her bedroom. Her suitcase and all her cash were missing.

An hour later, the phone rang again. It was Alice. He barely recognized her voice. She sounded beyond tired, but not hungover. There was determination under her muted tone. It was restrained at first, but then urgent, and very clear. After some resistance, he agreed to meet with her at Wally's at two. She told him to use the back entrance.

It was pouring outside. A sudden gust and then a deluge thundered at the walls and windows. He scurried to close the front windows and then stood at the back door screen to let the mist cool his face. He let his mind empty as he gazed into the little patch of backyard, where the soot and smoke washed from the air, and the dry soil erupted in puffs of gray vapor. The old oil drum they'd used as an incinerator—his untrusty sentinel—finally gave up and collapsed under the downpour. An unbidden surge of pleasure rushed through him as he watched the rusted drum wobble, roll, and then settle against the old, jagged, splintered fence. He had a passing urge to walk the streets, to take advantage of this earth and soul cleansing squall. But he just stood in the doorway and breathed, the cool wet air welcome on his lungs, bathing and sanitizing the clogged pathways of his body and mind.

He went upstairs. As he emerged from the bath, he remembered he'd made four hundred forty dollars from the estate bash. He decided to call a cab. As he hung up the phone, the downpour suddenly subsided, as if a dream had ended on a cue from an offstage director.

Wally greeted him at the back door with a bear hug. "She's not here yet, but come in, come in. Yes. You look good." He waved at Jade as he took hurried steps ahead of him toward the office. "Talk to me. It's so good to see you." Wally beamed his gap-toothed grin and slapped Jade's cheek tenderly with his thick gnarled hand, his old gray eyes swimming in sentiment.

The diner was quiet, reminding Jade of the many closing hours he'd spent cleaning up, chatting with Dee and Wally and Wilma. The place smelled like onions and garlic and sweet butter, as always. In the office, Wally told him to sit behind his desk, in his chair, while he took the guest chair. They chatted for nearly an hour, Wally grilling Jade for details of his post-diner life and work. Jade kept it simple, avoiding all the drama. He'd felt purified by the rain squall and did not want to pollute his mind, not yet. But Wally wasn't fooled. He told Jade he knew he'd had more difficulties than he'd expected at Macson, and Jade just nodded and smiled.

"I'll survive," he said, and Wally nodded, too, but not in agreement. It was in resignation.

By three fifteen, Jade decided Alice wasn't going to show up. He stood at the back door with Wally and promised him he'd come back to see him soon.

Suddenly, the outside door opened, nearly knocking them over. Alice gasped as she stepped inside, first apologizing, then blaming the rainstorm. The sky behind her had cleared, framing her shadowed face in a halo of azure and gold. She reached out and put her arms around Jade. He drank in the scent of her sweet perfume and put his hand on the back of her head and held her face close to his neck. Then he pushed her back just enough to look at her, holding her shoulders with his hands, never wanting to let her go.

"You're a redhead now?" he said, his smile glowing at her.

"I call it autumn," she said with a sly grin, lifting her face to look into his eyes.

It occurred to him that he should say, "I love you," but he knew it was something they'd never said to each other. It was understood, he assured himself. It was mutual.

He watched her let Wally make a fuss over her, the love between them familial, a woman with her uncle, or her surrogate father. Wally effused his praise of her appearance—she wore green and purple and gold, colors that gave her eyes luminance and her skin radiance—and then he adjured her to be safe, to be cautious, and she conceded to him with deferential nods and polite smiles, but Jade knew better. Something had changed in her; he could sense it more than know how to identify it. She was in charge now as she escorted Wally out of his own office and then turned to Jade. He sat forward in Wally's chair, anticipating the opening salvo of a challenging lecture, but she just smiled at him, a hint of mischief in her eyes, as she lowered herself onto the edge of the guest chair.

"I love and respect Wally Wolczynski more than any man I've ever known," she said, her chin and eyebrows elevated, her full lips pursed.

"He is my inspiration to keep going. He has the will and strength of a survivor of horrors, who will not be defeated by them." Her green eyes flashed and then settled easy on his. "And the heart of an angel." She lowered her chin, and her eyes widened. "You would do well in your life to always stay in touch with that man."

She relaxed her posture and sat back. She told him she'd learned hours earlier that Dennis Hafferty was going to offer him a job to work on his campaign for the U.S. Congress—Roland, as well. Jobs that might take them to Washington. She said these offers represented a wonderful opportunity, if only they'd been made by an honorable man. She urged him to reject the offer, and she said Roland's father will make the same recommendation.

Jade was stunned. He stumbled his way to a response, and it came out as a near-shout. "Why are you saying this? How did you know? *No one* knows about his plan to run for Congress!"

Her look was stern, her eyes steady on his. "Roland's father knows. And now I do."

Jade shifted in his chair and blinked her away for a moment. Then he felt his heat rise, and he leaned forward, his chin matching hers. "You've known Roland's father for a long time. How? Who is he to you?"

"It's complicated," she said, looking down at her hands as they brushed smooth her lime green slacks. "We were close a long time ago." She picked up her chin again and blinked twice before meeting his eyes. "And estranged for many years. But we are now united on this issue. You cannot accept Hafferty's offer. He is under investigation for serious crimes—corruption, racketeering, influence peddling in the U.S. Government. And his campaign will launch, and then stumble and fall, precipitously. And if you join him, he will take you down with him. Or rather, he will push you off the first cliff that crosses his path. You first, and then Roland. And then everyone else surrounding him. His code is the opposite of that of the captain of a ship. He's first, and everyone else is last."

Jade stood up, shaking, his eyes wild, his heart pounding. "It's too late!" he said, as if it were a victory. "He's already offered us the jobs. Yesterday at his estate."

Alice smirked, unmoved by Jade's premature celebration. "His estate, huh? Such a big, important man."

"Yes, he is. Very. And I will take the job! And Roland will, too. This is the chance of a lifetime for me, Alice. I can get out of this goddamn hell hole and never look back."

She lifted her head and pushed back her shoulders, her eyes fierce, setting him in stone. "You can*not*, Seamus. Your life will be ruined. You will be forever attached to a criminal who will be in federal prison for years to come."

428

Jade leaned across the desk, coming eye to eye with her in his best imitation of her ferocity. "Did Doctor Wilson tell you Roland had already been offered the job?"

"No," she said flatly. "He said Dennis had told him he was going to make the offers at his big party at the estate, and he demanded that James convince Roland to take the offer in order to keep him from quitting Penn State to join a radical political movement."

Jade began pacing around the small room, nodding and smiling to himself. "You know something, Alice. I know a lot more about you than you think I do. More than you ever told me, anyway." He watched her face as he paced. "Dennis Hafferty has kept you alive—*us* alive—for twenty years. All those mysterious cash payments you got from strange men? I didn't catch on for a long time, but I know all about it now. And I want to hear it from *you*. I want you to tell me what you are to Mr. Hafferty. And why you had so much of that cash hidden in your bedroom. And why it all disappeared yesterday, as if you were planning to take off for good this time. Is this your idea of a goodbye meeting with me, Alice? And is all that cash the reason you never really had a job at the Sheldon Library? Because you didn't need it? While I worked after school and on weekends here at the diner since I was twelve, and you were getting thousands of dollars in cash for doing *nothing*?! Why!?"

He stopped circling at Wally's chair, put his hands on the desk and leaned toward her. He looked through her blank stare, her icy indifference, searching for a breach. He knew this time he could win the stare-down contest they'd had so often.

But she didn't blink. So he resumed his prosecutor's pacing.

"Since we moved here, you've been away at least half the time, Alice. Where the hell do you go? And who are you with? And when you're home, instead of telling me what you do out there, you just get drunk and talk to your statues and scare the shit out of me with your visions and your premonitions.

"And now, you want to stop me from getting a good job—*again*, just like you wanted to stop me from working at Macson. You want to stop me from going out on my own, moving away from here. Don't you, Alice?" He slammed the palm of his hand on the desk, startling her from her trance-like gaze. "Why?!"

"I will explain," she said, her tone steady, calm. "But first, you must assure me you will not take that job."

This time, Jade used his fist on the desk. "No! No! No! I *will* take that job! And I don't believe your crap about an investigation. You made that up just to keep me here, tied down to *you*."

"Roland is your brother," she said, locking her wide green eyes onto his. The chin went out again. "He's my son."

Jade sputtered a laugh and pushed away from the desk. "You're insane, dear mother. Do you realize that? You are in*sane*!"

"Dennis Hafferty," she said, raising her voice, "is my stepbrother. I've known him all my life. He is the epitome of evil, Seamus. And he wants to take you away from me...you and Roland..."

"No! No! No! No! No!" Jade shouted. "You are crazy, Alice. Nutso. Coocoo. And I am getting out of this trap you've set for me today. Right now!"

He leaned into her face as he stepped toward the door. "Goodbye, mother. It was weird knowing you."

He flung open the door and nearly bounced off Wally's big chest. Then he plunged through the outside door and began to run.

The rain returned in full force as he ran through center city, his feet plowing through puddles near the bus station, then through a mob of umbrellas on the storefront sidewalk near the scene of the Mustang crash. He sloshed past the turn off to Macson, past the Sheeley Hotel and the train station, and into the neighborhood adjacent to Dickson College. Running, his legs pumping, his face into the rain, his mouth open in a silent scream, his arms flailing as he dodged cars and gusts of wind and walls of water.

By the time he reached Wally's home, his skin was water, and his bones were ice. He climbed the steps in delirium and someone short and blonde peeked out of the second-floor apartment, but he couldn't look at her eyes. In another moment, he was a retching, writhing heap, trembling and crying and muttering at the top of the steps, curled into a fetal ball on the rainbow-colored peace symbol adorning Tamara's welcome mat.

58
Squirrel's Secret Vault

Monday, July 14, 1969

He lay in bed, already at least a half-hour late for work. He hadn't slept much, having rested Sunday at Tamara's and then spending the night at home tossing around on his sweaty sheets, going over what she'd told him.

His recollection of her finding him on her doorstep was vague. He remembered standing naked in her bathroom, not sure why, and then her telling him through the door to put on her robe after his bath. He couldn't remember if she'd helped him out of his clothes, but that thought and the memory of awakening naked later in her bed, the robe on the floor, had fired up his relentless sexual heat, and later, in his own bedroom, the memory launched a long night of battle with sleeplessness.

As he tossed about his bed in the brilliant morning light, he remembered sitting on her back porch in her light blue robe, staring at his clothes drying in the sun on a line that stretched from her porch to a telephone pole in the alley behind Wally's garage. He remembered his embarrassment that she would have washed by hand the red shirt and beige shorts and jockey underpants and socks that dangled three stories above the small yard where Wilma's garden flourished. He remembered that Tamara had served him a meal, but he couldn't recall what it was. And when he reviewed the details of what she told him later in her front room, standing with him at the floor-to-ceiling windows with the rumbling fan at their backs, while they watched the streets of the city dry up in the hot sun, he relented and sat up in his bed, staring at the open window. He remembered arguing with her, and then sitting with her on the couch, his temper mollified by her hand holding his on her knees, her voice like a fresh wave of breathable air at last, explaining what she'd learned from Alice and James, and what he and Roland would need to do. After he reviewed all of this, over and over, sitting up in his bed, he felt the weight of it settle on his eyes, then his shoulders, and he lay down again, and his mind finally shut down. When the alarm went off, he'd swatted at it, knocking it to the floor. He lay awake for a long time just staring at the cracks in his old ceiling.

At work, a new guy was in Roland's place on The Line. He was civil to Jade, didn't reprimand him for being late, and told him Roland would be late as well. An hour later, Roland showed up. They worked side by side in silence. Jade knew Tamara had planned to speak with Roland after Jade had left her apartment, and now he wondered how much she had told Roland, and what he'd planned to do about it. But when Roland arrived, he said nothing to Jade. He just took the iron rod from his replacement and started pulling shells across the moving conveyor belts. Jade was used to Roland's stonewalling, but now he expected at least a fissure, a small opening to a common connection. Tamara's revelations had radically altered his view of his own life, and he was certain it must have done the same for Roland. But there was no sign of it.

At mid-morning break, Jade hit the head and saw that the library mode must have returned to the plant before the morning whistle. There were at least a dozen copies of *The Ebonton Clarion* scattered around the restroom, on the floor in the stalls, and under the sinks, piles of them on the windowsill, peeling into loose sheets and gathering in a mini tornado of hot air in the corner. The front-page stories revealed that Hafferty had already followed through on the demands he'd made at the estate meeting with his local leaders. Two stories shared a banner headline: The Ebonton police and the county sheriff announced a valley-wide crackdown on drugs, and Ralph Ismeltz had been released from prison. The DA declared the evidence against Ismeltz insufficient, but said Ismeltz would remain a prime suspect while the investigation continued. A photo of the DA at a podium was bordered in a thick black band. He was flanked by three stiff-jawed faces: The Ebonton mayor, Police Chief Haney, and Judge Albert Lewis, whose mustachioed mug looked much more sober without a cigar in his maw and bathtub bubbles tickling his heavy jowl.

Below the fold, another banner headline and story announced the launch of Hafferty's Civic Center moon flight celebration. The story was littered with flattering file photos of Hafferty in various scenes around the valley over the years, and a lengthy bold-faced call-out that used a quote from his statement: "Yoakna County has always been the backbone of America. Over the years, our Diamond Valley men have worked with their bare hands to produce the fuel of progress for this great nation. This same breed of Diamond Valley men have fought bravely overseas, time and time again, some making the ultimate sacrifice—all in service to America, history's greatest nation. And as we hail the courage and bravery of our astronauts on their journey, all God-loving people of this region are invited to the Civic Center over the next week to celebrate with me our inevitable space race victory over the Soviets and their sinister socialism. America will prevail, my friends! Because America is back!"

At lunch break, Roland joined Jade at the flagpole base and spoke his first words of the workday. "Jerry Jensen has been replaced by a new guy, and you probably already saw the new guy in Ren Belden's spot," he said. "Our new shop steward." Roland's tone was impassive. He opened his lunch pail, avoiding eye contact with Jade. "The new GM is from an ordnance plant in Tennessee, and Ren's replacement is from another plant in Wisconsin, where he was union steward." He turned to Jade, making eye contact for the first time. His hazel eyes seemed to sparkle, and his mouth hinted at a smile buried inside a grimace. "And, the word is out that Mutt and Jeff have vanished, along with their big brothers. Gone to unknown places."

Jade was uncertain how to respond. He felt lightheaded, in part from lack of sleep, but now from conflicting emotions. He was deeply relieved that the most impending threats to Alice and Lucy and him had been eliminated, but he was astounded once again that Hafferty could make people disappear so easily, and always with impunity. But Wilson seemed to take it in stride, as if he considered these sudden changes just another trick in the bottomless bag of surprises bestowed upon the stricken valley by the master manipulator, the self-declared behavior expert, Commissioner Dennis Hafferty, the valley's tacit ruler. Jade decided to greet Roland's news with a carefully stated positive response, but Roland held up his hand.

432

"Squirrel's still missing," he said. "Didn't show up for work. I called his mother at the break, and she told me to check his old hiding place—an abandoned trolley in the woods a half mile from their house. Hafferty wants his Caddy washed after work, but I'm taking it to Squirrel's trolley first. You with me?"

"In the woods? The Caddy in the woods again? Hafferty'll flip."

"I don't care. I need to find Squirrel. And, if Hafferty won't help me, I will use his car to do so."

After work, en route to the trolley, Jade tried to pry open the conversation that both had avoided so far. He considered dancing around it, and then decided to go right for the heart of it.

"What did you think of what Tamara had to say?"

Roland was stony in his black sunglasses, his jaw twitching, his broad mouth pinched. He shook his head slowly twice. "Can't think about all that right now," he said. "Every time I start to, I see Squirrel's face, his silly grin, and I hear his crazy laugh. He's out there somewhere. He better be alive, that's all I have to say."

They parked the Caddy at the end of a dirt road and walked the rest of the way on foot. The trolley was buried in a copse of scrub trees in what once was a clearing for a spur off the main line, where trolley cars that had broken down were pushed aside for later towing. Now, the old rusting relic was nearly engulfed by nature's revenge. And they found that Squirrel used that cover as camouflage. The trolley wasn't easy to spot, and at closer inspection, Jade and Roland could see that it appeared unworthy of an effort to break in. But, in the event of a persistent intruder, Squirrel had made adjustments to its exterior that made certain the interior was impenetrable.

Roland pounded on the side of the trolley and shouted Squirrel's name. He climbed up onto the roof and stomped on it, screaming for his buddy to answer. "God dammit, Squirrel. If you're in there, you better be alive."

Jade crawled underneath the trolley, through weeds and underbrush, and found a rusty hatch that had been rehabbed with newer hardware. "I found an entrance," he called out to Roland, "but we'd need some heavy tools to open it up. This looks Houdini-proof." He pounded on the hatch and called out for Squirrel. In a moment, Roland was pushing him aside and pounding on the hatch and shouting.

They stood in a sea of weeds and thorn bushes ten feet from the trolley, their hands on their hips, their faces blank as they stared at Squirrel's secret vault. Jade wondered out loud how Squirrel could get air in there.

"Those pipes on top," Roland said. "Squirrel's got something rigged up for ventilation, I guarantee it. He can rig up anything he puts his mad mind to."

"But if he's in there," Jade said, "and he won't let us in, he probably has his reasons. Maybe we should give him his privacy."

"No! He would not do that to me. If he could hear me, he'd open up. I've been there with him when he's down, and he always opens up for me. And no one else."

Roland turned and began to march through the brush and trees toward the path. As Jade started to follow him, he stopped when Roland screamed.

"Fu-u-u-u-u-u-uck!"

He was holding his arms out, his head tilted toward the sky, his big body trembling.

59
Hafferty in the Crosshairs

Tuesday, July 15, 1969

She saw Dell put down his fork without a sound, and she could feel him staring at her as she sampled her dinner tentatively, small bites, her thoughts far away. She glanced at his eyes and saw the moony look. She sighed and set her fork softly on her plate. She was about to conjure up her debutante schtick to quell his longing, but, at the last moment, she relented. He was nearly swooning, his Brahmin shell shattered, his broken heart on his sleeve. He told her he loved her new hair style and color—that it reminded him of her glory days at Barnard. He was so stricken with emotion that she thought he might pass out onto his plate, so she reluctantly put on a broad smile for him. When he reached out to touch her hand across the table, she withdrew hers and grabbed her napkin to dab at the corner of her mouth, where she felt the twinge of a smirk arising.

"You're thinking about the Apollo launch, I'm sure of it," she said, and he sputtered a laugh and pulled back his hand. He used his napkin to cover his embarrassed grin. The passive aggressive Dell was becoming the approach-avoidance Dell, she thought, and then she winked at him, and let her smirk erupt into a full smile.

He gathered his resolve and lifted his chin and began a soliloquy about the moon that first sounded almost giddy, and then he transitioned into a more rational and reflective dissertation about the meaning of the event, but he was still boyishly ebullient, and she knew it had more to do with her than it did the histrionic speech about the damn moon. He seemed to read her thoughts and slipped his hand across the table again and stopped talking. He leaned forward over his dinner, and she knew she had to urgently change course.

"I need to know what progress you've made, Dell," she said, her smile now an inscrutable thin line, neither yielding nor drawing him in.

He took a deep breath and pulled his hand away yet again. Disappointment flashed on his face, but he recovered quickly and shifted to his reporter persona. He told her preliminary phone calls had been made. She asked him who was making the calls.

"Tommy Brackman, a young reporter," Dell said, his eyes trying to sell her now, opening wide to seem convincing, but clearly hiding something. Tommy's a rookie, she thought. "But he's very smart," Dell said, "and very clever. He doesn't back down, and he knows how to make people talk."

He told her Brackman called all five munitions plants inquiring about MacInnes's ties to them. The plant managers played dumb as expected, but Brackman's tactic was all about setting up his call to MacInnes.

"He also called Henry Walsh," Dell said, reaching into his suit jacket pocket for his Raleighs and delicately pushing his dinner plate to the side. "He's not only the Republican congressman Hafferty intends to unseat, but he's a longtime member of the Appropriations Committee." She nodded and pursed her lips, her eyes implying that he should stop wasting her time with the obvious.

Dell caught her inference, lit a cigarette, and then offered the pack to her. She shook her head and resumed poking at her dinner.

"Walsh would not talk directly, so Tommy left separate messages with three of his legislative assistants. First message was that he needed to ask the Congressman about rumors that Hafferty, his longtime supporter, intends to run for his seat. The message for the second L.A. was that he needed to ask Walsh about his role in defense department contracts with ordnance manufacturers in five states, and he named them as well as MacInnes's colleagues in Congress connected to them. Third message was to offer an update he'd uncovered on the defense contracts—that he'd just learned that the same manufacturers have been getting contracts for the entirety of Walsh's tenure—twenty years—and that his would-be opponent, Hafferty, might use the contract controversy against him in the campaign for his seat."

Dell took a long drag on his cigarette and watched with a look of self-satisfaction as she set her fork on her plate and sat back, giving him a nod to continue.

"The messages," Dell said, "will surely have the L.A.'s scrambling to their boss, given that their jobs are in jeopardy if Hafferty wins the seat. Walsh may not be the brightest bulb, but he has a veteran congressman's radar, and he likely knows Kennedy has been fishing in his pond for his replacement, and that Hafferty, a Democrat, is the most obvious choice.

He also likely knows that Hafferty has already started the wheels in motion, but it seems Walsh hasn't yet informed his staff about the threat, so we're counting on Tommy's calls to raise those hackles, which would in turn get us a direct response from Walsh—probably in the form of a threat.

"Meanwhile, Tommy has also made calls to the other four congressmen in whose districts the other munitions plants reside. That should put a little more pressure on Walsh, as well. And, since Walsh must certainly see his fall from power as inevitable in the election of his long-time benefactor and co-conspirator, he'll likely make a move toward us, in either anger or in the hubristic conviction that he can derail Hafferty in time, given that Hafferty is the long-time deal maker behind the scenes for the defense contracts, and that he profits handily from them. On that score, Walsh may have to walk a thin line since he, too, has taken a share of the kickbacks, albeit peanuts compared to Hafferty's and MacInnes's take."

"Interesting," she said, reaching for his Raleighs. Dell stretched his long arm toward her, holding his lighter aflame and waiting for her to lean into it.

He let a small victory smile crawl across his mouth as she exhaled and sat back.

"Go on," she said, offering her best poker face.

Dell picked up his pace, enthusiastic now. "Tommy's also been sniffing around Salvatore Giallo, but he hasn't placed a direct call yet. Tommy's a Brooklyn native, so he knows how to dance around the mob without getting killed. I hope. He's learned from other sources that Giallo is old fashioned insofar as he's been a numbers, prostitution, and demolition guy, now moving away from those traditions into the more lucrative trucking, construction and land acquisitions arenas, but he's strongly opposed to the new money in drugs that his younger New Jersey and New York colleagues are making. He's already abandoned his prostitution game to a slew of local idiots, because he's a fierce bigot and knows hookers and drugs go together, and, to him, drugs mean an influx of Afro-Americans. He's also proficient at "disappearing" people, which has Tommy a little alarmed. As you indicated to me, we may be best off if we just push Giallo into a corner without directly confronting him, such that he'll turn on Hafferty in due course."

She nodded once and took another drag.

"At some point, we'll also want to talk with your sister, the cloistered nun, but, as you'd indicated, we'll need your assistance there."

She nodded again, exhaled toward the ceiling, and offered a smile that implied acquiescence.

"On the local front," he continued, leaning forward and turning his head slightly as if to ward off suspicion, "we haven't made any calls yet, but we will get to the insurance man, Freeman, who wants Hafferty's Commissioner seat, as well as one or two of Hafferty's self-proclaimed adversaries—malcontents he's damaged in his relentless accumulation of power over the years. There must be plenty of those types on the local front to back us up, but right now we're focusing on the big picture—the federal crimes and influence peddling, racketeering, and so forth. For now, we've triggered the alarms for Hafferty's partners, so we'll wait until Hafferty's announcement and the Senator's public endorsement, which we assume will happen simultaneously. We're quite certain it'll happen after the moon landing excitement subsides a bit, but not too long after, as Hafferty will surely want to bathe in the holy waters of jingoism after the successful moon landing and, as it were, the safe and dramatic splash down."

She wasn't entirely sold, but that last remark stirred a chuckle in her that she couldn't hold back. Dell the old Brahmin was pleased with himself.

"Tell me, Dell," she said, exhaling a cloud over his head, "have you considered that Walsh or the other congressmen might get word to Kennedy about your boy Brackman's inquiries, and thereby scare the Senator away from endorsing Hafferty."

Dell was shaking his head, already dismissing her concern before she finished.

"Why would Walsh and the others hand information to Kennedy that incriminates them?" he asked. "It's one thing to derail Hafferty's candidacy, and quite another to blow yourself up in the process."

Alice felt pleased. She hadn't expected him to have made much progress at all, but now it appeared as though he'd been taking her more seriously than she'd suspected. She let the pleasure of the moment sink in and then smiled at him, genuinely, her eyes wide as she bit her lower lip tenderly. For the first time, she felt close to real assurance that her venture might actually work.

Dell was tickled that he'd pleased her. They got drinks—"just this one," she said—and then he walked her to the Waldorf where, at the front door, he took her hand, and she let him. Inside, they turned toward the elevators, and Dell tugged her gently next to the pillar behind a giant floral arrangement and kissed her.

She battled her urges. She was suddenly thrown back twenty years to their rosy romantic encounters, to Dell's passion and his tenderness, the persistence of his need, his hands pressing on her now, the taste of him bringing her back to the long-lost luxury of being desired. She felt the need to have another drink, and she let the swirling in her chest and loins burst through. Deep down, she was flooded with a craving for contact.

She let him kiss her again, and this time she kissed him back. But as she pulled him closer and pushed her body up to meet his, something inside her sent out a different sort of urgency. A call to caution, an awareness of unwanted eyes, a sense that she was making a costly error.

She put her hand behind his neck and pulled him into her kiss, and then abruptly let go, pressing her palms on his chest and pushing back to stand on her own again, to take a deep, tremulous breath, to regain control. He was flustered and confused, his eyes swimming in a sea of dreams. She'd known this look so well so long ago, and she'd wanted then and now to give this man his release, to stop torturing him. But when she felt him resist her separation, she spoke.

"Dell, no," she heard herself say, recalling suddenly how Marte used to tell her to beware at all times, lest a public display bring havoc to their love, even violence.

"Wait, please," she whispered, her breath coming in spurts, as she tried to calm the rush of warmth in her loins and the trembling in her knees. "Not here," she said, pulling farther away, "not now."

She stood back and looked around her. Men were nearby, some in small groups, others alone, and then she saw a couple, a man and woman, looking toward them and smiling.

"Dell," she said, swallowing hard and stiffening her resolve. She put her hands up to warn him not to try to touch again. She wasn't certain yet that she could resist but Marte's voice was there, insistent.

She attempted a smile, but her mouth was trembling as much as her knees. "We should...we should celebrate the moon launch, Dell." She kept her hands up in a plea. "Yes," she said, swallowing hard. "We should not ruin that celebration with emotions. Private feelings."

Dell was breathing heavily, his eyes lost in delirium, but he lifted himself up to his full height and straightened his tie in a nervous gesture of compliance. She could see him trembling, too, and she nodded to him.

"Let's take a breather here," she said, letting out a little laugh. "Please, I need to—"

"Let's get another drink," Dell said, catching a falter in his voice and clearing his throat. "It's right over there. The bar. Come on, Issa. Please. We can celebrate the moon launch in a very special way."

"Wait," she said. "Listen, Dell—"

"Issa, you can't keep putting this off," he said, his voice nearly cracking. "It's meant to be. You and I were meant to be together. You know it's true. It has always been so." He reached for her, but she shook her head and stepped back further.

"Dell, wait." She looked around again, and then turned to him. "Our feelings are going to get in the way of this. It's too big. I cannot...*We* cannot let the enemy win here. Dell, you *know* he will win if he finds out about this. He will use it against us, against *you*." She held up her hands again. "Listen. We...we need to focus on the project, and you on the moon launch. For your job. Let's keep our heads for now. Perhaps later, when—"

Dell's laugh was sheepish, almost mournful. He smiled down at her, his eyes cooling over now.

"I will always love you, Issa," he said, trying to control his mouth from total collapse. "And you will always know that." He nodded and fumbled with his suit jacket and looked around him for the first time. Then he stepped back toward the elevator and pushed the wall button. "Go on upstairs," he said, his voice in command of himself now. "I'll be fine. Get a good night's rest. Come to my office at eight. I'll have danish and coffee and whatever else you want. And then we'll watch the launch. With my team."

She gave him a soft smile and nodded. She was still shaking when he gave a little wave as the elevator doors closed.

She took a long shower and then fell naked into bed. Alone and wondering.

60
No Man in the Moon

Wednesday, July 16, 1969

Jade woke up at 5:15 and checked Alice's room. The bed was undisturbed. He hadn't heard her come in, but he'd hoped she might have slipped upstairs while he was sleeping. He needed to talk with her. His apology would have to wait.

He stood at his alien observation post at the top of the weedy knoll in the empty lot across Reston Street from his house. The sky was still dark in the west, but a wash of gold from the rising sun at his back bathed the great charcoal mantis in a tone that reminded him of Tamara's eyes. He tried to ignore her voice in his head, telling him again about who he really was and why his mother wanted to protect him, not keep him for herself or hold him back from his freedom. He didn't want to deal with that yet. He was still wrestling with her other revelations, the ones that Wilson wasn't willing to talk about.

He looked above him to the moon, still visible in the smoky sky. He tried to see the mythical face on its surface but the burning culm smog left a smear of yellowy gauze over it, the silver sheen tainted with man's waste. There was no face there.

He wondered if the famous face would forever fail to return after men landed there in a few days. He wondered if the moon was prepared for the invasion, since it would naturally follow that more men would go there, and, soon enough, regular flights of human tourists would descend on the lunar surface, digging up moon soil to sell back on earth, perhaps a new form of fuel that would outstrip coal and oil, creating yet another kind of smog. And then they'd start leaving their trash behind on the moon, and then they'd build roads for moon cars, and then munitions plants and military stations from which they could launch attacks on other planets.

It would all start when the astronauts planted a flag there, laying claim to something that was not theirs. He wondered finally if the moon, in reaction to the invasion, might suddenly shift its course and head to another planet to escape the recklessly destructive ways of humans, which must be well known throughout the solar system by now.

Later, when he caught the 15 just in time, he ended up standing three people ahead of Gort, who was wearing sunshades over his aviator glasses—like a baseball player, or more appropriately for this day, like an astronaut. But, since Gort was actually a robot from outer space, perhaps he was allied with the Soviets, and, at precisely the right moment on this morning, Gort would zoom up in midair, miles above the Macson courtyard, take direct aim toward Florida, and send a cosmic ray across the sky to zap Apollo 11 at the precise moment it launched from Cape Canaveral.

At Macson, the mood was boisterous. Before the starting whistle, men arriving in the yard chattered and whooped like schoolboys. The moon launch was being celebrated as if it were the World Series. Jade heard one guy shout, "It's the Yankees versus the Reds!" and the man's cohort hooted with approval. Jade walked past other small groups and heard repeated conversations prompted by the newspaper stories, and he realized these stories and conversations were orchestrated by Dennis Hafferty, the man behind the curtain. There was buzz about the new wave of drug enforcement and jawboning over the new GM and union steward, but the real excitement surrounded the moon launch and the five-day party at the Civic Center. They're lambs, Jade thought.

The 10:30 break whistle blasted off more than an hour early. Workers rushed toward the open doorway to the yard. Jade and Roland were slow to follow, and, by the time they got to the doorway, a large crowd of workers had gathered at the flagpole, where the new GM stood on a small platform holding a bullhorn. A minute later, as the crowd thickened, the GM held up his hand, and the whistle sounded again, this time a short blast. He brought the bullhorn to his face and aimed it in Jade's and Roland's direction.

"Gentlemen, I have great news," the GM announced. "Just a few minutes ago, at zero nine thirty-two, Apollo Eleven launched successfully from Cape Canaveral. She's in the air, men, and on her way to the moon!"

The crowd erupted into cheers, and the men raised their arms to the sky and shook hands and slapped each other on the backs, and the GM was saying something else, but the roar of the crowd drowned him out.

Jade looked up into the sky above the Stars and Stripes, limp at the top of the pole. Gray haze and a low bank of yellowish clouds hovered over the yard. There was no sign of Gort rocketing into the air with his cosmic ray gun.

At lunch break, Roland told Jade he wasn't going outside to eat. He said the flagpole would be taken over by the moon launch revelers. He sat on a small stack of shells on the floor next to The Line and opened his lunch pail. Jade sat near him on another shell stack. Out in the yard, they could see Roland's prediction coming true, as their coworkers gathered around the centerpiece of the courtyard and chatted and shouted and pushed each other, laughing, as if the moonshot World Series was a *fait accompli* in their favor.

Roland's voice was low and flat. "Squirrel's been 'disappeared.' Made to vanish like the Jensen and Belden brothers, and Cheese, and who knows how many others."

"I don't think so, Roland," Jade said. "Not yet. Squirrel's not an easy one to nail down; you know that better than anyone. If he's being held somewhere, he's already figured out how he's going to escape."

"Hafferty better have an answer for me tomorrow after work," Roland said. "If he doesn't, I'm out of here. I will not take his job offer, and I will *not* do this job any longer. I'll find out where Squirrel is on my own."

Near the huge doorway, the loudest of their coworkers were jabbering and shouting, some of them jostling others, picking pretend fights. It was playful and high-spirited, the opposite of the mood at the base of The Line. When one group broke out in a song, Roland and Jade looked at each other. It was an off-key battle anthem of some kind.

"This place is turning into a boy scout camp," Jade said. "We better pick a permanent new spot for lunch from now on. These guys are so charged up, they'll probably spend their lunch every day in a circle around the flag singing 'God Bless America.'"

Roland didn't flinch. He didn't laugh or make a sound. He just stood up and headed for the men's room.

After the whistle, Roland stood on The Line with his head down. Production had slowed, but the conveyor belts continued to roll. That meant they'd be loading shells from the floor. At the sound of the horn, Roland hopped down to the floor, and Jade joined him, and, for the next ninety minutes, they lifted dozens of mortar shells onto the moving belts.

At the afternoon break, Roland said he was leaving for the day. He told Jade to let the foreman know. For a long few minutes working alone, Jade feared they'd send Dimmock to take Roland's place. But it was the guy who'd taken Ren Belden's spot on the honing machine. He was the new union steward, but he said nothing to Jade, just picked up where Roland had left off and pointed when he wanted Jade to take care of a problem.

It was clear to Jade there would be no discussion with Roland about Tamara until Squirrel was found.

61
9:32 a.m. ET

Wednesday, July 16, 1969

Her dream of flying with Marte like great cormorants soaring over the ocean was interrupted by music. She opened her eyes and frowned, looking around the room to get her bearings. She'd set the alarm but hadn't chosen the radio station. This one was playing a popular song she'd heard Jade sing along to on their kitchen radio—*Bad Moon Rising*.

She slapped her palm on the button, and the voice disappeared.

"Oh, God," she muttered, chuckling softly. "These FM Dee Jays think they're so clever."

It was 6:30. The walk to Dell's office would take five minutes. She had time to shower, pack, check out, leave her bag with the valet, and be there before eight. She selected one of her new outfits—a mauve pantsuit, white silk blouse, flats of soft pale leather. Conservative. Business only. She hoped Dell would be disappointed.

But, of course, the resilient Dell nearly swooned again at her arrival, waving from his office door like a boy spying Santa on the roof. She reconsidered her outfit, promising herself next time to wear a nun's habit. Of course, he'd probably tremble over that one, as well.

She strode toward him with her eyes down, walking quickly through the chaos of phones ringing, typewriters clacking, male voices creating a humming baseline that sounded like Gregorian Chant. The image of Tara's face flashed in her vision, the eyes in a trance, the sweet voice giving needed tone to the droning music. She blinked away the vision, but it left her disoriented, and she stopped short of Dell's office.

She could feel every reporter's eyes on her.

Dell embraced her at the office door, and then slowly closed the door behind her. The din of the reporters' pit was reduced to a muffled rumble. He'd embraced her like a lover, not a sister or a colleague. She was not Dell's wife. Marte's voice whispered to her. This was a bad idea.

Dell was acting half his age. He fawned over her, opening the napkin and sailing it down to her lap like a five-star waiter, and then serving her coffee and danish with dramatic gestures, the coffee poured with a bartender's flourish. The only piece missing was the pressed linen towel over his arm. He gave her a little bow and then, with a great sigh, he settled his long frame into his executive leather chair. The coffee's aroma filled her head, and she closed her eyes for a moment and considered telling him about the song that woke her.

"This is such an exciting morning, Issa," he said, barely containing his glee and oblivious to her dark humor, her sudden, inexplicable need to diminish what he wanted to elevate. "Think of it! We're witnessing history here, Issa. The greatest achievement of mankind, perhaps ever! And I'm so delighted you're here with me to experience it together."

"Thank you, Dell," she said, glancing out to the pit to confirm that many eyeballs were still on them. "Perhaps we should open the door."

"Oh, no," he said, his smile turning down, as he cut a piece of danish for himself. "They're used to it. I have guests all the time. Plus, we need a moment of privacy before we go out there. It'll be pandemonium soon enough."

"How will you introduce me to them?" She raised her dark eyebrows at him, and he smiled, and then covered his mouth as he chewed.

He cleared his throat and took a sip from his coffee, and then his Brahmin chin jutted out. "As my girlfriend, of course." He winked at her and grinned, and then turned serious. "You're a family member, Issa, that's all. I don't ever feel the need to explain my guests to my team. They're going to come to their own conclusions anyway. They're reporters, after all."

He announced to them that she was Isobel, and that she was his mother's second cousin. He didn't assign her a last name. "This is her first visit to New York, and she's never visited a big city newsroom before." He turned and smiled at her, his eyes revealing the frailty of his ruse. "Isobel will be joining us for the launch, and I know you're all going to be excited, with good reason. But, gentlemen, please watch your language."

Then he offered an oral editorial about the significance of the event, the recovery of the country from the stranglehold that has gripped everyone and weakened the nation—political strife, declining trust in civic leadership, an endless war in Southeast Asia, street riots, racial hatred, police abuse, sexual rebellion, drugs, student unrest, and the ever-threatening dominance of the USSR over the last decade of the space race.

"But gentlemen…and ladies," he nodded to her, and she quickly canvassed the big room for female faces, finding just two in the back. "This moment in history will be the turning point, the phoenix rising, the moment we've all waited for, when we can exhale, at last, and carry forward the momentum that will redirect this nation's attention toward a promising future. This, above all else, will unite us again as the United States of America."

The room was silent. Some of the reporters stared at Dell, some at her. Others turned to their desks and began working. One of them stood up and turned up the volume on a television, and the rest of the room turned toward it. The phones were silent. She realized that everyone in the country, and possibly around the world, was fixed to the same image. If someone tried to make a phone call, no one would answer.

On the television, Walter Cronkite was narrating a chronology of Apollo missions, while the screen showed the launchpad with a digital countdown clock and an Eastern Time Zone clock superimposed over the Saturn rocket and its small module containing three astronauts waiting for lift off. Cronkite's voice cut through the silence in the newsroom, as he detailed the facts of the scene before the world's eyes: In a moment, the Apollo 11 Saturn V space vehicle would lift off from Cape Canaveral Air Force Station Launch Complex on Merritt Island, Florida, with Astronauts Neil A. Armstrong, Michael Collins and Edwin E. Aldrin Jr. aboard.

She turned to Dell. His face was frozen, his eyes glazed over. He was teetering in a daze. His editorial had bombed. This was a newsroom, she thought, not a locker room. She wondered if her presence had thrown him off, had somehow transformed him from a respected political analyst into a college frat boy conflating principles and chauvinism.

She touched his hand, and he snapped out of his trance. "Let's find some seats and watch this," she said. He followed her as she navigated through the rows of desks to an empty one near the two women in the back. She sat in the side chair and pointed to the desk chair. Dell looked around the room one more time and then slumped into the cushioned chair.

As the countdown hit zero, and the clock read 9:32 ET, the TV screen seemed to shake with the eruption of the rocket. In the moment between the blast off and the sound of Cronkite's voice, she heard what sounded like a squeal emerge from Dell. She looked over at him. A tear was running down his long rosy cheek, and his head was shuddering.

62

Pictures

Jade and Roland marched through the Macson gate and headed up the hill toward center city. When they crossed over Canton Avenue, and Jade pointed out the mangled fire hydrant that had saved his life, Roland was silent. A block later, Jade pointed to the Sheeley Hotel calling it "Hafferty House," but Roland didn't laugh; he just kept walking in the direction of the Civic Center, leading with his jaw. Another block later, Jade decided to tell Roland what he knew about the Civic Center, starting with a brief background on the Judge and Jury at Wally's. Roland picked up his pace and kept marching.

Jade persisted. He recalled the much-ballyhooed grand opening two years earlier, and then gave a summary of The Judge and Jury debate over the dirty details of the renovation project. Self-appointed Judge Red Larkin had repeated his version more often than the others, so it became the version that eventually prevailed, verifiable truth notwithstanding.

The conversion of the sprawling World War II armory from a training facility for troops and a transfer station for arms and military vehicles into a massive performance and event space had started the year before Jade moved to the Black Diamond Valley, but, over the next several years, he had listened to so many arguments and inside scoops that the project had become a farce to Jade and nearly everyone else in the diner, except The Judge and Jury. To them, it was chum for the eager jaws of their conspiracy theorizing. The Judge and Jury debated most often the identity of the so-called "anonymous donor" who'd sponsored the renovation, with Hafferty and Giallo the top two guesses, and Red Larkin declaring, over and over in his redoubtable foghorn voice, that it was Hafferty.

The Judge and Jury took most of the meat for their theories from *The Clarion*, where it had been reported many times that the mystery donor had contributed two million dollars of his own funds to the County, which oversaw the renovation, and the federal government ponied up eight million in grant money, with overruns and plan changes eventually pushing the feds' part to twelve million. When it was revealed by the newspaper after the grand opening that the two million in seed money came back to the County in the form of a low interest federal loan, Judge Red exploded with excitement and made his irrefutable assertion that the donor was Hafferty.

Red's version solidified into accepted truth when it turned out that the sky suite, originally designed for use by community organizations, became Hafferty's second Ebonton office, for his exclusive use, justified by his claim that he wanted to keep the suite in impeccable condition for the community to host certain important out of town guests. Since the finishing date in 1967, the guests so far had been only those invited and hosted by Hafferty.

Judge Red's version found solid ground when Dirk Evans, the popular local TV reporter, was given a tour of the suite by Hafferty. According to Red, Evans was in Hafferty's pocket, which explained why the story ended up as a two-minute puff piece on the illustrious County Commissioner's history of benevolence to the valley, and ended with a fifteen-second quick pan of the inner workings of the sky suite. TV news watchers got their first and only glimpse of the suite with the modest entrance off the glass walkway opening onto a large waiting area with a small bar and then to a sprawling office, a conference room, and men's and women's full bathrooms, the interiors of which were not shown.

According to Red, his inside man told him other astounding features had been left out of the visual tour, including a back exit from the large office onto a private elevator and stairway, two bedrooms with king size beds, a sauna room, a fully stocked bar and barroom, which included two billiard tables, a dart room, and a small stage with nightclub style seating and a drop-down screen for movie viewing. The Jury debated for weeks over the validity of Red's claim, but his repeated assertions converted speculation into fact for anyone who cared to listen to the presentments at Wally's Diner.

Roland remained silent, unmoved by Jade's tale, until they rode up in the Civic Center elevator to the glass enclosed walkway and headed to the sky suite. "Your judge friend?" Roland said. "He was right. I've been here. You'll be stunned when you see this place."

Jade was first stunned by who was standing outside the door to the sky suite. His breath caught in his throat as the man with the slicked-back silver hair turned to them and scowled something about waiting right here for Hafferty. Jade exhaled. It was Ronnie, not Stanley.

The glass-encased walkway gave them a bird's eye view of the carnival atmosphere they'd walked through to get to the elevator. Roland and Jade stood a few feet away from Ronnie in silence, gazing over the enormous space below where hundreds of people weaved among a myriad of moon themed exhibits and carnival rides. They turned around when they heard Dennis Hafferty call to Ronnie from the open doorway behind them. He gave Ronnie instructions for an errand and told him he'd need his key to get back into the suite when he returns. "I'll be in my office in a private meeting with the boys. Not to be interrupted."

Jade met Ronnie's dark eyes as he started toward the elevators. His resemblance to Stanley worked up a knot in Jade's gut, and he clenched his fists as the scowling man passed him.

Roland stood rigid, his back to the glass wall, his eyes glazed over, the muscles in his jaw twitching. Hafferty signaled for Roland and Jade to stand by him as he started bloviating about the spectacle of wonder beneath them. A thirty-foot tall replica of the Apollo 11 stood at one end of the cavernous floor, surrounded by spectators, and, at the other end, an enormous three-dimensional moon floated above the floor with outsized replicas of the lunar module and an astronaut fixed to its side. On the huge stage set up for a ten-piece band, a small local rock band played in front of the big band setup, the sound filling the enormous arena, but slightly muffled by the glass walkway enclosure. Crowds of celebrants wove through open and tented exhibit spaces and game sites like ants swarming on sugar.

Hafferty raised his voice when he started describing the twenty-foot waterfalls on two sides of the arena, with huge fans blowing behind them to cool the air in the arena.

"Ancient Egyptian air conditioning engineering brought to the twentieth century," he proclaimed. "And those spritzing stations you see on the floor? They're all over the place, inside the tents, everywhere. No one is overheated at this incredible event. Look above you."

He pointed to ten huge ceiling fans pushing the cool air down but also adding their own coolant with mists of water that sprayed out of pipes above the fans. "It's a wonder of the world, fellas," he boasted.

At the foot of a towering Ferris wheel that Hafferty called "World's Fair class," the line of people awaiting their turns swirled around the tents and intersected with lines for moon-themed kiddie rides, including a train encircling the entire floor—the passenger cars designed as rocket ships. Men in spacesuits on stilts and wearing rocket ship top hats tossed mini lunar modules to the children. Dozens of young women in sparkling silver bikinis and silver high heels handed out mini American flags from trays around their necks, the spring-loaded rocket ships in their hair bobbing as they dished out the gifts. A half dozen other bikini-clad models wove through the crowds, waving American flags at the tops of long wooden poles. TVs mounted on kiosks throughout the arena played tapes on a loop, showing the launches of previous Apollo spaceships, the blast-off audio rising above the din in a hypnotizing metronomic tempo.

Hafferty pointed out all of these wonders with the boisterous braggadocio of a drunken teenager, oblivious to the fact that Roland and Jade were at first impressed by the scene, but quickly became disinterested, lost in their own thoughts. Roland had one thing on his mind. And Jade lost track of Hafferty's oration when the band broke into a song by The Byrds that had gotten stuck in his head recently: *Mr. Spaceman*. At the refrain, Jade heard his own voice whispering along with the lyrics, begging the spaceman to take him away on his spaceship.

During the warmup conversation in his office, Hafferty's desk phone erupted in a double ring, and he grabbed it. "What'd ya got, Louise," he barked. He held his hand over the receiver and told the boys to wait out in the anteroom, to help themselves to whatever they wanted in the bar. "But don't get too drunk," he said with a wink. "I'll be about ten minutes here. Don't answer the door if anyone knocks. Ronnie has his own key."

As Roland and Jade exited through the office door, Jade heard Hafferty shout into the phone.

"Attorney MacInnes! To what do I owe this great pleasure? How's the missus? How's the circus in DC? Are you still cracking the whip?"

He laughed, and then his voice was muffled by the closed office door. Jade went to the outer door, unlocked it, and checked the glass walkway to be sure Ronnie was gone, then locked the door and ambled over to the bar. "Beer?" he asked Roland. Roland shook his head, looking far away again, absent.

Jade was pouring a club soda into a glass, when he was startled by a bellowing roar from the office. He stepped close to the door and leaned against it to listen to Haffery's end of the phone conversation.

"*The New York Times!* Jesus fucking Christ. What's the reporter's name again? Blackman?

"*Brack*man! What the hell kind of name is that? Never heard of him. Gotta be a Jew.

"What! He called the plants?! Did he say he called Macson, too?

"That's bullshit, I didn't hear a thing from the new guy at Macson. When did he call?

"Jesus Christ, Friday! He could have talked to Jensen. That's not good."

He was silent, listening. Jade looked at Roland, seated near the bar, stoic. But Jade could tell he was listening to the one-sided conversation. It was hard to miss.

"Wait!" Hafferty shouted. "All five congressmen?! That motherfucker! What the hell is this? I'll find out who this Brackman is. Did he call *Walsh*?

"Goddammit, he what? Asked them about *me*? That kike son of a fucking bitch! Who does he work for there?

"Yeah, of course I mean the goddamn *Times*. What's the boss's name?

"Wait, you've got to be kidding me." He let out a boom of laughter. "Dell Cranstone!? What the hell is that limp-wristed princess doing at *The New York Times*?! I thought he'd be gathering moth balls in Boston by now, counting stacks of money for his family."

Jade sat in a chair next to the office door.

"Yes, I do know who he is," Hafferty bellowed, breathing heavily now. Jade figured he was walking back and forth behind his desk. "Long time ago. A spoiled Columbia snot from Boston shipbuilding money who spent a year trying to fuck my sister when she was at Barnard. He's behind this? I'll have his candy ass in a cement suit at the bottom of the goddamn Hudson! The fucking priss. I'm calling Giallo. I'll get back to you."

There was a moment of silence, and then his booming voice again, "Louise, get me Salvatore on the line. Immediately! Tell his girl it's urgent."

Two silent minutes went by before his voice shouted again, "Salvatore! Got a few problems here."

The voice lowered. Jade stood and put his ear to the door but could only hear fragments. Then Hafferty roared again, and Jade pulled away, startled.

"That goddamn *bitch*! That stupid fucking *cunt*! She has stretched her chain too far this time. Goddamn it, we should've cut her off from New York a long time ago. I knew it! Now, she's there sucking her old boyfriend's cock, so he can use his Commie newspaper to fuck me. I'll fucking *kill* her."

There was a crashing sound in the office. Jade and Roland exchanged looks and then Roland shrugged as if to say, who cares?

"Yeah, of course I know that," Hafferty boomed. "You had a guy on her the whole time, didn't you? You got pictures, I hope.

"Oh, Jesus Christ, that's beautiful! How many? What's the best one?" His laugh exploded, startling Jade.

"Oh God, the love clench. In the fucking Waldorf? That's it, that's the winner! Jesus Christ, I can almost hear that song from that sappy movie with that fag Ryan whathisname—you know the song. They play it over and over again on the radio.

"Yeah, that's it." He burst out laughing again.

"Yeah, yeah, Louise has it on all the time, drives me crazy. She goes through a box of Kleenex twice a day." He laughed and muttered something low. Then his foghorn voice erupted again.

"Aw, Sal, this is *beautiful* news. Thank God Almighty in heaven! Listen, we need to act fast. Tell your guy to print up the best ones and use three envelopes. Outside one addressed to Cranstone, and two inside envelopes with all the photos in each one—address one to Brackman and the other to Mrs. Dell Cranstone. Drop it off at his office at *The Times*. Tomorrow at the latest. Have your girl call Louise when it's done. And, Sal, I want copies ASAP. I'd love to see that panty waist's pompous face when he sees his life melt before his eyes.

"No, no. I won't make an appearance, but I'll make sure he knows where it came from. That blueblood cocksucker is gonna pay for this. And so is *she*. I'll take care of her pronto.

"No, no, no! No need for that. I can handle her. I just need those pictures first. I wanna see her lose her mind one last time. Right before I slap her silly and haul her away for good. That double-crossing little *cunt*."

At the door to the outside, someone tried the handle, and Jade quickly sat in the chair. Roland turned to Jade and shook his head. If it was Ronnie, he'd use his key. The handle moved again, and there was a brief muffled conversation and then silence.

Hafferty's voice blasted through the wall again. "Yeah, of course I know who the wife is," Then his voice was too low to hear. Jade assumed he was sitting in his chair again, so he got up, and rested his ear against the door.

"Yeah, right after my sister ditched him," Hafferty said, sputtering a laugh. "Probably a shotgun marriage. Couldn't keep it in his pants after a year of blue balls. She's an uppity bitch from Westchester, groveling after his family money, no doubt, just another greedy cunt in pearls." And then his voice rose again. "Rest assured, Sal, Cranstone's little blue balls will fall right off when he sees those pictures.

"What? No, of course I won't call Walsh! He wouldn't take the call anyway. By now, he's fucking ballistic over my Kennedy thing. The goddamn pussy. He's been sitting down there in DC for twenty years fiddling with his dick and counting the money we give him.

"No, I'm not waiting. I'm going through with everything as planned! This is a once-in-a-lifetime deal for me.

"Fuck *The New York Times*!" he shouted, in his loudest voice so far. "It will be handled. Cranstone will fold. And Ted'll give me the green light within the week. We're all set with Landers in New York and the DC PR guy, whatshisname.

"Yeah, him. We'll be ready as early as Wednesday, but it probably won't happen until Sunday at the earliest.

"No, we're going with local TV first.

"Oh, fuck *The Courier*! Those ungrateful crybabies. They'll have to run it anyway. Above the fold, banner headline. And they'll stoke it and make an advertising fortune on it with their follow up reports and editorials. Guaranteed. They'll milk it for a month. Biggest two stories they'll ever have. It's the one-two punch with the moon landing. Biggest local story together with the biggest national story. In history!

"You said it, Sal. That's right! We're gonna own that goddamn motherfucking town. Just gimme a year down there.

"Yeah, I guarantee it. What?

"Oh, fuck them, too! When it's their turn, I'll work with them. Hell, I'd even move over to their side when the time comes, what difference does it make? Right now, I'm a Democrat. That's all Ted cares about.

"All right, Sal. Let me know when the drop is made. You coming to the Center tonight?"

He laughed heartily. "Of course you won't. I'd be disappointed if you did." He laughed again, and there was a fumbling sound, and then the slam of the phone.

Jade got up and moved toward the bar, just as Hafferty opened the office door.

"Oh Jesus, fellas, I'm sorry," he said, his face red and sweaty and his voice hoarse. "I forgot you were here. Gimme a minute to hit the head and grab a drink, and then I'll be right back, and we'll seal the deal. Come on in and take a seat, and I'll be right there."

When Hafferty started into his pitch to the boys, Jade looked at Roland and saw that he was not on board. Hafferty noticed it, too, and stopped talking. He held out his hands to Roland and shrugged.

Roland's hazel eyes darkened, locking on Hafferty's. "I'm not talking about a new job until you tell me what happened to Squirrel," he said.

Hafferty stood up and went to his bar. "I'm getting a freshener. Anyone else?" He looked up at Jade and Roland. Jade shook his head. "I'll tell you what," Hafferty said, "I'll make you both a Scotch on the rocks, and you can let my twenty-five-year-old single malt melt into the ice like piss, or…you can join me for the best tasting Scotch you'll ever have in your lives." He shuffled quickly around the bar with the drinks and kept talking. "Meanwhile, Roland, I can tell you that your friend, Bozak, was detained for trespassing and is in custody, but he's safe."

"He's in jail?!" Roland fumed, gripping the arms of his chair.

"He *was*," Hafferty said, holding up a drink to Roland, "but not now." Roland was on his feet, his chest out, eyes blazing. Hafferty set the drinks on the desk and held up his palm. "Criminal law is made for two reasons, son. Retribution and deterrence. I have nothing against your friend, even though he's a pain in the ass. But I need to set an example. If not, the other lowlife idiots out there will take advantage of me. I'm out in the boondocks, and if a couple of those redneck dickheads get an idea my estate is an open target, well…you get the idea. Deterrence."

He pushed back his shoulders to meet Roland eye to eye.

Roland was seething. "You've had him all this time?!" he said, his voice rising. "I thought he was *dead*! I thought he *killed* himself. We couldn't get into his hiding place, and the cops wouldn't open it without a warrant. Don't you remember what I told you? His father had the same thing he has, and he *killed* himself!"

"He is not dead, I assure you, Roland," Hafferty said, pushing out his chin and picking up a drink and holding it out. "Take a drink and settle down now. I just found out last night where he is. So give me a goddamn break, son. Now sit down. Please. This'll calm your nerves."

Roland backed away from the desk, but he remained standing in front of his chair. "Where is he?"

Hafferty put Roland's drink back on the desk and offered his paternal smile, nodding and feigning patience. "Your friend's safe, son. He's out of jail now. Just spent the first couple nights there, over in Munsee County. Local sheriff intervened and made the call. It's what he has to do. We got him out, and he's in a comfortable place right now in our own county, safe and well taken care of. Three meals a day, all the television he wants, access to tennis courts, an outdoor pool, a billiards room, even a couple pinball machines…it's a nice set up. And no, he's not at my estate, so don't bother going there."

He threw back his drink in one gulp and sat down in his chair with a huff. "He'll return to work right after we make the announcement. And he will be paid for his time away from Macson." He held up his hand, and then got to his feet again with a grunt and stood at the corner of the desk.

"Look. Roland," he said, his voice softer, paternal again. "I know you care about Bozak, I do." He grabbed his cigarette box and quickly lit up and talked through his exhale. "But he broke the law by trespassing. *And* by eavesdropping on two private highly confidential conversations." He grinned at Roland and Jade and nodded.

"That's right, boys. I know where he was listening from during the first meeting I had with the men from Washington. We had him tagged from the moment he hit the entrance to the estate. And then he dragged you two along with him to spy on the second meeting."

He stepped around the desk and sat on the front corner, taking another drag and huffing the smoke toward the ceiling with a low growl in his throat. He gestured for Roland to sit. Roland remained standing, his hands on his hips, his eyes still burning.

"If you're going to be part of my team, Roland, you'll need to sit down and listen." He smiled and nodded toward the chair, but Roland remained on his feet. "You want to live in D.C., have your own pad, everything paid for? Access to Howard University as a part-time student? Which I will also pay for." He held out his hands and shrugged. "You want all of that—a new life for yourself, no football or school hassles, no more summers under your father's watch, but getting serious in your life as an independent man? If you want all that, you'll sit down and listen to me. If you're going to be a key teammate with us—and I mean that, a key player in my Washington office—you'll hear what I have to say."

Roland glared at Hafferty for a long moment and almost spoke. Then he sat down.

"Thank you, Roland." He turned on a low-beam version of his politician smile. "Your father knows the terms of my offer to you, even the part about Howard. Which, by the way, he is delighted about. His alma mater, as you know." He looked at Jade and then back to Roland. "You'll be second in command of the community outreach team in my office on Capitol Hill, Roland. A *huge* job. And a tremendous responsibility. You'll also be our liaison to the Afro-American community in the District, which is something I know you're interested in—expanding your contact with the coloreds. The *Black* people, I mean. God knows, you've been restricted in that area by living here in our lily-white valley, and I'm very aware of that hardship, son." He took another drag and then pointed the cigarette at Roland.

"Think about it, son. A key job in the nation's capital, all expenses paid, and an opportunity to open doors to the Afro-American community—doors they've never even seen, much less had access to. And you would be the guy in D.C. who would make that happen for them. Dr. King would be proud. It's all yours, son. You are in charge of your own future."

Roland's jaw twitched as he stared at Hafferty. His breathing had subsided, but he was still stiff-lipped. "I'd like to see Squirrel," he said. "I want to be sure he's ok."

Hafferty huffed and shook his head. "You're good, you know that?" He smiled—it was his rare genuine smile. "That's why I want you on my team, Roland. You are tough. You won't be put off. You have drive and purpose and principles." He nodded and broadened his smile, the fluorescence returning.

"Consider it done. I'll make arrangements for you to visit your friend. Of course, you must not tell him anything about this deal, and you must not tell anyone, even Jade here, where your friend is being held."

Roland looked at Jade and gave him one nod.

Hafferty punched out his cigarette in the crowded ashtray and stepped around his desk and stood before them.

"Can we have a handshake, gentlemen?" He extended his meaty hand to Roland. "Let's seal our deals."

63
Breathe

Saturday, July 19, 1969

After the moon launch on Wednesday, Dell had asked her to have dinner with him that evening, but she told him she had to return home. She called his office Friday evening from her room in the Fairhaven in Telford and left her hotel number. Then she called Tamara.

She told her the investigation into Hafferty was underway and that it will likely become public in the next week or so. She urged Tamara to speak with James and Roland and to get an exit plan together for all three of them. Tamara asked her if she'd given thought to her advice about forgiveness.

"It's too late for that," Alice said. "The die is cast. By now, he already knows they're talking to sources who can hurt him. And when they start calling local people, that's when he'll start reacting, taking people down. Like Roland and James. And Jade."

"Are you sure you want to go through with this?" Tamara asked.

"I've never been more sure of anything in my life. But even if I weren't, as I've said, it's out of my hands now. It's an avalanche aimed right at Dennis Hafferty, and it will bury him. Only the fickle finger of fate could save him at this point."

They spoke at length about what Tamara had told the boys, and Alice thanked her and said she'd need to provide each of them with more details. It was vital now, she said, that Jade and Roland would hear it all from the source—Alice herself.

Tamara proposed a meeting—Alice, Jade, Roland, and James. "All cards on the table," she said, sounding less like the philosopher and more like the dealmaker. Alice was surprised to discover her muse's exigent instinct, how quickly she dropped the theoretical and yielded to the urgency before her. She was of a form both projected and real, part-spirit, part-clay, but clearly possessing corporeal guards.

Alice insisted that Tamara be included in the meeting. Tamara resisted, but Alice convinced her. "If it weren't for you, we'd all be lost."

Tamara offered to organize the meeting, and she proposed that Alice would host it on Reston Street. Monday evening at seven.

Alice was resistant to hosting, embarrassed by the condition of her home.

"This is an all-cards-on-the-table meeting, Alice," Tamara said. "All cards. You needn't hide anything any longer. And it would be best for Jade to be at home and for Roland and James to see you as you are, to witness the truth of how you've lived, indeed survived, over all these years. It would be essential, too, that Roland and James see you in your home with Jade. Let them see you unguarded," Tamara said, her voice soft but certain. "It will leave them no choice but to be unguarded as well."

Alice told her about the statues and the drinking and the visions, even those in which Tamara had appeared, and Tamara said she found it fascinating, and that it was thrilling to know she'd been "seen" by someone. She told Alice she was not alone, that many women she'd known, including her relatives in The Caribbean, had the gift of visions, psychic projection, orphic communication, clairvoyance, and that she should embrace them, even the ones that frighten her.

"These are the voices of your own extended consciousness," Tamara said in her soothing, mesmerizing tone, the one Alice had heard in her daydreams. "These are your inherited thoughts from lifelines of the past, and perhaps the future, that are connected to yours. You have the gift, Alice. The gift of seeing your inner life wrought from your heritage and destiny—and to see it all through your dream life. Embrace it. Your physical gifts are prodigious, and your intellect is clearly extraordinary, so grant yourself space in your life for your rare spiritual and mystical gifts, as well."

Alice cried a little, and then laughed and told Tamara how easy it was to acquiesce to her, and Tamara said it wasn't acquiescence but merely agreeing to what she wanted for herself yet would not permit herself to have.

Alice told her about Marte, and then wondered out loud why she was saying all of that, and Tamara told her that she'd deserved that happiness, and that she should celebrate, not hide, the memories of it.

"You've discovered a new possibility for yourself," Tamara said, "perhaps another reason for you to let go of the bitter past, a sign that you must move forward. Focus on the open horizon of that breakthrough, and let it erase the limitations of other past experiences. You need balance in your life, Alice, and you now have the capacity for it."

Only Tamara could talk to her like this. Tamara, the mysterious harborer of truths. This stranger, this rapturously beautiful, enchanting Black muse. Just the sound of her voice was transcending. Where had she come from? The future? The ether world?

It was only minutes after she hung up with Tamara that Dell's call came through the front desk. Alice hesitated. She needed more time to reflect. She knew Dell would still be in his hopeless state of yearning, perhaps even insisting on coming to Telford, and she knew that time and space now was the only buffer she could rely on. She told the operator to tell him there was no answer in her room.

A half-hour later, she watched an envelope slip under her door. She knew what it was but was startled by what it said. In the frilly handwriting of the front desk operator, the message from Dell told her not to call his office again or his home, ever. He would call her when he had a chance. "Do not come to New York." That last sentence was underscored.

Something had gone wrong. She reached for the phone, but her hand froze over it. She closed her eyes and thought of Dell, of what would panic him. Behind her eyes, she saw shadows of men in the restaurants where they'd met, knowing now how she had sensed them but had ignored it. Even Dell's man at Arthur's Tavern. Was he just Dell's man? Then she saw those men in the Waldorf lobby and heard the voice of Marte warning her. And she knew. She knew. Fate was far from fickle.

She checked the lock on the door, pressed her ear to it for movement in the hallway, then dumped her purse on the bed and pulled the pistol from the false bottom. She held it at her shoulder and swept open the shower curtain, whisked aside the dust ruffle on the bed and pointed the pistol into the darkness there, flung open the closet door and took a wide-legged stance, aiming. Her hand trembled at the window, pinching aside the heavy drape. She scoured the street below. She watched every car, every walking and standing body, every window and doorway, every movement. For a long time.

The bottles in the fridge were tiny, so she relented. Just two of them. Straight, no water, no ice. Back-to-back. And then a third. She tried to wash away her shame in the shower, but Jade's haunting angry face and voice made it worse until she scrubbed the shampoo into her scalp so hard it stung, almost bleeding. Good old Sister Saint Joe. The punisher knew exactly when to apply the pain.

She stood naked before the mirror on the closet door. Her face was drawn, barely recognizable. Even her body, always so resilient, so reliably sturdy under so much neglect and torment, now looked exhausted, the shoulders sunken, thighs wilting, feet pink with aches. Her breasts were heavy, belly softened. She found a new razor and re-shaved the nubs of hair on her mons. For Marte. In case she was watching. In case she would appear. And soothe her. She smiled with the memory and closed her eyes and slid her fingers past the shaven mound, releasing her own cold touch to the gentle one she remembered so well.

She woke up on the bed on her back, and, through the slot in the drapes, she saw the blink and flash of nightlife lights. She looked down at herself. Naked. She yanked the sheet up to her neck and looked around the room. She pulled the sheet with her as she reached for the phone. She called Jade, but it just rang and rang and rang.

She spent the rest of Friday night in an empty trance, watching moon landing preparations on television. Walter Cronkite's voice droned on and on, until finally, at last, she let herself go, the familiar monotone numbing her into somnolence.

On Saturday morning, she checked out and took the train to Ebonton and a cab to Reston Street. Jade was not at home. She scurried about The Grotto moving her covered statues and shoving them into the corner. When she finished, she looked around and then shook her head, chuckling at herself, hearing the echo of Tamara's voice. She moved the statues back and uncovered them.

She spent the afternoon fixing the old television. She wanted to have it working for the landing, for Jade. If he came home.

She got it working, and she started putting away her tools, when she was distracted by special news coverage breaking into a dull network program. Photos of Senator Ted Kennedy and a young woman splashed across the screen. The announcer reported something about a bridge near Martha's Vineyard. There was a photo of the back end of a black sedan poking out of water next to the broken slats of the bridge, and the announcer said something about Kennedy swimming to safety, the girl dead.

The screwdriver slipped from her fingers and clattered to the floor next to the toolbox. Her breath came in short gasps, and her worst thoughts scurried into the corner of her mind as she searched the cupboard over the sink and then upstairs to her bedroom closet. There was nothing. Jade had tossed out everything.

She went downstairs to the Virgin and stood before her, waiting for the eyes to move, the voice to speak, the message to be delivered. She waited. She prayed. She dropped to her knees and asked for forgiveness. Still nothing. She looked at the other statues. All blank stares. She tried to will herself into that dreamlife Tamara had identified. Nothing.

She went to the kitchen and picked up the wall phone to call Dell, but then she set it back and rested her head against the kitchen door jamb. It was all clear to her now. It was over. She knew exactly how he would construct his lie about deep-sixing the investigation. It wasn't the findings of seamy sleuths on behalf of Giallo, he'd say. It wasn't the threats from Dennis to ruin his marriage, his career. He'd say it was Ted. There would be no endorsement, no announcement. Dell's national story on Dennis Hafferty died in the dark waters of Massachusetts with that girl.

She closed her eyes. "Breathe," she whispered, her heart searching for Marte's voice. Exhale. The bucket drops. Scoops up air from the bottom. Inhale ever slower. Rises to the top. Exhale. Repeat.

Repeat.

Repeat.

64
Lovers' Leap

Sunday, July 20, 1969

He stood on the slab of chipped and cracked concrete that served as a half-step outside the front door. Reston Street was Sunday morning silent, the pink sunrise warm on his face, the sweet scent of cut grass surprising him, defying his weary expectation of assault from the smoldering mountain of fire and ash behind him. He wouldn't look back there now, above his house, not today. He decided the mountain of culm that glowed at night in poison purples and yellows and oranges belonged there in the dark, belonged to the night and not to a day like this one. The light of this day would be his, and, for this day, he would not look back into the darkness, to the mantis, to the valley of ashes. He would look south and east toward the light.

He let his eyes settle on the big rambling ash tree across the street, on the twinkling edges of sunlight tickling at the leaves in their giant umbrella of green. His gaze drifted upward and there it was—the crescent still aglow, hanging like the seat on a tree swing, the shadowed circle above it a fading memory of its completeness. It would never be complete again after this day.

He looked down the street toward Gort's house. He could see only the rooftop and the chimney, and he wondered, just one more time, if robot man would act, if he would put on his aviator shades, grease his hair into sharp edges, and fix his shoulders into iron epaulets, and then shoot suddenly out of that chimney and rocket upward at ten times warp speed toward the crescent and its lonely shadow, to save that oh-so-sacred satellite of earth from its heedless invaders.

There was movement there. On the chimney. A black figure. Small at first, but it would grow, he could feel it. His breath caught in his chest; his heart pounded. The figure moved again, and he thought he saw a head with a sharp edge.

But no. This wasn't robot man. It was a huge crow. Its sharp beak jerked and jutted upward toward the moon and then it spread its wings and launched off the chimney and soared above Gort's house. Then it dove downward and disappeared, drawn to the earth, faithfully toward prey. There would be no rescue on this day or any other day. The moon romance was over.

Inside, he went back upstairs to reassure himself that she hadn't been an illusion, a dream. She was there. A rumpled form on the bed, covered in a sheet. In a shaft of sunlight her hair was the color of fallen autumn leaves peeking out from under the pillow. When she stirred, he backed away and crept down the stairs to the kitchen, where he set to the task of making her coffee, eggs over easy, toast with butter and jam, and strawberries and cantaloupe—fresh-picked fruit that Wally's grocer pal, Abe, had surprised him with Saturday morning.

He wanted to tell her what Tamara had told him, but he knew she knew, so he let her sit at the table in the silence of her slow awakening. Her mouth, so soft, her lips puffy, barely pursed. Her eyes were heavy, stuck somewhere between the unknown spaces before her and the broken ones behind her. Her hair was all over the place, a wild nest of springs and curls, growing out now, making him smile, wanting to tousle it. This child now adult, so lost and so far out at sea. But not too far for him to toss a ring to her.

She looked up at him at last and smiled, but it was weak, and he knew it wasn't because she was angry with him. She looked so tired, so stunned with sorrow.

He set the coffee and breakfast plate before her and sat across from her with his own plate of eggs and toast and fruit at their little wobbly

Formica table with the rusty once-silver edging, the fluorescent light over the sink blinking in a slow rhythm like an old lighthouse on the worn shores of a slate sea.

After breakfast, they sat side by side on the couch, facing the silent assembly of statues in The Grotto, and he reached across her shoulders and pressed his fingers softly on the wiry tense muscle between her neck and the knob of her shoulder, her skin warm beneath the sheer of her nightgown. She turned her face to his and reached her own hand around and toward him, and when it touched his neck, he brought his face to her hair and reached his other hand toward her, brushing her satiny breast with his fingers and drawing his breath as he settled the hand on her waist and whispered, "sorry," and she laughed a little as she brought her body around to clench his to hers, and he felt her breath on his neck and her other arm slip behind his back, and they rocked like that for a time that could not be measured.

She bathed while he cleaned up and made sandwiches and packed them into a paper bag with apples and cheese and set the bag on two hand towels on the kitchen table. He washed up in the bathroom while she dressed. They went to her '57 Chevy, and she let him drive, and he laughed like a child and said he felt like he was a sky pilot, an astronaut.

They pulled over at the lookout on the mountain road to the rez. They got out and stood together at the waist-high limestone wall and watched the valley change from waxen gray to sallow gray as the sun rose higher in the sky. He pointed north to the mountains in the clear blue above and beyond the jaundiced valley and told her he thought they looked like whales all in a row, blue-gray humps headed west, where the sky was clean and the air sweet, and she held onto his arm, telling him how much stronger he felt to her touch.

She held his bicep and forearm with both hands and pulled him close to her side, as she looked at the mountains with him, and told him about her childhood and teenage years and about her father and her siblings, and how Dennis had come into her life and that it was all explained in detail in the memoir she'd showed him months ago, under the pen name Jeannette Robbins. She said the manuscript was up to date, she was finished with it, and that it was now in the hands of Helen at the library if he wanted to read it. She told him what her real name was and what his real name was and why she had to change them, why she could never settle down anywhere with him. Why she could never settle down with herself.

She told him about Barnard and the brief thrill of being a scholar amid the ironic emptiness of high society, and how she'd met James, and where Roland was born and how he'd been taken away from her, and why James wasn't allowed to be with her. The deception, the cruelty, the lost love. She told him about meeting his father, and what they'd attempted together, and how he'd disappeared before she gave birth to her second son in Vermont, and that she fought to keep him, determined that she would not be fooled twice. She told him his father now lived in California, where she'd met with him just a few weeks ago for the first time since 1950, and how disappointed she was in him, but still she told Jade where to find him, if he ever wanted to meet him. She told him about the information his father had given her, and how she'd met with Giallo and what she'd tried to do with the information in order to stop Dennis. How it all took off more quickly than she'd expected and gave her hope for the first time in years, and then how, in the course of the last twenty-four hours, it unraveled completely. An undoing of the hope and redemption that she'd lived for over the years and then foolishly believed it would actually happen, finally, this time.

"I'd forgotten my scholarship, Seamus," she said with a wistful smile, pulling tighter on his bicep. "The impermanence of life, the fragility of what we believe is built to last." She turned and looked up at him, soreness in her eyes. "Your favorite literature professor, Seamus, forgot the lesson about the best laid schemes of mice and men. How it leaves you nothing but grief and pain for promised joy."

She shook off her self-indulgent pity, let go of his arm, and put her hands on the wall. She took a deep breath of the rarified air, so far above the miasmic spew of the valley. She turned to him and told him about the meeting planned for Monday, and that the wrath of Dennis Hafferty would come down hard now, and that they would have to leave this valley, quickly, Tuesday at the latest, and that he would need to be ready to go, taking very little with him.

Jade felt relief and joy and deep sorrow all at once, and he realized he was suddenly scared about putting his escape dreams into action. It was as if the moon landing had caused this breach, this sudden clean sweep of the soft, thin veil between his dreams and the hard surface of reality. The moon was occupied now, he couldn't fly there on phantom wings. And his quest for freedom was no longer a wishful fantasy; it was real. But he had hope now; she would be with him.

When he started to talk about Tamara and Roland, and how his sense of who they were had changed so much, he felt relief at last in his gut, a warmth that shored up his new hope. He said he'd been stunned to learn about Roland, but soon glad for it, even excited. He said he'd known there was something more to their connection, but he'd never considered what it turned out to be. And when he told her about meeting Tamara and how his feelings for her had escalated amid so much chaos, he broke down and wept.

His mother held him, and then wiped his cheek with a gentle hand, and said she understood, more than he would ever know.

460

He told her about the car wreck, and the rez with Roland and Lucy, and the body of the boy who was killed. He told her about what he saw at the wreck, and about Mutt and Jeff and Hafferty and Jensen and Detective Marion, and the party at the estate, and the jobs Dennis was offering Roland and him.

She tried to apologize for not knowing, for not being there for him during all of this, but he held up his hand and put his other hand around her waist and drew her to him, holding her sobbing head against his chest.

"No need for sorrow here. You gave me the strength to fight through it all. I watched you struggle and survive all my life. I learned from the master."

They held hands for a long quiet time, her head against his shoulder, and they looked at the lost valley and then up to the mountains of whimsical whales beyond it. They watched an eagle in the sky above them, and he pointed to a second one, and she laughed, the sound of a child's joy in her voice lifting him, and he turned her to him, and they held onto each other so tightly that eventually she had to pull away, at once laughing and gasping for air.

She said he did not have to stay with her wherever they go, but that she had resources for him, and that, if something should happen to her before they leave, he should contact Wally immediately. Go to him if it's safe.

They sat at the lookout picnic table and had lunch in silence. As they cleaned up and started for the car, Jade signaled for her to follow him to the stone wall again, where he told her, "They call this place 'Lovers' Leap.'" They leaned over the wall together and looked at the steep scree below, and he held onto her arm in a firm grip.

"Don't worry," she said, smiling at him. "This one has fallen many times. But she would never leap."

She asked him to show her the rez, and he was reluctant at first. But she pleaded and said he could drive the car, and he laughed at her charm, her relentless persuasiveness, and he said he wished he'd inherited even a little of that trait. At the water's edge, she took off her shoes and socks and rolled up her linen pants and waded up to her knees, whooping about how cold it was.

"It's July!" she shouted. "Does the ice ever melt?"

He laughed, and then hooted, and his echo came back to him. He pointed to the geese at the other end and called to them like Squirrel would, and then stripped down to his underpants and dove in. When he came up, he let out a howl that reverberated around the lake. She laughed at him and held out her arms and tipped her head to the sky and let out a howl of her own. Together they howled until they grew hoarse.

At home, he made them a light dinner, and they discussed a strategy for the next day's meeting. As they cleaned up the dishes together, she told him she'd fixed the television, so they could watch the moon landing together. He shook his head at her, and his smile twisted sideways.

"You knew how to fix that damn thing all this time?"

She shrugged and put her wet hands on his cheeks and poked him in the ribs. "Reading is your future," she said in her professor's voice. "Not that stupid thing."

Jade said they should watch the six o'clock news to catch up on the space flight, and Alice said she could wait, because the landing wouldn't happen for a few more hours, but he smiled down at her, and pleaded and coaxed her, rubbing her arms.

"Looks like that trait came through after all," she said, letting him pull her onto the couch next to him. He smiled, but his insides were exploding, so thrilled he was to have within him at least a modicum of her that he could always rely on.

The top story was the landing of the lunar module on the surface of the moon. It had happened at 4:17 p.m., and Alice laughed, and then apologized. "I don't know how I heard it wrong. Looks like we missed it."

"No sweat," Jade said. "They're saying it will take a few hours before they actually set foot on the surface, sometime around ten."

"Maybe that's what I heard," she said. "I don't know. I guess I wasn't paying attention. Gee, I wonder why."

The next story was about Ted Kennedy and the Chappaquiddick Bridge, and Alice said with a flat tone, "This is what I didn't want to watch, I guess. It's the same story all over again, like a recurring nightmare. And it's ruining our good day."

Jade put his arm around her and pulled her close. "I'll shut it off if you want."

"No," she said, smiling up at him. "I fixed it for you, and we'll watch it together." She kissed him on the cheek and settled in under his arm.

After a minute of updates and photos of the Kennedy crash, the newscaster said more will follow on the national news at 6:30, and that "live" coverage of the moon landing would continue into the night. The top local story was the Civic Center celebration. It opened with a tape of Dennis Hafferty speaking at a microphone on a stage in the massive building, with clips of moon-themed exhibits and moon-costumed characters on stilts and women in sparkly bikinis and high heels and a huge crowd of celebrants. Alice moaned and Jade turned to her.

"You're right," he said. "This *is* ruining our day. I'll change it to something else."

Before he could get up to turn the dial, the segment switched to a "live" interview with Hafferty. He was raving about the moon landing and seeming to take credit for the entire Apollo program. A reporter interrupted the soliloquy to ask him about rumors he'll be announcing a campaign to run for Congressman Walsh's seat.

Jade sat back, stunned.

"Absolutely, unequivocally false," Hafferty barked at the reporter. He leaned into the reporter's microphone and turned to the camera. His face turned crimson and his googly eyes bulged in a truculent glare. "Congressman Henry Walsh is a *very* close friend of mine and of the *people* he serves here in the Diamond Valley. He is a *dedicated* servant of this district, and, for the last two decades, he's been *instrumental* in helping us rebuild our infrastructure, bringing needed jobs here to Yoakna County. Never in a *million* years would I consider undermining my good friend by running for the seat he's held so honorably for all of us."

"Commissioner, you're the leading Democrat of this area," the reporter persisted. "What do you say to our viewers about the Chappaquiddick Bridge incident? Senator Kennedy is the national leader of the Democratic Party and the likely upcoming contender for the presidency. Are his chances spoiled now?"

"No, sir," Hafferty bellowed, his defiance transforming into unctuous brio. "I am convinced that the most honorable Senator Ted Kennedy is innocent in this unfortunate accident, and that he will emerge from this event stronger than ever. Right now, I'm sure he's not worried about himself, but about the family of that poor girl he tried to save. And I just want to clarify what I said earlier." He flashed his fluorescent teeth and his voice transformed yet again, softening to a melodramatic sincerity. "I have *no* intention of running for national office. I *love* this community. This is my home, and I will be here in the Commissioner's office for as long as the people of the county will have me. And look around you, here's the proof." He turned to the scene in the Civic Center. The camera panned the audience gathered nearby, the crowds at the exhibits, zooming in on the replicas of the launchpad and the moon. Hafferty filled in the narrative with a litany of platitudes, overpowering the tentative voice of the reporter.

"Look at how proud our Yoakna County citizens are of our national heroes—astronauts Armstrong, Aldrin, and Collins," Hafferty declaimed. "Look at this celebration! We're on the moon, folks! The world's first nation to land on the moon! And I will say this: it's all over for the Soviets. We beat them to it. We've proven again that God blesses a nation that strives to honor Him. Communism just took a fatal blow today, and now, hang in there, because we're about to set foot on the lunar surface, another landmark the Soviets will never catch up to. God in heaven, please watch over our men who've landed there, and let them return to us safe and sound. God bless the greatest country in the world—The United States of America!"

Jade launched himself from the couch and clicked off the TV.

"I'm sorry," he said to Alice. "Mom." He attempted a smile. "Is it okay if I call you that? Once in a while?"

She looked dazed, and, for a moment, he thought she hadn't heard him. Then she blinked twice and smiled at him. "There's nothing for you to feel sorry about, honey." Her smile widened, and she tilted her head. He could feel the warmth of her charm rising again; the light returning to her soft green eyes. "And yes, you may call me that any time you want. You will always be my son, and I will always be your mother."

She stood and stepped up to him, looking into his eyes and patting his chest with her hands. Her voice was firm; the mother was in charge. "You'll need to go to work tomorrow, Jade. Act as you always would. It'll be your last day. And Roland's, too. Don't bring attention to yourselves. We'll work out the details here at seven. We'll be free soon, my son." She made a fist and tapped the soft end of it on his sternum. "And you...Jade...Seamus...James...Jacob." She couldn't hold her laughter, which came out in a little huff. "Pick one. You can be whoever you want to be. You are a man now. You'll make good choices, I know you will. And I will always be with you, in your heart and in your spirit. And you in mine."

He wrapped his arms around her shoulders, gently pulled her head against him, and rested his chin on the softness of her auburn curls. He held her there with his eyes closed, thinking of nothing but what he felt— the pulse of her blood, the rhythm of her breathing, the warmth of her face on his chest, their heartbeats.

He brought her a piece of apple pie and iced tea, and she smiled and whispered, "Wilma."

"Let's watch something stupid until ten," he said. He switched to Channel 11, and there it was, his answer—*The Three Stooges*. Then came *Hogan's Heroes*, *Gilligan's Island*, and then more Stooges. They laughed, and they ate pie.

At ten, he switched over to the moon landing coverage, and the newscasters were still going over the same clip of the lunar module and the astronaut's voice, "The Eagle has landed." Then it switched to local coverage of the celebration at the Civic Center and an irrepressible Dennis Hafferty back-slapping on the floor, surrounded by local leaders, including many of the men Jade saw at the estate party.

Jade started rattling off a few of their names, and even made vague references to some of their dirty deeds at the party, but when he heard no response from Alice, he turned to her. She was asleep, her face peaceful, a look he saw years ago when they lived at the beach and he was a boy, and he watched her soft mouth as she sighed through her dreams and wished then, as now, that the dreams were sweet for her.

He put his hand on her hair, and he leaned over and kissed her on the forehead, and she did not stir.

At 10:56 p.m., he witnessed the first step of a man on the moon. He got up to turn off the TV after he heard the astronaut say "mankind." It was over. The moon, once a dream source, a fantastical, almost imaginary specter in the sky, to which he'd pinned all his boyish hopes, was now under occupation.

All around him, in the tiny house on Reston Street, there was silence, except for the steady, soft whisper of his mother, breathing right next to him, sweet dreaming.

A few minutes later, he heard horns blowing in the distance, and somebody nearby was banging pots and pans on a front porch. He wondered if the crescent was still there.

65
Summit on Reston Street

Monday, July 21, 1969

When Jade came home from work at 4:30, Alice was on her knees in the kitchen in her cutoffs and tee shirt scrubbing the last corner of the floor. She told him she was packed and asked him to do the same. When he was finished, they sorted out the few personal items they'd planned to take with them, and then Jade scoured the bathroom, while Alice dusted and vacuumed the first floor, even rubbing a shine to the statues of the Virgin and her comrade saints. She'd already cleaned most of the windows on the first floor, inside and out, and as she set out to clean the front windows, Jade convinced her to leave them untouched. "They'll come in the back way, mom. Please don't risk your life on that goddamn street, cleaning windows that no one will ever see."

As he worked, Jade began to worry. He was nervous about Tamara seeing him at home, witnessing how he and Alice lived—her golden-brown eyes taking in the shabby kitchen with its ancient appliances and wobbly Formica table and then The Grotto of statues and votive candles and crucifixes over the doors. She'd be choked by the sickness in the air surrounding this hovel. She'd seen him at his worst, but now she'd see him in his most private place—this crumbling little house on a noisy road at the foot of a smoking hill and a giant charcoal mantis, praying for its own extinction. He knew she would not judge all of this, but still, his heart felt like a fifty-pound weight in his chest. He was still in love with her. And he did not want her to feel embarrassed for him.

As the meeting time approached, his worries multiplied. He was clear about what Alice expected from Hafferty, and the urgency to escape before Dennis tracked her down, but he worried about meeting Roland's father for the first time since early high school. How odd it was to imagine that man with Alice. He couldn't picture it. He feared Dr. Wilson would be gruff and short with everyone, as he had been in Biology class. Would he be nasty to Alice? Try to chase her away, as he did before?

And he worried most about Roland. What would the stoic hero think of the woman he'd teased Jade about, now that he knew who she really was? What would she say to Roland, and what, if anything, would he say to her? He might just storm away, like he did whenever things went wrong for him. Would Roland think all of this—the house, the meeting, the mother—was wrong for him?

At seven, the guests filed in through the kitchen door in silence. They crowded awkwardly into the tiny space under the blinking fluorescent light, and then Alice welcomed them and led them to The Grotto, where two silver and vinyl kitchen chairs flanked a cushioned living room chair facing the couch. There was a pitcher of iced tea and five glasses and napkins on the coffee table. A small fan in the corner was blowing thick air around the room. Jade had proposed bringing it out to keep the culm dump stench from absorbing into the skin of the guests, and Alice had laughed in agreement. But he was serious.

Tamara and James sat in the kitchen chairs and Roland settled uneasily between them in the cushioned chair, crossing and uncrossing his long legs. Alice sat on the couch and poured the tea, and Jade was making his way to the other side of the couch, when he turned toward the kitchen. Someone was knocking on the back door.

Jade answered it, and smiled as he opened the door. He moved back to the doorway of The Grotto, cleared his throat and stood aside as Wally stepped forward, a sheepish grin on his round face and a fresh-baked pie in his hands. Thanks to Jade's fan, the sweet peach aroma took precedence over the culm stench, at least for a passing moment.

"I saw him this morning," Tamara explained in her velvet tone, smiling, "and it just occurred to me: of course he should be here."

"I am honored to be with you," Wally said haltingly in his Polish accent. "On behalf of Wilma, who must stay with the receipts and do the counting, I am here to listen and to provide sweets."

As Jade retrieved plates and utensils from the kitchen, Wally offered a monologue of praise for everyone, and the awkwardness soon evaporated amid the busy clicking of forks on plates and the battling aromas of honeyed peaches and hot sulfury breezes. Wally declared the meeting "a gathering of refugees."

"Everyone is a refugee," he said, nodding to each of them. "Not just everyone in this room, but everyone in the world. We all have our moments of comfort, some longer than others, even a lifetime for the very lucky. But, for most of us, we live in danger much of the time." He looked around at the faces, some busy with the pie, others pensive at his prompting. "But I am not here to make a speech. All of you know hardship in your own ways, in your own lives. I am here to offer support for whatever you need." He gestured toward the pie. "There's another one in the kitchen. Lemon meringue."

Roland led the laughter, and the awkward tension seemed to clear. "I'm definitely having a slice of that lemon pie," he declared. Jade let out a silent if cautious sigh.

Tamara set her fork gently next to her unfinished pie, and asked permission to begin the meeting. "Thank you, Alice, for inviting all of us here. And thank you, Wally, for the pies and for everything you and Wilma have done for me, and I believe, for others here as well. And you are correct; we are all refugees of one sort or another."

She cleared her throat and sat up tall in the kitchen chair. Her giant gold hoop earrings swayed as she made eye contact with everyone, starting the discussion with background on her own experiences, especially in Ebonton, and informing all that there was an opportunity for everyone to find new and safe footing in Canada.

"I'll get to the details in due course, but I think Alice would like to start us off."

Alice announced, with a charming smirk, that it was okay to speak one's mind in front of the statues, since the people whom the icons represented had been refugees themselves. Jade felt a rush of heat in his neck, but he was quieted when he heard James and Wally chuckle. Tamara's laugh came a little late, but it was genuine, and she nodded at Alice in approval. But when Jade turned to Roland, he saw the look he'd feared. The statues were weird. His mother sometimes speaks in tongues.

Jade felt the urge to say something, unsure what it would be.

"I've never heard those saints say anything, and I've tried many times to coax them," he said, and Alice laughed, and then everyone chuckled. Except Roland. His stern gaze at the Virgin was fixed.

Alice noticed and took the cue to switch gears. "Thank you, Tamara, for taking the time to tell Roland and Jade the truth that I, and perhaps James, could not adequately provide." She looked at Roland, her eyes seeking his approval. But Roland remained stoic.

Alice turned to Tamara. "Without you, we'd all still be wallowing in the darkness. Not that it isn't dark out there, with our nemesis hovering over us all. But you've brought so much light into the lives of everyone here; and I just wanted to say how grateful I am."

There was a pause, and Jade started to fill in the gap when Alice continued, her voice wavering, her eyes moist. "And, if I may say, on behalf of everyone here, we are so fortunate that you appeared here, in this difficult place, at the right time for all of us, Tamara. You have saved my life, for what it's worth, and you've saved our sons as well. And I guess

I need to thank James for dragging you here to this valley for everyone's benefit."

Tamara held up her hand, and her bracelets clinked like chimes. "Wally said it best, Alice. We are all refugees, and we must plan together for our escape from here. We all need each other now. And we are not out of that darkness yet."

Jade kept his eye on Roland, as Alice and James alternated the history of their relationship and filled in the areas of their separated lives that Tamara had not been able to provide Roland and Jade. Faces and eyes around the coffee table softened at first when Alice talked about the births of her sons but grew somber when she told them about why she was sent away for both pregnancies, her crimes being two births out of wedlock, one a mixed-race child, the other a mixed religion child. She fumed about Dennis orchestrating her first banishment, because he feared his political aspirations would be ruined if a mixed-race child were born into his family. "A mulatto," she said, "which is what White Americans called first generation offspring of Black and White parents back then. It's a Spanish word meaning 'mule.' "

James interrupted her with a loud clearing of his throat. Jade frowned at the stern face he'd remembered, and then glanced at Alice, searching for a sign of hurt.

"Dennis is not as transparent as you imply," James said to Alice, with a dim smile, his face now serene. He sat erect on the kitchen chair, his shoulders back and his dark eyes scanning the group and then returning to Alice. "It is true that a mixed marriage, or rather a mixed pregnancy, posed a threat to his political future, but don't forget: Dennis learned at the foot of your father, his stepfather. About money, power, and the importance of maintaining those through racial purity. It was a philosophy that he'd learned well. But, instead of following your father's irrational scheme for repatriating American Negroes to Africa, he saw the control of Blacks in this nation as an opportunity. There were too many of us to manage *en masse*, as your father's scheme had failed to recognize. But Dennis saw something else. Even back then, he had a gift for sensing shifts in political and social trends. He was way ahead of his time in sensing a post-war change in politicians' regard for Afro-Americans. He told me there would be a change in racial relations in America, and that he and I would be part of it. His intentions proved nefarious, of course, but his political instincts were correct. Slowly, over the next decade, the case for civil rights would build, and he would benefit from posing as a supporter.

"So, yes, Dennis banished you and your child-to-be, but, instead of ridding the family of the Black father and the Black child, as your father had directed, Dennis took on the risky task of privately and clandestinely sponsoring my U.S. education as a bet on what he sensed would be a rising tide of change in this thriving nation's attitudes toward education, liberal economics, and a recognition of the plight of its Negro population."

He looked around at the group as he continued in his steady, reasoned professorial tone. Jade heard the island accent seeping through, the British lilt seeming to give Dr. Wilson even more credibility and authority. He felt like he was back in Wilson's classroom at Pell Academy.

"Dennis was correct, of course," James continued. "And, at the right time, he was front and center with his props—myself, and later, Roland by my side—giving him the appearance of tolerance in concert with his liberal national party, while still enabling him to send the hidden message to his constituents that he would sponsor and support only the *good* Negroes, who would appear to thrive while remaining in their prescribed places in society.

"It is a position he's now moving rapidly away from, because it is no longer to his benefit, as the rise of Black people in this country becomes more strident and the inherent bigotry of his constituents, including his partner, Salvatore Giallo, is coming out from under the thin veil of artifice that Hafferty so expertly created for them. He's reading the signals, as always, and preparing to change his tune, sensing a backlash from the middle class and conservatives against the various liberation and anti-war movements. Of course, his financial interests are the priority for him, so his emerging standing will conveniently place him more openly among those who support the continuation of, not just the current war, but other wars to come."

He held up a finger, as if to signal a new idea suddenly occurring to him. Jade was awed by the professor's theatrics and, as if on cue, James's face revealed something Jade had not expected from him—vulnerability.

"I know Dennis well, for better or for worse. But I have been in denial. And it is only through the persistent advice of Tamara and…discussions with my son…and the urgency of…uh…Alice…that I have come to realize that the game is up for me, as well as for Roland, here in this economically, politically, and quite frankly, biologically bereft valley. Our usefulness to Dennis Hafferty has expired. We are disposable props."

He turned his finger into an open hand, summoning the next revelation.

"As such, I have agreed to join this exodus. I have lived under the cover of my work, but I have not been living an honest life. I've been merely surviving, under the delusion of comfort. In a home Dennis Hafferty owns. In a college so White that, until Tamara arrived, I'd forgotten what another Black colleague looked like. There is no longer a Black community in this valley. At one point, I actually owned property— my home—as did a few other Black men—the minister, the grocer, the clothing merchant, the barber, and other neighborhood colleagues. Our community was small and economically unstable at best. But a few years ago, the city secured federal redevelopment grants to tear down our community and someday, I'm told, replace it with government-sponsored apartments. Not for Black ownership, but for rent.

"My home was purchased for cents on the dollar by the city, and our merchants were bought out, and our families dispersed. It's called Urban Renewal. By my measure, it is purposeful dissolution, plain and simple. And a resounding success for its White architects. Today, there are zero Black businesses in this valley. And the same number of Black property owners. We are not welcome here."

He moved forward on the edge of his kitchen chair, and Jade thought he was going to stand, but he simply lifted his frame taller.

"My colleagues at Dickson have asked me repeatedly why Blacks in this country are rioting, burning down their homes and businesses. It doesn't make sense, they said. Well, Roland has provided me with insight on these questions, and I only wish he were there when I was left dumbfounded by my colleagues and by my own blindness to the truth. Blacks are not burning down their own homes or businesses; they don't own *any* of them. That's the point. They're burning the hovels where they've been corralled and the run-down ghetto businesses owned by Whites, because they're fed up with being denied access to property ownership. It's the single most important economic driver of a healthy community in this country. Home ownership and business ownership. And time and again, we are locked out of that privilege and locked into cages they call housing projects, renting from White landlords, and buying overpriced junk food and booze from sleazy White vendors. We don't own *any*thing in this country. We are not allowed to sit at the adult table with the White overlords. *That* is why people are revolting," he fumed, finally losing his stiff composure. "They are *not* rioting, they are *revolting*. There's a difference!"

He turned to Roland, clearly struggling with his raw emotions. "But I digress," he said, his voice still shaking. "My son has heard this lecture and knows my intentions, and I've asked him to join us in our exodus. But before Roland tells us his view on the Canada plan, I am compelled to tell all of you that I spoke with Dennis this morning by telephone. He confided in me that he privately blames Ted Kennedy for the cancellation of his congressional campaign."

Roland let out a sarcastic single syllabic laugh. James ignored him.

"But when he began peppering me with questions about whether I'd been contacted by *The New York Times*, and then asked me to report to him if I came in contact with Alice, I realized he was out for vindication. He obviously cannot take it out on Senator Kennedy publicly, so it appears he's after whoever tipped off *The Times* about his nefarious dealings, and he's quite certain it started with Alice. He asked me if I had met with her and, well, I have to say, he's very intimidating in person, and if it weren't a phone call, I don't think I could have convinced him I did not know about her plan to expose him. He's been my sponsor, as it were, for many years, and I find it difficult to evade his probing. So, while I could not see his face, I could hear it in his voice—he did not believe me."

Alice started to speak, but James held up his hand. "Please let me finish." She nodded. "Thank you," he said. "I have just one more thing to say, Alice, and it's for your sake more than anyone's." She nodded again, and Jade thought he saw a smile peek out of the corner of her soft mouth.

"I've urged Tamara to move immediately on the Canada plan," James continued. "Tamara has contacted her family in Toronto, and they're awaiting her follow up call, immediately after this meeting, to confirm. If we agree to leave tomorrow, they'll send a small aircraft, a six-seater, to an airfield an hour north of here. We can take very few belongings, but there is room for Tamara, Alice, Roland, Jade, and myself. I apologize, Wally. We did not—"

"No, no," Wally said, holding up his hand. "I do not expect to be included. I will stay with my Wilma and my diner. I have been in your situation many times, all of them most dangerous. I can help in whatever way you ask. But please, rest assured, we will survive."

"We can send another plane, Wally," Tamara said. "It's my fault that you've been dragged in on this."

"No, no," Wally repeated. "There was no dragging. I've known Alice and Jimmy—or, Jade, sorry—for many years. But they do not need me where they are going. Wilma and I would be a burden, and, what's more, I love my diner. I belong here."

"Wally," Alice said, her nostrils flaring, her face red with a look Jade had never seen. "I am the one who has dragged everyone into this. Including you. And Wilma. If he gives you trouble, I will find out. And I will make him pay." Her voice was shaking.

"Let's not get ahead of ourselves," Tamara warned. "James is correct. We need a consensus on our departure. If we can secure a car to get us to the airfield, we can leave as early as tomorrow, midday."

"They already know my Chevy," Alice said. "But I can trade it for another car. Leave that to me. Jade and I can be ready tomorrow."

Jade felt his stomach drop, and then wrench. "What about the draft?" he said, his voice wavering. "I'm putting everyone in danger in Canada if I go with you."

"My family is aware of that, for both you and Roland," Tamara said. "They have years of experience moving people to safety, no matter what the threat. They're prepared to deal with your situation, as well as with our own in terms of our status in Canada. You must come with us, Jade.

And you, as well, Roland. If you do not, you will be in greater danger from Dennis Hafferty and Salvatore Giallo than you will be from the U.S. Army."

Roland held up his hand, leaned forward and took a quick breath, glancing at his father, then at Tamara. "Leaving this valley for good has always been my plan," he said, "but I'm not interested in escaping to Canada or anywhere else outside the U.S. That strident uprising my father referred to is very real in the major cities in this country, places where change is already happening. And while some of you know that I had hoped to attend Howard University in the fall, that's impossible now. But I do see my place among my comrades in the Black liberation movement. I have close contacts in New York, and I am preparing to join them."

James cleared his throat to announce his disapproval. "Son, you'll be safe with us in Canada until we can get our bearings. Tamara's relatives are *our* people—many of them from the Islands, where she and I come from. For decades, her grandparents' trading business has enabled them to take in Caribbean people in danger, giving them respite and then directing them on to safer, more prosperous lives. This movement you speak of is doomed. It's already violent, and the Whites will continue to crush it, killing everyone involved. Look at King, and some of your heroes in the Panthers. All dead, jailed, or exiled. It's history repeating itself, and it never ends well for us. If they don't kill you, they'll put you in jail. And then ship you to the front lines in that slaughterhouse in Southeast Asia."

Roland shook his head, his mouth curled in a frown. "I've already made my contribution toward that war by creating thousands of bomb shells to kill Brown people. Enough of them have already died at my hands. No one can make me kill another one." He stood up and began to pace in front of the statues, his voice rising.

"Do we need to dwell on this any further? Really?" he said, waving his hand toward the group. "My father got a White woman pregnant. That's been a crime in this country for centuries. But if we want to sit here grousing about crimes against Black and Brown people, we are wasting our time. My father made the best of it, got his degrees and his teaching and research post, but it seems to me that he would have been strung up for his crime in 1949, if it weren't for our nemesis, as you called him, Alice. Dennis Hafferty. He's the elephant in the room, is he not? He's the great White man with all the power and the money, and we're mere pawns in his many games. He owns politicians who siphon money from the government into his pockets for his bombs to be used for whatever the latest war this country is waging. That's life here in the good old U.S.A. Always has been. But this is not the time to whine about it. There are men in this country who aim to change all of that, and they're not sitting around whining about it in a stuffy little room full of statues and candles and crosses. They're arming themselves and their people, and they're preparing for change by force. You can make your plans to run away to Canada, but I plan to stay and fight. Dennis Hafferty is not my enemy; he's my sponsor. Just as he has been your sponsor all these years, father. He is our owner. We are his slaves. When I join the fight, and Dennis and his ilk get in my way, they will fall. But I will not use a peashooter from Canada. I will join the forces who are taking the fight to the streets and bring justice to Black people once and for all. No more non-violent protests. No more begging the White gods in Washington for another handout, another unenforceable law, another double-cross like Doctor King got. If all of you are leaving this poisoned valley for the greener hills of Canada, good luck. I wish you well. I have different plans."

66
The New Deal

Tuesday, July 22, 1969

Jade stood at the stove in old khaki shorts, shirtless and barefoot, frying eggs for Alice. The house was hotter than usual, and he'd barely slept. His duffle bag was standing on end near the back door. When Alice came downstairs, she stood in the kitchen doorway and watched him. She was barefoot in a white tee shirt and blue boxers she'd permanently borrowed from Jade. She pushed the knot of curls from her forehead and smiled at him.

"It wasn't that long ago when I stood in your place making eggs on the morning of your first day at the bomb factory," she said, and Jade turned to her with his face in a question.

"You don't remember?" she said, her smile wider and her dark eyebrows arched high above her pale green eyes. "You pushed them around on the plate like they were army rations."

His questioning eyes turned soft, and he sighed. "Yeah. I remember. I was a jerk. All pumped up in my big boots like I was going off to war, a kid in men's clothing ready to slay all the dragons." He let out a sigh and pointed to her chair and place setting. "Have a seat, mom."

She stepped behind him and reached her arms around his middle, resting her cheek and chest on his bare back. "You're right. It felt like I was sending you off to war. I was terrified."

"That picture we fought over that day," Jade said, placing a hand on hers for a moment and then grabbing a plate for the eggs. "You always called him Big Mack. Was that really your father?"

Alice chuckled against his back and then let go, turning to sit down. "No," she said. "That was my grandfather. My father's father. That photo was taken on his family's land somewhere in Scotland or Northern Ireland. I never had a picture of my father. But he looked just like him. You probably noticed I took it down. Tossed it in the trash. It was a ghost I didn't need to rely on any longer, I guess. Either that, or I didn't need to let it continue to haunt me."

While they ate their last breakfast at the wobbly little table, she told him about her phone call with Tamara a few hours after the meeting had broken up. Tamara told her Roland's decision was not rash, as Alice had insisted.

"Tamara said he'd been living two lives since he left Penn State— making money here by day and speaking with his politically active friends in New York by night and going there most weekends. He'd shared his decision with her the night before the meeting, right after he'd shared it with his father, who didn't take it well. James knew in the meeting that his plea for Roland to go with us would fail, but he wanted what was too late for him—a chance to close the breach between them. Tamara believes now that Roland's decision is in line with where he feels needed and wanted and where he can make an impact. She's unhappy about it, as we all are, but she said it is an important step for Roland. A dangerous one, of course, but, as Wally said yesterday, many of us are always in danger. Roland has been protected from most of it, ironically, by a man who has been helping to create that very danger for decades. Roland finally accepted that truth and decided to choose. Tamara said it was a matter of his soul."

She set her fork next to her unfinished eggs and sighed, looking at Jade. "I just wish he and I had had a chance to talk. I wouldn't try to talk him out of his decision. I just wish I got to know him a little bit. He's why I dragged you here in the first place six years ago. I just wanted to know who he was."

Jade reached across the table and put his hand on hers. "I know some of who he is, mom. It took a long time, but he finally opened up to me once or twice, and he's a lot more complicated than the stiff-lipped tough guy role he's had to play. In some weird way, he actually reminded me of you once or twice."

Alice let out a little laugh and raised her eyebrows. "Weird being the operative word, Seamus."

She told him they needed to be prepared for alternatives, should something go wrong with their plan. She said she had cash for them, plenty of it for the trip and afterward, and, if they got split up, he should contact Wally. "He's prepared to take a call from anywhere and wire you what you need."

Jade asked her about the memoir now in Helen's possession, and she said Helen would send a copy to them in Canada when they get settled. She said Helen also has a copy of the information she'd given *The New*

York Times, and that she was prepared to get it to the right people if necessary.

"Right people?" he asked.

"I need to have some leverage in case Dennis interferes," she said. "And he will try. Rest assured. But I have a backup plan."

The phone rang. They looked at each other and let it ring two more times. Alice stood up and reached for it.

"It's Tamara," she said, holding her hand over the speaker.

When she hung up, she told Jade that Tamara said to scratch the idea of making a trade for the '57 Chevy. Transportation was already arranged.

"Tamara's family is connected with people in Scottsville, a village not far from the airfield," she said. "The airplane arrangements are shifting, so if the plane can't make the trip as scheduled for this evening, her family's friends would put up the group in their Scottsville home for tonight and, if necessary, tomorrow night.

"They'll pick up all of us this afternoon in the garage behind Wally's house. We'll need to get to Wally's well before then and wait. They have a windowless van to provide better cover than a car. The van will also take us from Scottsville to the airfield at the appropriate time, hopefully tonight."

While Alice was upstairs running the bath water, Jade cleaned up the dishes and took a final tour of the little house where he'd lived for the longest six years of his life. He allowed himself a laugh about the stone occupants of The Grotto, but he wasn't yet prepared for more turmoil and the empty feeling he had about leaving yet again with his mother, this time on the run. That thought made him realize something he hadn't considered—she was always on the run.

There was a knock at the front door. Jade jumped back two steps. He slipped to the window to peek outside and then quickly unlocked the door.

Roland stood there with a thin smile on his worried face. Jade waved him inside and locked the door.

"I need to see your mother—uh, I mean…Alice," he said, his voice sounding deeper than Jade had ever heard it. "I need to…apologize. I said some things yesterday that probably hurt her. I'm leaving today and I thought she'd—"

"Oh, man, yeah," Jade said, smiling. "She just told me minutes ago that she wished she had a chance to talk with you."

Roland smirked and his eyes widened. "There you go with that 'man' thing again."

They laughed, and then Jade pointed to the Virgin and the saints. "And here I thought you came back to see if we could let you take all these nice White people to New York with you."

Roland sighed. "Yeah, that would be a big treat for my comrades. Holy White people. They'd be thrilled."

In the kitchen, Jade told him Alice was upstairs taking a bath and would be down in a little while. He opened the refrigerator and offered Roland iced coffee, and Roland started in on him about being "fancy."

"Iced coffee. Wow. You been to New York while I wasn't looking?" he chided.

They sat together at the kitchen table with their iced coffees, and Roland told him about Squirrel.

"He said he was well taken care of, just like Hafferty said. For once, that man seems to have told the truth, but I'm sure there's more to it than that. Squirrel's not saying much more. He's on one of his mood upswings. Been making stupid jokes about his captivity, which I do not find funny. He's outside right now in his mother's Buick across the street under that big tree. He'll be driving me to New York. Not sure where he goes after that."

"What the hell is he doing outside? Tell him to come in."

Roland shook his head. "I asked him to wait. I need some privacy here. For when I talk to her."

"After you stormed out of here last night," Jade said, "everyone left like this was a house on fire."

"Yeah, well, I said what I had to say, and I didn't want to hear anymore grief about it, especially from my father." Jade saw fire in Roland's eyes. "I have work to do, and it's not at that damn bomb factory, and it's not with that motherfucker Hafferty who's been pulling my puppet strings my whole life. Those strings are cut. And I'm glad he lost his chance at Congress. I don't know why he wanted to go there anyway. He's god around here, and he'd be just another fat White guy in D.C., pillaging the government till for his bomb factories. Hell, he already gets that dough without being in Congress, so why go there? He probably thinks he can be the king of Washington, too. Pretty funny, if you ask me. I've been there. A lot of fat White guys just like him are already settled in there, and all of them think they're kings. He'd be at the bottom of the pile."

There was a loud pounding on the back door. Roland stood up. The back door opened as Jade stood and reached for the knob.

Dennis Hafferty's hefty frame filled the doorway. A scowl on his face morphed into his fluorescent smile when he saw Jade and Roland. He tucked his thumbs into his suspenders under his tan suit coat and stepped inside, his bulging red face matching his tie.

"Well," he said, his voice booming as he opened his arms and strode to the sink. "My boys are here. I came to see the old lady, but this is a very pleasant surprise." He ran his thick finger across the edge of the sink and then settled his googly eyes on Jade and Roland.

"Called in sick again today, boys? Is this where you're hiding out this time? You won't make much of an impression on your new general manager if you keep skipping work." His eyes shifted to the duffle bag behind the open door. "Somebody going away?" He looked from Jade to Roland and back again, his toothy smile on parade. "That's not momma's bag. She'd have something prettier and way more expensive than that thing. You joining the army after all, Jade?"

"It's my laundry," Jade said.

"Oh yeah? Washer's broken, huh?" Hafferty raised his eyebrows, and his smile turned into a half-frown. His eyes seemed to shrink a bit as they settled on Jade. "Place looks neat and tidy, Jade. Your mamma must be busy keeping this place so nice for you. Maybe she did it for your special guest, here. I did not realize you two were so close, Roland here looking comfortable with his coffee and all." He turned to Roland. "I'm assuming you've met Jade's mother, the lovely Alice Flynn."

Roland nodded once, his face frozen.

Dennis strolled into The Grotto, asking for Alice. Jade followed him, and said she was in the bath. "What did you want with her?"

"Well, I don't want to take a bath with her, that's for sure," he said, forcing a laugh at his lousy joke. He stood in front of the Blessed Virgin and looked her up and down. "Never been this close to the mother of God."

He turned around to face Jade and Roland standing next to the couch, his capped and gleaming teeth on full display. He reached into the inside pocket of his suit jacket and held up a blue envelope. "Got a little business to conduct with your mother, that's all. I can wait. Mind if I smoke?"

He lit up a Benson & Hedges and exhaled toward the boys, holding up the box. "Anybody else?" He motioned to the couch. "Take a seat, boys. I'm glad you're here, actually. I have great news for you two."

Jade and Roland remained standing. Hafferty began pacing among the statues and votive candles, smoking and waving his hand in the air. "Boys, the deal I offered you is still on, but it's gotten a lot better, if you can believe that's possible! A better deal for you and a better chance for me to win big." He stopped and faced them, grinning. "Not in the upcoming election, gentlemen, but in the election two years from now. By then, Henry Walsh will be retiring, or will be strongly encouraged to do so, and our team will have spent two years building a solid base for the campaign. And that building process will include you and you." He pointed to them, his teeth shining in the dim light.

He stood in front of them with his hands on his hips, looking at Roland. "Before I give you the details, Roland, how's your pal, Bozak? Did you tell Jade how great a job we did taking care of him?"

Roland nodded once and said, "Yes."

"And we will continue to take care of that boy, too," Hafferty said, nodding. "In fact, we're gonna have a place for Bozak in my campaign, but not right away. He'll have to work a little longer at Macson, where he can be my inside man there. Unlike you two, he's good at mixing it up and getting info. A real natural undercover man. Believe me, he'll be well compensated."

Then he segued into his new deal for the boys. They'd resign from Macson Wednesday morning and immediately join him in his private office at the Civic Center to begin the work on his '71 campaign for U.S. Congress, with the help of specialists from New York and Washington.

As he said this, Jade felt the fire of turmoil brewing in his gut. He'd marveled at this man's ability to cajole and persuade, realizing now how gullible he'd been. An easy mark. A kid without a father in awe of a man in charge of the world around him, so much so that the man could turn an entire room in five minutes with his performance, his theatrics, his charm, and his guile. And, for those who still hovered in doubt, he could always bring out his big purse and throw them a few coins. This was the same man who'd ruled secretly over Alice, keeping her in a constant state of fear and furor, crushing her every move, driving her to desperation. A man who could smile and swagger on the stage and then choke the life out of his own stepsister behind the curtain. Jade's gut was burning now, as the show continued.

"You boys would need to sign an oath of nondisclosure, of course," Hafferty said, pacing among the statues, "because we won't announce the campaign for another six to eight months. The Civic Center suite will be closed to the public and guarded day and night. For the campaign, it will be equipped with desks for you two, televisions and extra phones and other equipment, and you'll have the luxury of working in a first-rate environment. It's like a five-star hotel, isn't it, boys?"

He butted his cigarette in one of the votive candles, lit up another one, and stood a few feet in front of Jade and Roland. "In addition, you boys will share a place to live—a two-bedroom suite in the Sheeley Hotel on the same floor as my suite. We'll be a family, all together. The three of us. But still independent. You'll be paid twice the rate you're getting at Macson, with plenty of opportunity for overtime—at time and a half! As for college, you can attend Dickson part-time if you wish, but part-time would still leave both of you One-A for the draft. Of course, I would handle keeping you out of the army, as always. As long as you work for me, you're draft free." He let out a two-note laugh. "Don't go around saying that, but it's a pretty good slogan, isn't it? Work for me, you're draft free! Just warming up for the campaign, boys." He lifted his fists and shifted his shoulders like a boxer waiting for the first-round bell.

His smile expanded as he scanned their blank faces and then lit another cigarette. "After our victory in '71," he said as he began pacing

478

again, "we'll all move to Washington, where you'll work with me on Capitol Hill and have your own apartments. Roland, you can attend Howard part-time and, Jade, across the Potomac from Washington there's George Mason College, part of the University of Virginia, where you can continue or begin your college career, depending on whether or not you attend Dickson first. It's all worked out. I have good connections there. We're still a team, boys."

He stopped again and held out his arms, the fingers of one hand inches from the chest of the Blessed Virgin. His eyes followed his arm, and he looked at her face. "Don't worry, Mother. I won't hurt you. Just tell your boys here to lighten up, will ya?" He looked from Roland to Jade and held out his hands. "Are you boys with me?"

Jade held his breath as he pushed down on his roiling gut. He glanced over at Roland, who just stared at Hafferty's thick glasses, focusing on nothing. Jade finally understood Roland's buried rage. He'd been handled by this trickster his whole life and, in this very room just twelve hours earlier, he'd announced to those who loved him that he was going to risk his life to finally get a chance to be with people like him—men and women who'd been crushed their whole lives by a nation of men like Hafferty, while Roland had enjoyed the protection of that same man. Protection from the real world. Isolation. A lone Black face in a sea of White. A lone stranger in a strange land.

"I understand your hesitancy, boys," Hafferty said, his head turning to the side as he looked at them and then held up his hand. "I get it. I do. My last offer went south, and I didn't tell you guys it was over. You had to learn from someone else. That was my fault, and I apologize. I was a bit distracted, as you might imagine. But I can understand how you might think this offer will fall dead, too. But let me tell you this." He stepped closer to them and put his hands on his hips again, his eyes moving from face to face, his voice softening. He let the phony smile fall, as he took on that paternal look Jade had fallen for more than once.

"I think you boys are aware that I'm a wealthy man," he said, lifting his heavy chin and looking down his nose at Jade. "I'm only 41 years old, so I have a long life ahead of me. But I'm here to tell you that I don't have heirs. I don't have children. Or nephews or nieces. Or even a wife, thank God." He let out a little chuckle, but Jade and Roland remained mum. Jade lifted his eyes and met Hafferty's. He saw the fatherly face grow more sincere and realized he could be fooled by it yet again. But this time, the hoax set his gut afire. He could barely breathe. He felt the heat rising in his neck.

"As things stand, boys," Hafferty said, his voice soft and almost consoling. "I consider you two my family. And as such, you would be my heirs." He nodded in the affirmative to each of them and then leaned toward them and whispered. "We're talking about *lots* of money, gentlemen. And some wonderful properties. You'll be set. For. Life."

He froze there in front of them, letting his words sink in. Then his politician smile erupted on his face.

"Of course, I'd have to die first. Maybe you'd want to kill me." He exhaled a forced laugh, and Jade nearly choked on the acidic stench of cigarettes and booze. Hafferty stepped away and paced toward the Virgin and back again, his finger in the air. "You wouldn't be the first." His laugh seemed forced yet again.

"But seriously, boys—Roland, you're already like a son to me. I'm not saying I'm going to try to take you away from your dad; he's one of my closest friends. But I'm saying, regardless of his situation, *you* would be my *heir*. And as for you, Jade, same thing goes. I'm not sure what will happen to your mother, but if something should, well, I'd offer to adopt you as my son. I was adopted, too, when I was a boy, and it turned out to be a pretty good deal." He stopped in front of them again.

"So there it is. Roland. Jade. Stick with me, work on my campaign, win with me, come to Washington with me, go to college, stay with me, and be my heirs. Your life is set. If you're smart, you can turn my wealth into even greater wealth for yourselves one day. But I need you to be loyal to me. Be on my team. For good."

Jade felt the heat flushing his face, and he tried to remember what Alice had told him long ago about turning his rage into action before it was turned against him. He thought he heard movement upstairs and looked at Roland to see if he would respond. Roland's eyes seemed to be somewhere else.

"What is your business with my mother?" Jade said through gritted teeth. He clenched his fists, steadied his stance, and tightened the knot around his burning gut.

Hafferty closed his mouth, giving Jade a grim grin. "That's what's so special about you, do you know that, Jade? You just listened to the offer of a lifetime, and your first question is about your mother. You're dedicated, I can see that. And that's why I'm making you this incredible offer. Because once you're in, nothing can get in the way of your dedication. Your commitment."

"So what *is* your business with Alice?" Roland said, startling Jade. Roland's voice was deep and threatening. Hafferty turned to him with a sudden frown and lifted his frame to meet Roland's height and his dark eyes. Then he looked back at Jade and turned on his heel. He fumbled with his lighter and lit another cigarette, turned back to face them and held up his hand.

"My business, gentlemen, is that of the County Court." His mouth was flat and his googly eyes behind the thick lenses seemed to glow with flames. "Alice is not well, boys. She has alcohol and possibly drug addiction issues, and she needs psychiatric help as well. Look around this room. This is not the living room of a normal mother. She's been to my office recently, and I have to say, it was obvious to me that she's not right. I talked with her doctor, and he's convinced she is in the grips of a nervous breakdown and has been for months now—a condition she's suffered several times over the years. There's a hospital that specializes in caring for women in her condition, and, after a period of time, she should be ready to get back to her life as a healthy and independent woman."

He moved closer to them, and Jade took a half step back, his fists locked.

"Meanwhile," Hafferty said, his magic smile returning, "you boys will be well taken care of and on your way to a prosperous life of your own. I see both of you guys sailing through your Political Science degrees after your two years of work on my campaign. Roland, you could even set yourself up to run for office after you get out of Howard. God knows, we need some Afro-American representatives in Congress, and I see you as a natural. And Jade, you're more of a behind the scenes guy, so I see you as a key player in Roland's campaigns."

"So you're here to take her away, is that it?" Jade said, his voice shaking. His heart pounded as he struggled to keep his rage controlled. "You just stopped by without warning her, without calling? To take her to a hospital? What's in that envelope?"

Hafferty gave him the grim grin again and removed a long document from the blue envelope and held it up. "It's a court order, son, signed by Judge Albert Lewis. I'm sorry, son, but I've been asked to take her to the Valmont asylum for assessment. The order says she's a danger to herself, to you, and to the public."

Jade exploded. "You've been asked? You've been *asked*? No one *asks* you, Hafferty! You *tell* them what you want, and they give it to you!" He raised his fists halfway and stepped closer to Hafferty and pushed his chin toward the jowly crimson face. The fire was in his brain now, and it was raging. "You want my mother in an *asylum*? A mental institution! *Why*? Because she knows everything about you? Because she knows you're a thief and a liar and a fucking *monster*?! You've destroyed my mother's life?! And now you're here to finish the job? Is that what you've been *asked* to take care of, Hafferty? Asked by your*self*? To put her away for *good*?!"

As he hollered and spit the last words, Jade felt an iron grip on his arm. He thought it was Roland and was ready to punch his own brother. He turned around. Stanley Selczyk's scowling mask and dead eyes were inches from Jade's face.

67

Implore No More

S he's barefoot at the top of the stairs in her red silk robe, hand on the pistol in her pocket, listening to that voice. That sales pitch. Always hustling. Feigning generosity, beseeching trust. The voice scratches at her brain—a persistent, raspy rat. If only others knew his real voice.

She takes a step down and stops, hearing him say something that freezes her to her soul. He is offering Jade and someone else a place to live, with him. She heard clearly, *"A family, the three of us."* Roland? Yes, it was Roland's voice she'd heard earlier. Dennis is offering Jade and Roland another job and is asking them to move in with him.

She clenches the handle of the pistol and looks down at her feet, then her bare knees, the thin robe clinging to her body, her nipples showing through the silk. "No," she says. "No. I will not supplicate before him. No more."

She steps up and into her room, tossing the pistol on her bed. She yanks clothes from the floor and her dresser and throws them next to the pistol. She pulls the sash and lets the robe fall to her feet. She thinks she hears him say something about being his heirs, his family. Her heart races as she pulls her black jeans over her bare rear end, fastens the belt and then shoves the pistol into the small of her back. She yanks on the black tee shirt, stumbles into Jade's room and finds his old black Converse All-Stars and shoves her feet into them. She pauses when she hears him make his final pitch. He was saying something about coming with him to Washington, *go to college, be my heirs.* Her breath catches in her throat as she heads for the stairs. At the top, she is startled by Jade's voice asking Hafferty what business he has with her. Jade sounds angry. Enraged.

She makes her way down, tiptoeing closest to the wall where the treads don't squeak, listening to Dennis's announcement about a court order. As she reaches the bottom step, she hears Jade's voice howling. He's screaming. *Asylum. Mental institution. Liar. Monster. Destroyed my mother's life.*

She peeks around the corner of the wall at the base of the stairs and sees Stanley's face in the kitchen doorway. He grabs Jade by the arm and points a pistol at Roland.

She reaches back to her waistband and wraps her hand around the grip of her silver .38.

68
Unholy Specimen

Tuesday, July 22, 1969

"Sit down, Roland. Relax." Hafferty pointed to the couch. He was standing in front of it, his back to the Blessed Virgin. "Put Jade next to him, Stanley. Go easy with that gun, now. We don't want to damage these boys. They're already victims, been brainwashed by that coo-coo bird upstairs. We're gonna put an end to that nonsense right away. By way of Valmont State Hospital. Then we'll give the boys some time to recover from their brainwashing, so they can carry on with their lives in a productive way. The way I just outlined for you, boys."

Hafferty nodded to Stanley and waved his hand at Roland and Jade. "Just keep your weapon ready, Stanley, while I go upstairs and retrieve the coo-coo bird from her bath. She'll be nice and clean for her first night in Valmont. Maybe get a gold star from her shrink." He flashed the fluorescent smile at Jade, as if he were a member of his fawning audience, as if he'd laugh at the lame joke.

"Stanley, if you have to use the gun, aim to maim, please, not to kill. These boys are far more useful to me alive than dead. You know my rule, Stanley. Hurt 'em enough to remind 'em who's boss, but don't finish 'em off."

As he turned toward the stairway door, Hafferty called out to Alice in a childish singsong. "Oh, coo-coo bird, here I come. I hope you're all cleaned up and naked, cuz the shrinks at Valmont love to get their paws on naked patients. Especially pretty ones like you, coo-coo bird."

As he stepped toward the shadowed doorway, Alice emerged, startling Hafferty. "Jesus fucking Christ!" he bellowed, taking a step backward.

Alice offered a steely grin, her hands at her thighs, palms out. "It's quite clear the boys aren't falling for your sales pitch any longer, Dennis. And you'll never get elected to Congress, not this time, not next time, or even to County Commissioner again—not with all that information out there on you. Dell Cranstone backed down, but it's in the hands of others who can do even more damage than he could. All I have to do is give them the green light, and you're finished."

Hafferty glanced at Roland and Jade, his googly eyes swimming in rage. He turned to Alice. "You won't be giving any of your fantasy friends a green light or a red light or even a white flag, Alice. Because you'll be in the loony bin where you belong." He pulled out the blue envelope from his breast pocket and waved it at her. "Court order! You're certifiable.

And I'm taking you in." He stepped toward her, his hand reaching for her arm as she stepped back.

"You touch her, and I will kill you with my bare hands!"

Hafferty paused and turned, his face twisted. It was Roland. He was on his feet and right behind Hafferty with his fists clenched at his sides. Stanley swept around the end of the couch and cocked his gun and held it to the back of Roland's head.

Hafferty's face relaxed, and his mouth reflexively leapt into his Day-Glo smile, his red cheeks twitching at the corners. "Well, if it isn't the dark hero of the valley, Mister James Roland Wilson, *former* high school star and now *benchwarmer* on the college squad. Or did you quit that squad, quit that school altogether, Roland? Because you're not good enough. And now you plan to join your Black brothers in New York in their losing battle against the U.S. Government and Mr. Hoover's formidable COINTELPRO? Twenty-one New York Panthers are now sitting in Rikers Island cells, did you know that, Roland? Looks to me like a losing proposition all around, wouldn't you say, Roland? You're walking into a shitstorm with your eyes closed. You're hoping to play in the big leagues when you can't even make it off the bench in college."

Jade saw Alice lift her chin and grit her teeth. "James already told Roland everything, Dennis. He knows about me, and he knows all about you. The truth."

Hafferty wheeled around to her. "The truth!" he shouted. "You mean that I raised this boy, and that his mother died in childbirth, a sweet but hopeless little colored girl from the D.C. ghetto? Is that what you mean, Alice? Because *that's* the truth."

"That's the lie James has been telling me for years," Roland said, the gun still at his skull. "But he finally told me the truth two days ago. Alice, your stepsister, is my mother. And if you touch her—"

Stanley shoved him forward with the gun, and Hafferty stepped inches from Roland's face. "You'll what, Roland? With a gun to your head, you'll do what? Take a last swing at me while Stanley puts a bullet into your soft brain? Sounds about right, Roland. You'd fit in with your Panther brothers perfectly. Idiots taking pot shots at the greatest police forces in the world and expecting to win."

"Roland, sit down," Alice said in a steady tone. "Stanley will put his gun away if you just slowly sit down on the couch. Please. We can all just settle down and talk. I think Mr. Hafferty will agree that we can come to the end of our relationship in peace. He'll go his way, and we'll go ours."

Roland remained standing as Hafferty turned to her.

"Well, now, listen to the mother of the year," he snarled. "And what a mother you are. Dressed like a man, all in black, with your tits showing through that tee shirt like a slut. Like some hippie babe. You can't make up your mind, can you, Alice? Are you a girl, or are you a boy? Are you a mommy, or are you a hippie? And the only friends you have are a bunch of statues in your parlor. You were crazy enough to think your old flame, Dell Cranstone, was your friend, but all he wanted to do was to fuck you. God knows why. And now you want to sit down and talk? Alice, you can't complete a thought, much less a conversation. You've been having a nervous breakdown for months, Alice. You've completely lost your mind. And you've filled these boys' heads with your fantasies, and now you're threatening to throw away the best chance they have to become men of significance, men who will earn the respect of others and become something more than the losers you're trying to make of them."

Jade finally found his voice. "You should just leave, Hafferty. We're not coming with you. And our mother is not either."

He stood up, and Stanley turned the gun on him. Roland spun around, punched the gun out of Stanley's grasp and smashed his face with the other fist. Then he picked him up by the scruff of his shirt and slammed him to the floor. Stanley's head bounced twice, his eyes bulging with rage.

Hafferty stepped toward the gun on the floor, but Jade beat him to it. Alice froze Hafferty in place, her pistol at the back of his head. "One more step, Dennis, and you're dead. Take it from a crazy woman. I'll do it."

Jade held the gun on Stanley as Roland reared back and slammed Stanley's face with a hammer punch. The dead eyed man's mouth slackened, and he lay still, his eyes closed. Jade turned the gun on Hafferty.

"Put the gun down, Jade," Alice said calmly. "I've got him. Keep it on Stanley. You ok, Roland?"

"Never better," he said in his deep tone, his chest heaving, his eyes on Hafferty. He stepped up to him. "She tried to do this peaceably, Mr. Commissioner, but you would not have it. Jade, go get a kitchen chair, and set it next to that statue. We're gonna keep you quiet for a while, Hafferty, while we get ready to leave. It may be the first time in your life your mouth won't be flapping like you own everyone around you."

There was a rumbling noise in the kitchen and then a crashing sound. Jade turned the gun toward the kitchen door. Two voices grunting and then silence.

"Get behind the couch, Jade, and hold the gun steady," Alice said, as she shoved the barrel of her pistol deeper under the shelf of Hafferty's skull. "Just squeeze if you see a gun pointed at you."

"Ronnie!" Hafferty called out. "They have two guns. Stay where you are."

Alice shoved the pistol deeper into Hafferty's skull and his back arched. "Shut up, Dennis," she said through gritted teeth. "I know that's difficult for you, little boy, but I've got nothing to lose by pulling this trigger and a world to gain by watching your tiny brains leave a lovely tattoo on the ceiling of this hideous dungeon you've kept us in."

Jade heard a familiar voice from the kitchen. "Don't shoot, Jademan. I got him right here, and I have his gun." It was Squirrel. "I'll walk him toward the doorway. You'll see him first."

Ronnie appeared in the doorway with a scowl on his face, his back arched. A Bowie knife was at his throat, and next to his head was Squirrel's grinning mug. He had Ronnie's arm pulled up behind him, and Ronnie grunted as Squirrel pushed up harder. "He's a lousy lookout but a worse ambusher," Squirrel said. He sized up the room and nodded to Roland. "His pistol's on the floor in the kitchen, Ro."

Squirrel retrieved rope from his car, and he and Roland tied up Hafferty and Ronnie, gagging them with strips of the sheets Alice had used for the statues, and then binding them to kitchen chairs next to the Blessed Mother. Then Roland hogtied the unconscious Stanley as he lay face down. He wrapped Stanley's eyes in a sheet strip and pried open his mouth and secured a gag that stretched Stanley's leathery face into a wide grimace.

"Now you look like a brother in a Rikers Island cell, Stanley," Roland announced. "Take a look, Hafferty. This is how my brothers are being treated. The only difference is that they are courageous men. Your swine here is the lowest form of animal. Thanks to you and the powers you've given him. I hope you're proud."

Alice told them to take the gag off Hafferty so she could have a few last words with him. When Squirrel loosened the gag, Hafferty took the cue to snarl at Alice.

"If you think you'll get away with this, bitch, you're nuttier than I thought you were. Giallo's men are on their way here. They'll make your little band of boys here look like the pikers they really are. And they won't spare you either. Probably take turns on you before they slit your throat. And I'll get to watch. And it will be a beautiful thing."

"Giallo's not sending anyone to your rescue, little Denny," Alice said quietly to him, aiming the pistol at his face. "I've already covered that item. Giallo's scrambling to get his distance from you right now. The people I gave your story to? They have plenty on Giallo, too, and his connections to you. And, on top of that, they now have something I hadn't given Dell. The fact that thirty years ago, young Sallie Giallo killed your real daddy, Michael Hafferty, and there's proof. Giallo's moving fast to separate himself from you, because he knows you. When the questions come at you, you'll dime him out the first chance you get. He might even want you dead right now. If his men are coming here, they're coming for you, not me."

"What are you talking about, bitch? You really *are* insane. Look at you," he snapped, his foggy eyes flashing. "No wonder the judge wants you in the looney bin. You're just another bra burning dyke. I'll bet your boys here don't know you like the taste of pussy."

Alice struck him in the jaw with the barrel of her gun, and his glasses popped off his face and fell to the floor. He seemed shocked more than pained as he turned his big head toward her. His eyes—no longer swarms of blue behind thick lenses—were tiny pin holes at the center of a bloodied mass of fleshy jowl.

Alice picked up his glasses from the floor and tossed them in his lap. "Now *that's* the foul-mouthed Dennis that I know. That's the real menace coming out from behind your bloated phony veneer." She scraped the gun across his bloody cheek and wiped it off on the other cheek. "Gag him, Roland."

"What are you gonna do, shoot us, bitch?" Dennis barked, his tiny eyes searching blindly for her face. "I have people everywhere. You'll be caught, all four of you. Hunted down in no time. Amateurs up against my professionals. And then you'll be on your knees begging me for your lives."

Roland tore a strip of sheet and leaned close to Hafferty's face.

"You put that on me, boy, and I'll have you hung from the highest tree."

Roland grinned as he tightened the gag and spoke loudly into Hafferty's covered ear. "Well bless your pointed little head."

Hafferty's muffled shouts were muted by a loud groan from Stanley. He stirred on the floor, straining at his bindings. Alice hovered over him. "Please try to escape, Stanley. Because I won't miss this time." She put the barrel of the pistol against the top of his head. "Please, Mr. Rapist. Please make one more move to untie your hands and feet." She cocked the gun and shoved it into his scarred temple, and he lay still, a tremor in his limbs.

Alice's face had a look that Jade had never seen. Her eyes wild, her jaw jutted forward, her teeth clenched and bared. When she lowered the gun after a long minute, Jade's sigh came out in tremors.

She gave Stanley's head a last shove with the barrel of her pistol, stepped past Hafferty and Ronnie and put her arm around the Virgin's shoulder, her cheek pressed against the statue's head, the two faces joined, one real, one clay.

"I present before you, Queen Mother, three of the most pathetic excuses for humans in your vast realm," she said, a turned down smile on her face as she glared into Hafferty's cold, frightened eyes. Then she let go of the statue and started to pace among her captives, her gun swaying in her hand. The look in her eyes had changed again, at once distant and focused, fey and fierce. She stopped in front of Dennis, cocked the gun again and pushed it slowly toward his face until it rested in the notch at the top of his nose. His pinpoint eyes followed the barrel until they were crossed. His jowls jiggled. Spittle seeped from his quivering papery lips.

"This unholy specimen before you, Mother, is the feckless parasite known as Michael Dennis Hafferty," she said, as she used the barrel of the pistol to drag the spittle from Dennis's chin and poke it under his gag against the fragile veneer of his shiny front teeth. His head bucked backward, and he made a moaning sound.

She continued to pace, stopping occasionally to hover over Stanley for emphasis.

"He was named for his father," she declared, her tone now prosecutorial. "Unlike his indolent offspring, Michael Senior was actually a well-liked man who had worked diligently for his constituents during his decade in the twenties as Commissioner of this doomed county. His only son never had a job in his life, never worked for pay, but rather grifted for it—a natural born swindler. Stole millions from a dying man and even more from American taxpayers. But never once did he lift a finger in actual work. Always talking, but never working. Always having others do his bidding. Unlike his real father, little Dennis has no particular ideology. He's simply a narcissist, a cynical small man interested in others only if he can leverage them to his advantage.

"But poor old dad? Michael Senior? Despite his political skill and fortitude, he was the victim of his own wanton needs, his insatiable libido. And curiously, Mother Mary, he was indiscriminate in his choices. Young, old, female, male—it didn't matter. He confined his dalliances to New York City, but, when he was ten years into his new job here in the valley heading up my father's war machine interests, he was murdered in 1939. It was ruled a suicide—a note had been left, confessing to homosexual proclivity.

"Of course, it was a frame job, orchestrated by my own evil father, whose temperament was ruled by his rules—one in particular was his belief that sex with one's own gender was sinful, evil. So he hired a young greenhorn named Sally Giallo to set up the charade in a New York hotel. Sally was such a natural at the ruse that my father later took him under his wing, evidently inspired by his resourcefulness. He seemed more impressed than disappointed that Sally had kept all the money my father had given him to hire a hitman, and instead had done the deed himself. Of course, my father had his own furtive motives for having Michael murdered. He'd been screwing Michael's wife—Dennis's mother—for years. And he'd struck out on molding one of his *actual* sons to his suiting, so he had Michael murdered, set it up as a suicide, and then played the hero, saving Mhairi from her grief and embarrassment by marrying her and acquiring her young son—an intellectually and emotionally stunted boy he could easily manipulate."

She paused next to the Blessed Virgin and put her hand on the statue's shoulder. "You see, Mother, the sins of the fathers are, well, not always handed down in a straight line. But you certainly know more about that than I. In the case of our boy, Dennis, my father decided that the name Michael Dennis Junior was no longer fitting for the boy under his tutelage, so he called him by his middle name when he arrived in our household. By the time Dennis learned from his stepfather that his real father's suicide was actually a murder committed by Giallo, he was already well along on his own unique path—a path far more disturbing than that of his real father. Dennis, you see, Mother, did not follow his daddy's wanton ways; he did not love women *or* men. Just himself. That said, rumors did persist around New York about his pederastic tastes.

"And his feelings toward girls and, later, women? Well, Mother, for girls and women, Dennis had a rather vindictive and violent attitude. Not sure why. Perhaps his real momma disappointed him somehow. Who knows? In any case, he proved to be a poor student, bouncing around from Catholic elementary school to private boarding school, then one high school after another, same with colleges, failing at academics, failing at football despite his size—he never made the cut, complaining of injuries all the time—and then setting a pattern of getting kicked out of schools time and again for problems with girls, and young women. Not the kind of problems you usually hear about, dear Mother Mary. You see, he never touched them sexually. Instead, he beat them up. Regularly. Viciously."

She left the statue's side and moved to Stanley, setting the barrel of her pistol on his head for a moment.

"I'll bet that sounds exciting to you, Stanley. Giving your little balls a stir? Starting to become clear about your natural attraction to Dennis? About why you serve so faithfully as this dirty man's dirty man? Could it be that you, too, Stanley, hate women? Love to rough them up? Love to molest them, rape them? Even snuff them out? I'll bet that notion just sends your little testes into a frenzy, doesn't it, Stanley?"

She dragged the barrel of the gun across the scar on Stanley's temple and cheek. "If I'd only let Jade hit you again with that iron pan." She hissed at him through gritted teeth.

She returned to Hafferty and continued her prosecution.

"Sally Giallo and my twisted father kept the murder secret, but the new wife, Mhairi—what a name, huh, Mother?—found out one night when my father went on a rampage, abusing her in his own special way, and the secret was overheard by my brother, Tormud, who eventually wrote it all down in letters to my sister, Deirdre, a cloistered nun. And now, certain people have investigated the circumstances surrounding the so-called suicide, and our dear friend, Mr. Giallo is not happy about it. Of course, he's not afraid of prosecution, but he is quite wary now of his formerly close association with my father, and with father's acolyte, Dennis, and he's certain that information pointing to him as a murderer, if made public, would bring him unwanted attention. And he's even more certain Dennis would double-cross him the moment the heat turns on our noble County Commissioner. If and when Dennis does return to the scene, there will be a separation of church and state, as it were. Giallo being the church, of course. You should see Giallo swoon in front of his own version of your likeness, Mother Mary. Oh, it's so moving. Such a holy man is the murderer, Sally Giallo."

She stopped in front of Hafferty and glared at his pinpoint eyes. Sweat poured from his face and forehead. She grabbed his tie and wiped it on his eyes. "I know you can't see much past the bridge of your nose, little Denny—how symbolic for you. But all of us here can easily see those tiny rat-like blue coals in your face and the look of terror in them. Your bluster doesn't hold with us. You *are* terrified. *You* are now in the position of so many whom you've harmed over your malicious and vile existence. How does it feel, Denny? Scary?"

She pivoted toward the Virgin statue and began her pacing again.

"So, Mother Mary, if we set Dennis free, and he returns to his throne, he may turn around one day very soon and be face to face with his own Brutus, our beloved Sally Giallo, slipping the shiv into Dennis's heart for good old time's sake. You know how it goes with these bloodthirsty types, Mother. Kill the daddy, kill the son. After all, in the face of public pressure, Sally will have to keep Dennis quiet about Michael Hafferty's murder, and Giallo will know that the only way to keep a slime like Dennis quiet is to kill him."

She paused, a smirk at the edge of her mouth, her eyes wide on Jade and Roland.

Then she tugged at Hafferty's gag and pointed her pistol at his face. "I'm going to take this off you in a moment, Mister Commissioner, because you may want to give us your blessing as we depart from you and your esteemed colleagues. James and Roland and Jade and I are leaving this poisoned valley for good. And, if you try to thwart our exit or if you *ever* try to find us, there are certain very professional people who live here, and in other parts of the world, who are prepared, in the event of *anything* happening to anyone I love, *anything*—they are prepared to release to the press all of the information that Dell had failed to follow up on, plus much, much more."

Jade touched her arm, and she turned to him abruptly, her face almost unrecognizable. He saw pain and anguish there, worse than any he'd ever seen before.

"Let's go, mom," he said. "I'll get your bag. When we get to safety, we'll make the call."

490

Alice's face was still lost in her rage, her eyes wide with anger and venom. Jade thought she was going to turn and shoot Hafferty, so he put his hand gently on the arm that held her gun. She cleared her eyes and nodded her head. "I'm okay, honey." She gave him a thin smile, and he could see in her eyes that her composure was quickly returning. "I'm more than okay," she said, her smile edging wider.

She turned to Hafferty. "We'll alert someone to come get you in due course, little Denny. We won't leave you to die, just swelter a bit, perhaps piss in your pants, or worse, and get a little hungry and thirsty. But you haven't missed a meal in years. You could last a long time living off that hideous tumescence bursting at your belt. Not sure about your boyfriends here. But that's on you. They're *your* stooges."

She backed away and glared at him. "You smell like rot, Dennis. But then, you always did." She put her pistol in her back waistband and looked once more at his eyes, pointing a finger inches from his face. "If you *ever* try to interfere with any of our lives wherever we are in the world, Michael Dennis Hafferty's awful life, along with Stanley's nefarious deeds, will be known nationwide, perhaps worldwide. You will be known infamously as a sick, slovenly, craven man, who hated and persecuted women and gay people and stole millions from American taxpayers to enrich himself and his friends, millions made on the suffering victims of the weapons of war. *Your* wars. All for greed and power. A grandiose cover for the whimpering little coward that *you* truly are."

She unknotted his gag and held it away from him. He sputtered and coughed and found his voice, weakened but searing with hate.

"You mean your father's blood money, don't you, bitch?" he shouted. "Money you wallowed in as a rich girl. And now you're on your high horse, you two-faced whore. You hypocrite."

"Exactly," she said, quickly seething again. "My father's money and my father's assets that you stole from him. Blood money that you used to torture me and my sons and James and countless others, for your own sick pleasure. I should kill you right now and end the mayhem you will continue to bring to innocent others."

"Go ahead, pull the trigger. You worthless *cunt*. His capped and bloodied teeth showed through in a broken version of his once fluorescent smile, now a dark and slimy maw slithering in his own venom. "But no," he snarled, "you can't do that, can you? You don't have the balls."

She yanked the pistol from her waistband and jabbed it toward his face and then shoved it between his legs, and he gave out a loud groan. "You mean like these tiny testes here?" she growled at him, as she cocked the gun. "These little baby beans you call balls? These empty sperm bags that have withered up from uselessness over the years?" She shoved the gun up further, and he groaned even louder. "To think," she shouted over his wailing, "my father chose you because of these empty little sacs. He was a fool for falling for your lies, but he deserved it. You deserved each other. Equally evil. *Diavoli.*"

She shoved the gun further up his crotch, and he let out a howl. "Don't worry, Denny boy," she shouted inches from his face, "you will meet up with him again. In the darkest corner of Hell."

She spit in his eyes, and he shook his head and blinked fiercely, frowning, and gurgling something inaudible.

She slugged him on the side of the head with her pistol, and he passed out.

Alice stood up tall and swayed a little, and Jade caught her arm. She laid a hand on his and pulled away and stepped up to the Virgin statue.

She asked Jade and Roland to help her. They dragged the statue close to Hafferty's unconscious form slumped in the chair.

"Keep him in his place, dear Mother," she implored with practiced exaggeration. "He cringes at a woman's touch. Makes him even weaker than he is." She gently lowered the statue so that it rested securely on his neck, keeping his head bowed.

"There you are, big boy," she said, her voice sweet as it could be, coming as it was between gritted teeth. "Now you're nice and cozy with a holy woman. Don't whine too much when you wake up, little Denny. She doesn't like whiners." She grabbed his flabby cheeks and turned his unconscious head toward the Virgin statue.

"See that bloody green snake under her foot?" she whispered. "That was the last whiner she heard from."

Epilogue

August 1974

She was bareback on Lucky. The mane was black, but Lucky's head and body were wrong. Her golden-brown skin was now as black as the mane.

She held her head high as Lucky carried her through the open front doors, then making their way through the foyer into the open grand room with its sweeping double staircase and knight in shining armor and thousand-piece glass chandelier hung from the gilded dome ceiling so high over their heads.

She felt a smile growing on her mouth as Lucky walked past the library and stopped at the entrance to the dining room. Tormud was blocking the double doors. He was covered in black soot, his miner's cap bent and crumpled, his eyes and mouth white inside the mask of coal dust. His teeth were yellow, his tongue pink as he spoke to her.

"You can't go in there. He's in there, with his associates. You cannot go in."

"Step aside, Tormud," she said. "We are welcome here. We are all welcome here. You can come in with us, too. Open the doors for us, please."

When Tormud opened the first door, the voices and laughter of the men caught him by surprise, and he stepped back.

"The other door, too, Tormud. Go ahead."

She pressed her heels against Lucky's flank, and they moved forward into the dining room. Her father was at the head of the table, watching and listening, as the men laughed and talked loudly and drank whiskey from glass tumblers. He looked up at her and said nothing. She saw Tara seated on his left, her chin on her chest. She appeared to be sobbing. Her long blonde hair was undone from her customary knot and fell around her shoulders, fanning out around the sides of her face, a soft wall to hide herself from him. She was wearing her beige coverup over her nightgown, and her hands were in her lap where she seemed to have settled her sorrowful eyes.

Next to Tara, a young girl sat in silence, looking at Lucky. Her skin was rosy, and her soft reddish braids tumbled over her flat chest. She was dressed in tennis whites. She had green eyes.

"Why are you naked?" her father said casually, as he looked up at her on Lucky. She looked down at herself, her breasts bare, the nipples erect, her legs spread across Lucky's back, her mons pushed against the filly's neck. "Put your clothes on," he barked.

"Tara," she said to the sobbing teenager. "You can come with us. Stand up. Come now."

Her father scowled at Tara, and put his hand on her shoulder, pushing down. Tara easily wriggled out from under his hand, pushed her chair back and stood up.

"Come, Tara. We're going where you will be loved." She reached her hand out to Tara and Lucky nodded and snorted. The men did not notice her or Lucky; they went on talking and laughing and drinking.

Tara stood before her and Lucky and took off her coverup and dropped it behind her, then untied the bow at the top of her nightgown and pushed it off her shoulders. The gown fell to her bare feet in a ruffle of pink and beige. Her breasts were full and pale, the nipples bluish, belly concave under a delicate rib cage, the tuft of hair at her mons a wispy blonde, the soft folds of skin beneath it bright pink. Her legs were pale, the knees reddish and bruised.

She stepped toward Lucky and reached up her hand. The younger girl in tennis whites appeared next to her and held out her cupped hands for Tara to step into, and in an instant Tara was straddled across Lucky's back, behind her sister.

Tormud opened the French doors onto a huge stone patio that led to an endless rolling lawn of cut green grass.

The naked sisters loped through the doorway and onto the lawn and then cantered to the top of the first knoll near the tee boxes. She turned Lucky around. Tara pointed to a window on the top floor. The younger sister was there in her tennis whites, her braids bright in the sunlight and her green eyes crystalline.

They looked down at the patio below the girl and saw the father standing at the edge of it, pointing at them, shouting something they could not hear.

She turned Lucky and jabbed the filly's sides with her heels, and they took off over the top of the knoll, heading down into the field of cut grass and then up toward the higher knoll in the distance. Lucky was moving faster, and she squeezed Tara's hands locked tight at her waist and smiled, and for a moment she closed her eyes.

"Are we free?" Tara whispered in her ear. "Are we free?"

As Lucky settled into a full rhythmic gallop, she shouted a laugh to her sister and fastened her arms to Lucky's neck, squeezing her knees

494

against the filly's flanks. A moment later, a pulsating rush of current surged from that deep down point of contact against the rhythmic ripple of Lucky's muscular neck. Suddenly it was an electric wave coursing with volcanic thrust throughout her body, blood swelling in every inch of her skin, the wave roaring through every pore, all the way to her fingertips and her toes and to the very core of her brain. She cried out in a guttural wail, and the wave kept coming.

"Yes! Yes!" she called out. "We are free! We are free!"

Tara's arms and hands gripped tighter onto her stomach, their bodies in sync now, Lucky pounding out the rhythm. She heard Tara moan and then shout with joy, just as a crackling shot pierced the air around them.

Another shot was fired, and the wave disappeared as fear took over, and she pounded Lucky with her heels and held her tighter around her neck. But she felt Tara's hands let go and then a coolness on her back where Tara's hot body had been fused to her own. She pulled up on Lucky's neck, commanding her to stop.

She turned the black horse around and saw Tara lying in the grass. She and Lucky charged toward her, and she jumped off and landed next to Tara whose brilliant blonde hair was strewn wildly in the grass, and her white arms and legs were open like a starfish on the sand, her eyes wide at the bright sky above them. Dark purplish blood was spreading from Tara's vulva, smearing her inner thighs.

"No!" she screamed as loud as her voice would carry and fell to her knees next to her sister, clutching the girl's face. But no sound had come from the scream.

She saw boots next to them and looked up at their father standing above them holding a rifle in his arms.

"She was a Papist," he said to her. "She disgraced our family name. You will never speak of her again."

She looked down at Tara. The girl's eyes were closed, her mouth was pale, her breath gone.

"You murdered her!" she shouted at her dead sister and then looked up at her father. But it wasn't her father standing there with the rifle aimed at her face. It was Dennis, with a wide rictus grin and muddy blue smudges where his eyes should be.

She screamed and leapt to her feet and charged at him, her teeth bared, her hands like claws, a deep growl in her throat.

A shot went off.

"Colette! Colette! *Svegliati! Svegliati!* Wake up!"

She tried to scream again, but a face appeared inches from hers, and the scream stuck in her throat.

"Era solo un sogno, amore mio. Just a dream."

She felt a warm hand on her cheek, wiping away her tears. *"Svegliati, dolce amore. Hai un ospite al piano di sotto.* You have a guest downstairs. *Un giovane."*

In the bathroom, she was trembling, covered in sweat, her tee shirt and underpants saturated. She peeled them off her body and dried herself with a towel, taking deep breaths, the bucket dropping and slowly rising in her chest. As she calmed her heartbeat, she began to dress. In the bedroom mirror, she saw joy returning at the thought of him, and she bolted from the room and hurried downstairs to greet him. They held onto each other for an eternity. She would not let him go until the dream faded.

They strolled together, arm in arm, along a wide promenade under a tunnel of trees, heading for the old walled city. The air was warm, the sky brilliant, the sun splashing through the dappled awning of leaves. As they walked in step, they gazed out to their left onto an endless field far below, a dazzling dance of sunflowers that seemed to stretch all the way to *Monte Amiata*, its deep purple hue rising from the sunflowers like a curtain under the sapphire sky, its craggy peaks backlit by a blinding golden glow. They did not speak until they reached a grotto beyond which more people were walking along *via Nationale* toward the huge *porta* in the distance—the entrance to the enclosed thirteenth century city. In the grotto of low trees and a fountain with stone cupids with their bows fixed and their lips spewing water into a pool, the mother and the son sat on a stone bench overlooking the sunflower fields. He was the first to speak.

He asked her why she was living here now, why she'd left Paris. "Was it because of her? The woman I just met? Gabriella?"

She laughed softly and held his hand, her eyes on the sun-speckled red earth in front of them. "I met her near Reims, where I was touring and learning about the history of Champagne from a new Parisian friend. We met Gabriella at the *Moët et Chandon* tour in Epernay, and perhaps it was the Dom Perignon—I'm such a lightweight these days. But I wouldn't say it was love at first sight, because I'm over forty now, and I don't believe in such things any longer. Not sure if I ever did."

He laughed self-consciously and sighed. "I'm not old enough yet, I guess."

"Oh? Have you been shot by an arrow?"

"Yeah, it certainly feels as if I have," he said reluctantly, grinning at her. Then he held up a finger. "But let's not get off the subject of Gabriella. Are you living here now with her, your Italian mistress? She's absolutely stunning, by the way."

She told him she was staying on through autumn to help with the olive harvest, and that she'd been helping out with the family farm, especially the animals, and giving tennis lessons to Gabriella's nieces, learning how to make cheese and limoncello with Gabriella's older sister and her husband. She said the family has horses, and she's already fallen in love with one, so she wasn't sure if returning to Paris was still in the cards. At least not for a while.

"But I haven't given up my little flat near the *Bois de Boulogne*. Subletting it for now. And I made some good friends there, and I've done well giving music and tennis lessons to some rich kids, and free English lessons for a few African immigrant kids. So, we'll see."

"Don't give up your flat yet, Mademoiselle Willaumez. I may need it."

"Monsieur Poinsot, you're moving to Paris?!"

"I'm waiting to hear from The Sorbonne. I've applied for a seat in a new master's program in comparative literature, and I've been wait-listed, so if there's an opening, I'll be moving there in September."

She let out a scream, jumped to her feet, pulled him off the bench, and pushed him around in a little dance, yelping a French pop song.

At a café inside the little walled city, she ordered a bottle of Chianti, and they had a Tuscan feast: plates of *pappa al pomodoro*, then fresh fruit and cheese, followed by *espresso* and soft almond biscuits she called *ricciarelli di Siena*. He told her about his studies at McGill and life in Montreal and that he'd been writing, but it was not going well, and that his new girlfriend was a native of Paris, part French, part Trinidadian, and also a writer, but she wasn't sure about returning to France just yet, and that created a conflict.

"If I'm accepted into the program, I'll have to choose. It won't be easy."

"I'll hang on to my flat until you decide," she said, placing her hand on his and running the other hand through his hair. "Does she love your soft wild curls?"

He offered to pour her another glass of wine, but she declined. "I'm not quite a teetotaler, but two glasses a week is my maximum, usually only one when we dine with Gabriella's family. Other than sips of the limoncello we make, I never touch the hard stuff. The closest I come to Four Roses is when I'm pruning the garden. No more medication required."

He laughed, with relief in his voice, and then asked her about her visions.

"Yes, from time to time, I still have some, but I've learned to accept them. It was Tamara who encouraged me to embrace them as part of my consciousness, so I've done that. Dreams, on the other hand, are still haunting, although I have fewer daydreams intruding in my rather busy life. And I think that's the key—keeping active. That, and not having to look over my shoulder day and night."

He told her he, too, has visions from time to time, and that surprised her. "I can't quite figure out any patterns for them," he said, as he sipped his wine. "But I definitely have something going on. My girlfriend is a bit skeptical about it, so I try to keep them to myself."

"It's a difficult thing to share," she said. "Most people associate it with mental illness, but others dispute that limited view. I am among the latter. You'll be fine, if you can accept the idea that you're somehow in touch with your own heritage—voices, images, and ideas from your predecessors, as well as those you love now. Or hate. That's just part of the territory. Oh, and steer clear of statue worshiping. That's where the trouble starts."

His laugh exploded, and she was thrilled by it, pleased that he still found her funny.

He told her he did something crazy that he hadn't included in his letters to her, and she held her breath and closed her eyes. She flashed on her dream, shook it away, opened her eyes again and looked at him. "Nothing is too crazy, my love."

He told her that, by the spring following their escape from Ebonton, there was still no word from Roland or Squirrel. Tamara had declined her grandmother's offer to take over the import-export business and had instead, with financial help from the grandmother, set up a nonprofit to assist Caribbean immigrants the company had brought in from dangerous situations on their home islands. James, meanwhile, joined the grandmother's company to provide support on biological imports, flying back and forth to the Caribbean regularly. Everyone, of course, had new names and identities, most of them French Canadian, except for James, whose new identity had him as a native of Jamaica, which gave Tamara something to laugh about.

Meanwhile, with his new identity as Canadian born Xavier Poinsot, Jade had been accepted to McGill for fall 1970 semester to study English and French literature and had been preparing to move to Montreal for summer sessions, so he could begin to accelerate his matriculation toward a three-year completion. At the time, he still did not know where his mother had landed after leaving Toronto for Europe, which put him on edge again about losing contact with Roland and Squirrel. He knew he couldn't call Wally because of the taps on his phones; he did try to call Squirrel's home phone but got a recording that it was no longer in service. So, he accompanied Tamara's cousin, Rafael, on a flight to New York, where Rafael had two days of business meetings for the import-export business. Jade was nervous about his ID, but it worked like magic, thanks to Rafael's tutelage. From New York, Jade took a train to Ebonton and a cab to Squirrel's mother's house. It was empty. In the small front yard, a "For Sale" sign rested against the yews, tilted nearly on its side.

He called his friend, Dee, the diner waitress, at her home and arranged to meet Wally in Jade's hotel room. From Wally, he learned that Alice, now Colette Willaumez, had contacted Wally through back channels and was safe in France. Wally also told him that Hafferty had stepped down from his Commissioner post, closed his estate and moved to Washington, D.C. There was a special election to replace Hafferty, and Robert Freeman, with Giallo's backing, won the prize. But Wally had nothing on Roland's or Squirrel's whereabouts.

Jade sighed and took another drink from his Chianti. "So, having struck out on finding Roland and Squirrel, I had an afternoon to kill, so I decided to make a visit to Mell Hollow. I wanted to see the place, to be sure it wasn't a long nightmare that I'd had."

She harrumphed and nearly spit out her water, choking and laughing. "Well, it certainly was *that*, honey," she sputtered.

"I know," he said, smiling, "but I just had to see it, and I had to settle a score on something else there, too. Finish off something that had haunted me," he said. "Anyway, the place was still there—the little brown dump we called home. And, up on the culm heap on the other side of The Filthy, there it was, the coal breaker, the giant praying mantis, still standing on its wavering stilts, waiting for my return. So, I found my way up there to the breaker, and I set it on fire."

"You what?!" Alice said, her face turning red. She glanced around the café.

"I know, I know," he said, holding up his hand to her. "I warned you, mom; I told you it was crazy."

"Jesus, Seamus," she sighed.

"I really didn't expect it to catch, but, after I was through the woods and making my way across that rickety little foot bridge over The Filthy, I could see it was burning fast. By the time I got back to Reston Street and up on the little knoll across from our house, the whole thing was in flames. I heard sirens, and I didn't stick around to watch it much longer, but something inside me felt right about what I had done. It was as if I had put the final nail in the coffin of our lives in that dark valley."

Alice took a deep breath and exhaled. "The *real* valley of ashes."

"Yes," he said. "Not the fictitious one."

"*En garde*, Fitzgerald," she said, hoisting an imaginary sword, and they laughed, and she reached across the table and put her hand on his, imagining their skin blending.

"What about *your* version of that valley, mom? Your book?" he said with a curious look. "Why haven't you published your Jeannette Robbins memoir? Perhaps under your own name. The new manuscript you gave Roland and me was extraordinary. The writing was vastly improved over the original you'd asked me to read that winter."

She was shaking her head before he'd finished. "My own name?" She chuckled. "And which of my own names would you suggest I use?"

He chuckled along with her. "*Touché*, Colette."

"I did not write it for public consumption," she said. "I wrote it for myself. In order to hang on, barely, to reality, amidst all that had been transpiring over those two horrid decades. Then, after I shared the first version with you in late winter that year, I realized I had to rewrite it for another rather small audience—my two sons. And so, somehow, I managed to write the newer version in a span of a few weeks. I thought of it as more of a letter to you two. It was necessary to tell you and Roland about your origins, since James and I had kept them a secret for so long. And, at the time, I wasn't sure if I was going to survive in that valley, so I was determined to finish it, all while whirling in circles over trying to thwart Dennis from taking you two from me. And from yourselves. I'm glad you read it, Seamus. Roland told me he read it as well and was appreciative. He said it helped him come to terms with lots of things, not least significant being his relationship with women. So, I'm thankful for that. And I'm glad you found it interesting."

"No, I said *extraordinary*, Alice. And I meant it." He said he had enough of the wine, and they ordered two more espressos, and she told him how she'd met with Roland in Paris the previous spring. She apologized for not filling him in, but she was afraid to put it into writing, even though their letters went through a trusted third party. And all had agreed not to connect by telephone.

"I had to protect Roland. I didn't want to be the one who unwittingly tipped off the FBI about his location."

"Where had he been hiding? And what about Squirrel?"

She told him Roland and Squirrel never made it to New York that night in July '69. From somewhere in New Jersey, Roland had placed a call to his contact in New York and was told to stay away, that the feds were breaking down doors everywhere in the city and hauling people away. He was told to go to Boston.

"There, he parted company with Squirrel and was met with a cool reception—suspicion, paranoia, distrust, organizational chaos. He ended up a few weeks later in Chicago and worked with the Panthers there until Fred Hampton was murdered in December. Roland bailed out of there fast and went to Oakland, where he lived for a short time doing community work with the Panthers. He told me he met the woman of his dreams there—Angela Davis. He said she was the fountain of enlightenment, as he called it, and much more beautiful than she was in that photo I had of her."

"He *loved* that photo," Jade said, smiling. "With the wild hair. Talk about a *Beatrice*."

"Oh, my! You *have* been studying your literature. *La Vita Nuova.* Impressive."

"Yeah, well, that one came from Tamara."

500

"Ah," she said. "Yes, the incandescent Tamara Chautier." She winked at him. "Now known by her *nom de guerre*, like the rest of us."

"As for Roland," she continued, "he somehow got to Algiers in early 1970, which was still in a glow of sorts after the Pan-African Cultural Festival the previous summer, celebrating Black liberation movements across Africa as well as in the rest of the world—including the U.S.-based Black Panthers. Eventually, as the glow receded and then turned into infighting and threats from the Algiers government, Roland found his way to Guinea, where he spent time with a small group of anti-imperialists, including the one and only Stokely Carmichael, now known as Kwame Ture. Roland later returned to Algiers, where he met Eldridge Cleaver and that's how he got to Paris—as part of Cleaver's entourage last year."

"How was he?" Jade asked. "I mean, was he at least accepting of you? Of who you were to him?"

She smiled at him, her eyes softening with the memory. "I believe he was. But he was also very nervous, as well as somewhat full of himself, which—and you may think this is odd for me to say—but I found it exciting for him to be so sure of himself intellectually, even though he was rather distant emotionally. After all, as you remember, I never really knew him, so I didn't expect much in the way of maternal satisfaction. My goal, as you know, was to set you and Roland free from the slimy grip of Dennis Hafferty. So, in that regard, I was thrilled for Roland. Ecstatic, actually, to see him so true to himself."

"How did he know where to find you?"

"Through Tamara and her grandmother's incredible back channels. She got word to him about how to call me when in Paris and, well, I have to say, I nearly fell off my feet when I heard his voice. My visit with him was too brief, and under a cloud of secrecy and fear, but at least I got an hour of time with my older son. When we parted company, he kissed me and held me close, and, you know, Seamus, that's all I ever wanted. To hold him, to be held by him, to feel him alive and strong. So, I've been going forward on the wings of that encounter."

"Where was he headed after that?"

"No idea. I may never see him again. But I hope he connects somehow with his father. I think James would be proud of his son."

"What about Squirrel? Did Roland stay in touch with him?"

"Yes. Squirrel evidently has a built-in radar system, as Roland said, and he was able to contact Roland when he was in Oakland to let him know that he'd gone to that music festival near Woodstock that August, a few weeks after he left Boston, and he bamboozled his way backstage when the technical people were having a meltdown with the rain and all the electrical equipment, and Squirrel managed to provide enough expertise to keep one of the bands on stage and technically functioning, such that the band hired him to go on the road with him, and the last time Roland heard from him was early 1970."

"The amazing Squirrel," Jade said, smiling and shaking his head. "What band was it? Did Roland say?"

"Oh, I don't know," she said, shaking her head, looking tired. "As you know, I was never much interested in rock bands, especially after the world started exploding with them. But I think he said they were from San Francisco. Something about Great Death, or something like that."

"The Grateful Dead! Squirrel works for the fucking Dead!" Jade fell back into his chair laughing.

"Seamus!" Alice said, shushing him. "You'll *wake* the fucking dead with all that racket. Low profile. Remember?"

"Yeah, sorry," he said. "I just can't believe Squirrel's with the Dead."

Alice shook her head. "A peculiar notion to celebrate, but I'm glad you're happy for him."

She called for the bill, and they started back toward the city gate, heading for the hillside farm and the cottage she shared with Gabriella. The sun was setting behind *Amiata*, and she pointed out for him Lake Trasimeno in the distance reflecting the blood red sky.

"What about *him*, mom?" Jade asked as they strolled past the little grotto and gazed at the sunflowers, now a faded blanket of gold in the last light of the falling sun.

"Do you ever think about him? He's still out there, you know. Are you worried about him showing up someday, or sending somebody to, you know, get back at you? Tamara keeps tabs on him. Says he's involved somehow, probably as an investor, with a defense contractor in Virginia that is developing wartime reconnaissance communication systems and some kind of satellite surveillance technology."

Alice turned to him and smirked, the glow of the sunset giving her face a soft rosy tint and her bright green eyes a touch of gold.

"Tamara wrote to me about him recently," she said, stepping toward the edge of the promenade and stopping to look out at the sunset. "He hasn't had an easy time of it in D.C., poor thing. He invested heavily in that firm and was doubling as a lobbyist, no doubt to shore up his investment in his typical self-serving fashion. But it turns out that a former *New York Times* reporter named Thomas Brackman, whom I knew about as *Tommy* Brackman in New York, is on his case. Now with *The Washington Post*, Brackman wrote an investigative piece on our dear Dennis, and the thing just won't go away for him. There were several follow-up reports, and, well, Tamara says it looks like the big fish from the small pond is drowning in the shark-infested sea of Washington."

"So, are you worried about him tracking us down, tracking *you* down?"

"I never think of him," she lied, pulling tenderly at his collar and touching his cheek. "I stopped looking over my shoulder four years ago, my love. I don't expect to encounter that man ever again."

Jade, now Xavier, put his arm around her shoulder and looked out onto the sunflower fields fading in the light.

"I hope you're telling me the truth, Colette Willaumez."

She let out a little laugh and then, with her lips closed, breathed in a bucket of the sweet tasting air and let it drop into her middle. As she let it rise slowly, she felt the warmth of her core rising with it, and she held him tightly against her, letting go of everything but the feeling of his warm body against hers.

"What are you thinking about right now, mom?"

She smiled, as the last of that warm breath seeped from her. She closed her eyes and rested herself in the silence before taking in another breath.

Acknowledgments

I am most grateful to many friends, family members, and professional associates who helped me bring to life the long-held dream of this, my first novel. It started out as a short story, handwritten in a crosshatched notebook I bought at Shakespeare and Company, when we lived in The City of Light so many years ago. Twenty years later, thanks to the encouragement and support of writer and editor, Brenda Walsh, I resurrected the story into the first manuscript for a novel. That bundle of pages sat in an attic box for another twelve years, while life took over. In late 2018, I dusted off the story and gave it what it deserved—four years of concentrated dedication (and revision through five more manuscripts)—the most enjoyable and satisfying intellectual experience of my life. While I cannot say that I enjoyed the subsequent long year of administrative work required to self-publish, I am grateful to those who helped me limp to the finish line. Self-publishing is not for the faint of heart.

I am especially grateful to my "beta" readers—those friends and relatives who were the first to set eyes on the finished manuscript, to let me know if what I had labored over in isolation for four years was worthwhile. Thank you, all, for your willingness, honesty, and encouragement, without which I would not have ventured beyond the final manuscript: Tom, Larry, Celia J. K., Janet, Laila, Sheryl, Conor, Tim M., Suzanna, Anna W., and the ultimate pass-fail test: The Bean.

Many, many thanks to my editor, and one-person technical support group, Sheryl Lynn Sochoka. A wonderful writer and incomparable editor, Sheryl's contribution to my novel was critical not only for all the reasons a writer needs an editor, but for the unique gifts she brings to every project I've ever worked on with her: compassion, honesty, respect, thoughtful consideration of cultural nuances, unwavering attention to detail, and strict adherence to the rules of writing. Any breach of those rules evident in the novel are mine.

I am also grateful to Sheryl's colleague, Carolan Ivey, who performed the magic act of reducing a 250,000-word manuscript to 200 words, thus creating a palette of marketing phrases that succinctly summarize the story and, hopefully, entice readers to give "Alice" a try.

Thanks also to the artist, David Provolo, for his outstanding work in creating the cover for *Alice Was Not Her Name.*

I am also grateful to friends and colleagues who've encouraged me for years to make this dream come true. Among the most enthusiastic were Laila, Celia J. K., Greenie, Sherry, Todd, Maria F. S., and Jason (my tech guru). And a deeply felt thanks goes to my brother, Mike, my brilliant childhood and teenage roommate, who introduced me to great literature at a young age, inspiring me to a lifetime of passion for fiction that stokes the imagination and stirs the soul.

A most special thank you goes to Conor, Celia, and Kat, for their endless supply of love, confidence, humor, and support for my efforts to achieve this lifelong dream.

To Jerome Lawrence Schwab, my lifelong friend and comrade in writing, I extend my eternal gratitude. A steadfast student of literature, published author, teacher of writing and ESL, and master of several languages, Jerome read my first manuscript many years ago and delicately advised on its strengths and weaknesses, as only a sensitive professor of writing would do. He said my "voice" was missing, and he was right, of course. Twelve years later, he was an important beta reader of the final manuscript, providing insight, encouragement, and confirmation that my voice had been found and used with passion. Thanks, my friend, for decades of steady and enlightened exchanges of correspondence over so many mediums of writing. You've kept alive the passion we share for the written word, in a friendship of inspiration, great humor, and hope.

In that same spirit, I want to acknowledge the euphoric power of imagination that is the beating heart of fiction. After a lifetime of writing nonfiction, in all its myriad forms, ranging from the mundane to the creative, I am grateful to have lived long enough to experience the exhilaration of writing a long-form story almost exclusively and entirely from the imagination. As an example of the power of this experience, the writer is finally free when a character in a work of fiction takes over their own story, as if the story were writing itself. Little in the world of writing compares with such ecstatic liberation from the self.

For having reached that epiphanic pinnacle, I am most grateful to the gift of life itself. And for that gift, I thank my late parents, who were so generous with their love, especially my mother, an impassioned philosopher, counselor, writer, and dreamer.

Finally, here's to my best friend and love of my life, the one who shared that romantic adventure in Paris with me, in several happily tight spaces, oh so many years ago—an experience still as real and thrilling as if it all happened this past autumn. We were living a dream, and you stuck by me then to encourage my short story writing, out of which came the tale that has now become the realization of yet another dream. Thank you for your enduring love, endless support, unmatched patience, positive attitude in the face of my instinctive gloom, and most of all for your indelible sense of humor. As you know well, I'm not trying to prove anything; I just love the adventure of writing. And you've been gracious enough to give me the space and support to let me explore that internal world, with my imaginary friends, the characters of my fiction. My gratitude to you is endless even though the very word, "gratitude," is insufficient.

About the Author

P. K. Kilcullen is a former journalist and freelance writer, having published news reports, features, reviews, editorials, advertising copy, video scripts, leadership speeches, and political campaign communications. After working as a staff writer, production manager, and associate editor at a business magazine, he went on to careers in senior management in broadcast television and higher education administration.

The author's debut novel, *Alice Was Not Her Name*, is available at Amazon, Barnes and Noble, and wherever books are sold. He is working on a new novel to be published in 2026, followed by a collection of short stories.

The author earned a bachelor's degree in English from Fordham University. He lives in Northeast Pennsylvania, with his wife, Jean.

Contact: AliceWasNotHerName@gmail.com